D0094987

GREAT SHORT TALES OF MYSTERY AND TERROR

GREAT SHORT TALES OF MYSTERY AND TERROR

Selected by
the Editors of Reader's Digest
Condensed Books

ILLUSTRATIONS BY
LEO AND DIANE DILLON

THE READER'S DIGEST ASSOCIATION
PLEASANTVILLE, NEW YORK
CAPE TOWN, HONG KONG, LONDON, MONTREAL, SYDNEY

The following selections
appear in condensed form:

*The Red-Headed League, The Turn of the Tide,
The Summer People, The Cask of Amontillado,
The Man Who Liked Dickens, The Fourth Man, The Wendigo,
The Touch of Nutmeg Makes It, The Absence of Mr. Glass,
The Log of the "Evening Star," Casting the Runes, The Whole Town's Sleeping,
The Arrow of God, The Gettysburg Bugle, The Damned Thing,
Don't Look Now, The Hands of Mr. Ottermole, An Alpine Divorce,
The Incautious Burglar, The Ghost-Ship, The Rats in the Walls,
After-Dinner Story, For Your Eyes Only,
Leiningen Versus the Ants, The Case of the Irate Witness*
and *The Nine Billion Names of God.*

First Edition

Library of Congress Catalog Card Number: 80-52212
ISBN 0-89577-091-1
Printed in the United States of America

CONTENTS

THE RED-HEADED LEAGUE

SIR ARTHUR CONAN DOYLE

I CALLED UPON my friend Sherlock Holmes one day in the autumn of 1890 and found him in deep conversation with a stout, florid-faced gentleman with fiery red hair. With an apology for my intrusion, I was about to withdraw when Holmes pulled me abruptly into the room and closed the door behind me.

"You could not possibly have come at a better time, my dear Watson," he said cordially. He turned back to his visitor. "Mr. Wilson, this gentleman has been my partner in many of my most successful cases, and I have no doubt that he will be of the utmost use to me in yours."

The stout gentleman half rose from his chair and gave a bob of greeting, with a quick little questioning glance.

"I know, my dear Watson," said Holmes, relapsing into his armchair, "that you share my love of all that is bizarre and outside the humdrum routine of everyday life. You will remember my remark the other day that for strange effects and extraordinary combinations we must go to life itself, which is always far more daring than any effort of the imagination. Now, Mr. Jabez Wilson here has been good enough to call upon me this morning and to begin a narrative which promises to be one of the most singular I have heard for some time. Perhaps, Mr. Wilson, you would have the kindness to recommence your narrative."

The portly client puffed out his chest with an appearance of some little pride and pulled a dirty and wrinkled newspaper from the inside pocket of his greatcoat. As he glanced down at the advertisement column, I took a good look at the man and endeavored, after the fashion of my companion, to read the indications which might be presented by his dress or appearance.

I did not gain much, however, by my inspection. Our visitor bore every mark of being a commonplace British tradesman, obese, pompous, and slow. He wore rather baggy gray shepherd's check trousers, a not overclean black frock coat, unbuttoned in the front, and a drab waistcoat. Look as I would, there was nothing remarkable about the man save his blazing red hair.

Sherlock Holmes's quick eye took in my occupation, and he shook his head with a smile as he noticed my questioning glances. "Beyond the obvious facts that he has at some time done manual labor, that he has been in China, and that he has done a considerable amount of writing lately, I can deduce nothing else."

Mr. Jabez Wilson started up in his chair. "How, in the name of good fortune, did you know all that, Mr. Holmes?" he asked. "How did you know, for example, that I did manual labor? It's as true as gospel, and I began as a ship's carpenter."

"Your right hand is quite a size larger than your left. You have worked with it, and the muscles are more developed."

"Well, then, the writing?"

"What else can be indicated by that right cuff so very shiny for five inches, and the left sleeve with the smooth patch near the elbow, where you rest it upon the desk."

"Well, but China?"

"The fish which you have tattooed immediately above your right wrist could only have been done in China. I have made a small study of tattoo marks. That trick of staining the fishes' scales a delicate pink is quite peculiar to China."

Mr. Jabez Wilson laughed heavily. "Well, I never!" said he. "I thought at first you had done something clever, but I see that there was nothing in it, after all."

"I think, Watson," said Holmes, "that I made a mistake in explaining. My poor little reputation will suffer shipwreck if I am so candid. Can you not find the advertisement, Mr. Wilson?"

"Yes, I have got it now," he answered, with his thick, red finger planted halfway down the column. "Here it is. This is what began it all. You just read it for yourself, sir."

I took the paper from him and read as follows:

> TO THE RED-HEADED LEAGUE: On account of the bequest of the late Ezekiah Hopkins, of Lebanon, Pa., U.S.A., there is now another vacancy open which entitles a member of the League to a salary of four pounds a week for purely nominal services. All red-headed men who are sound in body and mind, and above the age of twenty-one years, are eligible. Apply in person on Monday, at eleven o'clock, to Duncan Ross, at the offices of the League, 7 Pope's Court, Fleet Street.

"What on earth does this mean?" I ejaculated, after I had twice read over the extraordinary announcement.

Holmes chuckled, and wriggled in his chair, as was his habit when in high spirits. "It is a little off the beaten track, isn't it?" said he. "And now, Mr. Wilson, tell us all about yourself, your household, and the effect which this advertisement had upon your fortunes. You will first make a note, Doctor, of the paper and the date."

"It is the *Morning Chronicle* of August 7, 1890. Just about two months ago."

"Very good. Now, Mr. Wilson?"

"Well, it is just as I have been telling you, Mr. Holmes," said Jabez Wilson. "I have a pawnbroker's business at Saxe-Coburg Square. It's not a very large affair, and of late years it has not done more than just give me a living. I used to be able to keep two assistants, but now I only keep one; and I would have a job to pay him, but he is willing to come for half wages so as to learn the business."

"What is the name of this obliging youth?" asked Holmes.

"His name is Vincent Spaulding, and he's not such a youth, either. It's hard to say his age. I should not wish a smarter assistant. I know he could earn twice what I give him. But if he is satisfied, why should I put ideas in his head?"

"Why, indeed? You seem most fortunate. I don't know that your assistant is not as remarkable as your advertisement."

"Oh, he has his faults, too," said Mr. Wilson. "Never was such a fellow for photography. Snapping away with a camera when he ought to be improving his mind, and then diving down into the cellar like a rabbit into its hole to develop his pictures; but on the whole he's a good worker. He and a girl of fourteen, who does a bit of simple cooking and keeps the place clean—that's all I have in the house, for I am a widower and never had any family. We live very quietly, sir, the three of us; and the first thing that put us out was that advertisement. Spaulding, he came down into the office eight weeks ago with this very paper in his hand, and he says, 'I wish to the Lord, Mr. Wilson, that I was a red-headed man.'

"'Why that?' I asks.

"'Why,' says he, 'here's a vacancy on the Red-headed League. It's worth quite a little fortune to any man who gets it.'

"'Why, what is it, then?' I asked. You see, Mr. Holmes, I am a very stay-at-home man, and as my business came to me instead of my having to go to it, I was often weeks on end without putting my foot over the doormat. In that way I didn't know much of what was going on outside, and I was always glad of a bit of news.

"'Have you never heard of the Red-headed League?' Spaulding asked me.

"'Never.'

"'Why, I wonder at that, for you are eligible yourself for one of the vacancies.'

"'And what are they worth?' I asked.

"'Oh, merely a couple of hundred a year, but the work is slight, and it need not interfere with one's other occupations.'

"Well, you can easily think how that made me prick up my ears. 'Tell me all about it,' said I.

"'Well,' said he, showing me the advertisement, 'there is the address where you should apply for particulars. As far as I can make out, the League was founded by an American millionaire, Ezekiah Hopkins, who was very peculiar in his ways. He was himself red-headed, and he had a great sympathy for all red-headed men; so when he died he left his enormous fortune in the hands of trustees, with instructions to apply the interest to the providing of easy berths to men whose hair is of that color.'

"'But,' said I, 'there would be millions of red-headed men who would apply.'

"'Not so many as you might think,' he answered. 'You see, it is really confined to Londoners, and to grown men. This American had started from London when he was young, and he wanted to do the old town a good turn. Then, again, I have heard it is no use applying if your hair is light red, or dark red, or anything but real bright, blazing, fiery red.'

"Now, gentlemen, as you may see for yourselves, my hair is of a very full and rich tint, so it seemed to me that I stood as good a chance as any. So I ordered Spaulding to put up the shutters for the day and to come right away with me. He was very willing to have a holiday, so we started off to the address in the advertisement.

"I never hope to see such a sight as that again, Mr. Holmes. From north, south, east, and west every man who had a shade of red in his hair had tramped into the city to answer the advertisement. Every shade of the color they were—straw, lemon, orange, brick, Irish setter, liver, clay; but there were not many who had the real vivid flame-colored tint. When I saw how many were waiting, I would have given it up in despair; but Spaulding would not hear of it. He pushed and pulled until he got me through the crowd and up the steps which led to the office. There was a double stream upon the stair, some going up in hope, and some coming back dejected; but we wedged in as well as we could and soon found ourselves in the office."

Mr. Wilson paused and refreshed his memory with a huge pinch of snuff.

"Pray continue," said Holmes.

"There was nothing in the office but a couple of wooden chairs and a deal table, behind which sat a small man with a head that was even redder than mine. He said a few words to each candidate as he came up, and then he always managed to find some fault in them which would disqualify them. However, when our turn came, the little man was more favorable to me than to any of the others, and he closed the door as we entered, so that he might have a private word with us.

"'This is Mr. Jabez Wilson,' said my assistant, 'and he is willing to fill a vacancy in the League.'

"'And he is admirably suited for it,' the other answered. 'I cannot recall when I have seen anything so fine.' He took a step backward, cocked his head on one side, and gazed at my hair until I felt quite bashful. Then suddenly he plunged forward, wrung my hand, and congratulated me warmly on my success.

"'It would be injustice to hesitate,' said he. 'You will, however, I am sure, excuse me for taking an obvious precaution.' With that he seized my hair in both hands, and tugged until I yelled with the pain. 'There is water in your eyes,' said he as he released me. 'I perceive that all is as it should be. But we have to be careful, for we have twice been deceived by wigs and once by paint.' He stepped over to the window and shouted through it that the vacancy was filled. A groan of disappointment came up from below, and the folk all trooped away.

"'My name,' said he, 'is Mr. Duncan Ross, and I am myself one of the pensioners upon the fund left by our noble benefactor. When can you enter upon your new duties, Mr. Wilson?'

"'Well, it is awkward, for I have a business,' said I.

"'Oh, never mind about that, Mr. Wilson!' said Vincent Spaulding. 'I shall be able to look after that for you.'

"'What would be the hours?' I asked.

"'Ten to two.'

"Now a pawnbroker's business is mostly done of an evening, Mr. Holmes, especially Thursday and Friday evening, which is just before payday; so it would suit me very well to earn a little in the mornings. Besides, I knew that my assistant was a good man, and that he would see to anything that turned up.

"'That would suit me very well,' said I. 'And the pay?'

"'Four pounds a week. You have to be in the office, or at least in the building, the whole time. If you leave, you forfeit your position. The will is very clear upon that point, and no excuse will avail.'

"'I should not think of leaving,' said I. 'And the work?'

"'Is to copy the *Encyclopaedia Britannica.* There is the first volume of it in that cupboard. You use your own ink, pens, and blotting paper, but we provide this table and chair. Will you be ready tomorrow?'

"'Certainly,' I answered.

"'Then, good-by, Mr. Jabez Wilson, and let me congratulate you once more on the important position which you have been fortunate enough to gain.' He bowed me out of the room, and I went home with my assistant, very pleased at my good fortune.

"Well, I thought over the matter all day, and by evening I had quite persuaded myself that the whole affair must be some great hoax, though what its object might be I could not imagine. It seemed altogether past belief that anyone could make such a will, or that they would pay such a sum for doing anything so simple as copying out the *Encyclopaedia Britannica.* However, in the morning I determined to have a look at it anyhow, so, with a bottle of ink, a quill pen, and seven sheets of foolscap paper, I started off for Pope's Court.

"Well, to my surprise and delight, everything was as right as possible, and Mr. Duncan Ross was there to see that I got fairly to work. He started me off upon the letter *A*, and then he left me; but he would drop in from time to time to see that all was right. At two o'clock he bade me good day, complimented me upon the amount I had written, and locked the door of the office after me.

"This went on day after day, Mr. Holmes, and on Saturday the manager planked down four golden sovereigns for my week's work. It was the same next week, and the week after. By degrees Mr. Ross took to coming in only once of a morning, and then, after a time, he did not come in at all. Still, I never dared to leave the room, for I was not sure when he might come, and the billet was such a good one that I would not risk the loss of it.

"Eight weeks passed away like this, and I had written about Abbots, and Archery, and Architecture, and Armor. It cost me something in foolscap, and I had pretty nearly filled a shelf with my writings. And then suddenly the whole business came to an end."

"To an end?"

"Yes, sir. This morning I went to my work as usual at ten o'clock, but the door was locked, with a little square of cardboard hammered onto the middle of the panel with a tack. Here it is." He held up a piece of white cardboard about the size of a sheet of notepaper. It read in this fashion:

THE RED-HEADED LEAGUE IS DISSOLVED. OCTOBER 10, 1890

Sherlock Holmes and I surveyed this curt announcement, and the rueful face behind it, until the comical side of the affair so completely overtopped every other consideration that we both burst out into a roar of laughter.

"I cannot see that there is anything very funny," cried our client, flushing up to the roots of his flaming head. "If you can do nothing better than laugh at me, I can go elsewhere."

"No, no," cried Holmes. "I wouldn't miss your case for the world. It is refreshingly unusual. But there is, if you will excuse me saying so, something just a little funny about it. Pray what did you do when you found the card upon the door?"

"I called at the offices around, but none of them seemed to know anything about it. Finally I went to the landlord, who is an accountant living on the ground floor, and I asked him if he could tell me what had become of the Red-headed League. He said that he had never heard of any such body. Then I asked him who Mr. Duncan Ross was. He answered that the name was new to him.

" 'Well,' said I, 'the gentleman at number four.'

" 'Oh,' said he, 'his name was William Morris. He was a solicitor and was using my room as a temporary convenience. He left yesterday.' "

"What did you do then?" asked Holmes.

"I went home, and I asked the advice of my assistant. But he could only say that if I waited I should hear by post. But that was not quite good enough, Mr. Holmes. I did not wish to lose such a place without a struggle, so, as I had heard that you were good enough to give advice to poor folk who were in need of it, I came right away to you."

"And you did very wisely," said Holmes. "From what you have told me I think that it is possible that graver issues hang from your case than might at first sight appear."

"Grave enough!" said Mr. Jabez Wilson. "Why, I have lost four pounds a week."

"On the contrary," remarked Holmes, "you are richer by some thirty pounds, to say nothing of the minute knowledge you have gained on every subject which comes under the letter *A*."

"But I want to find out who they are and what their object was in playing this prank—if it was a prank—upon me."

"We shall endeavor to clear up these points. And, first, one or two questions, Mr. Wilson. This assistant of yours who first called your attention to the advertisement—how long had he been with you?"

"About a month then."

"How did he come?"

"In answer to an advertisement."

"Was he the only applicant?"

"No, I had a dozen."

"Why did you pick him?"

"Because he was handy and would come at half wages."

"What is he like, this Vincent Spaulding?"

"Small, stout-built, very quick in his ways, no hair on his face. Has a white splash, from acid, upon his forehead."

"Hum!" said Holmes, sinking back in deep thought. "And has your business been attended to in your absence?"

"Nothing to complain of, sir. There's not much to do of a morning."

"That will do, Mr. Wilson. I shall be happy to give you an opinion upon the subject in a day or two. I hope that by Monday we may come to a conclusion."

"Well, Watson," said Holmes, when our visitor had left us, "what do you make of it all?"

"I make nothing of it," I answered frankly. "It is most mysterious."

"As a rule," said Holmes, "the more bizarre a thing is, the less mysterious it proves to be. It is your commonplace, featureless crimes which are really puzzling. But I must be prompt over this matter."

"What are you going to do?"

"To smoke," he answered. "It is quite a three-pipe problem, and I beg you not to speak to me for fifty minutes." He curled up in his chair, with his thin knees drawn up to his hawklike nose, and there he sat with his eyes closed and his black clay pipe thrusting out like the bill of some strange bird. I had come to the conclusion that he had dropped asleep, and indeed was nodding myself, when he sprang up with the gesture of a man who had made up his mind, and put his pipe down upon the mantelpiece.

"Sarasate plays at the St. James's Hall this afternoon," he remarked. "I observe that there is a good deal of German music on the program. It is introspective, and I want to introspect. Will you come? I am going to Saxe-Coburg Square first, and we can have some lunch on the way."

I agreed, and we traveled by the Underground as far as Aldersgate; and a short walk took us to the scene of the singular story which we had listened to in the morning. It was a shabby-genteel little place, where four lines of dingy two-storied brick houses looked out into a small railed-in lawn of weedy grass. Three gilt balls on a corner house, and a board with JABEZ WILSON in white letters, announced the place where our red-headed client carried on his business. Holmes stopped in front of it with his head on one side and looked it all over, with his eyes shining brightly between puckered lids. Then he walked slowly up and down the street, looking keenly at the houses. Finally he returned to the pawnbroker's, and, having thumped vigorously upon the pavement with his stick two or three times, he went up to the door and knocked. It was opened by a bright-looking, clean-shaven young fellow, who asked him to step in.

"Thank you," said Holmes. "I only wished to ask you how you would go from here to the Strand."

"Third right, fourth left," answered the assistant promptly.

"Smart fellow, that," observed Holmes as we walked away. "He is, in my judgment, the fourth smartest man in London, and for daring I am not sure that he has not a claim to be third. I have known something of him before."

"Evidently," said I, "Mr. Wilson's assistant counts for a good deal in this mystery of the Red-headed League. I am sure you inquired your way merely in order that you might see him."

"Not him—the knees of his trousers."

"And what did you see?"

"What I expected to see."

"Why did you beat the pavement?"

"My dear doctor, this is time for observation, not for talk. We are spies in an enemy's country. We know something of Saxe-Coburg Square. Let us now explore the paths which lie behind it."

The road in which we found ourselves as we turned around the corner from the secluded Saxe-Coburg Square presented as great a contrast to it as the front of a picture does to the back. It was one of the main arteries which convey the traffic of the city to the north and west. The roadway was blocked with the immense stream of commerce flowing in a double tide inward and outward.

"Let me see," said Holmes, standing at the corner. "I should like to remember the order of the houses here. It is a hobby of mine to have an exact knowledge of London. There is the tobacconist, the newspaper shop, the Vegetarian Restaurant, the Coburg branch of the City and Suburban Bank, and McFarlane's carriage-building depot. And now, Doctor, we've done our work, so it's time we had some play. A sandwich and a cup of coffee, and then off to violin land, where all is sweetness and harmony, and there are no red-headed clients to vex us."

All the afternoon my friend sat in the stalls wrapped in perfect happiness, waving his long thin fingers in time to the music, while his gently smiling face and his dreamy eyes were as unlike those of Holmes the relentless, keen-witted sleuthhound as it was possible to conceive. In his singular character the extreme exactness and astuteness represented a reaction against the poetic and contemplative mood which occasionally predominated in him; and he was never so formidable as when, for days on end, he had been lounging in his armchair amid his musical scores. Then it was that the lust of the chase would suddenly come upon him, and that his brilliant reasoning power would rise to the level of intuition. When I saw him that afternoon so enwrapped in the music at St. James's Hall, I felt that an evil time might be coming upon those whom he had set himself to hunt down.

"You want to go home, Doctor?" he asked as we emerged.

"Yes, it would be as well."

"And I have business to do which will take some hours. A considerable crime is in contemplation. I have reason to believe that we shall be in time to stop it. But today being Saturday complicates matters. I shall want your help tonight at ten."

"I shall be at Baker Street at ten."

"Very well. And, I say, Doctor, there may be some little danger, so kindly put your army revolver in your pocket." He waved his hand, turned, and disappeared among the crowd.

I trust that I am not more dense than my neighbors, but I was always oppressed with a sense of my own stupidity in my dealings with Sherlock Holmes. Here I had heard what he had heard, I had seen what he had seen, and yet from his words it was evident that he saw clearly not only what had happened but what was about to happen, while to me the whole business was still confused and grotesque.

As I drove home to my house in Kensington, I thought over it all, from the extraordinary story of the red-headed copier of the *Encyclopaedia* down to the visit to Saxe-Coburg Square, and the ominous words with which Holmes had parted from me. What was this nocturnal expedition, and why should I go armed? I had the hint from Holmes that this smooth-faced pawnbroker's assistant was a formidable man—a man who might play a deep game. I tried to puzzle it out, but gave it up in despair.

IT WAS A quarter past nine when I started from home and made my way to Baker Street. Two hansoms were standing at the door, and as I entered the passage I heard the sound of voices from above. On entering his room I found Holmes in animated conversation with two men, one of whom I recognized as Peter Jones, the official police agent, while the other was a long, thin, sad-faced man, with a very shiny hat and oppressively respectable frock coat.

"Ha! Our party is complete," said Holmes, buttoning up his pea jacket and taking his heavy hunting crop from the rack. "Watson, you know Mr. Jones of Scotland Yard? Let me introduce you to Mr. Merryweather, who is to be our companion in tonight's adventure."

"We're hunting in couples again, Doctor, you see," said Jones in his consequential way. "Our friend here is a wonderful man for starting a chase. All he wants is an old dog to help him to do the running down."

"I hope a wild goose may not prove to be the end of our chase," observed Mr. Merryweather gloomily.

"You may place considerable confidence in Mr. Holmes, sir," said the police agent loftily. "He has his own little methods, which are, if he won't mind my saying so, just a little too theoretical and fantastic, but he has the makings of a detective in him. It is not too much to say that once or twice he has been more nearly correct than the official force."

"If you say so, Mr. Jones," said the stranger with deference. "Still, I miss my whist. It is the first Saturday night for seven and twenty years that I have not had my rubber of whist."

"I think you will find," said Sherlock Holmes, "that the play tonight will be more exciting. For you, Mr. Merryweather, the stake will be some thirty thousand pounds; and for you, Jones, it will be the man upon whom you wish to lay your hands."

"John Clay, the murderer, thief, smasher, and forger," said Jones. "He's a young man, Mr. Merryweather, but he is at the head of his profession, and I would rather have my bracelets on him than on any other criminal in London. He's a remarkable man, is young John Clay. His grandfather was a royal duke, and he himself has been to Eton and Oxford. His brain is as cunning as his fingers; he'll crack a crib in Scotland one week, and be raising money to build an orphanage in Cornwall the next. I've been on his track for years and have never set eyes on him yet."

"I hope I may have the pleasure of introducing you tonight," said Holmes. "It is past ten, however, and quite time we started. If you two will take the first hansom, Watson and I will follow in the second."

Sherlock Holmes was not very communicative during the long drive, and lay back in the cab humming the tunes which he had heard in the afternoon. We rattled through an endless labyrinth of gaslit streets until we emerged into Farringdon Street.

"Our friend Merryweather is personally interested in the matter," Holmes remarked. "I thought it as well to have Jones with us also. He is not a bad fellow, and though he is an absolute imbecile in his profession, he has one positive virtue. He is as brave as a bulldog, and as tenacious as a lobster if he gets his claws upon anyone. Here we are, and they are waiting for us."

We had reached the same crowded thoroughfare in which we had found ourselves in the morning. Our cabs were dismissed, and, following Mr. Merryweather, we passed down a narrow passage and through a side door, which he opened for us. Within, there was a small corridor, which ended in a massive iron gate. This also was opened, and led down a flight of winding stone steps, which terminated at another formidable gate. Mr. Merryweather stopped to light a lantern, and then conducted us down a dark, earth-smelling passage, and so, after opening a third door, into a huge vault, or cellar, which was piled all around with crates and boxes.

"You are not very vulnerable from above," Holmes remarked as he gazed about him.

"Nor from below," said Mr. Merryweather, striking his stick upon the flags which lined the floor. "Why, dear me, it sounds quite hollow!" he remarked, looking up in surprise.

"I must really ask you to be a little more quiet," said Holmes severely. "You have just imperiled the success of our expedition. Would you please sit down upon one of those boxes and not interfere?"

The solemn Mr. Merryweather perched himself upon a crate, with a very injured expression upon his face, while Holmes fell to his knees on the floor and, with the lantern and a magnifying lens, began to examine minutely the cracks between the stones. A few seconds sufficed to satisfy him, for he sprang to his feet again and put his glass in his pocket.

"We have at least an hour before us," he remarked, "for they can hardly take any steps until the good pawnbroker is safely in bed. Then they will not lose a minute, for the sooner they do their work, the longer they will have for their escape. We are, Doctor—as no doubt you have divined—in the cellar of the branch of one of the principal London banks. Mr. Merryweather is the chairman of directors, and he will explain to you that there are reasons why the more daring criminals of London should take a considerable interest in this cellar at present."

"It is our French gold," whispered the director. "We have had several warnings that an attempt might be made upon it."

"Your French gold?"

"Yes. We had occasion some months ago to strengthen our resources, and borrowed thirty thousand napoleons from the Bank of France. It has become known that we have never unpacked the money; it is lying here in these crates. Our reserve of bullion is much larger at present than is usually kept in a single branch office, and the directors have had misgivings upon the subject."

"Which were very well justified," observed Holmes. "And now it is time that we arranged our little plans. Mr. Merryweather, we must put the screen over that lantern."

"And sit in the dark?"

"I am afraid so. I brought a pack of cards in my pocket, and I thought you might have your game of whist after all. But I see that the enemy's preparations have gone so far that we cannot risk a light. These are daring men, and though we shall take them at a disadvantage, they may do us some harm unless we are careful. I shall stand behind this crate; you conceal yourselves behind those. Then, when I flash a light upon them, close in swiftly. If they fire, Watson, have no compunction about shooting them down."

I placed my revolver, cocked, on top of the wooden case behind which I crouched. Holmes shot the slide across the front of the lantern and left us in pitch-darkness. To me there was something depressing and subduing in the sudden gloom.

"They have but one retreat," whispered Holmes. "That is back through the house into Saxe-Coburg Square. I hope that you have done what I asked you, Jones?"

"An inspector and two officers are waiting at the front door."

"Then we have stopped all the holes. Now we must be silent and wait."

What a time it seemed! From comparing notes afterward it was but an hour and a quarter, yet it appeared to me that the night must have gone, and the dawn be breaking above us. My limbs were weary and stiff, for I feared to change my position; yet my nerves were worked up to a high pitch of tension, and my hearing was so acute that I could not only hear the gentle breathing of my companions but I could distinguish the deeper, heavier inbreathing of the bulky Jones from the thin sighing note of the bank director. From my position I could look over the case in the direction of the floor. Suddenly my eyes caught a glint of light.

At first it was but a lurid spark upon the stone floor. Then it lengthened until it became a yellow line, and then, without any sound, a gash opened and a hand appeared, which felt about in the center of the little area of light. For a minute or more the hand, with its writhing fingers, protruded out of the floor. Then it was withdrawn, as suddenly as it had appeared, and all was dark again save the single lurid spark, which marked a chink between the stones.

Its disappearance, however, was but momentary. With a rending, tearing sound, one of the broad stones turned over upon its side and left a square, gaping hole, through which streamed the light of a lantern. Over the edge there peeped a clean-cut boyish face, which looked keenly about; and then, with a hand on either side of the aperture, the man drew himself shoulder-high and waist-high, until one knee rested upon the edge. In another instant he stood at the side of the hole and was hauling after him a companion, lithe and small like himself, with a pale face and a shock of very red hair.

"It's all clear," he whispered. "Have you the chisel and the bags? Great Scott! Jump, Archie, jump, and I'll swing for it!"

Holmes had sprung out and seized the intruder by the collar. The other dived down the hole, and I heard the sound of rending cloth as Jones clutched at his coat. The light flashed upon the barrel of a revolver, but Holmes's crop came down on the man's wrist, and the pistol clinked upon the stone floor.

"It's no use, John Clay," said Holmes blandly. "You have no chance at all."

"So I see," Clay answered with the utmost coolness. "I fancy that my pal is all right, though I see you've got his coattails."

"There are three men waiting for him at the door," said Holmes.

"Oh, indeed. You seem to have done the thing very completely. I must compliment you."

"And I you," Holmes answered. "Your red-headed idea was very new and effective."

"You'll see your pal again presently," said Jones. "Just hold out while I fix the derbies."

"I beg that you will not touch me with your filthy hands," remarked our prisoner, as the handcuffs clattered upon his wrists. "You may not be aware that I have royal blood in my veins. Have the goodness, also, when you address me to say 'sir' and 'please.'"

"All right," said Jones, with a stare and a snicker. "Well, would you please, sir, march upstairs, where we can get a cab to carry Your Highness to the police station?"

"That is better," said Clay serenely. He made a sweeping bow to the three of us and walked off in the custody of the detective.

"Really, Mr. Holmes," said Mr. Merryweather, as we followed them from the cellar, "I do not know how the bank can thank you or repay you. There is no doubt that you have defeated a most determined attempt at bank robbery."

"I have been at some small expense over this matter, which I shall expect the bank to refund," said Holmes, "but beyond that I am amply repaid by having had an experience which is in many ways unique."

"YOU SEE, WATSON," he explained in the early hours of the morning, as we sat over a glass of whiskey and soda in Baker Street, "it was obvious from the first that the only possible object of this rather fantastic business of the advertisement of the League, and the copying of the *Encyclopaedia*, must be to get this not overbright pawnbroker out of the way for a number of hours every day. It was a curious way of managing it, but it really would be difficult to suggest a better. The method was no doubt suggested to Clay's ingenious mind by the color of his accomplice's hair. The four pounds a week was a lure which must draw Wilson, and what was it to them, who were playing for thousands? They put in the advertisement; one rogue has the temporary office, the other incites the man to apply for it, and together they secure his absence every morning in the week. From the time that I heard of the assistant having come for half wages, it was obvious to me that he had strong motives for securing the situation."

"But how could you guess what the motive was?"

"Had there been women in the house, I should have suspected a mere vulgar intrigue. That, however, was out of the question. The man's business was a small one, and there was nothing in his house which could account for such elaborate preparations and such an expenditure as they were at. It must, then, be something out of the house. What could it be? I thought of the assistant's fondness for photography, and his trick of vanishing into the cellar. The cellar! That was the end of this tangled clue. Then I made inquiries as to this mysterious assistant, and found that I had to deal with one of the coolest and most daring criminals in London. He was doing something in the cellar which took many hours a day for weeks on end. I could think of nothing save that he was running a tunnel to some other building.

"When we visited the scene of action, I surprised you by beating upon the pavement with my stick. I was ascertaining whether the cellar stretched out in front or behind. It was not in front. Then I rang the bell, and, as I hoped, the assistant answered it. We have had some skirmishes, but we had never set eyes on each other before. I hardly looked at his face. His knees were what I wished to see. You must yourself have remarked how worn and stained they were. They spoke of those hours of burrowing. The only remaining point was what they were burrowing for. I walked around the corner, saw that the City and Suburban Bank abutted on our friend's premises, and felt that I had solved my problem. When you drove home after the concert, I called upon Scotland Yard and upon the chairman of the bank directors, with the result that you have seen."

"And how could you tell that they would make their attempt tonight?" I asked.

"Well, when they closed their League offices, that was a sign they cared no longer about Mr. Jabez Wilson's presence—in other words, they had completed their tunnel. But it was essential that they should use it soon, as it might be discovered, or the gold might be removed. Saturday would suit them better than any other day, as it would give them a full day for their escape. For all these reasons I expected them to come tonight."

"You reasoned it out beautifully," I exclaimed in unfeigned admiration. "It is a long chain, and yet every link rings true."

"It saved me from ennui," he answered, yawning. "Alas, I already feel it closing in upon me! My life is spent in one long effort to escape from the commonplaces of existence. These little problems help me to do so."

"And you are a benefactor of the race," said I.

He shrugged his shoulders. "Well, perhaps, after all, it is of some little use," he remarked. "*'L'homme c'est rien—l'oeuvre c'est tout,'* as Gustave Flaubert wrote to George Sand."

THE TURN OF THE TIDE

C. S. FORESTER

"WHAT ALWAYS BEATS them in the end," said Dr. Matthews, "is how to dispose of the body. But, of course, you know that as well as I do."

"Yes," said Slade. He had, in fact, been devoting far more thought to what Dr. Matthews believed to be this accidental subject of conversation than Dr. Matthews could ever guess.

"As a matter of fact," went on Dr. Matthews, warming to the subject to which Slade had so tactfully led him, "it's a terribly knotty problem. It's so difficult, in fact, that I always wonder why anyone is fool enough to commit murder."

All very well for you, thought Slade, but he did not allow his thoughts to alter his expression. You smug, self-satisfied old ass! You don't know the sort of difficulties a man can be up against.

"I've often thought the same," he said.

"Yes," went on Dr. Matthews, "it's the body that does it, every time. To use a poison calls for special facilities, which are good enough to hang you as soon as suspicion is roused. And that suspicion—well, of course, part of my job is to detect poisoning. I don't think anyone can get away with it nowadays, even with the most dunderheaded general practitioner."

"I quite agree with you." Slade had no intention of using poison.

"The only other way, if a man cares to stand the racket of having the body to give evidence against him, is to fake things to look like suicide," Dr. Matthews continued, developing his logical argument. "But you know, and I know, that it just can't be done. The mere fact of suicide calls for a close examination, and no one has ever been able to fix things so well as to get away with it. You're a lawyer. You've probably read a lot of reports of trials where the murderer has tried it. And you know what's happened to them."

"Yes," said Slade. He certainly had given a great deal of consideration to the matter, and had put aside the notion of disposing of young Spalding and concealing his guilt by a sham suicide.

"That brings us to where we started, then," said Dr. Matthews. "The only other thing left is to try and conceal the body. And that's more difficult still."

"Yes," said Slade. But he had a perfect plan for disposing of the body.

"A human body," said Dr. Matthews, "is a most difficult thing to get rid of. That chap Oscar Wilde, in that book of his—*Dorian Gray*, isn't it?—gets rid of one by the use of chemicals. Well, I'm a chemist as well as a doctor, and *I* wouldn't like the job."

"No?" said Slade politely.

"There's altogether too much of it," said Dr. Matthews. "It's heavy, and it's bulky, and it's bound to undergo corruption. Think of all those poor devils who've tried it. Bodies in trunks, and bodies in coal cellars, and bodies in chicken runs. You can't hide the thing, try as you will."

Can't I? That's all you know, thought Slade, but aloud he said, "You're quite right. I've never thought about it before."

"Of course, you haven't," agreed Dr. Matthews. "Sensible people don't. And yet, you know," he went on meditatively, "there's one decided advantage about getting rid of the body altogether. You're much safer, then. You can't have a trial for murder unless you can prove there's a victim. There's got to be a corpus delicti, as you lawyers say. A corpse, in other words, even if it's only a bit of one. No corpse, no trial. I think that's good law, isn't it?"

"By jove, you're right!" said Slade. No sooner were the words out of his mouth than he regretted having said them. He did his best to make his face immobile again; he was afraid lest his expression might have hinted at his pleasure at the mention of this very reassuring factor in the problem of killing young Spalding.

But Dr. Matthews had noticed nothing. "All the same, it's only a theoretical piece of law," he said. "The entire destruction of a body is practically impossible. But if a man could achieve it, he would be all right. However strong the suspicion was against him, the police couldn't get him without a corpse. There might be a story in that, Slade, if you or I were writers."

"Yes," assented Slade, and laughed harshly.

There never would be any story about the killing of young Spalding, the insolent pup.

"Well," said Dr. Matthews, "we've had a pretty gruesome conversation, haven't we? And I seem to have done all the talking, somehow. That's the result, I suppose, Slade, of the very excellent dinner you gave me. I'd better push off now. Not that the weather is very inviting."

Nor was it. As Slade saw Dr. Matthews into his car, the rain was driving down in a real winter storm, and there was a bitter wind blowing. Slade was glad it was such a tempestuous night. It meant that there would be no one out in the lanes, no one out on the sands when he disposed of young Spalding's body.

Back in his drawing room, Slade looked at the clock. There was still an hour to spare; he could spend it in making sure that his plans were all correct. He looked up the tide tables. Yes, that was right enough. Spring tides. The lowest of low water on the sands. There was not so much luck about that; young Spalding came back on the midnight train every Wednesday night, and it was not surprising that, sooner or later, the Wednesday night would coincide with a spring tide. But it was lucky that this particular Wednesday night should be one of tempest; luckier still that low water should be at one thirty, the best time for him.

He opened the drawing-room door and listened carefully. He could not hear a sound. Mrs. Dumbleton, his housekeeper, must have been in bed some time now. She was as deaf as a post, anyway, and would not hear his departure. Nor his return, when Spalding had been killed and disposed of.

The hands of the clock seemed to be moving very fast. He must make sure everything was correct. The plow chain and the other iron weights were already in the back seat of the car; he had put them there before old Matthews arrived to dine. He slipped on his overcoat.

From his desk Slade took a curious little bit of apparatus: eighteen inches of strong cord, tied at each end to a six-inch length of wood so as to make a ring. He made a last close examination to see that the knots were firm, and then he put it in his pocket; as he did so, he ran through, in his mind, the words—he knew them by heart—of the passage in the book about the Thugs of India, describing the method of strangulation employed by them. He could think quite coldly about all this. Young Spalding was a pestilent busybody. A word from him now could bring ruin upon Slade, could send him to prison.

Slade thought of other defaulting solicitors he had heard of, even one or two with whom he had come into contact professionally. He remembered his brother solicitors' remarks about them, pitying or contemptuous. He thought of having to beg his bread in the streets on his release from prison, of cold and misery and starvation. The shudder which shook him was succeeded by a hot wave of resentment. Never, never would he endure it.

What right had young Spalding, who had barely been qualified two years, to condemn a gray-haired man twenty years his senior to such a fate? If nothing but death would stop him, then he deserved to die. He clenched his hand on the cord in his pocket.

A glance at the clock told him he had better be moving. He turned out the lights and tiptoed out of the house, shutting the door quietly. The bitter wind flung icy rain into his face, but he did not notice it.

He backed the car out of the garage, and, contrary to his wont, he locked the garage doors, as a precaution against the infinitesimal chance that, on a night like this, someone should notice that his car was out. He drove cautiously down the road.

There were lights in the station as he drove over the bridge; they were on for the arrival of the twelve-thirty train. Spalding would be on that. Every Wednesday he went over to his subsidiary office, sixty miles away. Slade turned into the lane just beyond the station and then reversed his car so that it pointed toward the road. He put out the lights and settled himself to wait; his hand fumbled with the cord in his pocket.

THE TRAIN WAS A LITTLE LATE. Slade had been waiting a quarter of an hour when he saw the lights of the train as it drew up to the station. So wild was the night that he could hear nothing of it. Then the train moved slowly out again. As soon as it was gone, the lights in the station began to go out, one by one; Hobson, the porter, was making ready to go home, his turn of duty completed.

Next, Slade's straining ears heard footsteps.

Young Spalding was striding down the road. With his head bent before the storm, he did not notice the dark mass of the motorcar in the lane, and he walked past it.

Slade counted up to two hundred, slowly, and then he switched on his lights, started the engine, and drove the car out into the road in pursuit. He saw Spalding in the glare of the headlights and drew up alongside.

"Is that Spalding?" he said, striving to make the tone of his voice as natural as possible. "I'd better give you a lift, old man, hadn't I?"

"Thanks very much," said Spalding. "This isn't the sort of night to walk two miles in."

He climbed in and shut the door. No one had seen. No one would know.

Slade let in his clutch and drove slowly down the road. "Bit of luck, seeing you," he said. "I was just on my way home from bridge at Mrs. Clay's when I saw the train come in and remembered it was Wednesday and you'd be walking home. So I thought I'd turn a bit out of my way to take you along."

"Very good of you, I'm sure," said Spalding.

"As a matter of fact," said Slade, speaking slowly and driving slowly, "it wasn't altogether disinterested. I wanted to talk business to you."

"Rather an odd time to talk business," said Spalding. "Can't it wait till tomorrow?"

"No, it cannot," said Slade. "It's about the Lady Vere trust."

"Oh, yes. I wrote to remind you last week that you had to make delivery."

"Yes, you did. And I told you, long before that, that it would be inconvenient, with Hammond abroad."

"I don't see that," said Spalding sharply. "I don't see that Hammond's got anything to do with it. Why can't you just hand over and have done with it? I can't do anything to straighten things up until you do."

"As I said, it would be inconvenient."

Slade brought the car to a standstill at the side of the road. "Look here, Spalding," he went on desperately, "I've never asked a favor of you before. But now I ask you, as a favor, to forgo delivery for a bit. Just for three months."

But Slade had small hope that his request would be granted. So little hope, in fact, that he brought his left hand out of his pocket holding the piece of wood with the loop of cord dangling from its ends. He put his arm around the back of Spalding's seat.

"No, I can't, really I can't," said Spalding. "I've got my duty to my clients to consider. I'm sorry to insist, but you're quite well aware of what my duty is."

"Yes," said Slade. "But I beg you to wait. I implore you to wait, Spalding. There! Perhaps you can guess why, now."

"I see," said Spalding, after a long pause.

"I only want three months," pressed Slade. "Just three months. I can get straight again in three months."

Spalding had known other men who had had the same belief in their ability to get straight in three months. It was unfortunate for Slade—and for Spalding—that Slade had used those words. Spalding hardened his heart.

"No," he said. "I can't promise anything like that. I don't think it's any use continuing this discussion. Perhaps I'd better walk home from here."

He put out his hand to the latch of the door, and as he did so, Slade jerked the loop of cord over his head. A single turn of Slade's wrist—a thin, bony, old man's wrist, but as strong as steel in that wild moment—tightened the cord about Spalding's throat. Slade swung around in his seat, getting both hands to the piece of wood, twisting madly. His breath hissed between his teeth with the effort, but Spalding never drew breath at all. He lost consciousness long before he was dead. Only Slade's grip of the cord around his throat prevented the dead body from falling forward, doubled up.

Nobody had seen, nobody would know. And what that book had stated about the method of assassination practiced by Thugs was perfectly correct.

SLADE HAD GAINED, now, the time in which he could get his affairs into order. With all the promise of his current speculations, with all his financial ability, he would be able to recoup himself for his past losses. It only remained to dispose of Spalding's body, and he had planned to do that very satisfactorily. Just for a moment Slade felt as if all this were only some heated dream, some nightmare, but then he came back to reality and went on with the plan he had in mind.

He pulled the dead man's knees forward so that the corpse lay back in the seat, against the side of the car. He put the car in gear, let in his clutch, and drove rapidly down the road—much faster than when he had been arguing with Spalding. Low water was in three quarters of an hour's time, and the sands were ten miles away.

Slade drove fast through the wild night. There was not a soul about in those lonely lanes. He knew the way by heart—he had driven repeatedly over that route recently in order to memorize it.

The car bumped down the last bit of lane, and Slade drew up on the edge of the sands. It was pitch-dark, and the bitter wind was howling about him under the black sky. Despite the noise of the wind, he could hear the surf breaking far away, two miles away, across the level sands. He climbed out of the driver's seat and walked around to the other door. When he opened it the dead man fell sideways, into his arms.

With an effort, Slade held him up, while he groped in the back of the car for the plow chain and the iron weights. He crammed the weights into the dead man's pockets, and he wound the chain around and around the dead man's body, tucking in the ends to make it all secure. With that mass of iron to hold it down, the body would never be found again when dropped into the sea at the lowest ebb of spring tide.

Slade tried now to lift the body in his arms, to carry it over the sands. He reeled and strained, but he was not strong enough—Slade was a man of slight figure, and past his prime. The sweat on his forehead was icy in the icy wind.

For a second, doubt overwhelmed him, lest all his plans should fail for want of bodily strength. But he forced himself into thinking clearly; he forced his frail body into obeying the vehement commands of his brain.

He turned around, still holding the dead man upright. Stooping, he got the heavy burden on his shoulders. He drew the arms around his neck, and, with a convulsive effort, he got the legs up around his waist. The dead man now rode him piggyback. Bending nearly double, he was able to carry the heavy weight in that fashion.

He set off, staggering, down the imperceptible slope of the sands toward the sound of the surf. The sands were soft beneath his feet—it was because of this softness that he had not driven the car down to the beach. He could afford to take no chances of being embogged.

The icy wind shrieked around him all that long way. The tide was nearly two miles out. That was why Slade had chosen this place. In the depth of winter, no one would go out to the water's edge at low tide for months to come.

He staggered on over the sands, clasping the limbs of the body close about him. Desperately he forced himself forward, not stopping to rest, for he only just had time now to reach the water's edge before the flow began. He went on and on, driving his exhausted body with fierce urgings from his frightened brain.

Then, at last, he saw it: a line of white in the darkness. Farther out, the waves were breaking in an inferno of noise. Here, the fragments of the rollers were only just sufficient to move the surface a little.

He was going to make quite sure of things. Steadying himself, he stepped into the water, wading in farther and farther so as to be able to drop the body into comparatively deep water. He held to his resolve, staggering through the icy water, knee-deep, thigh-deep, until it was nearly at his waist. This was far enough. He stopped, gasping in the darkness.

He leaned over to one side to roll the body off his back. It did not move. He pulled at its arms. They were obstinate. He could not loosen them. He shook himself furiously. He tore at the legs around his waist. Still the thing clung to him. Wild with panic and fear, he flung himself about in a mad effort to rid himself of the burden. It clung on as though it were alive. He could not break its grip.

Then a breaker came in. It splashed about him, wetting him far above his waist. The tide had begun to turn now, and the tide on those sands comes in like a racehorse.

He made another effort to cast off the load, and when it still held him fast, he lost his nerve and tried to struggle out of the sea. But it was too much for his exhausted body. The weight of the corpse and of the iron with which it was loaded overbore him. He fell.

He struggled up again in the foam-streaked dark sea, staggered a few steps, fell again—and did not rise. The dead man's arms were around his neck, strangling him. Rigor mortis had set in and Spalding's muscles had refused to relax.

THE SUMMER PEOPLE

SHIRLEY JACKSON

THE ALLISONS' COUNTRY cottage, seven miles from the nearest town, was set prettily on a hill; from three sides it looked down on soft trees and grass that seldom, even at midsummer, lay still and dry. On the fourth side was the lake, which touched against the wooden pier the Allisons had to keep repairing, and which looked equally well from the Allisons' front porch, their side porch or any spot on the wooden staircase leading from the porch down to the water. Although the Allisons loved their summer cottage, looked forward to arriving in the early summer and hated to leave in the fall, they had not troubled themselves to put in any improvements, regarding the cottage itself and the lake as improvement enough for the life left to them. The cottage had no heat, no running water except the precarious supply from the backyard pump and no electricity. For seventeen summers Janet Allison had cooked on a kerosene stove, heating all their water; Robert Allison had brought bucketfuls of water daily from the pump and read his paper by kerosene light in the evenings and they had both, sanitary city people, become stolid and matter-of-fact about their backhouse.

In themselves, the Allisons were ordinary people. Mrs. Allison was fifty-eight years old and Mr. Allison sixty; they had seen their children outgrow the summer cottage and go on to families of their own and seashore resorts; their friends were either dead or settled in comfortable year-round houses, their nieces and nephews vague. In the winter they told one another they could stand their New York apartment while waiting for the summer; in the summer they told one another that the winter was well worth while, waiting to get to the country.

Since they were old enough not to be ashamed of regular habits, the Allisons invariably left their summer cottage the Tuesday after Labor Day, and were as invariably sorry when the months of September and early October turned out to be insufferably barren in the city. Each year they recognized that there was nothing to bring them back to New York, but it was not until this year that they overcame their traditional inertia. "There isn't really anything to take us back to the city," Mrs. Allison told her husband seriously, as though it were a new idea, and he told her, as though neither of them had ever considered it, "We might as well enjoy the country as long as possible."

Consequently, with much pleasure and a slight feeling of adventure, Mrs. Allison went into their village with her husband the day after Labor Day and told those natives with whom she had dealings, with a pretty air of breaking away from tradition, that they had decided to stay at least a month longer.

"Nobody ever stayed at the lake past Labor Day before," Mr. Babcock, her grocer, said. He was putting Mrs. Allison's groceries into a large cardboard carton, and he stopped to look reflectively into a bag of cookies. "Nobody," he added.

"But the city!" Mrs. Allison always spoke of the city to Mr. Babcock as though it were Mr. Babcock's dream to go there. "It's so hot—you've no idea. We're always sorry to leave here."

"I'd hate to leave myself," Mr. Babcock said, after deliberation, and both he and Mrs. Allison smiled. "But I never heard of anyone ever staying out at the lake after Labor Day before."

"Well, we're going to give it a try," Mrs. Allison said, and Mr. Babcock replied gravely, "Never know till you try."

Physically, Mrs. Allison decided, as she always did when leaving the grocery after one of her inconclusive conversations with Mr. Babcock, physically, Mr. Babcock could model for a statue of Daniel Webster, but mentally . . . it was horrible to think into what old New England

Yankee stock had degenerated. She said as much to Mr. Allison when she got into the car, and he said, "It's generations of inbreeding. That and the bad land."

Since this was their big trip into town, which they made only once every two weeks to buy things they could not have delivered, they spent all day at it.

After her grocery shopping, Mrs. Allison was tempted by a set of glass baking dishes in the hardware and clothing and general store. She had the dishes carefully wrapped, to endure the uncomfortable ride home over the rocky road that led up to the Allisons' cottage, and while Mr. Charley Walpole, who ran the store, laboriously unfolded newspapers to wrap around the dishes, Mrs. Allison said, informally, "Course, I *could* have waited and gotten those dishes in New York, but we're not going back so soon this year."

"Heard you was staying on," Mr. Charley Walpole said. His old fingers fumbled maddeningly with the thin sheets of newspaper, carefully trying to isolate only one sheet at a time, and he did not look up at Mrs. Allison as he went on, "Don't know about staying on up there to the lake. Not after Labor Day."

"Well, you know," Mrs. Allison said, quite as though he deserved an explanation, "it just seemed to us that we've been hurrying back to New York every year, and there just wasn't any need for it. You know what the city's like in the fall." And she smiled confidingly up at Mr. Charley Walpole.

Rhythmically he wound string around the package. He's giving me a piece long enough to save, Mrs. Allison thought, and she looked away quickly to avoid giving any sign of impatience. "I feel sort of like we belong here, more," she said. "Staying on after everyone else has left." To prove this, she smiled brightly across the store at a woman with a familiar face, who might have been the woman who sold berries to the Allisons one year, or the woman who occasionally helped in the grocery and was probably Mr. Babcock's aunt.

"Well," Mr. Charley Walpole said as he shoved the finished package across the counter. "Never been summer people before, at the lake after Labor Day."

Mrs. Allison gave him a five-dollar bill, and he made change methodically. "Never after Labor Day," he said, and nodded at Mrs. Allison, and went soberly along the store to deal with two women who were looking at cotton housedresses.

As Mrs. Allison passed on her way out she heard one of the women say acutely, "Why is one of them dresses one dollar and thirty-nine cents and this one here is only ninety-eight?"

"They're great people," Mrs. Allison told her husband when they met at the door of the hardware store. "They're so solid, and so reasonable, and so *honest.*"

"Makes you feel good, knowing there are still towns like this," Mr. Allison said.

"You know, in New York," Mrs. Allison said, "I might have paid a few cents less for these dishes, but there wouldn't have been anything sort of personal in the transaction."

"Staying on to the lake?" Mrs. Martin, in the newspaper and sandwich shop, said when the Allisons stopped by for lunch.

"Thought we'd take advantage of the lovely weather this year," Mr. Allison said.

Mrs. Martin was a comparative newcomer to the town; she had married into the newspaper and sandwich shop from a neighboring farm, and had stayed on after her husband's death. She served bottled soft drinks, and fried egg and onion sandwiches on thick bread.

"I don't guess anyone's ever stayed out there so long before," Mrs. Martin said. "Not after Labor Day, anyway."

"Surprised you're staying on," Mr. Hall, the Allisons' nearest neighbor, told them later, in front of Mr. Babcock's store, where the Allisons were getting into their car to go home.

"It seemed a shame to go so soon," Mrs. Allison said. Mr. Hall lived three miles away; he supplied the Allisons with butter and eggs, and occasionally, from the top of their hill, the Allisons could see the lights in his house in the early evening before the Halls went to bed.

The ride home was long and rough; it was beginning to get dark, and Mr. Allison had to drive very carefully over the dirt road by the lake. Mrs. Allison lay back against the seat, pleasantly relaxed after a day of what seemed whirlwind shopping compared with their day-to-day existence; the new glass baking dishes lurked agreeably in her mind, along with the half bushel of red eating apples, and the package of colored thumbtacks with which she was going to put up new shelf edging in the kitchen. "Good to get home," she said softly as they came in sight of their cottage, silhouetted above them against the sky.

"Glad we decided to stay on," Mr. Allison agreed.

Mrs. Allison spent the next morning lovingly washing her baking dishes, although in his innocence Charley Walpole had neglected to notice the chip in the edge of one. She decided, wastefully, to use some of the red eating apples in a pie for dinner, and, while the pie was in the oven and Mr. Allison was down getting the mail, she sat out on the little lawn the Allisons had made at the top of the hill and watched the changing lights on the lake, alternating gray and blue as clouds moved quickly across the sun.

Mr. Allison came back a little out of sorts; it always irritated him to walk the mile to the mailbox on the state road and come back with nothing, even though he assumed that the walk was good for his health. This morning there was nothing but a circular from a New York department store, and their New York paper, which arrived erratically by mail from one to four days later than it should, so that some days the Allisons might have three papers and frequently none. Mrs. Allison, although she shared with her husband the annoyance of not having mail when they so anticipated it, pored affectionately over the department store circular, and made a mental note to check on the sale of wool blankets when she finally went back to New York. Then she dropped the circular into the grass beside her chair and lay back, her eyes half closed.

"Looks like we might have some rain," Mr. Allison said, squinting at the sky.

"Good for the crops," Mrs. Allison said laconically, and they both laughed.

The kerosene man came the next morning while Mr. Allison was down getting the mail. The kerosene man also hauled garbage away for the summer people; this was only necessary for improvident city folk; country people had no garbage.

"I'm glad to see you," Mrs. Allison told him. "We were getting pretty low."

The kerosene man, whose name Mrs. Allison had never learned, used a hose attachment to fill the twenty-gallon tank which supplied light and heat and cooking facilities for the Allisons; but today, instead of swinging down from his truck and unhooking the hose from where it coiled around the cab of the truck, the man stared uncomfortably at Mrs. Allison, his truck motor still going. "Thought you folks'd be leaving," he said.

"We're staying on another month," Mrs. Allison said brightly. "The weather was so nice, and it seemed like—"

"That's what they told me," the man said. "Can't give you no oil, though."

"What do you mean?" Mrs. Allison raised her eyebrows. "We're just going to keep on with our regular—"

"After Labor Day," the man said. "I don't get so much oil myself after Labor Day."

Mrs. Allison reminded herself, as she had frequently to do when in disagreement with her neighbors, that city manners were no good with country people; you could not expect to overrule a country employee as you could a city worker. Mrs. Allison smiled engagingly as she said, "But can't you get extra oil, at least while we stay?"

"You see," the man said. He tapped his finger exasperatingly against the wheel as he spoke. "You see," he said slowly, "I order this oil. I order it down from maybe fifty, fifty-five miles away. I order back in June, how much I'll need for the summer. Then I order again . . . oh, about November. Round about now it's starting to get pretty short."

"But can't you give us *some?*" Mrs. Allison said. "Isn't there anyone else?"

"Don't know as you could get oil anywheres else right now," the man said consideringly. "*I* can't give you none." Before Mrs. Allison could speak, the truck began to move. It drove away, and Mrs. Allison, comforted by the thought that she could probably get kerosene from Mr. Babcock, watched it go with anger. "Just let *him* try coming around next summer!" she told herself.

There was no mail, and Mr. Allison was openly cross when he returned. When Mrs. Allison told him about the kerosene man he was not particularly impressed. "Probably keeping it all for a high price during the winter," he commented. "What's happened to Anne and Jerry, do you think?"

Anne and Jerry were their son and daughter, both married, one living in Chicago, one in the Far West. Their dutiful weekly letters were late; so late, in fact, that Mr. Allison's annoyance at the lack of mail was able to settle on a legitimate grievance. "Ought to realize how we wait for their letters," he said. "Thoughtless, selfish children. Ought to know better."

"Well, dear," Mrs. Allison said placatingly. Anger at Anne and Jerry would not relieve her emotions toward the kerosene man. After a few minutes she said, "Wishing won't bring the mail, dear. I'm going to go call Mr. Babcock and tell him to send up some kerosene with my order."

"At least a postcard," Mr. Allison said as she left.

As WITH MOST of the cottage's inconveniences, the Allisons no longer noticed the phone particularly, but yielded to its eccentricities without conscious complaint. It was a wall phone, of a type still seen in only few communities; in order to get the operator, Mrs. Allison had first to turn the side crank and ring once. She had to crank the phone three times this morning before the operator answered, and then it was still longer before Mr. Babcock picked up the receiver at his phone in the corner of the grocery behind the meat table. He said, "Store?" with the rising inflection that seemed to indicate suspicion of anyone who tried to communicate with him by means of this unreliable instrument.

"This is Mrs. Allison, Mr. Babcock. I thought I'd give you my order a day early because I wanted to get some—"

"What say, Mrs. Allison?"

Mrs. Allison raised her voice a little. "I said I thought I'd call in my order early so you could send me—"

"Mrs. Allison? You'll come and pick it up?"

"Pick it up?" In her surprise Mrs. Allison let her voice drop back to its normal tone and Mr. Babcock said loudly, "What's that, Mrs. Allison?"

"I thought I'd have you send it out as usual," Mrs. Allison said.

"Well, Mrs. Allison," Mr. Babcock replied, "my boy's been working for me went back to school yesterday and now I got no one to deliver. I only got a boy delivering summers, you see. You never been here after Labor Day before, so's you wouldn't know, of course."

"Well," Mrs. Allison said helplessly. Far inside her mind she was saying, over and over, Can't use city manners on countryfolk, no use getting mad. "Are you *sure?*" she asked finally. "Couldn't you just send out an order today?"

"I guess I couldn't, Mrs. Allison. It wouldn't hardly pay, delivering, with no one else out at the lake."

"What about Mr. Hall?" Mrs. Allison asked suddenly. "The people who live about three miles away from us out here? Mr. Hall could bring it out when he comes."

"Hall?" Mr. Babcock said. "John Hall? They've gone to visit her folks upstate, Mrs. Allison."

"But they bring all our butter and eggs," Mrs. Allison said, appalled.

"Left yesterday," Mr. Babcock said. "Probably didn't think you folks would stay on up there."

"But I told Mr. Hall . . ." Mrs. Allison started to say, and then stopped. "I'll send Mr. Allison in after some groceries tomorrow," she said.

After she hung up, Mrs. Allison went slowly out to sit again in her chair next to her husband. "He won't deliver," she said. "You'll have to go in tomorrow. We've got just enough kerosene to last till you get back."

"He should have told us sooner," Mr. Allison said.

It was not possible to remain troubled long in the face of the day; the country had never seemed more inviting, and the lake moved quietly below them, among the trees, with the almost incredible softness of a summer picture. Mrs. Allison sighed deeply, in the pleasure of possessing for themselves that sight of the lake, with the distant green hills beyond, the gentleness of the small wind through the trees.

THE WEATHER CONTINUED fair; the next morning Mr. Allison, duly armed with a list of groceries, with "kerosene" in large letters at the top, went down the path to the garage, and Mrs. Allison began another pie in her new baking dishes. She was paring the apples when Mr. Allison came rapidly up the path and flung open the screen door.

"Damn car won't start," he announced, with the end-of-the-tether voice of a man who depends on a car as he depends on his right arm.

"Can you fix it?" Mrs. Allison asked, stopping with the paring knife in one hand and an apple in the other.

"No," Mr. Allison said, "I cannot. Got to call someone."

"Who?" Mrs. Allison asked.

"Man runs the filling station, I guess." Mr. Allison moved toward the phone. "He fixed it last summer one time."

A little apprehensive, Mrs. Allison went on paring apples, while she listened to Mr. Allison with the phone, ringing, waiting, finally giving the number to the operator, then waiting again and giving the number again, giving the number a third time and then slamming down the receiver.

"No one there," he announced as he came into the kitchen.

"He's probably gone out for a minute," Mrs. Allison said nervously; she was not quite sure what made her so nervous, unless it was the probability of her husband's losing his temper completely. "He's there alone, I imagine, so if he goes, there's no one to answer the phone."

"That must be it," Mr. Allison said with heavy irony. He slumped into a kitchen chair and watched Mrs. Allison paring apples. After a minute she said soothingly, "Why don't you go get the mail and then call him again?"

Mr. Allison debated and then said, "Guess I might as well." He rose heavily and when he got to the kitchen door he turned and said, "But if there's no mail . . ." and leaving an awful silence behind him, he went off down the path.

Mrs. Allison hurried with her pie. Twice she went to the window to glance at the sky to see if there were clouds coming up. The room seemed unexpectedly dark, and she herself felt in the state of tension that preceded a thunderstorm. But both times when she looked the sky was clear and serene, smiling indifferently down on the Allisons' summer cottage as well as on the rest of the world. When Mrs. Allison, her pie ready for the oven, went a third time to look outside, she saw her husband coming up the path; he seemed more cheerful, and when he saw her, he waved eagerly and held a letter in the air.

"From Jerry," he called as soon as he was close enough for her to hear him, "at last—a letter!" Mrs. Allison noticed with concern that he was no longer able to get up the gentle slope of the path without breathing heavily; but then he was in the doorway, holding out the letter.

Mrs. Allison looked with an eagerness that surprised her on the familiar handwriting of her son; she could not imagine why the letter excited her so, except that it was the first they had received in so long. It would be a pleasant, dutiful letter, full of the doings of Alice and the children, reporting progress with his job, commenting on the recent weather in Chicago, closing with love from all. Both Mr. and Mrs. Allison could, if they wished, recite a pattern letter from either of their children.

Mr. Allison slit the letter open with great deliberation, and then he spread it out on the kitchen table and they leaned down and read it together.

"Dear Mother and Dad," it began, in Jerry's familiar, rather childish handwriting, "Am glad this goes to the lake as usual, we always thought you came back too soon and ought to stay up there as long as you could. Alice says that now that you're not as young as you used to be and have no demands on your time, fewer friends, etc., in the city, you ought to get what fun you can while you can. Since you two are both happy up there, it's a good idea for you to stay."

Uneasily Mrs. Allison glanced sideways at her husband; he was reading intently, and she reached out and picked up the empty envelope, not knowing exactly what she wanted from it. It was addressed quite as usual, in Jerry's handwriting, and was postmarked Chicago. Of course it's postmarked Chicago, she thought quickly. Why would they want to postmark it anywhere else? When she looked back down at the letter, her husband had turned the page, and she read on with him: "And of course if they get measles, etc., now, they will be better off later. Alice is well, of course, me too. Been playing a lot of bridge lately with some people you don't know, named Carruthers. Nice young couple, about our age. Well, will close now as I guess it bores you to hear about things so far away. Tell Dad old Dickson, in our Chicago office, died. He used to ask about Dad a lot. Have a good time up at the lake, and don't bother about hurrying back. Love from all of us, Jerry."

"Funny," Mr. Allison commented.

"It doesn't sound like Jerry," Mrs. Allison said in a small voice. "He never wrote anything like . . ." She stopped.

"Like what?" Mr. Allison demanded.

Mrs. Allison turned the letter over, frowning. It was impossible to find any sentence, any word, even, that did not sound like Jerry's regular letters. Perhaps it was only that the letter was so late, or the unusual number of dirty fingerprints on the envelope. "I don't *know*," she said impatiently.

"Going to try that phone call again," Mr. Allison said.

Mrs. Allison read the letter twice more, trying to find a phrase that sounded wrong. Then Mr. Allison came back and said, very quietly, "Phone's dead."

"What?" Mrs. Allison said, dropping the letter.

"Phone's dead," Mr. Allison said.

THE REST OF the day went quickly; after a lunch of crackers and milk, the Allisons went to sit outside on the lawn, but their afternoon was cut short by the gradually increasing storm clouds that came up over the lake to the cottage, so that it was as dark as evening by four o'clock. The storm delayed, however, as though in loving anticipation of the moment it would break over the summer cottage, and there was an occasional flash of lightning, but no rain.

In the evening Mr. and Mrs. Allison, sitting close together inside their cottage, turned on the battery radio they had brought with them from New York. There were no lamps lighted in the cottage, and the only light came from the lightning outside and the small square glow from the dial of the radio.

The slight framework of the cottage was not strong enough to withstand the city noises, the music and the voices, from the radio, and the Allisons could hear them far off, echoing across the lake, the saxophones in the New York dance band wailing over the water, the flat voice of the girl vocalist going inexorably out into the clean country air. Even the announcer, speaking glowingly of the virtues of razor blades, was no more than an inhuman voice sounding out from the Allisons' cottage and echoing back, as though the lake and the hills and the trees were returning it unwanted. During one pause between commercials, Mrs.

Allison turned and smiled weakly at her husband. "I wonder if we're supposed to . . . *do* anything," she said.

"No," Mr. Allison said consideringly. "I don't think so. Just wait."

Mrs. Allison caught her breath quickly, and Mr. Allison said, under the trivial melody of the dance band beginning again, "The car had been tampered with. Even I could see that."

Mrs. Allison hesitated a minute and then said very softly, "I suppose the phone wires were cut."

"I imagine so," Mr. Allison said.

After a while the dance music stopped and they listened attentively to a news broadcast, the announcer's rich voice telling them breathlessly of a marriage in Hollywood, the latest baseball scores, the estimated rise in food prices during the coming week. He spoke to them, in the summer cottage, quite as though they still deserved to hear news of a world that no longer reached them except through the fallible batteries of the radio, which were already beginning to fade, almost as though they still belonged, however tenuously, to the rest of the world.

Mrs. Allison glanced out the window at the smooth surface of the lake, the black masses of the trees, and the waiting storm, and said conversationally, "I feel better about that letter of Jerry's."

"I knew when I saw the light down at the Hall place last night," Mr. Allison said.

The wind, coming up suddenly over the lake, swept around the summer cottage and slapped hard at the windows. Mr. and Mrs. Allison involuntarily moved closer together, and with the first sudden crash of thunder, Mr. Allison reached out and took his wife's hand. And then, while the lightning flashed outside, and the radio faded and sputtered, the two old people huddled together in their summer cottage and waited.

THE CASK OF AMONTILLADO

EDGAR ALLAN POE

THE THOUSAND INJURIES of Fortunato I had borne as I best could; but when he ventured upon insult, I vowed revenge. You, who so well know the nature of my soul, will not suppose, however, that I gave utterance to a threat. *At length* I would be avenged; this was a point definitively settled; and I must not only punish, but punish with impunity. A wrong is unredressed when retribution overtakes its redresser. It is equally unredressed when the avenger fails to make himself felt as such to him who has done the wrong.

It must be understood that neither by word nor deed had I given Fortunato cause to doubt my goodwill. I continued, as was my wont, to smile in his face, and he did not perceive that my smile *now* was at the thought of his immolation.

He had a weak point—this Fortunato—although in other regards he was a man to be respected and even feared. He prided himself on his connoisseurship in wine. In this respect I did not differ from him materially: I was skillful in the Italian vintages myself, and bought largely whenever I could.

It was about dusk, one evening during the supreme madness of the carnival season, that I encountered my friend. He accosted me with excessive warmth, for he had been drinking much. The man wore motley. He had on a tight-fitting parti-striped dress, and his head was surmounted by the conical cap and bells. I was so pleased to see him that I thought I should never have done wringing his hand.

I said to him, "My dear Fortunato, you are luckily met. How remarkably well you are looking today! But I have received a pipe of what passes for Amontillado, and I have my doubts."

"How?" said he. "Amontillado? A pipe? Impossible! And in the middle of the carnival!"

"I have my doubts," I replied; "and I was silly enough to pay the full Amontillado price without consulting you in the matter. You were not to be found, and I was fearful of losing a bargain."

"Amontillado!"

"I have my doubts."

"Amontillado!"

"And I must satisfy them."

"Amontillado!"

"As you are engaged, I am on my way to Luchesi. If anyone has a critical turn, it is he. He will tell me—"

"Luchesi cannot tell Amontillado from Sherry."

"And yet some fools will have it that his taste is a match for your own."

"Come, let us go to your vaults."

"My friend, no; I will not impose upon you. I perceive you are afflicted with a cold. The vaults are insufferably damp."

"Let us go, nevertheless. The cold is merely nothing."

Thus speaking, Fortunato possessed himself of my arm. Putting on a mask of black silk, and drawing a roquelaure closely about my person, I suffered him to hurry me to my *palazzo.*

There were no attendants at home; they had absconded to make merry in honor of the time. I had told them I should not return until morning, and had given them explicit orders not to stir from the house. These orders were sufficient, I well knew, to ensure their immediate disappearance as soon as my back was turned.

I took from their sconces two flambeaux, and giving one to Fortunato, bowed him through several suites of rooms to the archway that led into the vaults. I passed down a long and winding staircase, requesting him to be cautious as he followed. We came at length to the foot of the descent, and stood together on the damp ground of the catacombs of the Montresors.

The gait of my friend was unsteady, and the bells upon his cap jingled as he strode. "The pipe," said he.

"It is farther on," said I.

He looked into my eyes with two filmy orbs that distilled the rheum of intoxication. "Ugh! Ugh! Ugh!"

"How long have you had that cough?"

My poor friend found it impossible to reply for many minutes. "It is nothing," he said at last.

"Come," I said with decision, "we will go back; your health is precious. You will be ill, and I cannot be responsible. Besides, there is Luchesi—"

"Enough," he said; "the cough will not kill me."

"True—true," I replied; "but you should use all proper caution. A draft of this Médoc will defend us from the damps."

Here I knocked off the neck of a bottle which I drew from a long row of its fellows that lay upon the mold. "Drink," I said, presenting him the wine.

He raised it to his lips. "I drink," he said, "to the buried that repose around us."

"And I to your long life."

He again took my arm, and we proceeded.

"These vaults," he said, "are extensive."

"The Montresors were a great and numerous family."

"I forget your arms."

"A huge human foot d'or, in a field azure; the foot crushes a serpent rampant whose fangs are embedded in the heel."

"And the motto?"

"Nemo me impune lacessit." *

The wine sparkled in his eyes and his bells jingled. We had passed through walls of piled bones, with casks and puncheons intermingling, into the inmost recesses of the catacombs.

---

*No one attacks me with impunity.

"We are below the river's bed," I said. "The drops of moisture trickle among the bones." I broke and reached him a flagon of De Grâve. He emptied it at a breath. His eyes flashed with a fierce light. He laughed and threw the bottle upward with a gesticulation I did not understand.

I looked at him in surprise. He repeated the movement.

"You do not comprehend?" he said. "Then you are not of the brotherhood."

"How?"

"You are not of the masons."

"Yes, yes," I said. "Yes, yes."

"You? Impossible! A mason?"

"A mason," I replied.

"A sign," he said. "A sign."

"It is this," I answered, producing a trowel from beneath the folds of my roquelaure.

"You jest," he exclaimed, recoiling a few paces. "But let us proceed to the Amontillado."

"Be it so," I said, replacing the tool beneath the cloak, and offering him my arm. He leaned upon it heavily. We passed through a range of low arches, descended, passed on, and descending again arrived at a deep crypt, in which the foulness of the air caused our flambeaux rather to glow than flame.

At the most remote end of the crypt there appeared another, less spacious. Its walls had been lined with human remains, piled to the vault overhead, in the fashion of the great catacombs of Paris. Three sides of this interior crypt were still ornamented in this manner. From the fourth the bones had been thrown down, and lay promiscuously upon the earth, forming at one point a mound of some size. Within the wall exposed by the displacing of the bones we perceived a still interior recess, in depth about four feet, in width three, in height six. It formed the interval between two of the supports of the roof of the catacombs, and was backed by one of their circumscribing walls of solid granite.

It was in vain that Fortunato, uplifting his dull torch, endeavored to pry into the depth of the recess. Its termination the feeble light did not enable us to see. "Proceed," I said; "herein is the Amontillado. As for Luchesi—"

"He is an ignoramus," interrupted my friend, as he stepped unsteadily forward, while I followed immediately at his heels. In an instant he had reached the extremity of the niche, and, finding his progress arrested by the rock, stood bewildered. A moment more and I had fettered him to the granite. In its surface were two iron staples, distant from each other about two feet, horizontally. From one of these depended a short chain, from the other a padlock. Throwing the links about his waist, it was but the work of a few seconds to secure it. He was too much astounded to resist. Withdrawing the key, I stepped back from the recess.

"Pass your hand," I said, "over the wall. Indeed it is *very* damp. Once more let me *implore* you to return. No? Then I must positively leave you. But I must first render you all the little attentions in my power."

"The Amontillado!" ejaculated my friend, not yet recovered from his astonishment.

"True," I replied; "the Amontillado." As I said this I busied myself among the pile of bones of which I have before spoken. Throwing them aside, I soon uncovered a quantity of building stone and mortar. With these materials and with my trowel, I began vigorously to wall up the entrance of the niche.

I had scarcely laid the first tier of masonry when I discovered that Fortunato's intoxication had in great measure worn off. The earliest indication I had of this was a low moaning cry from the depth of the recess. It was *not* the cry of a drunken man. There was then a long and obstinate silence. I laid the second tier, and the third, and the fourth; and then I heard the furious vibrations of the chain. The noise lasted for several minutes, during which, that I might hearken to it with the more satisfaction, I ceased my labors and sat down upon the bones. When the clanking subsided, I resumed the trowel and finished the fifth, the sixth, and the seventh tier. The wall was now upon a level with my breast. I again paused and, holding the flambeaux over the masonwork, threw a few feeble rays upon the figure within.

A succession of loud and shrill screams burst suddenly from the throat of the chained form. For a brief moment I hesitated—I trembled. Unsheathing my rapier, I began to grope with it about the recess, but the thought of an instant reassured me. I placed my hand upon the solid fabric of the catacombs and felt satisfied. I reapproached the wall. I replied to the yells of him who clamored. I reechoed—I aided—I surpassed them in volume and in strength. I did this, and the clamorer grew still.

It was now midnight, and my task was drawing to a close. I had completed the eighth, the ninth, and the tenth tier. I had finished a portion of the last and the eleventh; there remained but a single stone to be plastered in. I struggled with its weight; I placed it partially in its destined position. But now there came from out the niche a low laugh that erected the hairs upon my head. It was succeeded by a sad voice, which I had difficulty in recognizing as that of the noble Fortunato. The voice said—

"Ha! ha! ha!—he! he! he!—a very good joke indeed—an excellent jest. We will have many a rich laugh about it at the *palazzo*—he! he! he!—over our wine—he! he! he!"

"The Amontillado!" I said.

"He! he! he!—he! he! he!—yes, the Amontillado. But is it not getting late? Will not they be awaiting us at the *palazzo,* the Lady Fortunato and the rest? Let us be gone."

"Yes," I said, "let us be gone."

"For the love of God, Montresor!"

"Yes," I said. "For the love of God!"

But to these words I hearkened in vain for a reply. I grew impatient. I called aloud, "Fortunato!"

No answer. I called again, "Fortunato!"

No answer still. I thrust a torch through the remaining aperture and let it fall within. There came forth in return only a jingling of the bells. My heart grew sick—on account of the dampness of the catacombs. I hastened to make an end of my labor. I forced the last stone into its position; I plastered it up. Against the new masonry I reerected the old rampart of bones. For the half of a century no mortal has disturbed them. *In pace requiescat!*

THE THIRD FLOOR FLAT

AGATHA CHRISTIE

"BOTHER!" SAID PAT.

With a deepening frown she rummaged wildly in the silken trifle she called an evening bag. Two young men and another girl watched her anxiously. They were all standing outside the closed door of Patricia Garnett's flat.

"It's no good," said Pat. "It's not there. And now what shall we do?"

"What is life without a latchkey?" murmured Jimmy Faulkener.

He was a short, broad-shouldered young man, with good-tempered blue eyes.

Pat turned on him angrily.

"Don't make jokes, Jimmy. This is serious."

"Look again, Pat," said Donovan Bailey. "It must be there somewhere."

He had a lazy, pleasant voice that matched his lean, dark figure.

"If you ever brought it out," said the other girl, Mildred Hope.

"Of course I brought it out," said Pat. "I believe I gave it to one of you two." She turned on the men accusingly. "I told Donovan to take it for me."

But she was not to find a scapegoat so easily. Donovan put in a firm disclaimer, and Jimmy backed him up.

"I saw you put it in your bag, myself," said Jimmy.

"Well, then, one of you dropped it out when you picked up my bag. I've dropped it once or twice."

"Once or twice!" said Donovan. "You've dropped it a dozen times at least, besides leaving it behind on every possible occasion."

"I can't see why everything on earth doesn't drop out of it the whole time," said Jimmy.

"The point is—how are we going to get in?" said Mildred.

She was a sensible girl, who kept to the point, but she was not nearly so attractive as the impulsive and troublesome Pat.

All four of them regarded the closed door blankly.

"Couldn't the porter help?" suggested Jimmy. "Hasn't he got a master key or something of that kind?"

Pat shook her head. There were only two keys. One was inside the flat hung up in the kitchen and the other was—or should be—in the maligned bag.

"If only the flat were on the ground floor," wailed Pat. "We could have broken open a window or something. Donovan, you wouldn't like to be a cat burglar, would you?"

Donovan declined firmly but politely to be a cat burglar.

"A flat on the fourth floor is a bit of an undertaking," said Jimmy.

"How about a fire escape?" suggested Donovan.

"There isn't one."

"There should be," said Jimmy. "A building five storeys high ought to have a fire escape."

"I daresay," said Pat. "But what should be doesn't help us. How am I ever to get into my flat?"

"Isn't there a sort of thingummybob?" said Donovan. "A thing the tradesmen send up chops and Brussels sprouts in?"

"The service lift," said Pat. "Oh, yes, but it's only a sort of wire-basket thing. Oh! wait—I know. What about the coal lift?"

"Now that," said Donovan, "is an idea."

Mildred made a discouraging suggestion.

"It'll be bolted," she said. "In Pat's kitchen, I mean, on the inside."

But the idea was instantly negatived.

"Don't you believe it," said Donovan.

"Not in *Pat's* kitchen," said Jimmy. "Pat never locks and bolts things."

"I don't think it's bolted," said Pat. "I took the dust-bin off this morning, and I'm sure I never bolted it afterwards, and I don't think I've been near it since."

"Well," said Donovan, "that fact's going to be very useful to us to-night, but, all the same, young Pat, let me point out to you that these slack habits are leaving you at the mercy of burglars (non-feline) every night."

Pat disregarded these admonitions.

"Come on," she cried, and began racing down the four flights of stairs. The others followed her. Pat led them through a dark recess, apparently full to overflowing of perambulators, and through another door into the well of the flats, and guided them to the right lift. There was, at the moment, a dust-bin on it. Donovan lifted it off and stepped gingerly onto the platform in its place. He wrinkled up his nose.

"A little noisome," he remarked. "But what of that? Do I go alone on this venture or is anyone coming with me?"

"I'll come, too," said Jimmy.

He stepped on by Donovan's side.

"I suppose the lift will bear me," he added, doubtfully.

"You can't weigh much more than a ton of coal," said Pat, who had never been particularly strong on her weights-and-measures table.

"And anyway, we shall soon find out," said Donovan cheerfully, as he hauled on the rope.

With a grinding noise they disappeared from sight.

"This thing makes an awful noise," remarked Jimmy, as they passed up through blackness. "What will the people in the other flats think?"

"Ghosts or burglars, I expect," said Donovan. "Hauling this rope is quite heavy work. The porter of Friars Mansions does more work than I ever suspected. I say, Jimmy, old son, are you counting the floors?"

"Oh, Lord! no. I forgot about it."

"Well, I have, which is just as well. That's the third we're passing now. The next is ours."

"And now, I suppose," grumbled Jimmy, "we shall find that Pat did bolt the door after all."

But these fears were unfounded. The wooden door swung back at a touch and Donovan and Jimmy stepped out into the inky blackness of Pat's kitchen.

"We ought to have a torch for this wild night work," explained Donovan. "If I know Pat, everything's on the floor, and we shall smash endless crockery before I can get to the light switch. Don't move about, Jimmy, till I get the light on."

He felt his way cautiously over the floor, uttering one fervent "Damn!" as a corner of the kitchen table took him unawares in the ribs. He reached the switch, and in another moment another "Damn!" floated out of the darkness.

"What's the matter?" asked Jimmy.

"Light won't come on. Dud bulb, I suppose. Wait a minute. I'll turn the sitting-room light on."

The sitting-room was the door immediately across the passage. Jimmy heard Donovan go out of the door, and presently fresh muffled curses reached him. He himself edged his way cautiously across the kitchen.

"What's the matter?"

"I don't know. Rooms get bewitched at night, I believe. Everything seems to be in a different place. Chairs and tables where you least expected it. Oh, hell! here's another!"

But at this moment Jimmy fortunately connected with the electric-light switch and pressed it down. In another minute two young men were looking at each other in silent horror.

This room was not Pat's sitting-room. They were in the wrong flat.

To begin with, the room was about ten times more crowded than Pat's which explained Donovan's pathetic bewilderment at repeatedly cannoning into chairs and tables. There was a large round table in the centre of the room covered with a baize cloth, and there was an aspidistra in the window. It was, in fact, the kind of room whose owner, the young man felt sure, would be difficult to explain to. With silent horror they gazed down at the table, on which lay a little pile of letters.

"Mrs. Ernestine Grant," breathed Donovan, picking them up and reading the name. "Oh! help. Do you think she's heard us?"

"It's a miracle she hasn't heard you," said Jimmy. "What with your language and the way you've been crashing into the furniture. Come on, for the Lord's sake, let's get out of here quickly."

They hastily switched off the light and retraced their steps on tip-toe to the lift. Jimmy breathed a sigh of relief as they regained the fastness of its depths without further incident.

"I do like a woman to be a good, sound sleeper," he said approvingly. "Mrs. Ernestine Grant has her points."

"I see it now," said Donovan; "why we made the mistake in the floor, I mean. Out in that well we started up from the basement." He heaved on the rope, and the lift shot up. "We're right this time."

"I devoutly trust we are," said Jimmy, as he stepped out into another inky void. "My nerves won't stand many more shocks of this kind."

But no further nerve strain was imposed. The first click of the light showed them Pat's kitchen, and in another minute they were opening the front door and admitting the two girls who were waiting outside.

"You have been a long time," grumbled Pat. "Mildred and I have been waiting here ages."

"We've had an adventure," said Donovan. "We might have been hauled off to the police station as dangerous malefactors."

Pat had passed on into the sitting-room, where she switched on the light and dropped her wrap on the sofa. She listened with lively interest to Donovan's account of his adventures.

"I'm glad she didn't catch you," she commented. "I'm sure she's an old curmudgeon. I got a note from her this morning—wanted to see me sometime—something she had to complain about—my piano, I suppose. People who don't like pianos over their heads shouldn't come and live in flats. I say, Donovan, you've hurt your hand. It's all over blood. Go and wash it under the tap."

Donovan looked down at his hand in surprise. He went out of the room obediently and presently his voice called to Jimmy.

"Hullo," said the other, "what's up? You haven't hurt yourself badly, have you?"

"I haven't hurt myself at all."

There was something so queer in Donovan's voice that Jimmy stared at him in surprise. Donovan held out his washed hand and Jimmy saw that there was no mark or cut of any kind on it.

"That's odd," he said, frowning. "There was quite a lot of blood. Where did it come from?"

And then, suddenly, he realised what his quicker-witted friend had already seen.

"By Jove," he said. "It must have come from that flat."

He stopped, thinking over the possibilities his words implied.

"You're sure it was—er—blood?" he said. "Not paint?"

Donovan shook his head.

"It was blood, all right," he said, and shivered.

They looked at each other. The same thought was clearly in each of their minds. It was Jimmy who voiced it first.

"I say," he said awkwardly. "Do you think we ought to—well—go down again—and have—a—a look around? See it's all right, you know?"

"What about the girls?"

"We won't say anything to them. Pat's going to put on an apron and make us an omelet. We'll be back by the time they wonder where we are."

"Oh, well, come on," said Donovan. "I suppose we've got to go through with it. I daresay there isn't anything really wrong."

But his tone lacked conviction. They got into the lift and descended to the floor below. They found their way across the kitchen without much difficulty and once more switched on the sitting-room light.

"It must have been in here," said Donovan, "that—that I got the stuff on me. I never touched anything in the kitchen."

He looked round him. Jimmy did the same, and they both frowned. Everything looked neat and commonplace and miles removed from any suggestion of violence or gore.

Suddenly Jimmy started violently and caught his companion's arm.

"Look!"

Donovan followed the pointing finger, and in his turn uttered an exclamation. From beneath the heavy rep curtains there protruded a foot—a woman's foot in a gaping patent-leather shoe.

Jimmy went to the curtains and drew them sharply apart. In the recess of the window a woman's huddled body lay on the floor, a sticky dark pool beside it. She was dead, there was no doubt of that.

Jimmy was attempting to raise her up when Donovan stopped him.

"You'd better not do that. She oughtn't to be touched till the police come."

"The police. Oh! of course. I say, Donovan, what a ghastly business. Who do you think she is? Mrs. Ernestine Grant?"

"Looks like it. At any rate, if there's anyone else in the flat they're keeping jolly quiet."

"What do we do next?" asked Jimmy. "Run out and get a policeman or ring up from Pat's flat?"

"I should think ringing up would be best. Come on, we might as well go out the front door. We can't spend the whole night going up and down in that evil-smelling lift."

Jimmy agreed. Just as they were passing through the door he hesitated.

"Look here; do you think one of us ought to stay—just to keep an eye on things—till the police come?"

"Yes, I think you're right. If you'll stay I'll run up and telephone."

He ran quickly up the stairs and rang the bell of the flat above. Pat came to open it, a very pretty Pat with a flushed face and a cooking apron on. Her eyes widened in surprise.

"You? But how—Donovan, what is it? Is anything the matter?"

He took both her hands in his.

"It's all right, Pat—only we've made rather an unpleasant discovery in the flat below. A woman—dead."

"Oh!" She gave a little gasp. "How horrible. Has she had a fit or something?"

"No. It looks—well—it looks rather as though she had been murdered."

"Oh! Donovan."

"I know. It's pretty beastly."

Her hands were still in his. She had left them there—was even clinging to him. Darling Pat—how he loved her. Did she care at all for him! Sometimes he thought she did. Sometimes he was afraid that Jimmy Faulkener—remembrances of Jimmy waiting patiently below made him start guiltily.

"Pat, dear, we must telephone to the police."

"Monsieur is right," said a voice behind him. "And in the meantime, while we are waiting their arrival, perhaps I can be of some slight assistance."

They had been standing in the doorway of the flat, and now they peered out on to the landing. A figure was standing on the stairs a little way above them. It moved down and into their range of vision.

They stood staring at a little man with very fierce moustaches and an egg-shaped head. He wore a resplendent dressing-gown and embroidered slippers. He bowed gallantly to Patricia.

"Mademoiselle!" he said. "I am, as perhaps you know, the tenant of the flat above. I like to be up high—the air—the view over London. I take the flat in the name of Mr. O'Connor. But I am not an Irishman. I have another name. That is why I venture to put myself at your service. Permit me."

With a flourish he pulled out a card and handed it to Pat. She read it.

"M. Hercule Poirot. Oh!" She caught her breath. "*The* M. Poirot? The great detective? And you will really help?"

"That is my intention, Mademoiselle. I nearly offered my help earlier in the evening."

Pat looked puzzled.

"I heard you discussing how to gain admission to your flat. Me, I am very clever at picking locks. I could without doubt have opened your door for you, but I hesitated to suggest it. You would have had the grave suspicions of me."

Pat laughed.

"Now, Monsieur," said Poirot to Donovan. "Go in, I pray of you, and telephone to the police. I will descend to the flat below."

Pat came down the stairs with him. They found Jimmy on guard and Pat explained Poirot's presence. Jimmy, in his turn, explained to Poirot his and Donovan's adventures. The detective listened attentively.

"The lift door was unbolted, you say? You emerged into the kitchen, but the light it would not turn on."

He directed his footsteps to the kitchen as he spoke. His fingers pressed the switch.

"Tiens! Voilà ce qui est curieux!" he said as the light flashed on. "It functions perfectly now. I wonder—"

He held up a finger to ensure silence and listened. A faint sound broke the stillness—the sound of an unmistakable snore.

"Ah!" said Poirot. *"La chambre de domestique."*

He tiptoed across the kitchen into a little pantry, out of which led a door. He opened the door and switched on the light. The room was the kind of dog-kennel designed by the builders of flats to accommodate a human being. The floor space was almost entirely occupied by the bed. In the bed was a rosy-cheeked girl lying on her back with her mouth wide open snoring placidly.

Poirot switched off the light and beat a retreat.

"She will not wake," he said. "We will let her sleep till the police come."

He went back to the sitting room. Donovan had joined them.

"The police will be here almost immediately, they say," he said breathlessly. "We are to touch nothing."

Poirot nodded.

"We will not touch," he said. "We will look, that is all."

He moved into the room. Mildred had come down with Donovan, and all four young people stood in the doorway and watched him with breathless interest.

"What I can't understand, sir, is this," said Donovan. "I never went near the window—how did the blood come on my hand?"

"My young friend, the answer to that stares you in the face. Of what colour is the tablecloth? Red, is it not? and doubtless you did put your hand on the table."

"Yes, I did. Is that—" He stopped.

Poirot nodded. He was bending over the table. He indicated with his hand a dark patch on the red.

"It was here that the crime was committed," he said solemnly. "The body was moved afterwards."

Then he stood upright and looked slowly round the room. He did not move, he handled nothing, but nevertheless the four watching felt as though every object in that rather frowsty place gave up its secret to his observant eye.

Hercule Poirot nodded his head as though satisfied. A little sigh escaped him.

"I see," he said.

"You see what?" asked Donovan curiously.

"I see," said Poirot, "what you doubtless felt—that the room is overfull of furniture."

Donovan smiled ruefully.

"I did go barging about a bit," he confessed. "Of course, everything was in a different place to Pat's room, and I couldn't make it out."

"Not everything," said Poirot.

Donovan looked at him inquiringly.

"I mean," said Poirot apologetically, "that certain things are always fixed. In a block of flats the door, the window, the fireplace—they are in the same place in the rooms which are below each other."

"Isn't that rather splitting hairs?" asked Mildred. She was looking at Poirot with faint disapproval.

"One should always speak with absolute accuracy. That is a little—how do you say?—fad of mine."

There was the noise of footsteps on the stairs, and three men came in. They were a police inspector, a constable, and the divisional surgeon. The Inspector recognised Poirot and greeted him in an almost reverential manner. Then he turned to the others.

"I shall want statements from everyone," he began, "but in the first place—"

Poirot interrupted.

"A little suggestion. We will go back to the flat upstairs and Mademoiselle here shall do what she was planning to do—make us an omelet. Me, I have a passion for the omelets. Then, M. l'Inspecteur, when you have finished here, you will mount to us and ask questions at your leisure."

It was arranged accordingly, and Poirot went up with them.

"M. Poirot," said Pat, "I think you're a perfect dear. And you shall have a lovely omelet. I really make omelets frightfully well."

"That is good. Once, Mademoiselle, I loved a beautiful young English girl, who resembled you greatly—but alas! she could not cook. So perhaps everything was for the best."

There was a faint sadness in his voice, and Jimmy Faulkener looked at him curiously.

Once in the flat, however, he exerted himself to please and amuse. The grim tragedy below was almost forgotten.

The omelet had been consumed and duly praised by the time that Inspector Rice's footsteps were heard. He came in accompanied by the doctor, having left the constable below.

"Well, Monsieur Poirot," he said. "It all seems clear and aboveboard—not much in your line, though we may find it hard to catch the man. I'd just like to hear how the discovery came to be made."

Donovan and Jimmy between them recounted the happenings of the evening. The Inspector turned reproachfully to Pat.

"You shouldn't leave your lift door unbolted, Miss. You really shouldn't."

"I shan't again," said Pat, with a shiver. "Somebody might come in and murder me like that poor woman below."

"Ah! but they didn't come in that way, though," said the Inspector.

"You will recount to us what you have discovered, yes?" said Poirot.

"I don't know as I ought to—but seeing it's you, M. Poirot. . . ."

"Précisément," said Poirot. "And these young people—they will be discreet."

"The newspapers will get hold of it, anyway, soon enough," said the Inspector. "There's no real secret about the matter. Well, the dead woman's Mrs. Grant, all right. I had the porter up to identify her. Woman of about thirty-five. She was sitting at the table, and she was shot with an automatic pistol of small calibre, probably by someone sitting opposite her at table. She fell forward, and that's how the bloodstain came on the table."

"But wouldn't someone have heard the shot?" asked Mildred.

"The pistol was fitted with a silencer. No, you wouldn't hear anything. By the way, did you hear the screech the maid let out when we told her her mistress was dead? No. Well, that just shows how unlikely it was that anyone would hear the other."

"Has the maid no story to tell?" asked Poirot.

"It was her evening out. She's got her own key. She came in about ten o'clock. Everything was quiet. She thought her mistress had gone to bed."

"She did not look in the sitting-room, then?"

"Yes, she took the letters in there which had come by the evening post, but she saw nothing unusual—any more than Mr. Faulkener and Mr. Bailey did. You see, the murderer had concealed the body rather neatly behind the curtains."

"But it was a curious thing to do, don't you think?"

Poirot's voice was very gentle, yet it held something that made the Inspector look up quickly.

"Didn't want the crime discovered till he'd had time to make his getaway."

"Perhaps—perhaps—but continue with what you were saying."

"The maid went out at five o'clock. The doctor here puts the time of death as—roughly—about four to five hours ago. That's right, isn't it?"

The doctor, who was a man of few words, contented himself with jerking his head affirmatively.

"It's a quarter to twelve now. The actual time can, I think, be narrowed down to a fairly definite hour."

He took out a crumpled sheet of paper.

"We found this in the pocket of the dead woman's dress. You needn't be afraid of handling it. There are no fingerprints on it."

Poirot smoothed out the sheet. Across it some words were printed in small prim capitals.

I WILL COME TO SEE YOU THIS EVENING AT HALF-PAST SEVEN.—J.F.

"A compromising document to leave behind," commented Poirot, as he handed it back.

"Well, he didn't know she'd got it in her pocket," said the Inspector. "He probably thought she'd destroyed it. We've evidence that he was a careful man, though. The pistol she was shot with we found under the body—and there again no fingerprints. They'd been wiped off very carefully with a silk handkerchief."

"How do you know," said Poirot, "that it was a silk handkerchief?"

"Because we found it," said the Inspector triumphantly. "At the last, as he was drawing the curtains, he must have let it fall unnoticed."

He handed across a big white silk handkerchief—a good-quality handkerchief. It did not need the Inspector's finger to draw Poirot's attention to the mark on it in the centre. It was neatly marked and quite legible. Poirot read the name out.

"John Fraser."

"That's it," said the Inspector. "John Fraser—J.F. in the note. We know the name of the man we have to look for, and I daresay when we find out a little about the dead woman, and her relations come forward, we shall soon get a line on him."

"I wonder," said Poirot. "No, *mon cher*, somehow I do not think he will be easy to find, your John Fraser. He is a strange man—careful, since he marks his handkerchiefs and wipes the pistol with which he has committed the crime—yet careless since he loses his handkerchief and does not search for a letter that might incriminate him."

"Flurried, that's what he was," said the Inspector.

"It is possible," said Poirot. "Yes, it is possible. And he was not seen entering the building?"

"There are all sorts of people going in and out at that time. These are big blocks. I suppose none of you"—he addressed the four collectively—"saw anyone coming out of the flat?"

Pat shook her head.

"We went out earlier—about seven o'clock."

"I see." The Inspector rose. Poirot accompanied him to the door.

"As a little favour, may I examine the flat below?"

"Why, certainly, M. Poirot. I know what they think of you at headquarters. I'll leave you a key. I've got two. It will be empty. The maid cleared out to some relatives, too scared to stay there alone."

"I thank you," said M. Poirot. He went back into the flat thoughtful.

"You're not satisfied, M. Poirot?" said Jimmy.

"No," said Poirot. "I am not satisfied."

Donovan looked at him curiously. "What is it that—well, worries you?"

Poirot did not answer. He remained silent for a minute or two, frowning, as though in thought, then he made a sudden impatient movement of shoulders.

"I will say good-night to you, Mademoiselle. You must be tired. You have had much cooking to do—eh?"

Pat laughed.

"Only the omelet. I didn't do dinner. Donovan and Jimmy came and called for us, and we went out to a little place in Soho."

"And then without doubt, you went to a theatre?"

"Yes. *The Brown Eyes of Caroline.*"

"Ah!" said Poirot. "It should have been blue eyes—the blue eyes of Mademoiselle."

He made a sentimental gesture, and then once more wished Pat good-night, also Mildred, who was staying the night by special request, as Pat admitted frankly that she would get the horrors if left alone on this particular night.

The two young men accompanied Poirot. When the door was shut, and they were preparing to say good-bye to him on the landing, Poirot forestalled them.

"My young friends, you heard me say that I was not satisfied? *Eh bien*, it is true—I am not. I go now to make some little investigations of my own. You would like to accompany me—yes?"

An eager assent greeted this proposal. Poirot led the way to the flat below and inserted the key the Inspector had given him in the lock. On entering, he did not, as the others had expected, enter the sitting-room. Instead he went straight to the kitchen. In a little recess which served as a scullery a big iron bin was standing. Poirot uncovered this, and doubling himself up, began to rootle in it with the energy of a ferocious terrier.

Both Jimmy and Donovan stared at him in amazement.

Suddenly with a cry of triumph he emerged. In his hand he held aloft a small stoppered bottle.

"Voilà!" he said. "I find what I seek."

He sniffed at it delicately.

"Alas! I am *enrhumé*—I have the cold in the head."

Donovan took the bottle from him and sniffed in his turn, but could smell nothing. He took out the stopper and held the bottle to his nose before Poirot's warning cry could stop him.

Immediately he fell like a log. Poirot, by springing forward, partly broke his fall.

"Imbecile!" he cried. "The idea. To remove the stopper in that foolhardy manner! Did he not observe how delicately I handled it? Monsieur—Faulkener—is it not? Will you be so good as to get me a little brandy? I observed a decanter in the sitting-room."

Jimmy hurried off, but by the time he returned, Donovan was sitting up and declaring himself quite all right again. He had to listen to a short lecture from Poirot on the necessity of caution in sniffing at possibly poisonous substances.

"I think I'll be off home," said Donovan, rising shakily to his feet. "That is, if I can't be any more use here. I feel a bit wonky still."

"Assuredly," said Poirot. "That is the best thing you can do. M. Faulkener, attend me here a little minute. I will return on the instant."

He accompanied Donovan to the door and beyond. They remained outside on the landing talking for some minutes. When Poirot at last re-entered the flat he found Jimmy standing in the sitting-room gazing round him with puzzled eyes.

"Well, M. Poirot," he said, "what next?"

"There is nothing next. The case is finished."

"What?"

"I know everything—now."

Jimmy stared at him.

"That little bottle you found?"

"Exactly. That little bottle."

Jimmy shook his head.

"I can't make head or tail of it. For some reason or other I can see you are dissatisfied with the evidence against this John Fraser, whoever he may be."

"Whoever he may be," repeated Poirot softly. "If he is anyone at all—well, I shall be surprised."

"I don't understand."

"He is a name—that is all—a name carefully marked on a handkerchief!"

"And the letter?"

"Did you notice that it was printed? Now why? I will tell you. Handwriting might be recognised, and a typewritten letter is more easily traced than you would imagine—but if a real John Fraser wrote that letter those two points would not have appealed to him! No, it was written on purpose, and put in the dead woman's pocket for us to find. There is no such person as John Fraser."

Jimmy looked at him inquiringly.

"And so," went on Poirot, "I went back to the point that first struck me. You heard me say that certain things in a room were always in the same place under given circumstances. I gave three instances. I might have mentioned a fourth—the electric-light switch, my friend."

Jimmy still stared uncomprehendingly. Poirot went on.

"Your friend Donovan did not go near the window—it was by resting his hand on this table that he got it covered in blood! But I asked myself at once—why did he rest it there? What was he doing groping about this room in darkness? For remember, my friend, the electric-light switch is always in the same place—by the door. Why, when he came to this room, did he not at once feel for the light and turn it on? That was the natural, the normal thing to do. According to him, he tried to turn on the light in the kitchen, but failed. Yet when I tried the switch it was in perfect working order. Did he, then, not wish the light to go on just then? If it had gone on you would both have seen at once that you were in the wrong flat. There would have been no reason to come into this room."

"What are you driving at, M. Poirot? I don't understand. What do you mean?"

"I mean—this."

Poirot held up a Yale door-key.

"The key of this flat?"

"No, *mon ami*, the key of the flat above. Mademoiselle Patricia's key, which M. Donovan Bailey abstracted from her bag some time during the evening."

"But why—why?"

"*Parbleu!* so that he could do what he wanted to do—gain admission to this flat in a perfectly unsuspicious manner. He made sure that the lift door was unbolted earlier in the evening."

"Where did you get the key?"

Poirot's smile broadened.

"I found it just now—where I looked for it—in M. Donovan's pocket. See you, that little bottle I pretended to find was a ruse. M. Donovan is taken in. He does what I knew he would do—unstoppers it and sniffs. And in that little bottle is Ethyl Chloride, a very powerful instant anaesthetic. It gives me just the moment or two of unconsciousness I need. I take from his pocket the two things that I knew would be there. This key was one of them—the other—"

He stopped and then went on:

"I questioned at the time the reason the Inspector gave for the body being concealed behind the curtain. To gain time? No, there was more than that. And so I thought of just one thing—the post, my friend. The evening post that comes at half-past nine or thereabouts. Say the murderer does not find something he expects to find, but that something may be delivered by post later. Clearly, then, he must come back. But the crime must not be discovered by the maid when she comes in, or the police would take possession of the flat, so he hides the body behind the curtain. And the maid suspects nothing and lays the letters on the table as usual."

"The letters?"

"Yes, the letters." Poirot drew something from his pocket.

"This is the second article I took from M. Donovan when he was unconscious." He showed the superscription—a typewritten envelope addressed to Mrs. Ernestine Grant. "But I will ask you one thing first, M. Faulkener, before we look at the contents of this letter. Are you or are you not in love with Mademoiselle Patricia?"

"I care for Pat damnably—but I've never thought I had a chance."

"You thought that she cared for M. Donovan? It may be that she had begun to care for him—but it was only a beginning, my friend. It is for you to make her forget—to stand by her in her trouble."

"Trouble?" said Jimmy sharply.

"Yes, trouble. We will do all we can to keep her name out of it, but it will be impossible to do so entirely. She was, you see, the motive."

He ripped open the envelope that he held. An enclosure fell out. The covering letter was brief, and was from a firm of solicitors.

Dear Madam,

The document you enclose is quite in order, and the fact of the marriage having taken place in a foreign country does not invalidate it in any way.

Yours truly, etc.

Poirot spread out the enclosure. It was a certificate of marriage between Donovan Bailey and Ernestine Grant, dated eight years ago.

"Oh, my God!" said Jimmy. "Pat said she'd had a letter from the woman asking to see her, but she never dreamed it was anything important."

Poirot nodded.

"M. Donovan knew—he went to see his wife this evening before going to the flat above (a strange irony, by the way, that led the unfortunate woman to come to this building where her rival lived)—he murdered her in cold blood—and then went on to his evening's amusement. His wife must have told him that she had sent the marriage certificate to her solicitors, and was expecting to hear from them. Doubtless he himself had tried to make her believe that there was a flaw in the marriage."

"He seemed in quite good spirits, too, all the evening. M. Poirot, you haven't let him escape?" Jimmy shuddered.

"There is no escape for him," said Poirot gravely. "You need not fear."

"It's Pat I'm thinking about mostly," said Jimmy. "You don't think—she really cared."

"*Mon ami*, that is your part," said Poirot gently. "To make her turn to you and forget. I do not think you will find it very difficult!"

THE MAN WHO LIKED DICKENS

EVELYN WAUGH

ALTHOUGH MR. MCMASTER had lived in Amazonas for nearly sixty years, no one except a few families of Shirianá Indians was aware of his existence. His house stood in a small savanna, one of those little patches of sand and grass that crop up occasionally in that neighborhood, three miles or so across, bounded on all sides by forest.

The stream which watered it was not marked on any map; it ran through rapids, always dangerous and at most seasons impassable, to join the upper waters of the river Uraricoera, whose course, though boldly delineated in every atlas, is still largely conjectural. None of the inhabitants of the district, except Mr. McMaster, had ever heard of the republics of Colombia, Venezuela, Brazil, or Bolivia, each of whom had at one time or another claimed its possession.

Mr. McMaster's house was larger than those of his neighbors, but similar in character—a palm-thatch roof, breast-high walls of mud and wattle, and a mud floor. He owned a dozen or so head of puny cattle which grazed in the savanna, a plantation of cassava, some banana and mango trees, a dog, and, unique in the neighborhood, a single-barreled, breech-loading shotgun. The few commodities which he employed from the outside world came to him through a long succession of traders, passed from hand to hand, bartered for in a dozen languages at the extreme end of one of the longest threads in the web of commerce that spreads from Manaus into the remote fastness of the forest.

One day, while Mr. McMaster was engaged in filling a cartridge, a Shirianá came to him with the news that a white man was approaching through the forest, alone and very sick. He closed the cartridge, loaded his gun with it, and set out in the direction indicated.

Mr. McMaster found the man sitting on the ground, clearly in a bad way. He was without hat or boots, and his clothes were badly torn; his feet were cut and swollen; every exposed surface of skin was scarred by insect and bat bites; his eyes were wild with fever. He was talking to himself in delirium, but stopped when Mr. McMaster approached and addressed him in English.

"I'm tired," the man said; then: "Can't go on any farther. Anderson died. That was a long time ago."

"You are ill, my friend."

"It must be several months since I had anything to eat."

Mr. McMaster hoisted him to his feet and, supporting him by the arm, led him across the hummocks of grass toward the farm. "It is a very short way. When we get there I will give you something to make you better."

"Jolly kind of you." Presently he said, "I say, you speak English. I'm English, too. My name is Henty."

"Well, Mr. Henty, you aren't to bother about anything more. I'll take care of you."

They went very slowly, but at length reached the house.

"Lie in the hammock. I will fetch something for you."

Mr. McMaster went into the back room of the house and dragged a tin canister from under a heap of skins. It was full of a mixture of dried leaf and bark. He took a handful and went outside to the fire. When he returned he put one hand behind Henty's head and held up the concoction of herbs in a calabash for him to drink. He sipped, shuddering slightly at the bitterness. At last he finished it. Mr. McMaster threw out the dregs on the floor. Henty lay back in the hammock, sobbing quietly. Soon he fell into a deep sleep.

"Ill fated" was the epithet applied by the press to the Anderson expedition to the Parima and upper Uraricoera region of Brazil. Every stage of the enterprise was attacked by misfortune. It was due to one of the early setbacks that Paul Henty became connected with it.

He was not by nature an explorer; an even-tempered, good-looking young man of fastidious tastes and enviable possessions, unintellectual but appreciative of fine architecture and the ballet, well traveled in the more accessible parts of the world, a collector though not a connoisseur, popular among hostesses, revered by his aunts. He was married to a lady of exceptional charm and beauty, and it was she who upset the good order of his life by confessing her affection for another man for the second time in the eight years of their marriage. The first occasion had been a short-lived infatuation with a tennis professional, the second was a captain in the Coldstream Guards, and more serious.

Henty's first thought under the shock of this revelation was to go out and dine alone. He was a member of four clubs, but at three of them he was liable to meet his wife's lover. Accordingly he chose one which he rarely frequented, a semi-intellectual company composed of publishers, barristers, and men of scholarship.

Here he fell into conversation with Professor Anderson and heard of the proposed expedition to Brazil. The misfortune that was retarding arrangements was defalcation of the secretary with two thirds of the expedition's capital. The principals were ready—Professor Anderson, Dr. Simmons the anthropologist, Mr. Necher the biologist, Mr. Brough the surveyor, wireless operator, and mechanic. The scientific and sporting apparatus was packed in crates ready to be embarked, but unless twelve hundred pounds was forthcoming the whole thing would have to be abandoned.

Henty, as has been suggested, was a man of comfortable means; the expedition would last from nine months to a year; he could shut his country house—his wife, he reflected, would want to remain in London near her young man—and cover more than the sum required. There was a glamour about the whole journey which might, he felt, move even his wife's sympathies. There and then he decided to accompany Professor Anderson.

When he went home that evening he announced to his wife, "I have decided what I shall do."

"Yes, darling?"

"You are certain that you no longer love me?"

"*Darling*, you *know*, I *adore* you."

"But you love this guardsman, Tony what's-his-name, more?"

"Oh, yes, *ever* so much more. Quite a different thing."

"Very well, then. I do not propose to do anything about a divorce for a year. You shall have time to think it over. I am leaving next week for the Uraricoera."

"Golly, where's that?"

"In Brazil, I think. It is unexplored. I shall be away a year."

"But darling, how ordinary! Like people in books—big game, I mean, and all that."

"You have obviously already discovered that I am a very ordinary person."

"Now, Paul—oh, there's the telephone. It's probably Tony. D'you mind terribly if I talk to him alone for a bit?"

But in the ten days of preparation that followed she showed greater tenderness, putting off her soldier twice in order to accompany Henty to the shops where he was choosing his equipment. On his last evening she gave a supper party for him at the embassy to which she allowed him to ask any of his friends he liked; he could think of no one except Professor Anderson, who looked oddly dressed, danced tirelessly, and was something of a failure with everyone. Next day Mrs. Henty came with her husband to the boat train and presented him with a pale blue, extravagantly soft blanket, in a suede case of the same color furnished with a zip fastener and monogram. She kissed him good-by and said, "Take care of yourself in wherever it is."

Had she gone as far as Southampton she might have witnessed two dramatic passages. Mr. Brough got no farther than the gangway before he was arrested for a debt—a matter of thirty-two pounds; the publicity given to the dangers of the expedition was responsible for the action. Henty settled the account.

The second difficulty was not to be overcome so easily. Mr. Necher's mother was on the ship before them; she carried a missionary journal in which she had just read an account of the Brazilian forests. Nothing would induce her to permit her son's departure; she would remain on board until he came ashore with her. If necessary, she would sail with him, but go into those forests alone he should not. All argument was unavailing with the resolute old lady, who eventually bore her son off in triumph, leaving the company without a biologist.

Nor was Mr. Brough's adherence long maintained. The ship in which they were traveling was a cruising liner taking passengers on a round-trip voyage. Mr. Brough had not been on board a week before he was engaged to be married; he was still engaged, although to a different lady, when they reached Manaus and refused all inducements to proceed farther, borrowing his return fare from Henty and arriving back in Southampton engaged to the lady of his first choice, whom he immediately married.

In Brazil the officials to whom their credentials were addressed were all out of power. While Henty and Professor Anderson negotiated with the new administrators, Dr. Simmons proceeded upriver to Boa Vista, where he established a base camp with the greater part of the stores. These were instantly commandeered by the revolutionary garrison and he himself imprisoned for some days and subjected to various humiliations, which so enraged him that, when released, he made promptly for the coast, stopping at Manaus only long enough to inform his colleagues that he insisted on leaving his case personally before the central authorities at Rio.

Thus Henty and Professor Anderson found themselves alone and deprived of the greater part of their supplies. The ignominy of immediate return was not to be borne. For a short time they considered the advisability of going into hiding for six months in Madeira or Tenerife, but even there detection seemed probable; there had been too many photographs in the illustrated papers before they left London. Accordingly, in low spirits, the two explorers set out alone for the Uraricoera with little hope of accomplishing anything of any value.

For seven weeks they paddled through green, humid tunnels of forest. They took a few snapshots of naked, misanthropic Indians, bottled some snakes, and later lost them when their canoe capsized in the rapids; they overtaxed their digestions, imbibing nauseous intoxicants at native galas; they were robbed of their last sugar by a Guianese prospector. Finally, Professor Anderson fell ill with malignant malaria, chattered feebly for some days in his hammock, lapsed into a coma, and died, leaving Henty alone with a dozen Macú oarsmen, none of whom spoke a word of any language known to him. They reversed their course and drifted downstream with a minimum of provisions and no mutual confidence.

One day, a week or so after Professor Anderson's death, Henty awoke to find that his boys and his canoe had disappeared during the night, leaving him some two or three hundred miles from the nearest Brazilian habitation. He set himself to follow the course of the stream, at first in the hope of meeting a canoe. But presently the whole forest became peopled for him with frantic apparitions. He plodded on, now wading in the water, now scrambling through the bush.

Vaguely he had always believed that the jungle was a place full of food, that there was danger of snakes and savages and wild beasts, but not of starvation. Now he observed that the jungle consisted solely of immense tree trunks, embedded in a tangle of thorn and vine rope, all far from nutritious. On the first day he suffered hideously. Later he seemed anesthetized and was chiefly embarrassed by the behavior of the inhabitants, who came out to meet him in footmen's livery, carrying his dinner, and then irresponsibly disappeared or raised the covers of their dishes and revealed live tortoises. Many people who knew him in London appeared and ran around him with derisive cries, asking him questions to which he could not possibly know the answers. His wife came and he was pleased to see her, assuming that she had got tired of her guardsman and was there to fetch him back, but she, too, soon disappeared.

It was then he remembered that it was imperative for him to reach Manaus; he redoubled his energy, stumbling against boulders in the stream and getting caught up among the vines. He was conscious of nothing more until he found himself lying in a hammock in Mr. McMaster's house.

His recovery was slow. At first, days of lucidity alternated with delirium; then his temperature dropped and he was conscious even when most ill. Mr. McMaster dosed him regularly with herbal remedies.

"It's very nasty," said Henty, "but it does do good."

"There are medicines for everything in the forest," said Mr. McMaster. "My mother was an Indian and she taught me many of them. I have learned others from time to time from my wives. There are plants to cure you and give you fever, to kill you and send you mad, to keep away snakes, to intoxicate fish so that you can pick them out of the water with your hands. There are medicines even I do not know. They say that it is possible to bring dead people to life after they have begun to stink, but I have not seen it done."

"But surely you are English?"

"My father was—at least a Barbadian. He came to British Guiana as a missionary. He was married to a white woman, but he left her in Guiana to look for gold. Then he took my mother. The Shirianá women are ugly but very devoted. I have had many. Most of the men and women living in this savanna are my children. That is why they obey—for that reason and because I have the gun. My father lived to a great age. It is not twenty years since he died. He was a man of education. Can you read?"

"Yes, of course."

"It is not everyone who is so fortunate. I cannot. But I have a great many books. I will show you when you are better. Until five years ago there was an Englishman—a black man, but he was well educated in Georgetown. He used to read to me every day until he died. You shall read to me when you are better."

"I shall be delighted to."

During his convalescence Henty lay in the hammock staring up at the thatched roof and thinking about his wife, rehearsing over and over again different incidents in their life together, including her affairs with the tennis professional and the soldier. The days, exactly twelve hours each, passed without distinction. Mr. McMaster retired to sleep at sundown, leaving a little lamp burning—a handwoven wick drooping from a pot of beef fat—to keep away vampire bats.

The first time that Henty left the house Mr. McMaster took him for a little stroll around the farm.

"I will show you the black man's grave," he said, leading him to a mound among the mango trees. "He was very kind to me. Every afternoon until he died, for two hours, he used to read to me. I think I will put up a cross—to commemorate his death and your arrival—a pretty idea. Do you believe in God?"

"I've never really thought about it much."

"You are perfectly right. I have thought about it a *great* deal and I still do not know. . . . Dickens did. It is apparent in all his books. You will see."

That afternoon Mr. McMaster began the construction of a headpiece for the Negro's grave. He worked with a large spokeshave in a wood so hard that it grated and rang like metal.

At last, when Henty had passed six or seven consecutive days without fever, Mr. McMaster said, "Now I think you are well enough to see the books."

At one end of the hut there was a kind of loft formed by a rough platform erected up in the eaves of the roof. Mr. McMaster propped a ladder against it and mounted. Henty followed, still unsteady after his illness. Mr. McMaster sat on the platform and Henty stood at the top of the ladder looking over. There was a heap of small bundles there, tied up with rag, palm leaf, and rawhide.

"It has been hard to keep out the worms and ants," Mr. McMaster said. "Two are practically destroyed. But there is an oil the Indians know how to make that is useful." He unwrapped the nearest parcel and handed down a calfbound book. It was an early American edition of *Bleak House.* "It does not matter which we take first."

"You are fond of Dickens?"

"Why, yes, of course. More than fond, far more. You see, they are the only books I have ever heard. My father used to read them and then later the black man . . . and now you. I have heard them all several times by now but I never get tired; there is always more to be learned and noticed. I have all Dickens' books except those that the ants devoured. It takes a long time to read them all—more than two years."

"Well," said Henty lightly, "they will well last out my visit."

"Oh, I hope not. It is delightful to start again. Each time I think I find more to enjoy and admire."

They took down the first volume of *Bleak House* and that afternoon Henty had his first reading.

He had always rather enjoyed reading aloud and in the first year of marriage had shared several books in this way with his wife, until one day she remarked that it was torture to her. Sometimes after that he had thought it might be agreeable to have children to read to. But Mr. McMaster was a unique audience.

The old man sat astride his hammock opposite Henty, fixing him throughout with his eyes, and following the words, soundlessly, with his lips. Often when someone new was introduced he would say, "Repeat the name, I have forgotten him," or, "Yes, yes, I remember her well. She dies, poor woman." He would frequently interrupt with questions about the characters. "Now, why does she say that? Does she really mean it? Did she feel faint because of the heat of the fire or of something in that paper?" He laughed loudly at all the jokes, asking Henty to repeat them two or three times; and later at the description of the sufferings of the outcasts in "Tom-all-alone" tears ran down his cheeks into his beard. His comments on the story were usually simple. "I think that Dedlock is a very proud man," or, "Mrs. Jellyby does not take enough care of her children." Henty enjoyed the readings almost as much as he did.

At the end of the first day the old man said, "You read beautifully, with a far better accent than the black man. And you explain better. It is almost as though my father were here again." And always at the end of a session he thanked his guest courteously. "I enjoyed that very much. It was a distressing chapter. But, if I remember rightly, it will turn out well."

By the time that they were well into the second volume, however, the novelty of the old man's delight had begun to wane, and Henty was feeling strong enough to be restless. He touched more than once on the subject of his departure, asking about canoes and rains and the possibility of finding guides. But Mr. McMaster seemed obtuse and paid no attention to these hints.

One day, running his thumb through the pages of *Bleak House* that remained to be read, Henty said, "We still have a lot to get through. I hope I shall be able to finish it before I go."

"Oh, yes," said Mr. McMaster. "Do not disturb yourself about that. You will have time to finish it, my friend."

For the first time Henty noticed something slightly menacing in his host's manner. That evening at supper, a brief meal of farine and dried beef eaten just before sundown, Henty renewed the subject. "You know, Mr. McMaster, the time has come when I must be thinking about getting back to civilization. I have already imposed myself on your hospitality for too long."

Mr. McMaster bent over his plate, crunching mouthfuls of farine, but made no reply.

"I appreciate all your kindness more than I can say, but—"

"My friend, any kindness I may have shown is amply repaid by your reading of Dickens."

"Well, I'm very glad you have enjoyed it. I have, too. But I really must be thinking of getting back."

"Yes," said Mr. McMaster. "The black man was like that. He thought of it all the time. But he died here. . . ."

Twice during the next day Henty opened the subject, but his host was evasive. Finally he said, "Forgive me, Mr. McMaster, but I really must press the point. When can I get a boat?"

"There is no boat."

"Well, the Indians can build one."

"You must wait for the rains. There is not enough water in the river now."

"How long will that be?"

"A month . . . two months. . . ."

They had finished *Bleak House* and were nearing the end of *Dombey and Son* when the rain came.

"Now it is time to make preparations to go."

"Oh, that is impossible. The Indians will not make a boat during the rainy season—it is one of their superstitions."

"You might have told me."

"Did I not mention it? I forgot."

Next morning Henty went out alone and, looking as aimless as he could, strolled across the savanna to the group of Indian houses. There were four or five Shirianás sitting in one of the doorways. He addressed them in the few words of Macú he had acquired during the journey, but they made no sign whether they understood him or not. Then he drew a sketch of a canoe in the sand, he went through some vague motions of carpentry, pointed from them to him, then made motions of giving something to them and scratched out the outlines of a gun and a hat and a few other recognizable articles of trade. One of the women giggled, but no one gave any sign of comprehension, and he went away unsatisfied.

At their midday meal Mr. McMaster said, "Mr. Henty, the Indians tell me that you have been trying to speak with them. It is easier that you say anything you wish through me. You realize, do you not, that they would do nothing without my authority. They regard themselves, quite rightly in most cases, as my children."

"As a matter of fact, I was asking them about a canoe."

"So they gave me to understand. . . . And now if you have finished your meal perhaps we might have another chapter."

They finished *Dombey and Son;* nearly a year had passed since Henty had left England, and his foreboding of permanent exile became acute when, between the pages of *Martin Chuzzlewit*, he found a document written in pencil in irregular characters.

> Year 1919. I James McMaster of Brazil do swear to Barnabas Washington of Georgetown that if he finish this book in fact Martin Chuzzlewit I will let him go away back as soon as finished.

There followed a heavy penciled *X*, and after it, "Mr. McMaster made this mark signed Barnabas Washington."

"MR. MCMASTER," SAID Henty, "I must speak frankly. You saved my life, and when I get back to civilization I will reward you to the best of my ability. But at present you are keeping me here against my will. I demand to be released."

"But, my friend, what is keeping you? You are under no restraint. Go when you like."

"You know very well I can't get away without your help."

"In that case you must humor an old man. Read to me."

"Mr. McMaster, I swear by anything you like that when I get to Manaus I will find someone to take my place. I will pay a man to read to you all day."

"But I have no need of another man. You read so well."

"I have read for the last time."

"I hope not," said Mr. McMaster politely.

That evening at supper only one plate of dried meat and farine was brought in and Mr. McMaster ate alone. Henty lay without speaking, staring at the thatch.

Next day at noon a single plate was put before Mr. McMaster, but with it lay his gun, cocked, on his knee, as he ate. Henty resumed the reading of *Martin Chuzzlewit* where it had been interrupted.

Weeks passed hopelessly. They read *Nicholas Nickleby* and *Little Dorrit* and *Oliver Twist*. Then a stranger arrived in the savanna, a half-caste prospector, one of that lonely order of men who wander through the forests, tracing the streams, sifting the gravel and, ounce by ounce, filling the little leather sack of gold dust, more often than not dying of exposure and starvation with five hundred dollars' worth of gold hung around their necks. Mr. McMaster was vexed at his arrival, fed him, and sent him on his journey within an hour of his arrival, but in that hour Henty had scribbled his name on a slip of paper and put it into the man's hand.

From now on there was hope. The days followed their unvarying routine: coffee at sunrise, a morning of inaction while Mr. McMaster pottered about on the business of the farm, farine and *passo* at noon, Dickens in the afternoon, farine and *passo* and sometimes some fruit for supper, silence from sunset to dawn, with the small wick glowing in the beef fat and the palm thatch overhead dimly discernible. But Henty lived in quiet confidence and expectation.

Some time, this year or the next, the prospector would arrive at a Brazilian village with news of his discovery. The disasters to the Anderson expedition would not have passed unnoticed. Henty could imagine the headlines that must have appeared in the popular press; even now probably there were search parties working over the country he had crossed; any day English voices might sound over the savanna and a dozen friendly adventurers come crashing through the bush. Even as he was reading, while his lips mechanically followed the printed pages, his mind wandered away from his eager, crazy host opposite, and he began to narrate to himself incidents of his homecoming—he shaved and bought new clothes at Manaus, telegraphed for money, received wires of congratulation; he enjoyed the leisurely river journey to Belém, the big liner to Europe; savored fresh meat and spring vegetables; he was shy at meeting his wife and uncertain how to address. . . . "*Darling*, you've been much longer than you said. I quite thought you were lost—"

And then Mr. McMaster interrupted. "May I trouble you to read that passage again? It is one I particularly enjoy."

The weeks passed; there was no sign of rescue, but Henty endured the day for hope of what might happen on the morrow; he even felt a stirring of cordiality toward his jailer and was therefore quite willing to join him when, one evening after a long conference with an Indian neighbor, he proposed a celebration.

"It is one of the local feast days," he explained, "and they have been making *piwari.* You may not like it, but you should try some. We will go across to this man's home tonight."

Accordingly after supper they joined a party of Indians that was assembled around the fire in one of the huts at the other side of the savanna. They were singing in an apathetic, monotonous manner and passing a large calabash of liquid from mouth to mouth. Separate bowls were brought for Henty and Mr. McMaster, and they were given hammocks to sit in.

"You must drink it all without lowering the cup. That is the etiquette."

Henty gulped the dark liquid, trying not to taste it. It was not unpleasant, but hard and muddy on the palate, with a flavor of honey and brown bread. He leaned back in the hammock, feeling unusually contented. Perhaps at that very moment the search party was in camp a few hours' journey from them. Meanwhile he was warm and drowsy. The cadence of song rose and fell interminably, liturgically. Another calabash of *piwari* was offered him and he handed it back empty. He lay full length watching the play of shadows on the thatch as the Shirianás began to dance. Then he shut his eyes and thought of England and his wife and fell asleep.

HE AWOKE, STILL in the Indian hut. By the position of the sun he knew it was late afternoon. No one else was about. He looked for his watch and found to his surprise that it was not on his wrist. He had left it in the house, he supposed, before coming to the party.

I must have been tight last night, he reflected. Treacherous drink, that. He had a headache and feared a recurrence of fever. He found when he set his feet to the ground that he stood with difficulty; his walk was unsteady and his mind confused. On the way across the savanna he was obliged to stop more than once, shutting his eyes and breathing deeply. When he reached the house he found Mr. McMaster sitting there.

"Ah, my friend, how do you feel?"

"Rotten. That drink doesn't seem to agree with me."

"I will give you something to make you better. The forest has remedies for everything; to make you awake and to make you sleep."

"You haven't seen my watch anywhere?"

"You have missed it?"

"Yes. I thought I was wearing it. I say, I've never slept so long."

"Do you know how long? Two days. It is a pity because you missed our guests."

"Guests?"

"Why, yes. I have been quite gay while you were asleep. Three men from outside. Englishmen. It is a pity you missed them. A pity for them, too, as they particularly wished to see you. But what could I do? You were so sound asleep. They had come all the way to find you, so—I thought you would not mind—as you could not greet them yourself I gave them a little souvenir, your watch. They wanted something to take home to your wife, who is offering a great reward for news of you. They were very pleased with it. And they took some photographs of the little cross I put up to commemorate your coming. They were pleased with that, too. They were very easily pleased. But I do not suppose they will visit us again, our life here is so retired . . . no pleasures except reading. . . . Well, well, I will get you some medicine to make you feel better. Your head aches, does it not? . . . We will not have any Dickens today . . . but tomorrow, and the day after that, and the day after that. Let us read *Little Dorrit* again. There are passages in that book I can never hear without the temptation to weep."

WAS IT A DREAM?

GUY DE MAUPASSANT

I HAD loved her madly!

Why does one love? Why does one love? How queer it is to see only one being in the world, to have only one thought in one's mind, only one desire in the heart, and only one name on the lips—a name which comes up continually, rising, like the water in a spring, from the depths of the soul to the lips, a name which one repeats over and over again, which one whispers ceaselessly, everywhere, like a prayer.

I am going to tell you our story, for love only has one, which is always the same. I met her and loved her; that is all. And for a whole year I have lived on her tenderness, on her caresses, in her arms, in her dresses, on her words, so completely wrapped up, bound, and absorbed in everything which came from her that I no longer cared whether it was day or night, or whether I was dead or alive, on this old earth of ours.

And then she died. How? I do not know; I no longer know anything. But one evening she came home wet, for it was raining heavily, and the next day she coughed, and she coughed for about a week, and took to her bed. What happened I do not remember now, but doctors came, wrote, and went away. Medicines were brought, and some women made her drink them. Her hands were hot, her forehead was burning, and her eyes were bright and sad. When I spoke to her, she answered me, but I have forgotten what we said. She died, and I well remember her slight, feeble sigh. The nurse said, "Ah!" and I understood, I understood!

I knew nothing more, nothing. I saw a priest, who said, "Your mistress?" and it seemed to me as if he were insulting her. As she was dead, nobody had the right to say that any longer, and I turned him out. Another came who was very kind and tender, and I shed tears when he spoke to me about her.

They consulted me about the funeral, but I do not remember anything that they said, though I recollect the coffin, and the sound of the hammer when they nailed her down in it. Oh! God, God!

She was buried! Buried! She! In that hole! Some people came—female friends. I made my escape and ran away. I ran, and then walked through the streets, went home, and the next day started on a journey.

YESTERDAY I RETURNED to Paris, and when I saw my room again—our room, our bed, our furniture, everything that remains of the life of a human being after death—I was seized by such a violent attack of fresh grief that I felt like opening the window and throwing myself out into the street. I could not remain any longer among these things, between these walls which had enclosed and sheltered her, which retained a thousand atoms of her, of her skin and of her breath, in their imperceptible crevices. I took up my hat to make my escape, and just as I reached the door, I passed the large glass in the hall, which she had put there so that she might look at herself every day from head to foot as she went out, to see if her toilette looked well, and was correct and pretty, from her little boots to her bonnet.

I stopped short in front of that looking glass in which she had so often been reflected—so often, so often, that it must have retained her reflection. I was standing there, trembling, with my eyes fixed on the glass—on that flat, profound, empty glass—which had contained her entirely, and had possessed her as much as I, as my passionate looks had. I felt as if I loved that glass. I touched it; it was cold. Oh! The recollection! Sorrowful mirror, burning mirror, horrible mirror, to make men suffer such torments! Happy is the man whose heart forgets everything that it has contained, everything that has passed before it! How I suffer!

I went out without knowing it, without wishing it, and toward the cemetery. I found her simple grave, a white marble cross, with these few words:

She loved, was loved, and died.

She is there, below, decayed! How horrible! I sobbed with my forehead on the ground, and I stopped there for a long time, a long time. Then I saw that it was getting dark, and a strange, mad wish, the wish of a despairing lover, seized me. I wished to pass the night in weeping on her grave. But I should be seen and driven out. How was I to manage? I got up and began to roam about in that city of the dead. I walked and walked. How small this city is, in comparison with the other, the city in which we live. And yet, how much more numerous the dead are than the living. We want high houses, wide streets, and much room for the four generations who see the daylight at the same time, drink water from the spring and wine from the vines, and eat bread from the plains.

And for all the generations of the dead, for all that ladder of humanity that has descended down to us, there is scarcely anything! The earth takes them back, and oblivion effaces them.

At the end of the cemetery, I suddenly perceived that I was in its oldest part, where those who had been dead a long time are mingling with the soil, where the crosses themselves are decayed, where possibly newcomers will be put tomorrow. It is full of untended roses, of strong and dark cypress trees, a sad and beautiful garden, nourished on human flesh.

I was alone, perfectly alone. So I crouched in a green tree and hid myself there completely amid the thick and somber branches. I waited, clinging to the trunk like a shipwrecked man does to a plank.

When it was quite dark, I left my refuge and began to walk softly, slowly, inaudibly through that ground full of dead people. I wandered about for a long time, but could not find her tomb again. I went on with extended arms, knocking against the tombs with my hands, my feet, my knees, my chest, even with my head, without being able to find her. I groped about like a blind man finding his way. I felt the stones, the crosses, the iron railings, the metal wreaths, and the wreaths of faded flowers! I read the names with my fingers, by passing them over the letters. What a night! What a night! I could not find her again!

There was no moon. What a night! I was frightened, horribly frightened in these narrow paths between two rows of graves. Graves! Graves! Graves! Nothing but graves! On my right, on my left, in front of me, around me, everywhere there were graves! I sat down on one of them, for I could not walk any longer, my knees were so weak. I could hear my heart beat! And I heard something else as well. What? A confused, nameless noise.

Was the noise in my head, in the impenetrable night, or beneath the earth sown with human corpses? I looked all around me, but I cannot say how long I remained there; I was paralyzed with terror, cold with fright, ready to shout out, ready to die.

Suddenly, it seemed to me that the slab of marble on which I was sitting was moving. Certainly it was moving, as if it were being raised. With a bound, I sprang onto the neighboring tomb, and I saw, yes, I distinctly saw the stone which I had just quitted rise upright. Then the dead person appeared, a naked skeleton, pushing the stone up with its bent back. I saw it quite clearly, although the night was so dark. On the cross I could read:

> Here lies Jacques Olivant, who died at the age of fifty-one. He loved his family, was kind and honorable, and died in the grace of the Lord.

The dead man also read what was inscribed on his tombstone; then he picked up a stone off the path, a little, pointed stone, and began to scrape the letters carefully. He slowly effaced them, and with the hollows of his eyes he looked at the places where they had been engraved. Then with the tip of the bone that had been his forefinger, he wrote in luminous letters, like those lines which boys trace on walls with the tip of a lucifer match:

> Here reposes Jacques Olivant, who died at the age of fifty-one. He hastened his father's death by his unkindness, as he wished to inherit his fortune; he tortured his wife, tormented his children, deceived his neighbors, robbed everyone he could, and died wretched.

When he had finished writing, the dead man stood motionless, looking at his work. On turning around I saw that all the graves were open, that all the dead bodies had emerged from them, and that all had effaced the lies inscribed on the gravestones by their relations, substituting the truth instead. And I saw that all had been the tormentors of their neighbors—malicious, dishonest, hypocrites, liars, rogues, calumniators, envious; that they had stolen, deceived, performed every disgraceful, every abominable action, these good fathers, these faithful wives, these devoted sons, these chaste daughters, these honest tradesmen, these men and women who were called irreproachable. They were all writing at the same time, on the threshold of their eternal abode, the truth, the terrible and the holy truth of which everybody was ignorant, or pretended to be ignorant, while they were alive.

I thought that *she* also must have written something on her tombstone, and now running without any fear among the half-open coffins, among the corpses and skeletons, I went toward her, sure that I should find her immediately. I recognized her at once, without seeing her face, which was covered by the winding-sheet, and on the marble cross, where shortly before I had read:

She loved, was loved, and died.

I now saw:

> Having gone out in the rain one day, in order to deceive her lover, she caught cold and died.

It appears that they found me at daybreak, lying on the grave unconscious.

THE FOURTH MAN

JOHN RUSSELL

THE RAFT MIGHT have been taken for a swath of cut sedge or a drifting tangle of roots as it slid out of the shadowy river mouth at dawn and dipped into the first ground swell. But while the sky brightened and the breeze came fresh offshore it picked a way among shoals and swampy islets with purpose and direction, and when at last the sun leaped up and cleared his bright eye of the morning mist it had passed the wide entrance to the bay and stood to open sea.

It was a curious craft for such a venture, of a type that survives here and there in the obscure corners of the world. A mat of pandanus leaves served for its sail and a paddle of niaouli wood for its helm. But it had a single point of real seaworthiness. Its twin floats, paired as a catamaran, were woven of reed bundles and bamboo sticks upon triple rows of bladders. It was light as a bladder itself, elastic, fit to ride any weather. One other quality recommended this raft beyond all comfort and all safety to its present crew. It was very nearly invisible. They had only to unstep its mast and lie flat in the cup of its soggy platform and they could not be spied half a mile away.

Four men occupied the raft. Three were white. Their bodies had been scored with brambles and blackened with dried blood; on wrist and ankle they bore the dark and wrinkled stain of the gyves. Their hair was long and matted. They wore the rags of blue canvas uniforms. But they were whites—members of a highly superior race, according to those philosophers who rate criminal aberration as a form of genius.

The fourth was the man who had built the raft and was now sailing it. There was nothing superior about him. His skin was a layer of soot. His prognathous jaw carried out the angle of a low forehead. No line of beauty redeemed his lean limbs and knobby joints. He wore only a twist of bark about his middle and a prong of pig ivory through the cartilage of his nose. Altogether a very ordinary specimen of one of the lowest branches of the human family—the *canaques* of New Caledonia.

The three whites sat together well forward, and so they had sat in silence for hours. But at sunrise they stirred and breathed deep of the salt air and looked at one another with hope in their haggard faces, and then back toward the land, which was now no more than a gray-green smudge behind them. . . . "Friends," said the eldest, whose temples were bound with a scrap of crimson scarf, "friends—the thing is done." With a gesture like conjuring he produced from the breast of his tattered blouse three cigarettes, fresh and round, and offered them.

"Nippers!" cried the one at his right. "True nippers—and here? Doctor, I always said you were a marvel."

Dr. Dubosc smiled. Those who had known him in very different circumstances—about the boulevards, the lobbies, the clubs—would have known him again, and in spite of all disfigurement, by that smile. And here, at the bottom of the earth, it had set him still apart in the prisons, the cobalt mines, the chain gangs of a community not much given to mirth. Many a crowded lecture hall at Montpellier had seen him touch some intellectual firework with just such a twinkle behind his bristly gray brows, with just such a thin curl of lip.

"By way of celebration," he explained. "Consider. From Nouméa there are seventy-five evasions every six months, of which not more than one succeeds. I had the figures myself from Dr. Pierre at the infirmary. Could anybody win on that percentage without dissipating? I ask you."

"Therefore you prepared for this?"

"It is now three weeks since I bribed the night guard to get these same nippers."

The other regarded him with admiration. Sentiment came readily upon this beardless face, tender and languid, with eyes too large and soft. It was one of those faces familiar to the police which might serve as model for an angel were it not associated with some revolting piece of deviltry. Fenayrou himself had been condemned "to perpetuity" as an incorrigible.

"Is not our doctor a wonder?" he inquired as he handed a cigarette along to the third white man. "He thinks of everything. You should be ashamed to grumble. See—we are free. Free!"

The third was a gross, pockmarked man with hairless lids known as Perroquet—the Parrot—a name derived perhaps from his beaked nose, or from some perception of his jailbird character. He was a garroter by profession, who relied upon his fists only for the exchange of amenities. There is perhaps a tribute to the practical spirit of penal administration in the fact that while Dubosc was the most dangerous of these three and Fenayrou the most depraved, Perroquet was the one with the official reputation, whose escape would be signaled first among the "wanted."

He accepted the cigarette, but he said nothing until Dubosc passed a tin box of matches and the first gulp of picadura filled his lungs. "Wait till you've got your two feet on a *pavé*, my boy. That will be the time to talk of freedom. What? Suppose there came a storm."

"It is not the season of storms," observed Dubosc.

But the Parrot's word had given them a check. Such spirits as these, to whom the land had been a horror, would be slow to feel the terror of the sea. Back there they had left the festering limbo of a convict colony, oblivion. Out here they had reached the rosy threshold of the big round world again.

They were men raised from the dead, charged with all the furious appetites of lost years. And yet they paused and looked about in quickened perception, with the clutch at the throat that takes the landsman on big waters. The spaces were so wide and empty. The voices in their ears were so strange and murmurous. There was a threat in each wave that came from the depths, a sinister vibration. None of them knew the sea, what tricks it might play, what traps it might spread—more deadly than those of the jungle.

The raft was running now before a brisk chop with alternate spring and wallow, while the froth bubbled in over the prow and ran down among them as they sat. "Where is that cursed ship that was to meet us here?" demanded Fenayrou.

"It will meet us." Dubosc spoke carelessly, though behind the blown wisp of his cigarette he had been searching the horizon with keen glance. "This is the day, as agreed. We will be picked up off the mouth of the river."

"You say," growled Perroquet. "But where is any river now? Or any mouth? Sacred name! This wind will blow us to China if we keep on."

"We dare not lie in any closer. There is a government launch at Torrien. Also the traders go armed hereabouts, ready for chaps like us. And don't imagine that the native trackers have given us up. They are likely to be following still in their proas."

Fenayrou laughed, for the Parrot's dread of their savage enemies had a morbid tinge. "Take care, Perroquet. They will eat you yet."

"Is it true?" demanded the other, appealing to Dubosc. "I have heard it is even permitted these devils to keep all runaways they can capture—name of God!—to fatten on."

"An idle tale." Dubosc smiled. "They prefer the reward. But one hears of convicts being badly mauled. One who made a break from Baie du Sud came back lacking an arm. These people have not lost the habit of cannibalism."

"Piecemeal." Fenayrou chuckled. "Let them make a stew of your brains, Perroquet. You would miss nothing."

But the Parrot swore. "Name of a name—what brutes!" he said, and by a gesture recalled the presence of that fourth man who was of their party and yet so completely separated from them that they had almost forgotten him. The *canaque* was steering the raft. He sat crouched at the stern, his body glistening like varnished ebony with spray. He held the steering paddle, immobile as an image, his eyes fixed upon the course ahead.

There was no expression on his face, no hint of what he thought or felt or whether he thought or felt anything. He seemed unaware of their regard, and each of them experienced that twinge of uneasiness with which the white always confronts his brother of color—this enigma, brown or yellow or black, he is fated never wholly to understand or to fathom.

"It occurs to me," said Fenayrou, "that our friend here is able to steer us God knows where, to claim the reward."

"Reassure yourself," answered Dubosc. "He steers by my order. He is a simple creature—incapable of any treachery or deception. Also, he is bound by his duty. I made my bargain with his chief, up the river, who sent this one to deliver us on board our ship. And he will do it. Such is the nature of the native."

"I am glad you feel so," returned Fenayrou, adjusting himself indolently among the drier reeds. "For my part I wouldn't trust a figurehead like that for two sous."

"Brute!" repeated Perroquet, and this man, sprung from some vile riverfront slum of Argenteuil, whose home had been the dock pilings, the grogshop, and the jail, even this man viewed the black *canaque* with a look of hatred and contempt.

Under the heat of the day the two younger convicts lapsed presently into dozing. But Dubosc did not doze. He stood to sweep the skyline again under shaded hand. His theory had been so precise; the fact was so different. He had counted absolutely on meeting the ship—some small schooner, one of those flitting, half-piratical traders of the copra islands that can be hired like cabs in a dark street for any questionable enterprise. Now there was no ship, and here was no crossroads where one might sit and wait. Such a craft as the catamaran could not be made to lie to.

The doctor foresaw ugly complications for which he had not prepared. The escape had been directed by him from the start. He had picked his companions from the whole forced-labor squad, Perroquet for his great strength, Fenayrou as a ready echo. He had made it plain since their first dash from the mine, during their skirmish with the military guards, their wanderings in the brush, with bloodhounds and trackers on the trail—through every crisis—that he alone should be the leader.

For the others, they had understood well enough which of their number was the chief beneficiary. Those mysterious friends on the outside that were reaching half around the world to further their release had never heard of Fenayrou and the Parrot. Dubosc was the man who had pulled the wires: that brilliant physician whose conviction for murder had followed so sensationally, so scandalously, upon his sweep of academic and social honors. There would be clacking tongues in many a Parisian salon, and white faces in some, when news should come of his escape. Ah, yes, they knew the highflier of the band, and they submitted—as long as he led them to victory—while reserving a depth of jealousy, the inevitable remnant of caste persisting still in this democracy of stripes and shame.

By the middle of the afternoon the doctor had taken certain necessary measures.

"Ho," said Fenayrou sleepily. "Behold our colors at the masthead. What is that for, comrade?"

The sail had been lowered and in its place streamed the scrap of crimson scarf that had served Dubosc as a turban.

"To help them sight us when the ship comes."

"What wisdom!" cried Fenayrou. "He thinks of everything, our doctor—" He stopped, his hand outstretched toward the center of the platform. Here, in a damp depression among the reeds, had lain the wicker-covered bottle of green glass in which they carried their water. It was gone. "Where is that flask?" he demanded. "The sun has grilled me like a bone."

"This crew is put on rations," said Dubosc grimly.

From the shadow of a folded mat the Parrot thrust his purpled face. "What do you sing me there? Where is the water?"

"I have it," said Dubosc. He held the flask between his knees, along with their single packet of food in its wrapping of coconut husk.

"I want a drink," challenged Perroquet.

"Reflect a little. We must guard our supplies like reasonable men. One does not know how long we may be floating here."

A silence fell among them, heavy and strained, in which they heard only the squeaking of frail basketwork as their raft labored in the wash. They were being pushed steadily outward and onward, and the last cliffs of New Caledonia were no longer even a smudge in the west, but only a hazy line. And still they had seen no moving thing upon the great round breast of the sea that gleamed in its corselet of brass plates under a brazen sun. "So you do not know how long?" said the Parrot, half choking. "But you were sure enough when we started."

"I am still sure," returned Dubosc. "The ship will come. Only she cannot stay for us in one spot. She will be cruising to and fro until she intercepts us. We must wait."

"Ah, good! We must wait. And in the meantime, what? Fry here with our tongues hanging out while you deal us drop by drop—*hein?* Blood of God, there is no man big enough to feed me with a spoon!"

Fenayrou's chuckle came pat, as it had more than once.

"You laugh!" cried Perroquet, turning in fury. "But how about this lascar of a captain that lets us put to sea unprovided? He thinks of everything, does he? And now he bids us be reasonable! Tell that to the devils in hell."

"It is true," muttered Fenayrou, frowning. "A bad piece of work for a captain of runaways."

But the doctor faced mutiny with his thin smile. "All this alters nothing. Unless we would die very speedily, we must guard our water."

"By whose fault?"

"Mine," acknowledged the doctor. "I admit it. But we can't turn back. We must do our best with what we have."

"I want a drink," repeated the Parrot, whose throat was afire since he had been denied.

"You can claim your share, of course. But after it is gone do not think to sponge on us—on Fenayrou and me."

"He would be capable of it, the pig!" exclaimed Fenayrou, to whom this thrust had been directed. "I know him. See here, old man, the doctor is right. Fair for one, fair for all."

"I want a drink."

Dubosc removed the wooden plug from the flask.

"Very well," he said quietly.

With the delicacy that lent something of legerdemain to all his gestures, he took out a small canvas bag and drew out a thimble. Meticulously he poured a brimming measure, and Fenayrou gave a shout at the grumbler's fallen jaw as he accepted that tiny cup between his big fingers. Dubosc served Fenayrou and himself with the same amount before he recorked the bottle.

"In this manner we should have enough to last us three days—maybe more—with equal shares among the three of us."

It passed without comment, as a matter of course, that he should count as he did—ignoring that other who sat alone at the stern of the raft, the black *canaque*, the fourth man.

Perroquet had been outmaneuvered, but he listened sullenly while for the hundredth time Dubosc recited his plan for their rescue, as arranged with his secret correspondents.

"That sounds very well," observed the Parrot at last. "But what if these jokers only mock you? What if they count it good riddance to let you rot here? And us? That would be a jest! To let us wait for a ship and they have no ship!"

"My faith," said Dubosc with great good humor, "it would not be well for them to fail me. Figure to yourselves that there is a safety vault in Paris full of papers to be opened at my death. Certain friends of mine could hardly afford to have some little confessions published that would be found there. Such a tale as this, for instance . . ."

And to amuse them he told an indecent anecdote of high life, true or fictitious, it mattered nothing, so he could make Fenayrou's eyes glitter and the Parrot growl in wonder. Therein lay his means of ascendancy over such men, the knack of eloquence and vision. Harried, worn, oppressed by fears that he could sense so much more sharply than they, he must expend himself now in vulgar marvels to distract these ruder minds. He succeeded so far that when the wind fell at sunset they were almost cheerful, ready to believe that the morning would bring relief. They dined on dry biscuit and another thimbleful of water apiece and took watch by amiable agreement. And through that long, clear night of stars, whenever the one of the three who lay awake chanced to look aft, he could see the vague blot of another figure—the naked *canaque*, who slumbered there apart.

It was an evil dawning. Fenayrou, on the morning trick, was aroused by a foot as hard as a hoof, and started up at Perroquet's wrathful face, with the doctor's graver glance behind.

"Idler! Good-for-nothing! Name of God, here is a way to stand watch! A ship could have passed us a dozen times while you slept."

Perroquet knotted his great fist over Fenayrou, who crouched away catlike, his mobile mouth twisted to a snarl. Dubosc stood aside in watchful calculation until against the angry red sunrise in which they floated there flashed the naked red gleam of steel. Then he stepped between.

"Enough. Fenayrou, put up that knife. Perroquet! The harm is done. Listen now, both of you. Things are bad enough already. Look about."

They looked and saw the far, round horizon and the empty desert of the sea and nothing else. "Good God, how lonely it is!" breathed Fenayrou in a hush.

No more was said. Silently they shared their rations as before and made shift to eat something with their few drops of water.

A calm had fallen, as it does between trades in this flawed belt, an absolute calm. The air hung weighted. The sea showed no faintest crinkle, only the maddening, unresting heave and fall in polished undulations on which the lances of the sun broke and drove in under their eyelids as white, hot splinters; a savage sun that kindled upon them with the power of a burning glass, and sent them crawling to the shelter of their mats and brought them out again, gasping. The water, the world of water, seemed sleek and thick as oil. They came to loathe it and the rotting smell of it, and when the doctor made them dip themselves overside they found little comfort. It was warm, sluggish, slimed. But a curious thing resulted.

While they clung along the edge of the raft they all faced inboard, and there sat the black *canaque.* He did not glance at them. He sat hunkered on his heels in the way of the native, with arms hugging his knees. He stayed in his place at the stern, motionless under that shattering sun, gazing out into vacancy. Whenever they raised their eyes they saw him, and for the first time with direct interest, with thought of him as a fellow being—with the beginning of envy.

"He does not seem to suffer."

"What is going on in his brain? What does he dream of?"

"Perhaps he is waiting for us to die," suggested Fenayrou with a harsh chuckle. "Perhaps he is waiting for the reward. He would not starve on the way home, at least. And he could deliver us—piecemeal."

They studied him.

"How does he do it, Doctor? Has he no feeling?"

"I have been wondering," said Dubosc. "It may be that his fibers are tougher—his nerves."

"Yet we have had water and he none."

"But look at his skin, fresh and moist."

The Parrot hauled himself aboard. "Don't tell me this black beast knows thirst!" he cried with a strange excitement. "Is there any way he could steal our supplies?"

"Certainly not."

"Then what if he has hidden supplies of his own?"

The same monstrous notion struck them all. They knocked the black aside. They searched the platform where he had sat, burrowing among the rushes, seeking some secret cache, another bottle or a gourd. They found nothing.

"We were mistaken," said Dubosc.

But Perroquet had a different expression for disappointment. He turned on the *canaque* and caught him by his kinky mop of hair and proceeded to give him what is known as gruel in the cobalt mines. This was a little specialty of the Parrot's. He paused only when he himself was breathless and exhausted and threw the limp, unresisting body from him.

"There, lump of dirt! Maybe you're not so chipper now!"

The others looked on as at the satisfaction of a common grudge. The white trampled the black with or without cause, and that was natural. And the black crept away into his place with his hurts and his wrongs and struck no blow. And that was natural, too.

The sun declined into a blazing furnace, but when it was gone their blistered bodies still held the heat like things incandescent. The night closed down over them like a purple bowl, glazed and impermeable. They would have divided the watches again, but Fenayrou made a discovery.

"Idiots!" he rasped. "Why should we look and look? No ships can help us now. If we are becalmed, why so are they!"

"Is this true?" the Parrot asked Dubosc.

"Yes, we must hope for a breeze first."

"Then, name of God, why didn't you tell us so?" He pondered it for a time. "See here," he said. "You are wise. You know things we do not and you keep them to yourself." He leaned forward to peer into the doctor's face. "But if you think you're going to use that cursed smartness to get the best of us in any way—see here, my zig, I pull your gullet out like the string of an orange."

It was perhaps about this time that Dubosc began to regret his intervention in the knifeplay. For there was no breeze and there was no ship.

By the third morning each had sunk within himself. The doctor was lost in a profound depression, Perroquet in dark suspicion, and Fenayrou in bodily suffering, which he supported ill. Only two effective ties still bound their confederacy. One was the flask which Dubosc had slung at his side by a strip of the wickerwork. Every move he made with it, every drop he poured, was followed by burning eyes. Under his careful saving there still remained nearly half of their original store.

The other bond, as it had come to be by strange mutation, was the presence of the black *canaque.* There was no forgetting the fourth man now, no overlooking of him. He loomed upon their consciousness, more formidable, more mysterious, more exasperating with every hour. Their own powers were ebbing. The naked savage had yet to give the slightest sign of complaint or weakness.

During the night he had stretched himself out on the platform as before. Through the hours of darkness and silence, while each of the whites wrestled with despair, this black man had slept as placidly as a child. Since then he had resumed his place aft. And so he remained, a fixed fact and a growing wonder.

The brutal rage of Perroquet had been followed by superstitious doubts. "Doctor," he said at last, in awed huskiness, "is this a man or a fiend?"

"It is a man."

"A miracle," put in Fenayrou.

But the doctor lifted a finger in a way his pupils would have remembered. "It is a man," he repeated, "and a very poor and wretched example of a man. You will find no lower type anywhere. Observe his cranial angle, the high ears, the heavy bones of his skull. He is scarcely above the ape."

"Ah? Then what?"

"He has a secret," said the doctor.

That was a word to transfix them. "A secret! But we see every move he makes, every instant. What chance for a secret?"

The doctor rather forgot his audience, betrayed by chagrin and bitterness. "How pitiful!" he mused. "Here are we three—children of the century, products of civilization—I fancy none would deny that, at least. And here is this man who belongs before the Stone Age. In a set trial of fitness, of wits, of resource, is he to win? Pitiful!"

"What kind of secret?" demanded Perroquet, fuming.

"I cannot say," admitted Dubosc with a baffled gesture. "Possibly some method of breathing, some peculiar posture that operates to cheat the sensations of the body. Such things are known among primitive peoples—known and carefully guarded—like the properties of certain drugs, the uses of hypnotism and complex natural laws. Then, again, it may be psychologic—a mental attitude persistently held. Who knows?

"He will not tell his innermost secrets. Why should he? We scorn him. We give him no share with us. We abuse him. He simply falls back on his own expedients. His secrets are the means by which he has survived from the depth of time, by which he may yet survive when all our wisdom is dust."

"I know excellent ways of learning secrets," said Fenayrou as he passed his dry tongue over his lips. "Shall I begin?"

Dubosc came back with a start and looked at him. "He could stand any torture you could invent. No, that is not the way."

"You say he is a man?" said Perroquet with sudden violence. "Very well. If he is a man, he must have blood in his veins. That would be, anyway, good to drink."

"No," returned Dubosc. "It would be hot. Also it would be salt. For food—perhaps. But we do not need food."

"Well, sacred name, what do you want?"

"To beat him at the game," cried the doctor, curiously agitated. "For our own sakes, for our racial pride. To outlast him, to prove ourselves his masters. By better brain, by better organization and control. Watch him, friends—that we may ensnare him, that we may detect and defeat him in the end!"

But the doctor was miles beyond them. "Watch?" growled the Parrot. "I believe you, old windbag. It is all one watch. I sleep no more and leave any man alone with that bottle."

To this the issue finally sharpened. They watched. They watched the *canaque.* They watched each other. And they watched the falling level in their flask—until the tension gave.

Another dawn upon the same dead calm, rising like a conflagration through the puddled air, cloudless, hopeless! Another day of blinding, slow-drawn agony to meet. And Dubosc announced that their allowance must be cut to half a thimbleful.

There remained perhaps a quarter of a liter—a miserable reprieve of bare life among the three of them, but one good swallow for a yearning throat. At sight of the bottle, at the tinkle of its limpid content, so cool and silvery green inside the glass, Fenayrou's nerve snapped.

"More!" he begged with pleading hands. "I die. More!"

When the doctor refused him he groveled among the reeds, then rose suddenly to his knees and tossed his arms abroad with a hoarse cry: "A ship! A ship!"

The others spun about. They saw the thin unbroken ring of this greater and more terrible prison to which they had exchanged—and that was all they saw. They turned back to Fenayrou and found him in the act of tilting the bottle. A cunning slash of his knife had loosed it from its sling at the doctor's side. Even now he was sucking at the mouth, spilling the precious liquid.

With one sweep Perroquet caught up their paddle and flattened him, crushed him.

Springing across the prostrate man, Dubosc snatched the flask upright and put the width of the raft between himself and the big garroter who stood wide-legged, his bloodshot eyes alight, rumbling in his chest.

"There is no ship," said the Parrot. "There will be no ship. We are done. Because of you and your rotten promises that brought us here—doctor, liar, ass!"

Dubosc stood firm. "Come a step nearer and I break bottle and all over your head."

They stood regarding each other, and Perroquet's brows gathered in a slow effort of thought.

"Consider," urged Dubosc with his quaint touch of pedantry. "Why should you and I fight? We are rational men. We can win yet. Such weather cannot last forever. Besides, there are only two of us to divide the water now."

"That is true." The Parrot nodded. "That is true, isn't it? Fenayrou kindly leaves us his share. An inheritance—what? A famous idea. I'll take mine now, if you please."

The doctor smiled his grim, wan little smile. "So be it."

Without relinquishing the flask he brought out his canvas bag once more and rolled out the thimble by some swift sleight of his flexible fingers while he held Perroquet's glance with his own. "I will measure it for you."

He poured the thimbleful and handed it over quickly, and when Perroquet had tossed it off he filled again and again.

"Four—five," he counted. "That is enough."

But the Parrot's big grip closed quietly around his wrist at the last offering and pinioned him and held him helpless.

"No, it is not enough. Now I will take the rest."

There was no chance to struggle, and Dubosc did not try, only stayed smiling up at him, waiting.

Perroquet took the bottle.

"The best man wins," he remarked. "Eh, my zig? A bright notion . . . of yours. The . . . best . . ."

His lips moved, but no sound issued. A look of the most intense surprise spread upon his round face. He stood swaying a moment, and collapsed like a huge hinged toy when the string is cut.

Dubosc stooped and caught the bottle again, looking down at his big adversary, who sprawled in brief convulsion and lay still, a bluish scum oozing between his teeth.

"Yes, the best man wins," repeated the doctor, and laughed as he in turn raised the flask for a draft.

"The best wins!" echoed a voice in his ear.

Fenayrou, writhing up and striking like a wounded snake, drove the knife home between his shoulders.

The bottle fell and rolled to the middle of the platform, and there, while each strove vainly to reach it, it poured out its treasure in a tiny stream that trickled away and was lost.

IT MAY HAVE BEEN MINUTES or hours later—for time has no count in emptiness—when next a sound proceeded from that frail slip of a raft, hung like a mote between sea and sky. It was a phrase of song, a wandering strain in halftones and fluted accidentals, not unmelodious. The black *canaque* was singing. He sang without emotion or effort, quite casually and softly to himself. So he might sing by his forest hut to ease some hour of idleness. Clasping his knees and gazing out into space, untroubled, unmoved, enigmatic to the end, he sang—he sang.

And, after all, the ship came.

She came in a manner befitting the sauciest little topsail schooner between Nuku Hiva and the Palaus—as her owner often averred and none but the envious denied—in a manner worthy, too, of that able Captain Jean Guibert, the merriest little scamp that ever cleaned a pearl bank or snapped a cargo of labor from a scowling coast. Before the first whiff out of the west came the *Petite Suzanne*, curtsying and skipping along with a flash of white frill by her forefoot, and brought up startled and stood shaking her skirts and keeping herself quite daintily to windward.

"And 'ere they are sure enough, by dam'!" said Captain Jean in the language of commerce and profanity. "Zose passengers for us, hey? They been here all the time, not ten mile off—I bet you, Marteau. Ain't it 'ell? What you zink, my gar?"

His second, a tall and excessively bony individual of gloomy outlook, handed back the glasses.

"More bad luck. I never approved of this job. And now—see?—we have had our voyage for nothing. What misfortune!"

"Do I 'ire you to stand zere and cry about ze luck, Marteau?" retorted Captain Jean. "Get a boat over, and quicker zan zat!"

M. Marteau aroused himself sufficiently to take command of the boat's crew that presently dropped away to investigate.

"It is even as I thought," he called up from the quarter when he returned with his report. "We are too late. Bad luck, bad luck—that calm. What misfortune! They are all dead!"

"All ze better, they will cost nozing to feed."

"But how—"

"Hogsheads, my gar," said Captain Jean paternally. "Zose hogsheads in the afterhold. Fill them nicely with brine, and zere we are!" And, having drawn all possible satisfaction from the other's amazement, he sprang the nub of his joke with a grin. "Ze gentlemen's passage is all paid, Marteau. Before we left Sydney, Marteau. I contrac' to bring back three escape' convicts, and so by 'ell I do—in pickle! And now if you'll kindly get zose passengers aboard like I said an' bozzer less about ze dam' luck, I be much oblige'."

Marteau recovered himself in time to recall another trifling detail. "There is a fourth man on board that raft, Captain Jean. He is a *canaque*—still alive. What shall we do with him?"

"A *canaque?*" snapped Captain Jean. "A *canaque!* I had no word in my contrac' about any *canaque*. . . . Leave him zere. . . . He is only a dam' nigger. He'll do well enough where he is."

And Captain Jean was right, perfectly right, for while the *Petite Suzanne* was taking aboard her grisly cargo the wind freshened from the west, and just about the time she was shaping away for Australia the "dam' nigger" spread his own sail of pandanus leaves and twirled his own helm of niaouli wood and headed the catamaran eastward, back toward New Caledonia.

Feeling somewhat dry after his exertion, he plucked at random from the platform a hollow reed with a sharp end and, stretching himself at full length in his accustomed place at the stern, he thrust the reed down into one of the bladders underneath and drank his fill of sweet water. . . .

He had a dozen such storage bladders remaining, built into the floats at intervals above the waterline—quite enough to last him safely home again.

THE WENDIGO

ALGERNON BLACKWOOD

A CONSIDERABLE NUMBER of hunting parties were out that year without finding so much as a fresh trail, for the moose were uncommonly shy. Dr. Cathcart, among others, came back without a trophy; but he brought instead the memory of an experience which he declares was worth all the bull moose that had ever been shot. But then Cathcart, of Aberdeen, Scotland, was interested in other things besides moose—among them the vagaries of the human mind. This particular story, however, found no mention in his book on *Collective Hallucination* for the simple reason that he himself played too intimate a part in it to form a competent judgment of the affair as a whole. . . .

Besides himself and his guide, Hank Davis, there was Cathcart's nephew, young Simpson, a divinity student on his first visit to the Canadian backwoods, and Simpson's guide, Défago. Joseph Défago was a French Canuck who had strayed from his native Quebec years before, and had got caught in Rat Portage when the Canadian Pacific Railway was abuilding. He was deeply susceptible to that spell which the wilderness lays upon certain lonely natures, and he loved the wild solitudes with a romantic passion that amounted almost to an obsession.

On this particular expedition he was Hank's choice. Hank knew him and swore by him. He had, however, one objection to Défago, which was that the French Canadian sometimes exhibited what Hank described as "the output of a cursed and dismal mind." Apparently Défago suffered fits of silent moroseness when nothing could induce him to speak. Défago, that is to say, was imaginative and melancholy.

There was also Punk, an Indian, who acted as cook. His duty was merely to stay in camp, catch fish, and prepare venison steaks and coffee at a few minutes' notice.

This, then, was the party of five that found themselves in camp the last week in October of that "shy moose year" way up in the wilderness north of Rat Portage—a forsaken and desolate country.

The party around the blazing fire that night were despondent, for a week had passed without a single sign of recent moose. Défago had subsided into a sulky silence which nothing seemed likely to break. Dr. Cathcart and his nephew were fairly done after an exhausting day. Punk was washing up the dishes, grunting to himself under the lean-to of branches, where he also slept. No one troubled to stir the slowly dying fire. Overhead the stars were brilliant in a sky quite wintry, and ice was already forming along the shores of the still lake behind them. The silence of the vast listening forest stole forward and enveloped them.

Hank broke in suddenly with his nasal voice. "I'm in favor of breaking new ground tomorrow, Doc," he observed with energy, looking across at his employer.

"Agreed," said Cathcart. "Think the idea's good."

"Sure pop, it's good," Hank resumed with confidence. "S'pose, now, you and I strike west, up Garden Lake way for a change! None of us ain't touched that quiet bit o' land yet."

"I'm with you."

"And you, Défago, take Mr. Simpson along in the small canoe, skip across the lake, portage over into Fifty Island Water, and take a good squint down that thar southern shore. The moose yarded there like hell last year, and for all we know they may be doin' it agin this year jest to spite us."

Défago kept his eyes on the fire and said nothing.

"No one's been up that way this year, an' I'll lay my bottom dollar on *that!*" Hank added with emphasis. He looked over at his partner sharply. "Better take the little silk tent and stay away a couple o' nights," he concluded, as though the matter were definitely settled. For Hank was recognized as general organizer of the hunt, and in charge of the party.

It was obvious that Défago did not jump at the plan, but his silence seemed to convey something more than ordinary disapproval, and across his sensitive dark face there passed a curious expression like a flash of firelight—not so quickly, however, that the three men had not time to catch it.

Hank had been the first to notice it, and the odd thing was that instead of becoming explosive or angry over the other's reluctance, he at once began to humor him a bit. "But there ain't no *speshul* reason why no one's been up there this year," he said, with a perceptible hush in his tone; "not the reason *you* mean, anyway! Las' year it was the fires that kep' folks out, and this year I guess—I guess it jest happened."

Joseph Défago raised his eyes a moment, then dropped them. A breath of wind stole out of the forest and stirred the embers into a passing blaze. Dr. Cathcart again noticed the expression in the guide's face, and he did not like it. For in those eyes he caught the gleam of a man scared in his very soul. It disquieted him more than he cared to admit.

"Bad Indians up that way?" he asked, with a laugh to ease matters a little, while Simpson, too sleepy to notice this subtle byplay, moved off to bed with a prodigious yawn. "Or—or anything wrong with the country?" he added, when his nephew was out of hearing.

Hank met his eye with something less than his usual frankness. "He's just skeered," he replied good-humoredly, "skeered stiff about some ole feery tale! That's all, ain't it, ole pard?" And he gave Défago a friendly kick on the moccasined foot that lay nearest the fire.

Défago looked up quickly, as from an interrupted reverie. "Skeered, *nuthin'!*" he answered, with a flush of defiance. "There's nothin' in the bush that can skeer Joseph Défago, and don't you forget it!"

Hank was just going to add something when he stopped abruptly and looked around. A sound close behind them in the darkness made all three start. It was old Punk, who had come up from his lean-to while they talked and now moved in and warmed his feet, smiling darkly at the other's volubility.

Presently Dr. Cathcart, seeing that further conversation was impossible, followed his nephew's example and turned in, weariness and sleep still fighting in his mind with an obscure curiosity to know what it was that had scared Défago about the country up Fifty Island Water way. Then sleep overtook him. He would know tomorrow. Hank would tell him the story while they trudged after the elusive moose.

Deep silence fell about the little camp, planted there so audaciously in the jaws of the wilderness. The lake gleamed like a sheet of black glass beneath the stars. The cold air pricked. In the drafts of night that poured their silent tide from the depths of the forest, there lay already the faint, bleak odors of coming winter.

An hour later, when all slept like the dead, old Punk crept from his blankets and went down to the shore of the lake like a shadow—silently, as only Indian blood can move. He raised his head and looked about him, then sniffed the air. Motionless as a hemlock stem he stood there. After five minutes, again he lifted his head and sniffed, and yet once again. Then, merging his figure into the surrounding blackness in a way that only wild men and animals understand, he turned, still moving like a shadow, and went stealthily back to his bed.

Soon after he slept, the change of wind he had divined stirred gently the reflection of the stars within the lake. Rising among the far ridges of the country beyond Fifty Island Water, it came from the direction in which Punk had stared, and it passed over the sleeping camp with a faint and sighing murmur through the tops of the big trees. With it, down the desert paths of night, there passed a curious, thin odor, strangely disquieting, an odor of something that seemed unfamiliar—utterly unknown.

The French Canadian and the man of Indian blood each stirred uneasily in his sleep just about this time, though neither of them woke. Then the ghost of that unforgettably strange odor passed away and was lost among the leagues of tenantless forest beyond.

IN THE MORNING the camp was astir before the sun. There had been a light fall of snow during the night and the air was sharp. Punk had done his duty betimes, for the odors of coffee and fried bacon reached every tent. All were in good spirits.

"Wind's shifted!" cried Hank vigorously, watching Simpson and his guide already loading the small canoe. "It's across the lake, dead right for you fellers. And the snow'll make bully trails! If there's any moose mussing around up thar, they'll not get so much as a tail-end scent of you with the wind as it is. Good luck, Monsieur Défago!" he added facetiously. *"Bonne chance!"*

Défago returned the good wishes, apparently in the best of spirits, the silent mood gone. Before eight o'clock old Punk had the camp to himself. Cathcart and Hank were far along the trail that led westward, while the canoe that carried Défago and Simpson was already a dark speck bobbing on the bosom of the lake, going due east.

The wintry sharpness of the air was tempered now by a sun that topped the wooded ridges and blazed with a luxurious warmth upon the world of lake and forest below. Loons flew skimming through the sparkling spray that the wind lifted; and as far as eye could reach rose the leagues of endless, crowding bush, desolate in its lonely sweep and grandeur, and stretching its mighty and unbroken carpet right up to the frozen shores of Hudson Bay.

Simpson, who was seeing it all for the first time as he paddled hard in the bow of the dancing canoe, was enchanted by its austere beauty. Behind him in the stern seat, singing fragments of his native chanteys, Défago steered the craft of birch bark. Both were gay and lighthearted, and they reached the farther shore after a stiff paddle of twelve miles against a head wind.

Simpson held a new .303 rifle in his hands and looked along its pair of faultless, gleaming barrels. Now that he was about to plunge into the virgin heart of uninhabited regions as vast as Europe itself, the true nature of the situation was beginning to steal upon him with an effect of delight and awe that his imagination was fully capable of appreciating. The bleak splendors of these remote and lonely forests overwhelmed him with the sense of his own littleness. He understood the silent warning. Only Défago, as a symbol of a distant civilization where man was master, stood between him and a pitiless death by exhaustion and starvation.

It was thrilling to him, therefore, to watch Défago turn over the canoe upon the shore, pack the paddles carefully underneath, and then proceed to blaze the spruce stems for some distance on either side of an almost invisible trail, with the careless remark thrown in, "Simpson, boss, if anything happens to me, you'll find the canoe all correc' by these marks; then strike doo west into the sun to hit the home camp agin, see?"

It was the most natural thing in the world to say, and yet it expressed the youth's emotions at the moment with an utterance that was symbolic of the situation and of his own helplessness as a factor in it. He was alone with Défago in a primitive world; that was all. The canoe, another symbol of man's ascendancy, was now to be left behind. Those small yellow patches, made on the trees by the axe, were the only indications of its hiding place.

Meanwhile, shouldering the packs between them, they followed the slender trail over rocks and fallen trunks and across half-frozen swamps, skirting numerous lakes that fairly gemmed the forest, their borders fringed with mist. Toward five o'clock they found themselves suddenly on the edge of the woods, looking out across a large sheet of water in front of them, dotted with pine-clad islands of all describable shapes and sizes.

"Fifty Island Water," announced Défago wearily. "And the sun jest goin' to dip his bald old head into it!" he added. Immediately they set about pitching camp for the night.

In a very few minutes, under those skillful hands, the silk tent stood taut and cozy, the beds of balsam boughs ready laid, and a brisk cooking fire burned with a minimum of smoke. While young Simpson cleaned the fish they had caught trolling behind the canoe, Défago "guessed" he would "jest as soon" take a turn through the bush for indications of moose. "*May* come across a trunk where they bin and rubbed horns," he said as he moved off, "or feedin' on the last of the maple leaves." His small figure melted away like a shadow in the dusk. A few steps, it seemed, and he was no longer visible.

Yet there was little underbrush hereabouts; the trees stood somewhat apart, well spaced; and in the clearings grew silver birch and maple, spearlike and slender, against the immense stems of spruce and hemlock. A little to the right, however, began the great burned section, miles in extent—*brulé*, as it is called—where fires the previous year had raged for weeks. The blackened stumps now rose gaunt and ugly, bereft of branches, savage and desolate beyond words. The perfume of charcoal and rain-soaked ashes still hung faintly about it.

The dusk rapidly deepened; the glades grew dark; the crackling of the fire and the wash of little waves along the rocky lakeshore were the only sounds audible. The wind had dropped with the sun, and in all that vast world of branches nothing stirred.

In front lay the stretch of Fifty Island Water, a crescent-shaped lake some fifteen miles from tip to tip, and perhaps five miles across where they were camped. A sky of rose and saffron still dropped its pale streaming fires across the waves, where the islands—a hundred, surely, rather than fifty—floated like the fairy barques of some enchanted fleet.

The beauty of the scene was strangely uplifting. Simpson smoked the fish and tended the fire. Yet ever at the back of his thoughts lay that other aspect of the wilderness: the indifference to human life, the merciless spirit of desolation which took no note of man. The sense of his utter loneliness, now that even Défago had gone, came close as he looked about him and listened for the sound of his companion's returning footsteps. And instinctively the thought stirred him: What should I—*could* I—do if anything happened and he did not come back . . . ?

They enjoyed their well-earned supper, eating untold quantities of fish, and drinking unmilked tea strong enough to kill men who had not covered thirty miles of hard going. And when it was over, they smoked and told stories around the blazing fire, laughing, stretching weary limbs, and discussing plans for the morrow. Défago was in excellent spirits, though disappointed at having no signs of moose to report. But it was dark and he had not gone far. The *brulé*, too, was bad. His clothes and hands were smeared with charcoal. Simpson, watching him, realized with renewed vividness their position—alone together in the wilderness.

"Défago," he said presently, "these woods, you know, are a bit too big to feel quite at home in—to feel comfortable in . . . eh?"

"You've hit it right, Simpson, boss," Défago replied, fixing his searching brown eyes on Simpson's face. "There's no end to 'em—no end at all." Then he added in a lowered tone as if to himself, "There's lots found out *that*, and gone plumb to pieces!"

The man's gravity of manner was not quite to the other's liking; he was sorry he had broached the subject. He remembered suddenly how his uncle had told him that men were sometimes stricken with a strange fever of the wilderness, when the seduction of the uninhabited wastes caught them so fiercely that they went forth, half fascinated, half deluded, to their death. And he had a shrewd idea that his companion held something in sympathy with that queer type. He led the conversation on to other topics, on to Hank and the doctor, for instance, and the natural rivalry as to who should get the first sight of moose.

"If they went doo west," observed Défago carelessly, "there's sixty miles between us now—with ole Punk at halfway house eatin' himself full to bustin' with fish and corfee." They laughed together over the picture. But the casual mention of those sixty miles again made Simpson realize the prodigious scale of this land where they hunted; sixty miles was a mere step; two hundred little more than a step. Stories of lost hunters rose persistently before his memory. The passion and mystery of homeless and wandering men, seduced by the beauty of great forests, swept his soul in a way too vivid to be quite pleasant.

"Sing us a song, Défago, if you're not too tired," he asked; "one of those old *voyageur* songs you sang the other night." He handed his tobacco pouch to the guide and then filled his own pipe, while the Canadian sent his light voice across the lake in one of those plaintive, almost melancholy chanteys with which lumbermen and trappers lessen the burden of their labor.

It was in the middle of the third verse that Simpson noticed a curious change in the man's voice. Even before he knew what it was, uneasiness caught him, and looking up quickly, he saw that Défago, though still singing, was peering about him into the bush, as though he heard or saw something. His voice grew fainter, dropped to a hush, then ceased altogether. The same instant, with a movement amazingly alert, he started to his feet and stood upright—*sniffing the air.* Like a dog scenting game, he drew the air into his nostrils in short, sharp breaths, turning quickly as he did so in all directions, and finally "pointing" down the lakeshore, eastward. Simpson's heart fluttered disagreeably as he watched him.

"Lord, man! How you made me jump!" he exclaimed, and peered

over his shoulder into the sea of darkness. "What's up? D'you smell moose? Or anything queer, anything—wrong?"

Even before the questions were out of his mouth he knew they were foolish, for any man with a pair of eyes in his head could see that the Canadian had turned white down to his very gills. Not even sunburn and the glare of the fire could hide that.

The forest pressed around him with its encircling wall; the nearer tree stems gleamed like bronze in the firelight; beyond that—blackness and, so far as he could tell, a silence of death.

Défago turned abruptly; the livid hue of his face had turned to a dirty gray. "I never said I heered—or smelt—nuthin'," he said in an oddly altered voice that conveyed a touch of defiance. "I was only takin' a look around, so to speak." Then he added suddenly, in his more natural voice, "Have you got the matches, Boss Simpson?" and proceeded to light the pipe he had half filled just before he began to sing.

Without speaking another word, they sat down again by the fire, Défago settling so that he could face the direction the wind came from. Even a tenderfoot could tell that Défago changed his position in order to hear and smell whatever there was to be heard and smelled. "Guess now I don't feel like singing any," he explained presently of his own accord. "That song kinder brings back memories that's troublesome to me; I never oughter've begun it. It sets me on t' imagining things, see?"

Clearly the man was still fighting with some profoundly moving emotion. He wished to excuse himself in the eyes of the other. But nothing could explain away the livid terror that had dropped over his face while he stood there sniffing the air. And nothing—no amount of blazing fire, or chatting on ordinary subjects—could make that camp exactly as it had been before. The shadow of an unknown horror had flashed for an instant in the face and gestures of the guide and had also communicated itself, vaguely and yet more potently, to his companion.

Somehow or other, after another long spell of smoking, talking, and roasting themselves before the great fire, the shadow that had so suddenly invaded their peaceful camp began to lift. The feeling of immediate horror passed away as mysteriously as it had come, and Simpson began to feel that he had permitted himself the unreasoning terror of a child. He put it down partly to the wild and immense scenery, partly to the spell of solitude, and partly to overfatigue. The pallor of the guide's face was, of course, uncommonly hard to explain, yet it *might* have been due in some way to an effect of firelight, or his own imagination.

Simpson lit his pipe and tried to laugh to himself. Défago heard that low laughter and looked up with surprise on his face. "What's ticklin' yer?" he asked gravely.

"I—I was thinking of our little toy woods at home in Scotland," stammered Simpson, coming back to what really dominated his mind, "and comparing them to—to all this," and he swept his arm around to indicate the bush.

"I wouldn't laugh about it, if I was you," Défago said, looking over Simpson's shoulder into the shadows. "There's places in there nobody won't never see into—nobody knows what lives in there either."

"Too big—too far off?" The suggestion in the guide's manner was immense and horrible.

Défago nodded.

In a loud voice Simpson cheerfully suggested that it was time for bed. But the guide lingered.

"Say, you, Boss Simpson," he began suddenly, as the last shower of sparks went up into the air, "you don't smell nothing, do you—nothing pertickler, I mean?"

The commonplace question, Simpson realized, veiled a dreadfully serious thought in his mind. A shiver ran down his back. "Nothing but this burning wood," he replied, kicking at the embers.

"And all the evenin' you ain't smelt nothing?" persisted the guide, peering at him through the gloom. "Nothing extrordiny, and different to anything else you ever smelt before?"

"No, no, man; nothing at all!" he replied aggressively.

Défago's face cleared. "That's good!" he exclaimed, with evident relief. "That's good to hear."

"Have *you?*" asked Simpson sharply.

The Canadian came closer in the darkness. He shook his head. "I guess not," he said, without overwhelming conviction. "It must've been jest that song of mine that did it. It's the song they sing in lumber camps and godforsaken places like that, when they're skeered the Wendigo's somewheres around, doin' a bit of swift travelin'—"

"And what's the Wendigo, pray?" Simpson asked. He knew that he was close upon the man's terror and the cause of it.

Défago turned swiftly and looked at him as though he were suddenly about to shriek. His eyes shone, his mouth was wide open. Yet all he said, or whispered rather, for his voice sank very low, was, "It's nuthin' but what those lousy fellers believe when they've been hittin' the bottle too long—a sort of great animal that lives up yonder"—he jerked his head northward—"quick as lightning in its tracks, an' bigger'n anything else in the bush, an' ain't supposed to be very good to look at—*that's all!*"

"A backwoods superstition . . ." began Simpson, moving hastily toward the tent. "Come on and get the lantern going! It's time we were asleep if we're to be up with the sun tomorrow."

The guide was close on his heels. "I'm coming," he answered out of the darkness. "I'm coming." And after a slight delay he appeared with the lantern and hung it from a nail in the front pole of the tent.

The two men lay down upon their beds of soft balsam boughs. Inside, all was warm and cozy, but outside, the world of crowding trees pressed close about them, marshaling their million shadows, and smothering the little tent that stood there like a wee white shell facing the ocean of tremendous forest.

Between the two lonely figures within, however, there pressed another shadow that was *not* a shadow from the night. It was the shadow cast by the strange fear, never wholly exorcised, that had leaped suddenly upon Défago in the middle of his singing. And Simpson, as he lay there, watching the darkness through the open flap of the tent, knew first that unique and profound stillness of a primeval forest when no wind stirs . . . and when the night has weight and substance that enters into the soul to bind a veil about it. . . . Then sleep took him.

THUS IT SEEMED to him, at least until he realized that he was lying with his eyes open and listening to a sound. And long before he understood what this sound was, it had stirred in him the centers of pity and alarm. Did it come, he wondered, from the lake, or from the woods?

Then, suddenly, with a rush and a flutter of the heart, he knew that it was close beside him, not two feet away, in the tent. It was a sound of weeping: Défago was sobbing in the darkness as though his heart would break, the blankets stuffed against his mouth to stifle it.

"Défago," he whispered quickly, "what's the matter?" There was no reply, but the sounds ceased abruptly. He stretched his hand out and touched him. The body did not stir.

"Are you awake?" for it occurred to him that the man was crying in his sleep. "Are you cold?" He noticed that his feet, which were uncovered, projected beyond the mouth of the tent. He spread an extra fold of his own blankets over them. The guide had slipped down in his bed, and the branches seemed to have been dragged with him. He was afraid to pull the body back again, for fear of waking him.

He hardly knew what it all meant. Défago, of course, had been crying in his sleep; some dream had afflicted him. Yet never in his life would he forget that pitiful sobbing, and the feeling that the whole awful wilderness of woods listened.

His own mind busied itself for a long time with the recent events, and a sensation of uneasiness remained, resisting ejection, very deep seated—peculiar beyond ordinary.

But sleep, in the long run, proves greater than all emotions, and half an hour later he was oblivious of everything in the outer world about him. Yet sleep, in this case, was his great enemy, concealing all approaches, smothering the warning of his nerves.

SO FAR AS Simpson can recall, it was a violent movement that first woke him and made him aware that his companion was sitting bolt upright beside him, quivering. Hours must have passed, for it was the pale gleam of dawn that revealed his outline against the canvas. This time the man was not crying; he was quaking like a leaf; he felt the trembling plainly through the blankets down the entire length of his own body. Défago now huddled down against him for protection, shrinking away from something that apparently concealed itself near the door flaps of the little tent.

Simpson thereupon called out to Défago, but he made no reply. And next—almost simultaneous with his waking, it seemed—the profound stillness of the dawn outside was shattered by a most uncommon sound. It came without warning and it was unspeakably dreadful. It was a voice, Simpson declares, possibly a human voice; hoarse yet plaintive—a soft, roaring voice close outside the tent, overhead rather than upon the ground, of immense volume, while in some strange way most penetratingly and seductively sweet. It rang out, too, in three separate and distinct notes, or cries, that bore an odd resemblance to the name of the guide: "*Dé-fa-go!*" It was unlike any sound the divinity student had ever heard in his life. A sort of windy, crying voice, as of something lonely and untamed, wild and of abominable power.

And even before it ceased, the guide beside him had sprung to his feet with an answering cry. He blundered against the tent pole, shaking the whole structure and spreading his arms out frantically for more room. For a second he stood upright by the door, his outline dark against the pallor of the dawn; then, with a furious rushing speed, before his companion could move a hand to stop him, he plunged through the flaps of canvas and was gone. And as he went—so astonishingly fast that the voice could actually be heard dying in the distance—he called aloud in tones of anguished terror that at the same time held something strangely like the frenzied exultation of delight: "Oh! Oh! My feet of fire! My burning feet of fire! Oh! Oh! This height and fiery speed!"

And then the distance quickly buried it, and the deep silence of very early morning descended upon the forest as before.

It had all come about with such rapidity that, but for the empty bed beside him, Simpson could almost have believed it to have been the memory of a nightmare carried over from sleep. But the strange words rang in his ears, as though he still heard them in the distance. Moreover, he had become aware that a strange perfume, faint yet pungent, pervaded the interior of the tent. And it was at this point, as his nostrils were taking this distressing odor down into his throat, that he found his courage, sprang quickly to his feet, and went out.

The gray light of dawn revealed the scene tolerably well. There stood the tent behind him, soaked with dew; the dark ashes of the fire, still warm; the lake, white beneath a coating of mist, the islands rising darkly out of it like objects packed in wool; and patches of snow beyond, among the clearer spaces of the bush—everything cold, still, waiting for the sun. But nowhere a sign of the vanished guide. He had gone—utterly.

There was nothing; nothing but the sense of his recent presence, *and* this penetrating, all-pervading odor. It was unlike any smell he knew. Acrid rather, not unlike the odor of a lion, yet softer and not wholly unpleasing, with something almost sweet in it that reminded him of the scent of decaying garden leaves, earth, and the myriad, nameless perfumes that make up the odor of a big forest. Yet the "odor of lions" is the phrase with which he usually sums it all up.

Then it was gone. A great kiss of wind ran softly through the awakening forest, and a few maple leaves rustled tremblingly to earth. The sky grew suddenly much lighter. Simpson felt the cool air upon his cheek and realized that he was alone in the bush—*and* that he was called upon to take immediate steps to find his vanished companion.

Make an effort, accordingly, he did, though an ill-calculated and futile one. With that wilderness of trees about him, he ran about, without any sense of direction, like a frantic child, and called loudly without ceasing the name of the guide.

"Défago! Défago! Défago!" he yelled, and the trees gave him back the name as often as he shouted, only a little softened: "Défago! Défago! Défago!"

He followed the trail that lay for a short distance across the patches of snow, and then lost it again where the trees grew too thick for snow to lie. He shouted till he was hoarse, and till the sound of his own voice in all that unanswering world began to frighten him. His confusion increased. His distress became formidably acute, till at length he headed back to the camp again. It remains a wonder that he ever found his way.

Exhaustion then applied its own remedy, and he grew calmer. He made the fire and breakfasted. Hot coffee and bacon put a little sense into him again, and he realized that he had been behaving like a boy. He now decided that he must first make as thorough a search as possible, failing success in which, he must find his way to the home camp as best he could and bring help.

Taking food, matches, and rifle with him, and a small axe to blaze the trees against his return journey, he set forth. It was eight o'clock when he started, the sun shining over the tops of the trees in a sky without clouds. Pinned to a stake by the fire he left a note in case Défago returned while he was away.

This time he took a new direction, intending to make a wide sweep that must sooner or later cut into indications of the guide's trail. Before he had gone a quarter of a mile he came across the tracks of a large animal in the snow, and beside it the light and smaller tracks of what were beyond question human feet—the feet of Défago. The relief he at once experienced was natural, though brief; for at first he saw in these tracks a simple explanation of the whole matter: these big marks had surely been left by a bull moose that, wind against it, had blundered upon the camp, and uttered its singular cry of warning and alarm the moment its mistake was apparent. Défago had scented the brute coming downwind hours before. His excitement and disappearance were due, of course, to—to his . . .

Then the impossible explanation at which he grasped faded, as common sense showed him mercilessly that none of this was true. No guide, much less a guide like Défago, could have acted in so irrational a way, going off even without his rifle! Besides, now that he examined them closer, these were not the tracks of a moose at all! These were big, round, ample, and with no pointed outline as of sharp hoofs. He wondered for a moment whether bear tracks were like that. There was no other animal he could think of, for caribou did not come so far south at this season and, even if they did, would leave hoofmarks.

They were ominous signs—these mysterious writings left in the snow by the unknown creature that had lured a human being away from safety—and when he coupled them in his imagination with that haunting sound that broke the stillness of the dawn, a momentary dizziness shook his mind. Stooping down to examine the marks more closely, he caught a faint whiff of that sweet yet pungent odor that made him instantly straighten up again, fighting a sensation almost of nausea.

With the persistence of true pluck, however, Simpson went forward, following the tracks as best he could, smothering these ugly emotions that sought to weaken his will. He blazed innumerable trees as he went, ever fearful of being unable to find the way back, and he called aloud the name of the guide every few seconds. The dull tapping of the axe upon the massive trunks and the unnatural accents of his own voice at length became sounds that he even dreaded to hear. For they drew attention to his presence and exact whereabouts, and if something were really hunting himself down in the same way that he was hunting down another . . . With a strong effort he crushed the thought out the instant it rose.

Although the snow was not continuous, lying merely in shallow flurries over the more open spaces, he found no difficulty in following the tracks for the first few miles. They were straight as a ruled line wherever the trees permitted. The stride soon began to increase in length, till it finally assumed proportions that seemed absolutely impossible for an ordinary animal to have made. Like huge flying leaps they became. One of these he measured, and though he knew that a stretch of eighteen feet must be somehow wrong, he was at a complete loss to understand why he found no signs on the snow between the extreme points. But what perplexed him even more was that Défago's stride increased in the same manner, and finally covered the same incredible distances. It looked as if the great beast had lifted him with it and carried him across these astonishing intervals.

The sight of these huge tracks was profoundly shocking. It was the most horrible thing his eyes had ever looked upon. He began to follow them mechanically, absentmindedly almost, ever peering over his shoulder to see if he, too, were being followed by something with a gigantic tread.

Two things he presently noticed, while forging pluckily ahead. Both tracks, he saw, had undergone a change, and this change, so far as it concerned the footsteps of the man, was appalling.

It was in the bigger tracks he first noticed this, and for a long time he could not quite believe his eyes. Was it the blown leaves that produced odd effects of light and shade, or was it actually the fact that the great marks had become faintly colored? For round about the deep, plunging holes of the animal there now appeared a mysterious reddish tinge that was more like an effect of light than of anything that dyed the substance of the snow itself. Every mark had it, and had it increasingly—this indistinct fiery tinge that painted a new touch of ghastliness into the picture.

But when, wholly unable to explain or credit it, he turned his attention to the other tracks, he noticed that these had undergone a change that was infinitely worse, and charged with far more horrible suggestion. For, in the last hundred yards or so, he saw that they had grown gradually into the semblance of the parent tread. It was hard to see where the change first began. The result, however, was beyond question. Smaller, neater, more cleanly modeled, they formed now an exact and careful duplicate of the larger tracks beside them. The feet that produced them had, therefore, also changed. And something in his mind reared up with loathing and with terror as he saw it.

Simpson hesitated; then, ashamed of his alarm and indecision, took a few hurried steps ahead; the next instant he stopped dead in his tracks. Immediately in front of him all signs of the trail ceased; both tracks came to an abrupt end. On all sides, for a hundred yards and more, he searched in vain for the least indication of their continuance. There was nothing.

The trees were very thick just there, big trees all of them, spruce, cedar, hemlock; there was no underbrush. He stood looking about him, bereft of any power of judgment. Then he set to work to search again, and again, and yet again, but always with the same result: *nothing.* The feet that printed the surface of the snow thus far had now, apparently, left the ground!

And it was in that moment of distress and confusion that the whip of terror laid its most nicely calculated lash about his heart. Far overhead, muted by great height and distance, strangely thinned and wailing, he heard the crying voice of Défago.

"Oh! Oh! This fiery height! Oh, my feet of fire! My burning feet of fire. . . !" The sound dropped upon him out of that still, wintry sky with an effect of dismay and terror unsurpassed. Once it called—then silence through all the wilderness of trees.

Simpson, scarcely knowing what he did, presently found himself running wildly to and fro, searching, calling, tripping over roots and boulders, and flinging himself in a frenzy of undirected pursuit after the caller. For the panic of the wilderness had called to him in that far voice—the power of untamed distance—the enticement of the desolation that destroys. A vision of Défago, eternally hunted, driven and pursued across the skyey vastness of those ancient forests, fled like a flame across the dark ruin of his thoughts.

The cry was not repeated; his own hoarse calling brought no response; the inscrutable forces of the wild had summoned their victim beyond recall—and held him fast. Yet he searched and called, it seems, for hours afterward, for it was late in the afternoon when at length he decided to abandon a useless pursuit. He went with reluctance, that crying voice still echoing in his ears. With difficulty he found the homeward trail and headed back toward his camp on the shores of Fifty Island Water.

But the journey through the gathering dusk was miserably haunted. He heard innumerable following footsteps, voices that laughed and whispered, and saw figures crouching behind trees and boulders. The shadows of the woods had now become menacing, challenging, and the presentiment of a nameless doom lurked ill-concealed behind every detail.

Sleep being absolutely out of the question, and traveling an unknown trail in the darkness equally impracticable, he sat up the whole of that night in camp, rifle in hand, before a fire he never for a single moment allowed to die down. With the very first signs of dawn he set forth upon the long return journey to the home camp to get help. As before, he left a written note for Défago to explain his absence, and to indicate where he had left a plentiful cache of food and matches.

How Simpson found his way alone by lake and forest might well make a story in itself. He followed the almost invisible trail mechanically, relying upon instinct. Through all that tangled region he succeeded in reaching the exact spot where Défago had hidden the canoe nearly three days before with the remark, "Strike doo west across the lake into the sun to find the home camp."

There was not much sun left to guide him, but he used his compass to the best of his ability, embarking in the frail craft for the last twelve miles of his journey with a sensation of immense relief that the forest was at last behind him. Fortunately, too, the other hunters were back. The light of their fires furnished a steering point without which he might have searched all night long for the actual position of the camp.

It was close upon midnight all the same when his canoe grated on the sandy cove, and Hank, Punk, and his uncle, disturbed in their sleep by his cries, ran quickly down and helped a very exhausted and broken specimen of Scots humanity over the rocks toward a dying fire.

THE SUDDEN APPEARANCE OF HIS prosaic uncle, the sound of that crisp "Hulloa, my boy!" and the grasp of that vigorous hand introduced another standard of judgment. A revulsion of feeling washed through him. He realized that he had let himself go rather badly. He even felt vaguely ashamed of himself.

This doubtless explains why he found it so hard to tell that group around the fire everything. Thus, all the others gathered was that Défago had suffered in the night an acute and inexplicable attack of mania, had imagined himself called by someone or something, and had plunged into the bush after it without food or rifle. Simpson told enough, however, for the immediate decision to be arrived at that a relief party must start at the earliest possible moment, and that Simpson, in order to guide it capably, must first have food and, above all, sleep.

They were off by seven the following day, leaving Punk in charge of the home camp, with instructions to have food and fire always ready. By the time they reached the beginning of the trail, where the canoe was laid up against the return journey, Simpson had mentioned how Défago spoke vaguely of "something he called a Wendigo," how he cried in his sleep, and how he imagined an unusual scent about the camp. He also admitted the bewildering effect of "that extraordinary odor" upon himself, "pungent and acrid like the odor of lions." And by the time they were within an easy hour of Fifty Island Water he had let slip the further fact that he had heard the vanished guide "call for help." Also, while describing how the man's footsteps in the snow had gradually assumed an exact miniature likeness of the animal's plunging tracks, he left out the fact that they measured a *wholly* incredible distance. He mentioned the fiery tinge in the snow, yet shrank from telling that body and bed had been partly dragged out of the tent.

With the net result that Dr. Cathcart, adroit psychologist that he fancied himself to be, had assured him clearly enough exactly where his mind, influenced by loneliness, bewilderment, and terror, had yielded to the strain and invited delusion.

"The spell of these terrible solitudes," he said, "cannot leave any mind untouched. The animal that haunted your camp was undoubtedly a moose, for the 'belling' of a moose may sometimes have a very peculiar quality of sound. The size and stretch of the tracks we shall prove when we come to them. The hallucination of an audible voice, of course, is one of the commonest forms of delusion due to mental excitement. But the thing I find it uncommonly difficult to explain is that—damned odor."

"It made me feel sick," declared his nephew. "A kind of desolate and terrible odor is the only way I can describe it," he concluded, glancing at the quiet, unemotional man beside him.

AND SO AT last they came to the little camp and found the tent still standing, the remains of the fire, and the piece of paper pinned to a stake beside it—untouched. The cache, however, had been discovered and opened by muskrats, minks, and squirrels. The matches lay scattered about the opening, but the food had been taken to the last crumb.

"Well, fellers, he ain't here!" exclaimed Hank loudly after his fashion. "I propose that we start out at once an' hunt for 'm like hell!"

The gloom of Défago's probable fate oppressed the whole party with a sense of dreadful gravity. Simpson, feeling vaguely as if his word were somehow at stake, went about explaining particulars in a hushed tone. "And that's the direction he ran off in," he said to his two companions, pointing toward the woods where the guide had vanished that morning in the gray dawn. "Straight down there he ran like a deer, in between the birch and the hemlock."

Hank and Dr. Cathcart exchanged glances.

"And it was about two miles down there, in a straight line," continued the other, speaking with something of the former terror in his voice, "that I followed his trail to the place where it stopped—dead!"

It was early in the afternoon, for they had traveled quickly, and there were still a good two hours of daylight left. Dr. Cathcart and Hank lost no time in beginning the search, but Simpson was too exhausted to accompany them. They would follow the blazed marks on the trees and, where possible, his footsteps. Meanwhile, the best thing he could do was to keep a good fire going, and rest.

But after something like three hours' search, the darkness already down, the two men returned to camp with nothing to report. Fresh snow had covered all signs, and though they had followed the blazed trees to the spot where Simpson had turned back, they had not discovered the smallest indications of a human being, or, for that matter, of an animal. There were no fresh tracks of any kind; the snow lay undisturbed.

It was difficult to know what was best to do, though in reality there was nothing more they *could* do. They might stay and search for weeks without much chance of success. The fresh snow destroyed their only hope, and they gathered around the fire for supper, a gloomy and despondent party. The facts, indeed, were sad enough, for Défago had a wife at Rat Portage, and his earnings were the family's sole means of support.

On the suggestion of Hank, his old pal, however, they proposed to wait a little longer and devote the whole of the following day, from dawn to darkness, to the most systematic search they could devise. All that men could do they would do.

Meanwhile, they talked about the particular form in which the singular panic of the wilderness had made its attack upon the mind of the unfortunate guide. Hank admitted that a story ran over all this section of country to the effect that several Indians had "seen the Wendigo" along the shores of Fifty Island Water in the fall of last year, and that this was the true reason of Défago's disinclination to hunt there. "When an Indian goes crazy," Hank explained, "it's always put that he's 'seen the Wendigo.' An' pore old Défago was superstitious down to his very heels!"

A wall of silence wrapped them in, for the snow, though not thick, was sufficient to deaden any noise, and the frost held things pretty tight besides. Fear, to put it plainly, hovered close about that little camp, and though all three would have been glad to speak of other matters, the only thing they seemed able to discuss was this—the source of their fear.

No sound but their voices and the soft roar of the flames made itself heard. Only, from time to time, something soft as the flutter of a pine moth's wings went past them through the air. No one seemed anxious to go to bed. The hours slipped toward midnight.

"The legend is picturesque enough," observed the doctor after one of the longer pauses, "for the Wendigo is simply the call of the wild personified, which some natures hear to their own destruction."

"That's about it," Hank said presently. "An' there's no misunderstandin' when you hear it. It calls you by name right 'nough."

Another pause followed. Then Dr. Cathcart came back to the forbidden subject. "The allegory *is* significant," he remarked, looking about him into the darkness, "for the voice, they say, resembles all the minor sounds of the bush—wind, falling water, cries of animals, and so forth. And once the victim hears *that*, he's off for good, of course! His most vulnerable points, moreover, are said to be the feet and the eyes; the feet, you see, for the lust of wandering, and the eyes for the lust of beauty. The poor beggar goes at such a dreadful speed that he bleeds beneath the eyes, and his feet burn."

Dr. Cathcart, as he spoke, continued to peer uneasily into the surrounding gloom. His voice sank to a hushed tone.

"The Wendigo," he added, "is said to burn his feet—owing to the friction, apparently caused by its tremendous velocity—till they drop off, and new ones form exactly like its own."

"It don't always keep to the ground neither," came in Hank's slow, heavy drawl, "for it goes so high that he thinks the stars have set him all afire. An' it'll take great thumpin' jumps sometimes, an' run along the tops of the trees, carrying its partner with it, an' then droppin' him jest as a fish hawk'll drop a pickerel to kill it before eatin'. An' its food, of all the muck in the whole bush, is—moss!" And he laughed a short, unnatural laugh. "It's a moss eater, is the Wendigo," he added, looking up excitedly into the faces of his companions. "Moss eater," he repeated, with a string of outlandish oaths.

Simpson now understood the true purpose of all this talk. What these two men dreaded more than anything else was silence. They were talking against time. They were also talking against darkness, against the invasion of panic, against the admission that they were in an enemy's country—against anything, in fact, rather than allow their inmost thoughts to assume control. Thus the hours passed; and thus, with lowered voices, this little group of humanity sat in the jaws of the wilderness and talked foolishly of the terrible and haunting legend. The fate of their comrade hung over them with a steadily increasing weight of oppression that finally became insupportable.

It was Hank who first let loose all this pent-up emotion by springing suddenly to his feet and letting out an ear-shattering yell into the night. He could not contain himself any longer. To make it carry even beyond an ordinary cry, he interrupted its rhythm by shaking the palm of his hand before his mouth.

"That's for Défago," he said, looking down at the other two with a queer, defiant laugh, "for it's my belief that my ole partner's not far from us at this very minute."

There was a vehemence and recklessness about his performance that made Simpson start to his feet in amazement, and betrayed even the doctor into letting the pipe slip from between his lips. Hank's face was ghastly, but Cathcart's showed a sudden weakness. Then a momentary anger blazed into his eyes, and he, too, got to his feet and faced the excited guide. For this was unpermissible, foolish, dangerous, and he meant to stop it in the bud.

What might have happened in the next minute or two one may speculate about, yet never definitely know, for in the instant of profound silence that followed Hank's roaring voice, something went past through the darkness of the sky overhead at terrific speed—something very large, for it displaced much air, while down among the trees there fell a faint and windy cry of a human voice, calling in tones of indescribable anguish and appeal:

"Oh! Oh! This fiery height! Oh, oh! My feet of fire! My burning feet of fire!"

White to the very edge of his shirt, Hank looked stupidly about him like a child. Dr. Cathcart uttered some kind of unintelligible cry, turning with blind terror toward the protection of the tent, then halting in the act as though frozen. Simpson's own horror was too deep to allow of any immediate reaction. He had heard that cry before. Turning to his stricken companions, he said almost calmly, "That's exactly the cry I heard, the very words he used!"

Then, lifting his face to the sky, he cried aloud, "Défago, Défago! Come down here to us! Come down!"

Before there was time for anybody to take definite action, there came the sound of something dropping heavily among the trees, striking the branches on the way down, and landing with a dreadful thud upon the frozen earth below. The crash and thunder of it was terrific.

"That's him, s'help me the good Gawd!" came from Hank in a whispering cry half choked, his hand going automatically toward the hunting knife in his belt. "And he's coming! He's coming!" he added, with an irrational laugh of terror as the sounds of heavy footsteps crunching over the snow became distinctly audible, approaching through the blackness toward the circle of light.

And while the steps, with their stumbling motion, moved nearer and nearer, the three men stood around the fire, motionless and dumb. Like stricken children they seemed. And, meanwhile, their owner still invisible, the footsteps came closer, crunching the frozen snow. Then at length the darkness brought forth a figure. It drew forward into the zone of uncertain light where fire and shadow mingled, not ten feet away; then halted, staring at them fixedly. The same instant it started forward again with the spasmodic motion of a thing moved by wires; and as it came up closer to them, full into the glare of the fire, they perceived then that it was a man, and apparently that this man was Défago.

Something like a skin of horror drew down in that moment over every face. Défago advanced, his tread faltering and uncertain; he made his way straight up to them as a group first, then turned sharply and peered close into the face of Simpson. The sound of a voice issued from his lips.

"Here I am, Boss Simpson. I heered someone calling me." It was a faint, dried-up voice, made wheezy and breathless as by immense exertion. "I'm havin' a reg'lar hellfire kind of a trip, I am." And he laughed, thrusting his head forward into the other's face.

Hank immediately sprang forward with a stream of oaths so far-fetched that Simpson did not recognize them as English at all, but thought he had lapsed into Indian or some other lingo. Dr. Cathcart advanced behind him, heavily stumbling. Simpson merely stood still. He said nothing. Yet, through the torrent of Hank's meaningless phrases, he remembers hearing his uncle's tone of authority—hard and forced—saying several things about food and warmth, blankets, whiskey, and the rest . . . and, further, that whiffs of that penetrating, unaccustomed odor, vile, yet sweetly bewildering, assailed his nostrils during all that followed.

"It *is*—YOU, isn't it, Défago?" he asked under his breath, horror breaking his speech.

And at once Cathcart burst out with the loud answer before the other had time to move his lips. "Of course it is! Of course it is! Only—can't you see?—he's nearly dead with exhaustion, cold, and terror. Isn't *that* enough to change a man beyond all recognition?" It was said in order to convince himself as much as to convince the others. And continually, while he spoke and acted, he held a handkerchief to his nose. That odor pervaded the whole camp.

For the "Défago" who sat huddled by the big fire, wrapped in blankets, drinking hot whiskey and holding food in wasted hands, was no more like the guide they had last seen alive than the picture of a man of sixty is like a daguerreotype of his early youth. Nothing can describe that ghastly caricature masquerading there in the firelight as Défago. The face was more animal than human. The features were drawn about into wrong proportions, the skin loose and hanging, as though he had been subjected to extraordinary pressures and tensions.

It was Hank, though distraught and shaking with emotion, who brought things to a head. Without more ado, he went off a little distance from the fire and, shading his eyes for a moment with both hands, shouted in a loud voice that mingled anger and affection.

"You ain't Défago! You ain't Défago at all! I don't give a damn, but that ain't you, my ole pal of twenty years!" He glared upon the huddled figure as though he would destroy him with his eyes. It was impossible to silence him. He stood there shouting like one possessed, horrible to see, horrible to hear, *because it was the truth.* He repeated himself in fifty different ways. The woods rang with echoes. At one time it looked as if he meant to fling himself upon the intruder, for his hand continually jerked toward the long hunting knife in his belt.

But in the end Hank's voice suddenly broke, he collapsed on the ground, and Cathcart persuaded him at last to go into the tent and lie quiet. Then the doctor, followed by his nephew, went up with a determined air and stood opposite the figure of Défago. He looked him squarely in the face and spoke.

"Défago, tell us what's happened, so that we can know how best to help you," he said in a tone of authority, almost of command. At once the figure turned up to him a face so piteous and so terrible that the doctor shrank back from him as from something spiritually unclean. Simpson, close behind, got the impression of a mask that was on the verge of dropping off, and that underneath they would discover something black and diabolical revealed in utter nakedness. "Out with it, man, out with it!" Cathcart cried, terror running neck and neck with entreaty. "None of us can stand this much longer!"

Défago answered in a thin and fading voice. "I seen that great Wendigo thing," he whispered, sniffing the air about him exactly like an animal. "I been with it, too. . . ."

At that moment the voice of Hank was heard yelling from behind the canvas. "His feet! Oh, Gawd, his feet! Look at his great changed—feet!"

Défago, shuffling where he sat, had moved in such a way that for the first time his legs were in full light and his feet visible. Yet Simpson had no time, himself, to see properly what Hank had seen. That same instant Cathcart was upon him, bundling the folds of blanket about his legs with such speed that Simpson caught little more than a passing glimpse of something dark and oddly massed where moccasined feet ought to have been.

Then, before the doctor had time to do more, Défago was standing upright in front of them, with an expression so dark and malicious upon his twisted visage that it was, in the true sense, monstrous.

"Now *you* seen it, too," he wheezed. "You seen my fiery, burning feet! And now—that is, unless you kin save me an' prevent—it's 'bout time for—"

His piteous voice was interrupted by a sound that was like the roar of wind coming across the lake. The trees overhead shook their tangled branches. The blazing fire bent its flames as before a blast. And something swept with a terrific, rushing noise about the little camp and seemed to surround it entirely in a single moment of time. Défago shook the blankets from his body, turned toward the woods behind, and with the same stumbling motion that had brought him—was gone; gone, before anyone could move muscle to prevent him. The darkness positively swallowed him; and less than a dozen seconds later, above the roar of the swaying trees, all three men, watching and listening with stricken hearts, heard a cry that seemed to drop down upon them from a great height—"Oh, oh! This fiery height! Oh, oh! My feet of fire! My burning feet of fire . . . !" then died away, into untold space and silence.

Dr. Cathcart was just able to seize Hank violently by the arm as he tried to dash headlong into the bush. "But I want ter know!" shrieked the guide. "I want ter see! That ain't him at all, but some devil that's shunted into his place!"

Cathcart admits he never quite knew how he managed to keep him in the tent and pacify him. Certainly he managed Hank admirably. But it was his nephew who gave him most cause for anxiety, for the cumulative strain had now produced a condition of hysteria which made it necessary to isolate him upon a bed of boughs and blankets as far removed from Hank as was possible.

And there he lay, as the watches of that haunted night passed over the lonely camp, crying startled sentences into the folds of his blankets. A quantity of gibberish about speed and height and fire mingled with Biblical memories of the classroom. "People with broken faces all on fire are coming at a most awful, awful pace toward the camp!" he would moan one minute, and the next would sit up and stare into the woods, intently listening, and whisper, "How terrible in the wilderness are—are the feet of them that . . ." until his uncle came across to change the direction of his thoughts and comfort him.

The hysteria, fortunately, proved but temporary. Sleep cured him, just as it cured Hank.

Till the first signs of daylight came, Dr. Cathcart kept his vigil. His face was the color of chalk and there were strange flushes beneath his eyes. An appalling terror of the soul battled with his will all through those silent hours.

At dawn he lit the fire himself, made breakfast, and woke the others, and by seven they were well on their way back to the home camp—three perplexed and afflicted men, but each in his own way having reduced his inner turmoil to a condition of more or less systematized order again.

They talked little, and then only of the most wholesome and common things, for their minds were charged with painful thoughts, though no one dared refer to them. Hank, being nearest to primitive conditions, was the first to find himself, for he was also less complex.

Simpson, the student of divinity, arranged his conclusions probably with the best, though not most scientific, appearance of order. Out there, in the heart of unreclaimed wilderness, they had surely witnessed something crudely and essentially primitive. Something that had survived the advance of humanity and betrayed a scale of life still monstrous and immature. He envisaged it rather as a glimpse into prehistoric ages, when superstitions, gigantic and uncouth, oppressed the hearts of men; when the forces of nature were still untamed, the powers that may have haunted a primeval universe not yet withdrawn.

AT THE FALL of day, cold, exhausted, famished, the party came to the end of the long portage and dragged themselves into a camp that at first glimpse seemed empty. Fire there was none, and no Punk came forward to welcome them. But the cry that burst from the lips of Hank, as he rushed ahead of them toward the fireplace, came as a warning that the end of the amazing affair was not quite yet. And both Cathcart and his nephew confessed afterward that when they saw him kneel down in his excitement and embrace something that reclined, gently moving, beside the extinguished ashes, they felt in their very bones that this would prove to be Défago—the true Défago, returned.

And so, indeed, it was.

It is soon told. Exhausted to the point of emaciation, the French Canadian—what was left of him, that is—fumbled among the ashes, trying to make a fire. His body crouched there, the weak fingers obeying feebly the instinctive habit of a lifetime with twigs and matches. But there was no longer any mind to direct the simple operation. The mind had fled beyond recall. And with it, too, had fled memory. Not only recent events, but all previous life was a blank.

This time it was the real man, though incredibly and horribly shrunken. On his face was no expression of any kind whatever—fear, welcome, or recognition. He did not seem to know who it was that embraced him, or who it was that fed, warmed, and spoke to him the words of comfort and relief. Forlorn and broken beyond all reach of human aid, the little man did meekly as he was bidden. The something that had constituted him an individual had vanished forever.

In some ways it was more terribly moving than anything they had yet seen—that idiot smile as he drew wads of coarse moss from his swollen cheeks and told them that he was "a damned moss eater"; the continued vomiting of even the simplest food; and, worst of all, the piteous and childish voice of complaint in which he told them that his feet pained him—"burn like fire"—which was natural enough when Dr. Cathcart examined them and found that both were dreadfully frozen. Beneath the eyes there were faint indications of recent bleeding.

The details of how he survived the prolonged exposure, of where he had been, or of how he covered the great distance from one camp to the other, including an immense detour of the lake on foot, since he had no canoe—all this remains unknown. His memory had vanished completely. And before the end of the winter whose beginning witnessed this strange occurrence, Défago, bereft of mind, memory, and soul, had gone with it. He lingered only a few weeks. And what Punk later was able to contribute to the story throws no further light upon it. He was cleaning fish by the lakeshore about five o'clock in the evening—an hour, that is, before the search party returned—when he saw this shadow of the guide picking its way weakly into camp. In advance of him, he declares, came the faint whiff of a certain singular odor.

The same instant old Punk started for home. He covered the entire journey of three days as only Indian blood could have covered it. The terror of a whole race drove him. He knew what it all meant. Défago had "seen the Wendigo."

THE TOUCH OF NUTMEG MAKES IT

JOHN COLLIER

A DOZEN BIG firms subsidize our mineralogical institute, and most of them keep at least one man permanently on research there. The library has the intimate and smoky atmosphere of a club. Logan and I had been there longest and had the two tables in the big window bay. Against the wall, just at the edge of the bay, where the light was bad, was a small table which was left for newcomers or transients.

One morning a new man was sitting at this table. It was not necessary to look at the books he had taken from the shelves to know that he was on statistics rather than formulas. He had one of those skull-like faces on which the skin seems stretched painfully tight. These are almost a hallmark of the statistician. His mouth was intensely disciplined but became convulsive at the least relaxation. His hands were the focal point of a minor morbidity. When he had occasion to stretch them both out together—to shift an open book, for example—he would stare at them for a full minute at a time. At such times the convulsive action of his mouth muscles was particularly marked.

The newcomer crouched low over his table when anyone passed behind his chair, as if trying to decrease the likelihood of contact. At midmorning he dissolved a tablet in a glass of water. I guessed at a long-standing anxiety neurosis.

I mentioned this to Logan at lunchtime. He said, "The poor guy certainly looks as miserable as a wet cat."

I am never repelled or chilled, as many people are, by the cheerless self-centeredness of the nervous or the unhappy. Logan, who has less curiosity, has a superabundance of good nature. We watched this man sitting in his solitary cell of depression for several days while the pleasant camaraderie of the library flowed all around him. Then we asked him to lunch with us.

He took the invitation in the typical neurotic fashion, seeming to weigh half a dozen shadowy objections before he accepted it. However, he came along, and before the meal was over he confirmed my suspicion that he had been starving for company but was too tied up to make any move toward it. We had already found out his name—J. Chapman Reid—and that he worked for the Walls Tyman Corporation. He named a string of towns he had lived in, and told us that he came originally from Georgia. That was all the information he offered. He opened up very noticeably when the talk turned on general matters, and occasionally showed signs of having an intense and painful wit, which is the sort I like best. He was pathetically grateful for the casual invitation. He thanked us when we got up from the table, again as we emerged from the restaurant, and yet again on the threshold of the library. This made it all the more natural to suggest a quiet evening together sometime soon.

During the next few weeks we saw a good deal of J. Chapman Reid and found him a very agreeable companion. I have a great weakness for these dry, reserved characters who once or twice an evening come out with a vivid, penetrating remark. We might even have become friends if Reid himself hadn't prevented this final step, less by his reserve, which I took to be part of his nature, than by his unnecessary gratitude. He made no effusive speeches—he was not that type—but a lost dog has no need of words to show his dependence and his appreciation. It was clear our company was everything to J. Chapman Reid.

One day Nathan Trimble, a newspaperman friend of Logan's, looked in at the library. He sat on Logan's table facing the window, with his back to the rest of the room. I went around and talked to him and Logan. Trimble was just getting ready to leave when Reid came in and sat down at his table. Trimble happened to look around, and he and Reid saw each other.

I was watching Reid. After the first startled stare, he did not even glance at the visitor. He sat quite still, his head dropping lower and lower in little jerks, as if someone were pushing it down. Then he got up and walked out of the library.

"By God!" said Trimble. "Do you know who that is?"

"No," said we. "Who?"

"Jason C. Reid."

"Jason C.?" I said. "No, it's J. Chapman. Oh, yes, I see. So what?"

"Why, for God's sake, don't you read the news? Don't you remember the Pittsburgh cleaver murder?"

"No," said I.

"Wait a minute," said Logan. "Was it about a year or so ago?"

"Damn it!" said Trimble. "It was a front-page sensation. This guy was tried for it. They said he hacked a pal of his pretty nearly to pieces. I saw the body. Never seen such a mess in my life. Fantastic! Horrible!"

"However," said I, "it would appear this fellow didn't do it. Presumably he wasn't convicted."

"They tried to pin it on him," said Trimble, "but they couldn't. It looked hellish bad, I must say. Alone together. No trace of any outsider. But no motive. I don't know. I just don't know. I covered the trial. I was in court every day, but I couldn't make up my mind about the guy. Don't leave any meat cleavers around this library, that's all."

With that, he bade us good-by. I looked at Logan. Logan looked at me. "I don't believe it," said Logan. "I don't believe he did it."

"I don't wonder his nerves are eating him," said I.

"No," said Logan. "It must be damnable. And now it's followed him here, and he knows it."

"We'll let him know, somehow," said I, "that we're not even interested enough to look up the newspaper files."

"Good idea," said Logan.

A little later Reid came in again. He came over to where we were sitting. "Would you prefer to cancel our arrangement for tonight?" said he. "I think it would be better if we canceled it. I shall ask my firm to transfer me again. I—"

"Hold on," said Logan. "Who said so? Not us."

"Didn't he tell you?" said Reid. "Of course he did."

"He said you were tried," said I. "And he said you were acquitted. That's good enough for us."

"You're still acquitted," said Logan. "And the date's on. And we *won't* talk."

"Oh!" said Reid. "Oh!"

"Forget it," said Logan, returning to his papers.

I took Reid by the shoulder and gave him a friendly shove toward his table. We avoided looking at him for the rest of the afternoon.

That night, when we met for dinner, we were naturally a little self-conscious. Reid probably felt it. "Look here," he said when we had finished eating, "would you mind if we skipped the movie tonight?"

"It's okay by me," said Logan. "Shall we go to Chancey's?"

"No," said Reid, "I want you to come somewhere where we can talk. Come up to my place."

"Just as you like," said I. "It's not necessary."

"Yes, it is," said Reid. "We may as well get it over."

He was in a painfully nervous state, so we consented and went up to his apartment, where we had never been before. It was a single room with a pull-down bed and a bathroom and kitchenette opening off it. Though Reid had now been in town over two months, there was absolutely no sign that he was living there at all. It might have been a room hired for the uncomfortable conversation of this one night.

We sat down, but Reid immediately got up again and stood between us, in front of the imitation fireplace. "I should like to say nothing about what happened today," he began. "I should like to ignore it and let it be forgotten. But it can't be forgotten.

"It's no use telling me you won't think about it," said he. "Of course you'll think about it. Everyone did back there. The firm sent me to Cleveland. It became known there, too. Everyone was thinking about it, whispering about it, wondering. You see, it would be rather more exciting if the fellow *was* guilty after all, wouldn't it?

"In a way, I'm glad this has come out. With you two, I mean. Most people—I don't want them to know anything. You two—you've been decent to me—I want you to know all about it.

"I came up from Georgia to Pittsburgh, was there for ten years with the Walls Tyman people. While there I met—I met Earle Wilson. He came from Georgia, too, and we became very great friends. I've never been one to go about much. Earle was not only my best friend; he was almost my only friend.

"Very well. Earle's job with our company was a better paid one than mine. He was able to afford a small house just beyond the fringe of the town. I used to drive out there two or three evenings a week. We spent the evenings very quietly. I want you to understand that I was quite at home in the house. There was no host-and-guest atmosphere about it. If I felt sleepy, I'd make no bones about going upstairs and stretching out on a bed and taking a nap for half an hour. There's nothing so extraordinary about that, is there?"

"No, nothing extraordinary about that," said Logan.

"Some people seemed to think there was," said Reid. "Well, one night I went out there after work. We ate, we sat about a bit, we played a game of checkers. He mixed a couple of drinks, then I mixed a couple. Normal enough, isn't it?"

"It certainly is," said Logan.

"I was tired," said Reid. "I felt heavy. I said I'd go upstairs and stretch out for half an hour. That always puts me right. So I went up.

"I sleep heavily, very heavily, for half an hour, then I'm all right. This time I seemed to be dreaming, a sort of nightmare. I thought I was in an air raid somewhere, and heard Earle's voice calling me, but I didn't wake, not until the usual half hour was up, anyway.

"I went downstairs. The room below was dark. I called out to Earle and started across from the stairs toward the light switch. Halfway across, I tripped over something. I went down, and I fell on him.

"I knew he was dead. I got up and found the light. He was lying there. He looked as if he had been attacked by a madman. He was cut to pieces, almost. God!

"I got hold of the phone at once and called the police. While they were coming, I just walked about, dazed. It seems I must have gone up into the bedroom again. I've got no recollection of that, but they found a smear of blood on the pillow. Of course, I was covered with it. Absolutely covered; I'd fallen on him. You can understand a man being dazed, can't you? You can understand him going upstairs, even, and not remembering it? Can't you?"

"I certainly can," said Logan.

"It seems very natural," said I.

"They thought they had trapped me over that," said Reid. "They said so to my face. The idiots! Well, I remember looking around, and I saw what it had been done with. Earle had a great equipment of cutlery in his kitchen. One of the things was a meat cleaver, the sort of thing you see usually in a butcher's shop. It was there on the carpet.

"Well, the police came. I told them all I could. Earle was a quiet fellow. He had no enemies. I thought it must be some maniac. Nothing was missing. It wasn't robbery, unless some half-crazy tramp had got in and been too scared in the end to take anything.

"Whoever it was had made a very clean getaway. Too clean for the police. They looked for fingerprints, and they couldn't find any.

"They have an endless routine in this sort of thing, but it wasn't good enough—the fellow was too clever for them. They wanted an arrest. So they indicted me.

"Their case was nothing but a negative one. God knows how they thought it could succeed. Perhaps they didn't think so. But, you see, if they could build up a strong presumptive case, and I only got off because of a hung jury—well, that's different from having to admit they couldn't find the real murderer.

"What was the evidence against me? That they couldn't find traces of anyone else! That's evidence of their own damned inefficiency, that's all. Does a man murder his best friend for nothing? Could they find any reason, any motive? They were trying to find some woman first of all. They have the mentality of a ten-cent magazine. They combed our money affairs. They even tried to smell out some subversive tie-up. God, if you knew what it was to be confronted with faces out of a comic strip and with minds that match the faces!

"In the end they settled on our game of checkers. Our poor, harmless game of checkers! We talked all the while we were playing, you know, and sometimes even forgot whose turn it was. I suppose there are people who can go berserk in a dispute over a childish game, but to me that's something utterly incomprehensible. Can *you* understand a man murdering his friend over a game? I can't. As a matter of fact, I remember we had to start this game over again, not once but twice—first when Earle mixed the drinks, and then when I mixed them. Each time we forgot who was to move. But they fixed on that. They had to find some shadow of a motive, and that was the best they could do.

"Of course, my lawyer tore it to shreds. By the mercy of God there'd been quite a craze at the works for playing checkers at lunchtime. So he soon found half a dozen men to swear that neither Earle nor I ever played the game seriously enough to get het up about it.

"They had no other motive to put forward. Both our lives were simple, ordinary, and open as a book. What was their case? They couldn't find what they were paid to find. For that, they proposed to send a man to the death cell. Can you beat that?"

"It sounds pretty damnable," said I.

"Yes," said he passionately. "Damnable is the word. They got what they were after—the jury voted nine to three for acquittal, which saved the faces of the police. There was plenty of room for a hint that they were on the right track all the time. You can imagine what my life has been since! If you ever get into that sort of mess, my friends, hang yourselves the first night, in your cell."

"Don't talk like that," said Logan. "Look here, you've had a bad time. But what the hell? It's over. You're here now."

"And we're here," said I. "If that helps any."

"Helps?" said he. "God, if you could ever guess how it helped! I'll never be able to tell you. I'm no good at that sort of thing. See, I drag you here, the only human beings who've treated me decently, and I pour all this stuff out and don't offer you a drink, even. Never mind, I'll give you one now—a drink you'll like."

"I could certainly swallow a highball," said Logan.

"You shall have something better than that," said Reid, moving toward the kitchenette. "We have a little specialty down in our corner of Georgia. Only it's got to be fixed properly. Wait just a minute."

He disappeared through the door, and we heard corks being drawn and a great clatter of pouring and mixing. While this went on, he was still talking through the doorway. "I'm glad I brought you up here," he said. "I'm glad I put the whole thing to you. You don't know what it means—to be believed, understood, by God! I feel I'm alive again."

He emerged with three brimming glasses on a tray. "Try this," he said proudly.

"To the days ahead!" said Logan, as we raised our glasses.

We drank and raised our eyebrows in appreciation. The drink seemed to be a sort of sherry flip, with a heavy sprinkling of nutmeg.

"You like it?" cried Reid eagerly. "There's not many people know the recipe for that drink, and fewer still can make it well. There are one or two bastard versions which some damned fools mix up—a disgrace to Georgia. I could—I could pour the mess over their heads. Wait a minute. You're men of discernment. Yes, by God, you are! You shall decide for yourselves."

With that, he darted back into the kitchenette and rattled his bottles more furiously than before, still talking to us disjointedly, praising the orthodox version of his drink, and damning all imitations.

"Now, here you are," said he, appearing with the tray loaded with drinks very much like the first but rather differently garnished. "These abortions have mace and ginger on the top instead of nutmeg. Take them. Drink them. Spit them out on the carpet if you want to. I'll mix some more of the real thing to take the taste out of your mouth. Just try them. Just tell me what you think of a barbarian who could insist that *that* was a Georgian flip. Go on. Tell me."

We sipped. There was no considerable difference. However, we replied as was expected of us.

"What do you think, Logan?" said I. "The first has it, beyond doubt."

"Beyond doubt," said Logan. "The first is the real thing."

"Yes," said Reid, his face livid and his eyes blazing like live coals. "And *that* is hogwash. The man who calls *that* a Georgian flip is not fit to mix boot blacking. It hasn't the nutmeg. The touch of nutmeg makes it. A man who'd leave out the nutmeg . . . ! I could . . . !"

He put out both his hands to lift the tray, and his eyes fell on them. He sat very still, staring at them.

THE ABSENCE OF MR. GLASS

G. K. CHESTERTON

THE CONSULTING ROOMS of Dr. Orion Hood, the eminent criminologist and specialist in certain moral disorders, lay along the seafront at Scarborough in a series of very large and well-lighted French windows, which showed the North Sea like one endless outer wall of blue-green marble. There was luxury in Dr. Hood's apartments, and even poetry; but one felt that these things were never allowed out of their place. There stood upon a special table eight or ten boxes of the best cigars, but they were built upon a plan so that the strongest were always nearest the wall and the mildest nearest the window. A tantalus containing three kinds of excellent spirit stood always on this table of luxury; but the fanciful have asserted that the whiskey, brandy and rum seemed always to stand at the same level. The left-hand corner of the room was lined with as complete a set of English classics as the right hand could show of English and foreign physiologists. But if one took a volume of Chaucer or Shelley from that rank, its absence irritated the mind like a gap in a man's front teeth. And yet more of such heathen holiness protected the shelves that held the frail and even fairylike instruments of chemistry or mechanics.

Dr. Orion Hood paced the length of his string of apartments, clad in an artist's velvet, but with none of an artist's negligence; his hair was heavily shot with gray, but growing thick and healthy; his face was lean, but sanguine and expectant. Everything about him and his room indicated something at once rigid and restless, like that great northern sea by which he had built his home.

Fate, being in a funny mood, introduced into those apartments one who was the most startling opposite of them and their master. In answer to a curt but civil summons, the door opened and there shambled into the room a shapeless little figure, which seemed to find its own hat and umbrella as unmanageable as a mass of luggage. The umbrella was a black and prosaic bundle long past repair; the hat was a broad-curved black hat, clerical but not common in England; the man was the very embodiment of all that is homely and helpless.

The doctor regarded the newcomer with a restrained astonishment. The newcomer regarded the doctor with beaming but breathless geniality. His hat tumbled to the carpet, his heavy umbrella slipped between his knees with a thud; he reached after the one, ducked after the other and spoke as follows.

"My name is Brown. Pray excuse me. I come about that business of the MacNabs. I have heard you often help people out of such troubles. Pray excuse me if I am wrong." By this time he had settled himself in a chair.

"I fear you are mistaken," replied the scientist. "I am Dr. Hood, and my work is almost entirely literary and educational. It is true that I have sometimes been consulted by the police in cases of peculiar difficulty and importance, but—"

"Oh, this is of the greatest importance," broke in the little man called Brown. "Why, her mother won't let them get engaged." And he leaned back in his chair in radiant rationality.

The brows of Dr. Hood were drawn down darkly, but the eyes under them were bright with something that might be anger or might be amusement. "I do not quite understand," he said.

"You see, they want to get married," said the man with the clerical hat. "Maggie MacNab and young Todhunter want to get *married*. Now, what can be more important than that?"

A chuckle broke out of the great Orion Hood, and he threw himself into an armchair in an attitude of the consulting physician. "Mr.

Brown," he said gravely, "it is quite fourteen and a half years since I was asked to test a personal problem; then it was the case of an attempt to poison the French president at a lord mayor's banquet. It is now, I understand, a question of whether some friend of yours called Maggie is a suitable fiancée for some friend of hers called Todhunter. Well, Mr. Brown, I am a sportsman. I will take it on. I will give the MacNab family my best advice, as good as I gave the French Republic and the king of England. Tell me your story."

The little clergyman thanked him with unquestionable warmth, but still with a queer kind of simplicity. It was rather as if he were thanking a stranger in a smoking room for some trouble in passing the matches. Then he began his recital.

"I'm the priest of the little Catholic church I daresay you've seen beyond those straggly streets where the town ends toward the north. In the last and straggliest of those streets, which runs along the sea like a seawall, there is an honest but sharp-tempered member of my flock, a widow called MacNab. She has a daughter of marriageable age, and she lets lodgings. At present she has only one lodger, the young man called Todhunter; and he wants to marry the young woman of the house."

"And the young woman of the house," asked Dr. Hood with huge and silent amusement, "what does she want?"

"Why, she wants to marry him," cried Father Brown, sitting up eagerly. "That is just the awful complication."

"It is indeed a hideous enigma," said Dr. Hood.

"This young James Todhunter," continued the cleric, "is a very decent man so far as I know. He is a bright, brownish little fellow, agile like a monkey, clean-shaven and obliging. He seems to have a pocketful of money, but nobody knows what his trade is. Mrs. MacNab, therefore (being of a pessimistic turn), is quite sure it is something dreadful, and probably connected with dynamite. The dynamite must be of a shy and noiseless sort, for the poor fellow only shuts himself up for several hours of the day and studies something behind a locked door. He declares his privacy is temporary and justified, and promises to explain before the wedding. That is all that anyone knows for certain, but Mrs. MacNab will tell you a great deal more than even she is certain of. There are tales of two voices heard talking in the room; though when the door is opened, Todhunter is found alone. There are tales of a mysterious tall man in a silk hat, who once came out of the sea mists and apparently out of the sea, stepping softly through the small back garden at twilight, till he was heard talking to the lodger at his open back window. The colloquy seemed to end in a quarrel: Todhunter dashed down his window with violence, and the man in the high hat melted into the sea fog again. This story is told by the family with the fiercest mystification; but I really think Mrs. MacNab prefers her own original tale: that the other man (or whatever it is) crawls out every night from a big box in the corner, which is kept locked all day. Yet the little fellow in his respectable black jacket is as punctual and innocent as a parlor clock. He pays his rent to the tick; he is practically a teetotaler; he is tirelessly kind with the younger children, and can keep them amused for days on end; and, last and most urgent of all, he has made himself equally popular with the eldest daughter, who is ready to go to church with him tomorrow."

A man concerned with large theories always relishes applying them to any triviality. The great specialist having condescended to the priest's simplicity, condescended expansively. He settled himself in his armchair and began to talk.

"Even in a minute instance, it is best to look first to the main tendencies of nature. To the scientific eye all human history is a series of collective movements, destructions or migrations, like the massacre of flies in winter or the return of birds in spring. Now there is no stronger case than that of the wild, unworldly and perishing stock which we commonly call the Celts, of whom your friends the MacNabs are specimens. Small, swarthy and of this dreamy and drifting blood, they accept easily the superstitious explanation of any incidents. It is not remarkable that such people should put fantastic features into what are probably plain events. You, with your small parochial responsibilities, see only this particular Mrs. MacNab, terrified with this particular tale of two voices and a tall man out of the sea. But the man with the scientific imagination sees thousands of Mrs. MacNabs, in thousands of houses, dropping their little drop of morbidity in the teacups of their friends; he sees—"

Before the scientist could conclude his sentence, someone with swishing skirts was marshaled hurriedly down the corridor, and the door opened on a young girl, decently dressed but disordered and red-hot with haste. She had sea-blown blond hair, and would have been entirely beautiful if her cheekbones had not been, in the Scotch manner, a little high in color. "I'm sorry to interrupt you, sir," she said; "but I had to follow Father Brown at once; it's nothing less than life or death."

Father Brown began to get to his feet in some disorder. "Why, what has happened, Maggie?" he said.

"James has been murdered, for all I can make out," answered the girl, still breathing hard from her rush. "That man Glass has been with him again; I heard them talking through the door quite plain. Two separate voices; for James speaks low, with a burr, and the other voice was high and quavery."

"That man Glass?" repeated the priest in some perplexity.

"I heard the name Glass through the door," answered the girl. "They were quarreling—about money, I think—for I heard James say again and again, 'That's right, Mr. Glass,' or 'No, Mr. Glass,' and then, 'Two and three, Mr. Glass.' But we're talking too much; you must come at once."

"What is there about Mr. Glass and his money troubles that should impel such urgency?" asked Dr. Hood, who had been studying the young lady with marked interest.

"I tried to break down the door and couldn't," answered the girl. "Then I ran around to the backyard, and managed to climb onto the windowsill that looks into the room. It was all dim and seemed to be empty; but I swear I saw James lying huddled up in a corner, as if he were drugged or strangled."

"This is very serious," said Father Brown, gathering his errant hat and umbrella and standing up. "In point of fact, I was just putting your case before this gentleman, and his view—"

"Has been largely altered," said the scientist gravely. "I do not think this young lady is so Celtic as I had supposed. As I have nothing else to do, I will put on my hat and stroll down the town with you."

In a few minutes all three were approaching the dreary tail of the MacNabs' street. The scattered houses stood in a broken string along the seashore; the afternoon was closing with a lurid twilight; the sea was of an inky purple and murmuring ominously. In the back garden of the MacNabs' which ran down toward the sand, two black, barren-looking trees stood like demon hands held up in astonishment; and as Mrs. MacNab ran down the street to meet them, she was a little like a demon herself.

The doctor and the priest made scant reply to her shrill vows of vengeance against Mr. Glass for murdering, and against Mr. Todhunter for being murdered, or against the latter for having dared to want to marry her daughter, and for not having lived to do it. They passed through the narrow passages in the front of the house until they came to the lodger's door at the back, and there Dr. Hood, with the trick of an old detective, put his shoulder sharply to the panel and burst in the door.

It opened on a scene of silent catastrophe. Playing cards lay littered across the table or fluttered about the floor as if a game had been interrupted. Two wineglasses stood on a side table, but a third lay smashed upon the carpet. Near it lay a long knife, or short sword, with an ornamental handle. Toward the opposite corner was rolled a gentleman's silk top hat, as if it had just been knocked off his head. And in the corner behind it lay Mr. James Todhunter, with a scarf across his mouth and six or seven ropes knotted around his elbows and ankles. His brown eyes were alive and shifted alertly.

Dr. Orion Hood paused and drank in the whole scene. Then he stepped swiftly across the carpet, picked up the silk hat, and gravely put it upon the head of the yet pinioned Todhunter. It was so large for him that it almost slipped down onto his shoulders.

"Mr. Glass's hat," said the doctor, returning with it and peering into the inside with a pocket lens. "How to explain the absence of Mr. Glass and the presence of Mr. Glass's hat? For Mr. Glass is not a careless man with his clothes. This hat is of a stylish shape and systematically brushed and burnished, though not very new. An old dandy, I should think."

"But, good heavens!" called out Miss MacNab. "Aren't you going to untie the man first?"

"My reason for saying 'old' might seem a little farfetched," continued the expositor. "The hair of human beings falls out in varying degrees, but almost always falls out slightly, and with the lens I should see the tiny hairs in a hat recently worn. It has none, which leads me to guess that Mr. Glass is bald. Now when this is taken with the high-pitched and querulous voice which Miss MacNab described, when we take the hairless head together with the tone common in senile anger, I should think we may deduce some advance in years. Nevertheless, he was probably vigorous, and he was almost certainly tall. This wineglass has been smashed all over the place, but one of its splinters lies on the high bracket beside the mantelpiece. No such fragment could have fallen there if the vessel had been smashed in the hand of a comparatively short man like Mr. Todhunter."

"By the way," said Father Brown. "Might it not be as well to untie Mr. Todhunter?"

"I may say at once," proceeded the specialist, "that it is possible that the man Glass was bald or nervous through dissipation rather than age. Mr. Todhunter, as has been remarked, is a quiet, thrifty gentleman, essentially an abstainer. These cards and wine cups are no part of his normal habit; they have been produced for a particular companion. But we may go further. Mr. Todhunter may or may not possess this wine service, but there is no appearance of his possessing any wine. What, then, were these vessels to contain? I would suggest some brandy or whiskey from a flask in the pocket of Mr. Glass. We have thus a picture of the man: tall, elderly, fashionable but somewhat frayed, fond of play and strong waters, and perhaps rather too fond of them. Mr. Glass is a gentleman not unknown on the fringes of society."

"Look here," cried the young woman. "If you don't let me pass to untie him, I'll run outside and scream for the police."

"I should not advise *you*, Miss MacNab," said Dr. Hood gravely, "to be in any hurry to fetch the police. Father Brown, I ask you to compose your flock. Well, we have seen something of the figure and quality of Mr. Glass; what are the chief facts known of Mr. Todhunter? They are substantially three: he is economical, he is more or less wealthy, and he has a secret. Now it is obvious that these are the three chief marks of the kind of man who is blackmailed. And it is equally obvious that the faded finery, the profligate habits and the shrill irritation of Mr. Glass are the unmistakable marks of the kind of man who blackmails him. We have the two typical figures of a tragedy of hush money: on the one hand, the respectable man with a mystery; on the other, the west-end vulture with a scent for a mystery. These two men have met here today and have quarreled, using blows and a bare weapon."

"Are you going to take those ropes off?" asked the girl stubbornly.

Dr. Hood replaced the silk hat carefully on the side table and went across to the captive. He studied him intently, even moving him a little and half turning him around by the shoulders, but he only answered, "No, I think these ropes will do very well till your friends the police bring the handcuffs."

Father Brown, who had been looking dully at the carpet, lifted his round face and said, "What do you mean?"

The man of science had picked up the peculiar dagger sword from the carpet and was examining it intently as he answered.

"Because you find Mr. Todhunter tied up," he said, "you all jump to the conclusion that Mr. Glass had tied him up; and then, I suppose, escaped. There are four objections to this. First, why should a gentleman so dressy as our friend Glass leave his hat behind him, if he left of his own free will? Second, the window is the only exit, and it is locked on the inside. Third, this blade here has a tiny touch of blood at the point, but there is no wound on Mr. Todhunter. Mr. Glass took that wound away with him, dead or alive. Add to all this primary probability. It is much more likely that the blackmailed person would try to kill his incubus, rather than that the blackmailer would try to kill the goose that lays his golden eggs."

"But the ropes?" inquired the priest, whose eyes had remained open with a rather vacant admiration.

"Ah, the ropes. Miss MacNab very much wanted to know why I did not set Mr. Todhunter free from his ropes. Well, I will tell her. I did not do it because Mr. Todhunter can set himself free from them at any minute he chooses."

"What?" cried the audience on different notes of astonishment.

"I have looked at all the knots on Mr. Todhunter," reiterated Hood quietly. "Every one of those knots he has made himself and could loosen himself. The whole of this affair of the ropes is a clever fake, to make us think him the victim of the struggle instead of the wretched Glass, whose corpse may be hidden in the garden or stuffed up the chimney."

There was a rather depressed silence; the room was darkening, the sea-blighted boughs of the garden trees looked leaner and blacker than ever, and the whole air was dense with the morbidity of blackmail.

The face of the little Catholic priest had become knotted with a curious frown. It was not the blank curiosity of his first innocence. It was that creative curiosity which comes when a man has the beginnings of an idea. "Do you mean," he asked in a simple, bothered manner, "that Todhunter can tie himself up all alone and untie himself all alone?"

"That is what I mean," said the doctor.

"Jerusalem!" ejaculated Brown suddenly. "I wonder if it could possibly be that!" He scuttled across the room rather like a rabbit and peered into the partially covered face of the captive. Then he turned to the company. "Yes, that's it!" he cried. "Can't you see it in the man's face? Why, look at his eyes!"

Both the professor and the girl followed the direction of his glance. And though the broad black scarf completely masked the lower half of Todhunter's visage, they did grow conscious of something struggling and intense about the upper part of it.

"His eyes do look queer," cried the young woman, strongly moved. "You brutes. I believe it's hurting him!"

"The eyes have a singular expression," said Dr. Hood. "But I interpret those transverse wrinkles as expressing rather such slight psychological abnormality—"

"Oh, bosh!" cried Father Brown. "Can't you see he's laughing?"

"Laughing!" repeated the doctor with a start. "But what on earth can he be laughing at?"

"Well," replied the Reverend Mr. Brown apologetically, "not to put too fine a point on it, I think he is laughing at you. And indeed, I'm a little inclined to laugh at myself, now that I know the profession of Mr. Todhunter."

He shuffled about the room looking at one object after another. He laughed over the hat, still more over the broken glass; but the blood on the sword point sent him into mortal convulsions of amusement. Then he turned to the fuming specialist.

"Dr. Hood," he cried enthusiastically, "you are a great poet! You have called an uncreated being out of the void. How much more godlike that is than if you had only ferreted out the mere facts!"

"I have no notion what you are talking about," said Dr. Hood rather haughtily. "My facts are all inevitable, though necessarily incomplete. A place may be permitted to intuition, perhaps, but only because the corresponding details cannot as yet be ascertained. In the absence of Mr. Glass—"

"That's it, that's it," said the little priest, nodding quite eagerly. "The absence of Mr. Glass. He is so extremely absent. I suppose," he added reflectively, "that there was never anybody so absent as Mr. Glass."

"Do you mean he is absent from the town?" demanded the doctor.

"I mean he is absent from everywhere," answered Father Brown. "He is absent from the nature of things, so to speak."

"Do you seriously mean," said the specialist with a smile, "that there is no such person?"

The priest made a sign of assent. "It does seem a pity," he said.

Orion Hood broke into a contemptuous laugh. "Well," he said, "if there is no Mr. Glass, whose hat is this?"

"It is Mr. Todhunter's," replied Brown.

"But it doesn't fit him," cried Hood impatiently. "He couldn't possibly wear it!"

Father Brown shook his head with ineffable mildness. "I never said he could wear it. I said it was his hat. Or, if you insist on a shade of difference, a hat that is his."

"And where is the shade of difference?" asked the criminologist with a slight sneer.

"My good sir," cried the mild little man, with his first movement akin to impatience. "If you will go to a hatter's shop, you will see that there is, in common speech, a difference between a man's hat and the hats that are his."

"But a hatter," protested Hood, "can get money out of his stock of new hats. What could Todhunter get out of this one old hat?"

"Rabbits," replied Father Brown promptly, "ribbons, sweetmeats, goldfish, rolls of colored paper. Didn't you see it all when you found out the faked ropes? It's just the same with the sword. Mr. Todhunter hasn't got a scratch on him, as you say; but he's got a scratch in him, if you follow me."

"Do you mean inside Mr. Todhunter's clothes?" inquired Mrs. MacNab sternly.

"I do not mean inside Mr. Todhunter's clothes," said Father Brown. "I mean inside Mr. Todhunter."

"Well, what in the name of bedlam *do* you mean?"

"Mr. Todhunter," explained Father Brown placidly, "is learning to be a professional conjurer, as well as juggler, ventriloquist and expert in the rope trick. The conjuring explains the hat. It is without traces of hair, not because it is worn by the prematurely bald Mr. Glass, but because it has never been worn by anybody. The juggling explains the three glasses, which Todhunter was teaching himself to throw up and catch in rotation. But, being only at the practicing stage, he smashed one glass against the ceiling. And the juggling also explains the sword, which it was Mr. Todhunter's professional pride and duty to swallow. But, again, being at the practicing stage, he very slightly grazed the inside of his throat with the weapon. Hence he has a wound inside him, which I am sure (from the expression of his face) is not a serious one. He was also practicing the trick of a release from ropes, and he was just about to free himself when we all burst into the room. The cards, of course, are for card tricks, and they are scattered on the floor because he had just been practicing one of those dodges of sending them flying through the air. He kept his trade secret, because he had to keep his tricks secret, like any other conjurer. But the mere fact of an idler in a top hat having once looked in at his back window, and been driven away by him with great indignation, was enough to set us all on a wrong track."

"But what about the two voices?" asked Maggie, staring.

"Have you never heard a ventriloquist?" asked Father Brown. "Don't you know they speak first in their natural voice, and then answer themselves in just that shrill, squeaky, unnatural voice that you heard?"

There was a long silence, and Dr. Hood regarded the little man with a dark and attentive smile. "You are certainly a very ingenious person," he said; "but there is just one part of Mr. Glass you have not succeeded in explaining away, and that is his name. Miss MacNab distinctly heard him so addressed by Mr. Todhunter."

The Reverend Mr. Brown giggled. "Well, that," he said, "that's the silliest part of the whole silly story. When our juggling friend here threw up the three glasses in turn, he counted them aloud as he caught them, and also commented aloud when he failed to catch them. What he really said was 'One, two and three—missed a glass; one, two—missed a glass.' And so on."

There was a second of stillness in the room, and then everyone with one accord burst out laughing. As they did so, the figure in the corner complacently uncoiled all the ropes and let them fall with a flourish. Then, advancing into the middle of the room with a bow, he produced from his pocket a big bill printed in blue and red, which announced that Zaladin, the world's greatest conjurer, contortionist, ventriloquist and human kangaroo, would be ready with an entirely new series of tricks at the Empire Pavilion, Scarborough, on Monday next at eight o'clock precisely.

MIRIAM

TRUMAN CAPOTE

FOR SEVERAL YEARS, Mrs. H. T. Miller had lived alone in a pleasant apartment (two rooms with kitchenette) in a remodeled brownstone near the East River. She was a widow: Mr. H. T. Miller had left a reasonable amount of insurance. Her interests were narrow, she had no friends to speak of, and she rarely journeyed farther than the corner grocery. The other people in the house never seemed to notice her: her clothes were matter-of-fact, her hair iron-gray, clipped and casually waved; she did not use cosmetics, her features were plain and inconspicuous, and on her last birthday she was sixty-one. Her activities were seldom spontaneous: she kept the two rooms immaculate, smoked an occasional cigarette, prepared her own meals and tended a canary.

Then she met Miriam. It was snowing that night. Mrs. Miller had finished drying the supper dishes and was thumbing through an afternoon paper when she saw an advertisement of a picture playing at a neighborhood theater. The title sounded good, so she struggled into her beaver coat, laced her galoshes and left the apartment, leaving one light burning in the foyer: she found nothing more disturbing than a sensation of darkness.

The snow was fine, falling gently, not yet making an impression on the pavement. The wind from the river cut only at street crossings.

Mrs. Miller hurried, her head bowed, oblivious as a mole burrowing a blind path. She stopped at a drugstore and bought a package of peppermints.

A long line stretched in front of the box office; she took her place at the end. There would be (a tired voice groaned) a short wait for all seats. Mrs. Miller rummaged in her leather handbag till she collected exactly the correct change for admission. The line seemed to be taking its own time and, looking around for some distraction, she suddenly became conscious of a little girl standing under the edge of the marquee.

Her hair was the longest and strangest Mrs. Miller had ever seen: absolutely silver-white, like an albino's. It flowed waist-length in smooth, loose lines. She was thin and fragilely constructed. There was a simple, special elegance in the way she stood with her thumbs in the pockets of a tailored plum-velvet coat.

Mrs. Miller felt oddly excited, and when the little girl glanced toward her, she smiled warmly. The little girl walked over and said, "Would you care to do me a favor?"

"I'd be glad to, if I can," said Mrs. Miller.

"Oh, it's quite easy. I merely want you to buy a ticket for me; they won't let me in otherwise. Here, I have the money." And gracefully she handed Mrs. Miller two dimes and a nickel.

They went into the theater together. An usherette directed them to a lounge; in twenty minutes the picture would be over.

"I feel just like a genuine criminal," said Mrs. Miller gaily, as she sat down. "I mean that sort of thing's against the law, isn't it? I do hope I haven't done the wrong thing. Your mother knows where you are, dear? I mean she does, doesn't she?"

The little girl said nothing. She unbuttoned her coat and folded it across her lap. Her dress underneath was prim and dark blue. A gold chain dangled about her neck, and her fingers, sensitive and musical-looking, toyed with it. Examining her more attentively, Mrs. Miller decided the truly distinctive feature was not her hair, but her eyes; they were hazel, steady, lacking any childlike quality whatsoever and, because of their size, seemed to consume her small face.

Mrs. Miller offered a peppermint. "What's your name, dear?"

"Miriam," she said, as though, in some curious way, it were information already familiar.

"Why, isn't that funny—my name's Miriam, too. And it's not a terribly common name either. Now, don't tell me your last name's Miller!"

"Just Miriam."

"But isn't that funny?"

"Moderately," said Miriam, and rolled the peppermint on her tongue.

Mrs. Miller flushed and shifted uncomfortably. "You have such a large vocabulary for such a little girl."

"Do I?"

"Well, yes," said Mrs. Miller, hastily changing the topic to: "Do you like the movies?"

"I really wouldn't know," said Miriam. "I've never been before."

Women began filling the lounge; the rumble of the newsreel bombs exploded in the distance. Mrs. Miller rose, tucking her purse under her arm. "I guess I'd better be running now if I want to get a seat," she said. "It was nice to have met you."

Miriam nodded ever so slightly.

IT SNOWED ALL week. Wheels and footsteps moved soundlessly on the street, as if the business of living continued secretly behind a pale but impenetrable curtain. In the falling quiet there was no sky or earth, only snow lifting in the wind, frosting the window glass, chilling the rooms, deadening and hushing the city. At all hours it was necessary to keep a lamp lighted, and Mrs. Miller lost track of the days: Friday was no different from Saturday and on Sunday she went to the grocery: closed, of course.

That evening she scrambled eggs and fixed a bowl of tomato soup. Then, after putting on a flannel robe and cold-creaming her face, she propped herself up in bed with a hot-water bottle under her feet. She was reading the *Times* when the doorbell rang. At first she thought it must be a mistake and whoever it was would go away. But it rang and rang and settled to a persistent buzz. She looked at the clock: a little after eleven; it did not seem possible, she was always asleep by ten.

Climbing out of bed, she trotted barefoot across the living room. "I'm coming, please be patient." The latch was caught; she turned it this way and that way and the bell never paused an instant. "Stop it," she cried. The bolt gave way and she opened the door an inch. "What in heaven's name?"

"Hello," said Miriam.

"Oh . . . why, hello," said Mrs. Miller, stepping hesitantly into the hall. "You're that little girl."

"I thought you'd never answer, but I kept my finger on the button; I knew you were home. Aren't you glad to see me?"

Mrs. Miller did not know what to say. Miriam, she saw, wore the same plum-velvet coat and now she had also a beret to match; her white hair was braided in two shining plaits and looped at the ends with enormous white ribbons.

"Since I've waited so long, you could at least let me in," she said.

"It's awfully late. . . ."

Miriam regarded her blankly. "What difference does that make? Let me in. It's cold out here and I have on a silk dress." Then, with a gentle gesture, she urged Mrs. Miller aside and passed into the apartment.

She dropped her coat and beret on a chair. She was indeed wearing a silk dress. White silk. White silk in February. The skirt was beautifully pleated and the sleeves long; it made a faint rustle as she strolled about the room. "I like your place," she said. "I like the rug, blue's my favorite color." She touched a paper rose in a vase on the coffee table. "Imitation," she commented wanly. "How sad. Aren't imitations sad?" She seated herself on the sofa, daintily spreading her skirt.

"What do you want?" asked Mrs. Miller.

"Sit down," said Miriam. "It makes me nervous to see people stand."

Mrs. Miller sank to a hassock. "What do you want?" she repeated.

"You know, I don't think you're glad I came."

For a second time Mrs. Miller was without an answer; her hand motioned vaguely. Miriam giggled and pressed back on a mound of chintz pillows. Mrs. Miller observed that the girl was less pale than she remembered; her cheeks were flushed.

"How did you know where I lived?"

Miriam frowned. "That's no question at all. What's your name? What's mine?"

"But I'm not listed in the phone book."

"Oh, let's talk about something else."

Mrs. Miller said, "Your mother must be insane to let a child like you wander around at all hours of the night—and in such ridiculous clothes. She must be out of her mind."

Miriam got up and moved to a corner where a covered bird cage hung from a ceiling chain. She peeked beneath the cover. "It's a canary," she said. "Would you mind if I woke him? I'd like to hear him sing."

"Leave Tommy alone," said Mrs. Miller, anxiously. "Don't you dare wake him."

"Certainly," said Miriam. "But I don't see why I can't hear him sing." And then, "Have you anything to eat? I'm starving! Even milk and a jam sandwich would be fine."

"Look," said Mrs. Miller, arising from the hassock, "look—if I make some nice sandwiches will you be a good child and run along home? It's past midnight, I'm sure."

"It's snowing," reproached Miriam. "And cold and dark."

"Well, you shouldn't have come here to begin with," said Mrs. Miller, struggling to control her voice. "I can't help the weather. If you want anything to eat you'll have to promise to leave."

Miriam brushed a braid against her cheek. Her eyes were thoughtful, as if weighing the proposition. She turned toward the bird cage. "Very well," she said, "I promise."

How old is she? Ten? Eleven? Mrs. Miller, in the kitchen, unsealed a jar of strawberry preserves and cut four slices of bread. She poured a glass of milk and paused to light a cigarette. *And why has she come?* Her hand shook as she held the match, fascinated, till it burned her finger. The canary was singing; singing as he did in the morning and at no other time. "Miriam," she called, "Miriam, I told you not to disturb Tommy." There was no answer. She called again; all she heard was the canary. She inhaled the cigarette and discovered she had lighted the cork-tip end and—oh, really, she mustn't lose her temper.

She carried the food in on a tray and set it on the coffee table. She saw first that the bird cage still wore its night cover. And Tommy was singing. It gave her a queer sensation. And no one was in the room. Mrs. Miller went through an alcove leading to her bedroom; at the door she caught her breath.

"What are you doing?" she asked.

Miriam glanced up and in her eyes there was a look that was not ordinary. She was standing by the bureau, a jewel case opened before her. For a minute she studied Mrs. Miller, forcing their eyes to meet, and she smiled. "There's nothing good here," she said. "But I like this." Her hand held a cameo brooch. "It's charming."

"Suppose—perhaps you'd better put it back," said Mrs. Miller, feeling suddenly the need of some support. She leaned against the door frame; her head was unbearably heavy; a pressure weighted the rhythm of her heartbeat. The light seemed to flutter defectively. "Please, child—a gift from my husband . . ."

"But it's beautiful and I want it," said Miriam. *"Give it to me."*

As she stood, striving to shape a sentence which would somehow save the brooch, it came to Mrs. Miller there was no one to whom she might turn; she was alone; a fact that had not been among her thoughts for a long time. Its sheer emphasis was stunning. But here in her own room in the hushed snow-city were evidences she could not ignore or, she knew with startling clarity, resist.

MIRIAM ATE RAVENOUSLY, and when the sandwiches and milk were gone, her fingers made cobweb movements over the plate, gathering crumbs. The cameo gleamed on her blouse, the blonde profile like a trick reflection of its wearer. "That was very nice," she sighed, "though now an almond cake or a cherry would be ideal. Sweets are lovely, don't you think?"

Mrs. Miller was perched precariously on the hassock, smoking a cigarette. Her hair net had slipped lopsided and loose strands straggled down her face. Her eyes were stupidly concentrated on nothing and her cheeks were mottled in red patches, as though a fierce slap had left permanent marks.

"Is there a candy—a cake?"

Mrs. Miller tapped ash on the rug. Her head swayed slightly as she tried to focus her eyes. "You promised to leave if I made the sandwiches," she said.

"Dear me, did I?"

"It was a promise and I'm tired and I don't feel well at all."

"Mustn't fret," said Miriam. "I'm only teasing."

She picked up her coat, slung it over her arm, and arranged her beret in front of a mirror. Presently she bent close to Mrs. Miller and whispered, "Kiss me good night."

"Please—I'd rather not," said Mrs. Miller.

Miriam lifted a shoulder, arched an eyebrow. "As you like," she said, and went directly to the coffee table, seized the vase containing the paper roses, carried it to where the hard surface of the floor lay bare, and hurled it downward. Glass sprayed in all directions and she stamped her foot on the bouquet.

Then slowly she walked to the door, but before closing it she looked back at Mrs. Miller with a slyly innocent curiosity.

MRS. MILLER SPENT the next day in bed, rising once to feed the canary and drink a cup of tea; she took her temperature and had none, yet her dreams were feverishly agitated; their unbalanced mood lingered even as she lay staring wide-eyed at the ceiling. One dream threaded through the others like an elusively mysterious theme in a complicated symphony, and the scenes it depicted were sharply outlined, as though sketched by a hand of gifted intensity: a small girl, wearing a bridal gown and a wreath of leaves, led a gray procession down a mountain path, and among them there was unusual silence till a woman at the rear asked, "Where is she taking us?" "No one knows," said an old man marching in front. "But isn't she pretty?" volunteered a third voice. "Isn't she like a frost flower . . . so shining and white?"

Tuesday morning she woke up feeling better; harsh slats of sunlight, slanting through Venetian blinds, shed a disrupting light on her unwholesome fancies. She opened the window to discover a thawed, mild-as-spring day; a sweep of clean new clouds crumpled against a vastly blue, out-of-season sky; and across the low line of rooftops she could see the river and smoke curving from tugboat stacks in a warm wind. A great silver truck plowed the snow-banked street, its machine sound humming on the air.

After straightening the apartment, she went to the grocer's, cashed a check and continued to Schrafft's where she ate breakfast and chatted happily with the waitress. Oh, it was a wonderful day—more like a holiday—and it would be so foolish to go home.

She boarded a Lexington Avenue bus and rode up to Eighty-sixth Street; it was here that she had decided to do a little shopping.

She had no idea what she wanted or needed, but she idled along, intent only upon the passers-by, brisk and preoccupied, who gave her a disturbing sense of separateness.

It was while waiting at the corner of Third Avenue that she saw the man: an old man, bowlegged and stooped under an armload of bulging packages; he wore a shabby brown coat and a checkered cap. Suddenly she realized they were exchanging a smile: there was nothing friendly about this smile, it was merely two cold flickers of recognition. But she was certain she had never seen him before.

He was standing next to an El pillar, and as she crossed the street he turned and followed. He kept quite close; from the corner of her eye she watched his reflection wavering on the shopwindows.

Then in the middle of the block she stopped and faced him. He stopped also and cocked his head, grinning. But what could she say? Do? Here, in broad daylight, on Eighty-sixth Street? It was useless and, despising her own helplessness, she quickened her steps.

Now Second Avenue is a dismal street, made from scraps and ends; part cobblestone, part asphalt, part cement; and its atmosphere of desertion is permanent. Mrs. Miller walked five blocks without meeting anyone, and all the while the steady crunch of his footfalls in the snow stayed near. And when she came to a florist's shop, the sound was still with her. She hurried inside and watched through the glass door as the old man passed; he kept his eyes straight ahead and didn't slow his pace, but he did one strange, telling thing: he tipped his cap.

"SIX WHITE ONES, did you say?" asked the florist. "Yes," she told him, "white roses." From there she went to a glassware store and selected a vase, presumably a replacement for the one Miriam had broken, though the price was intolerable and the vase itself (she thought) grotesquely vulgar. But a series of unaccountable purchases had begun, as if by prearranged plan: a plan of which she had not the least knowledge or control.

She bought a bag of glazed cherries, and at a place called the Knickerbocker Bakery she paid forty cents for six almond cakes.

Within the last hour the weather had turned cold again; like blurred lenses, winter clouds cast a shade over the sun, and the skeleton of an early dusk colored the sky; a damp mist mixed with the wind and the voices of a few children who romped high on mountains of gutter snow seemed lonely and cheerless. Soon the first flake fell, and when Mrs. Miller reached the brownstone house, snow was falling in a swift screen and foot tracks vanished as they were printed.

THE WHITE ROSES were arranged decoratively in the vase. The glazed cherries shone on a ceramic plate. The almond cakes, dusted with sugar, awaited a hand. The canary fluttered on its swing and picked at a bar of seed.

At precisely five the doorbell rang. Mrs. Miller *knew* who it was. The hem of her housecoat trailed as she crossed the floor. "Is that you?" she called.

"Naturally," said Miriam, the word resounding shrilly from the hall. "Open this door."

"Go away," said Mrs. Miller.

"Please hurry . . . I have a heavy package."

"Go away," said Mrs. Miller. She returned to the living room, lighted a cigarette, sat down and calmly listened to the buzzer; on and on and on. "You might as well leave. I have no intention of letting you in."

Shortly the bell stopped. For possibly ten minutes Mrs. Miller did not move. Then, hearing no sound, she concluded Miriam had gone. She tiptoed to the door and opened it a sliver; Miriam was half-reclining atop a cardboard box with a beautiful French doll cradled in her arms.

"Really, I thought you were never coming," she said peevishly. "Here, help me get this in, it's awfully heavy."

It was not spell-like compulsion that Mrs. Miller felt, but rather a curious passivity; she brought in the box, Miriam the doll. Miriam curled up on the sofa, not troubling to remove her coat or beret, and watched disinterestedly as Mrs. Miller dropped the box and stood trembling, trying to catch her breath.

"Thank you," she said. In the daylight she looked pinched and drawn, her hair less luminous. The French doll she was loving wore an exquisite powdered wig and its idiot glass eyes sought solace in Miriam's. "I have a surprise," she continued. "Look into my box."

Kneeling, Mrs. Miller parted the flaps and lifted out another doll; then a blue dress which she recalled as the one Miriam had worn that first night at the theater; and of the remainder she said, "It's all clothes. Why?"

"Because I've come to live with you," said Miriam, twisting a cherry stem. "Wasn't it nice of you to buy me the cherries. . . ?"

"But you can't! For God's sake go away—go away and leave me alone!"

". . . and the roses and the almond cakes? How really wonderfully generous. You know, these cherries are delicious. The last place I lived was with an old man; he was terribly poor and we never had good things to eat. But I think I'll be happy here." She paused to snuggle her doll closer. "Now, if you'll just show me where to put my things . . ."

Mrs. Miller's face dissolved into a mask of ugly red lines; she began to cry, and it was an unnatural, tearless sort of weeping, as though, not having wept for a long time, she had forgotten how. Carefully she edged backward till she touched the door.

SHE FUMBLED THROUGH the hall and down the stairs to a landing below. She pounded frantically on the door of the first apartment she came to; a short, redheaded man answered and she pushed past him. "Say, what the hell is this?" he said. "Anything wrong, lover?" asked a young woman who appeared from the kitchen, drying her hands. And it was to her that Mrs. Miller turned.

"Listen," she cried, "I'm ashamed behaving this way but—well, I'm Mrs. H. T. Miller and I live upstairs and . . ." She pressed her hands over her face. "It sounds so absurd. . . ."

Thc woman guided her to a chair, while the man excitedly rattled pocket change. "Yeah?"

"I live upstairs and there's a little girl visiting me, and I suppose that I'm afraid of her. She won't leave and I can't make her and—she's going to do something terrible. She's already stolen my cameo, but she's about to do something worse—something terrible!"

The man asked, "Is she a relative, huh?"

Mrs. Miller shook her head. "I don't know who she is. Her name's Miriam, but I don't know for certain who she is."

"You gotta calm down, honey," said the woman, stroking Mrs. Miller's arm. "Harry here'll tend to this kid. Go on, lover." And Mrs. Miller said, "The door's open—5A."

After the man left, the woman brought a towel and bathed Mrs. Miller's face. "You're very kind," Mrs. Miller said. "I'm sorry to act like such a fool, only this wicked child . . ."

"Sure, honey," consoled the woman. "Now, you better take it easy."

Mrs. Miller rested her head in the crook of her arm; she was quiet enough to be asleep. The woman turned a radio dial; a piano and a husky voice filled the silence and the woman, tapping her foot, kept excellent time. "Maybe we oughta go up too," she said.

"I don't want to see her again. I don't want to be anywhere near her."

"Uh huh, but what you shoulda done, you shoulda called a cop."

Presently they heard the man on the stairs. He strode into the room frowning and scratching the back of his neck. "Nobody there," he said, honestly embarrassed. "She musta beat it."

"Harry, you're a jerk," announced the woman. "We been sitting here the whole time and we woulda seen . . ." she stopped abruptly, for the man's glance was sharp.

"I looked all over," he said, "and there just ain't nobody there. Nobody, understand?"

"Tell me," said Mrs. Miller, rising, "tell me, did you see a large box? Or a doll?"

"No, ma'am, I didn't."

And the woman, as if delivering a verdict, said, "Well, for cryinoutloud. . . ."

MRS. MILLER ENTERED HER apartment softly; she walked to the center of the room and stood quite still. No, in a sense it had not changed: the roses, the cakes, and the cherries were in place. But this was an empty room, emptier than if the furnishings and familiars were not present, lifeless and petrified as a funeral parlor. The sofa loomed before her with a new strangeness: its vacancy had a meaning that would have been less penetrating and terrible had Miriam been curled on it. She gazed fixedly at the space where she remembered setting the box and, for a moment, the hassock spun desperately. And she looked through the window; surely the river was real, surely snow was falling—but then, one could not be certain witness to anything: Miriam, so vividly *there*—and yet, where was she? Where, where?

As though moving in a dream, she sank to a chair. The room was losing shape; it was dark and getting darker and there was nothing to be done about it; she could not lift her hand to light a lamp.

Suddenly, closing her eyes, she felt an upward surge, like a diver emerging from some deeper, greener depth. In times of terror or immense distress, there are moments when the mind waits, as though for a revelation, while a skein of calm is woven over thought; it is like a sleep, or a supernatural trance; and during this lull one is aware of a force of quiet reasoning: well, what if she had never really known a girl named Miriam? that she had been foolishly frightened on the street? In the end, like everything else, it was of no importance. For the only thing she had lost to Miriam was her identity, but now she knew she had found again the person who lived in this room, who cooked her own meals, who owned a canary, who was someone she could trust and believe in: Mrs. H. T. Miller.

Listening in contentment, she became aware of a double sound: a bureau drawer opening and closing; she seemed to hear it long after completion—opening and closing. Then gradually, the harshness of it was replaced by the murmur of a silk dress and this, delicately faint, was moving nearer and swelling in intensity till the walls trembled with the vibration and the room was caving under a wave of whispers. Mrs. Miller stiffened and opened her eyes to a dull, direct stare.

"Hello," said Miriam.

THE LOG OF THE *EVENING STAR*

ALFRED NOYES

WE WERE SITTING on the porch of a low white bungalow with masses of purple bougainvillea embowering its eaves. A ruby-throated hummingbird, with green wings, flickered around it. The tall palms and the sea were whispering together. Over the water, the West was beginning to fill with that California sunset which is the most mysterious in the world, for one is conscious that it is the fringe of what Europeans call the East, and that, looking westward across the Pacific, our faces are turned toward the dusky myriads of Asia. All along the California coast there is a touch of incense in the air, and though it is probably caused by gardeners burning the dead leaves of the eucalyptus trees, one might well believe that one breathed the scent of the joss sticks, wafted across the Pacific from the land of paper lanterns.

A Japanese servant, in a white duck suit, marched like a ghostly little soldier across the lawn. The great hills behind us quietly turned to amethysts. The lights of Los Angeles, ten miles away to the north, began to spring out like stars, and the evening star itself, over the huge, slow breakers crumbling into lilac-colored foam, looked bright enough to be a companion of the city lights.

"I should like to show you the log of the *Evening Star*," said my visitor, who was none other than Moreton Fitch, president of the Insurance Company of San Francisco. "I think it may interest you as evidence that our business is not without its touches of romance. I don't mean what you mean," he added cheerfully, as I looked up smiling. "The *Evening Star* was a schooner running between San Francisco and Tahiti and other places in the South Seas. She was insured by our company. One April she was reported overdue. After search had been made, she was posted as lost. There was no clue to what had happened, and we paid the insurance money, believing she had foundered with all hands.

"Two months later we got word from Tahiti that the *Evening Star* had been found drifting about in a dead calm, with all sails set, but not a soul aboard. Everything was in perfect order, except that the ship's cat was lying dead in the bows, baked to a bit of seaweed by the sun. Otherwise there wasn't the slightest trace of any trouble. The tables below were laid for a meal, and there was plenty of water aboard."

"Were any of the boats missing?"

"No; she only carried three boats, and all were there. When she was discovered, two of the boats were on deck as usual, and the third was towing astern. None of the men has been heard of from that day to this. The amazing part of it was not only the absence of anything that would account for the disappearance of the crew, but the clear evidence that they had been intending to stay, in the fact that the tables were laid for a meal and then abandoned. Besides, where had they gone, and how? There are no magic carpets, even in the South Seas. And this wasn't in wartime, remember.

"The best brains of our company puzzled over the mystery for a year or more; but at the end of the time nothing had turned up. No theory, even, seemed to fit the case at all; and in most mysteries there is room for a hundred theories. There were twelve persons aboard, and we investigated the history of them all. There were three American seamen, all of the domesticated kind, with respectable old mothers in gold-rimmed spectacles at home. There were five Kanakas of the mildest type, as easy to handle as an infant school. There was a Japanese cook, who was something of an artist, used to spend his spare time in painting things to palm off on the unsuspecting connoisseur as the work of an obscure pupil of Hokusai, which I suppose he might have been in a way.

"Then there was Harper, the mate, rather an interesting young fellow, with the wanderlust. He had been pretty well educated. I believe he had spent a year or two at one of the California colleges. Altogether about the most harmless kind of ship's family that you could pick up anywhere between the Golden Gate and the Baltic. Then there was Captain Burgess, who was the most domesticated of them all, for he had his wife with him on this voyage. They had been married about three months. She was the widow of the former captain of the *Evening Star*, a fellow named Dayrell, and she had often been on the ship before.

"In fact, they were all old friends of the ship. Except one or two of the Kanakas, all the men had sailed on the *Evening Star* for something like two years under Captain Dayrell. Burgess himself had been his mate. Dayrell had been dead about six months, and the only criticism we ever heard against anybody aboard was made by some of Dayrell's relatives, who thought the widow might have waited more than three months before marrying the newly promoted Burgess. They suggested, of course, that there must have been something between them before Dayrell was out of the way. But I hardly believed it. In any case, it threw no light on the mystery."

"What sort of man was Burgess?"

"Big, burly fellow, with a fat white face and curious little black eyes, like huckleberries in a lump of dough. He was very silent and inclined to be religious. He used to read Emerson and Carlyle, quite an unusual sort of sea captain. There was a *Sartor Resartus* in the cabin, with a lot of the queerest passages marked in pencil. What can you make of it?"

"Nothing at all, except that there was a woman aboard. What was she like?"

"She was one of our special California mixtures—touch of Italian, touch of Irish, touch of American, but Italian predominated, I think. She was a good deal younger than Burgess, and one of the clerks in our office who had seen her described her as a peach.

"She had the dusky Italian beauty, black hair and eyes like black diamonds, but her face was very pale, the kind of pallor that makes you think of magnolia blossoms at dusk. She was fond of bright colors, tawny reds and yellows, but they suited her. If I had to give you my impression of her in a single word, I should say that she looked like a

Gypsy. She also had rather a fine voice. Used to sing sentimental songs to Dayrell and his friends in Frisco—'Love's Old Sweet Song' and that sort of stuff. Apparently they took it very seriously. Several of them told me that if she had been trained—well, you know the old story—every prima donna would have had to retire from business. I fancy they were all a little in love with her. The curious thing was that after Dayrell's death she gave up her singing altogether. Now, I think I have told you all the facts about the ship's company."

"Didn't you say there was a log you wanted to show me?"

"There were no ship's papers of any kind, and no log was found on the derelict; but a week or two ago we had a visit from the brother of the Japanese cook, who made us all feel like fifteen cents before the wisdom of the East. I have to go over and see him tomorrow afternoon. He is a fisherman, lives on the coast, not far from here. I'd like you to see what I call the log of the *Evening Star.* I won't say any more about it now. It isn't quite worked out yet, but it looks as if it's going to be interesting. Will you come tomorrow afternoon? I'll call for you at a quarter after two. It won't take us long."

Promptly at the time appointed on the following afternoon, Fitch called for me. We drove along the coast for a little way between palms and low white-pillared houses, all crimson poinsettias and marble, that looked as if they were meant for the gods and goddesses of Greece, but were only the homes of a few score lotus-eating millionaires. In a few minutes we turned off the highway and went along a narrow sandy road. On one side, rising from the road, were great desert hills covered with gray-green sagebrush, tinged at the tips with rusty brown; and on the other there was a strip of sandy beach where the big slow breakers tumbled, and the unmolested pelicans waddled and brooded like goblin sentries.

We sighted a cluster of tiny wooden houses ahead of us, and pulled up on the outskirts of a little Japanese fishing village built along the fringe of the beach itself. It was a single miniature street, nestling under the hill on one side of the narrow road, and built along the sand on the other. Japanese signs stood over quaint little stores, with here and there a curious tinge of Americanism. Rice cakes and candies were advertised by one black-haired and boyish-looking gentleman, who sat at the door of his hut playing with three children, one of whom squinted at us gleefully with bright sloe-black eyes. Every tiny house, even when it stood on the beach, had its own little festoon of flowers. Wisteria drooped from the jutting eaves, and—perhaps only the Japanese could explain the miracle—tall and well-nourished red geraniums rose out of the salt sea sand around their doors. In the center of the village, on the seaward side, there was a miniature mission house. A beautifully shaped bell swung over the roof, and there was a miniature notice board at the door. The announcements upon it were in Japanese, but it looked as if East and West had certainly met and kissed each other there.

Some of the huts had little oblong letter boxes of gray tin, perched on stumps of bamboo fishing poles, in front of their doors. We stopped before one that bore the name of Y. Kato. His unpainted wooden shack was the most Japanese of all in appearance; for the yellow placard underneath the window advertising Sweet Caporal was balanced by a single tall pole planted in the sand a few feet to the right, and lifting a beautiful little birdhouse high above the roof.

Moreton Fitch knocked at the door. It was opened at once by a dainty creature, four feet high, with a black-eyed baby on her back; and we were ushered, with smiles, into a very bare living room, to be greeted by Kato himself and Howard Knight, a professor at the University of California.

"Amazing, amazing, perfectly amazing," said Knight, who was wearing two elderly tea roses in his cheeks now from excitement. "I have just finished it. Sit down and listen."

"Wait a moment," said Fitch. "I want our friend here to see the original log of the *Evening Star*."

"Of course," said Knight. "A human document of the utmost value." Then, to my surprise, he took me by the arm and led me in front of a large *kakemono*, which was the only decoration on the walls.

"This is what Mr. Fitch calls the log of the *Evening Star*," he said. "It was found among the effects of Mr. Kato's brother on the schooner; and, fortunately, it was claimed by Mr. Kato himself. Take it to the light and examine it."

I took it to the window and looked at it with curiosity, though I did not quite see its bearing on the mystery of the *Evening Star*. It was a fine piece of work, one of those weird night pictures at which the Japanese are masters; for they know how to give you the single point of light that tells you of the unseen life around the lamp of the household or the temple. This was a picture of a little dark house, with jutting eaves, and a tiny rose light in one window, overlooking the sea. At the brink of the sea rose a ghostly figure that might only be a drift of mist, for the curve of the vague body suggested that the offshore wind was blowing it out to sea, while the great gleaming eyes were fixed on the lamp, and the shadowy arms outstretched toward it in hopeless longing. Sea and ghost and house were suggested in a very few strokes of the brush. All the rest, the peace and the tragic desire and a thousand other suggestions, according to the mood of the beholder, were concentrated into that single pinpoint of warm light in the window.

"Turn it over," said Fitch.

I obeyed him, and saw that the whole back of the *kakemono*, which measured about four feet by two, was covered with a fine scroll of Japanese characters in purple copying pencil. I had overlooked it at first, or accepted it, with the eye of ignorance, as a mere piece of Oriental decoration.

"That is what we all did," said Fitch. "We all overlooked the simple fact that Japanese words have a meaning. We didn't trouble about it—you know how vaguely one's eye travels over a three-foot sign on a Japanese teahouse. We didn't even think about it till Mr. Kato turned up in our office a week or two ago. You can't read it. No more can I. But we got Mr. Knight here to handle it for us."

"It turns out to be a message from Harper," said Knight. "Apparently he was lying helpless in his berth, and told the Japanese cook to write it down. I have made two versions, one a perfectly literal one, which requires a certain amount of retranslation. The other is an attempt to give as nearly as possible what Harper himself dictated. This is the version which I had better read to you now. The original has various repetitions, and shows that Harper's mind occasionally wandered, for he goes into trivial detail sometimes. But he seems to have been possessed with the idea of getting his account through to the owners; and whenever he got an opportunity, he made Kato take up his pencil and write, so that we have a very full account."

Knight took out a notebook, adjusted his glasses, and began to read, while the ghostly original fluttered in my hand as the night wind blew from the sea.

"A TERRIBLE THING has happened, and I think it my duty to write this, in the hope that it may fall into the hands of friends at home. I am not likely to live another twenty-four hours. The first hint that I had of anything wrong was on the night of March the fifteenth, when Mrs. Burgess came up to me on deck, looking worried, and said, 'Mr. Harper, I am in great trouble. I want to ask you a question, and I want you to give me an honest answer.' She looked around nervously, and her hands were fidgeting with her handkerchief, as if she were frightened to death. 'Whatever your answer may be,' she said, 'you'll not mention what I've said to you.' I promised her. She laid her hand on my arm and said, with the most piteous look in her face I have ever seen, 'I have no other friends to go to, and I want you to tell me. Mr. Harper, is my husband sane?'

"I had never doubted the sanity of Burgess till that moment. But there was something in the dreadfulness of that question from a woman who had only been married a few months that seemed like a door opening into the bottomless pit.

"It seemed to explain many things that hadn't occurred to me before. I asked her what she meant, and she told me that last night Burgess had come into the cabin and waked her up. His eyes were starting out of his head, and he told her that he had seen Captain Dayrell walking on deck. She told him it was nothing but imagination, and he laid his head on his arms and sobbed like a child. He said he thought it was one of the deckhands that had just come out of the forecastle, but all the men were short and smallish, and this was a big burly figure. It went ahead of him like his own shadow, and disappeared in the bows.

"Tonight, she said, half an hour ago, Burgess had come down to her, taking her by the throat, and sworn he would kill her if she didn't confess that Dayrell was still alive. She told him he must be crazy. 'My mind may be going,' he said, 'but you shan't kill my soul.' And he called her a name which she didn't repeat, but began to cry when she remembered it. He said he had seen Dayrell standing in the bows with the light of the moon full on his face, and he looked so brave and upright that he knew he must have been bitterly wronged.

"While she was telling me this she was looking around her in a very nervous kind of way, and we both heard someone coming up behind us very quietly. We turned around, and there—as God lives—stood the living image of Captain Dayrell looking at us in the shadow of the mast. Mrs. Burgess gave a shriek that paralyzed me for the moment, then she ran like a wild thing into the bows, and before anyone could stop her she climbed up and threw herself overboard.

"Evans and Barron were only a few yards away from her when she did it, and they both went overboard after her immediately, one of them throwing a life belt over ahead of him as he went. They were both good swimmers, and as the moon was bright, I thought we had only to launch a boat to pick them all up. I shouted to the Kanakas, and they all came up running. Two of the men and myself got into one of the starboard boats; and we were within three feet of the water when I heard the crack of a revolver from somewhere in the bows of the *Evening Star.* The men, who were lowering away, let us down with a rush that nearly capsized us. There were four more shots while we were getting our oars out. I called to the men on deck, asking them who was shooting, but got no reply. I believe they were panic-stricken and had bolted into cover. We pulled around the bows, and could see nothing. There was not a sign of the woman or the two men in the water.

"We could make nobody hear us on the ship, and all this while we had seen nothing of Captain Burgess. It must have been nearly an hour before we gave up our search and tried to get aboard again. We were still unable to get any reply from the ship, and we were about to try to climb on board by the boat's falls. The men were backing her in, stern first, and we were about ten yards from the ship when the figure of Captain Dayrell appeared, leaning over the side of the *Evening Star.* He stood there against the moonlight with his face in the shadow; but we all of us recognized him, and I heard the teeth of the Kanakas chattering. They had stopped backing, and we all stared at one another.

"Then, as casually as if it were a joke, Captain Dayrell stretched out his arm, and I saw the moonlight glint on his revolver. He fired at us deliberately, as if he were shooting at clay pigeons. I felt the wind of the first shot going past my head, and the two men at once began to pull hard to get out of range. The second shot missed also. At the third shot he got the man in the bows full in the face. He fell over backward, and lay there in the bottom of the boat. He must have been killed instantaneously. At the fourth shot I felt a stinging pain on the left side of my body, but hardly realized I had been wounded at the moment.

"A cloud passed over the moon just then, and the headway on the boat carried us too far for Dayrell to aim very accurately, so that I was able to get to the oars and pull out of range. The other man must have been wounded also, for he was lying in the bottom of the boat groaning, but I do not remember seeing him hit. I managed to pull fifty yards or so and then fainted, for I was bleeding very badly.

"When I recovered consciousness I found that the bleeding had stopped, and I was able to look at the two men. Both of them were dead and quite cold, so that I must have been unconscious for some time.

"The *Evening Star* was about a hundred yards away in the full light of the moon, but I could see nobody on deck. I sat watching her till daybreak, wondering what I should do, for there was no water or food in the boat, and I was unarmed. Unless Captain Burgess and the other men aboard could disarm Dayrell, I was quite helpless. Perhaps my wound had dulled my wits, for I was unable to think out any plan, and I sat there aimlessly for more than an hour.

"It was broad daylight, and I had drifted within fifty yards of the ship, when, to my surprise, Captain Burgess appeared on deck and hailed me. 'All right, Harper,' he said, 'come aboard.'

"I was able to scull the boat alongside, and Burgess got down into her without a word and helped me aboard. He took me down to my berth, with his arm around me, for I almost collapsed again with the effort, and he brought me some brandy. As soon as I could speak, I asked him what it all meant, and he said, 'The ship is his, Harper; we've got to give it up to him. That's what it means. I am not afraid of him by daylight, but what we shall do tonight, God only knows! Then, just as Mrs. Burgess had told me, he put his head down on his arms and began to sob like a child.

"'Where are the other men?' I asked him.

"'There's only you and I and Kato,' he said, 'to face it out aboard this ship.'

"With that he got up and left me, saying that he would send Kato to me with some food, if I thought I could eat. But I knew by this time that I was a dying man.

"There was only one thing I had to do, and that was to try to get this account written, and hide it in the hope of someone finding it later, for I felt sure that neither Burgess nor myself would live to tell it. There was no paper in my berth, and it was Kato who thought of writing it down in this way.

"*About an hour later.* Burgess has just been down to see me. He said that he had buried the two men who were shot in the boat. I wanted to ask him some questions, but he became so excited, it seemed useless. Neither he nor Kato seemed to have any idea where Dayrell was hiding. Kato believes, in fact, in ghosts, so it is no use questioning him.

"I must have lost consciousness or slept very heavily since the above was written, for I remembered nothing more till nightfall, when I woke up in the pitch-darkness. Kato was sitting by me, and gave me another drink of brandy. The ship was dead still, but I felt that something had gone wrong again.

"I do not know whether my own mind is going, but we have just heard the voice of Mrs. Burgess singing one of those sentimental songs that Captain Dayrell used to be so fond of. It seemed to be down in the cabin, and when she came to the end of it I heard Dayrell's voice calling out, 'Encore! Encore!' just as he used to do.

"I heard someone running down the deck like mad, and Captain Burgess came tumbling down to us with the whites of his eyes showing. 'Did you hear it?' he said. 'Harper, you'll admit you heard it. Don't tell me I'm mad. They're in the cabin together now. Come and look at them.' Then he looked at me with a curious, cunning look and said, 'No, you'd better stay where you are, Harper. You're not strong enough.' And he crept up on the deck like a cat.

"Something urged me to follow him, even if it took the last drop of my strength. Kato tried to dissuade me, but I drained the brandy flask, and managed to get out of my berth onto the deck by going very slowly, though the sweat broke out on me with every step. Burgess had disappeared, and there was nobody on deck. It was not so difficult to get to the skylight of the cabin. God knows what I had expected to see, but there I did see the figure of Captain Dayrell, dressed as I had seen him in life, with a big scarf around his throat and a peaked cap. There was an open sea chest in the corner, with a good many clothes scattered about, as if by someone who had been dressing in a hurry. It was an old chest belonging to Dayrell, and I often wondered why Burgess had left it lying there. The revolver lay on the table, and as Dayrell picked it up to load it the scarf unwound itself a little around his throat and the lower part of the face. Then, to my amazement, I recognized him."

"THERE," SAID KNIGHT, "the log of the *Evening Star* ends, except for a brief sentence by Kato himself, which I will not read to you now."

"I wonder if the poor devil did really see," said Moreton Fitch. "And what do you suppose he did when he saw who it was?"

"Crept back to his own berth, barricaded himself in with Kato's help, finished his account, died in the night with Dayrell tapping on the door, and was neatly buried by Burgess in the morning, I suppose."

"And Burgess?"

"Tidied everything up and then jumped overboard."

"Probably—in his own clothes; for it's quite true that we did find a lot of Dayrell's old clothes in a sea chest in the cabin. Funny idea, isn't it, a man ghosting himself like that?"

"Yes; but what did Harper mean by saying he heard Mrs. Burgess singing in the cabin that night?"

"Ah, that's another section of the log, recorded in a different way."

Moreton Fitch made a sign to the little Japanese, and told him to get a package out of his car. He returned with it in a moment.

"Dayrell was very proud of his wife's voice," said Fitch as he took the covers off the package. "Just before he was taken ill he conceived the idea of getting some records made of her songs to take with him on board ship. The phonograph was found among the old clothes. The usual sentimental stuff, you know. Like to hear it? She had rather a fine voice."

He turned a handle and, floating out into the stillness of the California night, we heard the full rich voice of the dead woman:

"Just a song at twilight, when the lights are low;
And the flick'ring shadows softly come and go."

At the end of the stanza a deep bass voice broke in with, "Encore! Encore!"

Then Fitch stopped it.

When we were in the car on our way home, I asked if there were any clue to the fate of the Japanese cook in the last sentence of the log of the *Evening Star.*

"I didn't want to bring it up before his brother," said Knight. "They are a sensitive folk. But the last sentence was to the effect that the *Evening Star* had now been claimed by the spirit of Captain Dayrell, and that the writer respectfully begged to commit hara-kiri."

Our road turned inland here, and I looked back toward the fishing village. The night was falling, but the sea was lilac-colored with the afterglow. I could see the hut and the little birdhouse, black against the water. On a sand dune just beyond them the fisherman Kato and his wife were sitting, still watching us. They must have been nearly a mile away by this time; but in the clear air they were carved out sharp and black as minute ebony images against the fading light of the Pacific.

CASTING THE RUNES

M. R. JAMES

April 15th, 190–

DEAR SIR—I am requested by the Council of the ____ Association to return to you the draft of a paper on "The Truth of Alchemy," which you have been good enough to offer to read at our forthcoming meeting, and to inform you that the council does not see its way to including it in the program.

April 18th

Dear Sir—I am sorry to say that my engagements do not permit of my affording you an interview on the subject of your proposed paper. Nor do our laws allow of your discussing the matter with a committee of our council, as you suggest. Please allow me to assure you that the fullest consideration was given to the draft which you submitted, and that it was not declined without having been referred to the judgment of a most competent authority. No personal question can have had the slightest influence on the decision of the council.

April 20th

The Secretary of the ____ Association begs respectfully to inform Mr. Karswell that it is impossible for him to communicate the name of any person or persons to whom the draft of Mr. Karswell's paper may have been submitted; also, that he cannot reply to any further letters on this subject.

"And who *is* Mr. Karswell?" inquired the Secretary's wife. She had called at his office, and (perhaps unwarrantably) had picked up the last of these three letters, which the typist had just brought in.

"Why, my dear, Mr. Karswell is a very angry man. But I don't know much about him otherwise, except that he is a person of wealth, his address is Lufford Abbey, Warwickshire, and he's an alchemist, apparently, and wants to tell us about it."

"What have you done to make him angry?" asked Mrs. Secretary.

"He sent in a draft of a paper he wanted to read at the next meeting, and we referred it to Edward Dunning—almost the only man in England who knows about these things. He said it was hopeless, so we declined it. Karswell has been pelting me with letters ever since. The last thing he wanted was the name of the man we referred his nonsense to; you saw my answer."

The Secretary and his wife were lunching out, and the friends to whose house they were bound were Warwickshire people. So Mrs. Secretary had already settled it in her own mind that she would question them judiciously about Mr. Karswell. But she was saved the trouble of leading up to the subject, for the hostess said to the host, before many minutes had passed, "I saw the Abbot of Lufford this morning. He was coming out of the British Museum gate as I drove past." It was not unnatural that Mrs. Secretary should inquire whether this was a real abbot who was being spoken of. "Oh no, my dear, only a neighbor of ours in the country who bought Lufford Abbey a few years ago. His real name is Karswell."

"Is he a friend of yours?" asked Mr. Secretary, with a private wink to his wife. The question let loose a torrent of declamation. There was really nothing to be said for Mr. Karswell. Nobody knew what he did with himself; his servants were a horrible set of people; he had invented a new religion for himself, and practiced no one could tell what appalling rites; he was very easily offended, and never forgave anybody; he had a dreadful face; he never did a kind action—

"You forget the treat he gave the schoolchildren, dear," the husband interrupted.

"Forget it, indeed! Now, Florence, listen to this. The first winter he was at Lufford this delightful neighbor of ours wrote to the clergyman of his parish and offered to show the schoolchildren some magic-lantern slides. Well, the clergyman was surprised, because Mr. Karswell had shown himself inclined to be unpleasant to the children—complaining of their trespassing, or something of the sort. But of course he accepted, the evening was fixed, and our friend went himself to see that everything went right.

"Mr. Karswell had evidently set out to frighten these poor village children out of their wits. He began with some comparatively mild things. Red Riding Hood was one, and even then, the wolf was so dreadful that several of the smaller children had to be taken out. Our friend said Mr. Karswell began the story by producing a noise like a wolf howling in the distance, which was the most gruesome thing he had ever heard. Well, the show went on, and the stories kept on becoming a little more terrifying each time, and the children were mesmerized into complete silence. At last he produced a series which represented a little boy passing through his own park—Lufford, I mean—in the evening. Every child in the room could recognize the place from the pictures. And this poor boy was followed, and at last pursued and overtaken, and either torn in pieces or somehow made away with, by a horrible hopping creature in white. Of course this was too much, and our friend spoke very sharply to Mr. Karswell and said it couldn't go on.

"All *he* said was, 'Oh, you think it's time to bring our little show to an end and send them home to their beds? *Very* well!' And then, if you please, he switched on another slide, which showed a great mass of snakes, centipedes, and disgusting creatures with wings, and somehow he made it seem as if they were climbing out of the picture and getting in among the audience; and this was accompanied by a sort of dry rustling noise which sent the children nearly mad, and of course they stampeded. A good many of them were rather hurt in getting out of the room, and I don't suppose one of them closed an eye that night. There was the most dreadful trouble in the village afterward, and if they could have got past the gates, I believe the fathers would have broken every window in the abbey. Well, now, that's Mr. Karswell; that's the Abbot of Lufford."

"He has all the possibilities of a distinguished criminal," said the host. "I'd be sorry for anyone who got into his bad books."

"Is he the man," asked the Secretary, "who brought out a *History of Witchcraft* some time back?"

"That's the man. Do you remember the reviews of it?"

"Certainly I do, and I knew the author of the most incisive of the lot. You must remember John Harrington."

"Oh, very well, and I remember the account of the inquest on him."

"Inquest?" said one of the ladies. "What happened to him?"

"Why, he fell out of a tree and broke his neck. But the puzzle was what could have induced him to get up there. Here was this man—not an athletic fellow, was he, and with no eccentric twist about him that was ever noticed?—walking home along a country road late in the evening—no tramps about, well known and liked in the place—and he suddenly begins to run like mad, loses his hat and stick, and finally shins up a tree. A dead branch gives way, and he comes down with it and breaks his neck, and there he's found next morning with the most dreadful face of fear on him that could be imagined. It was evident that he had been chased by something, and people talked of savage dogs, and beasts escaped out of menageries; but there was nothing to be made of that. That was in 1889, and I believe his brother Henry has been trying to get on the track of an explanation ever since. He insists there was malice in it, but I don't know."

After a time the talk reverted to the *History of Witchcraft*. "Did you ever look into it?" asked the host.

"Yes, I did," said the Secretary. "It was an evil book. The man believed every word of what he was saying, and I'm very much mistaken if he hadn't tried the greater part of his recipes."

"Well, I only remember Harrington's review of it, and I must say, if I'd been the author, it would have quenched my literary ambition for good."

"It hasn't had that effect in the present case. But come, it's half past three; I must be off."

On the way home the Secretary's wife said, "I do hope that horrible man won't find out that Mr. Dunning had anything to do with the rejection of his paper."

"I don't think there's much chance of that," said the Secretary. "Dunning won't mention it himself, for these matters are confidential, and none of us will for the same reason. The only danger is that Karswell might ask the British Museum people who was in the habit of consulting alchemical manuscripts. Let's hope it won't occur to him."

However, Mr. Karswell was an astute man.

THIS MUCH IS in the way of prologue. On an evening later in the same week, Mr. Edward Dunning was returning from the British Museum, where he had been engaged in research, to the comfortable house in a suburb where he lived alone, tended by two excellent women who had been long with him.

A train took him to within a mile or two of his house, and an electric streetcar a stage farther. The advertisements on the panes of glass that faced him as he sat were objects of his frequent contemplation. But on this particular night there was one at the corner of the car farthest from him which did not seem familiar. It was in blue letters on a yellow background, and all that he could read of it was a name—John Harrington—and something like a date. As the car emptied, he was curious enough to move along the seat until he could read it well. The advertisement was *not* of the usual type. It ran thus: IN MEMORY OF JOHN HARRINGTON, F.S.A., OF THE LAURELS, ASHBROOKE. DIED SEPTEMBER 18TH, 1889. THREE MONTHS WERE ALLOWED.

The car stopped. Mr. Dunning, still contemplating the blue letters on the yellow background, had to be stimulated to rise by a word from the conductor. "I beg your pardon," he said. "I was looking at that advertisement; it's a very odd one, isn't it?"

The conductor read it slowly. "Well, my word," he said. "I never saw that one before." He got out a duster and applied it, not without saliva, to the pane and then to the outside. "No," he said, returning, "that ain't no transfer; seems to me as if it was *in* the glass."

Mr. Dunning examined it and rubbed it with his glove, and agreed. "Who gives leave for these advertisements to be put up? I wish you would inquire. I will just take a note of the words."

"Well, sir, that's all done at the company's office. It's our Mr. Timms looks into that. When we put up tonight I'll leave word, and per'aps I'll be able to tell you tomorrer if you 'appen to be coming this way."

This was all that passed that evening. And next day Mr. Dunning went to town again. The car (it was the same car) was too full in the morning to allow of his getting a word with the conductor; he could only be sure that the curious advertisement had been made away with. At the close of the day he missed the streetcar, or else preferred walking home, but at a rather late hour, while he was at work in his study, one of the maids came to say that two men from the streetcar company were anxious to speak to him. He had the men in—they were the conductor and driver of the car—and when the matter of refreshment had been attended to, he asked what Mr. Timms had had to say.

"Well, sir, that's what we took the liberty to step round about," said the conductor. "'Cordin' to 'im there warn't no advertisement of that description sent in, nor ordered, nor paid for, nor put up, nor nothink. 'Well,' I says, 'if that's the case, all I ask of you, Mr. Timms,' I says, 'is to take and look at it for yourself,' I says. 'Of course if it ain't there, you may take and call me what you like.' 'Right, George,' he says, 'I will'; and we went straight off." The conductor paused.

"Well," said Mr. Dunning, "it was gone, I suppose. Broken?"

"Broke! Not it. There warn't, if you'll believe me, no trace of them letters on that piece o' glass!"

"And what did Mr. Timms say?"

"Why, 'e did what I give 'im leave to—called us pretty much anythink he liked. But William and me thought, as we seen you take down a bit of a note about that letterin'—"

"I certainly did that, and I have it now. Did you wish me to speak to Mr. Timms myself, and show it to him?"

"We 'adn't ought to take up your time this way, sir; but if it so 'appened you could find time to step round to the company's office in the morning and tell Mr. Timms what you seen for yourself, we should lay under a very 'igh obligation to you. If they got it into their 'ead at the office as we seen things as warn't there, why, one thing leads to another, and where we should be a twelvemunce 'ence—well, you can understand what I mean."

Amid further elucidations of the proposition, George and William left the room.

The incredulity of Mr. Timms was greatly modified on the following day by what Mr. Dunning could tell and show him; and any bad mark that might have been attached to the names of William and George was not suffered to remain on the company's books; but explanation there was none.

Mr. Dunning's interest in the matter was kept alive by an incident the following afternoon. He was walking from his club to the train, and he noticed some way ahead a man with a handful of leaflets such as are distributed to passersby by agents of enterprising firms. This agent had not chosen a very crowded street for his operations. In fact, Mr. Dunning did not see him get rid of a single leaflet before he himself reached the spot. Then one was thrust into his hand. He looked in passing at the giver, but the impression he got was so unclear that, however much he tried to reckon it up subsequently, nothing would come. As he went on, he glanced at the paper. It was a blue one. The name of Harrington in large capitals caught his eye. He stopped, startled, and felt for his glasses. The next instant the leaflet was twitched out of his hand by a man who hurried past. He ran back a few paces, but where was the passerby? And where the distributor?

It was in a pensive frame of mind that Mr. Dunning went on the following day into the Select Manuscript Room of the British Museum and filled out cards for Harley 3586 and some other volumes. After a few minutes they were brought to him, and he was settling the one he wanted first upon the desk when he thought he heard his own name whispered behind him. He turned around hastily and, in doing so, brushed his little portfolio of loose papers onto the floor. He saw no one he recognized except one of the staff in charge of the room, who nodded to him, and he proceeded to pick up his papers. He thought he had them all, and was turning to begin work when a stout gentleman at the table behind him, who was just rising to leave, touched him on the shoulder, saying, "May I give you this? I think it should be yours," and handed him a missing quire.

"It is mine, thank you," said Mr. Dunning. In another moment the man had left the room. Upon finishing his work, Mr. Dunning had some conversation with the assistant in charge and took occasion to ask who the stout gentleman was.

"Oh, he's a man named Karswell," said the assistant. "He was asking me a week ago who were the great authorities on alchemy, and of course I told him you were the only one in the country."

On the way home that day Mr. Dunning did not look forward with his usual cheerfulness to a solitary evening. He wanted to sit close up to his neighbors in the train and in the streetcar, but as luck would have it both train and car were markedly empty.

On arriving at his house he found Dr. Watson, his medical man, on his doorstep. "I've had to upset your household arrangements, I'm sorry to say, Dunning. Both your servants are *hors de combat.* In fact, I've had to send them to the hospital."

"Good heavens! What's the matter?"

"It's ptomaine poisoning, I think. You've not suffered yourself, I can see, or you wouldn't be walking about."

"Dear, dear! Have you any idea what brought it on?"

"Well, they tell me they bought some shellfish from a hawker at their dinnertime. It's odd. I've made inquiries, but I can't find that any hawker has been to other houses in the street. You come and dine with me tonight, anyhow, and we can make arrangements for a charwoman to come tomorrow."

The solitary evening was thus obviated. Mr. Dunning spent the time pleasantly enough with the doctor and returned to his lonely home at about eleven thirty. He was in bed and the light was out when he heard the unmistakable sound of his study door opening. He slipped out into the hall and leaned over the banister in his nightclothes, listening. No light was visible; no further sound came. Only a gust of warm air played for an instant around his shins. He went back and decided to lock himself in his room.

There was more unpleasantness, however. The electric light had stopped working. The obvious course was to find a match, and also to consult his watch; he might as well know how many hours of discomfort awaited him. So he put his hand into the well-known nook under the pillow—only, it did not get so far. What he touched was, according to his account, a mouth, with teeth, and with hair about it—and, he declares, not the mouth of a human being. I do not think it is any use to guess what he said or did; but he was in a spare room with the door locked and his ear to it before he was clearly conscious again. And there he spent the rest of a most miserable night, looking every moment for some fumbling at the door, but nothing came.

The venturing back to his own room in the morning was attended with many listenings and quiverings. The door stood open and there was no trace of an inhabitant. The watch, too, was in its usual place. A ring at the back door now announced the charwoman who had been ordered the night before, and nerved Mr. Dunning, after letting her in, to continue his search in other parts of the house. It was equally fruitless.

The day thus begun went on dismally enough. He dared not go to the museum. Karswell might turn up there, and Dunning felt he could not cope with a probably hostile stranger. His own house was odious; he hated sponging on the doctor. He spent some time in a call at the hospital, where he was slightly cheered by a good report of his housekeeper and maid. Toward lunchtime he betook himself to his club, again experiencing a gleam of satisfaction at seeing the Secretary of the association. At luncheon Dunning told his friend the more material of his woes, but could not bring himself to speak of those that weighed most heavily on his spirits.

"My poor dear man," said the Secretary, "what an upset! Look here—we're alone at home, absolutely. You must put up with us. Yes! No excuse. Send your things in this afternoon."

Dunning was unable to say no, for he was becoming acutely anxious as to what that night might have waiting for him. He was almost happy as he hurried home to pack up.

His friends were shocked at his lorn appearance and did their best to keep him up to the mark, not altogether without success. But when he and the Secretary were smoking alone later, Dunning suddenly said, "Gayton, I believe that alchemist man knows it was I who got his paper rejected."

Gayton whistled. "What makes you think that?" he said.

Dunning told of his conversation with the museum assistant. "Not that I care much," he went on, "only it might be a nuisance if we were to meet. He's a bad-tempered party, I imagine." Gayton became more and more strongly impressed with the desolateness that came over Dunning's face and bearing, and finally he asked him point-blank whether something serious was not bothering him.

Dunning gave an exclamation of relief. "I was perishing to get it off my mind," he said. "Do you know anything about a man named John Harrington?" Gayton was thoroughly startled, and could only ask why. Then the complete story of Dunning's experiences came out—what had happened in the streetcar, in his own house, and in the street. He ended with the question he had begun with. Gayton was at a loss how to answer him. To tell the story of Harrington's end would perhaps be right; only, Dunning was in a nervous state, the story was a grim one, and he could not help asking himself whether there were not a connecting link between these two cases, in the person of Karswell. In the end he decided that his answer should be guarded. So he said that he had known Harrington at Cambridge, and he had died suddenly in 1889, adding a few details about the man and his published work. Later he talked over the matter with Mrs. Gayton. She reminded him of a surviving brother, Henry Harrington, who might be got hold of through mutual friends.

It is not necessary to tell in further detail the steps by which Henry Harrington and Dunning were brought together. The next scene that does require to be narrated is a conversation that took place between the two. Dunning had told Harrington of the strange ways in which the dead man's name had been brought before him, and something of his subsequent experiences. Then he had asked if Harrington could recall the circumstances connected with his brother's death.

"John," Harrington said, "was in a very odd state for some weeks before the catastrophe. The principal notion he had was that he was being followed. I cannot get it out of my mind that there was ill will at work, and what you tell me about yourself reminds me of my brother. Can you think of any possible connecting link?"

"I've been told that your brother reviewed a book very severely not long before he died, and just lately I have crossed the path of the man who wrote that book in a way he would resent."

"Don't tell me the man was called Karswell."

"Why not? That is exactly his name."

Henry Harrington leaned back. "That is final to my mind. I feel sure that my brother John was beginning to believe—very much against his will—that Karswell was at the bottom of his trouble. My brother was a great musician and used to run up to concerts in town. He came back, three months before he died, from one of these, and gave me his program to look at—an analytical program. He always kept them. 'I nearly missed this one,' he said. 'I suppose I must have dropped it. Anyhow, I was looking for it under my seat, and my neighbor offered me his, said he had no further use for it, and he went away just afterward. I don't know who he was—a stout, clean-shaven man.'

"Then, not very long after, John was going over these programs, putting them in order, to have them bound up, and in this particular one he found a strip of paper with some very odd writing on it in red and black. It looked to me more like runic letters than anything else. 'Why,' he said, 'this must belong to my fat neighbor. It looks as if it might be worth returning to him; it may be a copy of something.' We agreed that my brother had better look out for the man at the next concert, to which he was going very soon.

"The paper was lying on the book and we were both by the fire; it was a cold, windy summer evening. I suppose the door blew open, though I didn't notice it. At any rate a gust—a warm gust it was—came quite suddenly between us, took the paper, and blew it straight into the fire. It was light, thin paper, and flared and went up the chimney in a single ash. 'Well,' I said, 'you can't give it back now.'

"I remember all that very clearly, without any good reason; and now to come to the point. I don't know if you looked at that book of Karswell's which my unfortunate brother reviewed. It was written in no style at all—split infinitives, and every sort of thing that makes an Oxford gorge rise. Then there was nothing that the man didn't swallow: mixing up classical myths with reports of savage customs of today—all very proper, no doubt, if you know how to use them, but he didn't.

"Well, after the misfortune, I looked over the book again. It was no better than before, but the impression which it left this time on my mind was different. I suspected—as I told you—that Karswell had borne ill will to my brother, even that he was in some way responsible for what had happened; and now his book seemed to me to be a very sinister performance indeed. In one chapter he spoke of 'casting the runes' on people, either for the purpose of gaining their affection or of getting them out of the way. He spoke of all this in a way that seemed to imply actual knowledge. By now I am sure that the civil man at the concert was Karswell; I suspect that the paper was of importance; and I do believe that if my brother had been able to give it back, he might have been alive now. Therefore, it occurs to me to ask you whether you have anything to put beside what I have told you."

By way of answer, Dunning had the episode in the manuscript room at the British Museum to relate. "Then he did actually hand you some papers. Have you examined them? No? Because we must look at them at once, and very carefully."

They went to the house, where Dunning's portfolio of papers was gathering dust on the writing table. In it were the quires of small-sized scribbling paper which he used for his transcripts, and from one of these, as he took it up, there slipped and fluttered out into the room a strip of thin, light paper. The window was open, but Harrington slammed it to, just in time to intercept the paper, which he caught. "I thought so," he said. "It might be the identical thing that was given to my brother. You'll have to look out, Dunning; this may mean something quite serious for you."

The paper was narrowly examined. As Harrington had said, the characters on it were more like runes than anything else, but not decipherable by either man, and both hesitated to copy them, for fear, as they confessed, of perpetuating whatever evil purpose they might conceal. So it has remained impossible to ascertain what was conveyed in this curious message. Both Dunning and Harrington are convinced that it had the effect of bringing its possessors into very undesirable company. That it must be returned to the source whence it came they were agreed, and further, that the only certain way was that of personal service; and here contrivance would be necessary, for Dunning was known by sight to Karswell. He must alter his appearance by shaving his beard.

But then might not the blow fall first? Harrington thought they could time it. He knew the date of the concert at which the "black spot" had been put on his brother: it was June eighteenth. The death had followed on September eighteenth. Dunning reminded him that three months had been mentioned in the inscription on the car window. "Perhaps," he added, "mine may be a bill at three months too. I believe I can fix it by my diary. Yes, April twenty-third was the day at the museum; that brings us to July twenty-third. Now, you know, it becomes extremely important to me to know anything you can tell me about the progress of your brother's trouble."

"Of course. Well, the sense of being watched whenever he was alone was the most distressing thing to him. Also, two items came for him by mail during those weeks, both with a London postmark, and addressed in a commercial hand. One was a woodcut of Bewick's, roughly torn out of the page: one which shows a moonlit road and a man walking along it, followed by an awful demon creature. Under it were written the lines out of 'The Ancient Mariner' (which I suppose the cut illustrates) about one who, having once looked around—

> *'walks on,*
> *And turns no more his head;*
> *Because he knows a frightful fiend*
> *Doth close behind him tread.'*

The other was a calendar, such as tradesmen often send. My brother paid no attention to this, but I looked at it after his death and found that everything after September eighteenth had been torn out."

The end of the consultation was this. Harrington, who knew a neighbor of Karswell's, thought he saw a way of keeping a watch on his movements. It would be Dunning's part to be in readiness to try to cross Karswell's path at any moment, to keep the paper safe and in a place of ready access.

They parted. The next weeks were a severe strain upon Dunning's nerves. The intangible barrier which had seemed to rise about him on the day when he received the paper gradually developed into a brooding blackness. He waited with inexpressible anxiety for a mandate from

Harrington as May, June, and early July passed on. But all this time Karswell remained immovable at Lufford.

At last, in less than a week before the date he had come to look upon as the end of his earthly activities, came a telegram: LEAVES VICTORIA BY BOAT TRAIN THURSDAY NIGHT. DO NOT MISS. I COME TO YOU TONIGHT. HARRINGTON.

He arrived accordingly, and they concocted plans. The train left Victoria at nine, and its last stop before Dover was Croydon West. Harrington would keep close watch on Karswell at Victoria, and look out for Dunning at Croydon, calling to him, if need were, by a name agreed upon. Dunning, disguised as far as might be, must have the paper with him.

Dunning's suspense as he waited on the Croydon platform I need not attempt to describe. Finally the train came, and Harrington was at the window. It was important that there should be no recognition; so Dunning got in at the farther end of the corridor carriage, and only gradually made his way to the compartment where Harrington and Karswell were. He was pleased to see that the train was far from full.

Karswell was on the alert, but gave no sign of recognition. Dunning took the seat not immediately facing him, and attempted, vainly at first, then with increasing command of his faculties, to reckon the possibilities of making the desired transfer. Opposite Karswell, and next to Dunning, was a heap of Karswell's coats on the seat. It would be of no use to slip the paper into these—he would not be safe, or would not feel so, unless in some way it could be proffered by him and accepted by the other. The minutes went on. Karswell rose and went out into the corridor. As he did so, something slipped off his seat and fell with hardly a sound to the floor. When Karswell had gone out, Dunning picked up what had fallen, and saw that the key was in his hands in the form of one of Cook's ticket cases, with tickets in it. These cases have a pocket in the cover, and within very few seconds the paper of which we have heard was in the pocket of this one. To make the operation more secure, Harrington stood in the doorway of the compartment and fiddled with the blind. It was done, and done at the right time, for the train was now slowing down toward Dover.

In a moment more Karswell reentered the compartment. As he did so, Dunning, managing, he knew not how, to suppress the tremble in his voice, handed him the ticket case, saying, "May I give you this, sir? I believe it is yours."

After a brief glance at the ticket inside, Karswell uttered the hoped-for response, "Yes, it is; much obliged to you, sir," and he placed it in his breast pocket.

Even in the few moments that remained—moments of tense anxiety, for they knew not to what a premature finding of the paper might lead—both men noticed that the carriage seemed to darken about them and to grow warmer; that Karswell was fidgety and oppressed; that he sat upright and glanced anxiously at both. They, with sickening anxiety, busied themselves in collecting their belongings; but they both thought that Karswell was on the point of speaking when the train stopped at Dover pier.

There they got out, but so empty was the train that they were forced to linger on the platform until Karswell should have passed ahead of them with his porter on the way to the boat, and only then was it safe for them to exchange a pressure of the hand and a word of congratulation. The effect upon Dunning was to make him almost faint. Harrington made him lean up against the wall, while he himself went forward a few yards within sight of the gangway to the boat, at which Karswell had now arrived.

The man at the head of it examined Karswell's ticket, and he passed down into the boat. Suddenly the official called after him, "You, sir, beg pardon, did the other gentleman show his ticket?"

"What the devil do you mean by the other gentleman?" Karswell's snarling voice called back from the deck.

The man bent over and looked at him. "The devil? Well, I don't know, I'm sure," Harrington heard him say to himself, and then loudly, "My mistake, sir." And then, to a subordinate near him, "'Ad he got a dog with him, or what? Funny thing—I could 'a' swore 'e wasn't alone." In five minutes more there was nothing but the lessening lights of the boat, the night breeze, and the moon.

Long and long the two sat in their room at the Lord Warden. In spite of the removal of their greatest anxiety, they were oppressed with a doubt, not of the lightest. Had they been justified in sending a man to his death, as they believed they had? Ought they not to warn him, at least?

"No," said Harrington. "If he is the murderer I think him, we have done no more than is just. Still, if you think it better—but how and where can you warn him?"

"He was booked to Abbeville only," said Dunning. "I saw that. If I wired to the hotels there in Joanne's Guide, 'Examine your ticket case. Dunning,' I should feel happier. This is the twenty-first; he will have a day. But I am afraid he has gone into the dark." So telegrams were left at the hotel office.

It is not clear whether these reached their destination or whether, if they did, they were understood. All that is known is that, on the afternoon of the twenty-third, an English traveler, examining the front of St. Wulfram's Church at Abbeville, then under extensive repair, was struck on the head and instantly killed by a stone falling from the scaffold erected around the northwestern tower, there being, as was clearly proved, no workman on the scaffold at that moment. And the traveler's papers identified him as Mr. Karswell.

Only one detail shall be added. At Karswell's sale a set of Bewick, sold with all faults, was acquired by Harrington. The page with the woodcut of the traveler and the demon was, as Harrington had expected, mutilated.

MAN FROM THE SOUTH

ROALD DAHL

IT WAS GETTING on toward six o'clock so I thought I'd buy myself a beer and go out and sit in a deck chair by the swimming pool and have a little evening sun.

I went to the bar and got the beer and carried it outside and wandered down the garden toward the pool.

It was a fine garden with lawns and beds of azaleas and tall coconut palms, and the wind was blowing strongly through the tops of the palm trees making the leaves hiss and crackle as though they were on fire. I could see the clusters of big brown nuts hanging down underneath the leaves.

There were plenty of deck chairs around the swimming pool and there were white tables and huge brightly colored umbrellas and sunburned men and women sitting around in bathing suits. In the pool itself there were three or four girls and about a dozen boys, all splashing about and making a lot of noise and throwing a large rubber ball at one another.

I stood watching them. The girls were English girls from the hotel. The boys I didn't know about, but they sounded American and I thought they were probably naval cadets who'd come ashore from the U.S. naval training vessel which had arrived in harbor that morning.

I went over and sat down under a yellow umbrella where there were four empty seats, and I poured my beer and settled back comfortably with a cigarette. It was very pleasant sitting there in the sunshine with beer and cigarette. It was pleasant to sit and watch the bathers splashing about in the green water.

The American sailors were getting on nicely with the English girls. They'd reached the stage where they were diving under the water and tipping them up by their legs.

Just then I noticed a small, oldish man walking briskly around the edge of the pool. He was immaculately dressed in a white suit and he walked very quickly with little bouncing strides, pushing himself high up onto his toes with each step. He had on a large creamy Panama hat, and he came bouncing along the side of the pool, looking at the people and the chairs.

He stopped beside me and smiled, showing two rows of very small, uneven teeth, slightly tarnished. I smiled back.

"Excuse pleess, but may I sit here?"

"Certainly," I said. "Go ahead."

He bobbed around to the back of the chair and inspected it for safety, then he sat down and crossed his legs. His white buckskin shoes had little holes punched all over them for ventilation.

"A fine evening," he said. "They are all evenings fine here in Jamaica." I couldn't tell if the accent were Italian or Spanish, but I felt fairly sure he was some sort of a South American. And old too, when you saw him close. Probably around sixty-eight or seventy.

"Yes," I said. "It is wonderful here, isn't it."

"And who, might I ask, are all dese? Dese is no hotel people." He was pointing at the bathers in the pool.

"I think they're American sailors," I told him. "They're Americans who are learning to be sailors."

"Of course dey are Americans. Who else in de world is going to make as much noise at dat? You are not American, no?"

"No," I said. "I am not."

Suddenly one of the American cadets was standing in front of us. He was dripping wet from the pool and one of the English girls was standing there with him.

"Are these chairs taken?" he said.

"No," I answered.

"Mind if I sit down?"

"Go ahead."

"Thanks," he said. He had a towel in his hand and when he sat down he unrolled it and produced a pack of cigarettes and a lighter. He offered the cigarettes to the girl and she refused; then he offered them to me and I took one. The little man said, "Tank you, no, but I tink I have a cigar." He pulled out a crocodile case and got himself a cigar, then he produced a knife which had a small scissors in it and he snipped the end off the cigar.

"Here, let me give you a light." The American boy held up his lighter.

"Dat will not work in dis wind."

"Sure, it'll work. It always works."

The little man removed his unlighted cigar from his mouth, cocked his head on one side and looked at the boy.

"*All*-ways?" he said slowly.

"Sure, it never fails. Not with me anyway."

The little man's head was still cocked over on one side and he was still watching the boy. "Well, well. So you say dis famous lighter it never fails. Iss dat you say?"

"Sure," the boy said. "That's right." He was about nineteen or twenty with a long freckled face and a rather sharp birdlike nose. His chest was not very sunburned and there were freckles there too, and a few wisps of pale reddish hair. He was holding the lighter in his right hand, ready to flip the wheel. "It never fails," he said, smiling now because he was purposely exaggerating his little boast. "I promise you it never fails."

"One momint, pleess." The hand that held the cigar came up high, palm outward, as though it were stopping traffic. "Now juss one momint." He had a curiously soft, toneless voice and he kept looking at the boy all the time.

"Shall we not perhaps make a little bet on dat?" He smiled at the boy. "Shall we not make a little bet on whether your lighter lights?"

"Sure, I'll bet," the boy said. "Why not?"

"You like to bet?"

"Sure, I'll always bet."

The man paused and examined his cigar, and I must say I didn't much like the way he was behaving. It seemed he was already trying to make something out of this, and to embarrass the boy, and at the same time I had the feeling he was relishing a private little secret all his own.

He looked up again at the boy and said slowly, "I like to bet, too. Why we don't have a good bet on dis ting? A good big bet."

"Now wait a minute," the boy said. "I can't do that. But I'll bet you a quarter. I'll even bet you a dollar, or whatever it is over here—some shillings, I guess."

The little man waved his hand again. "Listen to me. Now we have some fun. We make a bet. Den we go up to my room here in de hotel where iss no wind and I bet you you cannot light dis famous lighter of yours ten times running without missing once."

"I'll bet I can," the boy said.

"All right. Good. We make a bet, yes?"

"Sure. I'll bet you a buck."

"No, no. I make you very good bet. I am rich man and I am sporting man also. Listen to me. Outside de hotel iss my car. Iss very fine car. American car from your country. Cadillac—"

"Hey, now. Wait a minute." The boy leaned back in his deck chair and he laughed. "I can't put up that sort of property. This is crazy."

"Not crazy at all. You strike lighter successfully ten times running and Cadillac is yours. You like to have dis Cadillac, yes?"

"Sure, I'd like to have a Cadillac." The boy was still grinning.

"All right. Fine. We make a bet and I put up my Cadillac."

"And what do I put up?"

The little man carefully removed the red band from his still unlighted cigar. "I never ask you, my friend, to bet something you cannot afford. You understand?"

"Then what do I bet?"

"I make it very easy for you, yes?"

"Okay. You make it easy."

"Some small ting you can afford to give away, and if you did happen to lose it you would not feel too bad. Right?"

"Such as what?"

"Such as, perhaps, de little finger of your left hand."

"My *what!*" The boy stopped grinning.

"Yes. Why not? You win, you take de car. You looss, I take de finger."

"I don't get it. How d'you mean, you take the finger?"

"I chop it off."

"Jumping jeepers! That's a crazy bet. I think I'll just make it a dollar."

The little man leaned back, spread out his hands palms upward and gave a tiny contemptuous shrug of the shoulders. "Well, well, well," he said. "I do not understand. You say it lights but you will not bet. Den we forget it, yes?"

The boy sat quite still, staring at the bathers in the pool. Then he remembered suddenly he hadn't lighted his cigarette. He put it between his lips, cupped his hands around the lighter and flipped the wheel. The wick lighted and burned with a small, steady, yellow flame and the way he held his hands the wind didn't get to it at all.

"Could I have a light, too?" I said.

"Gee, I'm sorry. I forgot you didn't have one."

I held out my hand for the lighter, but he stood up and came over to do it for me.

"Thank you," I said, and he returned to his seat.

"You having a good time?" I asked.

"Fine," he answered. "It's pretty nice here."

There was a silence then, and I could see that the little man had succeeded in disturbing the boy with his absurd proposal. He was sitting there very still, and it was obvious that a small tension was beginning to build up inside him. Then he started shifting about in his seat, and rubbing his chest, and stroking the back of his neck, and finally he placed both hands on his knees and began tapping with his fingers against the kneecaps. Soon he was tapping with one of his feet as well.

"Now just let me check up on this bet of yours," he said at last. "You say we go up to your room and if I make this lighter light ten times running I win a Cadillac. If it misses just once then I forfeit the little finger of my left hand. Is that right?"

"Certainly. Dat is de bet. But I tink you are afraid."

"What do we do if I lose? Do I have to hold my finger out while you chop it off?"

"Oh, no! Dat would be no good. And you might be tempted to refuse to hold it out. What I should do I should tie one of your hands to de table before we started and I should stand dere with a knife ready to go *chop* de momint your lighter missed."

"What year is the Cadillac?" the boy asked.

"Excuse. I not understand."

"What year—how old is the Cadillac?"

"Ah! How old? Yes. It is last year. Quite new car. But I see you are not betting man. Americans never are."

The boy paused for just a moment and he glanced first at the English girl, then at me. "Yes," he said sharply. "I'll bet you."

"Good!" The little man clapped his hands together quietly, once. "Fine," he said. "We do it now. And you, sir," he turned to me, "you would perhaps be good enough to, what you call it, to—to referee." He had pale, almost colorless eyes with tiny bright black pupils.

"Well," I said. "I think it's a crazy bet. I don't think I like it very much."

"Nor do I," said the English girl. It was the first time she'd spoken. "I think it's a stupid, ridiculous bet."

"Are you serious about cutting off this boy's finger if he loses?" I said.

"Certainly I am. Also about giving him Cadillac if he win. Come now. We go to my room."

He stood up. "You like to put on some clothes first?" he said.

"No," the boy answered. "I'll come like this." Then he turned to me. "I'd consider it a favor if you'd come along and referee."

"All right," I said. "I'll come along, but I don't like the bet."

"You come too," he said to the girl. "You come and watch."

The little man led the way back through the garden to the hotel. He was animated now, and excited, and that seemed to make him bounce up higher than ever on his toes as he walked along.

"I live in annex," he said. "You like to see car first? Iss just here."

He took us to where we could see the front driveway of the hotel and he stopped and pointed to a sleek pale green Cadillac parked close by.

"Dere she iss. De green one. You like?"

"Say, that's a nice car," the boy said.

"All right. Now we go up and see if you can win her."

We followed him into the annex and up one flight of stairs. He unlocked his door and we all trooped into what was a large pleasant double bedroom. There was a woman's dressing gown lying across the bottom of one of the beds.

"First," he said, "we 'ave a little Martini."

The drinks were on a small table in the far corner, all ready to be mixed, and there was a shaker and ice and plenty of glasses. He began to make the Martini, but meanwhile he'd rung the bell and now there was a knock on the door and a colored maid came in.

"Ah!" he said, putting down the bottle of gin, taking a wallet from his pocket and pulling out a pound note. "You will do something for me now, pleess." He gave the maid the pound.

"You keep dat," he said. "And now we are going to play a little game in here and I want you to go off and find for me two—no tree tings. I want some nails; I want a hammer, and I want a chopping knife, a butcher's chopping knife which you can borrow from de kitchen. You can get, yes?"

"A *chopping knife!*" The maid opened her eyes wide and clasped her hands in front of her. "You mean a *real* chopping knife?"

"Yes, yes, of course. Come on now, pleess. You can find dose tings surely for me."

"Yes, sir, I'll try, sir. Surely I'll try to get them." And she went.

The little man handed round the Martinis. We stood there and sipped them, the boy with the long freckled face and the pointed nose, bare-bodied except for a pair of faded brown bathing shorts; the English girl, a large-boned, fair-haired girl wearing a pale blue bathing suit, who watched the boy over the top of her glass all the time; the little man with the colorless eyes standing there in his immaculate white suit drinking his Martini and looking at the girl in her pale blue bathing dress. I didn't know what to make of it all. The man seemed serious about the bet and he seemed serious about the business of cutting off the finger. But hell, what if the boy lost? Then we'd have to rush him to the hospital in the Cadillac that he hadn't won. That would be a fine thing. Now wouldn't that be a really fine thing? It would be a damn silly unnecessary thing so far as I could see.

"Don't you think this is rather a silly bet?" I said.

"I think it's a fine bet," the boy answered. He had already downed one large Martini.

"I think it's a stupid, ridiculous bet," the girl said. "What'll happen if you lose?"

"It won't matter. Come to think of it, I can't remember ever in my life having had any use for the little finger on my left hand. Here he is." The boy took hold of the finger. "Here he is and he hasn't ever done a thing for me yet. So why shouldn't I bet him. I think it's a fine bet."

The little man smiled and picked up the shaker and refilled our glasses.

"Before we begin," he said, "I will present to de—to de referee de key of de car." He produced a car key from his pocket and gave it to me. "De papers," he said, "de owning papers and insurance are in de pocket of de car."

Then the colored maid came in again. In one hand she carried a small chopper, the kind used by butchers for chopping meat bones, and in the other a hammer and a bag of nails.

"Good! You get dem all. Tank you, tank you. Now you can go." He waited until the maid had closed the door, then he put the implements on one of the beds and said, "Now we prepare ourselves, yes?" And to the boy "Help me, pleess, with dis table. We carry it out a little."

It was the usual kind of hotel writing desk, just a plain rectangular table about four feet by three with a blotting pad, ink, pens and paper. They carried it out into the room away from the wall, and removed the writing things.

"And now," he said, "a chair." He picked up a chair and placed it beside the table. He was very brisk and very animated, like a person organizing games at a children's party. "And now de nails. I must put in de nails." He fetched the nails and he began to hammer them into the top of the table.

We stood there, the boy, the girl, and I, holding Martinis in our hands, watching the little man at work. We watched him hammer two nails into the table, about six inches apart. He didn't hammer them right home; he allowed a small part of each one to stick up. Then he tested them for firmness with his fingers.

Anyone would think the son of a bitch had done this before, I told myself. He never hesitates. Table, nails, hammer, kitchen chopper. He knows exactly what he needs and how to arrange it.

"And now," he said, "all we want is some string." He found some string. "All right, at last we are ready. Will you pleess to sit here at de table," he said to the boy.

The boy put his glass away and sat down.

"Now place de left hand between dese two nails. De nails are only so I can tie your hand in place. All right, good. Now I tie your hand secure to de table—so."

He wound the string around the boy's wrist, then several times around the wide part of the hand, then he fastened it tight to the nails. He made a good job of it and when he'd finished there wasn't any question about the boy being able to draw his hand away. But he could move his fingers.

"Now pleess, clench de fist, all except for de little finger. You must leave de little finger sticking out, lying on de table.

"*Ex*-cellent! *Ex*-cellent! Now we are ready. Wid your right hand you manipulate de lighter. But one momint, pleess."

He skipped over to the bed and picked up the chopper. He came back and stood beside the table with the chopper in his hand.

"We are all ready?" he said. "Mister referee, you must say to begin."

The English girl was standing there in her pale blue bathing costume right behind the boy's chair. She was just standing there, not saying anything. The boy was sitting quite still, holding the lighter in his right hand, looking at the chopper. The little man was looking at me.

"Are you ready?" I asked the boy.

"I'm ready."

"And you?" to the little man.

"Quite ready," he said and he lifted the chopper up in the air and held it there about two feet above the boy's finger, ready to chop. The boy watched it, but he didn't flinch and his mouth didn't move at all. He merely raised his eyebrows and frowned.

"All right," I said. "Go ahead."

The boy said, "Will you please count aloud the number of times I light it."

"Yes," I said. "I'll do that."

With his thumb he raised the top of the lighter, and again with the thumb he gave the wheel a sharp flick. The flint sparked and the wick caught fire and burned with a small yellow flame.

"One!" I called.

He didn't blow the flame out; he closed the top of the lighter on it and he waited for perhaps five seconds before opening it again.

He flicked the wheel very strongly and once more there was a small flame burning on the wick.

"Two!"

No one else said anything. The boy kept his eyes on the lighter. The little man held the chopper up in the air and he too was watching the lighter.

"Three!

"Four!

"Five!

"Six!

"Seven!" Obviously it was one of those lighters that worked. The flint gave a big spark and the wick was the right length. I watched the thumb snapping the top down onto the flame. Then a pause. Then the thumb raising the top once more. This was an all-thumb operation. The thumb did everything. I took a breath, ready to say eight. The thumb flicked the wheel. The flint sparked. The little flame appeared.

"Eight!" I said, and as I said it the door opened. We all turned and we saw a woman standing in the doorway, a small, black-haired woman, rather old, who stood there for about two seconds then rushed forward shouting, "Carlos! Carlos!" She grabbed his wrist, took the chopper from him, threw it on the bed, took hold of the little man by the lapels of his white suit and began shaking him very vigorously, talking to him fast and loud and fiercely all the time in some Spanish-sounding language. She shook him so fast you couldn't see him any more. He became a faint, misty, quickly moving outline, like the spokes of a turning wheel.

Then she slowed down and the little man came into vicw again and she hauled him across the room and pushed him backward onto one of the beds. He sat on the edge of it blinking his eyes and testing his head to see if it would still turn on his neck.

"I am so sorry," the woman said. "I am so terribly sorry that this should happen." She spoke almost perfect English.

"It is too bad," she went on. "I suppose it is really my fault. For ten minutes I leave him alone to go and have my hair washed and I come back and he is at it again." She looked sorry and deeply concerned.

The boy was untying his hand from the table. The English girl and I stood there and said nothing.

"He is a menace," the woman said. "Down where we live at home he has taken altogether forty-seven fingers from different people, and he has lost eleven cars. In the end they threatened to have him put away somewhere. That's why I brought him up here."

"We were only having a little bet," mumbled the little man from the bed.

"I suppose he bet you a car," the woman said.

"Yes," the boy answered. "A Cadillac."

"He has no car. It's mine. And that makes it worse," she said, "that he should bet you when he has nothing to bet with. I am ashamed and very sorry about it all." She seemed an awfully nice woman.

"Well," I said, "then here's the key of your car." I put it on the table.

"We were only having a little bet," mumbled the little man.

"He hasn't anything left to bet with," the woman said. "He hasn't a thing in the world. Not a thing. As a matter of fact I myself won it all from him a long while ago. It took time, a lot of time, and it was hard work, but I won it all in the end." She looked up at the boy and she smiled, a slow sad smile, and she came over and put out a hand to take the key from the table.

I can see it now, that hand of hers; it had only one finger on it, and a thumb.

THE WHOLE TOWN'S SLEEPING

RAY BRADBURY

IT WAS A warm summer night in the middle of Illinois country. The little town was deep far away from everything, kept to itself by a river and a forest and a ravine. In the town the sidewalks were still scorched. The stores were closing and the streets were turning dark. There were two moons: a clock moon with four faces in four night directions above the solemn black courthouse, and the real moon that was slowly rising in vanilla whiteness from the dark east.

In the downtown drugstore, fans whispered in the high ceiling air. In the rococo shade of porches, invisible people sat. On the purple bricks of the summer twilight streets, children ran. Screen doors whined their springs and banged. The heat was breathing from the dry lawns and trees.

On her solitary porch, Lavinia Nebbs, aged thirty-seven, very straight and slim, sat with a tinkling lemonade in her white fingers, tapping it to her lips, waiting.

"Here I am, Lavinia."

Lavinia turned. There was Francine, at the bottom porch step, in the smell of zinnias and hibiscus. Francine was all in snow white and didn't look thirty-five.

Miss Lavinia Nebbs rose and locked her front door, leaving her lemonade glass standing empty on the porch rail. "It's a fine night for the movie."

"Where you going, ladies?" cried Grandma Hanlon from her shadowy porch across the street.

They called back through the soft ocean of darkness: "To the Elite Theater to see Harold Lloyd in *Welcome, Danger!*"

"Won't catch *me* out on no night like this," wailed Grandma Hanlon. "Not with the Lonely One strangling women. Lock myself in with my *gun!*" Grandma's door slammed and locked.

The two maiden ladies drifted on. Lavinia felt the warm breath of the summer night shimmering off the oven-baked sidewalk. It was like walking on a hard crust of freshly warmed bread. The heat pulsed under your dress and along your legs with a stealthy sense of invasion.

"Lavinia, you don't believe all that gossip about the Lonely One, do you?"

"Those women like to see their tongues dance."

"Just the same, Hattie McDollis was killed a month ago. And Roberta Ferry the month before. And now Eliza Ramsell has disappeared. . . ."

"Walked off with a traveling man, I bet."

"But the others—strangled—four of them, their tongues sticking out their mouths, they say."

They stood upon the edge of the ravine that cut the town in two. Behind them were the lighted houses and faint radio music; ahead was deepness, moistness, fireflies and dark.

"Maybe we shouldn't go to the movie," said Francine. "The Lonely One might follow us. I don't like that ravine. Look how black, smell it, and *listen.*"

The ravine was a dynamo that never stopped running. Night or day there was a great moving hum among the secret mists, and the odors of a rank greenhouse. Always the black dynamo was humming, with green electric sparkles where fireflies hovered.

"And it won't be *me,*" said Francine, "coming back through this terrible dark ravine tonight, late. It'll be you, Lavinia, you down the steps and over that rickety bridge and maybe the Lonely One standing behind a tree. I'd never walk through here all alone, even in daylight."

"Bosh," said Lavinia Nebbs.

"It'll be you alone on the path, listening to your shoes, not me. And shadows. You *all alone* on the way back home. Lavinia, don't you get lonely living by yourself in that house?"

"Old maids love to live alone," said Lavinia. She pointed to a hot shadowy path. "Let's walk the shortcut."

"I'm afraid."

"It's early. The Lonely One won't be out till late."

Lavinia, as cool as mint ice cream, took the other woman's arm and led her down the dark winding path.

"Let's run," gasped Francine.

"No."

If Lavinia hadn't turned her head just then, she wouldn't have seen it. But she did turn her head, and it was there. And then Francine looked over and she saw it too, and they stood there on the path, not believing what they saw.

In the singing deep night, back among a clump of bushes—half hidden, but laid out as if she had put herself down there to enjoy the soft stars—lay Eliza Ramsell.

Francine screamed.

The woman lay as if she were floating there, her face moon-freckled, her eyes like white marble, her tongue clamped in her lips.

Lavinia felt the ravine turning like a gigantic black merry-go-round underfoot. Francine was gasping and choking, and a long while later Lavinia heard herself say, "We'd better get the police."

"HOLD ME, LAVINIA, please hold me, I'm cold. Oh, I've never been so cold since winter." Lavinia held Francine, and the policemen were all around in the ravine grass. Flashlights darted about, voices mingled, and the night grew toward eight thirty.

"It's like December, I need a sweater," said Francine, eyes shut against Lavinia's shoulder.

The policeman said, "I guess you can go now, ladies. You might drop by the station tomorrow for a little more questioning." Lavinia and Francine walked away from the police and the delicate sheet-covered thing upon the ravine grass.

A police voice called, "You want an escort, ladies?"

"No, we'll make it," said Lavinia, and they walked on. I can't remember anything now, she thought. I can't remember how she looked lying there, or anything. I don't believe it happened. Already I'm forgetting, I'm making myself forget.

"I've never *seen* a dead person before," said Francine.

Lavinia looked at her wristwatch, which seemed impossibly far away. "It's only eight thirty. We'll pick up Helen and get on to the show."

"The show!"

"It's what we *need.*"

"Lavinia, you don't *mean* it!"

"We've got to forget this. It's not good to remember."

"But Eliza's back there now and—"

"We'll go to the show as if nothing happened."

"But Eliza was once your friend, *my* friend—"

"We can't help her; we can only help ourselves forget. I insist. I won't go home and brood over it."

They started up the side of the ravine on a stony path in the dark. They heard voices and stopped.

Below, near the creek waters, a voice was murmuring, "I am the Lonely One. I am the Lonely One. I *kill* people."

"And I'm Eliza Ramsell. Look. And I'm dead, see my tongue sticking out my mouth, see!"

Francine shrieked. "You, there! Children, you nasty children! Get home, get out of the ravine, you hear me?"

The children fled from their game. The night swallowed their laughter away up the distant hills into the warm darkness.

Francine sobbed again and walked on.

"I THOUGHT YOU ladies'd never come!" Helen Greer tapped her foot atop her porch steps. "You're only an hour late, that's all."

"We—" started Francine.

Lavinia clutched her arm. "There was a commotion. Someone found Eliza Ramsell dead in the ravine."

Helen gasped. "Who found her?"

"We don't know."

The three maiden ladies stood in the summer night looking at one another. "I've a notion to lock myself in my house," said Helen at last.

But finally she went to fetch a sweater, and while she was gone Francine whispered frantically, "Why didn't you *tell* her?"

"Why upset her? Time enough tomorrow," replied Lavinia.

The three women moved along the street under the black trees through a town that was slamming and locking doors, pulling down windows and shades and turning on blazing lights.

How strange, thought Lavinia Nebbs, with the children all scooped indoors. Baseballs and bats lie on the unfootprinted lawns. A half-drawn white chalk hopscotch line is there on the steamed sidewalk.

"We're crazy to be out on a night like this," said Helen.

"Lonely One can't kill three ladies," said Lavinia. "There's safety in numbers. Besides, it's too soon. The murders come a month separated."

A shadow fell across their faces. A figure loomed. As if someone had struck an organ a terrible blow, the three women shrieked.

"*Got* you!" the man jumped from behind a tree. Rearing into the moonlight, he leaned on the tree and laughed.

"Hey, I'm the Lonely One!"

"Tom Dillon!" said Lavinia. "If you ever do a childish thing like that again, may you be riddled with bullets by mistake!"

Francine began to cry.

Tom Dillon stopped smiling. "Hey, I'm sorry."

"Haven't you heard about Eliza Ramsell?" snapped Lavinia. "She's dead, and you scaring women. You should be ashamed. Don't speak to us again."

"Aw—" He moved to follow them.

"Stay right there, Mr. Lonely One, and scare yourself," said Lavinia. "Go see Eliza Ramsell's face and see if it's funny!" She pushed the other two on along the street of trees and stars, Francine holding a handkerchief to her face.

"Francine," pleaded Helen, "it was only a joke. Why's she crying so hard?"

"I guess we better tell you, Helen. *We* found Eliza. And it wasn't pretty. And we're trying to forget. We're going to the show to help, and let's not talk about it. Enough's enough."

THE DRUGSTORE WAS A SMALL pool of sluggish air which the great wooden fans stirred in tides of arnica and tonic and soda smell out into the brick streets.

"A nickel's worth of green mint chews," said Lavinia to the druggist. His face was set and pale, like all the faces they had seen on the half-empty streets. "For eating in the show," she explained.

"Sure look pretty tonight," said the druggist. "You looked cool this noon, Miss Lavinia, when you was in here for chocolates. So cool and nice that someone asked after you."

"Oh?"

"You're getting popular. Man sitting at the counter"— he dropped the mints in a sack—"watched you walk out and he said to me, 'Say, who's *that?*' Man in a dark suit, thin pale face. 'Why, that's Lavinia Nebbs,' *I* said. 'Beautiful,' *he* said. 'Where's she live?'" Here the druggist paused and looked away.

"You *didn't?*" wailed Francine. "You didn't give him her address, I hope? You *didn't!*"

"Sorry, guess I didn't think. I said, 'Oh, over on Park Street, you know, near the ravine.' Casual remark. But now, tonight, them finding the body. I heard a minute ago, I suddenly thought, What've I *done!*" He handed over the package, much too full.

"You fool!" cried Francine, and tears were in her eyes.

"I'm sorry. Course maybe it was nothing."

Lavinia stood with the three people looking at her, staring at her. She felt the slightest prickle of excitement in her throat. She held out her money automatically.

"No charge for those pepperiments." The druggist turned down his eyes and shuffled some papers.

"Well, I know what we're going to do right *now!*" Helen stalked out of the drugstore. "We're going right straight home. I'm not going to be part of any hunting party for you, Lavinia. That man asking for you. You're *next!* You want to be dead in that ravine?"

"It was just a man," said Lavinia slowly, eyes on the streets. "We're all overwrought. I won't miss the movie now. If I'm the next victim, let me *be* the next victim. A lady has all too little excitement in her life, especially an old maid, a lady thirty-seven like me, so don't you mind if

I enjoy it. And I'm being sensible. Stands to reason he won't be out tonight, so soon after a murder. A month from now, yes, when he *feels* like another murder. You've got to *feel* like murdering people, you know. At least that kind of murderer does. And anyway I'm not going home to stew in my juices."

"But Eliza's face, there in the ravine!"

"After the first look I never looked again. I didn't *drink* it in, if that's what you mean. I can see a thing and tell myself I never saw it, that's how strong *I* am. And the whole argument's silly anyhow, because I'm not beautiful."

"Oh, but you are, Lavinia. You're the loveliest maiden lady in town, now that Eliza's—" Francine stopped. "If you'd only relaxed, you'd been married years ago—"

"Stop sniveling, Francine. Here's the box office. You and Helen go on home. I'll sit alone and go home alone."

"Lavinia, you're crazy. We can't leave you here."

They argued for five minutes. Helen started to walk away but came back when Lavinia thumped down her money for a movie ticket. Helen and Francine followed her silently into the theater.

The first show was over. In the dim auditorium, as they sat in the odor of ancient brass polish, the manager appeared before the worn red velvet curtains for an announcement:

"The police have asked for an early closing tonight. So everyone can be home at a decent hour. So we're cutting our short subjects and putting on our feature film again now. The show will be over at eleven. Everyone's advised to go straight home after it's over."

"That means us, Lavinia. *Us!*" Lavinia felt the hands tugging at her elbows on either side.

"Harold Lloyd in *Welcome, Danger!*" said the screen in the dark.

"Lavinia," Helen whispered.

"What?"

"As we came in, a man in a dark suit, across the street, crossed over. He just came in and sat in the row behind us."

"Oh, Helen."

"He's right behind us *now*."

Lavinia looked at the screen.

Helen turned slowly and glanced back. "I'm calling the manager!" she cried, and leaped up. "Stop the film! Lights!"

"Helen, come back!" said Lavinia, eyes shut.

WHEN THEY SET down their empty soda glasses, each of the ladies had a chocolate mustache on her upper lip. They removed them with their tongues, laughing.

"You see how *silly* it was?" said Lavinia. "All that riot for nothing. How embarrassing!"

The drugstore clock said eleven twenty-five. They had come out of the theater and the laughter and the enjoyment feeling new. And now they were laughing at Helen and Helen was laughing at herself.

Lavinia said, "When you ran up that aisle crying 'Lights!' I thought I'd die!"

"That poor man!"

"The theater manager's brother from Racine!"

The great fans still whirled and whirled in the warm night air, stirring and restirring the smells of vanilla, raspberry, peppermint and disinfectant in the drugstore.

"We shouldn't have stopped for these sodas."

Lavinia laughed. "I'm not afraid. The Lonely One is a million miles away now. He won't be back for weeks, and the police'll get him then, just wait. Wasn't the film *funny!*"

The streets were clean and empty. Not a car or a truck or a person was in sight. The bright lights were still lit in the small store windows where the hot wax dummies stood. Their blank blue eyes watched as the ladies walked past them, down the night street.

"Do you suppose if we screamed, they'd do anything?"

"Who?"

"The dummies, the window people."

"Oh, Fran*cine*."

"Well . . ."

There were a thousand people in the windows, stiff and silent, and three people on the street, the echoes following like gunshots when they tapped their heels on the baked pavement.

A red neon sign flickered dimly, buzzing like a dying insect. They walked past it. Baked and white, the long avenue lay ahead. The trees stood tall on either side of the three small women.

"First we'll walk you home, Francine."

"No, I'll walk *you* home."

"Don't be silly. You live the nearest. If you walked me home, you'd have to come back across the ravine alone yourself. And if so much as a leaf fell on you, you'd drop dead."

Francine said, "I can stay the night at your house. You're the *pretty* one!"

"No."

SO THEY DRIFTED like three prim clothes forms over a moonlit sea of lawn and concrete and tree. To Lavinia, watching the black trees flit by, listening to the voices of her friends, the night seemed to quicken. They seemed to be running while walking slowly. Everything seemed fast, and the color of hot snow.

"Let's sing," said Lavinia.

They sang sweetly and quietly, arm in arm, not looking back. They felt the hot sidewalk cooling underfoot.

"Listen," said Lavinia.

They listened to the summer night, to the crickets and the far-off tone of the courthouse clock making it fifteen minutes to twelve.

"Listen."

A porch swing creaked in the dark. And there was Mr. Terle, silent, alone on his porch as they passed, having a last cigar. They could see the pink cigar fire idling to and fro.

Now the lights were going, going, gone. The little house lights and big house lights, the yellow lights and green hurricane lights, the candles and oil lamps and porch lights. Everything, thought Lavinia, is boxed and wrapped and shaded. She imagined the people in their moonlit beds, and their breathing in the summer night rooms, safe and together. And here we are, she thought, listening to our solitary footsteps on the baked summer evening sidewalk. And above us the lonely streetlights shining down, making a million wild shadows.

"Here's your house, Francine. Good night."

"Lavinia, Helen, stay here tonight. It's late, almost midnight now.

Mrs. Murdock has an extra room. I'll make hot chocolate. It'd be ever such fun!" Francine was holding them both close to her.

"No, thanks," said Lavinia.

And Francine began to cry.

"Oh, not *again*, Francine," said Lavinia.

"I don't want you dead," sobbed Francine, the tears running straight down her cheeks. "You're so fine and nice, I want you alive. Please, oh, please."

"Francine, I didn't realize how much this has affected you. But I promise you I'll phone when I get home, right away."

"Oh, *will* you?"

"And tell you I'm safe, yes. And tomorrow we'll have a picnic lunch at Electric Park, all right? You'll see; I'm going to live forever!"

"You'll phone?"

"I promised, didn't I?"

"Good night, good night!" Francine was gone behind her door, locked tight in an instant.

"Now," said Lavinia to Helen, "I'll walk *you* home."

THE COURTHOUSE CLOCK struck the hour. The sounds went across an empty town.

"Ten, eleven, *twelve*," counted Lavinia, with Helen on her arm.

"Don't you feel *funny?*" asked Helen.

"How do you mean?"

"When you think of us being out here on the sidewalk, under the trees, and all those people safe behind locked doors lying in their beds. We're practically the only walking people out in the open in a thousand miles, I bet." The sound of the deep warm dark ravine came near.

In a minute they stood before Helen's house, looking at each other for a long time. The moon was high in a sky that was beginning to cloud over. "I don't suppose it's any use asking you to stay, Lavinia?"

"I'll be going on."

"Sometimes . . ."

"Sometimes what?"

"Sometimes I think people *want* to die. You've certainly acted odd all evening."

"I'm just not afraid," said Lavinia. "And I'm curious, I suppose. And I'm using my head. Logically, the Lonely One can't be around. The police and all."

"*Our* police? *Our* little old force? They're home in bed too, the covers up over their ears."

"Let's just say I'm enjoying myself, precariously but safely. If there were any *real* chance of anything happening to me, I'd stay here with you, you can be sure of that."

"Maybe your subconscious doesn't want you to live anymore."

"You and Francine, honestly."

"I feel so guilty. I'll be drinking hot coffee just as you reach the ravine bottom and walk on the bridge in the dark."

"Drink a cup for me. Good night."

Lavinia Nebbs walked down the midnight street, down the late summer night silence. Far away she heard a dog barking. In five minutes, she thought, I'll be safe home. In five minutes I'll be phoning silly little Francine. I'll—

She heard a man's voice singing far away among the trees.

She walked a little faster.

Coming down the street toward her in the dimming moonlight was a man. He was walking casually.

I can run and knock on one of these doors, thought Lavinia. If necessary.

The man was singing "Shine On, Harvest Moon," and he carried a long club in his hand. "Well, look who's here! What a time of night for you to be out, Miss Nebbs!"

"Officer Kennedy!"

And that's who it was, of course—Officer Kennedy on his beat.

"I'd better see you home."

"Never mind, I'll make it."

"But you live across the ravine."

Yes, she thought, but I won't walk the ravine with *any* man. How do I know *who* the Lonely One is? "No, thanks," she said.

"I'll wait right here, then," he said. "If you need help, give a yell. I'll come running."

She went on, leaving him under a light, humming to himself.

Here I am, she thought.

The ravine.

She stood on the top of the one hundred and thirteen steps down the steep, brambled bank that led across the creaking bridge one hundred yards and up through the black hills to Park Street. And only one lantern to see by. Three minutes from now, she thought, I'll be putting my key in my house door. Nothing can happen in just one hundred and eighty seconds.

She started down the steps into the deep ravine night.

"One, two, three, four, five, six, seven, eight, nine steps," she whispered.

She felt she was running, but she was not running.

"Fifteen, sixteen, seventeen, eighteen, nineteen steps," she counted aloud.

"One fifth of the way!" she announced to herself.

The world was gone, the world of safe people in bed. The locked doors, the town, the drugstore, the theater, the lights, everything was gone. Only the ravine existed and lived, black and huge about her.

"Nothing's happened, has it? No one around, *is* there? Twenty-four, twenty-five steps. Remember that old ghost story you told each other when you were children?"

She listened to her feet on the steps.

"The story about the dark man coming in your house and you upstairs in bed. And now he's at the *first* step coming up to your room. Now he's at the second step. Now he's at the third and the fourth and the *fifth* step! Oh, how you laughed and screamed at that story! And now the horrid dark man is at the twelfth step, opening your door, and now he's standing by your bed. I *got you!*"

She screamed. It was like nothing she had ever heard, that scream. She had never screamed that loud in her life. She stopped, she froze, she clung to the wooden banister. Her heart exploded in her. The sound of its terrified beating filled the universe.

"There, there!" she screamed to herself. "At the bottom of the steps. A man, under the light! No, now he's gone! He was *waiting* there!"

She listened.

Silence. The bridge was empty.

Nothing, she thought, holding her heart. Nothing. Fool. That story I told myself. How silly. What shall I do?

Her heartbeats faded.

Shall I call the officer, did he hear my scream? Or was it only loud to *me?* Was it really just a small scream after all?

She listened. Nothing. Nothing.

I'll go back to Helen's and sleep the night. But even while she thought this she moved down again. No, it's nearer home now. Thirty-eight, thirty-nine steps, careful, don't fall. Oh, I *am* a fool. Forty steps. Forty-one. Almost halfway now. She froze again.

"Wait," she told herself. She took a step.

There was an echo.

She took another step. Another echo—just a fraction of a moment later.

"Someone's following me," she whispered to the ravine, to the black crickets and dark green frogs and the black steam. "Someone's on the steps behind me. I don't dare turn around."

Another step, another echo.

Every time I take a step, *they* take one.

A step and an echo.

"Officer Kennedy? Is that *you?*"

The crickets were suddenly still. The crickets were listening. The night was listening to *her.* For a moment, all of the far summer night meadows and close summer night trees were suspending motion. And perhaps a thousand miles away, across locomotive-lonely country, in an empty way station a lonely night traveler reading a dim newspaper under a naked light bulb might raise his head, listen, and think, What's that! and decide, Only a woodchuck, surely, beating a hollow log. But it was Lavinia Nebbs, it was most surely the heart of Lavinia Nebbs.

Faster. Faster. She went down the steps.

Run!

SHE HEARD MUSIC. In a mad way, a silly way, she heard the huge surge of music that pounded at her, and she realized as she ran—as she ran in panic and terror—that some part of her mind was dramatizing, borrowing from the turbulent score of some private film. The music was rushing and plunging her faster, faster, plummeting and scurrying, down and down into the pit of the ravine!

"Only a little way," she prayed. "One hundred ten, eleven, twelve, thirteen steps! The bottom! Now, run! Across the bridge!"

She spoke to her legs, her arms, her body; she advised all parts of herself in this white and terrible instant. Over the roaring creek waters, on the hollow, swaying, almost alive bridge planks she ran, followed by the wild footsteps behind, with the music following too, the music shrieking and babbling!

He's following. Don't turn, don't look—if you see him, you'll not be able to move! You'll be frightened, you'll freeze! Just run, run, *run!*

She ran across the bridge.

Oh, God! God, please, please let me get up the hill! Now up, up the path, now between the hills. Oh, God, it's dark, and everything so far away! If I screamed now, it wouldn't help; I can't scream anyway! Here's the top of the path, here's the street. Thank God I wore my low-heeled shoes. I can run, I can run! Oh, God, please let me be safe! If I get home safe, I'll never go out alone. I was a fool, let me admit it, a fool! If you let me get home from this, I'll never go out without Helen or Francine again! Across the street now!

She crossed the street and rushed up the sidewalk.

Oh, God, the porch! My house!

In the middle of her running, she saw the empty lemonade glass where she had left it on the railing hours before. She wished she were back in that time now, drinking from it, the night still young and not begun.

"Oh, please, please, give me time to get inside and lock the door and I'll be safe!"

SHE HEARD HER clumsy feet on the porch, felt her hands scrabbling and ripping at the lock with the key. She heard her heart. She heard her inner voice shrieking.

The key fitted. The door opened.

"Now inside. *Slam* it!"

She slammed the door.

"Now lock it!" she cried wretchedly. "Lock it *tight!*"

The door was locked.

The music stopped. She listened to her heart again and the sound of it diminishing into silence.

Home. Oh, safe at home. Safe, safe, and safe at home! She slumped against the door. Safe, safe. Listen. Not a sound. Oh, thank God, safe at home. I'll never go out at night again. Safe, oh safe inside, the door locked. *Wait.* Look out the window.

She gazed out the window for a full half minute.

"Why there's no one there at all! Nobody! There was no one following me at all. Nobody running after me." She caught her breath and almost laughed at herself. "It stands to reason. If a man *had* been following me, he'd have *caught* me. I'm not a fast runner. There's no one on the porch or in the yard. How silly of me. I wasn't running from anything except *me.* That ravine was safer than safe. Just the same, though, it's nice to be home. Home's the really good warm safe place, the *only* place to be."

She put her hand out to the light switch and stopped.

"What?" she asked. "What? *What?*"

Behind her, in the black living room, someone cleared his throat. . . .

THE ARROW OF GOD

LESLIE CHARTERIS

ONE OF SIMON Templar's stock criticisms of the classic type of detective story is that the victim of the murder, the reluctant spark plug of all the entertaining mystery and strife, is usually a mere nonentity who wanders vaguely through the first few pages with the sole purpose of becoming a convenient body in the library by the end of Chapter One. But whatever his own feelings and problems may have been, the personality that has to provide so many people with adequate motives for desiring him to drop dead is largely a matter of hearsay, retrospectively brought out in the process of drawing attention to various suspects.

"Actually," Simon has said, "the physical murder should be the midpoint of the story. The things that led up to it are at least as interesting as the mechanical solution of who done it."

Coming from a man who is generally regarded as almost a detective-story character himself, this comment is at least worth recording for reference; but it did not apply to the shuffling off of Mr. Floyd Vosper, which caused a commotion in the Bahamas in the spring of that year.

WHY SIMON TEMPLAR should have been in Nassau at the time is one of those questions that can only be answered by repeating that he liked to travel and was just as likely to show up there as in Nova Zembla or

Namaqualand. As for why he should have been invited to the house of Mrs. Herbert H. Wexall, that is another irrelevancy; he had friends in many places, legitimate and otherwise. But Mrs. Wexall had some international renown as a social lion hunter, and it was not to be expected that the advent of such a creature as Simon Templar would have escaped her attention.

Thus one noontime Simon found himself strolling up the driveway and into what little was left of the life of Floyd Vosper. Naturally he did not know this at the time; nor did he know Floyd Vosper, except by name. In this he was no different from at least fifty million other people; for Floyd Vosper was one of the most widely syndicated pundits of the day, and his books (*Feet of Clay*, *As I Saw Them*, and *The Twenty Worst Men in the World*) had sold by the millions. For Mr. Vosper specialized in the ever popular sport of shattering reputations. He had met, and apparently had unique opportunities to study, practically every great name in the national and international scene, and could remember everything in their biographies that they would prefer forgotten, leaving them naked and squirming on the operating table of his vocabulary. But what this merciless professional iconoclast was like as a person, Simon had never heard or bothered to wonder about. So the first impression Vosper made on him was a voice, a dry and deliberate and needling voice, which came from behind a bank of riotous hibiscus and oleander.

"My dear Janet," it said, "you must not let your innocent admiration for Reggie's bulging biceps color your estimate of his perspicacity in world affairs. The title of all-American, I hate to disillusion you, has no reference to statesmanship."

There was a rather strained laugh that must have come from Reggie, and a girl's clear young voice said, "That isn't fair, Mr. Vosper. Reggie doesn't pretend to be a genius, but he's bright enough to have a wonderful job waiting for him on Wall Street."

"I don't doubt that he will make an excellent contact man for the more stupid clients," conceded the voice with the measured nasal gripe. "And I'm sure that his education can cope with the simple arithmetic of the stock exchange, just as I'm sure it can grasp the basic figures of your father's Dun and Bradstreet. This should not dazzle you with his brilliance, any more than it should make you believe that you have some spiritual fascination that lured him to your feet."

At this point Simon rounded a curve in the driveway and caught his first sight of the speakers. There was no difficulty in assigning them to their lines—the young redheaded giant with the pleasantly rugged face and the slim pretty blond girl, who sat at a wrought-iron table on the terrace in front of the house, with a broken deck of cards in front of them that established an interrupted game of gin rummy, and the thin stringy man reclining in a long cane chair with a cigarette holder in one hand and a highball glass in the other.

Simon smiled and said, "Hullo. This is Mrs. Wexall's house, is it?" The girl said yes, and he added, "My name's Templar, and I was invited here."

The girl jumped up. "Oh, yes. Lucy told me. I'm her sister, Janet Blaise. This is my fiancé, Reg Herrick. And Mr. Vosper."

Simon shook hands with the two men, and Janet said, "I think Lucy's on the beach. I'll take you around."

Vosper unwound his bony length from the long chair, looking like a slightly dissolute mahatma in his white shorts and burnt-chocolate tan. "Let me do it," he said. "I'm sure you two ingenues would rather be alone. And I need another drink."

He led the way around the house by a flagged path that struck off to the side and meandered through a bower of scarlet poinciana. A breeze rustled in the leaves and mixed flower scents with the sweetness of the sea. Vosper smoothed down his sparse gray hair; and Simon was aware that the man's beady eyes and sharp thin nose were cocked toward him with brash speculation.

"Templar," he said. "Of course, you must be the Saint—the fellow they call the Robin Hood of modern crime."

"I see you read the right papers," said the Saint pleasantly.

"I read all the papers," Vosper said, "in order to keep in touch with the vagaries of vulgar taste. I've often wondered why the Robin Hood legend should have so much romantic appeal. Robin Hood, as I understand it, was a bandit who indulged in some well-publicized charity—but not, as I recall, at the expense of his own stomach. A good many unscrupulous promoters have also become generous—and with as much shrewd publicity—when their ill-gotten gains exceeded their personal spending capacity, but I don't remember that they succeeded in being glamorized for it."

"There may be some difference," Simon suggested, "in who was robbed to provide the surplus spoils."

"Then," Vosper challenged, "you consider yourself an infallible judge of who should be penalized and who should be rewarded."

"Oh, no," said the Saint modestly. "Not at all. No more, I'm sure, than you would call yourself the infallible judge of all the people whom you dissect so definitively in print."

He felt the other's probing glance stab at him suspiciously and with puzzled incredulity, as if Vosper couldn't quite accept the idea that anyone had dared to cross swords with him, and moreover might have scored on the riposte. But before anything further could develop, there was a distraction.

This took the form of a man seated on top of a truncated column which had been incorporated into the design of a wall that curved out from the house to encircle a portion of the shore like a possessive arm. The man had long curly hair that fell to his shoulders, delicate ascetic features, and an equally curly and silken beard. He sat cross-legged and upright, his hands folded in his lap, staring straight out into the blue sky. He was so motionless that he might easily have been taken for a tinted statue except for the fluttering of his long white robe.

"That fugitive from a Turkish bath," Vosper said, "calls himself Astron. He's a nature boy from the Dardanelles who just concluded a very successful season in Hollywood. He wears a beard to cover a receding chin, and long hair to cover a hole in the head. He purifies his soul with a diet of boiled grass and prune juice. Whenever this diet permits him, he meditates. After he was brought to the attention of the Western world by some engineers of the Anglo-Mongolian Oil Company, whom he cured of stomach ulcers by persuading them not to spike their sacramental wine with rubbing alcohol, he began to meditate about the evils of earthly riches. He maintains that the only way for the holders of worldly wealth to purify themselves is to get rid of as much as they can spare. Being pure himself, he is unselfishly ready to become the custodian of this corrupting cabbage, parking it in a shrine in the Sea of

Marmara, which he plans to build as soon as there is enough kraut in the kitty."

Without any waste motion the figure on the column expanded its crossed legs like a lazy tongs until it towered at its full height. "You have heard the blasphemer," it said. "But I say to you that his words are dust in the wind, as he himself is dust among the stars that I see."

"So if you have this direct pipeline to the Almighty," Vosper said, "why don't you strike me dead?"

"Death can only come from the hands of the Giver of all Life," Astron replied in a confident voice. "In His own good time He will strike you down, and the arrow of God will silence your mockeries."

"Quaint, isn't he?" Vosper said, and opened the gate between the wall and the beach.

Beyond the wall a few steps led down to a kind of open Grecian courtyard, where the paving merged directly into the white sand of the beach. The courtyard was furnished with gaily colored lounging chairs and a well-stocked pushcart bar, to which Vosper directed himself.

"You have visitors, Lucy," he said, without letting it interfere with the important work of reviving his highball.

Out on the sand, on a towel spread under an enormous beach umbrella, Mrs. Wexall rolled over and said, "Oh, Mr. Templar."

Simon went over and shook hands with her as she stood up. It was hard to think of her as Janet Blaise's sister, for there were at least twenty years between them and hardly any physical resemblances. She was a big woman with an open homely face, sun-bleached hair, and a sloppy figure, but she made a virtue of those disadvantages by the cheerfulness with which she ignored them.

"Good to see you," she said, and gestured to the man who had been sitting beside her as he struggled to his feet. "Do you know Arthur Gresson?"

Mr. Gresson was a full head shorter than the Saint's six feet two, but he weighed a good deal more. Unlike anyone else that Simon had encountered on the premises so far, his skin looked as if it was unaccustomed to exposure. His round body and balding brow, under a liberal sheen of oil, had the hot rosy blush which the kiss of the sun evokes in virgin epidermis.

"Glad to meet you, Mr. Templar." His hand was soft and earnestly adhesive.

"I expect you'd like a drink," Lucy Wexall said. "Let's keep Floyd working." As they joined Vosper at the bar wagon, she turned to the Saint and added, "Just make yourself at home. I'm so glad you could come."

"I'm sure Mr. Templar will be happy," Vosper said. "He's a man of the world like me. We enjoy Lucy's food and liquor, and in return we give her the pleasure of hitting the society columns with our names. A perfectly businesslike exchange."

"That's progress for you," Lucy Wexall said breezily. "In the old days I'd have had a court jester. Now all I get is a professional stinker."

"That's no way to refer to Arthur," Vosper said, handing Simon a long cold glass. "For your information, Templar, Mr. Gresson—Mr. Arthur *Granville* Gresson—is a promoter. He has a long history of selling phony oil stock. He is just about to take Herb Wexall for another sucker; but since Herb married Lucy, he can afford it."

Arthur Gresson's elbow nudged Simon's ribs. "What a character!" he said, almost proudly.

"I only give out with facts," Vosper answered. "My advice, Templar, is, never be an elephant. Because when you reach back into that memory, the people who should thank you will call you a stinker."

"Would you like to get in a swim before lunch?" Lucy Wexall said. "Floyd, show him where he can change."

"A pleasure," Vosper said. He thoughtfully refilled his glass before he steered Simon, by way of the veranda, into the beachward side of the house and into a bedroom, where Simon stripped down and pulled on the trunks he had brought with him.

As they were starting back through the living room, a small birdlike man in a dark and incongruous business suit bustled in by another door. He had bright baggy eyes behind rimless glasses, slack but fleshless jowls, and a wide tight mouth. He was followed by a statuesque brunette who carried a notebook and a sheaf of papers and whose severe tailoring failed to disguise an outstanding combination of curves.

"Herb!" Vosper said. "I want you to meet Lucy's latest addition to the menagerie which already contains Astron and me—Mr. Simon

Templar, known as the Saint. Templar—your host, Mr. Wexall."

"Pleased to meet you," said Wexall, shaking hands briskly.

"And this is Pauline Stone," Vosper went on, indicating the nubile brunette. "The tired businessman's consolation. Whatever Lucy can't supply, she can."

"How do you do," said the girl stoically.

Her dark eyes lingered momentarily on the Saint's torso, and he noticed that her mouth was very full and soft.

"Going for a swim?" Wexall said, as if he had heard nothing. "Good. Then I'll see you at lunch in a few minutes."

He trotted busily on his way, and Vosper ushered the Saint to the beach by another flight of steps that led directly down from the veranda. The house commanded a small half-moon bay, and both ends of the crescent of sand were guarded by abrupt rises of jagged coral rock.

"Herbert is the living example of how really stupid a successful businessman can be," Vosper said tirelessly. "He was just an office boy of some kind in the Blaise outfit when he got smart enough to woo and win the boss's daughter. And from that flying start he was clever enough to really pay his way by making Blaise Industries twice as big as even the old man himself had been able to do. Yet he's dumb enough to think that Lucy won't catch on to the extracurricular functions of that busty secretary sooner or later—or that when she does, he won't be out on a cold doorstep in the rain. . . . No, I'm not going in. I'll hold your drink for you."

Simon ran down into the surf and churned seaward for a couple of hundred yards, then paddled lazily back. The balmy water was still refreshing after the heat of the morning, and when he came out, the breeze had become brisk enough to give him the luxury of a fleeting shiver as the wetness evaporated from his tanned skin.

He crossed the sand to the Greek patio, where Floyd Vosper was on duty again at the bar. Discreet servants were setting up a buffet table. Janet Blaise and Reg Herrick had transferred their gin rummy game to a table right under the column where Astron had resumed his seat and his cataleptic meditations.

Simon took Lucy Wexall a martini and said with a glance at the figure on the column, "Where did you find him?"

"The people who brought him to California sent him to me when he had to leave the States. They gave me such a good time when I was out there, I couldn't refuse. He's writing a book, you know, and of course he can't go back to that dreadful place he came from before he has a chance to finish it in reasonable comfort."

Simon avoided discussing this assumption, but he said, "What's it like, having a resident prophet in the house?"

"He's very interesting. And quite as drastic as Floyd, in his own way, in summing up people. You ought to talk to him."

Arthur Gresson came over with a plate of smoked salmon and stuffed eggs from the buffet. He said, "Anyone you meet at Lucy's is interesting, Mr. Templar. But you have it all over the rest. Who'd ever think we'd find the Saint looking for crime in the Bahamas?"

"I hope no one will think I'm looking for crime," Simon answered deprecatingly, "any more than I take it for granted that you're looking for oil."

"That's where you'd be wrong," Gresson said. "I am."

The Saint raised an eyebrow. "Well, I can always learn something. I'd never heard of oil in the Bahamas."

"But you will, Mr. Templar, you will. Just think about some of the places you have heard of where there *is* oil. Let me mention them in a certain order: Mexico, Texas, Louisiana, and the Florida Everglades. We might even include Venezuela in the south. Does that suggest anything to you?"

"Hm-mm," said the Saint thoughtfully.

"A pattern," Gresson went on. "A vast central pool of oil somewhere under the Gulf of Mexico, with oil wells dipping into it from the edges of the bowl. Now think of the islands of the Caribbean as the eastern edge of the same bowl. Why not?"

"It's an interesting theory," said the Saint.

"Mr. Wexall thinks so too, and I hope he's going into partnership with me."

"Herbert can afford it," intruded the metallic sneering voice of Floyd Vosper. "But before you decide to buy in, Templar, you'd better check with New York about the time when Mr. Gresson thought he could dig gold in the Catskills."

Arthur Gresson chuckled like a happy Buddha. "What a ribber!" he said. "He kills me!"

Herbert Wexall came down from the veranda and beamed around. As a sort of tacit announcement that he had put aside his work for the day, he had changed into a sport shirt on which various exotic fish were depicted wandering through vines of seaweed, but he retained his business trousers and business shoes and business face.

"Well," he said, inspecting the buffet and addressing the world at large. "Let's come and get it whenever we're hungry."

As if a spell had been snapped, Astron removed himself from the contemplation of the infinite, descended from his pillar, and began to help himself to cottage cheese and caviar on a foundation of lettuce leaves.

Simon drifted in the same direction, and found Pauline Stone beside him, saying, "What do you feel like, Mr. Templar?"

Her indication of having come off duty was a good deal more radical than her employer's. In fact, the bathing suit that she had changed into seemed based more on the French minimums of the period than on any British tradition. She filled it opulently, and her question amplified its suggestiveness with undertones that the Saint felt it wiser not to challenge at the moment.

"There's so much," he said, referring studiously to the buffet table. "But that green turtle aspic looks pretty good to me."

She stayed with him when he carried his plate to a table as far as possible from that chosen by Vosper, though Astron had already settled there in temporary solitude. They were joined by Reg Herrick and Janet Blaise, and slipped into an easy exchange of banalities.

But it was impossible to escape Vosper's tongue. His saw-edged voice whined across the patio above the general level of harmless chatter: "When are you going to tell the Saint's fortune, Astron? That ought to be worth hearing."

Astron looked at the Saint with a gentle smile and said quietly, "You are a seeker after truth, Mr. Templar, as I am. But when instead of truth you find falsehood, you destroy it with a sword. I only say, 'This is falsehood, and God will destroy it. Do not come too close, lest you be destroyed with it.'"

"Okay," Herrick growled, just as quietly. "But if you're talking about Vosper, it's about time someone destroyed it."

"Sometimes," Astron said, "God places His arrow in the hand of a man."

For a few moments that seemed unconscionably long nobody said anything; then the Saint said casually, "Talking of arrows—I hear the sport this season is to hunt sharks with bow and arrow."

Herrick nodded. "It's fun. Would you like to try it?"

"Reggie's terrific," Janet Blaise said, "but of course he uses a bow that nobody else can pull."

"I'd like to try," said the Saint, and the conversation slid harmlessly along the tangent he had provided.

After lunch everyone went back to the beach, except Astron, who retired to put his morning's meditations on paper. Chatter surrendered to an afternoon torpor which even subdued Vosper.

An indefinite while later, Herrick arose with a yell and plunged roaring into the sea, followed by Janet Blaise. They were followed by others, including the Saint. An interlude of aquatic brawling developed somehow into a pickup game of touch football on the beach. This boisterous nonsense churned up sand for the still freshening breeze to spray over Floyd Vosper, who by that time had drunk enough to be trying to sleep under the big beach umbrella.

"Perhaps," he said witheringly, "I had better get out of the way of you perennial juveniles before you convert me into a dune."

He rose, stalked off along the beach, and lay down again about a hundred yards away. Simon noticed him still there, flat on his face and presumably unconscious, when the game eventually broke up. It was the last time he saw the unpopular Mr. Vosper alive.

"Well," Arthur Gresson observed, toweling his round body, "one of us seems to have enough sense to know when to lie down."

Herbert Wexall glanced along the beach in the direction Gresson referred to, then glanced at his waterproof watch.

"It's almost cocktail time," he said. "How about it, anyone?"

His wife shivered and said, "Let's all go in and get some clothes on first—then we'll be set for the evening. You'll stay for supper of course, Mr. Templar?"

"I hadn't planned to make a day of it," Simon protested diffidently, and was promptly overwhelmed from all quarters.

He found his way back to the room where he had left his clothes, and made leisured use of the freshwater shower and monogrammed towels. When he sauntered back into the living room, he almost had the feeling of being lost in a strange and empty house, for all the varied individuals who had peopled the stage so vividly a short time before had vanished into other and unknown seclusions and had not yet returned.

He lit a cigarette and strolled idly toward the picture window that overlooked the veranda and the sea. Everything around him was so still that he was tempted to walk on tiptoe; and yet outside the broad pane of plate glass the fronds of coconut palms were fluttering in a thin febrile frenzy, and there were lacings of white cream on the incredible jade of the short waves simmering on the beach.

He noticed that the big beach umbrella was no longer where he had first seen it, off to his right outside the patio. He saw, as his eye wandered on, that it had been moved a hundred yards or so to his left—to the place where Floyd Vosper was still lying. It occurred to him that Vosper must have moved it himself, except that no shade was needed in the brief and darkening twilight. After that he noticed that Vosper seemed to have turned over on his back; and then as the Saint focused his eyes he saw with a weird thrill that the shaft of the umbrella stood straight up out of the left side of Vosper's scrawny brown chest, not in the sand beside him at all, but like a gigantic pin that had impaled a strange and inelegant insect—or, in a fantastic phrase that was not Simon's at all, like the arrow of God.

MAJOR RUPERT FANSHIRE, the senior superintendent of police, paid tribute to the importance of the case by taking personal charge of it. He was a slight pinkish blond man with large, very bright blue eyes and a discreetly modulated voice that commanded attention through the basic effort of trying to hear what it was saying. He sat at a desk in the living room, with a Bahamian sergeant standing stiffly beside him, and contrived to turn the whole room into an office in which seven previously happy-go-lucky adults wriggled like guilty schoolchildren.

He said, with impersonal conciseness, "You all know by now that

Mr. Vosper was found on the beach with the steel spike of an umbrella through his chest. My job is to find out how it happened. The topography suggests that the person responsible came from or through this house. I've heard your statements, and all they seem to amount to is that each of you was going about his own business at the time when this might have occurred."

"All I know," Herbert Wexall said, "is that I was in my study, reading and signing the letters that I dictated this morning."

"And I was getting dressed," said his wife.

"So was I," said Janet Blaise.

"I guess I was in the shower," said Reginald Herrick.

"I was having a bubble bath," said Pauline Stone.

"I was still working," said Astron. "This morning I started a new chapter of my book—in my mind, you understand. I do not write by putting everything on paper. For me it is necessary to meditate, to feel, to open floodgates in my mind, so that—"

"Quite," Major Fanshire assented politely. "The point is that none of you have alibis, if you need them. You were all going about your own business, in your own rooms."

"I wasn't here," Arthur Gresson said recklessly. "I drove to my own place—I'm staying at the Montagu Beach Hotel. I wanted a clean shirt. When I got back, all this had happened."

"There's not much difference," Major Fanshire said. "Dr. Rassin tells me we couldn't establish time of death within an hour or two, anyway. So the next thing we come to is motive. Did anyone here have any serious trouble with Mr. Vosper?"

There was an uncomfortable silence, which the Saint finally broke by saying, "I'm an outsider, so I'll take the rap. I'll answer for everyone."

"Very well, sir. What would you say?"

"My answer," said the Saint, "is—everybody."

There was another silence, in which it seemed, surprisingly, as if all of them relaxed as unanimously as they had stiffened before. Yet, in its own way, this relaxation was as self-conscious and uncomfortable as the preceding tension had been. Only the Saint, who had every attitude of the careless onlooker, and Major Fanshire, whose patience was impregnably correct, seemed immune to the strain.

"Would you care to go any further?" Fanshire asked.

"Certainly," said the Saint. "I'll go on record with my opinion that the late Mr. Vosper was one of the most unpleasant characters I've ever met. He made a specialty of needling everyone he spoke to or about. He goaded everyone with nasty little things that he knew, or thought he knew, about them. I wouldn't blame anyone here for wanting, at least theoretically, to kill him."

"You will have to be more specific," Fanshire said.

"Okay," said the Saint. "I apologize in advance to anyone it hurts. Remember, I'm only repeating the kind of thing that made Vosper a good murder candidate. In my hearing he called Reg Herrick a dumb athlete who was trying to marry Janet Blaise for her money. He suggested that Janet was a stupid juvenile for taking him seriously. He called Astron a commercial charlatan. He implied that Lucy Wexall was a dope and a snob. He inferred that Herb Wexall had more use for his secretary's sex than for her stenography, and he thought out loud that Pauline was amenable. He called Mr. Gresson a crook to his face."

"And during all this," Fanshire remarked, "he had nothing to say about you?"

"He did indeed," said the Saint. "He analyzed me, more or less, as a flamboyant phony."

"And you didn't object to that?"

"I hardly could," Simon replied blandly, "after I'd hinted to him that I thought he was even phonier."

Fanshire drew down his upper lip with one forefinger and nibbled it inscrutably. "I expect this bores you as much as it does me, but this is the job I'm paid for. I've got to say that all of you had the opportunity, and from what Mr. Templar says you could all have had some sort of motive. Well, now I've got to look into what you might call the problem of physical possibility. Dr. Rassin says that to drive that umbrella shaft clean through a man's chest must have taken exceptional strength. It seems to be something that no woman, and probably no ordinary man, could have done."

His bright eyes came to rest on Herrick, and the Saint found his own eyes following others in the same direction.

The picture formed in his mind: the young giant towering over a prostrate Vosper, the umbrella raised in his mighty arms like a fantastic spear and the setting sun flaming on his red head, like an avenging angel, as he thrust downward with all the power of those herculean shoulders. . . . And then, as Herrick's face began to flush under the awareness of so many stares, Janet Blaise suddenly cried out, "No! No—it couldn't have been Reggie!"

Fanshire's gaze transferred itself to her curiously, and she said in a stammering rush, "You see, we didn't quite tell the truth, I mean about being in our own rooms. As a matter of fact, Reggie was in my room most of the time. We were—talking."

The superintendent cleared his throat and continued to gaze at her stolidly for a while. He didn't make any comment. But presently he looked at the Saint in the same dispassionately thoughtful way that he had first looked at Herrick.

Simon said calmly, "Yes, I was just wondering myself whether I could have done it. And I had a rather interesting thought. Certainly it must take a lot of strength to drive a spike through a man's chest with one blow. But remember that this wasn't just a spike, or a spear. It had an enormous umbrella on top of it. Think what would happen if you were stabbing down with a thing like that."

"Well, what would happen?"

"The umbrella would be like a parachute holding the shaft back. The air resistance would be so great that I'm wondering how anyone, even a very strong man, could get much momentum into the thrust. And the more force he put into it, the more likely he'd be to lift himself off the ground, rather than drive the spike down."

Fanshire digested this, blinking, and took his time to do it. "But it was done," he admitted. "So it must have been possible."

"There's something backward about that logic," said the Saint. "Suppose we say, if it was impossible, maybe it wasn't done."

"Now you're being a little ridiculous," Fanshire snapped. "We saw—"

"We saw a man with the sharp iron-tipped shaft of a beach umbrella through his chest. We jumped to the natural conclusion that somebody stuck it into him like a sword. And that may be just what a clever murderer meant us to think."

Arthur Gresson leaped out of his chair like a bouncing ball. "I've got it!" he yelped. "Believe me, everybody, I've got it! This'll kill you! I knew something rang a bell somewhere, but I couldn't place it. Now it all comes back to me. Some of you must have heard it before. It happened about a year ago, when Gregory Peck was visiting here. He stayed at the same hotel where I am, and one afternoon he was on the beach, and the wind came up, just like it did today, and it picked up one of those beach umbrellas and carried it right to where he was lying, and the point just grazed his ribs and gave him a nasty gash, but what the people who saw it happen were saying was that if he'd been just a few inches the other way, it could have gone smack into his heart, and you'd've had a film star killed in the most sensational way that ever was. Didn't you ever hear about that, Major?"

"Now that you mention it," Fanshire said slowly, "I think I did hear something about it."

"Well," Gresson said, "*what if it happened again this afternoon, to someone who wasn't as lucky as Peck?*"

There was an electric silence of assimilation, out of which Lucy Wexall said, "Yes, I heard about that." And Janet said, "Remember, I told you about it! I was at the hotel that day. I didn't see it happen, but I heard the commotion."

Gresson spread out his arms, his round face gleaming with excitement and perspiration. "That's it!" he said. "Vosper was lying under the umbrella outside the patio when we started playing touch football, and he got sore because we were kicking sand over him, and he went off to the other end of the beach. But he didn't take the umbrella with him. The wind did that, after we all went off to change. And this time it didn't miss!"

Suddenly Astron stood up; but where Gresson had risen like a jumping bean, this was like the growth and unfolding of a tree. "I have heard many words," Astron said in his firm gentle voice, "but now I am hearing truth. No man struck the blasphemer down. The arrow of God smote him, in his wickedness and pride."

"You can say that again," Gresson proclaimed triumphantly. "He sure had it coming."

The Saint lit a cigarette and created his own vision behind half-closed eyes. He saw the huge umbrella plucked from the sand by the invisible fingers of the wind, picked up and hurled spinning along the deserted twilight beach, its great mushroom spread of gaudy canvas now a sail for the wind to get behind, the whole thing transformed into a huge unearthly dart flung with literally superhuman power—the arrow of God indeed. A fantastic, an almost unimaginable solution; and yet it did not have to be imagined, because there were witnesses that it had almost happened once before. . . .

Fanshire was saying, "By Jove, that's the best suggestion I've heard yet—without any religious implication, of course."

Simon's eyes opened on him fully for an instant, almost pityingly, and then closed completely as the true and complete answer rolled through his mind like a long peaceful wave.

"I have one question to ask," said the Saint.

"What's that?" Fanshire said, too polite to be irritable, yet with a trace of impatience, as if he hated the inconvenience of even defending such a divinely tailored theory.

"Does anyone here have a gun?" asked the Saint.

"I have a revolver," Wexall said with some perplexity. "But what about it?"

"Could we see it, please?" said the Saint.

"I'll get it," said Pauline Stone, and left the room.

"You know I have a gun, Fanshire," Wexall said. "You gave me my permit. But I don't see—"

"Neither do I," Fanshire said.

The Saint said nothing. He devoted himself to his cigarette, with impregnable detachment, until the voluptuous secretary came back. Then he put out the cigarette and extended his hand.

Pauline looked at Wexall, hesitantly, and at Fanshire. The superintendent nodded a sort of grudging aquiescence.

Simon took the gun and broke it expertly. "A Colt thirty-eight detective special," he said. "Unloaded." He sniffed the barrel. "But fired quite recently." He handed the gun to Fanshire.

"I used it myself this morning," Lucy Wexall said cheerfully. "Janet and Reg and I were shooting at the Portuguese men-of-war. There were quite a lot of them around before the breeze came up."

"I wondered what the noise was," Wexall said vaguely.

"I was coming up the drive when I heard it first," Gresson said, "and I thought the next war had started."

"This is all very int'resting," Fanshire said, removing the revolver barrel from the proximity of his nostrils with a trace of exasperation, "but I don't see what it has to do with the case. Nobody has been shot—"

"Major Fanshire," said the Saint quietly, "may I have a word with you, outside? And will you keep that gun in your pocket so that at least we can hope there will be no more shooting?"

The superintendent stared at him for several seconds, then unwillingly got up. "Very well, Mr. Templar." He stuffed the revolver into the side pocket of his rumpled white jacket and glanced back at his impassive sentinel. "Sergeant, see that nobody leaves here, will you?"

He followed Simon out on the veranda and said almost peremptorily, "Come on now, what's this all about?"

The Saint took Fanshire's arm and led him down the front steps to the beach. Off to their left a tiny red glowworm blinked low down under the silver stars.

"You still have somebody watching the place where the body was found?" Simon asked.

"Of course," Fanshire grumbled. "As a matter of routine. But the sand's much too soft to show any footprints, and—"

"Will you walk over there with me?"

Fanshire sighed briefly and trudged beside him. "I don't know what you're getting at," he said, "but why *couldn't* it have been an accident?"

"I never heard a better theory in my life," said the Saint equably, "with one insuperable flaw. The wind wasn't blowing the right way."

Major Fanshire kept his face straight ahead to the wind and said nothing more after that until they reached the glowworm that they were making for and it became a cigarette end that a constable dropped as he came to attention.

The place where Floyd Vosper had been lying was marked off in a square of tape, but there was nothing out of the ordinary about it except some small stains that showed almost black under the flashlight that the constable produced.

"May I mess up the scene a bit?" Simon asked.

"I don't see why not," Fanshire said doubtfully. "It doesn't show anything, really."

Simon went down on his knees and began to dig with his hands, around and under the place where the stains were. Minutes later he stood up, with sand trickling through his fingers, and showed Fanshire the mushroomed scrap of metal that he had found.

"A thirty-eight bullet," Fanshire said, and whistled.

"And I think you'll be able to prove it was fired from the gun you have in your pocket," said the Saint. "Also you'd better have a sack of sand picked up from where I was digging. I think a laboratory examination will find that it also contains fragments of bone and human flesh."

"You'll have to explain this to me," Fanshire said quite humbly.

Simon dusted his hands and lit a cigarette. "Vosper was lying on his face when I last saw him," he said, "and I think he was as much passed out as sleeping. With the wind and the surf and the soft sand, it was easy for the murderer to creep up on him and shoot him in the back. But the murderer didn't want you looking for guns and comparing bullets. The umbrella was the inspiration. I don't have to remind you that the exit hole of a bullet is much larger than the entrance. By turning Vosper's body over, the murderer found a hole in his chest into which it couldn't have been too difficult to force the umbrella shaft—thus obliterating the original wound and confusing everybody in one operation."

"Let's get back to the house," said the superintendent abruptly.

As they walked, he said, "It's going to feel awfully funny having to arrest Herbert Wexall."

"Good God!" said the Saint in honest astonishment. "You weren't thinking of doing that?"

Fanshire stopped and blinked at him. "Why not?"

"Did Herbert seem at all guilty when he admitted he had a gun? Did he seem uncomfortable about having it produced? Was he ready with the explanation of why it still smelled of being fired?"

"But if anyone else used Wexall's gun, why should they go to such lengths to make it look as if no gun was used at all, when Wexall would obviously have been suspected?"

"*Because it was somebody who didn't want Wexall to take the rap.* Because Wexall is the goose who could still lay golden eggs."

The superintendent pulled out a handkerchief and wiped his face. "My God," he said. "You mean you think Lucy—"

"I think we have to go back to the question of motive," said the Saint. "Floyd Vosper was a nasty man who made dirty cracks about everyone here. But few people become murderers because of a dirty crack. Vosper called us all variously dupes, phonies, cheaters, and fools. But since he had roughly the same description for all of us, we could all laugh it off. There was only one person about whom he made the unforgivable accusation. . . . Now shall we rejoin the mob?"

"You'd better do this your own way," Fanshire muttered.

Simon took him up the steps to the veranda and into the living room, where all eyes turned to them in deathly silence.

"A paraffin test will prove who fired that revolver in the last twenty-four hours, aside from those who have already admitted it," Simon said, as if there had been no interruption. "And you'll remember who supplied that handy theory about the arrow of God."

"Astron!" Fanshire gasped.

"Oh, no," said the Saint a little tiredly. "He only said that God sometimes places His arrow in the hands of a man. And I feel quite sure that a wire to New York will establish that there is actually a criminal file under the name of Granville, with fingerprints and photos that should match Mr. Gresson's—as Vosper's fatally elephantine memory remembered. . . . That was the one crack he shouldn't have made—mentioning Granville as Gresson's middle name—because it was the only one that was more than gossip or shrewd insult, the only one that could be easily proved, and the only one that had a chance of upsetting an operation which was all set—if you'll excuse the phrase—to make a big killing."

Major Fanshire fingered his upper lip.

"I don't know," he began; and then, as Arthur Granville Gresson began to rise like a floating balloon from his chair, and the sergeant moved to intercept him like a well-disciplined automaton, he knew.

THE TWO BOTTLES OF RELISH

LORD DUNSANY

SMITHERS IS MY name. I'm what you might call a small man and in a small way of business. I travel for Num-numo, a relish for meats and savories—the world-famous relish I ought to say. It's really quite good, no deleterious acids in it, and does not affect the heart; so it is quite easy to push. I wouldn't have got the job if it weren't. But I hope someday to get something that's harder to push, as of course the harder they are to push, the better the pay. At present I can just make my way, with nothing at all over; but then I live in a very expensive flat. It happened like this, and that brings me to my story. And it isn't the story you'd expect from a small man like me, yet there's nobody else to tell it. Those that know anything of it besides me are all for hushing it up. Well, I was looking for a room to live in in London when first I got my job. It had to be in London, to be central; and I went to a block of buildings, very gloomy they looked, and saw the man that ran them and asked him for what I wanted. Flats they called them; just a bedroom and a sort of a cupboard. Well, he was showing a man around at the time who was a gent, in fact more than that, so he didn't take much notice of me—the man that ran all those flats didn't, I mean. So I just ran behind for a bit, seeing all sorts of rooms and waiting till I could be shown my class of thing. We came to a very nice flat, a sitting room, bedroom and bathroom, and a sort of little place that they called a hall. And that's how I came to know Linley. He was the bloke that was being shown around.

"Bit expensive," he said.

And the man that ran the flats turned away to the window and picked his teeth. It's funny how much you can show by a simple thing. What he meant to say was that he'd hundreds of flats like that, and thousands of people looking for them, and he didn't care who had them or whether they all went on looking. There was no mistaking him, somehow. And yet he never said a word, only looked away out of the window and picked his teeth. And I ventured to speak to Mr. Linley then; and I said, "How about it, sir, if I paid half, and shared it? I wouldn't be in the way, and I'm out all day, and whatever you said would go, and really I wouldn't be no more in your way than a cat."

You may be surprised at my doing it; and you'll be much more surprised at him accepting it—at least, you would if you knew me, just a small man in a small way of business. And yet I could see at once that Mr. Linley was taking to me more than he was taking to the man at the window.

"But there's only one bedroom," he said.

"I could make up my bed easy in that little room there," I said.

"The hall," said the man, looking around from the window, without taking his toothpick out.

"And I'd have the bed out of the way and hid in the cupboard by any hour you like," I said.

He looked thoughtful, and the other man looked out over London; and in the end, do you know, he accepted.

"Friend of yours?" said the flat man.

"Yes," answered Mr. Linley.

It was really very nice of him.

I'll tell you why I did it. Able to afford it? Of course not. But I heard him tell the flat man that he had just come down from Oxford and wanted to live for a few months in London. It turned out he wanted just to be comfortable and do nothing for a bit while he looked things over and chose a job, or probably just as long as he could afford it. Well, I said to myself, what's the Oxford manner worth in business, especially a business like mine? Why, simply everything you've got. If I picked up only a quarter of it from this Mr. Linley, I'd be able to double my sales, and that would soon mean I'd be given something a lot harder to push, with perhaps treble the pay. Worth it every time. And you can make a quarter of an education go twice as far again, if you're careful with it. I mean you don't have to quote the whole of the *Inferno* to show that you've read Milton; half a line may do it.

Well, about that story I have to tell. And you mightn't think that a little man like me could make you shudder. Well, I soon forgot about the Oxford manner when we settled down in our flat. I forgot it in the sheer wonder of the man himself. You didn't notice whether he was educated or not. Ideas were always leaping up in him, things you'd never have thought of. And not only that, but if any ideas were about, he'd sort of catch them. Time and again I've found him knowing just what I was going to say. Not thought reading, but what they call intuition. I used to try to learn a bit about chess, just to take my thoughts off Num-numo in the evening, when I'd done with it. But problems I never could do. Yet he'd come along and glance at my problem and say, "You probably move that piece first," and I'd say, "But where?" and he'd say, "Oh, one of those three squares." And I'd say, "But it will be taken on all of them." And the piece a queen all the time, mind you. And he'd say, "Yes, it's doing no good there: you're probably meant to lose it."

And, do you know, he'd be right.

You see, he'd been following out what the other man had been thinking. That's what he'd been doing.

Well, one day there was that ghastly murder at Unge. I don't know if you remember it. A man named Steeger had gone down there to live with a girl in a bungalow on the North Downs, and that was the first we had heard of him. The girl had two hundred pounds, and he got every penny of it, and she utterly disappeared. And Scotland Yard couldn't find her.

Well, I'd happened to read that Steeger had bought two bottles of Num-numo; for the Otherthorpe police had found out everything about him, except what he did with the girl; and that of course attracted my attention, or I should have never thought again about the case or said a word of it to Linley. Num-numo was always on my mind, as I always spent every day pushing it, and that kept me from forgetting the other thing. And so one day I said to Linley, "I wonder with all that knack you have for seeing through a chess problem, and thinking of one thing and another, that you don't have a go at that Otherthorpe mystery. It's a problem as much as chess," I said.

"There's not the mystery in ten murders that there is in one game of chess," he answered.

"It's beaten Scotland Yard," I said.

"Has it?" he asked.

"Knocked them endwise," I said.

"It shouldn't have done that," he said. "What are the facts?"

We were both sitting at supper, and I told him the facts, as I had them straight from the papers. She was a pretty blonde, she was small, she was called Nancy Elth, she had two hundred pounds, they lived at the bungalow for five days. After that he stayed there for another fortnight, but nobody ever saw her alive again. Steeger said she had gone to South America, but later said he had never said South America, but South Africa. None of her money remained in the bank where she had kept it, and Steeger was shown to have come by at least a hundred and fifty pounds just at that time. Then Steeger turned out to be a vegetarian, getting all his food from the greengrocer, and that made the constable in the village of Unge suspicious of him, for a vegetarian was something new to the constable. He watched Steeger after that, and it's well he did, for there was nothing that Scotland Yard asked him that he couldn't tell them about him, except of course the one thing. And he told the police at Otherthorpe five or six miles away, and they came and took a hand at it too. They were able to say for one thing that he never went outside the bungalow and its tidy garden ever since she disappeared. You see, the more they watched him the more suspicious they got, as you naturally do if you're watching a man; so that very soon they were watching every move he made, but if it hadn't been for his being a vegetarian, they'd never have started to suspect him, and there wouldn't have been enough evidence even for Linley. Not that they found out anything much against him, except that hundred and fifty pounds dropping in from nowhere, and it was Scotland Yard that found that, not the police of Otherthorpe. No, what the constable of Unge found out was about the larch trees, and that beat Scotland Yard utterly, and beat Linley up to the very last, and of course it beat me. There were ten larch trees in the bit of a garden, and he'd made some sort of an arrangement with the landlord, Steeger had, before he took the bungalow, by which he could do what he liked with the larch trees. And then from about the time that little Nancy Elth must have died he cut every one of them down. Three times a day he went at it for nearly a week, and when they were all down he cut them all up into logs no more than two foot long and laid them all in neat heaps. You never saw such work. And what for? To give an excuse for the axe was one theory. But the excuse was bigger than the axe; it took him a fortnight, hard work every day. And he could have killed a little thing like Nancy Elth without an axe, and cut her up too. Another theory was that he wanted firewood, to make away with the body. But he never used it. He left it all standing there in those neat stacks. It fairly beat everybody.

Well, those are the facts I told Linley. Oh yes, and he bought a big butcher's knife. Funny thing, they all do. And yet it isn't so funny after all; if you've got to cut a woman up, you've got to cut her up, and you can't do that without a knife. Then, there were some negative facts. He hadn't burned her. Only had a fire in the small stove now and then, and only used it for cooking. They got on to that pretty smartly, the Unge constable did, and the men that were lending him a hand from Otherthorpe. There were some little woody places lying around, and they could climb a tree handy and unobserved and get a sniff at the smoke in almost any direction it might be blowing. They did that now and then, and there was no smell of flesh burning, just ordinary cooking. Pretty smart of the Otherthorpe police that was, though of course it didn't help to hang Steeger. Then later on the Scotland Yard men went down and got another fact—negative, but narrowing things down all the while. And that was that the chalk under the bungalow and under the little garden had none of it been disturbed. And he'd never been outside it since Nancy disappeared. Oh yes, and he had a big file besides the knife. But there was no sign of any ground bones found on the file, or any blood on the knife. He'd washed them of course. I told all that to Linley.

Now I ought to warn you before I go any further. I am a small man myself and you probably don't expect anything horrible from me. But I ought to warn you this man was a murderer, or at any rate somebody was; the woman had been made away with, a nice pretty little girl too, and the man that had done that wasn't necessarily going to stop at things you might think he'd stop at. With the mind to do a thing like that, and with the long thin shadow of the rope to drive him further, you can't say what he'll stop at. Murder tales seem nice things sometimes for a lady to sit and read all by herself by the fire. But murder isn't a nice thing, and when a murderer's desperate and trying to hide his tracks he isn't even as nice as he was before. I'll ask you to bear that in mind. Well, I've warned you.

So I says to Linley, "And what do you make of it?"

"Drains?" said Linley.

"No," I says, "you're wrong there. Scotland Yard has been into that. And the Otherthorpe people before them. They've had a look in the drains, such as they are, a little thing running into a cesspool beyond the garden; and nothing has gone down it—nothing that oughtn't to have, I mean."

He made one or two other suggestions, but Scotland Yard had been before him in every case. That's really the crab of my story, if you'll excuse the expression. You want a man who sets out to be a detective to take his magnifying glass and go down to the spot; to go to the spot before everything; and then to measure the footmarks and pick up the clues and find the knife that the police have overlooked. But Linley never even went near the place, and he hadn't got a magnifying glass, not as I ever saw, and Scotland Yard were before him every time.

In fact they had more clues than anybody could make head or tail of. Every kind of clue to show that he'd murdered the poor little girl; every kind of clue to show that he hadn't disposed of the body; and yet the body wasn't there. It wasn't in South America either, and not much more likely in South Africa. And all the time, mind you, that enormous bunch of chopped larch wood, a clue that was staring everyone in the face and leading nowhere. No, we didn't seem to want any more clues, and Linley never went near the place. The trouble was to deal with the clues we'd got. I was completely mystified; so was Scotland Yard; and

Linley seemed to be getting no further; and all the while the mystery was hanging on me. I mean if it were not for the trifle I'd chanced to remember, and if it were not for one chance word I said to Linley, that mystery would have gone the way of all the other mysteries that men have made nothing of, a darkness, a little patch of night in history.

Well, the fact was Linley didn't take much interest in it at first, but I was so absolutely sure that he could do it that I kept him to the idea. "You can do chess problems," I said.

"That's ten times harder," he said, sticking to his point.

"Then why don't you do this?" I said.

"Then go and take a look at the board for me," said Linley.

That was his way of talking. We'd been a fortnight together, and I knew it by now. He meant for me to go down to the bungalow at Unge. I know you'll say why didn't he go himself; but the plain truth of it is that if he'd been tearing about the countryside, he'd never have been thinking, whereas sitting there in his chair by the fire in our flat, there was no limit to the ground he could cover, if you follow my meaning. So down I went by train next day, and got out at Unge station. And there were the North Downs rising up before me, somehow like music.

"It's up there, isn't it?" I said to the porter.

"That's right," he said. "Up there by the lane; and mind to turn to your right when you get to the old yew tree, a very big tree, you can't mistake it, and then . . ." and he told me the way so that I couldn't go wrong. I found them all like that, very nice and helpful. You see, it was Unge's day at last. Everyone had heard of Unge now; you could have got a letter there anytime just then without putting the county or post town; and this was what Unge had to show. I daresay if you tried to find Unge now . . . Well, anyway, they were making hay while the sun shone.

Well, there the hill was, going up into sunlight, going up like a song. You don't want to hear about the spring, and all the mayflowers rioting, and the color that came down over everything later on in the day, and all those birds; but I thought, What a nice place to bring a girl to. And then when I thought he'd killed her there, well, I'm only a small man, as I said, but when I thought of her on that hill with all the birds singing, I said to myself, Wouldn't it be odd if it turned out to be me after all that got that man killed, if he did murder her. So I soon found my way up to the bungalow and began prying about, looking over the hedge into the garden. And I didn't find much, and I found nothing at all that the police hadn't found already, but there were those heaps of larch logs staring me in the face and looking very queer.

I did a lot of thinking, leaning against the hedge, breathing the smell of the mayflowers, and looking at the larch logs, and the neat little bungalow the other side of the garden. Lots of theories I thought of, till I came to the best thought of all; and that was that if I left the thinking to Linley, with his Oxford and Cambridge education, and only brought him the facts, as he had told me, I should be doing more good in my way than if I tried to do any big thinking. I forgot to tell you that I had gone to Scotland Yard in the morning. Well, there wasn't really much to tell. What they asked me was what I wanted. And, not having an answer exactly ready, I didn't find out very much from them. But it was quite different at Unge; everyone was most obliging; it was their day there, as I said. The constable let me go indoors, so long as I didn't touch anything, and he gave me a look at the garden from the inside. And I saw the stumps of the ten larch trees, and I noticed one thing that Linley said was very observant of me, not that it turned out to be any use, but anyway I was doing my best: I noticed that the stumps had been all chopped anyhow. And from that I thought that the man that did it didn't know much about chopping. The constable said that was a deduction. So then I said that the axe was blunt when he used it; and that certainly made the constable think, though he didn't actually say I was right this time. Did I tell you that Steeger never went outdoors, except to the little garden to chop wood, ever since Nancy disappeared? I think I did. Well, it was perfectly true. They'd watched him night and day, one or another of them, and they'd never have done it if the news hadn't gone around that the man was a vegetarian and only dealt at the greengrocer's. Likely as not even that was only started out of pique by the butcher. It's queer what little things may trip a man up. Best to keep straight is my motto. But perhaps I'm straying a bit away from my story. I should like to do that forever—forget that it ever was; but I can't.

Well, I picked up all sorts of information; clues I suppose I should call it in a story like this, though they none of them seemed to lead anywhere. For instance, I found out everything he ever bought at the village. I could even tell you the kind of salt he bought, quite plain with no phosphates in it, that they sometimes put in to make it tidy. And then he got ice from the fishmonger's, and plenty of vegetables, as I said, from the greengrocer, Mergin & Sons. And I had a bit of a talk over it all with the constable. Slugger he said his name was. I wondered why he hadn't come in and searched the place as soon as the girl was missing.

"Well, you can't do that," he said. "And besides, we didn't suspect at once, not about the girl, that is. We only suspected there was something wrong about him on account of him being a vegetarian. He stayed a good fortnight after the last that was seen of her. And then we slipped in like a knife. But, you see, no one had been inquiring about her, there was no warrant out."

"And what did you find," I asked Slugger, "when you went in?"

"Just a big file," he said, "and the knife and the axe that he must have got to chop her up with."

"But he got the axe to chop trees with," I said.

"Well, yes," he said, but rather grudgingly.

"And what did he chop them for?" I asked.

"Well, of course, my superiors has theories about that," he said, "that they mightn't tell to everybody."

You see, it was those logs that were beating them.

"But did he cut her up at all?" I asked.

"Well, he said that she was going to South America," he answered. Which was really very fair-minded of him.

I don't remember now much else that he told me. Steeger left the plates and dishes all washed up and very neat, he said.

Well, I brought all this back to Linley, going up by the train that started just about sunset. I'd like to tell you about the late spring evening, so calm over that grim bungalow, closing in with a glory all around it, as though it were blessing it; but you'll want to hear of the murder. Well, I told Linley everything. The trouble was that the moment I began to leave anything out, he'd know it, and make me drag it in. "You can't tell what may be vital," he'd say. "A tin tack swept away by a housemaid might hang a man."

All very well, but be consistent, even if you are educated at Eton and Harrow, and whenever I mentioned Num-numo, which after all was the beginning of the whole story, because he wouldn't have heard of it if it hadn't been for me, and my noticing that Steeger had bought two bottles of it, why then he said that things like that were trivial and we should keep to the main issues. I naturally talked a bit about Num-numo, because only that day I had pushed close on fifty bottles of it in Unge. A murder certainly stimulates people's minds, and Steeger's two bottles gave me an opportunity that only a fool could have failed to make something of. But of course all that was nothing at all to Linley.

You can't see a man's thoughts, and you can't look into his mind, so that all the most exciting things in the world can never be told of. But what I think happened all that evening with Linley, while I talked to him before supper, and all through supper, and sitting smoking afterward in front of our fire, was that his thoughts were stuck at a barrier there was no getting over. And the barrier wasn't the difficulty of finding ways and means by which Steeger might have made away with the body, but the impossibility of finding why he chopped those masses of wood every day for a fortnight, and paid, as I'd just found out, twenty-five pounds to his landlord to be allowed to do it. That's what was beating Linley. As for the ways by which Steeger might have hidden the body, it seemed to me that every way was blocked by the police. If you said he buried it, they said the chalk was undisturbed; if you said he carried it away, they said he never left the place; if you said he burned it, they said no smell of burning was ever noticed when the smoke blew low, and when it didn't, they climbed trees after it.

Did anyone come to the house? he asked me once or twice. Did anyone take anything away from it? But we couldn't account for it that way. Then perhaps I made some suggestion that was no good, or perhaps I started talking of Num-numo again, and he interrupted me rather sharply.

"But what would you do, Smithers?" he said. "What would you do yourself?"

"If I'd murdered poor Nancy Elth?" I asked.

"Yes," he said.

"I can't ever imagine doing such a thing," I told him.

He sighed at that, as though it were something against me.

"I suppose I should never be a detective," I said. And he just shook his head.

Then he looked broodingly into the fire for what seemed an hour. And then he shook his head again. We both went to bed after that.

I shall remember the next day all my life. I was till evening, as usual, pushing Num-numo. And we sat down to supper about nine. You couldn't get things cooked at those flats, so of course we had it cold. And Linley began with a salad. I can see it now, every bit of it. Well, I was still a bit full of what I'd done in Unge, pushing Num-numo. Only a fool, I know, would have been unable to push it there; but, still, I *had* pushed it; and about fifty bottles, forty-eight to be exact, are something in a small village, whatever the circumstances. So I was talking about it a bit; and then all of a sudden I realized that Num-numo was nothing to Linley, and I pulled myself up with a jerk. It was really very kind of him; do you know what he did? He must have known at once why I stopped talking, and he just stretched out a hand and said, "Would you give me a little of your Num-numo for my salad?"

I was so touched I nearly gave it to him. But of course you don't take Num-numo with salad. Only for meats and savories. That's on the bottle.

So I just said to him, "Only for meats and savories." Though I don't know what savories are. Never had any.

I never saw a man's face go like that before.

He seemed still for a whole minute. And nothing speaking about him but that expression. Like a man that's seen a ghost, one is tempted to write. But it wasn't really at all. I'll tell you what he looked like. Like a man that's seen something that no one has ever looked at before, something he thought couldn't be.

And then he said in a voice that was all quite changed, more low and gentle and quiet it seemed, "No good for vegetables, eh?"

"Not a bit," I said.

And at that he gave a kind of sob in his throat. I hadn't thought he could feel things like that. Of course I didn't know what it was all about; but, whatever it was, I thought all that sort of thing would have been knocked out of him at Eton and Harrow, an educated man like that. There were no tears in his eyes, but he was feeling something horribly.

And then he began to speak with big spaces between his words, saying, "A man might make a mistake perhaps, and use Num-numo with vegetables."

"Not twice," I said. What else could I say?

And he repeated that after me, as though I had told of the end of the world, and adding an awful emphasis to my words, till they seemed all clammy with some frightful significance, and shaking his head as he said it.

Then he was quite silent.

"What is it?" I asked.

"Smithers," he said.

"Yes," I said.

"Look here, Smithers," he said, "you must phone down to the grocer at Unge and find out from him whether Steeger bought those two bottles, as I expect he did, on the same day, and not a few days apart."

I waited to see if any more was coming, and then I ran out and did what I was told. It took me some time, being after nine o'clock, and only then with the help of the police. About six days apart they said; and so I came back and told Linley. He looked up at me so hopefully when I came in, but I saw that it was the wrong answer by his eyes.

You can't take things to heart like that without being ill, and when he didn't speak I said, "What you want is a good brandy, and go to bed early."

And he said, "No. I must see someone from Scotland Yard. Phone around to them to send someone here at once."

But I said, "I can't get an inspector from Scotland Yard to call on us at this hour."

His eyes were all lit up. He was all there all right.

"Then tell them," he said, "they'll never find Nancy Elth. Tell one of them to come here, and I'll tell him why." And he added, I think only for me, "They must watch Steeger, till one day they get him over something else."

And, do you know, Inspector Ulton, he came himself.

While we were waiting I tried to talk to Linley. Partly curiosity, I admit. But I didn't want to leave him to those thoughts of his, brooding away by the fire. I tried to ask him what it was all about. But he wouldn't tell me. "Murder is horrible," is all he would say. "And as a man covers his tracks up, it only gets worse."

He wouldn't tell me. "There are tales," he said, "that one never wants to hear."

That's true enough. I wish I'd never heard this one. I never did actually. But I guessed it from Linley's last words to Inspector Ulton, the only ones that I overheard. And perhaps this is the point at which to stop reading my story, so that you don't guess it too; even if you think you want murder stories. For don't you rather want a murder story with a bit of a romantic twist, and not a story about real foul murder? Well, just as you like.

In came Inspector Ulton, and Linley shook his hand in silence, and pointed the way to his bedroom; and they went in there and talked in low voices, and I never heard a word.

A fairly hearty-looking man was the inspector when they went into that room.

When they came out, they walked through our sitting room in silence, and together they went into the hall, where I heard the only words they said to each other. It was the inspector that first broke that silence.

"But why," he said, "did he cut down the trees?"

"Solely," said Linley, "in order to get an appetite."

THE GETTYSBURG BUGLE

ELLERY QUEEN

THIS IS A very old story as Queen stories go. It happened in Ellery's salad days, when he was tossing his talents about like a Sunday chef and a redheaded girl named Nikki Porter had just attached herself to his typewriter. But it has not staled, this story; it has an unwithering flavor which those who partook of it relish to this day.

There are gourmets in America whose taste buds leap at any concoction dated 1861–1865. To such, the mere recitation of ingredients like Bloody Angle, minié balls, "Tenting Tonight," the brand of Ulysses Grant's whiskey, not to mention Father Abraham, is sufficient to start the passionate flow of juices. These are the misty-hearted to whom the Civil War is "the War" and the blue and gray armies rather more than men. It is they who keep the little flags flying and the ivy ever green on the graves of the old men.

Ellery is of this company, and that is why he regards the case of the old men of Jacksburg, Pennsylvania, with particular affection. He and Nikki came upon the village of Jacksburg as people often come upon the best things, unpropitiously. They had been driving back to New York from Washington, where Ellery had had some sleuthing to do among the stacks of the Library of Congress. Perhaps the Potomac, Arlington's eternal geometry, and giant Lincoln frozen in sadness all brought their weight to bear upon Ellery's decision to veer toward Gettysburg. And Nikki had never been there, and May was coming to its end. There was a climate of sentiment.

They crossed the Maryland-Pennsylvania line and spent timeless hours wandering over Culp's Hill and Seminary Ridge and Little Round Top and Spangler's Spring among the watchful monuments. When they left they were in a mood of wonder, oblivious to the darkening sky. So they were disagreeably surprised when it opened on their heads, drenching them to the skin. From the horizon behind them Gettysburg was a battlefield again, sending great flashes of fire through the darkness to the din of celestial cannon. Ellery stopped the car and put the top up, but the mood was drowned when he discovered that something had happened to the ignition system. They were marooned, Nikki moaned; making Ellery angry, for it was true.

"We can't go on in these wet clothes, Ellery!"

"Do you suggest that we stay here in them? I'll get this crackerbox started if—" But at that moment the watery lights of a house wavered on somewhere ahead, and Ellery became cheerful again. "At least we'll find out where we are. There may even be a garage."

It was a little white house on a little swampy road marked off by a little stone fence covered with rambler rose vines, and the man who opened the door to the dripping wayfarers was little, too, and weather-skinned and gallused. He smiled hospitably, but the smile became concern when he saw how wet they were.

"Won't take no for an answer," he said in a remarkably deep voice, and he chuckled. "That's doctor's orders, though I expect you didn't see my shingle—mostly overgrown with ivy. Got a change of clothing in your car?"

"Oh, yes!" said Nikki.

Ellery hesitated. The house looked neat and clean, there was an enticing fire, and the rain at their backs was coming down with a roar. "Well, thank you . . . but if I might use your phone to call a garage—"

"You just give me the keys to your car trunk."

"But we can't turn your home into a tourist house—"

"It's that, too, when the good Lord sends a wanderer my way. This storm's going to keep up most of the night, and the roads hereabout get mighty soupy." The little man was bustling into waterproof and overshoes. "I'll get Lew Bagley over at the garage to pick up your car. Now let's have those keys."

So an hour later, while the elements warred outside, they were toasting safely in a pleasant little parlor, full of Dr. Martin Strong's home-made poppy-seed twists, scrapple, and coffee. The doctor, who lived alone, was his own cook. He was also, he said with a chuckle, mayor of the village of Jacksburg and its chief of police. "Lot of us in the village run double harness. Bill Yoder of the hardware store's our undertaker. Lew Bagley's also the fire chief. Ed MacShane—"

"Jacksburger-of-all-trades you may be, Dr. Strong," said Ellery, "but to me you're the Good Samaritan."

"Hallelujah," said Nikki, piously wiggling her toes.

"And make it Doc," said their host. "Why, it's just selfishness on my part, Mr. Queen. We're off the beaten track here, and you do get a hankering for a new face. I guess I know every dimple and wen on the five hundred and thirty-four in Jacksburg."

"I don't suppose your police chiefship keeps you very busy."

Doc Strong laughed. "Not any. Though last year . . ." His eyes puckered and he got up to poke the fire. "Did you say, Miss Porter, that Mr. Queen is sort of a detective?"

"Sort of a!" began Nikki. "Why, Dr. Strong, he's solved some simply unbeliev—"

"My father is an inspector in the New York police department," interrupted Ellery, curbing Nikki's enthusiasm with a glance. "I stick my nose into a case once in a while. What about last year, Doc?"

"What put me in mind of it," said Jacksburg's mayor thoughtfully, "was your saying you'd been to Gettysburg today. And also you being interested in crimes . . . Memorial Day's tomorrow, and for the first time in my life I'm not looking forward to it. Jacksburg makes quite a fuss about Memorial Day. It's not every village can brag about three living veterans of the Civil War."

"Three!" exclaimed Nikki. "How thrilling."

"Gives you an idea what the Jacksburg doctoring business is like." Doc Strong grinned. "We run to longevity. . . . I ought to have said we *had* three Civil War veterans—Caleb Atwell, ninety-seven—there are dozens of Atwells in the county; Zach Bigelow, ninety-five, who lives with his grandson Andy and Andy's wife and seven kids; and Abner Chase, ninety-four, Cissy Chase's great-grandpa. This year we're down to two. Caleb Atwell died last Memorial Day."

"*A, B, C,*" murmured Ellery. "*A* died last Memorial Day. Is that why you're not looking forward to this one? *B* following *A* sort of thing?"

"I'm afraid it isn't as simple as all that," said Doc Strong. "Maybe I better tell you how Caleb Atwell died. Every year he, Zach, and Abner have been the star performers of our Memorial Day exercises, which are held at the old burying ground on the Hookerstown road. As the oldest of the three, Caleb always blew taps on a cracked old bugle that's most as old as he was. Caleb, Zach, and Abner were in the Pennsylvania Seventy-second. They covered themselves with immortal glory—the Seventy-second, I mean—at Gettysburg when they fought back Pickett's charge, and that bugle played a big part in their fighting. Ever since it's been known as the Gettysburg bugle—in Jacksburg, anyway."

The little mayor of Jacksburg looked softly down the years. "It's been a tradition, the oldest living vet tootling that bugle, far back as I remember. I recollect as a boy standing around with my mouth open watching the GARs—there were lots more then—take turns in front of the general store practicing on the bugle, so any one of 'em would be ready when his turn came." Doc Strong sighed. "And Zach Bigelow, as the next oldest to Caleb Atwell, he'd be the standard-bearer, and Ab Chase, as the next-next oldest, he'd lay the wreath on the memorial monument in the burying ground.

"Well, last Memorial Day, while Zach was holding the regimental colors and Ab the wreath, Caleb blew taps the way he'd done nigh onto twenty times before. All of a sudden, in the middle of a high note, he dropped in his tracks, deader than church on Monday."

"But surely, Doc," said Ellery with a smile, "you can't have been suspicious about the death of a man of ninety-seven?"

"Maybe I was, because I'd given old Caleb a thorough physical checkup only the day before he died. I'd have staked my medical license he'd live to break a hundred and then some."

"Just what was it you suspected, Doc?" Ellery forbore to smile now, but only because of Dr. Strong's evident distress.

"Didn't know what to suspect," said the country doctor shortly. "Fooled around with the notion of an autopsy, but the Atwells wouldn't hear of it. Said I was a blame jackass to think a man of ninety-seven would die of anything but old age. The upshot was we buried Caleb whole."

"But Doc, at that age the human economy can go to pieces without warning, like the one-hoss shay. You must have had another reason for uneasiness. A motive you knew about?"

"Well . . . maybe."

"He was a rich man," said Nikki sagely.

"He didn't have a pot he could call his own," said Doc Strong. "But somebody stood to gain by his death just the same. That is, if the old yarn's true. You see, there's been kind of a legend in Jacksburg about those three old fellows, Mr. Queen. Folks say that back in '65 they found some sort of treasure."

"Treasure . . ." Nikki began to cough.

"Treasure," repeated Doc Strong doggedly. "Fetched it home to Jacksburg with them, the story goes, hid it, and swore they'd never tell a living soul where it was buried. Now there's lots of tales like that came out of the War"—he fixed Nikki with a stern and glittering eye—"and most folks either cough or go into hysterics, but there's something about this one I've always half believed. So I'll breathe a lot easier when tomorrow's ceremonies are over and Zach Bigelow lays Caleb Atwell's bugle away till next year. As the older survivor, Zach does the tootling tomorrow."

"They hid the treasure and kept it hidden for considerably over half a century?" Ellery was smiling again. "Doesn't strike me as a very sensible thing to do with a treasure, Doc."

"The story goes that they'd sworn an oath—"

"Not to touch any of it until they all died but one," said Ellery, laughing outright now. "Last-survivor-takes-all department. Doc, that's the way most of these fairy tales go." Ellery rose, yawning. "I think I hear the feather bed in that other guest room calling. Nikki, your eyeballs are hanging out. Take my advice, Doc, and follow suit. You haven't a thing to worry about but keeping the kids quiet tomorrow while you read the Gettysburg Address!"

Ellery and Nikki awakened to a splendid world, risen from its night's ablutions with a shining eye and a scrubbed look; and they went downstairs within seconds of each other to find the mayor of Jacksburg pottering about the kitchen.

"Morning, morning," said Doc Strong, welcoming but abstracted. "Just fixing your breakfast before catching an hour's nap."

"You lamb," said Nikki. "But what a shame, Doctor. Didn't you sleep well last night?"

"Didn't sleep at all. Tossed around a bit and just as I was dropping off my phone rings and it's Cissy Chase. Emergency sick call. Hope it didn't disturb you."

"Cissy Chase." Ellery looked at their host. "Wasn't that the name you mentioned last night of—"

"Of Abner Chase's great-granddaughter. That's right. Cissy's an orphan and Ab's only kin. She's kept house for the old fellow and taken care of him since she was ten."

Ellery said peculiarly, "It was old Abner . . . ?"

"I was up with Ab all night. This morning, at six thirty, he passed away."

"On Memorial Day!" Nikki sounded like a little girl in her first experience with a fact of life.

There was a silence, fretted by the sizzling of Doc Strong's bacon.

Ellery said at last, "What did Abner Chase die of?"

Doc Strong looked at him. He seemed angry. "I know a cerebral hemorrhage when I see one, Mr. Queen, and that's what Ab Chase died of. In a man of ninety-four, that's as close to natural death as you can come. . . . No, there wasn't any funny business in this one."

"Except," mumbled Ellery, "that—again—it happened on Memorial Day."

"Man's a contrary animal. Tell him lies and he swallows 'em whole. Give him the truth and he gags on it." Doc Strong said it as if he were addressing not them but himself. "Any special way you like your eggs?"

"Leave the eggs to me, Doctor," Nikki said firmly. "You go on up those stairs and get some sleep."

"Reckon I better if I'm to do my usual dignified job today," said the mayor of Jacksburg with a sigh. "Though Abner Chase's death is going to make the proceedings solemner than ordinary. By the way, Mr. Queen, I talked to Lew Bagley this morning and he'll have your car ready in an hour. When you planning to leave?"

"I *was* intending . . ." Ellery stopped with a frown. "I wonder," he murmured, "how Zach Bigelow's going to take the news."

"He's already taken it, Mr. Queen. Stopped in at Andy Bigelow's place on my way home. Kind of a detour, but I figured I'd better break the news to Zach early as possible."

"Poor thing," said Nikki. "I wonder how it feels to learn you're the only one left."

"Can't say Zach carried on about it," said Doc Strong dryly. "About all he said was, 'Doggone it, now who's goin' to lay the wreath after I toot the Gettysburg bugle?' I guess when you reach the age of ninety-five, death don't mean what it does to young squirts of sixty-three like me. What time'd you say you were leaving, Mr. Queen?"

"Nikki," muttered Ellery, "are we in any particular hurry?"

"I don't know. Are we?"

"Besides, it wouldn't be patriotic. Doc, do you suppose Jacksburg would mind if a couple of New York Yanks invited themselves to your Memorial Day exercises?"

THE BUSINESS DISTRICT of Jacksburg consisted of a single paved street bounded at one end by the sightless eye of a broken traffic signal and at the other by the twin gas pumps before Lew Bagley's garage. In between were some stores in need of paint. Red, white, and blue streamers crisscrossed the thoroughfare overhead. A few seedy frame houses, each decorated with an American flag, flanked the main street at both ends.

Ellery and Nikki found the Chase house exactly where Doc Strong had said it would be—just around the corner from Bagley's garage, between the ivy-hidden church and the firehouse of the Jacksburg Volunteer Pump and Hose Company No. 1. But the mayor's directions were a superfluity; it was the only house with a crowded porch.

A heavy-shouldered young girl in a black Sunday dress sat in a rocker, the center of the crowd. She was trying to smile at the cheerful words of sympathy winged at her from all sides.

"Thanks, Mis' Plum. . . . That's right, Mr. Schmidt, I know. . . . But he was such a spry old soul. . . ."

"Miss Cissy Chase?"

Had the voice been that of a Confederate spy, a deeper silence could not have drowned the noise. Jacksburg eyes examined Ellery and Nikki with cold curiosity, and feet shuffled.

"My name is Queen and this is Miss Porter. We're attending the Jacksburg Memorial Day exercises as guests of Mayor Strong"—a warming murmur, like a zephyr, passed over the porch—"and he asked us to wait here for him. I'm sorry about your great-grandfather, Miss Chase."

"You must have been very proud of him," said Nikki.

"Thank you, I was. It was so sudden. . . . Won't you set? I mean, do come into the house. Great-grandpa's not here. . . . He's over at Bill Yoder's."

The girl was flustered and began to cry, and Nikki took her arm and led her into the house. Ellery lingered a moment to exchange appropriate remarks with the neighbors, who, while no longer cold, were still curious; and then he followed. It was a dreary little house with a dark and damp parlor.

"Now, now, this is no time for fussing. . . . May I call you Cissy?" Nikki was saying soothingly. "Besides, you're better off away from all those folks. Why, Ellery, she's only a child!"

And a very plain child, Ellery thought, with a pinched face and empty eyes; and he almost wished he had gone on past the broken traffic light and turned north.

"I understand the parade to the burying ground is going to form outside your house, Cissy," he said. "By the way, have Andrew Bigelow and his grandfather Zach arrived yet?"

"Oh, I don't know," said Cissy Chase dully. "It's all such a dream, seems like."

"Of course. And you're left alone. Haven't you any family at all, Cissy?"

"No."

"Isn't there some young man . . . ?"

Cissy shook her head bitterly. "Who'd marry me? This is the only decent dress I got, and it's four years old. We lived on Great-grandpa's pension and what I could earn hiring out by the day. Which ain't much, nor often. Now . . ."

"Cissy." Ellery spoke casually. "Doc Strong mentioned something about a treasure. Do you know anything about it?"

"Oh, that." Cissy shrugged. "Just what Great-grandpa told me, and he hardly ever told the same story twice. Near as I was able to make out, one time during the War him and Caleb Atwell and Zach Bigelow got separated from the army—scouting, or foraging, or something. It was down south somewhere, and they spent the night in an old empty mansion that was half burned down. Next morning they went through the ruins to see what they could pick up, and buried in the cellar they found the treasure. A big fortune in money, Great-grandpa said.

"They were afraid to take it with them, so they buried it in the same place in the cellar and made a map of the location, and after the War they went back, the three of 'em, and dug it up again. They swore they'd hold on to it till only one of them remained alive, I don't know why; then the last one was to get it all. Leastways, that's how Great-grandpa told it."

"Did he ever say how much of a fortune it was?"

Cissy laughed. "Couple of hundred thousand dollars. I ain't saying Great-grandpa was cracked, but you know how an old man gets."

"Did he ever give you a hint as to where he and Caleb and Zach hid the money after they got it back north?"

"No, he'd just slap his knee and wink at me."

"Maybe," said Ellery suddenly, "maybe there's something to that yarn after all."

But Cissy only drooped. "If there is, it's all Zach Bigelow's now."

Then Doc Strong came in, fresh as a daisy in a pressed blue suit and a stiff collar and a bow tie, and a great many other people came in, too. Ellery and Nikki surrendered Cissy Chase to Jacksburg.

"If there's anything to the story," Nikki whispered to Ellery, "and if Mayor Strong is right, then that old scoundrel Bigelow's been murdering his friends to get the money!"

"After all these years, Nikki? At the age of ninety-five?" Ellery shook his head.

"But then what—"

"I don't know." But when the little mayor happened to look their way, Ellery caught his eye and took him aside and whispered in his ear.

THE PROCESSION—NEAR every car in Jacksburg, Doc Strong announced, over a hundred of them—got under way at exactly two o'clock.

Nikki found herself being handed into the leading car, an old but brightly polished convertible contributed for the occasion by Lew Bagley. In the front seat she spied an ancient, doddering head under a Union Army hat. Zach Bigelow held his papery frame fiercely if shakily erect between the driver and a powerful red-necked man with a brutal face, who, Nikki surmised, was the old man's grandson, Andy. Nikki looked back, peering around the flapping folds of the flag stuck in the corner of the car. Cissy Chase was in the second car in a black veil, weeping on a stout woman's shoulder. So the female Yankee from New York sat back between Ellery and Mayor Strong, against the bank of flowers in which the flag was set, and glared at the necks of the two Bigelows, having long since taken sides in this matter.

Ellery, however, was all deference and cordiality, even to the brute grandson. He leaned forward, talking into a hairy ear. "How do I address your grandfather, Mr. Bigelow? I don't want to make a mistake about his rank."

"Gramp's a general," said Andy Bigelow loudly. "Ain't you, Gramp?" He beamed at the ancient, but Zach Bigelow was staring proudly ahead, holding fast to something in a rotted musette bag on his lap. "Went through the War a private," the grandson confided, "but he don't like to talk about that."

"General Bigelow—" began Ellery.

"Hey?" The old man turned his trembling head, glaring. "Speak up, bub. Ye're mumblin'."

"General Bigelow," shouted Ellery, "now that all the money is yours, what are you going to do with it?"

"Hey? Money?"

"The treasure, Gramp," roared Andy Bigelow. "They've even heard about it in New York. What are you goin' to do with it, he wants to know."

"Does, does he?" Old Zach sounded grimly amused. "Can't talk, Andy. Hurts m' neck."

"How much does it amount to, General?" cried Ellery.

Old Zach eyed him. "Mighty nosy, ain't ye?" Then he cackled. "Last time we counted it—Caleb, Ab, and me—came to nigh on a million dollars. Yes, sir, one million dollars." The old man's left eye drooped startlingly. "Goin' to be a big surprise to the smart alecks and the doubtin' Thomases. You wait an' see."

Andy Bigelow grinned, and Nikki could have strangled him.

"According to Cissy," Nikki murmured to Doc Strong, "Abner Chase said it was only two hundred thousand."

"Zach makes it more every time he talks about it," said the mayor unhappily.

"I heard ye, Martin Strong!" yelled Zach Bigelow, swiveling his twig of a neck so suddenly that Nikki winced, expecting it to snap. "You wait! I'll show ye who's a lot o' wind!"

"Now, Zach," said Doc Strong pacifyingly. "Save your wind for that bugle."

Zach Bigelow cackled and clutched the musette bag in his lap, glaring ahead in triumph, as if he had scored a great victory.

Ellery said no more. Oddly, he kept staring not at old Zach but at Andy Bigelow, who sat beside his grandfather, grinning at invisible audiences along the empty countryside as if he, too, had won—or were on his way to winning—a triumph.

THE SUN WAS hot. Men shucked their coats and women fanned themselves with handkerchiefs and pocketbooks.

"It is for us the living, rather to be dedicated . . ."

Children dodged among the graves, pursued by shushing mothers. On most of the graves there were fresh flowers.

". . . that from these honored dead . . ."

Little American flags protruded from the graves, too.

". . . gave the last full measure of devotion . . ."

Doc Martin Strong's voice was deep and sure, not at all like the voice of that tall ugly man, who had spoken the same words apologetically.

". . . that these dead shall not have died in vain . . ."

Doc was standing on the pedestal of the Civil War monument, which was decorated with flags and bunting and faced the weathered stone ranks like a commander in full-dress uniform.

". . . that this nation, under God . . ."

A color guard of the American Legion, Jacksburg Post, stood at attention between the mayor and the people. A file of legionnaires carrying old Sharps rifles faced the graves.

". . . and that government of the people . . ."

Beside the mayor, disdaining the simian shoulder of his grandson, stood General Zach Bigelow. Straight as the barrel of a Sharps, musette bag held tightly to his blue tunic.

". . . shall not perish from the earth."

The old man began to fumble with the bag.

"Comp-'ny! Present—arms!"

"Go ahead, Gramp!" Andy Bigelow bellowed.

The old man muttered. He was having difficulty extricating the bugle from the bag.

"Here, lemme give ye a hand!"

"Let the old man alone, Andy," said the mayor of Jacksburg quietly. "We're in no hurry."

Finally the bugle was free. It was an old army bugle, as old as Zach Bigelow, dented and scarred in a hundred places.

The old man raised it to his earth-colored lips.

Now his hands were not shaking.

Now even the children were quiet.

Now the legionnaires stood more rigidly.

And the old man began to play taps.

It could hardly have been called playing. He blew, and out of the bugle's bell came cracked sounds. And sometimes he blew and no sounds came out at all. Then the veins of his neck swelled and his face turned to burning bark. Or he sucked at the mouthpiece, in and out, to clear it of his spittle. But still he blew, and the people stood at attention, listening, as if the butchery of sound were sweet music.

And then, suddenly, the butchery faltered. Old Zach Bigelow stood with bulging eyes. The Gettysburg bugle fell to the pedestal with a tiny clatter.

For an instant everything seemed to stop—the slight movements of the children, the breathing of the people. Then into the vacuum rushed a murmur of horror, and Nikki unbelievingly opened the eyes which she had shut to glimpse the last of Jacksburg's GAR veterans crumpling at the feet of Doc Strong and Andy Bigelow.

"YOU WERE RIGHT the first time, Doc," Ellery said.

They were in Andy Bigelow's house, where old Zach's body had been taken from the cemetery. The house was full of chittering women and scampering children, but in this room there were only a few, and they talked in low tones. The old man was laid out on a settee with a patchwork quilt over him. Doc Strong sat in a rocker beside the body, looking very old.

"It's my fault," he mumbled. "I didn't examine Caleb's mouth last year. I didn't examine the mouthpiece of that bugle."

Ellery soothed him. "It's not an easy poison to spot, Doc. And after all, the whole thing was so ludicrous. You'd have caught it in autopsy, but the Atwells laughed you out of it."

"They're all gone. All three." Doc Strong looked up fiercely. "Who poisoned their bugle?"

"God Almighty, don't look at me," said Andy Bigelow. "Anybody could of, Doc."

"Anybody, Andy?" the mayor cried. "When Caleb Atwell died, Zach took the bugle and it's been in this house for a year!"

"Anybody could of," said Bigelow stubbornly. "The bugle was hangin' over the fireplace and anybody could of snuck in durin' the night. . . . Anyway, it wasn't here before old Caleb died; *he* had it up to last Memorial Day. Who poisoned it in *his* house?"

"We won't get anywhere on this tack, Doc," Ellery murmured. "Bigelow. Did your grandfather ever let on where that Civil War treasure is hidden?"

"Suppose he did." The man licked his lips, blinking, as if he had been surprised into the half admission. "What's it to you?"

"That money is behind the murders, Bigelow."

"Don't know nothin' about that. Anyway, nobody's got no right to that money but me." Andy Bigelow spread his thick chest. "When Ab

Chase died, Gramp was the last survivor. That money was Zach Bigelow's. I'm his next o' kin, so now it's mine!"

"You know where it's hid, Andy." Doc was on his feet, eyes glittering. "Where?"

"I ain't talkin'. Git outen my house!"

"I'm the law in Jacksburg, too, Andy," Doc said softly. "This is a murder case. Where's that money?"

Bigelow laughed.

"You didn't know, Bigelow, did you?" said Ellery.

"Course not." He laughed again. "See, Doc? He's on your side, and he says I don't know, too."

"That is," said Ellery, "until a few minutes ago."

Bigelow's grin faded. "What are ye talkin' about?"

"Zach Bigelow wrote a message this morning, immediately after Doc Strong told him about Abner Chase's death."

Bigelow's face went ashen.

"And your grandfather sealed the message in an envelope—"

"Who told ye that?" yelled Bigelow.

"One of your children. And the first thing you did when we got home from the burying ground with your grandfather's corpse was to sneak up to the old man's bedroom. Hand it over."

Bigelow made two fists. Then he laughed again. "All right, I'll let ye see it. Hell, I'll let ye dig the money up for me! Why not? It's mine by law. Here, read it. See? He wrote my name on the envelope!"

And so he had. And the message in the envelope was also written in ink, in the same wavering hand.

Dere Andy now that Ab Chase is ded to—if sumthin happins to me you wil find the money we been keepin all these long yeres in a iron box in the coffin *wich we beried Caleb Atwell in.* I leave it all to you my beluved grandson cuz you been sech a good grandson to me. Yours truly Zach Bigelow.

"In Caleb's coffin," choked Doc Strong.

Ellery's face was impassive. "How soon can you get an exhumation order, Doc?"

"Right now!" exclaimed Doc. "I'm also deputy coroner of this district!"

They took some men and went back to the old burying ground, and in the darkening day they dug up the remains of Caleb Atwell. They opened the casket and found, on the corpse's knees, a flattish box of iron with a hasp but no lock. Doctor-Mayor-Chief of Police-Deputy Coroner Martin Strong held his breath and raised the lid of the box. It was crammed to the brim with moldy bills of large denominations.

In Confederate money.

No one said anything for some time, not even Andy Bigelow.

Then Ellery said, "It stood to reason. They found it buried in the cellar of an old southern mansion—would it be northern greenbacks? When they dug it up again after the War and brought it up to Jacksburg, they probably hoped it might have some value. When they realized it was worthless, they decided to have some fun with it. This had been a private joke of those three old rascals since, roughly, 1865. When Caleb died, Abner and Zach probably decided that, as the first of the trio to go, Caleb ought to have the honor of being custodian of their Confederate treasure in perpetuity. So one of them managed to slip the iron box into the coffin before the lid was screwed on. Zach's note bequeathing his 'fortune' to his 'beloved grandson'—in view of what I've seen of his beloved grandson today—was the old fellow's final joke."

Everybody chuckled; but the corpse stared mirthlessly and the silence fell again, to be broken by a weak curse from Andy Bigelow and Doc Strong's puzzled, "But Mr. Queen, that doesn't explain the murders."

"Well, now, Doc, it does," said Ellery. And then he said in a very different tone, "Suppose we put old Caleb back the way we found him, for your reexhumation later for autopsy, Doc—and then we'll close the book on your Memorial Day murders."

ELLERY CLOSED THE book in town, in the dusk, on the porch of Cissy Chase's house, which was central and convenient for everybody. Ellery and Nikki and Doc Strong and Cissy and Andy Bigelow—still clutching the iron box dazedly—were on the porch, and Lew Bagley and Bill

Yoder and everyone else in Jacksburg, it seemed, stood about on the lawn and sidewalk, listening. There was a touch of sadness to the soft twilight air, for something vital and exciting in the life of the village had come to an end.

"There's no trick to this," began Ellery, "and no joke, either, even though the men who were murdered were so old that death had grown tired waiting for them. The answer is as simple as the initials of their last names. Who knew that the supposed fortune was in Confederate money and therefore worthless? Only the three old men. One or another of the three would hardly have planned the deaths of the other two for possession of some scraps of valueless paper. So the murderer has to be someone who believed the fortune was legitimate and who—since until today there was no clue to the money's hiding place—knew he could claim it legally.

"Now of course that last-survivor-takes-all business was pure moonshine, invented by Caleb, Zach, and Abner for their own amusement and the mystification of the community. But the would-be murderer didn't know that. The would-be murderer went on the assumption that the *whole* story was true, or he wouldn't have planned murder in the first place.

"Who would be able to claim the fortune legally if the last of the three old men—the survivor who presumably came into possession of the fortune on the deaths of the other two—died in his turn?"

"Last survivor's heir," said Doc Strong, and he rose.

"And who is the last survivor's heir?"

"Zach Bigelow's grandson, Andy." And the little mayor of Jacksburg stared hard at Bigelow, and a grumbling sound came from the people below, and Bigelow shrank against the wall behind Cissy, as if to seek her protection. But Cissy only looked at him and moved away.

"You thought the fortune was real," Cissy said scornfully, "so you killed Caleb Atwell and my great-grandpa so your grandfather'd be the last survivor so you could kill him the way you did today and get the fortune."

"That's it, Ellery," cried Nikki.

"Unfortunately, Nikki, that's not it at all. You all refer to Zach Bigelow as the last survivor—"

"Well, he was," said Nikki in amazement.

"Literally, that's true," said Ellery, "but what you've all forgotten is that Zach Bigelow was the last survivor *only by accident.* When Abner Chase died early this morning, was it through poisoning, or some other violent means? No, Doc, you were absolutely positive he'd died of a simple cerebral hemorrhage—not by violence, but a natural death. Don't you see that if Abner Chase hadn't died a natural death early this morning, *he'd still be alive this evening?* Zach Bigelow would have put the bugle to his lips this afternoon, just as he did, just as Caleb Atwell did a year ago. . . . *And at this moment Abner Chase would have been the last survivor.*

"And who was Abner Chase's only living heir, the girl who would have fallen heir to Abner's 'fortune' when, in time, or through her assistance, he joined his cronies in the great bivouac on the other side?

"You lied to me, Cissy," said Ellery to the shrinking girl in his grip, as horror came over the crowd of mesmerized Jacksburgers. "You pretended you didn't believe the story of the fortune. But that was only after your great-grandfather had inconsiderately died of a stroke just a few hours before old Zach would have died of poisoning, and you couldn't inherit that great, great fortune, anyway!"

NIKKI DID NOT speak until they were twenty-five miles from Jacksburg. Then all she said was, "And now there's nobody left to blow the Gettysburg bugle," and she continued to stare into the darkness toward the south.

THE DAMNED THING

AMBROSE BIERCE

BY THE LIGHT of a tallow candle which had been placed on one end of a rough table a man was reading something written in a book. It was an old account book, greatly worn; and the writing was not, apparently, very legible, for the man sometimes held the page close to the flame of the candle to get a stronger light on it. The shadow of the book would then throw into obscurity a half of the room, darkening a number of faces and figures; for besides the reader, eight other men were present. Seven of them sat against the rough log walls, silent, motionless, and the room being small, not very far from the table. By extending an arm any one of them could have touched the eighth man, who lay on the table, face upward, partly covered by a sheet. He was dead.

The man with the book was not reading aloud, and no one spoke; all seemed to be waiting for something to occur; the dead man only was without expectation. From the blank darkness outside came in, through the aperture that served for a window, all the ever unfamiliar noises of night in the wilderness—the long nameless note of a distant coyote; the stilly pulsing trill of tireless insects in trees; strange cries of night birds, so different from those of the birds of day; the drone of great blundering beetles. But nothing of all this was noted in that company; its members were not overmuch addicted to idle interest in matters of no practical importance; that was obvious in every line of their rugged faces—obvious even in the dim light of the single candle. They were evidently men of the vicinity—farmers and woodsmen.

The person reading was a trifle different; one would have said of him that he was of the world, worldly, albeit there was that in his attire which attested a certain fellowship with the organisms of his environment. His coat would hardly have passed muster in San Francisco; his footgear was not of urban origin, and the hat that lay by him on the floor (he was the only one uncovered) was such that if one had considered it as an article of mere personal adornment he would have missed its meaning. In countenance the man was rather prepossessing, with just a hint of sternness; though that he may have assumed or cultivated, as appropriate to one in authority. For he was a coroner. It was by virtue of his office that he had possession of the book in which he was reading; it had been found among the dead man's effects—in his cabin, where the inquest was now taking place.

When the coroner had finished reading he put the book into his breast pocket. At that moment the door was pushed open and a young man entered. He, clearly, was not of mountain birth and breeding: he was clad as those who dwell in cities. His clothing was dusty, however, as from travel. He had, in fact, been riding hard to attend the inquest.

The coroner nodded; no one else greeted him.

"We have waited for you," said the coroner. "It is necessary to have done with this business tonight."

The young man smiled. "I am sorry to have kept you," he said. "I went away, not to evade your summons, but to post to my newspaper an account of what I suppose I am called back to relate."

The coroner smiled.

"The account that you posted to your newspaper," he said, "differs, probably, from that which you will give here under oath."

"That," replied the other, rather hotly and with a visible flush, "is as you please. I used manifold paper and have a copy of what I sent. It was not written as news, for it is incredible, but as fiction. It may go as a part of my testimony under oath."

"But you say it is incredible."

"That is nothing to you, sir, if I also swear that it is true."

The coroner was silent for a time, his eyes upon the floor. The men about the sides of the cabin talked in whispers, but seldom withdrew their gaze from the face of the corpse. Presently the coroner lifted his eyes and said: "We will resume the inquest."

The men removed their hats. The witness was sworn.

"What is your name?" the coroner asked.

"William Harker."

"Age?"

"Twenty-seven."

"You knew the deceased, Hugh Morgan?"

"Yes."

"You were with him when he died?"

"Near him."

"How did that happen—your presence, I mean?"

"I was visiting him at this place to shoot and fish. A part of my purpose, however, was to study him and his odd, solitary way of life. He seemed a good model for a character in fiction. I sometimes write stories."

"I sometimes read them."

"Thank you."

"Stories in general—not yours."

Some of the jurors laughed. Against a somber background humor shows highlights. Soldiers in the intervals of battle laugh easily, and a jest in the death chamber conquers by surprise.

"Relate the circumstances of this man's death," said the coroner. "You may use any notes or memoranda that you please."

The witness understood. Pulling a manuscript from his breast pocket he held it near the candle and turning the leaves until he found the passage that he wanted began to read.

"THE SUN HAD hardly risen when we left the house. We were looking for quail, each with a shotgun, but we had only one dog. Morgan said that our best ground was beyond a certain ridge that he pointed out, and we crossed it by a trail through the chaparral. On the other side was comparatively level ground, thickly covered with wild oats. As we emerged from the chaparral Morgan was but a few yards in advance.

Suddenly we heard, at a little distance to our right and partly in front, a noise as of some animal thrashing about in the bushes, which we could see were violently agitated.

"'We've started a deer,' I said. 'I wish we had brought a rifle.'

"Morgan, who had stopped and was intently watching the agitated chaparral, said nothing, but had cocked both barrels of his gun and was holding it in readiness to aim. I thought him a trifle excited, which surprised me, for he had a reputation for exceptional coolness, even in moments of sudden and imminent peril.

"'Oh, come,' I said. 'You are not going to fill up a deer with quail shot, are you?'

"Still he did not reply; but catching a sight of his face as he turned it slightly toward me I was struck by the intensity of his look. Then I understood that we had serious business in hand and my first conjecture was that we had jumped a grizzly. I advanced to Morgan's side, cocking my piece as I moved.

"The bushes were now quiet and the sounds had ceased, but Morgan was as attentive to the place as before.

"'What is it? What the devil is it?' I asked.

"'That Damned Thing!' he replied, without turning his head. His voice was husky and unnatural. He trembled visibly.

"I was about to speak further, when I observed the wild oats near the place of the disturbance moving in the most inexplicable way. I can hardly describe it. It seemed as if stirred by a streak of wind, which not only bent it, but pressed it down—crushed it so that it did not rise; and this movement was slowly prolonging itself directly toward us.

"Nothing that I had ever seen had affected me so strangely as this unfamiliar and unaccountable phenomenon, yet I am unable to recall any sense of fear. I remember—and tell it here because, singularly enough, I recollected it then—that once in looking carelessly out of an open window I momentarily mistook a small tree close at hand for one of a group of larger trees at a little distance away. It looked the same size as the others, but being more distinctly and sharply defined in mass and detail seemed out of harmony with them. It was a mere falsification of the law of aerial perspective, but it startled, almost terrified me. We so rely upon the orderly operation of familiar natural laws that any seeming suspension of them is noted as a menace to our safety, a warning of unthinkable calamity. So now the apparently causeless movement of the herbage and the slow, undeviating approach of the line of disturbances were distinctly disquieting. My companion appeared actually frightened, and I could hardly credit my senses when I saw him suddenly throw his gun to the shoulder and fire both barrels at the agitated grain! Before the smoke of the discharge had cleared away I heard a loud savage cry—a scream like that of a wild animal—and flinging his gun upon the ground Morgan sprang away and ran swiftly from the spot. At the same instant I was thrown violently to the ground by the impact of something unseen in the smoke—some soft, heavy substance that seemed thrown against me with great force.

"Before I could get upon my feet and recover my gun, which seemed to have been struck from my hands, I heard Morgan crying out as if in mortal agony, and mingling with his cries were such hoarse, savage sounds as one hears from fighting dogs. Inexpressibly terrified, I struggled to my feet and looked in the direction of Morgan's retreat; and may Heaven in mercy spare me from another sight like that! At a distance of less than thirty yards was my friend, down upon one knee, his head thrown back at a frightful angle, hatless, his long hair in disorder and his whole body in violent movement. His right arm was lifted and seemed to lack the hand—at least, I could see none. The other arm was invisible. At times, as my memory now reports this extraordinary scene, I could discern but a part of his body; it was as if he had been partly blotted out—I cannot otherwise express it—then a shifting of his position would bring it all into view again.

"All this must have occurred within a few seconds, yet in that time Morgan assumed all the postures of a determined wrestler vanquished by superior weight and strength. I saw nothing but him, and him not always distinctly. During the entire incident his shouts and curses were heard, as if through an enveloping uproar of such sounds of rage and fury as I had never heard from the throat of man or brute!

"For a moment only I stood irresolute, then throwing down my gun I ran forward to my friend's assistance. I had a vague belief that he was suffering from a fit, or some form of convulsion. Before I could reach his side he was down and quiet. All sounds had ceased, but with a feeling of such terror as even these awful events had not inspired I now saw again the mysterious movement of the wild oats, prolonging itself from the trampled area about the prostrate man toward the edge of a wood. It was only when it had reached the wood that I was able to withdraw my eyes and look at my companion. He was dead."

THE CORONER ROSE from his seat and stood beside the dead man. Lifting an edge of the sheet he pulled it away, exposing the entire body, altogether naked and showing in the candlelight a claylike yellow. It had, however, broad maculations of bluish black, obviously caused by extravasated blood from contusions. The chest and sides looked as if they had been beaten with a bludgeon. There were dreadful lacerations; the skin was torn in strips and shreds.

The coroner moved around to the end of the table and undid a silk handkerchief which had been passed under the chin and knotted on the top of the head. When the handkerchief was drawn away it exposed what had been the throat. Some of the jurors who had risen to get a better view repented their curiosity and turned away their faces. Witness Harker went to the open window and leaned out across the sill, faint and sick. Dropping the handkerchief upon the dead man's neck the coroner stepped to an angle of the room and from a pile of clothing produced one garment after another, each of which he held up a moment for inspection. All were torn, and stiff with blood. The jurors did not make a closer inspection.

"Gentlemen," the coroner said, "we have no more evidence, I think. Your duty has been already explained to you; if there is nothing you wish to ask you may go outside and consider your verdict."

The foreman rose—a tall, bearded man of sixty, coarsely clad.

"I should like to ask one question, Mr. Coroner," he said. "What asylum did this yer last witness escape from?"

"Mr. Harker," said the coroner, gravely and tranquilly, "from what asylum did you last escape?"

Harker flushed crimson again, but said nothing, and the seven jurors rose and solemnly filed out of the cabin.

"If you have done insulting me, sir," said Harker, as soon as he and the officer were left alone with the dead man, "am I at liberty to go?"

"Yes."

Harker started to leave, but paused, with his hand on the door latch. The habit of his profession was strong in him—stronger than his sense of personal dignity. He turned about and said: "The book that you have there—I recognize it as Morgan's diary. You seemed greatly interested in it; you read in it while I was testifying. May I see it? The public would like—"

"The book will cut no figure in this matter," replied the official, slipping it into his coat pocket; "all the entries in it were made before the writer's death."

As Harker passed out of the house the jury reentered and stood about the table, on which the now covered corpse showed under the sheet with sharp definition. The foreman seated himself near the candle, produced from his breast pocket a pencil and scrap of paper and wrote rather laboriously the following verdict, which with various degrees of effort all signed:

"We, the jury, do find that the remains come to their death at the hands of a mountain lion, but some of us thinks, all the same, they had fits."

IN THE DIARY of the late Hugh Morgan are certain interesting entries having, possibly, a scientific value as suggestions. At the inquest upon his body the book was not put in evidence; possibly the coroner thought it not worthwhile to confuse the jury. The date of the first of the entries mentioned cannot be ascertained; the upper part of the leaf is torn away; the part of the entry remaining follows:

". . . would run in a half circle, keeping his head turned always toward the center, and again he would stand still, barking furiously. At last he ran away into the brush as fast as he could go. I thought at first that he had gone mad, but on returning to the house found no other alteration in his manner than what was obviously due to fear of punishment.

"Can a dog see with his nose? Do odors impress some cerebral center with images of the thing that emitted them? . . .

"Sept. 2—Looking at the stars last night as they rose above the crest of the ridge east of the house, I observed them successively disappear—

from left to right. Each was eclipsed but an instant, and only a few at the same time, but along the entire length of the ridge all that were within a degree or two of the crest were blotted out. It was as if something had passed along between me and them; but I could not see it, and the stars were not thick enough to define its outline. Ugh! I don't like this."

Several weeks' entries are missing, three leaves being torn from the book.

"Sept. 27—It has been about here again—I find evidences of its presence every day. I watched again all last night in the same cover, gun in hand, double-charged with buckshot. In the morning the fresh footprints were there, as before. Yet I would have sworn that I did not sleep—indeed, I hardly sleep at all. It is terrible, insupportable! If these amazing experiences are real I shall go mad; if they are fanciful I am mad already.

"Oct. 3—I shall not go—it shall not drive me away. No, this is *my* house, *my* land. God hates a coward. . . .

"Oct. 5—I can stand it no longer; I have invited Harker to pass a few weeks with me—he has a level head. I can judge from his manner if he thinks me mad.

"Oct. 7—I have the solution of the mystery; it came to me last night—suddenly, as by revelation. How simple—how terribly simple!

"There are sounds that we cannot hear. At either end of the scale are notes that stir no chord of that imperfect instrument, the human ear. They are too high or too grave. I have observed a flock of blackbirds occupying an entire treetop—the tops of several trees—and all in full song. Suddenly—in a moment—at absolutely the same instant—all spring into the air and fly away. How? They could not all see one another—whole treetops intervened. At no point could a leader have been visible to all. There must have been a signal of warning or command, high and shrill above the din, but by me unheard. I have observed, too, the same simultaneous flight when all were silent, among not only blackbirds, but other birds—quail, for example, widely separated by bushes—even on opposite sides of a hill.

"It is known to seamen that a school of whales basking on the surface of the ocean, miles apart, with the convexity of the earth between, will sometimes dive at the same instant—all gone out of sight in a moment. The signal has been sounded—too grave for the ear of the sailor at the masthead and his comrades on the deck—who nevertheless feel its vibrations in the ship as the stones of a cathedral are stirred by the bass of the organ.

"As with sounds, so with colors. At each end of the solar spectrum the chemist can detect the presence of rays which we are unable to discern. The human eye is an imperfect instrument; its range is but a few octaves of the real chromatic scale. I am not mad; there are colors that we cannot see.

"And, God help me! The Damned Thing is of such a color!"

DON'T LOOK NOW

DAPHNE DU MAURIER

"DON'T LOOK NOW," John said to his wife, "but there are a couple of old girls two tables away who are trying to hypnotize me. They're right behind you."

Laura dropped her napkin, then bent to scrabble for it under her feet, shooting a glance over her left shoulder as she straightened once again. "They're not old girls at all," she said. "They're male twins in women's clothes."

Her voice broke, the prelude to uncontrolled laughter, and John poured some Chianti into her glass. "Pretend to choke," he said, "then they won't notice. You know who they are—they're criminals doing the sights of Europe, changing disguise at each stop. Twin sisters here on Torcello. Twin brothers tomorrow in Venice. Just a matter of switching clothes and wigs."

"Jewel thieves or murderers?" asked Laura.

"Oh, murderers, definitely. But why, I ask myself, have they picked on me?"

The waiter made a diversion by bringing coffee and bearing away the fruit.

"Oh, God," said John, "the one with the shock of white hair has got her eye on me again."

Laura took the compact from her bag and held it in front of her face, the mirror acting as a reflector. "I think it's me they're looking at, not you," she said. She dabbed the sides of her nose with powder. "The thing is, we've got them wrong. They're a couple of retired schoolmistresses on holiday, who've saved up all their lives to visit Venice. And they're called Tilly and Tiny."

Her voice, for the first time since they had come away, took on the old bubbling quality he loved. At last, he thought, at last she's beginning to get over it. If I can keep this going, if we can pick up the familiar routine of jokes shared, ridiculous fantasies about people at other tables, or wandering in art galleries and churches, then life will become as it was before.

"You know," said Laura, "that really was a very good lunch."

Thank God, he thought, thank God. . . . Then he leaned forward, speaking in a whisper. "One of them is going to the ladies' room," he said. "Do you suppose she is going to change her wig?"

"I'll follow her," Laura murmured, "and find out."

"She's about to pass our table now," John said.

Seen on her own, the woman was not so remarkable. She was tall, angular, and had aquiline features and close-cropped hair. She would be in her middle sixties, he supposed, noting the masculine shirt with collar and tie, sport jacket, gray tweed skirt. He had seen the type on golf courses and at dog shows. But the striking point about this particular individual was that there were two of them, identical twins.

Laura squared her shoulders and rose to her feet. "I simply must not laugh," she said. "Whatever you do, don't look at me when I come back." She picked up her bag and strolled self-consciously in pursuit of her prey.

The sun blazed down upon the little garden of the restaurant. The other diners had left, and all was peace. The identical twin was sitting back in her chair with her eyes closed. Thank heaven, he thought, for this moment. The holiday could yet turn into the cure Laura needed, blotting out, if only temporarily, the numb despair that had seized her since their child had died.

"She'll get over it," the doctor said. "They all get over it, in time. And you have the boy."

"I know," John had said, "but the girl meant everything. A boy of school age is someone in his own right. Not a baby of five. Laura literally adored her."

"Give her time," repeated the doctor. "You're both young still. There'll be others."

So easy to talk . . . How replace the life of a loved lost child?

He looked up over his coffee, and the woman was staring at him again, her prominent, light blue eyes oddly penetrating, giving him a sudden feeling of discomfort. Damn her! All right, stare, if you must. Two can play at that game. He smiled at her, he hoped offensively. She did not register. The blue eyes continued to hold his, so that he was obliged to look away himself, glance over his shoulder for the waiter and call for the bill. Settling for this brought composure, but a prickly feeling on his scalp remained, and an odd sensation of unease.

There was a crunch of feet on the gravel. Laura's twin walked slowly past, alone. She went to her table and stood there a moment. She was saying something, but he couldn't catch the words. What was the accent, though—Scottish? Then she bent, offering an arm to the seated twin, and they moved away together across the garden. The twin who had stared at John was not quite so tall, and she stooped more—perhaps she was arthritic. John, becoming impatient, got up and was about to look for Laura when she returned.

"Well, I must say, you took your time," he began, and then stopped, because of the expression on her face.

"What's the matter, what's happened?" he asked.

She blundered toward the table and sat down, almost as if she were in a state of shock. He drew up his chair beside her, taking her hand. "Darling, what is it? Tell me. . . ."

She turned and looked at him. The dazed expression had given way to one of dawning confidence, almost of exaltation. "It's quite wonderful," she said slowly, "the most wonderful thing that could possibly be. You see, she isn't dead, she's still with us. That's why they kept staring at us, those two sisters. They could see Christine."

Oh, God, he thought. It's what I've been dreading. She's going off her head. "Laura, sweet," he began, forcing a smile, "look, shall we go? I've paid the bill; we can go and look at the cathedral and stroll around, and then it will be time to take off in that launch again for Venice."

She wasn't listening.

"John, love," she said, "I've got to tell you what happened. I followed her, as we planned, into the ladies' room. She was combing her hair and I went into the toilet, and then came out and washed my hands in the basin. Suddenly she turned and said to me, in a strong Scottish accent, 'Don't be unhappy anymore. My sister has seen your little girl. She was sitting between you and your husband, laughing.' Darling, I thought I was going to faint. Luckily there was a chair, and I sat down, and the woman bent over me and patted my head. I'm not sure of her exact words, but she said something about the moment of truth and joy being sharp as a sword, and not to be afraid, all was well, but the sister's vision had been so strong they knew I had to be told. Oh, John, don't look like that. I swear I'm not making it up; this is what she told me, it's all true."

The urgency in her voice made his heart sicken. He had to play along with her, agree, soothe, do anything to bring back some sense of calm. "Laura, darling, of course I believe you," he said, "only I'm upset because you're upset—"

"But I'm not upset," she interrupted. "I'm happy. You know what it's been like all these weeks. Now it's lifted, because I know that the woman was right. Oh, Lord, how awful of me, but I've forgotten their name—she did tell me. You see, the thing is that she's a retired doctor, they come from Edinburgh, and the one who saw Christine went blind a few years ago. Although she's studied the occult all her life, it's only since going blind that she has really seen things, like a medium. They've had the most wonderful experiences. But to describe Christine even down to the little blue-and-white dress that she wore at her birthday party, and to say she was smiling happily . . . Oh, darling, it's made me so happy I think I'm going to cry."

She took a tissue from her bag and blew her nose, smiling at him. "I'm all right, you see, you don't have to worry. Give me a cigarette."

He took one from his packet and lighted it for her. If this sudden belief was going to keep her happy, he couldn't possibly begrudge it. But . . . but . . . he wished, all the same, it hadn't happened. There was something uncanny about thought reading, about telepathy, and this is what must have happened just now. And the one who had been staring at him was blind. That accounted for the fixed gaze. Which somehow was unpleasant in itself, creepy.

"You didn't arrange to meet them again or anything, did you?" he asked, trying to sound casual.

"No, darling, why should I?" Laura answered. "I mean, there was nothing more they could tell me. The sister had had her wonderful vision, and that was that. Anyway, they're moving on. They're going round the world before returning to Scotland."

She stood up and looked about her. "Come on," she said. "Having come to Torcello, we must see the cathedral."

They made their way from the restaurant across the open piazza, where stalls had been set up with scarves and trinkets, and along the path to the cathedral. One of the ferryboats had just decanted a crowd of sightseers, many of whom had already found their way into Santa Maria Assunta. Laura, undaunted, asked her husband for the guide-book, and started to walk slowly through the cathedral, studying mosaics, columns, panels, while John followed close behind, keeping a weather eye alert for the twin sisters. He could not concentrate, the cold clear beauty of what he saw left him unmoved, and when Laura touched his sleeve, pointing to the mosaic of the Virgin and Child, he nodded in sympathy yet saw nothing. The long, sad face of the Virgin seemed infinitely remote. Turning on sudden impulse, he stared back over the heads of the tourists toward the door.

The twins were standing there, the blind one with her sightless eyes fixed firmly upon him. He felt himself held, unable to move, and an impending sense of doom, of tragedy, came upon him. Then both sisters turned and went out of the cathedral and the sensation vanished, leaving indignation in its wake, and rising anger. How dare those two old fools practice their tricks on him? It was fraudulent, unhealthy; this was probably the way they lived, touring the world, making everyone they met uncomfortable.

Laura touched his sleeve again. "Isn't she beautiful?"

"Who? What?" he asked.

"The Madonna," she answered. "She has a magic quality. It goes right through to one. Don't you feel it too?"

"I suppose so. I don't know. There are too many people around."

She looked up at him, astonished. "What's that got to do with it? Well, all right, let's get away from them." Disappointed, she began to thread her way through the crowd to the door.

"Come on," he said abruptly, once they were outside, "let's explore a bit," and he struck off from the path, which would have taken them back to the center, to a narrow way among uncultivated ground, beyond which he could see a canal.

"I don't think this leads anywhere much," said Laura. "It's a bit muddy too. Besides, there are more things the guidebook says we ought to see."

"Oh, forget the book," he said impatiently, and pulling her down beside him on the bank above the canal, he put his arms around her.

"Do you think Christine is sitting here beside us?" Laura said suddenly.

He did not answer at once. What was there to say? Would it be like this forever?

"I expect so," he said slowly, "if you feel she is."

The point was, remembering Christine before the onset of the fatal meningitis, she would have been running along the bank, throwing off her shoes, wanting to paddle, giving Laura a fit of apprehension.

"The woman said she was looking so happy, sitting beside us, smiling," said Laura. She got up, brushing her dress. "Come on, let's go back."

He followed her with a sinking heart. He knew she did not really want to see what remained to be seen; she wanted to go in search of the women again. When they came to the piazza he noticed that there were only a few stragglers left, and the sisters were not among them. They must have joined the tourists who had come to Torcello by the ferryboat. A wave of relief seized him.

"Look, there's a mass of scarves at the second stall," he said quickly. "Let me buy you one."

"Darling, I've so many!" she protested.

"I'm in a buying mood. What about a basket? Or some lace?"

She allowed herself, laughing, to be dragged to the stall. While he rumpled through the goods spread out before them, he knew it would give the tourists time to catch the ferryboat, and the twin sisters would be out of sight and out of their life.

"Never," said Laura, some twenty minutes later, "has so much junk been piled into so small a basket," her bubbling laugh reassuring him that all was well. The launch that had brought them from Venice was waiting by the boat landing. The passengers who had arrived with them were already assembled. They stepped down into the launch, and the boat chugged away down the canal and into the lagoon.

He put his arm around Laura once more, and this time she responded, smiling up at him. "It's been a lovely day," she said. "I shall never forget it. You know, darling, now at last I can begin to enjoy our holiday."

He wanted to shout with relief. It's going to be all right, he decided, let her believe what she likes. The beauty of Venice rose before them, sharply outlined against the glowing sky, and there was still so much to see that might now be perfect because of her change of mood. Aloud he began to discuss the evening to come, where they would dine.

Their hotel by the Grand Canal had a welcoming, comforting air. The bedroom was familiar, but with it the little festive atmosphere of strangeness, of excitement, that only a holiday bedroom brings. This is ours for the moment. While we are in it we bring it life. When we have gone it no longer exists. Now, he thought, now at last is the moment to make love, and she understood, and opened her arms and smiled. Such blessed relief after all those weeks of restraint.

"The thing is," she said later, fixing her earrings before the looking glass, "I'm not really terribly hungry. Shall we just be dull and eat in the dining room here?"

"God, no!" he exclaimed. "With all those rather dreary couples at the other tables? Let's find some small, dark, intimate cave full of lovers with other people's wives."

"Hm," sniffed Laura. "You'll spot some Italian lovely of sixteen and smirk at her all through dinner."

They went out laughing into the warm soft night. "Let's walk," he said, and inevitably they found themselves by the Molo and the gondolas dancing upon the water. There were other couples strolling for the same sake of aimless enjoyment, and the inevitable sailors in groups, noisy, gesticulating, and dark-eyed girls whispering, clicking on high heels.

"The trouble is," said Laura, "walking in Venice becomes compulsive. Just over the next bridge, you say, and then the next one beckons. I'm sure there are no restaurants down here. Let's turn back. I know there's a place somewhere near the Church of San Zaccaria."

"If we go down here by the Arsenal," said John, "and cross that bridge at the end and head left, we'll come upon San Zaccaria from the other side. We did it the other morning."

"Yes, but it was daylight then. We may lose our way; it's not very well lit."

"Don't fuss. I have an instinct for these things."

They crossed the little bridge short of the Arsenal, and so on past the Church of San Martino. There were two canals ahead, one bearing right, the other left, with narrow streets beside them. John hesitated. Which one was it they had walked beside the day before?

"You see," protested Laura, "we shall be lost."

"Nonsense," replied John firmly. "It's the left-hand one."

The canal was narrow, and the houses on either side seemed to close in upon it. In the daytime, with the sun's reflection on the water, there had been an impression of warmth. Now, almost in darkness, the windows of the houses shuttered, the scene appeared altogether different, neglected, poor, and the long, narrow boats moored to the slippery steps looked like coffins.

"I swear I don't remember this bridge," said Laura, pausing, "and I don't like the look of that alleyway beyond."

"There's a lamp halfway up," John told her. "I know exactly where we are, not far from the Greek quarter."

They crossed the bridge, and were about to plunge into the alleyway when they heard the cry. It came, surely, from one of the shuttered houses on the opposite side.

"What was it?" whispered Laura.

"Some drunk or other," said John briefly. "Come on."

Less like a drunk than someone being strangled, and the choking cry suppressed as the strangler's grip held firm.

"We ought to call the police," said Laura.

"Oh, for heaven's sake," said John.

"Well, it's sinister," she replied, and began to hurry up the twisting alleyway. John hesitated, his eye caught by a small figure which suddenly crept from a cellar entrance in one of the opposite houses, and then jumped into a narrow boat below. It was a child, a little girl, wearing a short coat over her minute skirt, a pixie hood covering her head. There were four boats moored side by side, and she proceeded to jump from one to the other with surprising agility, intent, it would seem, upon escape. Bending, she tugged at the rope of the farthest boat, swinging its afterend across the canal, almost touching another cellar entrance. Then she jumped again, landing upon the cellar steps, and vanished into the house. Now he heard the quick patter of feet. Laura had returned. She had seen none of it.

"What are you doing?" she called. "I daren't go on without you."

"Sorry," he told her. "I'm coming."

He took her arm and they walked briskly along the alley. It led to a deserted *campo* behind a church, and he led the way across, along another street and over a farther bridge.

The place was like a maze. They might circle around and around forever. Doggedly he led her on, and then with relief he saw people walking in the lighted street ahead; there was a spire of a church, and the surroundings became familiar.

"There, I told you," he said. "That's San Zaccaria. Your restaurant can't be far away."

At least here was the cheering glitter of lights, of movement. The letters RISTORANTE, in blue lights, shone like a beacon down a left-hand alley.

And so they went into the sudden blast of heated air and hum of voices, waiters, jostling customers, laughter. "For two? This way, please," in English. Why, he thought, was one's British nationality always so obvious? They sat down at a cramped little table with an enormous menu, and the waiter hovering.

"Two very large Camparis with soda," John said. "*Then* we'll study the menu."

He handed the bill of fare to Laura and looked about him. Mostly Italians—that meant the food would be good. Then he saw them. At the opposite side of the room. The twin sisters. They were just sitting down, shedding their coats. John was seized with the irrational thought that this was no coincidence. Why, in the name of hell, should they have picked on this particular spot, in the whole of Venice, unless . . . unless Laura herself had suggested a further encounter? It was she, before the walk, who had mentioned San Zaccaria. . . .

She was intent upon the menu, but any moment now she would raise her head and look across the room.

"You know, I was thinking," he said quickly, "we really ought to get the car tomorrow, and do that drive to Padua. We could lunch there, see the cathedral and look at the Giotto frescoes, and come back by way of those various villas along the Brenta."

It was no use, though. She was looking across the restaurant, and she gave a little gasp of surprise. He could have sworn it was genuine.

"Look," she said, "how extraordinary! There they are. My wonderful old twins. They've seen us." She waved her hand, radiant, delighted. The sister she had spoken to at Torcello bowed and smiled.

"Oh, darling, I must go and speak to them," she said, "just to tell them how happy I've been all day, thanks to them."

"Oh, for heaven's sake!" he said. "We haven't ordered yet. Surely you can wait."

"I won't be a moment. And I want scampi. Nothing first."

She got up and, brushing past the waiter with the drinks, crossed the room. He watched her bend over the table and shake them both by the hand, and because there was a vacant chair at their table, she drew it up and sat down, talking, smiling.

All right, thought John savagely, then I'm going to get sloshed, and he proceeded to down his Campari and soda and order another, while he pointed out something on the menu as his own choice. "Scampi for the signora. And a bottle of Soave," he added, "with ice."

The evening was ruined. What was to have been an intimate, happy celebration would now be heavy-laden with spiritualistic visions. The bitter taste of the Campari suited his mood of sudden self-pity, and all the while he watched Laura, apparently listening while the more active sister held forth and the blind one sat silent, her sightless eyes turned in his direction.

She's phony, he thought. She's not blind at all. They're both of them frauds, and they're after Laura.

He began on his second Campari and soda. The two drinks, taken on an empty stomach, had an instant effect. The waiter appeared with the scampi and John's own order, which was totally unrecognizable, heaped with a livid sauce.

John pointed across the room. "Tell the signora," he said carefully, "her scampi will get cold."

He stared down at the offering placed before him and forked a portion to his mouth. It was pork, steamy, rich, the spicy sauce having turned it curiously sweet. He pushed the plate away, and became aware of Laura, returning across the room and sitting beside him. She said nothing, and began to eat her scampi. The waiter, hovering at his elbow, seemed aware that John's choice was somehow an error and discreetly removed the plate. Laura did not register surprise. Finally, when she had finished her scampi and was sipping her wine, she began to speak.

"Darling," she said, "I know you won't believe it, and it's rather frightening in a way, but after they left the restaurant in Torcello, the sisters went to the cathedral, as we did, and the blind one had another vision. She said Christine was trying to tell her something about us, that we should be in danger if we stayed in Venice. Christine wanted us to go away as soon as possible."

So that's it, he thought. They think they can run our lives for us. Do we eat? Do we get up? Do we go to bed? Henceforth we must get in touch with the twin sisters.

"Well?" she said. "Why don't you say something?"

"Because," he answered, "quite frankly, I judge your old sisters as being a couple of freaks. They're obviously unbalanced, and they've found a sucker in you."

"You're being unfair," said Laura. "They are genuine, I know it. They were completely sincere in what they said."

"All right. They're sincere. But that doesn't make them well balanced. Honestly, darling, anyone with a gift for telepathy could read your unconscious mind in an instant—and then, pleased at her success with her vision of Christine, she flings a further mood of ecstasy and wants to boot us out of Venice. Well, I'm sorry, but to hell with it."

"I knew you would take it like this," said Laura unhappily. "I told them you would. They said not to worry. As long as we left Venice tomorrow, everything would come out all right."

"Oh, for God's sake," said John. He poured himself a glass of wine.

"After all," Laura went on, "we have really seen the cream of Venice. And if we stayed—I know it sounds silly, but I should keep thinking of Christine being unhappy and trying to tell us to go."

"Right," said John with ominous calm, "that settles it. Go we will."

"Oh, dear," sighed Laura, "don't take it like that. Look, why not come over and meet them? Perhaps you would take them seriously then. Especially as you are the one it most concerns. Christine is more worried over you than me. And the extraordinary thing is that the blind sister says you're psychic and don't know it. You are somehow *en rapport* with the unknown, and I'm not."

"Well, that's final," said John. "I'm psychic, am I? Fine. My psychic intuition tells me to get out of this restaurant at once, and we can decide what we do about leaving Venice when we are back at the hotel."

He signaled to the waiter for the bill and they waited for it, not speaking to each other. John glanced furtively at the twins' table and noticed that they were tucking into plates piled high with spaghetti, in very unpsychic fashion. The bill disposed of, John pushed back his chair. "Are you ready?" he asked.

"I'm going to say good-by to them first," said Laura, her mouth set sulkily, reminding him instantly of their poor lost child.

"Just as you like," he replied, and walked ahead of her out of the restaurant.

The soft humidity of the evening had turned to rain. The strolling tourists had melted away. One or two people hurried by under umbrellas. This is what the inhabitants who live here see, he thought. Empty streets by night, and the dank stillness of stagnant canals beneath shuttered houses.

Laura joined him and they walked in silence to the Piazza San Marco. The rain was heavy now, and they sought shelter under the colonnades. The orchestras had packed up for the evening. The café tables were bare. The experts are right, he thought. Venice is sinking. The whole city is slowly dying. One day the tourists will travel here to peer down into the waters, and they will see pillars and columns and marble far, far beneath them, a lost underworld of stone.

When they came to their hotel, Laura made straight for the elevator while John asked the night porter for the key. The man handed him a telegram at the same time. It was from the headmaster of Johnnie's preparatory school.

JOHNNIE UNDER OBSERVATION SUSPECTED APPENDICITIS IN CITY HOSPITAL HERE. NO CAUSE FOR ALARM BUT SURGEON THOUGHT WISE ADVISE YOU. CHARLES HILL.

He read the message twice, then walked slowly toward the elevator, where Laura was waiting for him. He gave her the telegram. "This came when we were out," he said. "Not awfully good news." She read the telegram as the elevator ascended to the second floor.

"Well, this decides it," she said. "We have to leave Venice because we're going home. It's Johnnie who's in danger, not us. This is what Christine was trying to tell the twins."

THE FIRST THING John did the following morning was to put a call through to the headmaster at Johnnie's school. They packed while they waited for the call. John knew the arrival of the telegram and the foreboding of danger from the sisters was coincidence, nothing more, but it was pointless to start an argument about it. Intuitively Laura realized it was best to keep her feelings to herself. During breakfast they discussed ways and means of getting home. It should be possible to get themselves and the car onto the special car train that ran from Milan through to the English Channel, since it was early in the season.

The call from England came while John was in the bathroom. Laura answered it. He came into the bedroom a few minutes later. She was still speaking, but he could tell from the expression in her eyes that she was anxious.

"It's Mrs. Hill," she told him. "Mr. Hill is in class. She says they reported from the hospital that Johnnie had a restless night and the surgeon may have to operate, but he doesn't want to unless it's absolutely necessary. They've taken X rays and the appendix is in a tricky position."

"Here, give it to me," John said.

The voice of the headmaster's wife came down the receiver. "I'm so sorry this may spoil your plans," she said, "but both Charles and I felt you might feel rather easier if you were on the spot. The surgeon's going to decide about operating this evening. Please do tell your wife not to worry too much. The hospital is excellent, and we have every confidence in the surgeon."

"Yes," said John, "yes—" and then broke off because Laura was making gestures beside him.

"If we can't get the car on the train, I can fly," she said. "Then at least one of us would be there this evening."

He nodded agreement. "Thank you so much, Mrs. Hill," he said. "We'll manage to get back all right. I'm sure Johnnie is in good hands. Good-by."

He replaced the receiver and looked around him at the tumbled beds, suitcases on the floor, tissue paper strewn. Maps, books, coats, everything they had brought with them in the car.

"Oh, God," he said, "all this junk." The telephone rang again. It was the hall porter to say he had succeeded in booking a sleeper for them both, and a place for the car, on the following night.

"Look," said Laura, who had seized the telephone, "could you book one seat on the midday plane from Venice to London today, for me? It's imperative one of us gets home this evening—"

"Here, hang on," interrupted John. "No need to panic. Surely twenty-four hours wouldn't make all that difference?"

She turned to him, distraught. "It mightn't to you, but it does to me," she said. "I've lost one child. I'm not going to lose another."

"All right, darling, all right. . . ."

Laura continued giving directions to the porter. He turned back to his packing. No use saying anything. Better for it to be as she wished. They could, of course, both go by air, and then when Johnnie was better, he could come back and fetch the car, driving home through France as they had come.

"We could, if you like, both fly," he began tentatively after she had hung up. But she would have none of it.

"That really *would* be absurd," she said impatiently. "As long as I'm there this evening, and you follow by train, it's all that matters. Besides, we shall need the car, going backward and forward to the hospital. And we couldn't just go off and leave our luggage here."

He saw her point. It was only—well, he was as worried about Johnnie as she was.

"I'm going downstairs to stand over the porter," said Laura. "They always make more effort if one is actually on the spot. I'll just take my overnight case. You can bring everything else in the car." She hadn't been out of the bedroom five minutes before the telephone rang. It was Laura. "Darling," she said, "the porter has got me on a charter flight that leaves in less than an hour. A motor launch takes the party direct from San Marco in about ten minutes."

"I'll be down right away," he told her.

At the reception desk, she no longer looked anxious, but full of purpose. She was on her way. He kept wishing they were going together. The thought of driving to Milan and spending a dreary night there alone filled him with intolerable depression. They walked along to the San Marco boat landing, the Molo bright and glittering after the rain, a little breeze blowing.

"I'll ring you from Milan," he told her. "The Hills will give you a bed, I suppose. And if you're at the hospital, they'll tell me the latest news. That must be your charter party."

The passengers descending into the waiting launch were mostly middle-aged, with what appeared to be two Methodist ministers in charge. One of them advanced toward Laura, showing a gleaming row of dentures when he smiled. "You must be the lady joining us for the homeward flight," he said. "Welcome aboard, and to the Union of Fellowship. We are all delighted to make your acquaintance."

Laura turned swiftly and kissed John. "Do you think they'll break into hymns?" she whispered.

The pilot sounded a curious little toot upon his horn, and in a moment Laura had climbed down into the launch and was standing among the crowd of passengers, her scarlet coat a gay patch of color next to the more sober suiting of her companions. The launch moved away from the landing, and he stood there watching it, a sense of immense loss filling his heart. Then he turned and walked back to the hotel, the bright day all about him desolate, unseen.

There was nothing, he thought, as he looked about his hotel bedroom, so melancholy as a vacated room, especially when the recent signs of occupation were still visible: Laura's suitcases on the bed, a second coat she had left behind, traces of powder on the dressing table. He finished packing and went downstairs to pay the bill.

He decided to have an early lunch on the hotel terrace overlooking the Grand Canal and then have the porter carry the baggage to one of the ferries that steamed direct between San Marco and the Piazzale Roma, where the car was garaged. The fiasco meal of the night before had left him empty, and he was ready for the trolley of hors d'oeuvres when they brought it to him, around midday.

Lunch over, his desire was to get away as soon as possible, to be en route to Milan. He made his farewells at the reception desk and, escorted by a porter with a wheeled trolley, made his way once more to the boat landing at San Marco. When he was on the ferry, his luggage heaped beside him, he had one momentary pang to be leaving Venice. When, if ever, he wondered, would they come again?

The water glittered in the sunshine, buildings shone, tourists in dark glasses paraded up and down as the ferry churned its way up the Grand Canal. So many impressions to seize and hold, familiar façades, balconies, water lapping the cellar steps of decaying palaces—and soon the ferry would be turning left on the direct route to the Piazzale Roma.

Another ferry, filled with passengers, was heading downstream to pass them, and for a brief foolish moment he wished he could change places, be among the happy tourists bound for Venice. Then he saw her. Laura, in her scarlet coat, the twin sisters by her side, the active sister with her hand on Laura's arm, talking earnestly, and Laura herself gesticulating, on her face a look of distress. He stared, too astonished to shout, and anyway they would never have heard him, for his own ferry had already passed in the opposite direction.

What the hell had happened? There must have been a holdup with the charter flight, but in that case why had Laura not telephoned him at the hotel? And what were those damned sisters doing with her? Had she run into them at the airport? And why did she look so anxious? He could think of no explanation.

Laura, of course, would go straight to the hotel, intending, doubtless, to drive with him after all to Milan. What a blasted mix-up. The only thing to do was to telephone the hotel immediately when his ferry reached the Piazzale Roma and tell her to wait—he would return and fetch her.

When the ferry arrived at the landing, he had to find a porter to collect his baggage, and then he had to locate a telephone. He succeeded at last in getting through, and luckily the reception clerk he knew was still at the desk.

"Look, there's been some frightful muddle," he began, and explained how Laura was even now on her way back to the hotel. Would the reception clerk tell her to wait? He would be back by the next available service to collect her. The reception clerk understood perfectly, and John rang off.

It seemed simplest to walk with the porter to the garage, hand the baggage over to the chap in charge until he returned in an hour to pick up the car. Then he went back to the boat landing to await the next ferry to Venice. The minutes dragged, and he kept wondering all the time what had gone wrong at the airport and why in heaven's name Laura hadn't telephoned. One thing was certain: he would not allow himself to be saddled with the sisters. He could imagine Laura saying that they also had missed the flight, and could they have a lift to Milan?

Finally the ferry chugged alongside the landing and he stepped aboard. He didn't even look about him at the familiar sights, he was so intent on reaching his destination.

He came to the hotel, expecting to see Laura waiting in the lounge to the left of the entrance. She was not there. He went to the desk. The reception clerk was standing there, talking to the manager.

"Has my wife arrived?" John asked.

"No, sir, not yet."

"What an extraordinary thing. Are you sure?"

"Absolutely certain, sir. I have been here at the desk ever since you telephoned me."

"I just don't understand it. She was on one of the *vaporetti* passing by the Accademia. She would have landed at San Marco about five minutes later and come on here."

The clerk seemed nonplussed. "I don't know what to say. The signora was with friends, did you say?"

"Yes. Two ladies we had met at Torcello yesterday. I assumed that the flight had been canceled, and she had somehow met up with them at the airport and decided to return here with them, to catch me before I left."

"Perhaps the signora went with her friends to their hotel instead. Do you know where they are staying?"

"No," said John. "What's more, I don't even know the names of the two ladies."

The manager broke into the conversation. "I tell you what I will do," he said. "I will telephone the airport and check about the flight. Then at least we will get somewhere."

"Yes, do that," said John. He began to pace up and down the entrance hall. What a bloody mix-up! And how unlike Laura, who surely would have telephoned at once, on arrival at the airport, had the flight been canceled. The manager was ages telephoning, and his Italian was too rapid for John to follow the conversation. Finally he replaced the receiver.

"It is more mysterious than ever, sir," he said. "The charter flight was not delayed, it took off on schedule with a full complement of passengers. The signora must simply have changed her mind." His smile was more apologetic than ever.

"Changed her mind," John repeated. "But why on earth should she do that? She was so anxious to be home tonight."

The manager shrugged. "You know how ladies can be, sir," he said. "Your wife may have thought that after all she would prefer to take the train to Milan with you."

"Is it possible," the reception clerk ventured, "that you made a mistake, and it was not the signora that you saw on the *vaporetto?*"

"Oh, no," replied John, "it was my wife, I assure you. She was wearing her red coat, she was hatless, just as she left here. I saw her as plainly as I can see you."

"It is unfortunate," said the manager, "that we do not know the names of the two ladies, or the hotel where they were staying. You say you met these ladies at Torcello yesterday?"

"Yes . . . but only briefly. I am certain they were not staying there. We saw them at dinner in Venice later."

"Excuse me. . . ." Guests were arriving; the clerk was obliged to attend to them.

John turned in desperation to the manager. "Do you think it would be any good telephoning the hotel in Torcello in case the people there know the names of the ladies?"

"We can try," replied the manager. "It is a small hope, but we can try."

"Tell them twin sisters," said John. "Two elderly ladies dressed in gray, both exactly alike. One lady was blind," he added.

The manager nodded. There followed what seemed an interminable telephone conversation. Yet when the manager hung up he shook his head. "At the hotel in Torcello, the maître remembers the two ladies well," he told John, "but they were only there for lunch. He never learned their names."

"Well, that's that. There's nothing to do now but wait."

John went out onto the terrace, to resume his pacing there. He stared across the canal, searching among the people on passing steamers, motorboats, even drifting gondolas. There was no sign of Laura. A terrible foreboding nagged at him that Laura had never intended to catch the aircraft, that last night in the restaurant she had made an assignation with the sisters. Oh, God, he thought, that's impossible, I'm going paranoiac. . . . More likely the encounter at the airport was fortuitous, and they had persuaded Laura not to board the aircraft, trotting out one of their psychic visions, that the aircraft would crash, that she must return with them to Venice. And Laura, in her sensitive state, swallowed it all without question.

But granted all these possibilities, why had she not come back to the hotel? What was she doing? Four o'clock, half past four; the sun no longer dappled the water. He went back to the reception desk.

"I just can't hang around," he said. "Even if she does turn up, we shall never make Milan this evening. I might see her walking with these ladies, in the Piazza San Marco, anywhere. If she arrives while I'm out, will you explain?"

"Indeed, yes," the clerk said. "Would it perhaps be prudent, sir, if we booked you in here tonight?"

John gestured helplessly. "Perhaps, yes . . ."

He went out the swing door and began to walk toward the Piazza San Marco. He looked into every shop up and down the colonnades, crossed the piazza a dozen times. He joined the crowd of shoppers in the Merceria, shoulder to shoulder with window gazers, knowing instinctively that it was useless. They wouldn't be here. Why should Laura have deliberately missed her flight to return to Venice for such a purpose?

The only thing left to him was to try to track down the sisters. Their hotel could be any one of the hundreds scattered through Venice. More likely they were staying in a *pensione* somewhere near San Zaccaria, handy to the restaurant where they had dined last night. The blind one would surely not go far afield in the evening. He had been a fool not to have thought of this before, and he turned back and walked quickly toward the narrow, cramped quarter where they had dined last evening. He found the restaurant without difficulty, but the waiter preparing tables for dinner was not the one who had served them. John asked to see the padrone.

"My wife and I had dinner here last night," he explained to the somewhat disheveled-looking proprietor. "There were two ladies sitting at that table there in the corner." He pointed to it. "Do you remember? Two ladies, *sorelle vecchie* . . ."

"Ah," said the man. "*Si, si,* signore. *La povera signorina.*" He put his hands to his eyes to feign blindness. "Yes, I remember."

"Do you know their names?" asked John. "Where they were staying? I am very anxious to trace them."

The proprietor spread out his hands in a gesture of regret. "I am ver' sorry, signore, I do not know the names of the signorinas; they have been here once, twice, perhaps, for dinner; they do not say where they were staying. Perhaps if you come again tonight, they might be here? Would you like to book a table?"

John shook his head. "Thank you, no. I am sorry to have troubled you. If the signorinas should come . . ." He paused. "Possibly I may return later. I am not sure."

"In Venice the whole world meets," the proprietor said, smiling. "It is possible the signore will find his friends tonight. *Arrivederci*, signore," he said, smiling.

Friends? John walked out into the street. More likely kidnappers. . . . Anxiety had turned to panic. Should he find the consulate? What would he say when he got there? He began walking without purpose, finding himself in streets he did not know, and suddenly came upon a tall building with the word QUESTURA above it. This is it, he thought. I'm going inside. Addressing himself to a policeman behind a glass partition, he asked if there was anyone who spoke English. The man pointed to a flight of stairs and John went up, entering a door to a room where he saw that a couple were sitting, waiting. With relief he recognized them as fellow countrymen, obviously man and wife.

"Come and sit down," said the man. "We've waited half an hour, but they can't be much longer."

John found a chair beside them.

"What's your trouble?" he asked.

"My wife had her handbag pinched in one of those shops in the Merceria," said the man. "She put it down one moment to look at something, and the next moment it had gone. She insists it was the girl behind the counter. But who's to say? I'm certain we shan't get it back. What have you lost?"

"Suitcase stolen," John lied rapidly. How could he say he had lost his wife? He couldn't even begin . . .

The man nodded in sympathy. "They're not going to bother with our troubles much, not with this murderer at large. They're all out looking for him."

"Murderer? What murderer?" asked John.

"Don't tell me you've not heard about it?" The man stared at him in surprise. "It's been in all the papers, on the radio. A grisly business. One woman found with her throat slit last week, and some old chap discovered with the same sort of knife wound this morning. They seem to think it must be a maniac, because there doesn't seem to be any motive. Nasty thing to happen in Venice in the tourist season."

The door of the inner room opened and a police officer asked the couple to pass through.

"I bet we don't get any satisfaction," murmured the husband, winking at John. The door closed behind them. John lighted a cigarette. He asked himself what he was doing here, what was the use of it? Laura was no longer in Venice but had disappeared, perhaps forever, with those diabolical sisters. She would never be traced. The women might even be the murderers whom the police sought. Who would ever suspect two elderly women living quietly in some second-rate hotel?

This, he thought, is really the start of paranoia. This is the way people go off their heads. He glanced at his watch. It was half past six. Better pack this in, this futile quest here in police headquarters, and keep to the single link of sanity remaining. Return to the hotel, put a call through to the school in England and ask about the latest news of Johnnie.

Too late, though. The inner door opened, the couple were ushered out.

"Usual claptrap," said the husband sotto voce to John. "They'll do what they can. Not much hope. So many foreigners in Venice, all of 'em thieves! Well, I wish you better luck."

John followed the police officer into the inner room. Formalities began. Name, address, length of stay in Venice, etc., etc. Then John, the sweat beginning to appear on his forehead, launched into his interminable story. When he had finished he felt as exhausted as after a severe bout of flu.

His interrogator spoke excellent English with a strong Italian accent. "You say," he began, "that your wife was suffering the aftereffects of shock. This had been noticeable during your stay here in Venice?"

"Well, yes," John replied, "she had really been quite ill. It was only when she met these two women at Torcello yesterday that her mood changed. This belief that our little girl was watching over her appeared to restore her to normality."

"It would be natural," said the police officer, "in the circumstances. But no doubt the telegram last night was a further shock to you both."

"Yes. That was the reason we decided to return home."

"No argument between you? No difference of opinion?"

"None. We were in complete agreement. My one regret was that I could not go with my wife on this charter flight."

The police officer nodded. "It could well be that your wife had a sudden attack of amnesia, and meeting the two ladies served as a link; she clung to them for support. You have described them with great accuracy, and they should not be too difficult to trace. I suggest you return to your hotel, and we will get in touch with you as soon as we have news."

At least, John thought, they believed his story. "You appreciate," he said, "that I am extremely anxious. These women may have some criminal design upon my wife. One has heard of such things. . . ."

The police officer smiled for the first time. "Please don't concern yourself," he said. "I am sure that there will be some satisfactory explanation."

"I'm sorry," John said, "to have taken up so much of your time. Especially as I gather the police have their hands full hunting down a murderer who is still at large." No harm in letting the fellow know that there might be some connection between Laura's disappearance and this other hideous affair.

"Ah, that," said the police officer, rising to his feet. "We hope to have the murderer under lock and key very soon."

His tone of confidence was reassuring. Murderers, missing wives, lost handbags were all under control. They shook hands, and John was ushered out the door and so downstairs. He could do nothing more. All he wanted to do right now was to collapse on a bed at the hotel with a stiff whiskey, and then put through a call to Johnnie's school.

The page took him up in the elevator to a modest room on the fourth floor at the rear of the hotel. "Ask them to send me up a double whiskey, will you?" John said to the boy. He flung off his shoes, hung his coat over the back of a chair and threw himself down on the bed. He reached for the telephone and asked the exchange to put through the call to England.

Presently there was a tap at the door. It was the waiter with his drink. He gulped it down, and in a few moments his anxiety was eased, numbed, the whiskey bringing, if only momentarily, a sense of calm. The telephone rang, and he braced himself for ultimate disaster, the final shock, Johnnie dying, or already dead. In which case nothing remained. Let Venice be engulfed. . . .

The exchange told him that the connection had been made, and in a moment he heard the voice of Mrs. Hill at the other end of the line. "Hullo?" she said. "Oh, I am so glad you rang. All is well. Johnnie has had his operation. The surgeon decided to do it at midday rather than wait, and it was completely successful. So you don't have to worry anymore."

"Thank God," he answered.

"I know," she said. "We are all so relieved. Now I'll get off the line and you can speak to your wife."

John sat up on the bed, stunned. What the hell did she mean? Then he heard Laura's voice, cool and clear.

"Darling? Darling, are you there?"

He felt the hand holding the receiver go clammy with sweat. "I'm here," he whispered.

"It's not a very good line," she said, "but never mind. As Mrs. Hill told you, all is well. I came straight down here after landing at Gatwick—the flight okay, by the way—and I went to the hospital, and Johnnie was coming round. Very dopey, of course, but so pleased to see me. And the Hills are being wonderful. I've got their spare room, and it's only a short taxi drive into the town and the hospital. How was the drive to Milan? And where are you staying?"

John did not recognize the voice that answered as his own. "I'm not in Milan," he said. "I'm still in Venice."

"Still in Venice? What on earth for?"

"I can't explain," he said. "There was a stupid sort of mix-up. . . ." He felt suddenly so exhausted that he nearly dropped the receiver, and, shame upon shame, he could feel tears pricking behind his eyes.

"A mix-up?" Her voice was suspicious. "You weren't in a crash?"

"No . . . no . . . nothing like that."

A moment's silence, and then she said, "Your voice sounds very slurred. Don't tell me you went and got sloshed."

Oh, God. . . . If she only knew!

"I thought," he said slowly, "I thought I saw you in a *vaporetto* with those two sisters."

"How could you have seen me with the sisters?" she said. "You knew I'd gone to the airport. Really, darling, you are an idiot. I hope you didn't say anything to Mrs. Hill just now."

"No."

"Well, what are you going to do? You'll catch the train at Milan tomorrow, won't you?"

"Yes, of course," he told her.

"I still don't understand what kept you in Venice," she said. "However . . . Thank God Johnnie is going to be all right and I'm here."

"Yes," he said, "yes." He could hear the distant sound of a gong from the headmaster's hall. "You had better go," he said. "My regards to the Hills, and my love to Johnnie."

"Well, take care of yourself, darling, and for goodness' sake, don't miss the train tomorrow."

The telephone clicked and she had gone. He got up and, crossing the room, threw open the shutters and leaned out the window. His sense of relief, enormous, overwhelming, was somehow tempered with a curious feeling of unreality, almost as though the voice speaking from England had not been Laura's after all but a fake, and she was still in Venice, hidden with the two sisters.

The point was, he *had* seen all three of them on the *vaporetto.* So what was the explanation? That he was going off his head? Or something more sinister? The sisters, possessing psychic powers of formidable strength, had seen him as their two ferries had passed, and in some inexplicable fashion had made him believe Laura was with them. But why, and to what end? It didn't make sense.

And what did he do now? Go downstairs and tell the management that his wife, after all, had arrived in England safe and sound from her charter flight? He glanced at his watch. It was ten minutes to eight. If he nipped into the bar and had a quick drink, it would be easier to face the manager. Then, perhaps, they would get in touch with the police. Profuse apologies all around for putting everyone to enormous trouble.

He made his way to the ground floor and went straight to the bar, feeling self-conscious, a marked man. Luckily the bar was full and there wasn't a face he knew. He downed his whiskey and glanced over his shoulder to the reception hall. The desk was momentarily empty. He could see the manager's back framed in the doorway of an inner room, talking to someone within. On impulse, cowardlike, he crossed the hall and passed through the swing door to the street outside.

I'll have some dinner, he decided, and then go back and face them. I'll feel more like it once I've some food inside me.

He went to the restaurant nearby where he and Laura had dined once or twice. She was safe. He could enjoy his dinner, and think of her sitting down with the Hills to a dull, quiet evening, early to bed, and on the following morning going to the hospital to sit with Johnnie. No more worries, only the awkward explanations and apologies to the manager at the hotel. He took his time, enjoying his food but eating in a kind of haze, a sense of unreality still with him.

He saw by the clock on the wall that it was nearly half past nine. No use delaying matters any further. He drank his coffee, lighted a cigarette and paid his bill. After all, he thought, as he walked back to the hotel, the manager would be greatly relieved to know that all was well.

When he pushed through the swing door, the first thing he noticed was a policeman talking to the manager at the desk. The reception clerk was there too. As John approached, the manager's face lighted up with relief.

"*Eccolo!*" he exclaimed. "Things are moving, signore. The two ladies have been traced, and they very kindly agreed to accompany the police to the *questura.* If you will go there at once, this *agente di polizia* will escort you."

John flushed. "I have given everyone a lot of trouble," he said. "I meant to tell you before going out to dinner, but you were not at the desk. The fact is that I have contacted my wife. She did make the flight to London after all, and I spoke to her on the telephone. It was all a great mistake."

The manager looked bewildered. "The signora is in London?" he repeated. He exchanged a rapid conversation in Italian with the policeman. "It seems that the two old ladies maintain they did not go out for the day, except for a little shopping in the morning," he said, turning back to John. "Then who was it the signore saw on the *vaporetto?*"

John shook his head. "A very extraordinary mistake on my part which I still don't understand," he said. "Obviously I did not see either my wife or the two ladies. I really am extremely sorry."

More rapid conversation in Italian. John noticed the clerk watching him with a curious expression in his eyes. The manager was obviously apologizing on John's behalf to the policeman, who looked annoyed and gave tongue to this effect. The whole business had undoubtedly given enormous trouble to a great many people, not least the two unfortunate sisters.

"Look," said John, interrupting the flow, "will you tell the *agente* I will go with him to headquarters and apologize in person to the ladies?"

The manager looked relieved. "If the signore would take the trouble," he said. "Naturally, the ladies were much distressed when a policeman interrogated them at their hotel, and they offered to accompany him to the *questura* only because they were so disturbed about the signora."

John felt more and more uncomfortable. He wondered if there were some penalty for giving the police misleading information involving a third party. His error began, in retrospect, to take on criminal proportions.

He crossed the Piazza San Marco, now thronged with after-dinner strollers, while his companion kept a discreet two paces to his left and never uttered a word.

They arrived at the police station and mounted the stairs to the same room where he had been before. Behind the desk sat a sallow-faced officer with a sour expression, while the two sisters, obviously upset, were seated on chairs nearby. John's escort went at once to the police officer, speaking in rapid Italian, while John himself, after a moment's hesitation, advanced toward the sisters.

"There has been a terrible mistake," he said. "I don't know how to apologize to you both. It's all my fault, mine entirely. The police are not to blame."

"We don't understand," the active sister said, her mouth twitching nervously. "We said good night to your wife last night at dinner, and we have not seen her since. The police came to our *pensione* more than an hour ago and told us your wife was missing and you had filed a complaint against us. My sister is not very strong. She was considerably disturbed."

"A mistake. A frightful mistake," he repeated.

He turned toward the desk. The police officer was addressing him, his English very inferior to that of the previous interrogator. He had John's earlier statement on the desk in front of him, and tapped it with a pencil.

"So?" he queried. "This document all lies? You not speak the truth?"

"I believed it to be true at the time," said John. "I could have sworn in a court of law that I saw my wife with these two ladies on a *vaporetto* in the Grand Canal this afternoon. Now I realize I was mistaken."

"We have not been near the Grand Canal all day," protested the sister. "We made a few purchases in the Merceria this morning, and remained indoors all afternoon. My sister was a little unwell. I have told the police officer this a dozen times, and the people at the *pensione* would corroborate our story. He refused to listen."

"And the signora?" rapped the police officer angrily. "What happen to the signora?"

"The signora, my wife, is safe in England," explained John patiently. "I talked to her on the telephone just after seven."

"Then who you see on the *vaporetto* in the red coat?" asked the furious police officer. "And if not these signorinas here, then what signorinas?"

"My eyes deceived me," said John, aware that his English was likewise becoming strained. "I think I see my wife and these ladies, but no, it was not so." It was like talking stage Chinese. In a moment he would be bowing and putting his hands in his sleeves.

The police officer thumped the table. "So all this work for nothing," he said. "Hotels and *pensioni* searched for the signorinas when we have plenty, plenty other things to do." He stood up, rumpling the papers on his desk. "And you, signorinas," he said, "you wish to make complaint against this person?" He was addressing the active sister.

"Oh, no," she said, "no, indeed. I quite see it was all a mistake."

The police officer pointed at John. "You very lucky man," he said. "These signorinas could file complaint against you."

"I'm sure," began John, "I'll do anything in my power . . ."

"Please don't think of it," exclaimed the sister, horrified. "We would not hear of such a thing."

The police officer waved a hand of dismissal and spoke in Italian to the underling. "This man walk with you to the *pensione,*" he said. "*Buona sera*, signorinas," and, ignoring John, he sat down again at his desk.

"I'll come with you too," said John. "I want to explain exactly what happened."

They trooped down the stairs and out of the building, the blind sister leaning on her twin's arm. Once outside, she turned her sightless eyes to John.

"You saw us," she said, "and your wife too. But not today. You saw us in the future."

"I don't follow," replied John, bewildered.

The active sister shook her head at him, frowning, and put her finger on her lips. "Come along, dear," she said to her twin. "You know you're very tired, and I want to get you home." Then, sotto voce to John, "She's psychic. But I don't want her to go into trance here in the street."

God forbid, thought John, and the little procession began to move slowly along the street.

"I must explain," said John softly. "My wife would never forgive me if I didn't." As they walked he went over the whole inexplicable story once again, beginning with the telegram received the night before and the conversation with Mrs. Hill. It no longer sounded as dramatic as it had when he had made his statement to the police officer, when the description of the two *vaporetti* passing one another on the Grand Canal had held a sinister quality, suggesting abduction on the part of the sisters. Now that neither of the women had any further menace for him, he spoke more naturally, feeling for the first time that they were somehow both in sympathy with him.

"You see," he explained, in a final endeavor to make amends, "I truly believed I had seen you with Laura, and I thought"—he hesitated, because this had been the police officer's suggestion and not his—"I thought that perhaps Laura had some sudden loss of memory, had met you at the airport, and you had brought her back to Venice to wherever you were staying."

They had crossed a large square and were approaching a house at one end of it, with a sign PENSIONE above the door.

"Is this it?" asked John.

"Yes," said the sister. "I know it is nothing much from the outside, but it is clean and comfortable." She turned to the police escort. "*Grazie,*" she said to him, "*grazie tanto.*"

The man nodded briefly and disappeared across the *campo.*

"Will you come in?" asked the sister.

"No, really." John thanked her. "I'm making an early start in the morning. I just want to make quite sure you do understand what happened, and that you forgive me."

"There is nothing to forgive," she replied. "It is one of the many examples of second sight that my sister and I have experienced time and time again."

"I myself find it hard to understand," he told her. "It has never happened to me before."

"So many things happen to us of which we are not aware," she said. "My sister felt you had psychic understanding. She also told your wife last night in the restaurant that you were to experience trouble, danger, that you should leave Venice. Well, don't you believe now that the telegram was proof of this? Your son was ill, possibly dangerously ill, and so it was necessary for you to return home immediately."

"Yes," said John, "but why should I see her on the *vaporetto* with you and your sister when she was actually on her way to England?"

"Thought transference, perhaps," she answered. "Your wife may have been thinking about us. We gave her our address, should you wish to get in touch with us. We shall be here another ten days. And she knows that we would pass on any message that my sister might have from your little one in the spirit world."

"Yes," said John awkwardly, "yes, I see. It's very good of you." He had a sudden picture of the two sisters putting on headphones in their bedroom, listening for a coded message from poor Christine. "Look, this is our address in London," he said. "I know Laura will be pleased to hear from you."

He scribbled their address on a sheet torn from his pocket diary, even, as a bonus thrown in, the telephone number, and handed it to her.

"Well, I must be off," he said. "Good night, and apologies, once again, for all that has happened this evening." He shook hands with the first sister, then turned to her blind twin. "I hope," he said, "that you are not too tired."

She held his hand fast and would not let it go. "The child," she said, speaking in an odd staccato voice, "the child . . . I can see the child. . . ." And then, to his dismay, a bead of froth appeared at the corner of her mouth, her head jerked back and she half collapsed in her sister's arms.

"We must get her inside," said the sister hurriedly. "It's the beginning of a trance state."

Between them they helped the twin into the house and sat her down on the nearest chair. A woman came running from some inner room. "Don't worry," the sister said to John. "The signorina and I can manage. I think you had better go."

"I'm most frightfully sorry . . ." John began, but the sister had already turned her back, and with the signorina was bending over her twin. He was obviously in the way, and he turned on his heel and began walking across the square.

What a finale to the evening! And all his fault. Poor old girls, first dragged to police headquarters, and then a psychic fit on top of it all. More likely epilepsy. Not much of a life for the other sister, but she seemed to take it in her stride.

Meanwhile, where the devil was he? He could not remember which way they had come from police headquarters, there had been so many turnings.

Wait a minute, the church itself had a familiar appearance. He drew nearer to it. San Giovanni in Bragora—that rang a bell. He and Laura had gone inside one morning to look at a painting by Cima da Conegliano. Surely it was only a stone's throw from the San Marco lagoon, with all the bright lights of civilization. He remembered taking a small turning. Wasn't that the alleyway ahead? He plunged along it, but halfway down he hesitated. It didn't seem right, although it was familiar for some unknown reason.

Then he realized that it was the narrow alley they had walked along the previous evening, only he was approaching it from the opposite direction. In that case it would be quicker to go on and cross the little bridge, and he would find the Arsenal on his left. Simpler than retracing his steps and getting lost once more in the maze of back streets.

He had almost reached the end of the alley, and the bridge was in sight, when he saw the child. It was the same little girl with the pixie hood who had leaped between the tethered boats the preceding night. This time she was running from the direction of the church on the other side, making for the bridge. She was running as if her life depended on it, and in a moment he saw why. A man was in pursuit, and when she glanced backward for a moment, he flattened himself against a wall, believing himself unobserved. The child came on across the bridge, and John, fearful of alarming her further, backed into an open doorway that led into a small court.

He remembered the drunken yell of the night before. The fellow's after her again, he thought, and with a flash of intuition he connected the two events, the child's terror then and now, and the murders reported in the newspapers. It could be coincidence, a child running from a drunken relative, and yet, and yet . . . His heart thumped in his chest, instinct warning him to run back along the alley the way he had come—but what about the child? What was going to happen to her?

Then he heard her running steps. She hurtled into the court in which he stood, not seeing him, making for the rear of the house that flanked it. She was sobbing as she ran, not the ordinary cry of a frightened child but the panic-stricken breath of a helpless being in despair. Were there parents in the house who would protect her? He hesitated a moment, then followed her down the steps to the house and through the door at the bottom.

"It's all right," he called. "I won't let him hurt you," cursing his poor Italian. But it was no use—she ran sobbing up another flight of stairs, which were spiral, leading to the floor above. Already it was too late for him to retreat. He could hear sounds of the pursuer in the courtyard behind, someone shouting, a dog barking. This is it, he thought, we're in it together, the child and I. Unless we can bolt some inner door above, he'll get us both.

He ran up the stairs after the child, who had darted into a room leading off a small landing, and followed her inside and slammed the door. Merciful heaven, there was a bolt which he rammed into its socket. The child was crouching by the open window. There was no one but themselves, no parents, and the room was bare except for a mattress on an old bed, and a heap of rags in one corner. But if he shouted for help, someone would surely hear, someone would surely come before the man in pursuit threw himself against the door.

"It's all right," he panted, "it's all right."

The child struggled to her feet and stood before him, the pixie hood falling from her head. He stared at her, incredulity turning to horror, to fear. It was not a child at all, but a little thickset woman dwarf, about three feet high, with a great square head too big for her body, gray locks hanging shoulder length, and she wasn't sobbing anymore, she was grinning at him, nodding her head up and down.

Then he heard the footsteps on the landing outside and the hammering on the door, and a barking dog, and not one voice but several voices, shouting, "Open up! Police!" The creature fumbled in her sleeve and drew out a knife. She threw it at him with hideous strength, piercing his throat; he stumbled and fell, the sticky mess covering his protecting hands.

And he saw the *vaporetto* with Laura and the two sisters steaming down the Grand Canal, and he knew why they were together and for what purpose they had come. The creature was gibbering in its corner. The hammering and the voices and the barking dog grew fainter, and, Oh, God, he thought, what a bloody silly way to die. . . .

THE HANDS OF MR. OTTERMOLE

THOMAS BURKE

AT SIX O'CLOCK of a January evening Mr. Whybrow was walking home through the cobweb alleys of London's East End. He had left the golden clamor of the great High Street to which the tram had brought him from the river and his daily work, and was now in the chessboard of byways that is called Mallon End. None of the rush and gleam of the High Street trickled into these byways. A few paces south—a flood tide of life, foaming and beating. Here—only slow, shuffling figures and muffled pulses. He was in the sink of London, the last refuge of European vagrants.

As though in tune with the street's spirit, he too walked slowly, with head down. It seemed that he was pondering some pressing trouble, but he was not. He had no trouble. He was walking slowly because he had been on his feet all day, and he was wondering whether the missus would have herrings for his tea, or haddock; and he was trying to decide which would be the more tasty on a night like this. A wretched night it was, of damp and mist, and the mist wandered into his throat and his eyes, and the damp had settled on pavement and roadway, and where the sparse lamplight fell it sent up a greasy sparkle.

His eye turned from the glum bricks that made his horizon, and went forward half a mile. He saw a gaslit kitchen, a flamy fire and a spread tea table. The vision gave his aching feet a throb of energy. He shook imperceptible damp from his shoulders, and hastened toward its reality.

But Mr. Whybrow wasn't going to get any tea that evening—or any other evening. Mr. Whybrow was going to die. Somewhere within a hundred yards of him another man was walking, a man much like any other, outwardly, but who had said within himself that Mr. Whybrow should never taste another herring. Not that Mr. Whybrow had injured him. Not that he had any dislike of Mr. Whybrow. Indeed, he knew nothing of him save as a familiar figure about the streets. But he had picked on Mr. Whybrow with that blind choice that makes us pick one restaurant table that has nothing to mark it from four or five other tables, or one apple from a dish of half a dozen equal apples. So this man had picked on Mr. Whybrow, as he might have picked on you or me, had we been within his daily observation; and even now he was creeping through the blue-toned streets, nursing his large white hands, moving ever closer to Mr. Whybrow's tea table, and so closer to Mr. Whybrow himself.

He wasn't, this man, a bad man. Indeed, he had many social and amiable qualities, and passed as a respectable man, as most successful criminals do. But the thought had come into his moldering mind that he would like to murder somebody, and, as he held no fear of God or man, he was going to do it, and would then go home to *his* tea. I don't say that flippantly, but as a statement of fact. Strange as it may seem to the humane, murderers must and do sit down to meals after a murder. There is no reason why they shouldn't, and many reasons why they should.

Walk on, then, Mr. Whybrow, walk on. Follow your jack-o'-lantern tea table. Don't annoy your burning feet by hurrying, for the more slowly you walk, the longer you will breathe the green air of this January dusk, and see the dreamy lamplight and the little shops, and hear the agreeable commerce of the London crowd and the haunting pathos of the street organ. These things are dear to you, Mr. Whybrow. You don't know it now, but in fifteen minutes you will have two seconds in which to realize how inexpressibly dear they are.

Walk on, then. You are in Lagos Street now, among the wanderers of Eastern Europe. A minute or so, and you are in Loyal Lane, among the lodging houses that shelter the useless and the beaten of London's camp followers. The lane holds the smell of them, and its soft darkness seems heavy with the wail of the futile. But you plod through it, unseeing, as you do every evening, and come to Blean Street, and plod through that. From basement to sky rise the tenements of an alien colony. Their windows slot the ebony of their walls with lemon. Behind those windows strange life is moving. From high above you comes a voice crooning "The Song of Katta." Through a window you see a family keeping a religious rite. Through another you see a woman pouring out tea for her husband. You see a man mending a pair of boots; a mother bathing her baby. You have seen all these things before, and never noticed them. You do not notice them now, but if you knew that you were never going to see them again, you would notice them. You never *will* see them again, not because your life has run its natural course, but because a man whom you have often passed in the street has at his own solitary pleasure decided to usurp the awful authority of nature, and destroy you.

Closer to you this shadow of massacre moves, and now he is twenty yards behind you. You can hear his footfall, but you do not turn your head. You are familiar with footfalls. You are in London, in the easy security of your daily territory, and footfalls behind you, your instinct tells you, are no more than a message of human company.

But can't you hear something in those footfalls? Something that says, *Look out, look out. Beware, beware.* No, the foot of villainy falls with the same quiet note as the foot of honesty. But those footfalls, Mr. Whybrow, are bearing on to you a pair of hands, and there *is* something in hands. Behind you that pair of hands is even now stretching its muscles in preparation for your end. Every minute of your days you have been seeing human hands. Have you ever realized the sheer horror of hands—those appendages that are a symbol for our moments of trust and affection and salutation? Have you thought of the sickening potentialities that lie within the scope of that five-tentacled member?

No, you never have; for all the human hands that you have seen have been stretched to you in kindness or fellowship. Yet, though the eyes can hate, and the lips can sting, it is only that dangling member that can gather the accumulated essence of evil, and electrify it into currents of destruction. Satan may enter into man by many doors, but in the hands alone can he find the servants of his will.

Another minute, Mr. Whybrow, and you will know all about the horror of human hands.

You are nearly home now. You have turned into your street—Caspar Street. You can see the front window of your little four-roomed house. The street is dark, and its three lamps give only a smut of light that is more confusing than darkness. It is dark—empty, too. Nobody about; no lights in the front parlors of the houses, for the families are at tea in their kitchens; and only a random glow in a few upper rooms occupied by lodgers. Nobody about but you and your following companion, and you don't notice him. You see him so often that he is never seen. Even if you turned your head and saw him, you would only say good evening to him, and walk on. A suggestion that he was a possible murderer would not even make you laugh. It would be too silly.

And now you are at your gate. You have found your door key. And now you are in, and hanging up your hat and coat. The missus has just called a greeting from the kitchen, and you have answered it, when the door shakes under a sharp knock.

Go away, Mr. Whybrow. Go away from that door. Don't touch it. Get right away from it. Get out of the house. Run with the missus to the back garden, and over the fence. Or call the neighbors. But don't touch that door. Don't, Mr. Whybrow, don't open . . .

Mr. Whybrow opened the door.

THAT WAS THE beginning of what became known as London's Strangling Horrors. Horrors they were called because they were something more than murders; they were motiveless, and there was an air of black magic about them. Each murder was committed at a time when the street where the bodies were found was empty of any perceptible or possible murderer. There would be an empty alley. There would be a policeman at its end. He would turn his back on the empty alley for less than a minute. Then he would look around and run into the night with news of another strangling. And in any direction he looked, nobody to be seen and no report to be had of anybody being seen. Or he would be on duty in a long-quiet street, and suddenly be called to a house of dead people whom a few seconds earlier he had seen alive. And, again, whichever way he looked, nobody to be seen; and although police whistles put an immediate cordon around the area, and searched all houses, no possible murderer was to be found.

The first news of the murder of Mr. and Mrs. Whybrow was brought by the station sergeant. He had been walking through Caspar Street on his way to the station for duty when he noticed the open door of number 98. Glancing in, he saw by the gaslight of the passage a motionless body on the floor. After a second look he blew his whistle, and when the constables answered him he took one to join him in a search of the house, and sent others to watch all neighboring streets, and make inquiries at adjoining houses. But neither in the house nor in the streets was anything found to indicate the murderer. Neighbors on either side, and opposite, were questioned, but they had seen nobody about, and had heard nothing. One had heard Mr. Whybrow come home—the scrape of his latchkey in the door was so regular an evening sound, he said, that you could set your watch by it for half past six—but he had heard nothing more than the sound of the opening door until the sergeant's whistle. Nobody had been seen to enter the house or leave it, by front or back, and the necks of the dead people carried no fingerprints or other traces. The little money in the house was untouched, and there were no signs of any disturbance of the property, or even of struggle. No signs of anything but brutal and wanton murder.

Mr. Whybrow was known to neighbors and workmates as a quiet, likable, home-loving man; such a man as could not have any enemies. So the police were left with an impossible situation: no clue to the murderer and no motive for the murders.

The first news of the affair sent a tremor through London generally, and an electric thrill through all Mallon End. Here was a murder of two inoffensive people, not for gain and not for revenge; and the murderer, to whom, apparently, killing was a casual impulse, was at large.

The doss houses and saloons and other places were combed and set with watches, and it was made known by whispers that good money and protection were assured to those with information, but nothing attaching to the Whybrow case could be found. The murderer clearly had no friends and kept no company. Known men of this type were called up and questioned, but each was able to give a good account of himself; and in a few days the police were at a dead end. Against the constant public gibe that the thing had been done almost under their noses, they became restive, and for four days each man of the force was working his daily beat under a strain. On the fifth day they became still more restive.

It was the season of annual teas and entertainments for the children of the Sunday schools, and on an evening of fog, when London was a world of groping phantoms, a small girl, in the bravery of best Sunday frock and shoes, shining face and new-washed hair, set out from Logan Passage for St. Michael's Parish Hall. She never got there. She was not actually dead until half past six, but she was as good as dead from the moment she left her mother's door. Somebody like a man, pacing the street from which Logan Passage led, saw her come out; and from that moment she was dead. Through the fog somebody's large white hands reached after her, and in fifteen minutes they were about her.

At half past six a whistle screamed trouble, and those answering it found the body of little Nellie Vrinoff in a warehouse entry in Minnow Street. The sergeant was first among them, and he posted his men to useful points, ordering them here and there in the tart tones of repressed rage, and berating the officer whose beat the street was. "I saw you, Magson, at the end of the lane. What were you up to there? You were there ten minutes before you turned." Magson began an explanation about keeping an eye on a suspicious-looking character at that end, but the sergeant cut him short. "Suspicious characters be damned. You don't want to look for suspicious characters. You want to look for *murderers.* Messing about . . . and then this happens right where you ought to be. Now think what they'll say."

With the speed of ill news came the crowd, pale and perturbed; and on the story that the unknown monster had appeared again, and this time to a child, their faces streaked the fog with spots of hate and horror. Then came the ambulance and more police, and swiftly they broke up the crowd; and, as it broke, low murmurs of "right under their noses" came from all sides. Later inquiries showed that four people of the district, above suspicion, had passed that entry at intervals of seconds before the murder, and had seen nothing and heard nothing. Again the police were left with no motive and with no clue.

And now the district was given over not to panic, for the London public never yields to that, but to apprehension and dismay. If these things were happening in their familiar streets, then anything might happen. Wherever people met—in the streets, the markets and the shops—they debated the one topic. Women took to bolting their windows and doors at the first fall of dusk. They kept their children closely under their eye. They did their shopping before dark, and watched anxiously, while pretending they weren't watching, for the return of their husbands from work. By the whim of one man with a pair of hands the structure and tenor of their daily lives were shaken. They began to realize that the pillars that supported the peaceable society in which they lived were mere straws that anybody could snap; that the police were potent only so long as they were feared.

And then, while it was yet gasping under this man's first two strokes, he made a third. Conscious of the horror that his hands had created, and hungry as an actor who has once tasted the thrill of the multitude, he made fresh advertisement of his presence. At 9:32 on Tuesday night a constable was on duty in Jarnigan Road, and at that time he spoke to a fellow officer named Petersen at the top of Clemming Street. He had seen this officer walk down that street. He had the habit, as all constables had just then, of looking constantly behind him and around him, and he was certain that the street was empty. He passed his sergeant at 9:33, reported that he had seen nothing, and passed on. His beat ended at a short distance from Clemming Street, and, having paced it, he turned and came again at 9:34 to the top of the street. He had scarcely reached it before he heard the hoarse voice of the sergeant. "Gregory! You there? Quick. Here's another. My God, it's Petersen! Garroted. Quick, call 'em up!"

That was the third of the Strangling Horrors, of which there were to be a fourth and a fifth; and the five horrors were to pass into the unknown and unknowable. That is, unknown as far as authority and the public were concerned. The identity of the murderer *was* known, but to two men only. One was the murderer himself; the other was a young journalist.

THIS YOUNG MAN, WHO WAS covering the affairs for his paper, was no smarter than the other zealous newspapermen who were hanging about these byways in the hope of a sudden story. But he was patient. He hung a little closer to the case than the other fellows, and by continually staring at it he at last raised the figure of the murderer like a genie from the stones on which he had stood to do his murders.

After the first few days the men had given up any attempt at exclusive stories, for there was none to be had. They met regularly at the local police station, and what little information there was they shared. The officials were cooperative, but no more. The sergeant discussed with them the details of each murder; suggested possible explanations of the man's methods; recalled from the past those cases that had some similarity; and hinted that work was being done which would soon bring the business to an end. The business had fallen heavily upon the police, and only through a capture made by their own efforts could they rehabilitate themselves in official and public esteem. Scotland Yard, of course, was at work, and had all the local station's material; but the station's hope was that they themselves would have the honor of settling the affair.

The young man soon gave up these morning lectures on the philosophy of crime, and took to wandering about the streets and making bright stories out of the effect of the murders on the normal life of the people. A melancholy job made more melancholy by the littered roadways, the crestfallen houses and the bleared windows of the district.

There was little to be picked up. All he saw and heard were indignant faces, and wild conjectures of the murderer's identity and of the secret of his trick of appearing and disappearing unseen. Men eyed other men, as though thinking, It might be *him*. It might be *him*. They were no longer looking for a man who had the air of a Madame Tussaud murderer; they were looking for a man, or perhaps some harridan woman, who had done these particular murders. They were sure that the murderer was a magician, a power able to hold them in subjection and to hold himself untouchable. He could do anything he chose; he would never be discovered. These two points they settled, and they went about the streets in a mood of resentful fatalism.

Almost was their belief in his invincibility justified; for, five days after the murder of the policeman Petersen, when the experience and inspiration of the whole detective force of London were turned toward the identification and capture of the murderer, he made his fourth and fifth strokes.

At nine o'clock that evening, the young newspaperman was strolling along Richards Lane. Richards Lane is a narrow street, partly a stall market and partly residential. The young man was in the residential section, which carries on one side small working-class cottages, and on the other the wall of a railway freightyard. The great wall hung a blanket of shadow over the lane, and the shadow and the cadaverous outline of the now deserted market stalls gave it the appearance of a living lane that had been turned to frost in the moment between breath and death. The very lamps, that elsewhere were nimbuses of gold, had here the rigidity of gems. The journalist, feeling this message of frozen eternity, was telling himself that he was tired of the whole thing, when in one stroke the frost was broken. Silence and darkness were racked by a high scream and through the scream a voice: "Help! Help! *He's here!*"

Before he could think what movement to make, the lane came to life. As though its invisible populace had been waiting on that cry, the door of every cottage was flung open, and from them and from the alleys poured shadowy figures. For a second or so they stood as rigid as the lamps; then a police whistle gave them direction, and the flock of shadows sloped up the street. The journalist followed them, and others followed him. From the main street and from surrounding streets they came, some risen from unfinished suppers, some disturbed in their ease of slippers and shirt sleeves, some stumbling on infirm limbs, and some armed with pokers or the tools of their trade. Here and there above the wavering cloud of heads moved the bold helmets of policemen. In one dim mass they surged upon a cottage whose doorway was marked by the sergeant and two constables; and voices of those behind urged them on with "Get in! Find him! Run round the back!" and those in front cried, "Keep back! Keep back!"

And now the fury of a mob held in thrall by unknown peril broke loose. He was here—on the spot. Surely this time he *could not* escape. All minds were bent upon the cottage; all energies thrust toward its doors and windows and roof; all thought was turned upon one unknown man and his extermination. So that no one man saw any other man. No man saw the narrow, packed lane and the mass of struggling shadows, and all forgot to look among themselves for the monster who never lingered upon his victims. All forgot, indeed, that they, by their mass crusade of vengeance, were affording him the perfect hiding place. They saw only the house, and they heard only the rending of woodwork and the smash of glass at back and front, and the police giving orders. But they found no murderer.

The journalist managed to struggle through to the cottage door, and to get the story from the constable stationed there. The cottage was the home of a pensioned sailor and his wife and daughter. They had been at supper, and at first it appeared that some noxious gas had smitten all three in mid-action. The daughter lay dead on the hearthrug, with a piece of bread and butter in her hand. The father had fallen sideways from his chair, leaving on his plate a filled spoon of rice pudding. The mother lay half under the table, her lap filled with the pieces of a broken cup and splashes of cocoa. But in three seconds the idea of gas was dismissed. One glance at their necks showed that this was the Strangler again; and the police stood and looked at the room and momentarily shared the fatalism of the public. They were helpless.

This was his fourth visit, making seven murders in all. He was to do one more—and to do it that night; and then he was to pass into history as the unknown London horror, and return to the decent life that he had always led, remembering little of what he had done, and worried not at all by the memory. Why did he stop? Impossible to say. Why did he begin? Impossible again. It just happened like that; and if he thinks at all of those days and nights, I surmise that he thinks of them as we think of foolish or dirty little sins that we committed in childhood. We say that they were not really sins, because we were not then consciously ourselves; we had not come to realization. And we look back at that foolish little creature that we once were, and forgive him because he didn't know. So, I think, with this man. There are plenty like him. More murderers than we guess are living decent lives today, and will die in decency, undiscovered and unsuspected. As this man will.

But he had a narrow escape, and it was perhaps this narrow escape that brought him to a stop. The escape was due to an error of judgment on the part of the journalist. As soon as he had the full story of the affair, which took some time, he spent fifteen minutes on the telephone, sending the story through, and at the end of the fifteen minutes he felt physically tired and mentally disheveled; so he turned into a bar for a drink and some sandwiches.

It was then that his mind received from nowhere a spark of light. He was not thinking about the Strangling Horrors; his mind was on his sandwich. It turned to the inventor of this refreshment, the Earl of Sandwich, and then to George the Fourth, and then to the Georges, and to the legend of that George who was worried to know how the apple got into the apple dumpling. He wondered whether George would have been equally puzzled to know how the ham got into the ham sandwich, and how long it would have been before it occurred to him that the ham could not have got there unless somebody had put it there. And in that moment a little active corner of his mind settled the affair. If there was ham in his sandwich, somebody must have put it there. If seven people had been murdered, somebody must have been there to murder them. There was no airplane or automobile that would go into a man's pocket; therefore that somebody must have escaped either by running away or standing still; and again therefore—

HE WAS VISUALIZING the front-page story his paper could carry if his theory were correct when a cry of "Time, gentlemen, please! All out!" reminded him of the hour. He went out into a world of mist, broken by the ragged disks of roadside puddles and the streaming lightning of motor buses. He was certain that he had *the* story, but even if it were proved, he was doubtful whether the policy of his paper would permit him to print it. It had one great fault. It was truth, but it was impossible truth. It rocked the foundations of everything that newspaper readers believed and that newspaper editors helped them to believe.

As it happened, they were not asked to, for the story was never written. As he was nourished by his refreshment and stimulated by his theory, he thought he might put in an extra half hour by testing that theory. So he began to look about for the man he had in mind—a man with white hair and large white hands; otherwise an everyday figure whom nobody would look twice at. He wanted to spring his idea on this man without warning, and he was going to placc himsclf within reach of a man armored in legends of dreadfulness and grue. He didn't think about the risk. He was moved simply by an instinct to follow a story to its end.

He walked slowly from the tavern and crossed into Fingal Street, making for Deever Market, where he had hope of finding his man. But his journey was shortened. At the corner of Lotus Street he saw him—or a man who looked like him. This street was poorly lit, and he could see little of the man; but he *could* see white hands. For some twenty paces he stalked him; then drew level with him; and at a point where the arch of a railway crossed the street, he saw that this was his man. He approached him with the current conversational phrase of the district: "Well, seen anything of the murderer?"

The man stopped to look sharply at him; then, satisfied that the journalist was not the murderer, said, "Eh? No, nor's anybody else. Doubt if they ever will."

"I don't know. I've got an idea."

"So?"

"Yes. Came to me all of a sudden. Quarter of an hour ago. And I'd felt that we'd all been blind. It's been staring us in the face."

The man turned again to look at him, and the look and the movement held suspicion of this man who seemed to know so much. "Oh? Has it? Well, why not give us the benefit of it?"

"I'm going to." They walked level, and were nearly at the end of the little street where it meets Deever Market when the journalist turned casually to the man. He put a finger on his arm. "Yes, it seems to me quite simple now. But there's still one point I don't understand. One little thing I'd like to clear up. I mean the motive. Now, as man to man, tell me, Sergeant Ottermole, just *why* did you kill all those inoffensive people?"

The sergeant stopped. There was just enough light from the sky, which held the reflected light of London, to give the journalist a sight of the sergeant's face, and the sergeant's face was turned to him with a wide smile of such urbanity and charm that the journalist's eyes were frozen as they met it.

The smile stayed for some seconds. Then said the sergeant, "Well, to tell you the truth, Mr. Newspaperman, I don't know. I really don't know. In fact, I've been worried about it myself. But I've got an idea—just like you. Everybody knows that we can't control the workings of our minds. Don't they? Ideas come into our minds without asking. But everybody's supposed to be able to control his body. Why? Eh? We get our minds from Lord knows where—from people who were dead hundreds of years before we were born. Mayn't we get our bodies in the same way? Our faces—our legs—our heads—they aren't completely ours. We don't make 'em. They come to us. And couldn't ideas come into our bodies like ideas come into our minds? Eh? Can't ideas live in nerve and muscle as well as in brain? Couldn't it be that parts of our bodies aren't really us, and couldn't ideas come into those parts all of a sudden, like ideas come into . . . into"—he shot his arms out, showing the great white-gloved hands and hairy wrists; shot them out so swiftly to the journalist's throat that his eyes never saw them—"into *my hands!*"

AN ALPINE DIVORCE

ROBERT BARR

IN SOME NATURES there are no halftones; nothing but raw primary colors. John Bodman was a man who was always at one extreme or the other. This probably would have mattered little had he not married a wife whose nature was an exact duplicate of his own.

Doubtless there exists in this world precisely the right woman for any given man to marry, and vice versa. But when you consider that a human being has the opportunity of being acquainted with only a few hundred people, and out of the few hundred that there are but a dozen or less whom he knows intimately, and out of the dozen, one or two friends at most, it will easily be seen, when we remember the number of millions who inhabit this world, that probably, since the earth was created, the right man has never yet met the right woman. The mathematical chances are all against such a meeting, and this is the reason that divorce courts exist. Marriage at best is but a compromise, and if two people happen to be united who are of an uncompromising nature, there is trouble.

In the lives of these two young people there was no middle distance. The result was bound to be either love or hate, and in the case of Mr. and Mrs. Bodman it was hate of the most bitter kind.

In some parts of the world incompatibility of temper is considered a just case for obtaining a divorce, but for years in England no such subtle distinction was made. And so, until the wife became criminal, or the man became both criminal and cruel, the two were linked together by a bond that only death could sever. The matter was only made the more hopeless by the fact that Mrs. Bodman lived a blameless life, and her husband was no worse, but rather better, than the majority of men. Perhaps, however, that statement held only up to a certain point, for John Bodman had reached a state of mind in which he resolved to get rid of his wife at all hazards. If he had been a poor man, he would probably have deserted her, but he was rich, and a man cannot freely leave a prospering business because his domestic life happens not to be happy.

When a man's mind dwells too much on any one subject, no one can tell just how far he will go. The mind is a delicate instrument, and even the law recognizes that it is easily thrown from its balance. Bodman's friends claim that his mind was unhinged, but neither his friends nor his enemies suspected the truth.

Whether John Bodman was sane or insane at the time he made up his mind to murder his wife will never be known, but there was certainly craftiness in the method he devised to make the crime appear the result of an accident. Nevertheless, cunning is often a quality in a mind that has gone wrong.

Mrs. Bodman well knew how much her presence afflicted her husband, but her nature was as relentless as his, and her hatred of him was, if possible, more bitter than his hatred of her. Wherever he went she accompanied him, and perhaps the idea of murder would never have occurred to him if she had not been so persistent in forcing her presence upon him on all occasions.

So, when he announced to her that he intended to spend the month of July in Switzerland, she said nothing, but made her preparations. On this occasion he did not protest, as was usual with him, and so to Switzerland this silent couple departed.

There is a hotel near the mountaintops which stands on a ledge over one of the great glaciers. It is a mile and a half above the level of the sea, and it stands alone, reached by a toilsome road that zigzags up the mountain for six miles. There is a wonderful view of snow peaks and glaciers from the verandas of this hotel, and in the neighborhood are many picturesque walks to points more or less dangerous.

John Bodman knew the hotel well, and in happier days he had been intimately acquainted with the vicinity. Now that the thought of murder arose in his mind, a certain spot two miles distant from this inn continually haunted him. It was a point of view overlooking everything, and its extremity was protected by a low and crumbling wall. He arose one morning at four o'clock, slipped unnoticed out of the hotel, and went to this point, which was locally named the Hanging Outlook. His memory had served him well. It was exactly the spot, he said to himself. The mountain which rose up behind it was wild and precipitous. There were no inhabitants near to overlook the place. The distant hotel was hidden by a shoulder of rock. Far down in the valley the only town in view seemed like a collection of little toy houses.

One glance over the crumbling wall at the edge was generally sufficient for a visitor of even the strongest nerves. There was a sheer drop of more than a mile straight down, and at the distant bottom were jagged rocks and stunted trees that looked, in the blue haze, like shrubbery.

This is the spot, said the man to himself, and tomorrow morning is the time.

John Bodman had planned his crime as grimly and relentlessly, and as coolly, as ever he had concocted a deal on the stock exchange. There was no thought in his mind of mercy for his unconscious victim. His hatred had carried him far.

The next morning after breakfast, he said to his wife, "I intend to take a walk in the mountains. Do you wish to come with me?"

"Yes," she answered briefly.

"Very well, then," he said. "I shall be ready at nine o'clock."

"I shall be ready at nine o'clock," she repeated after him.

At that hour they left the hotel together. They spoke no word to each other on their way to the Hanging Outlook. The path was practically level, skirting the mountains, for the Hanging Outlook was not much higher above the sea than the hotel.

John Bodman had formed no fixed plan for his procedure when the place was reached. He resolved to be guided by circumstances. Now and then a strange fear arose in his mind that she might cling to him and possibly drag him over the precipice with her. He found himself wondering whether she had any premonition of her fate, and one of his reasons for not speaking was the fear that a tremor in his voice might possibly arouse her suspicions. He decided that his action should be sharp and sudden, that she might have no chance either to help herself or to drag him with her.

Curiously enough, when they came within sight of the Hanging Outlook, Mrs. Bodman stopped and shuddered. Bodman looked at her and wondered again if she had any suspicion. "What is the matter?" he asked gruffly. "Are you tired?"

"John," she cried with a gasp in her voice, calling him by his Christian name for the first time in years, "don't you think that if you had been kinder to me at first, things might have been different?"

"It seems to me," he answered, not looking at her, "that it is rather late in the day for discussing that question."

"I have much to regret," she said quaveringly. "Have you nothing?"

"No," he answered.

"Very well," replied his wife, with the usual hardness returning to her voice. "I was merely giving you a chance. Remember that."

Her husband looked at her suspiciously. "What do you mean," he asked, "giving me a chance? I want no chance, nor anything else from you. A man accepts nothing from one he hates. My feeling toward you is, I imagine, no secret to you. We are tied together, and you have done your best to make the bondage insupportable."

"Yes," she answered, with her eyes on the ground, "we are tied together—we are tied together!"

She repeated these words under her breath as they walked the few remaining steps to the Outlook. Bodman sat down upon the crumbling wall. The woman dropped her alpenstock on the rock and walked nervously to and fro, clasping and unclasping her hands. Her husband caught his breath as the terrible moment drew near.

"Why do you walk about like a wild animal?" he cried. "Come here and sit down beside me, and be still."

She faced him with a light he had never before seen in her eyes—a light of insanity and of hatred.

"I walk like a wild animal," she said, "because I am one. You spoke a moment ago of your hatred of me; but you are a man, and your hatred is nothing to mine. Bad as you are, much as you wish to break the bond which ties us together, there are still things which I know you would not stoop to. I know there is no thought of murder in your heart, but there is in mine. I will show you, John Bodman, how much I hate you."

The man gave a guilty start as she mentioned murder.

"Yes," she continued, "I have told all my friends in England that I believed you intended to murder me in Switzerland."

"Good God!" he cried. "How could you say such a thing?"

"I say it to show how much I hate you—how much I am prepared to give for revenge. I have warned the people at the hotel, and when we left, two men followed us. The proprietor tried to persuade me not to accompany you. In a few moments those two men will come in sight of the Outlook. Tell them, if you think they will believe you, that it was an accident."

The madwoman tore from the front of her dress shreds of lace and scattered them around.

Bodman started up to his feet, crying, "What are you doing?" But before he could move toward her she precipitated herself over the wall, and went shrieking and whirling down the awful abyss.

The next moment two men came hurriedly around the edge of the rock and found the man standing alone. Even in his bewilderment he realized that if he told the truth, he would not be believed.

THE INCAUTIOUS BURGLAR

JOHN DICKSON CARR

TWO GUESTS, WHO were not staying the night at Cranleigh Court, left at shortly past eleven o'clock. Marcus Hunt saw them to the front door. Then he returned to the dining room, where the poker chips were now stacked into neat piles of white, red, and blue.

"Another game?" suggested Rolfe.

"No good," said Derek Henderson. His tone, as usual, was weary. "Not with just three of us."

Their host stood by the sideboard and watched them. The long, low house, overlooking The Weald of Kent, was so quiet that their voices rose with startling loudness. The dining room, large and paneled, was softly lighted by electric wall candles which brought out the somber colors of the paintings. It is not often that anybody sees, in one room of an otherwise commonplace country house, two Rembrandts and a Vandyke. There was a kind of defiance about those paintings.

To Arthur Rolfe—the art dealer—they represented enough money to make him shiver. To Derek Henderson—the art critic—they represented a problem. What they represented to Marcus Hunt was not apparent.

Hunt stood by the sideboard, his fists on his hips, smiling, a middle-sized, stocky man, with a full face and a high complexion. He watched with ironic amusement while Henderson picked up a pack of cards in long fingers, cut them into two piles, and shuffled with a flick that made the cards melt together like a conjuring trick.

"My boy," said Hunt, "you surprise me."

"That's what I try to do," answered Henderson, still wearily. He looked up. "But why do you say so?"

Henderson was young, he was long, he was lean, he was immaculate; and he wore a reddish beard with an air of complete naturalness.

"I'm surprised," said Hunt, "you enjoy anything so bourgeois—so plebeian—as poker."

"I enjoy reading people's characters," said Henderson. "Poker's the best way to do it, you know."

Hunt's eyes narrowed. "Oh? And can you read my character, for instance?"

"With pleasure," said Henderson. Absently he dealt himself a poker hand, face up. It contained a pair of fives, and the last card was the ace of spades. Henderson remained staring at it for a few seconds before he glanced up again.

"And I can tell you," he went on, "that *you* surprise *me*. Do you mind if I'm frank? I had always thought of you as the colossus of business; the smasher; the plunger; the fellow who took the long chances. Now, you're not like that at all."

Marcus Hunt laughed. But Henderson was undisturbed.

"You're tricky, but you're cautious. I doubt if you ever took a long chance in your life. Another surprise"—he dealt himself a new hand—"is Mr. Rolfe here. He's the man who, given the proper circumstances, would take the long chances."

Arthur Rolfe considered this. He looked startled, but rather flattered. Though in height and build not unlike Hunt, he had a square, dark face, with thin shells of eyeglasses, and a worried forehead.

"I doubt that," he declared. "A person who took long chances in my business would find himself in the soup." He glanced around the room. "Anyhow, I'd be too cautious to have three pictures, worth millions, hanging in an unprotected downstairs room with French windows giving on a terrace." An almost frenzied note came into his voice. "Great Scott! Suppose a burglar—"

"Damn!" said Henderson unexpectedly.

Even Hunt jumped. "You nearly made me slice my thumb off!" he said. Hunt had picked up an apple from a silver fruit bowl on the sideboard and had started to pare it with a fruit knife, a sharp wafer-thin blade which glittered in the light of the wall lamps. He put down the knife. "What's the matter with you?"

"It's the ace of spades," said Henderson languidly. "That's the second time it's turned up in five minutes."

Arthur Rolfe chose to be dense. "Well? What about it?"

"I think our young friend is being psychic," said Hunt, good-humored again. "Are you reading characters, or only telling fortunes?"

Henderson hesitated. His eyes moved to Hunt, and then to the wall over the sideboard, where Rembrandt's *Old Woman with Cap* stared back. Then Henderson looked toward the French windows opening on the terrace.

"None of my affair." Henderson shrugged. "It's your house and your collection and your responsibility. But this fellow Butler—what do you know about him?"

Marcus Hunt looked boisterously amused. "Butler? He's a friend of my niece's. Harriet picked him up in London and asked me to invite him down here. Nonsense! Butler's all right. What are you thinking, exactly?"

"Listen!" said Rolfe, holding up his hand.

The noise they heard, from the direction of the terrace, was not repeated. It was not repeated because the person who had made it, a very bewildered and uneasy young lady, had run lightly and swiftly to the far end, where she leaned against the balustrade.

Lewis Butler hesitated before going after her. The moonlight was so clear that one could see the mortar between the tiles which paved the terrace. Harriet Davis wore a white gown with long and filmy skirts, which she lifted clear of the ground as she ran.

Then she beckoned to him.

She was half sitting, half leaning against the rail. Her white arms were spread out, fingers gripping the stone. He could see the rapid rise and fall of her breast; he could even trace the shadow of her eyelashes.

"That was a lie, anyhow," she said.

"What was?"

"What my uncle Marcus said. You heard him." Harriet Davis nodded her head vehemently, with fierce accusation. "About my knowing you. And inviting you here. I never saw you before this weekend. Either Uncle Marcus is going out of his mind, or . . . Will you answer me just one question?"

"If I can."

"Very well. Are you by any chance a crook?"

She spoke with as much simplicity and directness as though she had asked him whether he might be a doctor or a lawyer.

"To be quite frank about it," he said, "I'm not. Will you tell me why you asked?"

"This house," said Harriet, "used to be guarded with burglar alarms. If you so much as touched a window, the whole place started clanging like a fire station. He had all the burglar alarms removed last week. Last week." She took her hands off the balustrade and pressed them together hard. "The pictures used to be upstairs, in a locked room next to his bedroom. He had them moved downstairs—last week. It's almost as though my uncle *wanted* the house to be burgled."

Butler knew that he must use great care here.

"Perhaps he does. For instance," he went on idly, "suppose one of his famous Rembrandts turned out to be a fake? It might be a relief not to have to show it to his expert friends."

The girl shook her head. "No," she said. "They're all genuine. You see, I thought of that too."

Now was the time to hit, and hit hard. Lewis Butler took out his cigarette case and turned it over without opening it.

"Look here, Miss Davis, you're not going to like this. But I can tell you of cases in which people were rather anxious to have their property 'stolen.' If a picture is insured for more than its value, and then it is mysteriously 'stolen' one night . . . ?"

"That might be all very well too," answered Harriet calmly. "Except that not one of those pictures has been insured."

The cigarette case slipped through Butler's fingers and fell with a clatter on the tiles. As he bent over to pick it up, he could hear a church clock across The Weald strike the half hour after eleven.

"You're sure of that?"

"I'm perfectly sure. He hasn't insured any of his pictures for as much as a penny. He says it's a waste of money."

"But—"

"Oh, I know! And I don't know why I'm talking to you like this. You're a stranger, aren't you?" She folded her arms, drawing her shoulders up as though she were cold. "But then Uncle Marcus is a stranger too. Do you know what I think? *I* think he's going mad."

"Hardly as bad as that, is it?"

"Yes, go on," the girl suddenly stormed at him. "*Say* it; go on and say it. That's easy enough. But you don't see him when his eyes seem to get smaller and all that genial-country-squire look goes out of his face. He's not a fake; he hates fakes, and goes out of his way to expose them. But, if he hasn't gone clear out of his mind, what can he be up to?"

In something over three hours they found out.

A CHILLY WIND stirred at the turn of the night, in the hour of suicides and bad dreams. When the burglar glanced over his shoulder, the last of the moonlight distorted his face; it showed less a face than the blob of a black cloth mask under a greasy cap pulled down over his ears.

He slipped up the outside steps to the French windows of the dining room and then went to work on the middle window with the contents of a small folding tool kit. He fastened two short strips of adhesive tape to the glass just beside the catch. Then his glass cutter sliced out a small semicircle inside the tape.

It was done not without noise; the cutter crunched like a dentist's drill in a tooth, and the man stopped to listen.

There was no answering noise. No dog barked.

With the adhesive tape holding the glass so that it did not fall and smash, he slid his gloved hand through the opening and twisted the catch. The weight of his body deadened the creaking of the window when he pushed inside. He knew exactly what he wanted. He put the tool kit into his pocket and drew out an electric torch. Its beam moved across to the sideboard; it touched gleaming silver, a bowl of fruit, and a wicked little knife thrust into an apple as though into someone's body; finally it moved up to the hag face of the *Old Woman with Cap.*

This was not a large picture, and the burglar lifted it down easily. He pried out glass and frame. Though he tried to roll up the canvas with great care, the brittle paint cracked across in small stars. The burglar was so intent on this that he never noticed the presence of another person in the room.

He was an incautious burglar; he had no sixth sense which smelled murder.

Up on the second floor of the house, Lewis Butler was awakened by a muffled crash like that of metal objects falling.

He had not fallen into more than a half doze all night. He knew with certainty what must be happening, though he had no idea of why, or how, or to whom.

Butler was out of bed and into his dressing gown and slippers as soon as he heard the first faint clatter from downstairs. A little flashlight was ready in his pocket.

That noise seemed to have roused nobody else. With certain possibilities in his mind, he had never in his life moved so fast.

Not using his light, he was down two flights of deep-carpeted stairs without noise. In the lower hall he could feel a draft, which meant that a window or door had been opened somewhere. He made straight for the dining room.

But he was too late.

Once the pencil beam of Butler's flashlight had swept around, he switched on a whole blaze of lights. The burglar was still here, right enough. But the burglar was lying very still in front of the sideboard; and, to judge by the amount of blood on his sweater and trousers, he would never move again.

"That's done it," Butler said aloud.

A silver service, including a tea urn, had been toppled off the sideboard. Where the fruit bowl had fallen, the dead man lay on his back among a litter of oranges, apples, and a squashed bunch of grapes. The mask still covered the burglar's face; his greasy cap was flattened still further on his ears; his gloved hands were thrown wide.

Fragments of smashed picture glass lay around him, together with the empty frame, and the *Old Woman with Cap* had been half crumpled up under his body. From the position of the most conspicuous bloodstains, one judged that he had been stabbed through the chest with the stained fruit knife beside him.

"What is it?" said a voice almost at Butler's ear.

He had not heard Harriet Davis approach. She was standing just behind him, wrapped in a Japanese kimono, with her dark hair around her shoulders. When he explained what had happened, she would not look into the dining room; she backed away, shaking her head violently, like an urchin ready for flight.

"You had better wake up your uncle," Butler said briskly. "I must use your telephone." Then he looked her in the eyes. "Yes, you're quite right. I think you've guessed it already. I'm a police officer."

She nodded. "Yes. I guessed. Who are you? And is your name really Butler?"

"I'm a sergeant of the Criminal Investigation Department. And my name really is Butler. Your uncle brought me here."

"Why?"

"I don't know. He hasn't got round to telling me."

This girl's intelligence, even when overshadowed by fear, was direct and disconcerting. "But, if he wouldn't say why he wanted a police officer, how did they come to send you? He'd have to tell them, wouldn't he?"

Butler insisted, "I must see your uncle. Will you go upstairs and wake him, please?"

"I can't," said Harriet. "Uncle Marcus isn't in his room. I knocked at the door on my way down. He's gone."

Butler took the stairs two treads at a time. Harriet had turned on all the lights on her way down, but nothing stirred in the bleak, over-decorated passages.

Marcus Hunt's bedroom was empty. His dinner jacket had been hung up neatly on the back of a chair, shirt laid across the seat with tie on top of it. Hunt's watch ticked loudly on the dressing table. His money and keys were there too. But he had not gone to bed, for the bedspread was undisturbed.

The suspicion which came to Lewis Butler, listening to the thin insistent ticking of that watch in the drugged hour before dawn, was so fantastic that he could not credit it.

He started downstairs again, and on the way he met Arthur Rolfe blundering out of another bedroom down the hall. The art dealer's stocky body was wrapped in a flannel dressing gown. He planted himself in front of Butler and refused to budge.

"Yes," said Butler. "You don't have to ask. It's a burglar."

"I knew it," said Rolfe calmly. "Did he get anything?"

"No. He was murdered."

For a moment Rolfe said nothing, but his hand crept into the breast of his dressing gown, as though he felt pain there.

"Murdered? You don't mean the *burglar* was murdered?"

"Yes."

"But why? By an accomplice, you mean? Who is the burglar?"

"That," snarled Lewis Butler, "is what I intend to find out."

In the lower hall he found Harriet Davis, who was now standing in the doorway of the dining room and looking steadily at the body by the sideboard.

"You're going to take off the mask, aren't you?" she asked, without turning around.

Stepping with care to avoid squashed fruit and broken glass, Butler leaned over the dead man. He pushed back the peak of the greasy cap; he lifted the black cloth mask, which was clumsily held by an elastic band; and he found what he expected to find.

The burglar was Marcus Hunt—stabbed through the heart while attempting to rob his own house.

"YOU SEE, SIR," Butler explained to Dr. Gideon Fell on the following afternoon, "that's the trouble. However you look at it, the case makes no sense."

Again he went over the facts. "Why should the man burgle his own house and steal his own property? Every one of those paintings is valuable, and not a single one is insured! Consequently, why? Was the man a simple lunatic? What did he think he was doing?"

The village of Sutton Valence, straggling like a gray-white Italian town along the very peak of The Weald, was full of hot sunshine. In the apple orchard behind the inn, the Tabard, Dr. Gideon Fell sat at a garden table with a pint tankard at his elbow. Dr. Fell's vast bulk was clad in a white linen suit. His pink face smoked in the heat, and his wary lookout for wasps gave him a regrettably walleyed appearance as he pondered.

"Superintendent Hadley suggested that I might—harrumph—look in here," he said. "The local police are in charge, aren't they?"

"Yes. I'm merely standing by."

"Hadley's exact words to me were, 'It's so crazy that nobody but you will understand it.' The man's flattery becomes more nauseating every day." Dr. Fell scowled. "I say. Does anything else strike you as queer about this business?"

"Well, why should a man burgle his own house?"

"No, no, no!" growled Dr. Fell. "Don't be obsessed with that point. Don't become hypnotized by it. For instance"—a wasp hovered near his tankard, and he distended his cheeks and blew it away with one vast puff, like Father Neptune—"for instance, the young lady seems to have raised an interesting question. If Marcus Hunt wouldn't say why he wanted a detective in the house, why did the CID consent to send you?"

Butler shrugged his shoulders. "Because," he said, "Chief Inspector Ames thought Hunt was up to funny business and meant to stop it."

"What sort of funny business?"

"A faked burglary to steal his own pictures for the insurance. It looked like the old game of appealing to the police to divert suspicion. In other words, sir, exactly what this appeared to be—until I learned (and today proved) that not one of those pictures has ever been insured for a penny.

"It can't have been a practical joke," Butler went on. "Look at the elaborateness of it! Hunt put on old clothes from which all tailors' tabs and laundry marks were removed. He put on gloves and a mask. He got hold of a torch and an up-to-date kit of burglar's tools. He went out of the house by the back door; we found it open later. He smoked a few cigarettes in the shrubbery below the terrace; we found his footprints in the soft earth. He cut a pane of glass. . . . But I've told you all that."

"And then," mused Dr. Fell, "somebody killed him."

"Yes. Why should anybody have killed him?"

"Hm. Clues?"

"Negative." Butler took out his notebook. "According to the police surgeon, he died of a direct heart wound from a blade (presumably that fruit knife) so thin that the wound was difficult to find. There were a number of his fingerprints, but nobody else's. We did find one odd thing, though. A number of pieces in the silver service off the sideboard were scratched in a queer way. It looked almost as though, instead of being swept off the sideboard in a struggle, they had been piled up on top of each other like a tower, and then pushed—"

Butler paused, for Dr. Fell was shaking his big head back and forth with an expression of gargantuan distress.

"Well, well, well," he was saying. "Well, well, well. And you call that negative evidence?"

"Isn't it? It doesn't explain why a man burgles his own house."

"Look here," said the doctor mildly. "I should like to ask you just one question. What is the most important point in this affair? One moment! I did not say the most interesting; I said the most important. Surely it is the fact that a man has been murdered?"

"Yes, sir. Naturally."

"I mention the fact"—the doctor was apologetic—"because it seems in danger of being overlooked. It hardly interests you. You are concerned only with Hunt's senseless masquerade. You don't mind a throat being cut, but you can't stand a leg being pulled. Why not try working at it from the other side, asking who killed Hunt?"

Butler was silent for a long time. "The servants are out of it," he said at length. "They sleep in another wing on the top floor; and for some reason, somebody locked them in last night." His doubts, even his dreads, were beginning to take form. "There was a fine blowup over that when the house was roused. Of course, the murderer could have been an outsider."

"You know it wasn't," said Dr. Fell. "Would you mind taking me to Cranleigh Court?"

THEY CAME OUT on the terrace in the hottest part of the afternoon.

Dr. Fell sat down on a wicker settee, with a dispirited Harriet beside him. Derek Henderson, in flannels, perched his long figure on the balustrade. Arthur Rolfe alone wore a dark suit and seemed out of place. For the pale green and brown of the Kentish lands, which rarely acquired harsh color, now blazed. No air stirred, no leaf moved in that brilliant thickness of heat; and down in the garden, toward their left, the water of the swimming pool sparkled with hot, hard light. Butler felt it like a weight on his eyelids.

"It's no good," Henderson said. "Don't keep on asking me why Hunt should have burgled his own house. But I'll give you a tip."

"Which is?" inquired Dr. Fell.

"Whatever the reason was," returned Henderson, sticking out his neck, "it was a good reason. Hunt was much too canny and cautious ever to do anything without a good reason. I told him so last night."

Dr. Fell spoke sharply. "Cautious? Why do you say that?"

"Well, for instance. I take three cards on the draw. Hunt takes one. I bet; he sees me and raises. I cover that, and raise again. Hunt drops out. In other words, it's fairly certain he's filled his hand, but not so certain I'm holding much more than a pair. Yet Hunt drops out. So with my three sevens I bluff him out of his straight. He played a dozen hands last night just like that."

Henderson began to chuckle. Seeing the expression on Harriet's face, he checked himself.

"But then, of course," Henderson added, "he had a lot on his mind last night."

Nobody could fail to notice the change of tone.

"So? And what did he have on his mind?"

"Exposing somebody he had always trusted," replied Henderson coolly. "That's why I didn't like it when the ace of spades turned up so often."

"You'd better explain that," said Harriet after a pause. "He told you he intended to expose somebody he had always trusted?"

"No. He hinted at it."

It was the stolid Rolfe who stormed into the conversation then. "Listen to me," he snapped. "I have heard a great deal, at one time or another, about Mr. Hunt's passion for exposing people. Very well!" He slid one hand into the breast of his coat, in a characteristic gesture. "But where in the name of sanity does that leave us? He wants to expose someone. And to do that, he puts on outlandish clothes and masquerades as a burglar. Is that sensible? I tell you, the man was mad! There's no other explanation."

"There are five other explanations," said Dr. Fell. "However, I will not waste your time with four of them. We are concerned with only one explanation: the real one."

"And you know the real one?" asked Henderson sharply.

"I rather think so."

"Since when?"

"Since I had the opportunity of looking at all of you," answered Dr. Fell.

He settled back massively in the wicker settee, so that its frame creaked like a ship's bulkhead in a heavy sea. His vast chin was outthrust, and he nodded absently, as though to emphasize some point that was quite clear in his own mind.

"I've already had a word with the local inspector," he went on suddenly. "He will be here in a few minutes. And, at my suggestion, he will have a request for all of you. I sincerely hope nobody will refuse."

"Request?" said Henderson. "What request?"

"It's a very hot day," said Dr. Fell, blinking toward the swimming pool. "He's going to suggest that you all go in for a swim."

Harriet uttered a kind of despairing mutter and turned as though appealing to Lewis Butler.

"That," continued Dr. Fell, "will be the politest way of drawing attention to the murderer. In the meantime, let me call your attention to one point in the evidence which seems to have been generally overlooked. Mr. Henderson, do you know anything about direct heart wounds, made by a thin steel blade?"

"Like Hunt's wound? No. What about them?"

"There is practically no exterior bleeding," answered Dr. Fell.

"But—" Harriet was beginning, when Butler stopped her.

"The police surgeon, in fact, called attention to that wound which was so 'difficult to find.' The victim dies almost at once; and the edges of the wound compress. But in that case," argued Dr. Fell, "how did the late Mr. Hunt come to have so much blood on his sweater, and even splashed on his trousers?"

"Well?"

"He didn't," answered Dr. Fell simply. "Mr. Hunt's blood never got on his clothes at all."

"I can't stand this," said Harriet, jumping to her feet. "I—I'm sorry, but have you gone mad yourself? Are you telling us we didn't see him lying by that sideboard, with blood on him?"

"Oh, yes. You saw that."

"Let him go on," said Henderson, who was rather white around the nostrils. "Let him rave."

"It is, I admit, a fine point," said Dr. Fell. "But it answers your question, repeated to the point of nausea, as to why the eminently sensible Mr. Hunt chose to dress up in burglar's clothes and play burglar. The answer is short and simple. He didn't."

"It must be plain to everybody," Dr. Fell went on, "that Mr. Hunt was deliberately setting a trap for someone—the real burglar.

"He believed that a certain person might try to steal one or several of his pictures. He probably knew that this person had tried similar games before, in other country houses: that is, an inside job which was carefully planned to look like an outside job. So he made things easy for this thief, in order to trap him, with a police officer in the house.

"The burglar, a sad fool, fell for it. This thief, a guest in the house, waited until well past two o'clock in the morning. He then put on his old clothes, mask, and gloves. He let himself out by the back door. He went through all the motions we have erroneously been attributing to Marcus Hunt. Then the trap snapped. Just as he was rolling up the Rembrandt, he heard a noise. He swung his light around. And he saw Marcus Hunt, in pajamas and dressing gown, looking at him.

"Yes, there was a fight. Hunt flew at him. The thief snatched up a fruit knife and fought back. In that struggle, Marcus Hunt forced his opponent's hand back. The fruit knife slashed the thief's chest, inflicting a superficial but badly bleeding gash. It sent the thief over the edge of insanity. He wrenched Marcus Hunt's wrist half off, caught up the knife, and stabbed Hunt to the heart.

"Then, in a quiet house, with a little beam of light streaming out from the torch on the sideboard, the murderer sees something that will hang him. He sees the blood from his own superficial wound seeping down his clothes.

"How is he to get rid of those clothes? He cannot destroy them or get them away from the house. Inevitably the house will be searched, and they will be found. Without the bloodstains, they would seem ordinary clothes in his wardrobe. But with the bloodstains—"

"There is only one thing he can do." Harriet Davis was standing behind the wicker settee, shading her eyes against the glare of the sun. Her hand did not tremble when she said, "He changed clothes with my uncle."

"That's it," growled Dr. Fell. "That's the whole sad story. The murderer dressed the body in his own clothes, making a puncture with the knife in sweater, shirt, and undervest. He then slipped on Mr. Hunt's pajamas and dressing gown, which at a pinch he could always claim as his own. Hunt's wound had bled hardly at all. His dressing gown, I think, had come open in the fight, so that all the thief had to trouble him was a tiny puncture in the jacket of the pajamas.

"But once he had done this, he had to hypnotize you all into the belief that there would have been no time for a change of clothes. He had to make it seem that the fight occurred just *then*. He had to rouse the house. So he brought down echoing thunders by pushing over a pile of silver, and slipped upstairs."

Dr. Fell paused. "The burglar could never have been Marcus Hunt, you know," he added. "We learn that Hunt's fingerprints were all over the place. Yet the murdered man was wearing gloves."

There was a swishing of feet in the grass below the terrace, and a tread of heavy boots coming up the terrace steps. The local inspector of police, buttoned up and steaming in his uniform, was followed by two constables.

Dr. Fell turned around a face of satisfaction.

"Ah!" he said, breathing deeply. "They've come to see about that swimming party, I imagine. It is easy to patch up a flesh wound with lint and cotton, or even a handkerchief. But such a wound will become infernally conspicuous in anyone who is forced to climb into bathing trunks."

"But it couldn't have been—" cried Harriet.

"Exactly," agreed the doctor, wheezing with pleasure. "It could not have been a long, thin, gangling fellow like Mr. Henderson. It assuredly could not have been a small and slender girl like yourself.

"There is only one person who, as we know, is just about Marcus Hunt's height and build; who could have put his own clothes on Hunt without any suspicion. That is the same person who, though he managed to stanch the wound in his chest, has been constantly running his hand inside the breast of his coat to make certain the bandage is secure. Just as Mr. Rolfe is doing now."

Arthur Rolfe sat very quietly, with his right hand still in the breast of his jacket. His face had grown smeary in the hot sunlight, but the eyes behind those thin shells of glasses remained inscrutable. He spoke only once, through dry lips, after they had cautioned him.

"I should have taken the young pup's warning," he said. "After all, he told me I would take long chances."

THANATOS PALACE HOTEL

ANDRÉ MAUROIS

Translated by Adrienne Foulke

"HOW'S AMSTEEL DOING?" Jean Monnier asked.

"Fifty-nine and a quarter," one of the typists in the pool answered.

The clattering typewriters were beating out a syncopated jazz rhythm. Through the windows one glimpsed the concrete giants of Manhattan. Telephones shrilled, ribbons of ticker tape unfurled and, at incredible speed, littered the office floor with sinister streamers speckled with letters and figures.

"AmSteel?" Jean Monnier asked again.

"Fifty-nine," Gertrude Owen answered.

She stopped a moment to glance at the young Frenchman. Sunk in a chair, his head in his hands, he looked utterly devastated.

One more who's played the market, she thought. Too bad for him! . . . And too bad for Fanny . . .

For Jean Monnier, assigned to the New York branch of the Holmann Bank, had married his American secretary two years before.

"Kennecott?" Jean Monnier asked.

"Twenty-eight," Gertrude Owen answered.

A voice shouted outside the door. Harry Cooper came in. Jean Monnier stood up.

"What a day downtown!" Harry Cooper said. "A twenty percent

drop across the board. And still there are some fools saying this isn't a crisis!"

"It's a crisis," Jean Monnier said, and he went out.

"That one's been hit," Harry Cooper said.

"Yes," Gertrude Owen said. "He risked his shirt. Fanny told me. She's leaving him tonight."

"There's nothing for it," Harry Cooper said. "It's the crisis."

THE HANDSOME BRONZE doors of the elevator slid open.

"Down," Jean Monnier said.

"How's AmSteel doing?" the elevator boy asked.

"Fifty-nine," Jean Monnier said.

He had bought it at a hundred and twelve. Loss: fifty-three dollars a share. And his other investments faring no better. The little fortune amassed earlier in Arizona had been poured into buying on margin. Fanny had never had a cent. He was finished.

Out in the street, hurrying for his train, he tried to visualize the future. Begin again? If Fanny would have the courage for it, it might be possible. He remembered his early struggles, the period of tending sheep in the desert, his rapid rise. After all, he was barely thirty. But he knew Fanny would be merciless.

She was.

The next morning, when Jean Monnier awoke alone, he felt drained of all courage. He had loved Fanny, despite her flinty coldness. The Negro maid served his slice of melon and bowl of cereal, and asked for money.

"Where's Mrs. Monnier?"

"Away on a trip."

He gave the woman fifteen dollars and figured out his bank balance. He had a little less than six hundred dollars left. Enough to live on two months, maybe three . . . And then? He looked out the window. Almost every day for a week, the papers had carried accounts of suicides. Bankers, brokers, speculators preferred death to a battle already lost. A twenty-story fall? How many seconds? Three? Four? And then the crushing thud . . . But suppose the force of it didn't kill you? He imagined the hideous pain, the broken limbs, and shattered bodies. He sighed and then, tucking a newspaper under his arm, he went out to a restaurant, where he was surprised to discover that he still had an appetite for waffles drowned in maple syrup.

"THANATOS PALACE HOTEL, New Mexico . . . Who's writing me from that queer address?"

He also had a letter from Harry Cooper, which he read first. The boss was asking why he had not shown up at the office. His account was short eight hundred and ninety-three dollars. What did he intend to do about it? The question was either cruel or naïve. But naïveté was not one of Harry Cooper's vices.

The other letter. Under an engraved design of three cypresses appeared the letterhead: THANATOS PALACE HOTEL. *Director: Henry Boerstecher.*

Dear Mr. Monnier:

The fact of our writing you today is not a matter of chance but is the result of our having certain information about you, which leads us to hope that our services can be useful to you.

You have not failed to notice, certainly, how in the life of the most courageous of men, such completely adverse circumstances can arise that further struggle becomes impossible, and death assumes the aspect of deliverance.

To close our eyes, to fall asleep, never to wake again, to hear no more questions, no more reproaches . . . Many of us have had this dream or actually formulated such a wish. However, except in very rare cases, men do not dare break free of their troubles, which is understandable when one observes those among us who have tried to do so. For the majority of suicides are ghastly failures. The man who wants to put a bullet through his head manages only to sever the optic nerve and blind himself. Another, who thinks that some barbiturate will put him permanently to sleep, mistakes the dosage and comes to three days later, his brain liquefied, his memory destroyed, and his body paralyzed. Suicide is an art that allows for neither mediocrity nor amateurism and yet, because of its nature, does not allow one to acquire experience.

This experience, dear Mr. Monnier, we are prepared to supply if, as we believe, the problem interests you. As founders of a hotel situated on the U.S.-Mexican border, removed from all inconvenient control thanks to the desertlike character of the region, we have considered it our duty to offer those of our human brothers who, for serious and irrefutable reasons, might want to quit this life, the means of doing so without pain and, if we may put it so, without danger.

At Thanatos Palace Hotel, death will await you in your sleep, and in the most gentle form. Our technical skill, acquired over fifteen years of uninterrupted success (we welcomed last year more than two thousand guests), allows us to guarantee a minimal dosage and immediate results. May we add that for visitors who would be troubled by legitimate religious scruples, we do, by an ingenious method, eliminate all moral responsibility.

We realize quite well that the majority of our clients have limited funds at their disposal, and that the frequency of suicides is inversely proportional to a credit balance in the bank. Therefore we have tried, with no sacrifice of comfort, to bring the rates at the Thanatos down to the lowest possible figure. It will be sufficient for you to deposit, on arrival, three hundred dollars. This amount will cover all your expenses for the duration of your stay with us, the extent of which must remain unknown to you, and it will defray the costs of the operation, funeral, and interment. For obvious reasons, service charges are included in this down payment and no gratuities will be asked of you.

It is important to add that the Thanatos is situated in a region of great natural beauty, that it provides four tennis courts, an eighteen-hole golf course, and a fine swimming pool. Its clientele includes both men and women, almost all of whom come from cultivated backgrounds; as a result, the social pleasures of one's stay, quickened as they are by the unusual situation, are incomparable. Travelers are requested to get off the train at the station in Deeming, where the hotel bus will meet them. They are also requested to announce their arrival, by letter or wire, two days in advance. The telegraph address is Thanatos, Coronado, New Mexico.

Jean Monnier took a pack of cards and laid out a game of patience that Fanny had taught him.

THE TRIP WAS very long. For hours on end, the train passed through fields of cotton where the dark heads of Negro workers bobbed above the white foam. Snatches of sleep and reading filled two days and two nights. Finally, the landscape turned rocky, titanic, dreamlike. The train ran through a deep ravine, between rock walls of prodigious height. Immense horizontal bands of violet, yellow, and red swathed the mountains. Halfway up floated a long scarf of cloud. In the little stations where the train paused, the traveler saw Mexicans in broad-brimmed sombreros and embroidered leather vests.

"Next station Deeming," the Pullman porter said to Jean Monnier. "Shine your shoes, suh?"

The Frenchman collected his books and closed his valises. The simplicity of his last trip astonished him. He heard the sound of rushing water. The brakes screeched. The train ground to a halt.

"Thanatos, sir?" asked the Indian porter running alongside the train.

This man had already piled on his cart the luggage of two blond young women who were following him.

Can it be, Jean Monnier thought, that those charming girls have come here to die?

They were looking at him, too, very seriously, and murmuring something he could not hear.

The Thanatos bus did not, as one might have feared, look like a hearse. Painted a bright blue, its seats upholstered in blue and orange, it gleamed in the sun among the broken-down cars that made the station yard, swarming with swearing Indians and Mexicans, look like a junkyard. The rocks lining the road were covered with lichen that enfolded the stone in a blue-gray film. Higher up, metallic multicolored rocks glinted in the sun. The chauffeur, wearing a gray uniform, was a heavyset man with bulging eyes. Jean Monnier, out of discretion and also so as to allow his companions some privacy, took the place beside him; presently, as the car undertook the assault of the mountain along a series of hairpin curves, the Frenchman tried to draw his neighbor out.

"Have you been driving for the Thanatos a long time?"

"Three years," the man muttered.

"It must be a strange sort of job."

"Strange?" the man said. "Why strange? I drive my bus. What's strange about that?"

"Do the passengers you take up ever come down again?"

"Not often," the man said, with a trace of constraint. "Not often . . . but it does happen. I'm one, for example."

"You! Really?. . . You came originally as a—a client?"

"Look, sir," the chauffeur said, "I took this job on so I wouldn't have to talk about myself, and these curves are rough going. You wouldn't want me to kill you, you and these young ladies, now would you?"

"Obviously not," Jean Monnier said.

Then his answer struck him as rather droll, and he smiled.

Two hours later, without a word, the chauffeur pointed to the silhouette of the Thanatos on a high plateau.

THE HOTEL WAS built in Indian and Spanish style, very low, with terraced roofs and red walls of cement that roughly approximated the native clay. The rooms faced south, across sunny balconies. An Italian doorman welcomed the visitors. His shaved face suddenly evoked for Jean Monnier another world—the streets, the flowering boulevards of a great city. "Where in the devil have I seen you before?" he asked the doorman, as a bellhop picked up his bag.

"At the Ritz in Barcelona, sir. My name is Sarconi. . . . I left when the civil war broke out."

"From Barcelona to New Mexico! Quite a change!"

"Oh, a doorman's job is the same everywhere, sir. Only the papers that I must ask you to fill out are a little more complicated here than anywhere else. I'm sorry, sir. . . ."

The printed forms presented to the three arrivals were indeed crammed full of questions, spaces for answers, and explanatory notes. One was requested to indicate with great exactness the date and place of one's birth, the names and addresses of those who should be notified in case of accident.

> Please give at least two addresses of relatives or friends, and copy out by hand and in your native language the following Statement A: "I the undersigned ________________, being of sound mind and body, certify that I renounce life of my own free will and, in case of accident, discharge the management and staff of the Thanatos Palace Hotel of all responsibility."

Seated facing each other at the table, the two young women were carefully filling out Statement A; Jean Monnier observed that they were writing in German.

HENRY B. BOERSTECHER, the manager, was a quiet, gold-bespectacled man, very proud of his establishment.

"Does the hotel belong to you?" Jean Monnier asked.

"No, sir, the hotel belongs to a corporation, but it was my idea, and I am manager here for life."

"How is it that you don't have the worst kind of difficulties with the local authorities?"

"Difficulties?" Mr. Boerstecher sounded surprised and shocked. "But we do nothing here, sir, that is out of line with our duties as hotelkeepers. We provide our clients with what they want, all that they want, and nothing more. Furthermore, sir, there are no local authorities here. Boundaries in this area have been so vaguely defined that no one knows for sure whether it belongs to Mexico or to the United States. For a long time this particular plateau was considered inaccessible. A legend hereabouts has it that a group of Indians gathered here—this was two or three hundred years ago—to die together and escape the European settlers. People here used to claim that the spirits of the dead forbade access to the mountain. That's why we were able to acquire the land for a very reasonable price and to live a perfectly independent existence."

"The families of your clients never get after you?"

"Get after us!" Mr. Boerstecher cried indignantly. "And merciful God, why? What courts would they go to? The families of our clients, sir, are only too happy to have such delicate and almost always painful matters taken care of without publicity. . . . No, no, M. Monnier, everything here goes along pleasantly, correctly, and to us our clients are like friends. . . . Would you like to see your room? It is, if you have no objections, number one thirteen. You're not superstitious?"

"Not at all," Jean Monnier said. "But I was brought up in the church, and I must tell you that the idea of suicide—"

"But there is, and there will be, no question of suicide, sir!" Mr. Boerstecher said in such a peremptory tone that the other man did not press the matter. "Sarconi, show number one thirteen to the gentleman. And the three hundred dollars, sir—will you be kind enough to deposit them on your way with the cashier, whose office is next to mine."

In room number 113, illuminated by a splendid sunset, Jean Monnier searched in vain for some trace of a lethal machine.

"WHAT TIME IS dinner?"

"Eight thirty, sir," the valet said.

"Does one have to dress?"

"Most of the gentlemen do, sir."

"Well, then, so will I. . . . Will you lay out a white shirt and black tie."

When he came down into the lobby, he saw that the women were indeed in evening dresses and the men in tuxedos. Mr. Boerstecher came up to him, officious and deferential.

"Ah, M. Monnier, I was looking for you. Since you are alone, I thought it might be pleasant for you to share your table with one of our guests, Mrs. Kirby-Shaw."

Monnier shook his head wearily.

"I haven't come here," he said, "to lead a social life. But . . . could you show me the lady without introducing me?"

"Of course, M. Monnier. Mrs. Kirby-Shaw is the young lady in the white satin dress sitting near the piano and leafing through a magazine. I don't think her appearance could be displeasing. Far from it . . . And she is a very pleasant woman, well bred, intelligent. . . . An artist."

Definitely Mrs. Kirby-Shaw was a very pretty woman. Soft brown curls were pulled back, revealing a high, strong forehead, and gathered together in a chignon low on the neck. Her eyes were warm and full of humor. Now why in the devil would such an attractive creature want to die?

"Is this Mrs. Kirby-Shaw—well, is this lady one of your clients on the same basis and for the same reason as I?"

"Cer-tain-ly," Mr. Boerstecher said, and he seemed to invest the word with profound meaning. "Cer-tain-ly."

"Then introduce me."

By the time dinner—simple but excellent and well served—was over, Jean Monnier already knew at least the essential outline of Clara Kirby-Shaw's life. She had been married to a rich man, who was very good to her, but whom she had never loved and whom she had left six months before to follow a young writer to Europe, an attractive, cynical fellow she'd met in New York. She had supposed he was ready to marry her as soon as she had got a divorce, but no sooner had they arrived in England than he indicated very definitely that he intended to get rid of her as fast as possible. Surprised and hurt by his harshness, she had tried to make him understand how much she had given up for him, and the dreadful situation she was now in. He had laughed heartily.

"Clara, really!" he had said to her. "You are a woman from another age. If I'd known you were Victorian to this degree, I'd have left you with your husband and your children. . . . You must go back to them, my dear. You are made to bring up a big and proper family."

She had then conceived one final hope—to persuade her husband, Norman Kirby-Shaw, to take her back. She was sure that if she had been able to see him again alone, she would easily have won him back. But, surrounded by family and associates who exerted a constant pressure on him that was hostile to Clara, he had proved inflexible. After several humiliating, futile attempts, one morning in her mail she had found the Thanatos prospectus and had understood that here was the one immediate and easy solution to her painful problem.

"And you're not afraid of death?" Jean Monnier asked.

"Yes, of course . . . But less afraid than I am of life."

"A good answer," Jean Monnier said.

"I didn't mean it that way," Clara said. "And now tell me why *you* are here."

When she had heard Jean Monnier's story, she reproached him warmly.

"It's almost beyond belief!" she said. "What do you mean? You want to die because your stocks have gone down! Don't you see that in a year, or in two or three or more years, if you have the courage to live, you will have forgotten, and perhaps even made up, your losses?"

"My losses are only an excuse. They'd be nothing, it's true, if I still had some reason to live. But I told you, too, that my wife has left me. I have no close family back in France, and I left no woman friend behind. . . . To be completely honest, I left France after a love affair had broken up. . . . Whom would I be fighting for now?"

"For yourself! For people who will come to love you later, and whom you're sure, sure to meet. Because several painful experiences have shown you how despicable some women can be, you mustn't judge all the others unfairly—"

"Do you really believe that there are women in this world—women whom I could love, I mean—who would be capable of accepting, at least for a few years, a life of struggle and poverty?"

"I am sure of it," she said. "There are women who love a struggle and who find some kind of romantic attraction in poverty. I do, for example."

"You?"

"Oh, I only meant . . ." She stopped, hesitated, then went on. "I think we should go back to the lobby. We're the last people in the dining room, and the headwaiter is prowling around us in despair."

"You don't suppose," he said, as he placed an ermine cape around Clara Kirby-Shaw's shoulders, "you don't suppose that—that tonight . . ."

"Oh, no," she said. "You just arrived."

"And you?"

"I've been here two days."

When they left each other, it was agreed that next morning they would meet and take a walk up the mountain.

THE MORNING SUN was bathing the balcony with a slanting sheen of light and warmth. Jean Monnier, who had just taken an ice-cold shower, was surprised to find himself thinking, How great to be alive! Then he reminded himself that he had only a few dollars and a few days ahead of him. He sighed.

"Ten o'clock! Clara will be waiting for me."

He dressed quickly, and felt very buoyant in his white linen suit. When he joined Clara Kirby-Shaw near the tennis courts, she, too, was dressed in white and was walking up and down, flanked by the two Austrian girls, who fled at the sight of the Frenchman.

"Did I frighten them?"

"You startled them. . . . They were telling me their stories."

"Interesting?. . . Tell me about them later. Were you able to get a little sleep?"

"I slept wonderfully well. I suspect the ominous Boerstecher of slipping a little chloral hydrate in our drinks."

"I don't believe it," he said. "I slept like a log, but it was a natural sleep, and this morning I feel perfectly clearheaded."

After a moment, he added, "And perfectly happy."

She looked at him, smiling, and said nothing.

"Let's take this path," he said, "and now tell me about the little Austrian girls. You are going to be my Scheherazade here."

"But our nights will not be a thousand and one."

"Unfortunately . . . *Our* nights?"

She interrupted him. "Those infants are sisters, twins. They were brought up together, first in Vienna, then in Budapest, and they have never had any other close friends. When they were eighteen, they met a Hungarian from an old and noble family, handsome as a demigod, musical as a Gypsy, and they both, the same day, fell madly in love with him. After a few months, he asked one of the sisters to marry him. The other sister, in despair, tried to drown herself but failed. Then the one who had been chosen resolved to renounce Count Nicky, and they worked out a plan to die together. . . . That's when—like you, like me—they received the Thanatos prospectus."

"They're mad!" Jean Monnier said. "They're young, they're ravishing. Let them live in America, and some other men will fall in love with them. A few weeks of patience . . ."

"It is always," she said sadly, "for lack of patience that one is here. . . . Each of us is wise about the others. Who was it who said that we always have the courage to bear other people's troubles?"

All day long, the guests of the Thanatos saw a couple dressed in white wandering along the paths of the hotel park, skirting the rocks and strolling the length of the ravine. The man and woman were talking passionately. When night fell, they turned back to the hotel and the Mexican gardener, seeing them locked in each other's arms, turned his head away.

AFTER DINNER, JEAN MONNIER spent the rest of the evening in the small, deserted salon, whispering to Clara Kirby-Shaw, who seemed moved by whatever he was saying. Then, before going up to his room, he sought out Mr. Boerstecher. He found the manager seated before a great black ledger. Mr. Boerstecher was checking figures and, from time to time, he drew a red line through an entry.

"Good evening, M. Monnier. Can I do something for you?"

"Yes, Mr. Boerstecher. At least, I hope so. . . . What I have to say will surprise you. . . . The change is so sudden. . . . But life is like that. In a word, I've come to tell you that I've changed my mind. I don't want to die anymore."

Mr. Boerstecher looked up in surprise.

"Are you serious, M. Monnier?"

"I know," the Frenchman said, "that I'm going to seem incoherent, indecisive to you. But isn't it natural that when circumstances change, our intentions change, too? A week ago, when I got your letter, I felt absolutely hopeless and all alone in the world. I didn't believe that the battle was worth the effort. . . . Today everything is changed. And at bottom that is thanks to you, Mr. Boerstecher."

"Thanks to me, M. Monnier?"

"Yes, because that young woman you sat me down opposite at table is the one who has brought this miracle about. . . . Mrs. Kirby-Shaw is a delicious woman, Mr. Boerstecher."

"I told you so, M. Monnier."

"Delicious and heroic. . . . When she learned about my difficult situation, she agreed—she is willing to share it with me. Does that surprise you?"

"Not at all. We are familiar here with these dramatic reversals. And I am delighted for it, M. Monnier. You are young, very young—"

"So, if you see nothing in the way, we will leave tomorrow, Mrs. Kirby-Shaw and I, for Deeming."

"Am I then to understand that Mrs. Kirby-Shaw, like you, is renouncing—"

"Yes, naturally. Furthermore, she will confirm it herself presently. There is just one rather delicate matter to settle. The three hundred dollars that I deposited with you, which was about all I had to my name—does that money belong irrevocably to the Thanatos, or could I get a part of it back to pay for our tickets?"

"We are honest people, M. Monnier. We never insist on payment for services that have not been rendered. Tomorrow morning, the cashier will make out your bill on the basis of twenty dollars a day for room and meals, plus service, and the balance will be returned to you."

"That is very courteous and generous of you. Ah, Mr. Boerstecher, how much I owe you! Happiness rediscovered . . . A new life . . ."

"At your service," Mr. Boerstecher said.

He watched Jean Monnier go out and walk down the corridor. Then he pressed a button and said, "Send Sarconi in."

In a few minutes, the doorman appeared.

"Did you call for me, signore?"

"Yes, Sarconi. It will be necessary to supply the gas to number one thirteen this evening. Around two a.m."

"Should we give the Somnial before the Lethal, signore?"

"I don't think it will be necessary. He's going to sleep very well. . . . That's all for this evening, Sarconi. And tomorrow, the two sisters in number seventeen, as scheduled."

As the doorman was leaving, Mrs. Kirby-Shaw appeared at the office door.

"Come on in," Mr. Boerstecher said. "I was just going to send for you. Your client's been in to announce his departure."

"It seems to me," she said, "that compliments are in order. That was a job well done."

"Well and quickly done. I shan't forget it."

"Then it's for tonight?"

"It's for tonight."

"Poor boy," she said. "He was sweet, and so romantic. . . ."

"They are all romantic," Mr. Boerstecher said.

"You're cruel, all the same," she said. "The very moment they find a new taste for life, you make them disappear."

"Cruel? On the contrary, all the humanity of our method lies here. This fellow had religious scruples. I've quieted them for him."

He consulted his ledger.

"Tomorrow, a day off . . . But the next day, I have another new arrival for you. A banker again, but a Swede this time . . . and no longer young."

"I liked that young Frenchman," she said dreamily.

"We do not choose our work," the manager said severely. "Here is your ten dollars, plus a ten-dollar bonus."

"Thanks," said Clara Kirby-Shaw.

As she slipped the bank notes into her purse, she sighed.

When she had gone out, Mr. Boerstecher reached for his red pencil, and using a small steel ruler as a guide, he carefully crossed a name from his ledger.

THE GHOST-SHIP

RICHARD MIDDLETON

FAIRFIELD IS A little village lying near the Portsmouth Road about halfway between London and the sea. Strangers who find it by accident, now and then, call it a pretty, old-fashioned place; we who live in it and call it home don't find anything very pretty about it, but we should be sorry to live anywhere else. Our minds have taken the shape of the inn and the church and the green, I suppose. At all events we never feel comfortable out of Fairfield.

Of course the cockneys, with their vasty houses and noise-ridden streets, can call us rustics if they choose, but for all that, Fairfield is a better place to live in than London. Doctor says that when he goes to London his mind is bruised with the weight of the houses, and he was a cockney born. He had to live there himself when he was a little chap, but he knows better now. You gentlemen may laugh—perhaps some of you come from London way—but it seems to me that a witness like that is worth a gallon of arguments.

Dull? Well, you might find it dull, but I assure you that I've listened to all the London yarns you have spun tonight, and they're absolutely nothing to the things that happen at Fairfield. It's because of our way of thinking and minding our own business. If one of your Londoners were set down on the green of a Saturday night when the ghosts of the lads who died in the war keep tryst with the lasses who lie in the churchyard, he couldn't help being curious and interfering, and then the ghosts would go where it was quieter. But we just let them come and go and don't make any fuss, and in consequence Fairfield is the ghostiest place in all England. Why, I've seen a headless man sitting on the edge of the well in broad daylight, and the children playing about his feet as if he were their father. Take my word for it, spirits know when they are well off as much as human beings.

Still, I must admit that the thing I'm going to tell you about was queer even for our part of the world, where three packs of ghost-hounds hunt regularly during the season, and blacksmith's great-grandfather is busy all night shoeing the dead gentlemen's horses. Now that's a thing that wouldn't happen in London, because of their interfering way, but blacksmith he lies up aloft and sleeps as quiet as a lamb. Once when he had a bad head he shouted down to them not to make so much noise, and in the morning he found an old guinea left on the anvil as an apology. He wears it on his watch chain now. But I must get on with my story; if I start telling you about the queer happenings at Fairfield I'll never stop.

It all came of the great storm in the spring of '97, the year that we had two great storms. This was the first one, and I remember it very well, because I found in the morning that it had lifted the thatch of my pigsty into widow Lamport's garden as clean as a boy's kite. After a little I went down to the Fox and Grapes to tell landlord what she had said to me. Landlord he laughed, being a married man and at ease with the sex. "Come to that," he said, "the tempest has blowed something into my field. A kind of a ship I think it would be."

I was surprised at that until he explained that it was only a ghost-ship and would do no hurt to the turnips. We argued that it had been blown up from the sea at Portsmouth, and then we talked of something else. There were two slates down at the parsonage and a big tree in Lumley's meadow. It was a rare storm.

I reckon the wind had blown our ghosts all over England. They were coming back for days afterward with foundered horses and as footsore as possible, and they were so glad to get back to Fairfield that some of them walked up the street crying like little children. What with one thing and another, I should think it was a week before we got straight again, and then one afternoon I met the landlord on the green and he had a worried face. "I wish you'd come and have a look at that ship in my field," he said to me. "It seems to me it's leaning real hard on the turnips. I can't bear thinking what the missus will say when she sees it."

I walked down the lane with him, and sure enough there was a ship in the middle of his field, but such a ship as no man had seen on the water for three hundred years, let alone in the middle of a turnip field. It was all painted black and covered with carvings, and there was a great bay window in the stern for all the world like the squire's drawing room. There was a crowd of little black cannon on deck and looking out of her portholes, and she was anchored at each end to the hard ground. I have seen the wonders of the world on picture postcards, but I have never seen anything to equal that.

"She seems very solid for a ghost-ship," I said, seeing the landlord was bothered.

"I should say it's a betwixt and between," he answered, puzzling it over, "but it's going to spoil a matter of fifty turnips, and missus she'll want it moved." We went up to her and touched the side, and it was as hard as a real ship. "Now there's folks in England would call that very curious," he said.

Now I don't know much about ships, but I should think that that ghost-ship weighed a solid two hundred tons, and it seemed to me that she had come to stay, so that I felt sorry for landlord.

"All the horses in Fairfield won't move her out of my turnips," he said, frowning at her.

Just then we heard a noise on her deck, and we looked up and saw that a man had come out of her front cabin and was looking down at us very peaceably. He was dressed in a black uniform set out with rusty gold lace, and he had a great cutlass by his side in a brass sheath. "I'm Captain Bartholomew Roberts," he said, in a gentleman's voice, "put in for recruits. I seem to have brought her rather far up the harbor."

"Harbor!" cried landlord. "Why, you're fifty miles from the sea."

Captain Roberts didn't turn a hair. "So much as that, is it?" he said coolly. "Well, it's of no consequence."

Landlord was a bit upset at this. "I don't want to be unneighborly," he said, "but I wish you hadn't brought your ship into my field. You see, my wife sets great store on these turnips."

The captain took a pinch of snuff out of a fine gold box that he pulled out of his pocket, and dusted his fingers with a silk handkerchief. "I'm only here for a few months," he said, "but if a testimony of my esteem would pacify your good lady, I should be content," and with the words he loosed a great gold brooch from the neck of his coat and tossed it down to landlord.

Landlord blushed as red as a strawberry. "I'm not denying she's fond of jewelry," he said, "but it's too much for half a sackful of turnips." And indeed it was a handsome brooch.

The captain laughed. "Tut, man," he said, "it's a forced sale, and you deserve a good price. Say no more about it," and nodding good day to us, he turned on his heel and went into the cabin. Landlord walked back up the lane like a man with a weight off his mind. "That tempest has blowed me a bit of luck," he said; "the missus will be main pleased with that brooch. It's better than blacksmith's guinea, any day."

Ninety-seven was Jubilee year, the year of the second Jubilee, you remember, and we had great doings at Fairfield, so that we hadn't much time to bother about the ghost-ship, though anyhow it isn't our way to meddle in things that don't concern us. Landlord, he saw his tenant once or twice when he was hoeing his turnips and passed the time of day, and landlord's wife wore her new brooch to church every Sunday. But we didn't mix much with the ghosts at any time, all except an idiot lad there was in the village, and he didn't know the difference between a man and a ghost, poor innocent! On Jubilee Day, however, somebody told Captain Roberts why the church bells were ringing, and he hoisted a flag and fired off his guns like a loyal Englishman.

It wasn't till our celebrations were over that we noticed that anything was wrong in Fairfield. 'Twas shoemaker who told me first about it one morning at the Fox and Grapes. "You know my great-great-uncle?" he said to me.

"You mean Joshua, the quiet lad," I answered, knowing him well.

"Quiet!" said shoemaker indignantly. "Quiet you call him, coming home at three o'clock every morning as drunk as a magistrate and waking up the whole house with his noise."

"Why, it can't be Joshua!" I said, for I knew him for one of the most respectable young ghosts in the village.

"Joshua it is," said shoemaker, "and one of these nights he'll find himself out in the street if he isn't careful."

This kind of talk shocked me, I can tell you, for I don't like to hear a man abusing his own family, and I could hardly believe that a steady youngster like Joshua had taken to drink. But just then in came butcher Aylwin in such a temper that he could hardly drink his beer. "The young puppy! The young puppy!" he kept on saying; and it was some time before shoemaker and I found out that he was talking about his ancestor that fell at Senlac.

"Drink?" said shoemaker hopefully, for we all like company in our misfortunes, and butcher nodded grimly.

"The young noodle," he said, emptying his tankard.

Well, after that I kept my ears open, and it was the same story all over the village. There was hardly a young man among all the ghosts of Fairfield who didn't roll home in the small hours of the morning the worse for liquor. I used to wake up in the night and hear them stumble past my house, singing outrageous songs. The worst of it was that we couldn't keep the scandal to ourselves, and the folk at Greenhill began to talk of "sodden Fairfield" and taught their children to sing a song about us:

"Sodden Fairfield, sodden Fairfield, has no use for bread-and-butter,
Rum for breakfast, rum for dinner, rum for tea, and rum for supper!"

We are easygoing in our village, but we didn't like that.

Of course we soon found out where the young fellows went to get the drink, and landlord was terribly cut up that his tenant should have turned out so badly. As time went on, things grew from bad to worse, and at all hours of the day you would see those young reprobates sleeping it off on the village green. Nearly every afternoon a ghost-wagon used to jolt down to the ship with a lading of rum, and though the older ghosts seemed inclined to give the captain's hospitality the go-by, the youngsters were neither to hold nor to bind.

So one afternoon when I was taking my nap I heard a knock at the door, and there was parson looking very serious, like a man with a job before him that he didn't altogether relish. "I'm going down to talk to the captain about all this drunkenness in the village, and I want you to come with me," he said straight out.

I can't say that I fancied the visit much myself, and I tried to hint to parson that as, after all, they were only a lot of ghosts, it didn't very much matter.

"Dead or alive, I'm responsible for their good conduct," he said, "and I'm going to do my duty and put a stop to this continued disorder. And you are coming with me, John Simmons." So I went, parson being a persuasive kind of man.

We went down to the ship, and as we approached her I could see the captain tasting the air on deck. When he saw parson he took off his hat very politely, and I can tell you that I was relieved to find that he had a proper respect for the cloth. Parson acknowledged his salute and spoke out stoutly enough. "Sir, I should be glad to have a word with you."

"Come on board, sir; come on board," said the captain, and I could tell by his voice that he knew why we were there. Parson and I climbed up an uneasy kind of ladder, and the captain took us into the great cabin at the back of the ship, where the bay window was. It was the most wonderful place you ever saw in your life, all full of gold and silver plate, swords with jeweled scabbards, carved oak chairs, and great chests that looked as though they were bursting with guineas. Even parson was surprised, and he did not shake his head very hard when the captain took down some silver cups and poured us out a drink of rum. I tasted mine, and I don't mind saying that it changed my view of things entirely. There was nothing betwixt and between about that rum, and I felt that it was ridiculous to blame the lads for drinking too much of stuff like that. It seemed to fill my veins with honey and fire.

Parson put the case squarely to the captain, but I didn't listen much to what he said; I was busy sipping my drink and looking through the window at the fishes swimming to and fro over landlord's turnips. Just then it seemed the most natural thing in the world that they should be there, though afterward, of course, I could see that that proved it was a ghost-ship.

All the time I was regarding the wonders of the deep, parson was telling Captain Roberts how there was no peace or rest in the village owing to the curse of drunkenness, and what a bad example the youngsters were setting to the older ghosts. The captain listened very attentively, and only put in a word now and then about boys being boys and young men sowing their wild oats. But when parson had finished his speech, the captain filled up our silver cups and said to parson, with a flourish, "I should be sorry to cause trouble anywhere I have been made welcome, and you will be glad to hear that I put to sea tomorrow night. And now you must drink me a prosperous voyage." So we all stood up and drank the toast with honor, and that noble rum was like hot oil in my veins.

After that, captain showed us some of the curiosities he had brought back from foreign parts, and we were greatly amazed, though afterward I couldn't clearly remember what they were. And then I found myself walking across the turnips with parson, and I was telling him of the glories of the deep that I had seen through the window of the ship. He turned on me severely. "If I were you, John Simmons," he said, "I should go straight home to bed." He has a way of putting things that wouldn't occur to an ordinary man, has parson, and I did as he told me.

Well, next day it came on to blow, and it blew harder and harder, till about eight o'clock at night I heard a noise and looked out into the garden. I daresay you won't believe me, it seems a bit tall even to me, but the wind had lifted the thatch of my pigsty into the widow's garden a second time. I thought I wouldn't wait to hear what widow had to say about it, so I went across the green to the Fox and Grapes, and the wind was so strong that I danced along on tiptoe like a girl at the fair. When I got to the inn, landlord had to help me shut the door.

"It's a powerful tempest," he said, drawing the beer. "I hear there's a chimney down at Dickory End."

"It's a funny thing how these sailors know about the weather," I answered. "When captain said he was going tonight, I was thinking it would take a capful of wind to carry the ship back to sea, but now here's more than a capful."

"Ah, yes," said landlord, "it's tonight he goes true enough and, mind you, though he treated me handsome over the rent, I'm not sure it's a loss to the village. I don't hold with gentrice who fetch their drink from London instead of helping our local traders to get their living."

"But you haven't got rum like his," I said, to draw him out.

His neck grew red above his collar, and I was afraid I'd gone too far, but after a while he got his breath with a grunt.

"John Simmons," he said, "if you've come down here this windy night to talk a lot of fool's talk, you've wasted a journey."

Well, of course, then I had to smooth him down with praising his rum, and heaven forgive me for swearing it was better than captain's. For the like of that rum no living lips have tasted save mine and parson's. But somehow I brought landlord around, and presently we must have a glass of his best to prove its quality.

"Beat that if you can!" he cried, and we both raised our glasses to our mouths, only to stop halfway and look at each other in amaze. For the wind that had been howling outside like an outrageous dog had all of a sudden turned as melodious as the carol boys of a Christmas Eve.

We went to the door, and the wind burst it open so that the handle was driven clean into the plaster of the wall. But we didn't think about that at the time; for over our heads, sailing very comfortably through the windy stars, was the ship that had passed the summer in landlord's field. Her portholes and her bay window were blazing with lights, and there was a noise of singing and fiddling on her decks. "He's gone," shouted landlord above the storm, "and he's taken half the village with him!" I could only nod in answer, not having lungs like bellows of leather.

In the morning we were able to measure the strength of the storm, and over and above my pigsty there was damage enough wrought in the village to keep us busy. Many of our ghosts were scattered abroad, but this time very few came back, all the young men having sailed with captain; and not only ghosts, for the poor half-witted lad was missing, and we reckoned that he had stowed himself away or perhaps shipped as cabin boy, not knowing any better.

What with the lamentations of the ghost-girls and the grumbling of families who had lost an ancestor, the village was upset for a while, and the funny thing was that it was the folk who had complained most of the carryings-on of the youngsters who made most noise now that they were gone. I hadn't any sympathy with shoemaker or butcher, who ran about saying how much they missed their lads, but it made me grieve to hear the poor bereaved girls calling their lovers by name on the village green at nightfall. It didn't seem fair to me that they should have lost their men a second time.

Still, not even a spirit can be sorry forever, and after a few months we made up our minds that the folk who had sailed in the ship were never coming back, and we didn't talk about it anymore.

And then one day, I daresay it would be a couple of years after, when the whole business was quite forgotten, who should come traipsing along the road from Portsmouth but the daft lad who had gone away with the ship, without waiting till he was dead to become a ghost. You never saw such a boy as that in all your life. He had a great rusty cutlass hanging on a string at his waist, and he was tattooed all over in fine colors, so that even his face looked like a girl's sampler. He had a handkerchief in his hand full of foreign shells and old-fashioned pieces of small money, very curious, and he walked up to the well outside his mother's house and drew himself a drink as if he had been nowhere in particular.

The worst of it was that he had come back as softheaded as he went, and try as we might we couldn't get anything reasonable out of him. He talked a lot of gibberish about keelhauling and walking the plank and crimson murders—things which a decent sailor should know nothing about, so that it seemed to me that for all his manners captain had been more of a pirate than a gentleman mariner. But to draw sense out of that boy was as hard as picking cherries off a crab tree. One silly tale he had that he kept on drifting back to, and to hear him you would have thought that it was the only thing that happened to him in his life. "We was at anchor," he would say, "off an island called the Basket of Flowers, and the sailors had caught a lot of parrots and we were teaching them to swear. Up and down the decks, up and down the decks, and the language they used was dreadful. Then we looked up and saw the masts of the Spanish ship outside the harbor. Outside the harbor they were, so we threw the parrots into the sea and sailed out to fight. And all the parrots were drowned in the sea and the language they used was dreadful." That's the sort of boy he was, nothing but silly talk of parrots when we asked him about the fighting. And we never had a chance of teaching him better, for two days after, he ran away again and hasn't been seen since.

That's my story, and I assure you that things like that are happening at Fairfield all the time. The ship has never come back, but somehow as people grow older they seem to think that one of these windy nights she'll come sailing in over the hedges with all the lost ghosts on board. Well, when she comes, she'll be welcome. There's one ghost-lass that has never grown tired of waiting for her lad to return. Every night you'll see her out on the green, straining her poor eyes with looking for the mast lights among the stars. A faithful lass you'd call her, and you'd be right.

Landlord's field wasn't a penny the worse for the visit, but they do say that since then the turnips that have been grown in it have tasted of rum.

THE RATS IN THE WALLS

H. P. LOVECRAFT

On July 16, 1923, I moved into Exham Priory after the last workman had finished his labors. The restoration had been a stupendous task, for little had remained of the deserted pile but a shell-like ruin; yet because it had been the seat of my ancestors, I let no expense deter me. The place had not been inhabited since the reign of James the First, when a tragedy of intensely hideous, though largely unexplained, nature had struck down the master, five of his children, and several servants; and driven forth under a cloud of suspicion and terror the third son, my lineal progenitor and the only survivor of the abhorred line.

With this sole heir denounced as a murderer, the estate had reverted to the crown, nor had the accused man made any attempt to exculpate himself or regain his property. Shaken by some horror greater than that of conscience or the law, and expressing only a frantic wish to exclude the ancient edifice from his sight and memory, Walter de la Poer, eleventh Baron Exham, fled to Virginia and there founded the family which by the next century had become known as Delapore.

Exham Priory had remained untenanted, though later allotted to the estates of the Norrys family and much studied because of its peculiarly composite architecture; an architecture involving Gothic towers resting on a Saxon or Romanesque substructure, whose foundation in turn was of a still earlier order or blend of orders—Roman, and even druidic or native Cymric, if legends speak truly. This foundation was a very singular thing, being merged on one side with the solid limestone of the precipice from whose brink the priory overlooked a desolate valley three miles west of the village of Anchester.

Architects and antiquarians loved to examine this strange relic of forgotten centuries, but the countryfolk hated it. They had hated it hundreds of years before, when my ancestors lived there, and they hated it now, with the moss and mold of abandonment on it. I had not been a day in Anchester before I knew I came of an accursed house. And this week workmen have blown up Exham Priory and are busy obliterating the traces of its foundations.

The bare statistics of my ancestry I had always known, together with the fact that my first American forebear had come to the colonies under a strange cloud. Of details, however, I had been kept wholly ignorant through the policy of reticence always maintained by the Delapores. Unlike our planter neighbors, we seldom boasted of crusading ancestors or other medieval and Renaissance heroes; nor was any kind of tradition handed down except what may have been recorded in the sealed envelope left before the Civil War by every squire to his eldest son for posthumous opening. The glories we cherished were those achieved since the migration; the glories of a proud and honorable, if somewhat reserved and unsocial Virginia line.

During the war our fortunes were extinguished and our whole existence changed by the burning of Carfax, our home on the banks of the James. My grandfather, advanced in years, had perished in that incendiary outrage, and with him the envelope that bound us all to the past. I can recall that fire today as I saw it then at the age of seven, with the Federal soldiers shouting, the women screaming, and the Negroes howling and praying. My father was in the army, defending Richmond, and after many formalities my mother and I were passed through the lines to join him.

When the war ended we all moved north, whence my mother had come; and I grew to manhood, middle age, and ultimate wealth as a stolid Yankee. Neither my father nor I ever knew what our hereditary envelope had contained, and as I merged into the grayness of Massachusetts business life I lost all interest in the mysteries which evidently lurked far back in my family tree. Had I suspected their nature, how gladly I would have left Exham Priory to its moss, bats, and cobwebs!

My father died in 1904, but without any message to leave to me, or to my only child, Alfred, a motherless boy of ten. It was this boy who reversed the order of family information, for although I could give him only jesting conjectures about the past, he wrote me of some very interesting ancestral legends when the late war took him to England in 1917 as an aviation officer. Apparently the Delapores had a colorful and perhaps sinister history, for a friend of my son's, Captain Edward Norrys of the Royal Flying Corps, dwelt near the family seat at Anchester and related some peasant superstitions which few novelists could equal for wildness and incredibility. Norrys himself, of course, did not take them seriously; but they amused my son and made good material for his letters to me. It was this legendry which definitely turned my attention to my transatlantic heritage and made me resolve to purchase and restore the family seat, which Norrys offered to get for a reasonable figure, since his own uncle was the present owner.

I bought Exham Priory in 1918, but was almost immediately distracted from my plans of restoration by the return of my son as a maimed invalid. During the two years that he lived I thought of nothing but his care, having even placed my business under the direction of partners.

In 1921, as I found myself bereaved and aimless, a retired manufacturer no longer young, I resolved to divert my remaining years with my new possession. Visiting Anchester in December, I was entertained by Captain Norrys, a plump, amiable young man who had thought much of my son, and secured his assistance in the coming restoration. Exham Priory itself I saw without emotion, a jumble of tottering medieval ruins covered with lichens, and denuded of floors or other interior features save the stone walls of the separate towers.

As I began to hire workmen for the reconstruction I was forced in every case to go outside the immediate locality, for the Anchester villagers had an almost unbelievable fear and hatred of both the priory and its ancient family. This sentiment was so great that it was sometimes communicated to the outside laborers, causing numerous desertions.

My son had told me that he was somewhat avoided during his visits because he was a de la Poer, and I now found myself subtly ostracized, so that I had to collect most of the village traditions through the mediation of Norrys. What the people could not forgive, perhaps, was that I had come to restore a symbol so abhorrent to them; for, rationally or not, they viewed Exham Priory as nothing less than a haunt of fiends and werewolves.

Piecing together the tales which Norrys collected for me, and supplementing them with the accounts of several savants who had studied the ruins, I deduced that Exham Priory stood on the site of a prehistoric temple, a druidic or antedruidic thing which must have been contemporary with Stonehenge. That indescribable rites had been celebrated there, few doubted, and there were unpleasant tales of the transference of these rites into the Cybele worship the Romans had introduced.

Inscriptions still visible in the subcellar bore such unmistakable letters as DIV . . . OPS . . . MAGNA MAT . . . sign of the Magna Mater, whose dark worship was once vainly forbidden to Roman citizens. Anchester had been the camp of the third Augustan legion, as many remains attest, and it was said that the temple of the Cybele was splendid and thronged with worshippers who performed nameless ceremonies at the bidding of a Phrygian priest. Tales added that the rites did not vanish with the Roman power, and that certain among the Saxons added to what remained of the temple and gave it the essential outline it subsequently preserved, making it the center of a cult feared through half the heptarchy. About AD 1000 the place is mentioned in a chronicle as being a substantial stone priory housing a strange and powerful monastic order and surrounded by extensive gardens which needed no walls to exclude a frightened populace. It was never destroyed by the Danes, though after the Norman Conquest it must have declined tremendously; since there was no impediment when Henry the Third granted the site to my ancestor, Gilbert de la Poer, first Baron Exham, in 1261.

Of my family before this date there is no evil report, but something strange must have happened then. In one chronicle there is a reference to a de la Poer as "cursed of God" in 1307. The fireside tales represented my ancestors as a race of hereditary demons beside whom the Marquis de Sade would seem the veriest tyro, and hinted whisperingly at their responsibility for the occasional disappearances of villagers through several generations.

The worst characters, apparently, were the barons and their direct heirs; at least, most was whispered about these. If of healthier inclinations, it was said, an heir would early and mysteriously die to make way for another, more typical scion. There seemed to be an inner cult in the family, presided over by the head of the house, and sometimes closed except to a few members. Temperament rather than ancestry was evidently the basis of this cult, for it was entered by several who married into the family. Lady Margaret Trevor from Cornwall, wife of Godfrey, the second son of the fifth baron, became a favorite bane of children all over the countryside, and the demon heroine of a particularly horrible old ballad not yet extinct near the Welsh border. Preserved in balladry, too, though not illustrating the same point, is the hideous tale of Lady Mary de la Poer, who shortly after her marriage to the Earl of Shrewsfield was killed by him and his mother, both of the slayers being absolved and blessed by the priest to whom they confessed what they dared not repeat to the world.

These myths and ballads, typical as they were of crude superstition, repelled me greatly. Their persistence and their application to so long a line of my ancestors were especially annoying.

I was much less disturbed by the vaguer tales of wails and howlings in the barren, windswept valley beneath the limestone cliff; of the graveyard stenches after the spring rains; of the floundering, squealing white thing on which Sir John Clave's horse had trodden one night in a lonely field; and of the servant who had gone mad at what he saw in the priory in the full light of day. These things were hackneyed spectral lore, and I was at that time a pronounced skeptic. The accounts of vanished peasants were less to be dismissed, though not especially significant in view of medieval custom. Prying curiosity meant death, and more than one severed head had been publicly shown on the bastions, now effaced, around Exham Priory.

A few of the tales were exceedingly picturesque, and made me wish I had learned more of comparative mythology in my youth. There was, for instance, the belief that a legion of bat-winged devils kept witches' sabbath each night at the priory—a legion whose sustenance might explain the disproportionate abundance of coarse vegetables harvested in the vast gardens. And, most vivid of all, there was the dramatic epic of the rats—the scampering army of obscene vermin which had burst forth from the castle three months after the tragedy that doomed it to desertion—the lean, filthy, ravenous army which had swept all before it and devoured fowl, cats, dogs, hogs, sheep, and even two hapless human beings before its fury was spent.

Such was the lore that assailed me as I pushed to completion, with an elderly obstinacy, the work of restoring my ancestral home. It must not be imagined for a moment that these tales formed my principal psychological environment. On the other hand, I was constantly praised and encouraged by Captain Norrys and the antiquarians who surrounded and aided me. When the task was done, over two years after its commencement, I viewed the great rooms, wainscoted walls, vaulted ceilings, mullioned windows, and broad staircases with a pride which fully compensated for the prodigious expense of the restoration.

Every attribute of the Middle Ages was cunningly reproduced, and the new parts blended perfectly with the original walls and foundation. The seat of my fathers was complete. I looked forward to residing here permanently, and proving that a de la Poer (for I had adopted again the original spelling of the name) need not be a fiend. My comfort was perhaps augmented by the fact that, although Exham Priory was medievally fitted, its interior was in truth wholly new and free from old vermin and old ghosts alike.

As I have said, I moved in on July 16, 1923. My household consisted of seven servants and nine cats, of which latter species I am particularly fond. My eldest, an old black cat, had come with me from my home in Bolton, Massachusetts; the others I had accumulated while living with Captain Norrys' family during the restoration of the priory.

For five days our routine proceeded with the utmost placidity, my time being spent mostly in the codification of old family data. I had now obtained some very circumstantial accounts of the final tragedy and flight of Walter de la Poer. It appeared that my ancestor was accused with much reason of having killed all the other members of his household, except four servant confederates, in their sleep, about two weeks after a shocking discovery which he disclosed to no one.

This deliberate slaughter, which included a father, three brothers, and two sisters, was partly condoned by the villagers, and so slackly treated by the law that its perpetrator escaped, unharmed and undisguised, to Virginia, some whispered sentiment being that he had purged the land of an immemorial curse. What discovery had prompted an act so terrible I could scarcely even conjecture. Walter de la Poer must have known for years the sinister tales about his family, so that this material could have given him no fresh impulse. Had he, then, witnessed some appalling ancient rite, or stumbled upon some frightful and revealing symbol in the priory or its vicinity?

On July 22 occurred the first incident, which, though lightly dismissed at the time, takes on a preternatural significance in relation to later events. What I afterward remembered is merely this—that my old black cat, whose moods I know so well, was undoubtedly alert and anxious to an extent wholly out of keeping with his natural character. He roved from room to room, restless and disturbed, and sniffed constantly about the walls which formed part of the Gothic structure. I realize how trite this sounds—like the inevitable dog in the ghost story, which always growls before his master sees the sheeted figure—yet I cannot suppress it.

The following day a servant complained of restlessness among all the cats in the house. He came to me in my study, a lofty west room on the second story, with groined arches, black oak paneling, and a triple Gothic window overlooking the limestone cliff and desolate valley; and even as he spoke I saw the black form of the old cat creeping along the wall and scratching at the panels which overlaid the ancient stone.

I told the man that there must be some singular odor or emanation from the old stonework, imperceptible to human senses, but affecting the delicate organs of cats even through the new woodwork. This I truly believed, and when the fellow suggested the presence of mice or rats, I mentioned that there had been no rats there for three hundred years, and that even the field mice of the surrounding country could hardly be found in these high walls. That afternoon I called on Captain Norrys, and he assured me that it would be quite incredible for field mice to infest the priory in such a sudden fashion.

That night, dispensing as usual with a valet, I retired in the west tower chamber which I had chosen as my own, reached from the study by a stone staircase and short gallery—the former partly ancient, the latter entirely restored. This room was circular, very high, and without wainscoting, being hung with Flemish tapestries which I had myself chosen in London.

Seeing that the black cat was with me, I shut the heavy Gothic door and retired by the light of the electric bulbs which so cleverly counterfeited candles, finally switching off the light and sinking onto the carved and canopied four-poster, with the venerable cat in his accustomed place across my feet. I did not draw the curtains, but gazed out at the narrow north window which I faced. There was a suspicion of aurora in the sky, and the delicate traceries of the window were pleasantly silhouetted.

At some time I must have fallen quietly asleep, for I recall a distinct sense of waking from strange dreams, when the cat started violently from his placid position. I saw him in the faint auroral glow, head strained forward, looking intensely at a point on the wall, which to my eye had nothing to mark it but toward which all my attention was now directed.

And as I watched, I knew the cat was not vainly excited. Whether the tapestry actually moved I cannot say. I think it did, very slightly. But I can swear that behind it I heard a low, distinct scurrying as of rats or mice. In a moment the cat had jumped on the tapestry, bringing a section to the floor with his weight and exposing a damp, ancient wall of stone, patched here and there by the restorers and devoid of any trace of rodent prowlers.

The old cat raced up and down the floor by this part of the wall, clawing the fallen cloth and seemingly trying at times to insert a paw between the wall and the oaken floor. He found nothing, and after a time returned wearily to his place across my feet. I had not moved, but I did not sleep again that night.

In the morning I questioned all the servants, and found that none of them had noticed anything unusual, save that the cook remembered the actions of a cat which had rested on her windowsill. This cat had howled at some unknown hour of the night, awaking the cook in time for her to see him dart purposefully out of the open door down the stairs. In the afternoon I called on Captain Norrys, who became exceedingly interested in what I told him. The odd incidents—so slight yet so curious—appealed to his sense of the picturesque and elicited from him a number of reminiscences of local ghostly lore. We were genuinely perplexed at the presence of rats, and Norrys lent me some traps and Paris green, which I had the servants place in strategic localities when I returned.

I retired early, being very sleepy, but was harassed by dreams of the most horrible sort. I seemed to be looking down from an immense height upon a twilit grotto, knee-deep with filth, where a white-bearded demon swineherd drove about with his staff a flock of fungous, flabby beasts whose appearance filled me with unutterable loathing. Then, as the swineherd paused and nodded over his task, a mighty swarm of rats rained down on the stinking abyss and fell to devouring beasts and man alike.

From this terrific vision I was abruptly wakened by the motions of my old cat, who had been sleeping as usual across my feet. This time I did not have to question the source of his snarls and hisses; for on every side of the chamber the walls were alive with nauseous sound—the verminous slithering of ravenous, gigantic rats. There was now no aurora to show the state of the tapestry—the fallen section of which had been replaced—but I was not too frightened to switch on the light.

As the bulbs leaped into radiance I saw a hideous shaking all over the tapestry, causing the somewhat peculiar designs to execute a singular dance of death. This motion disappeared almost at once, and the sound with it. Springing out of bed, I poked at the cloth and lifted one section to see what lay beneath. There was nothing but the patched stone wall. When I examined the circular rattrap that had been placed in the room, I found all of the openings sprung, though no trace remained of what had been caught and had escaped.

Further sleep was out of the question; so I opened the door and went out in the gallery toward the stairs to my study, the cat following at my heels. Before we had reached the stone steps, however, the cat darted ahead of me down the ancient flight. As I descended the stairs myself, I became suddenly aware of sounds in the great room below; sounds of a nature which could not be mistaken.

The oak-paneled walls were alive with rats, scampering and milling, while the cat was racing about with the fury of a baffled hunter. Reaching the bottom, I switched on the light, which did not this time cause the noise to subside. The rats continued their riot, stampeding with such force and distinctness that I could finally assign to their motions a definite direction. These creatures, in numbers apparently inexhaustible, were engaged in one stupendous migration from inconceivable heights to some depth conceivably or inconceivably below.

I now heard steps in the corridor, and in another moment two servants pushed open the massive door. They were searching the house for some unknown source of disturbance which had thrown all the cats into a snarling panic and caused them to plunge precipitately down several flights of stairs and squat, yowling, before the closed door to the subcellar. I asked the servants if they had heard the rats, but they replied in the negative. And when I turned to call their attention to the sounds in the panels, I realized that the noise had ceased.

With the two men, I went down to the door of the subcellar, but found the cats already dispersed. Later I resolved to explore the crypt below, but for the present I merely made a round of the traps. All were sprung, yet all were tenantless. Satisfying myself that no one had heard the rats save the felines and me, I sat in my study till morning, thinking profoundly and recalling every scrap of legend I had unearthed concerning the building I inhabited.

I slept some in the forenoon, leaning back in the one comfortable library chair which my medieval plan of furnishing could not banish. Later I telephoned to Captain Norrys, who came over and helped me explore the subcellar.

Absolutely nothing untoward was found, although we could not repress a thrill at the knowledge that this vault was built by Roman hands. Every low arch and massive pillar was Roman—not the debased Romanesque of the bungling Saxons, but the severe and harmonious classicism of the age of the Caesars; indeed, the walls abounded with inscriptions familiar to the antiquarians who had repeatedly explored the place—things like P. GETAE. PROP . . . TEMP . . . DONA . . . and L. PRAEC . . . VS PONTIFI . . . ATYS. . . ."

The reference to Atys made me shiver, for I had read Catullus and knew something of the hideous rites of the Eastern god whose worship was so mixed with that of Cybele. Norrys and I, by the light of lanterns, tried to interpret the odd and nearly effaced designs on certain irregularly rectangular blocks of stone generally held to be altars, but could make nothing of them. We remembered that one pattern, a sort of rayed sun, was held by students to imply a non-Roman origin, suggesting that these altars had merely been adopted by the Roman priests from some older temple on the same site. On one of these blocks were some brown stains which made me wonder. The largest block, in the center of the room, had certain features on the upper surface which indicated its connection with fire—probably burnt offerings.

Such were the sights in that crypt where Norrys and I now determined to pass the night. Couches were brought down by the servants, and the old black cat was admitted as much for help as for companionship. We decided to keep the great oaken door—a modern replica with slits for ventilation—tightly closed; and, with this attended to, we retired with lanterns still burning to await whatever might occur.

The vault was very deep in the foundations of the priory, and undoubtedly far down on the face of the beetling limestone cliff overlooking the waste valley. That it had been the goal of the scuffling and unexplainable rats I could not doubt, though why, I could not tell. As we lay there expectantly, I found my vigil occasionally mixed with half-formed dreams from which the uneasy motions of the cat across my feet would rouse me.

These dreams were not wholesome, but horribly like the one I had had the night before. I saw again the twilit grotto, and the swineherd with his unmentionable fungous beasts wallowing in filth, and as I looked at these things they seemed nearer and more distinct—so distinct that I could almost observe their features. Then I did observe the flabby features of one of them—and awoke with such a scream that the cat started up, while Captain Norrys, who had not slept, laughed considerably. Norrys might have laughed more—or perhaps less—had he known what it was that made me scream. But I did not remember till later. Ultimate horror often paralyzes memory in a merciful way.

Norrys wakened me when the phenomena began. Out of the same frightful dream I was called by his gentle shaking and his urging to listen to the cats. Indeed, there was much to listen to, for beyond the closed door at the head of the stone steps was a veritable nightmare of feline yelling and clawing, while my black cat, unmindful of his kindred outside, was running excitedly around the bare stone walls.

An acute terror now rose within me, for here were anomalies which nothing normal could well explain. These rats, if not the creatures of a madness which I shared with the cats alone, must be burrowing and sliding in Roman walls I had thought to be of solid limestone blocks. But if these were living vermin, why did not Norrys hear their disgusting commotion? Why did he urge me to watch the black cat and listen to the cats outside, and why did he guess wildly and vaguely at what could have aroused them?

By the time I had managed to tell him, as rationally as I could, what I thought I was hearing, my ears gave me the last fading impression of the scurrying; which had retreated *still downward*, far underneath this deepest of subcellars, till it seemed as if the whole cliff below were riddled with questing rats. Norrys was not as skeptical as I had anticipated, but instead seemed profoundly moved. He motioned me to notice that the cats at the door had ceased their clamor, as if giving up the rats for lost; while the black cat was now clawing frantically around the bottom of the large stone altar in the center of the room, which was nearer Norrys' couch than mine.

My fear of the unknown was at this point very great. Something astounding had occurred, and I saw that Captain Norrys, a younger, stouter, and presumably more naturally materialistic man, was affected fully as much as I—perhaps because of his lifelong and intimate familiarity with local legend. We could for the moment do nothing but watch the cat as he pawed with decreasing fervor at the base of the altar, occasionally looking up and mewing to me in that persuasive manner which he used when he wished me to perform some favor for him.

Norrys now took a lantern close to the altar and examined the place where the cat was pawing; silently kneeling and scraping away the lichens of centuries which joined the massive pre-Roman block to the tessellated floor. He did not find anything, and was about to abandon his efforts when I noticed a trivial circumstance which made me shudder. It was only this—that the flame of the lantern set down near the altar was slightly but certainly flickering from a draft of air which came indubitably from the crevice between floor and altar where Norrys was scraping away the lichens.

We spent the rest of the night in the brilliantly lighted study, nervously discussing what we should do next. The discovery that some vault deeper than the deepest known masonry of the Romans underlay this accursed pile, some vault unsuspected by the curious antiquarians of three centuries, would have been sufficient to excite us without any background of the sinister. As it was, the fascination became twofold; and we paused in doubt whether to abandon our search and quit the priory forever in superstitious caution, or to gratify our sense of adventure and brave whatever horrors might await us in the depths.

By morning we had compromised, and decided to go to London to gather a group of archaeologists and scientific men fit to cope with the mystery. It should be mentioned that before leaving the subcellar we had vainly tried to move the central altar. What secret would open the gate wiser men would have to find.

During many days in London Captain Norrys and I presented our facts, conjectures, and legendary anecdotes to five eminent authorities, all men who could be trusted to respect any family disclosures which future explorations might develop. We found most of them little disposed to scoff, but, instead, intensely interested and sincerely sympathetic. It is hardly necessary to name them all, but I may say that they included Sir William Brinton, whose excavations in the Troad excited most of the world in their day. As we all took the train for Anchester I felt myself poised on the brink of frightful revelations, a sensation symbolized by the air of mourning among the many Americans at the unexpected death of President Harding on the other side of the world.

On the evening of August 7 we reached Exham Priory, where the servants assured me that nothing unusual had occurred. The cats, even the old black cat, had been perfectly placid; and not a trap in the house had been sprung. We were to begin exploring on the following day, awaiting which I assigned well-appointed rooms to all my guests.

I myself retired in my own tower chamber, with the cat across my feet. Sleep came quickly, but hideous dreams assailed me. There was a vision of a Roman feast like that of Trimalchio, with a horror in a covered platter. Then came that damnable, recurrent thing about the swineherd and his filthy drove in the twilit grotto. Yet when I awoke, it was full daylight, with normal sounds in the house below. The rats, living or spectral, had not troubled me, and the black cat was still quietly asleep. On going down, I found that the same tranquillity had prevailed elsewhere, a condition which one of the assembled savants—a fellow named Thornton, devoted to the psychic—rather absurdly laid to the fact that I had now been shown the thing which certain forces had wished to show me.

All was now ready, and at eleven a.m. our entire group of seven men, bearing powerful electric searchlights and implements of excavation, went down to the subcellar and bolted the door behind us. The cat was with us, for the investigators were anxious that he be present in case of obscure rodent manifestations. We noted the Roman inscriptions and unknown altar designs only briefly, for three of the savants had already seen them, and all knew their characteristics. Prime attention was paid to the momentous central altar, and within an hour Sir William Brinton had caused it to tilt backward, balanced by some unknown species of counterweight.

There now lay revealed such a horror as would have overwhelmed us had we not been prepared. Through a nearly square opening in the tiled floor, sprawling on a flight of stone steps so prodigiously worn that it was little more than an inclined plane at the center, was a ghastly array of human or semihuman bones. Those which retained their collocation as skeletons showed attitudes of panic fear, and over all were the marks of rodent gnawing. The skulls denoted nothing short of utter idiocy, cretinism, or primitive semiapedom.

Above the hellishly littered steps arched a descending passage seemingly chiseled from the solid rock, and conducting a current of air. This current was not a sudden and noxious rush as from a closed vault, but a cool breeze with something of freshness in it. We did not pause long, but shiveringly began to clear a passage down the steps.

I must be very deliberate now, and choose my words.

After plowing down a few steps amid the gnawed bones we saw that there was light ahead; not any mystic phosphorescence, but a filtered daylight which could not come except from unknown fissures in the cliff that overlooked the waste valley. That such fissures had escaped notice from the outside was hardly remarkable, for not only is the valley wholly uninhabited, but the cliff is so high and beetling that only an aeronaut could study its face in detail. A few steps more, and our breaths were literally snatched from us by what we saw; so literally that Thornton, the psychic investigator, actually fainted in the arms of the dazed man who stood behind him. Norrys, his plump face utterly white and flabby, simply cried out inarticulately, while I think that what I did was to gasp or hiss, and cover my eyes.

The man behind me—the only one of the party older than I—croaked the hackneyed "My God!" in the most cracked voice I ever heard. Of seven cultivated men, only Sir William Brinton retained his composure, a thing the more to his credit because he led the party and must have seen the sight first.

It was a twilit grotto of enormous height, stretching away farther than any eye could see; a world of limitless mystery and horrible suggestion. There were buildings and other architectural remains—in one terrified glance I saw a weird pattern of tumuli, a savage circle of monoliths, a low-domed Roman ruin, a sprawling Saxon pile, and an early English edifice of wood—but all these were dwarfed by the ghoulish spectacle presented by the general surface of the ground. For yards about the steps extended an insane angle of human bones, or bones at least as human as those on the steps. Like a foamy sea they stretched, some fallen apart, but others wholly or partly articulated as skeletons; these latter invariably in postures of demoniac frenzy, either fighting off some menace or clutching other forms with cannibal intent.

When Dr. Trask, the anthropologist, stooped to classify the skulls, he found a degraded mixture which utterly baffled him. They were mostly lower than the Piltdown man in the scale of evolution, but in every case definitely human. Many were of higher grade, and a very few were the skulls of supremely and sensitively developed types. All the bones were gnawed, mostly by rats, but somewhat by others of the half-human drove. Mixed with them were many tiny bones of rats—fallen members of the lethal army which closed the ancient epic.

I wonder that any man among us lived and kept his sanity through that hideous day of discovery through which we seven staggered; each stumbling on revelation after revelation, and trying to keep for the nonce from thinking of the events which must have taken place there three hundred, or a thousand, or two thousand, or ten thousand years ago. It was the antechamber of hell, and poor Thornton fainted again when Trask told him that some of the skeleton things must have descended as quadrupeds through the last twenty or more generations.

Horror piled on horror as we began to interpret the architectural remains. The quadruped things—with their occasional recruits from the biped class—had been kept in stone pens, out of which they must have broken in their last delirium of hunger or rat fear. There had been great herds of them, evidently fattened on the coarse vegetables whose remains could be found as a sort of poisonous ensilage at the bottom of huge stone bins older than Rome. I knew now why my ancestors had had such excessive gardens—would to heaven I could forget! The purpose of the herds I did not have to ask.

Sir William, standing with his searchlight in the Roman ruin, translated aloud the most shocking ritual I have ever known, and told of the diet of the antediluvian cult which the priests of Cybele found and mingled with their own. Norrys, used as he was to the trenches, could not walk straight when he came out of the English building. It was a butcher shop and kitchen—he had expected that—but it was too much to see familiar English implements in such a place, and to read familiar English graffiti there, some as recent as 1610. I could not go in that building—that building whose demon activities were stopped only by the dagger of my ancestor Walter de la Poer.

What I did venture to enter was the low Saxon building, whose oaken door had fallen, and there I found a terrible row of ten stone cells with rusty bars. Three had tenants, all skeletons of high grade, and on the bony forefinger of one I found a seal ring with my own coat of arms. Sir William found a vault with far older cells below the Roman chapel, but these cells were empty. Below them was a low crypt with cases of formally arranged bones, some of them bearing terrible parallel inscriptions carved in Latin, Greek, and the tongue of Phrygia.

Meanwhile, Dr. Trask had opened one of the prehistoric tumuli, and brought to light skulls which were slightly more human than a gorilla's and which bore indescribable ideographic carvings. Through all this horror my old cat stalked unperturbed. Once I saw him monstrously perched atop a mountain of bones, and wondered at the secrets that might lie behind his yellow eyes.

Having grasped to some slight degree the frightful revelations of this twilit area—an area so hideously foreshadowed by my recurrent dream—we turned to that apparently boundless depth of midnight cavern where no ray of light from the cliff could penetrate. We shall never know what sightless Stygian worlds yawn beyond the little distance we went, for it was decided that such secrets are not good for mankind. But there was plenty to engross us close at hand, for we had not gone far before the searchlights showed that accursed infinity of pits in which the rats had feasted, and whose sudden lack of replenishment had driven the ravenous rodent army first to turn on the living herds of starving things, and then to burst forth from the priory in that historic orgy of devastation which the peasants will never forget.

God! Those carrion black pits of sawed, picked bones and opened skulls! Those nightmare chasms choked with the pithecanthropoid, Celtic, Roman, and English bones of countless unhallowed centuries! Some of them were full, and none can say how deep they had once been. Others were still bottomless to our searchlights, and peopled by unnameable fancies.

Once my foot slipped near a horribly yawning brink, and I had a moment of ecstatic fear. I must have been musing a long time, for I could not see any of the party but the plump Captain Norrys. Then there came a sound from that inky, boundless, farther distance that I thought I knew, and I saw my old black cat dart past me, straight into the illimitable gulf of the unknown. But I was not far behind, for there was no doubt after another second. It was the eldritch scurrying of those fiend-born rats, always questing for new horrors, and determined to lead me on even unto those grinning caverns of earth's center where Nyarlathotep, the mad faceless god, howls blindly in the darkness to the piping of two amorphous idiot flute players.

My searchlight expired, but still I ran. I heard voices, and yowls, and echoes, but above all there gently rose that impious, insidious scurrying; gently rising, rising, as a stiff bloated corpse gently rises above an oily river that flows under endless onyx bridges to a black, putrid sea.

Something soft and plump bumped into me. It must have been the rats; the viscous, ravenous army that feasts on the dead and the living. . . . Why shouldn't rats eat a de la Poer as a de la Poer eats forbidden things?. . . The war ate my boy, damn them all . . . and the Yanks ate Carfax with flames and burned Grandsire Delapore and the secret. . . . No, no, I tell you, I am *not* that demon swineherd in the twilit grotto! It was *not* Edward Norrys' fat face on that flabby fungous thing! Who says I am a de la Poer? He lived, but my boy died! Shall a Norrys hold the lands of a de la Poer?. . . Curse you, Thornton, I'll teach you to faint at what my family do! 'Sblood, thou stinkard, I'll learn ye how to gust . . . wolde ye swynke me thilke wys?. . . *Magna Mater! Magna Mater!. . . Atys . . . Dia ad aghaidh's ad aodaun . . . agus bas dunach ort! Dhonas's dholas ort, agus leat-sa!. . . Ungl . . . ungl . . . rrlh . . . chchch . . .*

That is what they say I said when they found me in the blackness after three hours—found me crouching in the blackness over the plump, half-eaten body of Captain Norrys, with my own cat leaping and tearing at my throat. Now they have blown up Exham Priory, taken my cat away from me, and shut me into this barred room at Hanwell with fearful whispers about my heredity and experiences. Thornton is in the next room, but they prevent me from talking to him. They are trying, too, to suppress most of the facts concerning the priory. When I speak of poor Norrys they accuse me of a hideous thing, but they must know that I did not do it. They must know it was the rats; the slithering scurrying rats whose scampering will never let me sleep; the demon rats that race behind the padding in this room and beckon me down to greater horrors than I have ever known; the rats they can never hear; the rats, the rats in the walls.

AFTER-DINNER STORY

WILLIAM IRISH

MACKENZIE GOT ON the elevator at the thirteenth floor. He was a water-filter salesman and had stopped in at his home office to make out his accounts before going home for the day. Later on that night he told his wife, half laughingly, that that must have been why it happened to *him*, his getting on at the thirteenth floor. A lot of buildings omit them.

The red bulb bloomed and the car stopped for him. It was an express, omitting all floors, both coming and going, below the tenth. There were two other men in it when he got on, not counting the operator. It was late in the day, and most of the offices had already emptied themselves. One of the passengers was a scholarly-looking man with rimless glasses, tall and slightly stooped. The time came when MacKenzie learned all their names. This was Kenshaw. The other was stout and cherubic-looking, one of two partners in a struggling concern that was trying to market fountain pens with tiny light bulbs in their barrels—without much success. He was fiddling with one of his own samples on the way down, clicking it on and off with an air of proud ownership. He turned out to be Lambert.

The car was smooth running, sleek with bronze and chrome. It appeared very safe. It stopped at the twelfth floor, and a surly-looking individual with bushy brows stepped in, Prendergast. Then the number eleven on the operator's call-board lit up, and it stopped there too. A man about MacKenzie's age and an older man with a trim white mustache were standing there when the door opened. Only the young man got on; the elder man gripped him by the arm in parting and remarked loudly, "Tell Elinor I was asking for her."

The younger answered, "By, Dad," and stepped in. Hardecker was his name. He turned to face the door. MacKenzie happened to glance at the sour-pussed man with the bushy brows at that moment; the latter was directly behind the newest arrival. He was glaring at the back of Hardecker's head with baleful intensity. MacKenzie imagined this was due to the newcomer's having inadvertently trodden on the other's toe in turning to face forward.

Ten was still another single passenger, a bill collector judging by the sheaf of pink, green, and canary slips he kept riffling through. He hadn't, by the gloomy look he wore, been having much luck today; or maybe his feet hurt. This was Megaffin.

There were now seven people in the car, counting the operator, standing in a compact little group facing the door, and no more stops due until it reached street level. Not a very great crowd; far from the maximum the mechanism was able to hold. The framed notice, tacked to the panel just before MacKenzie's eyes, showed that it had been last inspected barely ten days before.

It never stopped at the street floor.

MacKenzie, trying to reconstruct the sequence of events for his wife that night, said that the operator seemed to put on added speed as soon as they had left the tenth floor behind. It was an express, so he didn't think anything of it. He remembered noticing at this point that the operator had a boil on the back of his neck, just above his uniform collar, with a Maltese cross of adhesive over it. He got that peculiar sinking sensation at the pit of his stomach many people get from a too precipitate drop. The man near him, the young fellow from the eleventh, turned and gave him a half-humorous, half-pained look, so he knew that he must be feeling it too. Someone farther back whistled slightly to show his discomfort.

The car was a closed one, all metal, so you couldn't see the shaft doors flashing by. But MacKenzie began to get a peculiar ringing in his ears, and his knee joints seemed to loosen up, trying to buckle under him. What really first told him—and all of them—that something had gone wrong was the sudden, futile, jerky way the operator was wangling the control lever to and fro. It traveled the short arc of its orbit readily enough, but the car refused to answer to it. He kept slamming it into the socket at one end of the groove, marked STOP, and nothing happened. The velocity of the descent became sickening. Then they heard the operator say in a muffled voice, "Look out! We're going to hit!" And that was all there was time for.

There was a tremendous bang like a cannon, an explosion of blackness, and of bulb glass showering down as the light went out.

They all toppled together in a heap. MacKenzie was the luckiest of the lot; he could feel squirming bodies bedded under him, didn't touch the hard-rubber floor of the car at all. However, his hip and shoulder were badly wrenched, and the sole of his foot went numb, through shoe and all, from the stinging impact it got flying up and slapping the bronze wall of the car.

Then they were going up again—on springs or something. It was a little sickening too, but not as bad as the coming down had been. The car slackened, reversed into a drop, and they banged a second time, a sort of cushioned bang that scrambled them up even more than they were already. Somebody's shoe grazed MacKenzie's skull.

The car finally settled, after a second slight bounce that barely cleared the springs under it at all, and a third and almost unnoticeable jolt. The rest was pitch-darkness, a sense of suffocation, a commingling of threshing bodies, groans from the badly hurt, and an ominous sigh or two from those beyond groaning.

Somebody directly under MacKenzie was not moving at all. He put his hand on him, felt an upright, stiff collar, and just above it a small swelling, crisscrossed by plaster. The operator was dead, and the rubber matting beneath his skull was sticky.

MacKenzie felt then for the sleek metal wall of the enclosure and reached up it with the heels of his hands and the points of his elbows. He squirmed the rest of his body up after these precarious grips. Upright again, he leaned against cold bronze.

A voice was begging with childish vehemence: "Get me outa here! For the love of Mike, I've got a wife and kids. Get me outa here!"

MacKenzie had the impression it was the surly-looking fellow with the bushy eyebrows. Such visible truculence and toughness are usually all hollow inside, a mask of weakness."Shut up," he said. "I've got a wife too. What's that got to do with it?"

The most dangerous thing, he recognized, was not the darkness, nor their trapped position at the bottom of a sealed-up shaft, nor even any possible injuries any of them had received. It was that vague sense of stuffiness, of suffocation. Something had to be done about that at once. The operator had opened the front panel of the car at each floor, simply by latch motion. There was no reason why that could not be repeated down here, even though there was no accompanying opening in the shaft wall facing it. Enough air would filter down the crack between the jammed-in car and the wall, narrow though it was, to keep them breathing until help came. They were going to need that air before this was over.

MacKenzie's arms executed interlocking circles against the satiny metal face of the car, groping for the indented grip used to unlatch it. "Match," he ordered. "Somebody light a match. I'm trying to get this thing open. We're practically airtight in here."

The immediate, and expected, reaction was a howl of dismay from the tough-looking bird, like a dog's craven yelp.

Another voice, more self-controlled, said, "Wait a minute." Then nothing happened.

In exasperation MacKenzie hollered out, "For the love of— Haven't any of you got a match to give me?" Which was unfair, considering that he himself had run short just before he left his office and had been meaning to get a folder at the cigar store when he got off the car. "Hey, you, the guy that was fiddling with that trick fountain pen coming down, how about that?"

A new voice, unfrightened but infinitely crestfallen, answered disappointedly, "It—it broke." And then with a sadness that betokened there were other, greater tragedies than what had happened to the car: "It shows you can't drop it without breakage. And that was the chief point of our whole advertising campaign."

"Never mind!" MacKenzie exclaimed suddenly. "I've got it." His fingertips had found the slot at the far end of the seamless cast-bronze panel. He pulled back the latch, leaning over the operator's lifeless body to do so, and tugged at the slide. It gave, fell back about a third of its usual orbit along the groove, then stalled unmanageably. That was sufficient for their present needs, though there was no question of egress through it. The rough-edged bricks of the shaft wall were only a finger's width beyond the lips of the car's orifice, but they wouldn't asphyxiate now, no matter how long it took to raise the mechanism.

"It's all right, fellows," he called reassuringly to those behind him. "I've got some air into the thing now."

If there was light farther up the shaft, it didn't reach down this far. The shaft wall opposite the opening was as black as the inside of the car itself.

He said, "They've heard us. They know what's happened. No use yelling at the top of your voice like that, only makes it tougher for the rest of us. They'll get an emergency crew on the job. We'll just have to sit and wait, that's all."

The nerve-tingling bellows for help, probably the tough guy again, were silenced shamefacedly. A groaning still kept up intermittently from someone else. "My arm, oh, Gawd, it hurts!" The sighing, from an injury that had gone deeper still, had quieted suspiciously some time before. Either the man had fainted, or he, too, was dead.

MacKenzie, matter-of-factly but not callously, reached down for the operator's outflung form, shifted it into the angle between two of the walls, and propped it upright there. Then he sat in the clear floor space provided, tucked up his legs, wrapped his arms around them. He wouldn't have called himself a brave man; he was just a realist.

There was a momentary silence from all of them at once. Then, because there was also, or seemed to be, a complete stillness from overhead in the shaft, panic stabbed at the tough guy again. "They gonna leave us here all night?" he whimpered. "What you guys sit there like that for? Don't you wanna get out?"

"For Pete's sake, somebody clip that loudmouth on the chin!" urged MacKenzie truculently.

There was an indrawn whistle. "My arm! Oh, my arm!"

"Must be busted," suggested MacKenzie sympathetically. "Try wrapping your shirt tight around it to kill the pain."

Time seemed to stand still. The rustle of a restless body, a groan, an exhalation of impatience, an occasional cry from the craven in their midst. The waiting, the sense of trapped helplessness, began to tell on them far more than the accident had.

"They may think we're all dead and take their time," someone said.

"They never do in a case like this," MacKenzie answered. "They're doing whatever they're doing as fast as they can."

A new voice, which he hadn't heard until then, said to no one in particular, "I'm glad my father didn't get on here with me."

Somebody chimed in, "If I hadn't gone back after that damn phone call . . . It was a wrong number, and I coulda ridden down the trip before this."

MacKenzie had a wristwatch with a luminous dial. He wished it had gone out of commission like the trick fountain pen. It was too nerve-racking; every minute his eyes sought it, and when it seemed like half an hour had gone by, it was only five minutes. He refrained from mentioning it to the others; they would have kept asking him, "How long is it now?" until he went screwy.

When they'd been down twenty-two and one half minutes from the time he'd first looked at it, and were all in a state of nervous instability bordering on frenzy, including himself, there was a sudden unexpected thump directly overhead, as though something heavy had landed on the roof of the car.

MacKenzie leaped up, pressed his cheek flat against the brickwork outside the open panel, and funneled up the paper-thin gap: "Hello! Hello!"

"We're coming to you," a voice came down. "Take it easy!"

More thumping for a while. Then a sudden metallic din, like a boiler factory going full blast. The whole car seemed to vibrate with it. The confined space of the shaft magnified the noise into a torrent of sound, drowning out all their remarks.

A blue electric spark shot down the narrow crevice outside the door from above. Then another, then a third. They all went out too quickly to cast any light inside.

Acetylene torches! They were having to cut a hole through the car roof to get at them. If there was a basement opening in the shaft, and there must have been, the car must have plunged down even beyond that, to the bottom of the elevator pit.

A spark materialized eerily through the ceiling. Then another, then a semicircular gush of them. A curtain of fire descended halfway into their midst, illuminating their faces wanly for a minute.

The noise broke off short and the silence in its wake was deafening. A voice shouted just above them: "Look out for sparks, you guys below. We're coming through. Keep your eyes closed, get back against the walls!"

The noise came on again, nearer at hand, louder than before. MacKenzie's teeth were on edge from the incessant vibration. Being rescued was worse than being stuck down there. He thought he heard a voice scream: "Elinor! Elinor!" twice, like that, but you couldn't be sure of anything in that infernal din.

The sparks kept coming down like a dripping waterfall; MacKenzie squinted his eyes cagily. He thought he saw one spark shoot across horizontally, instead of down vertically, like all the others; it was a different color too, more orange. He thought it must be an optical illusion produced by the alternating glare and darkness they were all being subjected to, or a detached splinter of combusted metal from the roof, ricocheting off the wall.

The noise and sparks stopped abruptly. They pried up the crescent-shaped flap they had cut in the roof with crowbars, to keep it from toppling inward and crushing those below. The cool beams of flashlights flickered through. A cop jumped down into their midst and ropes were sent snaking down after him. "All right, who's first?" he said briskly. "Who's the worst hurt?"

His flashlight showed three forms motionless at the feet of the others in the confined space. The operator, huddled in the corner where MacKenzie had propped him; the scholarly-looking man with the rimless glasses (minus them now, and a deep gash under one eye to show what had become of them) lying senseless on his side; and the young fellow who had got on at the eleventh, tumbled partly across him, face down.

"The operator's dead," MacKenzie answered as spokesman for the rest, "and these two're out of their pain now. There's a guy with a busted arm here, take him first."

The cop deftly looped the rope under the armpits of the ashen-faced bill collector. "Haul away!" he shouted toward the opening. "And take your time, the guy's hurt."

The bill collector went up through the ceiling, groaning, legs drawn up under him like a trussed-up fowl.

The scholarly-looking man went next, head bobbing down in unconsciousness. When the noose came down empty, the cop bent over to fasten it around the young fellow still on the floor.

MacKenzie saw him change his mind, pry open one eyelid, pass the rope on to the tough-looking mug who had been such a crybaby and who was shaking all over from the reaction to the fright he'd had.

"What's the matter with him?" MacKenzie butted in, pointing to the floor.

"He's dead," the cop answered briefly. "He can wait."

"Dead! Why, I heard him say he was glad his father didn't get on with him, long after we hit!"

"He coulda said it, and still be dead now," the cop answered. "Are you telling me my business? You seem to be pretty chipper for a guy that's just come through an experience like this!"

"Skip it," said MacKenzie placatingly. He figured it was no business of his anyway, if the guy had seemed all right at first and now was dead. He might have had a weak heart.

He and the disheartened fountain-pen entrepreneur seemed to be the only two of the lot who were totally unharmed. The latter, however, was so brokenhearted over the failure of his appliance to stand up under an emergency that he seemed hardly to care what became of him. He kept examining the defective gadget even on his way up through the aperture in the car roof, with the expression of a man who has just bitten into a very sour lemon.

MacKenzie was the last one up the shaft, except the two fatalities. He was pulled in over the lip of the basement opening, from which the sliding doors had been taken down bodily. It was a bare four feet above the roof of the car; in other words the shaft continued on down past it for little more than the height of the car. He couldn't understand why it had been built that way, and not ended flush with the basement, in which case their long imprisonment could have been avoided. It was explained to him later, by the building superintendent, that it was necessary to give the car additional clearance underneath, else it would have run the risk of jamming each time it came down to the basement.

There were stretchers there in the basement passageway, and the bill collector and the studious-looking man were being given first aid by a pair of interns. The hard-looking egg was shuddering as he was being revived with a large whiff of spirits of ammonia. MacKenzie let one of the interns look him over, at the latter's insistence; was told what he knew already, that he was okay. He gave his name and address to the police lieutenant in charge, and walked up a flight of stairs to the street level, thinking, The old-fashioned way's the best after all.

He found the lobby of the building choked with a milling crowd, warded off a number of ambulance chasers who tried to tell him how badly hurt he was. "There's money in it, buddy, don't be a sucker!" MacKenzie phoned his wife from a nearby booth to shorten her anxiety; then he left the scene for home.

His last fleeting impression was of a forlorn figure standing in the lobby, a man with a trim white mustache, the father of the young fellow lying dead below, buttonholing every cop within reach, asking over and over again, "Where's my son? Why haven't they brought my son up yet?" And not getting any answer from any of them—which was an answer in itself.

Friday, that was four days later, the doorbell rang right after supper and he had a visitor. "MacKenzie? You were in that elevator Monday night, weren't you, sir?"

"Yes." MacKenzie grinned; he sure was.

"I'm from police headquarters. Mind if I ask you a few questions? I've been going around to all of 'em, checking up."

"Come in and sit down," said MacKenzie interestedly. His first guess was that they were trying to track down labor sabotage, or some violation of the building code. "Anything phony about it?"

"Not for our money," said the dick. "The young fellow that was lying dead there in the bottom of the car—not the operator but young

Wesley Hardecker—was found by the medical examiner to have a bullet embedded in his heart."

MacKenzie, jolted, gave a long-drawn whistle. "Whew! You mean somebody shot him while we were all cooped up down there?"

The dick showed, without being too pugnacious, that he was there to ask the questions, not answer them. "Did you know him at all?"

"Never saw him in my life before, until he got on the car that night. I know his name by now, because I read it in the papers next day; I didn't at the time."

The visitor nodded. "Did you hear anything like a shot?"

"No, not before they started the blowtorches. And after that, you couldn't have heard one anyway. I did see a flash, though. At least I remember seeing one of the sparks shoot *across* instead of dropping down, and it was more orange in color."

Again the dick nodded. "Yeah, a couple of others saw that too. That was probably it, right there. Did it light up anyone's face behind it, anything like that?"

"No," MacKenzie admitted. "My eyes were all pinwheels, between the blackness and these flashing sparks coming down through the roof." He paused thoughtfully, went on: "It doesn't hang together. Why should anyone pick such a time and place to—"

"It hangs together beautifully," contradicted the dick. "It's his old man, the elder Hardecker, that's trying to read something phony into it. It's suicide while of unsound mind; and that's what the coroner's inquest is going to find. Old man Hardecker himself hasn't been able to identify any of you as having known or seen his son—or himself—before six o'clock last Monday evening. The gun was the fellow's own, and he had a license for it. He had it with him when he got in the car. It was under his body when it was picked up. The only fingerprints on it were his. The examiner finds the wound a contact wound, powder burns all around it."

"The way we were crowded together, any kind of a shot at anyone would have been a contact," MacKenzie tried to object.

The dick waved this aside. "The nitrate test shows that his fingers fired the shot. It's true that we neglected to give it to anyone else at the time, but since there'd been only one shot fired out of the gun, and no other gun was found, that don't stack up to much. The bullet was from that gun and no other, ballistics has told us. The guy was a nervous, high-strung young fellow. He went hysterical down there, cracked up, and when he couldn't stand it anymore, took himself out of it. Against this, his old man is beefing that he was happy, he had a lovely wife, they were expecting a kid, and he had everything to live for."

"All right," objected MacKenzie mildly. "But why should he do it when they were already working on the roof over us, and it was just a matter of minutes before they got to us? Why not before?"

The detective got up, as though the discussion were ended, but condescended to enlighten him on his way to the door. "People don't crack up at a minute's notice; it was after he'd been down there twenty minutes, half an hour, it got him. Any psychiatrist will tell you what noise'll do to someone already under a strain or tension. The noise of the blowtorches gave him the finishing touch; that's why he did it then, couldn't think straight anymore. As far as having a wife and expecting a kid is concerned, that would only make him lose his head all the quicker. A man without ties or responsibilities is always more cold-blooded in an emergency."

"It's a new one on me, but maybe you're right. I only know water filters."

"It's my job to be right about things like that. Good night, Mr. MacKenzie."

THE VOICE ON the wire said, "Mr. MacKenzie? Is this the Mr. Stephen MacKenzie who was in an elevator accident a year ago last August? The newspapers gave—"

"Yes, I was."

"Well, I'd like you to come to dinner at my house next Saturday evening, at exactly seven o'clock."

MacKenzie cocked his brows at himself in the wall mirror. "Hadn't you better tell me who you are, first?"

"Sorry," said the voice crisply. "I thought I had. I've been doing this for the past hour or so, and it's beginning to tell on me. This is Harold Hardecker. I'm head of the Hardecker Import and Export Company. My son was on that elevator with you. He lost his life."

"Oh," said MacKenzie. He remembered now. A man with a trim white mustache, standing in the milling crowd, buttonholing the cops as they hurried by. . . .

"Can I expect you, then, at seven next Saturday, Mr. MacKenzie? I'm at —— Park Avenue."

"Frankly," said MacKenzie, who was a plain soul not much given to social hypocrisy, "I don't see any point to it. Why single me out?"

Hardecker explained patiently, even good-naturedly. "I'm not singling you out, Mr. MacKenzie. I've already contacted each of the others who were on the car that night with my son, and they've all agreed to be there. I don't wish to disclose what I have in mind beforehand; I'm giving this dinner for that purpose. However, I might mention that my son died intestate, and his poor wife passed away in childbirth in the early hours of the following morning. His estate reverted to me, and I am a lonely old man, without friends or relatives, and with more money already than I know what to do with. It occurred to me to bring together five perfect strangers, who shared a common hazard with my son, who were with him during the last few moments of his life." The voice paused insinuatingly to let this sink in. Then it resumed: "If you'll come to my house for dinner Saturday, I'll have an important announcement to make. It's to your interest to be present."

MacKenzie scanned his water-filter salesman's salary with his mind's eye and found it altogether unsatisfactory, as he had done not once but many times before. "All right," he agreed.

Saturday at six he was still saying, "The guy isn't in his right mind. Five people that he doesn't know from Adam and that don't know each other. I wonder if it's a practical joke?"

"Well, if you feel that way, why didn't you refuse him?" said his wife, brushing off his dark blue coat.

"I'm curious to find out what it's all about. I want to see what the gag is."

At the door his wife said with belated anxiety, "Steve, I know you can take care of yourself, but if you don't like the looks of things, I mean if none of the others show up, don't stay there alone."

He laughed. "You make me feel like one of those innocents in the old silent pictures, that were always being invited to a big blowout and when they got there they were alone with the villain and just supper for two. Don't worry, Toots. If there's no one else there, I turn around and come back."

THE BUILDING HAD a Park Avenue address, but was actually on one of the exclusive side streets just off that thoroughfare. A small ultra-ultra cooperative with only one apartment to a floor. "Mr. Harold Hardecker?" asked Mr. MacKenzie in the lobby. "Stephen MacKenzie."

He saw the hall man take out a small typed list of five names, four of which already had been penciled out, and cross out the last one. "Go right up, Mr. MacKenzie. Third floor."

A butler opened the door in the elevator foyer for him, greeted him by name, and took his hat. A single glance at the money this place spelled would restore anyone's confidence. People that lived like this were perfectly capable of having five strangers in to dinner, subdividing a dead son's estate among them, and chalking it off as just that evening's little whimsy.

Hardecker came toward him along the central gallery that seemed to bisect the place like a bowling alley. The man had aged appreciably from the visual snapshot that was all MacKenzie had had of him at the scene of the accident. He was slightly stooped, very thin at the waist, looked as though he'd suffered. But the white mustache was as trim as ever, and he had on one of the new turned-over soft collars under his dinner jacket, which gave him a peculiarly boyish look in spite of the almost blinding white of his undiminished hair, cropped close as a Prussian's.

Hardecker held out his hand, said with just the right mixture of dignity and warmth, "How do you do, Mr. MacKenzie. I'm very glad to know you. Come in and meet the others and have a pick-me-up."

There were no women present in the living room, just the four men sitting around at ease. There was no sense of strain, of stiffness; an advantage that stag gatherings are apt to have over mixed parties anyway, not through the fault of women but through men's consciousness of them.

Kenshaw, the scholarly-looking man, had a white scar still visible under his left eye where his glasses had broken. The cherubic Lambert had deserted the illuminated fountain-pen business, he hurriedly confided, unasked, to MacKenzie, for the ladies' foundation-girdle business. No more mechanical gadgets for him. The hard-bitten mug was introduced as Prendergast, occupation undisclosed. Megaffin, the bill collector, was no longer a bill collector. "I send out my own now," he explained, swiveling a synthetic diamond around on his pinkie.

MacKenzie selected Scotch, and when he'd caught up with the rest the butler came to the door, as though he'd been timing him through a knothole. He just looked in, then went away again.

"Let's get down to business now, gentlemen, shall we?" Hardecker grinned. He had the happy faculty, MacKenzie said to himself, of making you feel perfectly at home, without overdoing it.

No flowers, candles, or fripperies like that were on the table set for six; just good substantial man's board. Hardecker said, "Just sit down anywhere you choose, only keep the head for me." Lambert and Kenshaw took one side, Prendergast and Megaffin the other. MacKenzie sat down at the foot. It was obvious that whatever announcement their host intended making was being kept for the end of the meal, as was only fitting.

The butler had closed a pair of sliding doors beyond them after they were all in, and he stayed outside. The waiting was done by a man. It was a typical bachelor's repast, plain and marvelously cooked. Each course had its vintage corollary. And at the end no cloying sweets—Roquefort cheese, and coffee with the blue flame of Courvoisier flickering above each glass. It was a masterpiece. And each man, as it ended, relaxed in his chair in a haze of golden daydreams. They anticipated coming into money, money they hadn't had to work for, maybe more money than they'd ever had before. It wasn't such a bad world after all.

One thing had struck MacKenzie, but since he'd never been waited on by servants in a private home before, he couldn't determine whether it was unusual or customary. There was an expensive mahogany buffet running across one side of the dining room, but the waiter had done no serving or carving on it, had brought in each portion separately, always individually, even the roast. The coffee and the wines, too, had been poured behind the scenes, the glasses and the cups brought in already filled. It gave the man a lot more work and slowed the meal somewhat, but if that was the way it was done in Hardecker's house, that was the way it was done.

When they were already luxuriating with their cigars and cigarettes, and the cloth had been cleared of all but the emptied coffee cups, an additional dish was brought in. It was a silver chalice, a sort of stemmed bowl. The waiter placed it in the exact center of the table, even measuring with his eye its distance from both sides, and from the head and foot, and shifting its position to conform. Then he took the lid off. The bowl held a thick yellowish substance that looked like mayonnaise. Threads of steam rose sluggishly from it. Every eye was on it.

"Is it well mixed?" they heard Hardecker ask.

"Yes, sir," said the waiter.

"That will be all, don't come in again."

The man left by the pantry door he had been using, and it clicked slightly after it had closed behind him.

Somebody—Megaffin—asked cozily, "What's *that* got in it?" evidently on the lookout for still more treats.

"Oh, a number of things," Hardecker answered carelessly. "Egg whites, mustard, and other ingredients all beaten up together."

MacKenzie, trying to be funny, said, "Sounds like an antidote."

"It is an antidote," Hardecker answered, looking steadily down the table at him. He must have pushed a call button or something under the table, for the butler opened the sliding doors and stood between them, without coming in.

Hardecker didn't turn his head. "You have that gun I gave you? Stand on the other side of those doors, please, and see that no one comes out of here. If they try, you know what to do."

The doors slipped to again, effaced the butler, but not before MacKenzie had seen something glimmer in his hand.

Hardecker spoke. Not loudly, not angrily, but in a steely, pitiless voice. "Gentlemen, there's a murderer in our midst."

Five breaths were sharply indrawn together. Not so much aghast at the statement itself as at the implication of retribution that lurked behind it.

No one said anything.

Hardecker was smoking a long, slim cigar. He pointed it straight out before him, indicated them all with it, like a dark finger of doom. "Gentlemen, one of you killed my son." Pause. "On August 31, 1936." Pause. "And hasn't paid for it yet."

The words were like a stone going down into a deep pool of transparent water, and the ripples spreading out from them spelled fear.

MacKenzie said slowly, "You setting yourself above the properly constituted authorities? The findings of the coroner's inquest were suicide while of unsound mind—"

Hardecker cut him short like a whip. "This isn't a discussion. It's"—a long pause, then very low, but very audible—"an execution."

There was another of those strangling silences. MacKenzie just kept staring at him, startled. Apprehensive, but not inordinately frightened, any more than he had been that night on the elevator. The scholarly-looking Kenshaw had a rebuking look on his face, that of a teacher for an unruly pupil, and the scar on his cheek stood out whitely. Megaffin looked shifty, like some small weasel at bay, planning its next move. The pugnacious-looking guy was going to cave in again in a minute, judging by the wavering of his facial lines. Lambert pinched the bridge of his nose momentarily, dropped his hand, mumbled something that sounded like, "*Oy,* I give up my pinochle club to come here, yet!"

Hardecker resumed, as though he hadn't said anything unusual just now. "I know which one among you the man is. It's taken me a year to find out, but now I know, beyond the shadow of a doubt." He was looking at his cigar now, watching the ash drop off of its own weight onto his coffee saucer. "The police wouldn't listen to me; they insisted it was suicide. The evidence was insufficient to convince them the first time, and for all I know it still may be." He raised his eyes. "But I demand justice for the taking of my son's life." He took an expensive octagonal watch out of his pocket, placed it face up on the table before him. "Gentlemen, it's now nine o'clock. In half an hour, at the most, one of you will be dead. Did you notice that you were all served separately? One dish, and one alone out of all of them, was deadly. It's putting in its slow, sure work right as we sit here." He pointed to the silver tureen, equidistant from all of them. "There's the answer. There's the antidote. I have no wish to set myself up as executioner above the law. Let the murderer be the chooser. Let him reach out and save his life and stand convicted before all of you. Or let him keep silent and go down to his death without confessing, privately executed for what can't be publicly proved."

It was Lambert who voiced the question in all their minds. "But are you sure you did this to the right—"

"I haven't made any mistake, the waiter was carefully rehearsed, you are all perfectly unharmed but the killer."

Lambert didn't seem to derive much consolation from this. "Now he tells us! A fine way to digest a meal."

"Shut up," somebody said terrifiedly.

"Twenty minutes to go," Hardecker said, tonelessly as a chime signal over the radio.

MacKenzie said, without heat, "You can't be sane, you know, to do a thing like this."

"Did you ever have a son?" was the answer.

Something seemed to snap in Megaffin. His chair jolted back. "I'm getting out of here," he said hoarsely.

The doors parted about two inches, silently as water, and a black metal cylinder peered through. "That man there," directed Hardecker. "Shoot him where he stands if he doesn't sit down."

Megaffin shrank down in his seat like a whipped cur. The doors slipped together again into a hairline crack.

"I couldn't feel more at home," sighed the cherubic-faced Lambert.

"Eighteen minutes," was the comment from the head of the table.

Prendergast suddenly grimaced uncontrollably, flattened his fore-arms on the table, and ducked his head onto them. He sniveled aloud. "I can't stand it! Lemme out of here! *I* didn't do it!"

A wave of revulsion went around the table. It was not because he'd broken down, analyzed MacKenzie, it was just that he didn't have the face for it. It should have been Lambert with his Kewpie physiognomy, if anyone. The latter, however, was having other troubles. He touched the side of his head, tapped himself on the chest. "Whoof!" he murmured. "What heartburn!"

"This is no way," said MacKenzie surlily. "If you had any kind of a case—"

"This is my way," was Hardecker's crackling answer. "I've given the man his choice. He needn't have it this way; he has his alternative. Fourteen minutes. Let me remind you, the longer the antidote's delayed, the more doubtful its efficiency will be."

MacKenzie felt as though a mass of concrete had lodged in his stomach. There is such a thing as nervous indigestion, he knew, but— He eyed the silver goblet reflectively.

They were all doing that almost incessantly. Prendergast had raised his head again, but it remained a woebegone mask of infantile fretfulness. Megaffin was green in the face and kept moistening his lips. Kenshaw had folded his arms and just sat there, as though waiting to see which one of the others would reach for the salvation in the silver container.

MacKenzie could feel a painful pulsing under his solar plexus now; he was in acute discomfort that verged on cramp. The thought of what this might be was bringing out sweat on his forehead.

Lambert reached out abruptly, and they all quit breathing for a minute. But his hand dodged the silver tureen, plunged into a box of perfectos to one side of it. He grabbed up two, stuck one in his breast pocket, the other between his teeth. "On you," he remarked resentfully to Hardecker.

Somebody gave a strained laugh at the false alarm they had all had. Kenshaw took off his glasses, wiped them ruefully, as though disappointed it hadn't been the payoff after all.

MacKenzie said, "You're alienating whatever sympathy's due you by pulling a stunt like this."

"I'm not asking for sympathy," was Hardecker's coldly ferocious answer. "It's atonement I want. Three lives were taken from me: my only son, my daughter-in-law, their prematurely born child. I demand payment for that!"

Prendergast clutched his throat all at once, whimpered, "I can't breathe! He's done it to *me*, so help me!"

MacKenzie, hostile now to Hardecker, tried to steady him just on general principle. "Gas around the heart, maybe. Don't fall for it if you're not sure."

"Don't fall for it," was the ungrateful yelp. "And if I drop dead, are *you* gonna bring me back?"

"He ought to be arrested for this," said Kenshaw, displaying emotion for the first time. His glasses had clouded over, giving him a peculiarly sightless look.

"Arrested?" snapped Lambert. He wagged his head from side to side. "He's going to be sued like no one was ever sued before! When I get through with him he'll go on relief."

Hardecker threw him a contemptuous look. "About ten minutes," he said. "He seems to prefer the more certain way. Stubborn, eh? He'd rather die than admit it."

MacKenzie gripped the seat of his chair, his churning insides heaving. He thought, If this is the McCoy that I'm feeling now, I'm going to bash his head in with a chair before I go. I'll give him something to poison innocent people about!

Megaffin was starting to swear at their tormentor, in a whining, guttural singsong.

"Five minutes. It will almost certainly fail if it's not downed within the next thirty seconds." Hardecker pocketed his watch, as though there were no further need for consulting it.

MacKenzie gagged, hauled at the knot of his tie, undid his collar button. A needle of suffocating pain had just splintered into his heart.

Only the whites of Prendergast's eyes showed; he was going off into some fit or fainting spell. Even Lambert quit pulling at his cigar, as though it sickened him. Kenshaw took off his glasses for the third time in five minutes, to clear them.

A pair of arms suddenly shot out, grasped the silver bowl, swung it. It was uptilted over someone's face and there was a hollow, metallic groaning coming from behind it, infinitely gruesome to hear. It had happened so quickly, MacKenzie couldn't be sure who it was for a minute. He had to do it by a quick process of elimination. Man sitting beside Lambert—Kenshaw, the scholarly-looking one, the man who had had the least to say since the ordeal had begun! He was gulping with a convulsive rising and falling of his Adam's apple, visible in the shadow just below the lower rim of the bowl.

Then suddenly he flung it aside, his face was visible again, the drained receptacle clanged against the wall where he'd cast it, dropped heavily to the floor. He couldn't talk for a minute or two, and neither could anyone else, except possibly Hardecker, and he didn't. Just sat staring at the self-confessed culprit with pitiless eyes.

Finally Kenshaw panted, his cheeks twitching, "Will it—will it—save me?"

Hardecker folded his arms, said to the others, but without taking his eyes off Kenshaw, "So now you know. So now you see whether I was right or not."

Kenshaw was holding his hands pressed tightly to the sides of his head. A sudden flood of words was unloosed from him, as though he found it a relief to talk now, after the long, unbearable tension he'd been through. "Sure you were right, and I'd do it over again! The rich man's son that had everything. But that wasn't enough for him, was it? He had to show off how good he was—paddle your own canoe from riches to more riches! He couldn't take a job with your own firm, could he? No, people might say you were helping him. He had to come to the place *I* worked and ask for a job. Not just anonymously. No, he had to mention whose son he was, to swing the scales in his favor! They thought maybe they'd get a pull with you, through him. It didn't count that I'd been with them all the best years of my life, that I had someone home too, just like he had, that I couldn't go anywhere else and mention the name of an influential father! They fired me."

His voice rose shrilly. "D'you know what happened to me? D'you know or care how I tramped the streets in the rain, at my age, looking for work? D'you know my wife had to get down on her knees and scrub dirty office corridors? D'you know how I washed dishes, carried sandwich boards through the streets, all on account of a smart aleck with Rover Boy ideas? Yes, it preyed on my mind, why wouldn't it? I suppose you found the threatening letters I wrote him."

Hardecker just shook his head slightly in denial.

"Then he got on the elevator that day. He didn't see me, probably wouldn't have known me if he had, but I saw him. Then we fell—and I hoped he was dead! But he wasn't. The idea took hold of me slowly, waiting down there in the dark. The torches started making noise, and I grabbed him, I was going to choke him. But he wrenched himself free and took out his gun to defend himself against what I guess he thought was a fear-crazed man. I wasn't fear crazed, I was revenge crazed!

"I grabbed his hand. Not the gun, but the hand that was holding it. I turned it around the other way, into his own heart. He said, 'Elinor, Elinor!' But that didn't save him; that was the wrong name, that was *his* wife, not mine. I squeezed the finger he had on the trigger with my own, and he fired his own weapon. So the police were right, it was suicide in a way.

"He leaned against me; there wasn't room enough in there to fall. I flung myself down first under him, so they'd find us that way, and eased him down on top of me. He bled on me a little while and then he quit. And when they came through I pretended I'd fainted."

Hardecker said, "Murderer. Murderer." Like drops of ice water. "He didn't *know* he'd done all that to you; oh, why didn't you give him a chance at least, why weren't you a man?"

Kenshaw started reaching downward to the floor, where he'd dropped his glasses when he had seized the antidote. His face was on a level with the tabletop. He scowled. "No matter what they've all heard me say just now, you'll never be able to prove I did it. Nobody saw me. Only the dark."

A whisper sounded: "And that's where you're going. Into the dark."

Kenshaw's head vanished suddenly below the table. His empty chair whirled over sidewise, cracked against the floor.

They were all on their feet now, bending over him. All but Hardecker. MacKenzie straightened up. "He's dead!" he said. "The antidote didn't work in time!"

Hardecker said, "That wasn't the antidote, that was the poison itself. He hadn't been given any until he gulped that down. He convicted himself and carried out sentence upon himself with one and the same gesture. I hadn't known which one of you it was until then. I'd only known it hadn't been my son's own doing, because, you see, the noise of those torches wouldn't have affected him much; he was partly deaf from birth."

He pushed his chair back and stood up. "I didn't summon you here under false pretenses; his estate will be divided in equal parts among the four of you that are left. And now I'm ready to take my own medicine. Call the police, let them and their prosecutors and their courts of law decide whether I killed him or his own guilty conscience did!"

ANOTHER SOLUTION

GILBERT HIGHET

JUST BEFORE THE boat capsized, Victor noticed that the sun was beginning to touch the water. He had never seen a sunset from the level of the sea: now he turned to watch the glow sucked down into that motionless green; but one of the girls, at the bow, screamed. Her long appalling cry echoed back instantly from the cliffs.

Within the same moment there was a shock. Everyone in the boat seemed to be struck by an enormous fist. The boom whipped around and smashed Pedro in the face. Concha, sitting on the bulwark, was hurled backward into the water; her head must have struck something, for Victor did not see her again. Pepa was always afraid of the sea—she could swim only a little, and she had been sitting in the hold with her knees below the deck planking to make herself feel safe. As it turned over, the boat took her with it into the depths.

The last thin sector of the sun was exactly on Victor's eye level as he kicked his way to the surface. There was nothing else on the whole face of the sea except Concha's handkerchief. He dived several times as well as he could. He was not a good swimmer, and all he could do was to duck his head under the surface, trying to kick his way down through the vague luminous water, in the hope of finding one of his friends, struggling or unconscious. Once he got down about fifteen feet and saw dim shapes near him. Concha and Pedro? He could touch nothing when he swam across underwater, and afterward he thought it was only reflected light slanting down from the surface. There was nothing else within his reach.

Then he swam around and around in great circles, sometimes cutting across and turning back on his course, in case a body floated up to the surface. Nothing. He swam farther out to sea, dived again and again, until he felt sick. Nothing, nothing. His friends, Pedro, Pepa, Concha, were all drowned. He was suddenly alone.

HIS MIND WAS clear. His friends were dead. He had to save himself. He had to save himself—that was the problem. He had often heard of threatened men thinking clearly and swiftly; it was true that they could. Think.

He was alone, without a boat, in the Mediterranean, at nightfall, below the enormous cliffs of Majorca. He had eaten a good meal an hour before and was not tired. After the boat capsized, he had kicked off his clothes easily enough. It was summer, so the water would not be unbearably cold at any time during the night. The weather was calm: cloudless sky, no moon, but the first stars were appearing. It would be quite dark in about fifteen minutes. Already the cliffs seemed to exude a brown vapor, and above them the sky of night was luminous.

The first way of escape was to bring help by shouting. Difficult. As far as he knew, this coast was made of solid lava blocks cast up and shorn off in one abrupt and forbidding front. When the water was bright and still, the cliffs could be seen continuing down, far beneath it, to horrible depths. The island was only an incident in the Mediterranean; it rested on the seafloor, and under its cliffs were miles of water, the waves of the deep. There were no coastwise villages, no houses nearer than the archduke's deserted villas high on the hill. Over the water a shout will carry for miles; but Victor knew it would be useless to shout until much later, when a boat might be out for night fishing. He must try other solutions. Meanwhile, he was slowly treading water and beginning to feel a little tired.

Second, then. Was it possible to swim to the cliffs and climb them?

He looked up. Gulfs of dark space opened before him—a smooth wall with one long slow crack extending diagonally upward, out of sight. Leaving Concha's handkerchief still floating, he swam toward the lower end of the fissure. Every stroke took him into a deeper angle of midnight. The water was a quiet purple darkness all around him. He reached the black rock, and gripped. But he might as well have tried to climb an iceberg. For yards above his head the protuberances were all rounded off by years of waves. His hands slipped off every grip he took. The cliff was impossible. Dark and deathly, it towered above him, forcing him down.

Involuntarily he struck out into the open sea, away from the black echoing mass of stone. He could see the floating handkerchief as a tiny interruption in that smooth water in which his own movements made only large ripples. It was so small and lonely that he was glad when he reached it. Now, a third way of escape . . .

The last light was being sucked out of the air. Victor stopped treading water and began to jump. Standing upright in the water, he drew up his legs and jerked them sharply downward. At the same time, he thrust his hands into the face of the sea, palms under. This relieved his muscles, and raised him above the surface with every leap. He looked southward, in the direction of Otonozar, where his friends lived—had lived. Nothing there; not a light, not even a movement in the surface glimmer of the sea. Ten miles lay between him and home. Paddling slowly on his back, he considered the third escape. Could he swim back to Otonozar? Could he swim all night? Could he even float until he was rescued?

As the night breeze blew in from the sea, he knew that he could do neither. He was not a good swimmer, like poor Pedro. Once, with Pedro and two other Majorcans, he had swum out a mile to meet their motorboat at La Foradada; but he was exhausted and sick after it, and had had to come home in the boat. Now the distances lengthened out in the darkness before him. Ten miles. Twenty thousand strokes. To count them, and hear yourself panting, and count, and kick and plunge in the darkness, for hours, for hours, still to struggle on, through the water always colder and stranger, and at last to be engulfed in an unknown place, forever lost, not even beside his friends. No.

It was quite dark. Eleven. The quiet stars shone to one another without a thrill of movement. Silent night. The sea lay in leaden stillness, broken only by the recurrent thrust of Victor's strokes. They were slower now.

He turned over and swam ahead. He must think of some way to keep alive, not to die after a few hours of ignominious and futile survival. Four solutions: all useless. Could he swim along the coast to find a landing place?

No, not even that. The cliffs were never less than five hundred feet high, and always beaten smooth by the stormy waves. There was no place where they could be climbed. He remembered that his friends had never been able to go swimming except at the village: there was no way down, no way up the cliffs. They were broken sharp off by the volcano, and smoothed by the busy sea which now waited so quietly. The fifth solution was hopeless. Only one remained.

Victor felt something brush his head, and knew it for Concha's handkerchief, floating just below the surface. This was where to die. He grasped the little rag; he said a prayer for the souls of his friends and one for himself; he let himself sink. He would wait until he had sunk some distance before breathing the water into his lungs. Drowning was, they said, a blend of sickness and sleep.

Slowly, on his back, he sank. Above him the dark-shining surface would become smooth again; when it was beyond reach, he would breathe. First, the sickness; then, the sleep.

It seemed he was hardly underwater before his back felt a pain. There was something firm and sharp beneath him. It was a rock.

Victor sprang into movement—his lungs were still full of air. In his struggles he ground his shoulder on the rock with a welcome pang, and his first gasp after he reached the surface was choked by his splashing. He swallowed a great deal of water, which made him shiver and cough with nausea. But he was happy, breathing in great gulps of air. Escape was found; a solution was found. It was only one tall thin wedge of rock rising from the seafloor, or from some deep-sunken buttress of the cliff. If there had been a wide shelf, he would have touched it long before as he swam about; but it was easy enough to miss this—he felt it now with his feet—this blade six inches wide. After swimming over and over this place, he had thought of it only as a chasm of deep sea, with his friends buried far below. The boat was sunk and he had never thought of the rock which had sunk it.

As he cautiously put his weight on his feet, he felt ill with relief and hope and horror to think that he might have drowned two fathoms away from his safety. Here was the seventh, the unexpected solution. Now he had a firm foothold, his head and shoulders were out of the water, and there were no waves, so he could stand still and rest. The tide would not rise more than an inch. He could stand all night on this rock and bear the chill—never so dreadful. And in the morning there would be fishermen; in the morning, at the earliest light of dawn. Night was not long. For a moment the whole scene was friendly, and the stars were companions. He felt the solid grateful rock with his feet, bent his strained muscles. This night was a terrible adventure; but he would live to tell about it.

A piece of seaweed touched his foot, and he pushed it away. It drifted back, and he kicked it off. When it returned and glided along his knee, he lowered one arm to catch it. Perhaps it was not seaweed; perhaps it was poor Concha's handkerchief.

As he felt about in the water, something gripped his knee. Instantly the same grip was on his hand. He could not move. He glared down into the dark water, where beside his own body he saw nothing. But it was not necessary to see the gray shape with the long arms, the great octopus which clung to the rock and now grasped both his wrists and threw another tentacle around his waist and drew him down. He had not thought of that.

THE WAXWORK

A. M. BURRAGE

WHILE THE UNIFORMED attendants of Marriner's Waxworks were ushering the last stragglers through the great glass-paneled double doors, the manager sat in his office interviewing Raymond Hewson.

The manager was a youngish man, stout, blond, and of medium height. He wore his clothes well and contrived to look extremely smart without appearing overdressed. Raymond Hewson looked neither. His clothes, which had been good when new and which were still carefully brushed and pressed, were beginning to show signs of their owner's losing battle with the world. He was a small, spare, pale man, with lank, errant brown hair, and although he spoke plausibly and even forcibly, he had the defensive and somewhat furtive air of a man who was used to rebuffs. He looked what he was, a man gifted somewhat above the ordinary, who was a failure through his lack of self-assertion.

The manager was speaking. "There is nothing new in your request," he said. "In fact we refuse it to different people—mostly young bloods who have tried to make bets—about three times a week. We have nothing to gain and something to lose by letting people spend the night in our Murderers' Den. If I allowed it, and some young idiot lost his senses, what would be my position? But your being a journalist somewhat alters the case."

Hewson smiled. "I suppose you mean that journalists have no senses to lose."

"No, no." The manager laughed. "But one imagines them to be responsible people. Besides, here we have something to gain: publicity and advertisement."

"Exactly," said Hewson, "and there I thought we might come to terms."

The manager laughed again. "Oh!" he exclaimed. "I know what's coming. You want to be paid twice, do you? It used to be said years ago that Madame Tussaud's would give a man a hundred pounds for sleeping alone in the Chamber of Horrors. I hope you don't think that we have made any such offer. Er—what is your paper, Mr. Hewson?"

"I am free-lancing at present," Hewson confessed, "working on space for several papers. However, I should find no difficulty in getting the story printed. The *Morning Echo* would use it like a shot. 'A Night with Marriner's Murderers.' No live paper could turn it down."

The manager rubbed his chin. "Ah! And how do you propose to treat it?"

"I shall make it gruesome, of course; gruesome with just a saving touch of humor."

The other nodded and offered Hewson his cigarette case. "Very well, Mr. Hewson," he said. "Get your story printed in the *Morning Echo*, and there will be a five-pound note waiting for you here when you care to come and call for it. But first of all, it's no small ordeal that you're proposing to undertake. I'd like to be quite sure about you, and I'd like you to be quite sure about yourself. I know I shouldn't care to take it on. I've seen those figures dressed and undressed, I know all about the process of their manufacture, I can walk about in company downstairs as unmoved as if I were walking among so many skittles, but I should hate having to sleep down there alone among them."

"Why?" asked Hewson.

"I don't know. There isn't any reason. I don't believe in ghosts. If I did, I should expect them to haunt the scene of their crimes or the spot where their bodies were laid, instead of a cellar which happens to contain their waxwork effigies. It's just that I couldn't sit alone among them all night, with their seeming to stare at me in the way they do.

After all, they represent the lowest and most appalling types of humanity, and—although I would not say it publicly—the people who come to see them are not generally charged with the very highest motives. The whole atmosphere of the place is unpleasant, and if you are susceptible to atmosphere, I warn you that you are in for a very uncomfortable night."

Hewson had known that from the moment when the idea had first occurred to him. His soul sickened at the prospect, even while he smiled casually upon the manager. But he had a wife and family to keep, and for the past month he had been living on paragraphs, eked out by his rapidly dwindling store of savings. Here was a chance not to be missed—the price of a special story in the *Morning Echo*, with a five-pound note to add to it. It meant comparative wealth and luxury for a week, and freedom from the worst anxieties for a fortnight. Besides, if he wrote the story well, it might lead to an offer of regular employment.

"The way of transgressors—and newspapermen—is hard," he said. "I have already promised myself an uncomfortable night, because your Murderers' Den is obviously not fitted up as a hotel bedroom. But I don't think your waxworks will worry me much."

"You're not superstitious?"

"Not a bit." Hewson laughed.

"But you're a journalist; you must have a strong imagination."

"The news editors for whom I've worked have always complained that I haven't any. Plain facts are not considered sufficient in our trade, and the papers don't like offering their readers unbuttered bread."

The manager smiled and rose. "Right," he said. "I think the last of the people have gone. Wait a moment. I'll give orders for the figures downstairs not to be draped, and let the night people know that you'll be here. Then I'll take you down and show you round."

He picked up the receiver of a house telephone, spoke into it, and presently replaced it.

"One condition I'm afraid I must impose on you," he remarked. "I must ask you not to smoke. We had a fire scare down in the Murderers' Den this evening. I don't know who gave the alarm, but whoever it was, it was a false one. Fortunately there were very few people down there at the time, or there might have been a panic. And now, if you're ready, we'll make a move."

Hewson followed the manager through half a dozen rooms, where attendants were busy shrouding the kings and queens of England, the generals and prominent statesmen of this and other generations, all the mixed herd of humanity whose fame or notoriety had rendered them eligible for this kind of immortality. The manager stopped once and spoke to a man in uniform, saying something about an armchair in the Murderers' Den.

"It's the best we can do for you, I'm afraid," he said to Hewson. "I hope you'll be able to get some sleep."

He led the way through an open barrier and down ill-lit stone stairs which conveyed a sinister impression of giving access to a dungeon. In a passage at the bottom were a few preliminary horrors, such as relics of the Inquisition, a rack taken from a medieval castle, branding irons, thumbscrews, and other mementos of man's onetime cruelty to man. Beyond the passage was the Murderers' Den.

It was a room of irregular shape with a vaulted roof, and dimly lit by electric lights burning behind inverted bowls of frosted glass. It was, by design, an eerie and uncomfortable chamber—a chamber whose atmosphere invited its visitors to speak in whispers. There was something of the air of a chapel about it, but a chapel no longer devoted to the practice of piety and given over now for base and impious worship.

The waxwork murderers stood on low pedestals, with numbered tickets at their feet. Seeing them elsewhere, and without knowing whom they represented, one would have thought them a dull-looking crew, chiefly remarkable for the shabbiness of their clothes and as evidence of the changes of fashion even among the unfashionable.

Recent notorieties rubbed dusty shoulders with the old favorites. Thurtell, the murderer of Weir, stood as if frozen in the act of making a shopwindow gesture to young Bywaters. There was Lefroy, the poor half-baked little snob who killed for gain so that he might ape the gentleman. Within five yards of him sat Mrs. Thompson, that erotic romanticist, hanged to propitiate British middle-class matronhood. Charles Peace, the only member of that vile company who looked uncompromisingly and entirely evil, sneered across an aisle at Norman

Thorne. Browne and Kennedy, the two most recent additions, stood between Mrs. Dyer and Patrick Mahon.

The manager, walking around with Hewson, pointed out several of the more interesting of these unholy notabilities. "That's Crippen; I expect you recognize him. Insignificant little beast who looks as if he couldn't tread on a worm. That's Armstrong. Looks like a decent, harmless country gentleman, doesn't he? There's old Vaquier; you can't miss him because of his beard. And of course this—"

"Who's that?" Hewson interrupted in a whisper, pointing.

"Oh, I was coming to him," said the manager in a light undertone. "Come and have a good look at him. This is our star turn. He's the only one of the bunch that hasn't been hanged."

The figure which Hewson had indicated was that of a small, slight man not much more than five feet in height. It wore little waxed mustaches, large spectacles, and a caped coat. There was something so exaggeratedly French in its appearance that it reminded Hewson of a stage caricature. He could not have said precisely why the mild-looking face seemed to him so repellent, but he had already recoiled a step, and even in the manager's company, it cost him an effort to look again.

"But who is he?" he asked.

"That," said the manager, "is Dr. Bourdette."

Hewson shook his head doubtfully. "I think I've heard the name," he said, "but I forget in connection with what."

The manager smiled. "You'd remember better if you were a Frenchman," he said. "For some long while that man was the terror of Paris. He carried on his work of healing by day, and of throat cutting by night, when the fit was on him. He killed for the sheer devilish pleasure it gave him to kill, and always in the same way—with a razor. After his last crime he left a clue behind him which set the police upon his track. One clue led to another, and before very long they knew that they were on the track of the Parisian equivalent of our Jack the Ripper, and had enough evidence to send him to the madhouse or the guillotine on a dozen capital charges.

"But even then our friend here was too clever for them. When he realized that the toils were closing about him he mysteriously disappeared, and ever since, the police of every civilized country have been looking for him. There is no doubt that he managed to make away with himself, and by some means which has prevented his body coming to light. One or two crimes of a similar nature have taken place since his disappearance, but he is believed almost for certain to be dead, and the experts believe these recrudescences to be the work of an imitator. It's queer, isn't it, how every notorious murderer has imitators?"

Hewson shuddered and fidgeted with his feet. "I don't like him at all," he confessed. "Ugh! What eyes he's got!"

"Yes, this figure's a little masterpiece. You find the eyes bite into you? Well, that's excellent realism, then, for Bourdette practiced mesmerism, and was supposed to mesmerize his victims before dispatching them. Indeed, had he not done so, it is impossible to see how so small a man could have done his ghastly work. There were never any signs of a struggle."

"I thought I saw him move," said Hewson with a catch in his voice.

The manager smiled. "You'll have more than one optical illusion before the night's out, I expect. You shan't be locked in. You can come upstairs when you've had enough of it. There are watchmen on the premises, so you'll find company. Don't be alarmed if you hear them moving about. I'm sorry I can't give you any more light, because all the lights are on. For obvious reasons we keep this place as gloomy as possible. And now I think you had better return with me to the office and have a tot of whiskey before beginning your night's vigil."

THE MEMBER OF the night staff who placed the armchair for Hewson was inclined to be facetious. "Where will you have it, sir?" he asked, grinning. "Just 'ere, so as you can 'ave a little talk with Crippen when you're tired of sitting still? Or there's old Mother Dyer over there, making eyes and looking as if she could do with a bit of company. Say where, sir."

Hewson smiled. The man's chaff pleased him if only because, for the moment at least, it lent the proceedings a much desired air of the commonplace.

"I'll place it myself, thanks," he said. "I'll find out where the drafts come from first."

"You won't find any down here. Well, good night, sir. I'm upstairs if you want me. Don't let 'em sneak up be'ind you and touch your neck with their cold and clammy 'ands. And you look out for that old Mrs. Dyer; I b'lieve she's taken a fancy to you."

Hewson laughed and wished the man good night. It was easier than he had expected. He wheeled the armchair—a heavy one upholstered in plush—a little way down the central aisle, and deliberately turned it so that its back was toward the effigy of Dr. Bourdette. For some undefined reason he liked Dr. Bourdette a great deal less than his companions. Busying himself with arranging the chair, he was almost lighthearted, but when the attendant's footfalls had died away and a deep hush stole over the chamber, he realized that he had no slight ordeal before him.

The dim unwavering light fell on the rows of figures, which were so uncannily like human beings that the silence and the stillness seemed unnatural and even ghastly. He missed the sound of breathing, the rustling of clothes, the hundred and one minute noises one hears when even the deepest silence has fallen upon a crowd. But the air was as stagnant as water at the bottom of a standing pond. There was not a breath in the chamber to stir a curtain or rustle a hanging drapery or start a shadow. His own shadow, moving in response to a shifted arm or leg, was all that could be coaxed into motion. All was still to the gaze and silent to the ear. It must be like this at the bottom of the sea, he thought, and wondered how to work the phrase into his story on the morrow.

He faced the sinister figures boldly enough. They were only waxworks. So long as he let that thought dominate all others, he promised himself, all would be well. It did not, however, save him long from the discomfort occasioned by the waxen stare of Dr. Bourdette, which, he knew, was directed upon him from behind. The eyes of the little Frenchman's effigy haunted and tormented him, and he itched with the desire to turn and look.

Come! he thought. My nerves have started already. If I turn and look at that dressed-up dummy, it will be an admission of fear.

And then another voice in his brain spoke to him. It's because you're afraid that you won't turn and look at him.

The two voices quarreled silently for a moment or two, and at last

Hewson turned his chair around a little and looked behind him. Among the many figures standing in stiff, unnatural poses, the effigy of the dreadful little doctor stood out with a queer prominence, perhaps because a steady beam of light beat straight down upon it. Hewson flinched before the parody of mildness which some fiendishly skilled craftsman had managed to convey in wax, met the eyes for one agonized second, and turned again to face the other direction.

"He's only a waxwork like the rest of you," Hewson muttered defiantly. "You're all only waxworks."

They were only waxworks, yes, but waxworks don't move. Not that he had seen the least movement anywhere, but it struck him that, in the moment or two while he had looked behind him, there had been the least, subtle change in the grouping of the figures in front. Crippen, for instance, seemed to have turned at least one degree to the left. Or, thought Hewson, perhaps the illusion was due to the fact that he had not swung his chair back into its exact original position. And there were Field and Grey, too; surely one of them had moved his hands. Hewson held his breath for a moment, and then drew his courage back to him as a man lifts a weight. He remembered the words of more than one news editor and laughed savagely to himself.

"And they tell me I've got no imagination!" he said beneath his breath.

He took a notebook from his pocket and wrote quickly. "Memo—Deathly silence and unearthly stillness of figures. Like being bottom of sea. Hypnotic eyes of Dr. Bourdette. Figures seem to move when not being watched."

He closed the book suddenly over his fingers and looked around quickly and awfully over his right shoulder. He had neither seen nor heard a movement, but it was as if some sixth sense had made him aware of one. He looked straight into the vapid countenance of Lefroy, which smiled vacantly back as if to say, It wasn't I!

Of course it wasn't he, or any of them; it was his own nerves. Or was it? Hadn't Crippen moved again during that moment when his attention was directed elsewhere? You couldn't trust that little man! Once you took your eyes off him, he took advantage of it to shift his position. That was what they were all doing, if he only knew it, he told himself, and half rose out of his chair. This was not quite good enough! He was going. He wasn't going to spend the night with a lot of waxworks which moved while he wasn't looking. . . .

Hewson sat down again. This was very cowardly and very absurd. They *were* only waxworks and they *couldn't* move; let him hold that thought and all would yet be well. Then why all that silent unrest about him?—a subtle something in the air which did not quite break the silence and happened, whichever way he looked, just beyond the boundaries of his vision.

He swung around quickly to encounter the mild but baleful stare of Dr. Bourdette. Then, without warning, he jerked his head back to stare straight at Crippen. Ha! He'd nearly caught Crippen that time! "You'd better be careful, Crippen—and all the rest of you! If I do see one of you move, I'll smash you to pieces! Do you hear?"

He ought to go, he told himself. Already he had experienced enough to write his story, or ten stories, for that matter. Well, then, why not go? The *Morning Echo* would be none the wiser as to how long he had stayed, nor would it care, so long as his story was a good one. Yes, but that night watchman upstairs would chaff him. And the manager—one never knew—perhaps the manager would quibble over that five-pound note which he needed so badly. He wondered if Rose were asleep or if she were lying awake and thinking of him. She'd laugh when he told her that he had imagined . . .

This was a little too much! It was bad enough that the waxwork effigies of murderers should move when they weren't being watched, but it was intolerable that they should *breathe.* Somebody was breathing. Or was it his own breath, which sounded to him as if it came from a distance? He sat rigid, listening and straining, until he exhaled with a long sigh. His own breath after all—or, if not, something had divined that he was listening, and had ceased breathing simultaneously.

Hewson jerked his head swiftly around and looked all about him out of haggard and haunted eyes. Everywhere his gaze encountered the vacant waxen faces, and everywhere he felt that by just some least fraction of a second he had missed seeing a movement of hand or foot, a silent opening or compression of lips, a flicker of eyelids, a look of human intelligence now smoothed out. They were like naughty children in a class, whispering, fidgeting, and laughing behind their teacher's back, but blandly innocent when his gaze was turned upon them.

This would not do! This distinctly would not do! He must clutch at something, grip with his mind upon something which belonged essentially to the workaday world, to the daylight London streets. He was Raymond Hewson, an unsuccessful journalist, a living and breathing man, and these figures grouped around him were only dummies, so they could neither move nor whisper. What did it matter if they were supposed to be lifelike effigies of murderers? They were only made of wax and sawdust, and stood there for the entertainment of morbid sightseers and orange-sucking tourists. That was better! Now what was that funny story which somebody had told him in the Falstaff yesterday? . . .

He recalled part of it, but not all, for the gaze of Dr. Bourdette urged, challenged, and finally compelled him to turn.

Hewson half turned, and then swung his chair so as to bring him face to face with the wearer of those dreadful hypnotic eyes. His own eyes were dilated, and his mouth, at first set in a grin of terror, lifted at the corners in a snarl. Then Hewson spoke and woke a hundred sinister echoes. "You moved, damn you!" he cried. "Yes, you did, damn you! I saw you!"

Then he sat quite still, staring straight before him, like a man found frozen in the Arctic snows.

Dr. Bourdette's movements were leisurely. He stepped off his pedestal with the mincing care of a lady alighting from a bus. The platform stood about two feet from the ground, and above the edge of it a plush-covered rope hung in arclike curves. Dr. Bourdette lifted up the rope until it formed an arch for him to pass under, stepped off the platform, and sat down on the edge, facing Hewson. Then he nodded and smiled and said, "Good evening.

"I need hardly tell you," he continued in perfect English, in which was traceable only the least foreign accent, "that not until I overheard the conversation between you and the worthy manager of this establishment did I suspect that I should have the pleasure of a companion here for the night. You cannot move or speak without my bidding, but you can hear me perfectly well. Something tells me that you are—shall I say nervous? My dear sir, have no illusions. I am not one of these contemptible effigies miraculously come to life. I am Dr. Bourdette himself." He paused, coughed, and shifted his legs.

"Pardon me," he resumed, "but I am a little stiff. And let me explain. Circumstances with which I need not fatigue you have made it desirable that I should live in England. I was close to this building this evening when I saw a policeman regarding me a thought too curiously. I guessed that he intended to follow and perhaps ask me embarrassing questions, so I mingled with the crowd and came in here. An extra coin bought my admission to the chamber in which we now meet, and an inspiration showed me a certain means of escape.

"I raised a cry of fire, and when all the fools had rushed to the stairs, I stripped my effigy of the caped coat which you behold me wearing, donned it, hid my effigy under the platform at the back, and took its place on the pedestal.

"I own that I have since spent a very fatiguing evening, but fortunately I was not always being watched, and had opportunities to draw an occasional deep breath and ease the rigidity of my pose. One small boy screamed and exclaimed that he saw me moving. I understood that he was to be whipped and put straight to bed on his return home, and I can only hope that the threat has been executed to the letter.

"The manager's description of me, which I had the embarrassment of being compelled to overhear, was biased but not altogether inaccurate. Clearly I am not dead, although it is as well that the world thinks otherwise. His account of my hobby, which I have indulged for years, although, through necessity, less frequently of late, was in the main true, although not intelligently expressed. The world is divided between collectors and noncollectors. With the noncollectors we are not concerned. The collectors collect anything, according to their individual tastes, from money to cigarette cards, from moths to matchboxes. I collect throats." He paused again and regarded Hewson's throat with interest mingled with disfavor.

"I am obliged to the chance which brought us together tonight," he continued, "and perhaps it would seem ungrateful to complain. From motives of personal safety my activities have been somewhat curtailed of late years, and I am glad of this opportunity of gratifying my somewhat unusual whim. But you have a skinny neck, sir, if you will overlook a personal remark. I should never have selected you from choice. I like men with thick necks . . . thick red necks. . . ."

He fumbled in an inside pocket and took out something which he tested against a wet forefinger and then proceeded to pass gently to and fro across the palm of his left hand. "This is a little French razor," he remarked blandly. "They are not much used in England, but perhaps you know them? One strops them on wood. The blade, you will observe, is very narrow. They do not cut very deep, but deep enough. In one moment you shall see for yourself. I shall ask you the little civil question of all the polite barbers: Does the razor suit you, sir?"

He rose up, a diminutive but menacing figure of evil, and approached Hewson with the silent, furtive step of a hunting panther. "You will have the goodness," he said, "to raise your chin a little. Thank you, and a little more. Just a little more. Ah, thank you! . . . *Merci, m'sieur. . . . Ah, merci . . . merci.*"

OVER ONE END of the chamber was a thick skylight of frosted glass which, by day, let in a few sickly and filtered rays from the floor above. After sunrise these began to mingle with the subdued light from the electric bulbs, and this mingled illumination added a certain ghastliness to a scene which needed no additional touch of horror.

The waxwork figures stood apathetically in their places, waiting to be admired or execrated by the crowds who would presently wander fearfully among them. In their midst, in the center aisle, Hewson sat still, leaning far back in his armchair. His chin was uptilted, as if he were waiting to receive attention from a barber, and although there was not a scratch upon his throat, nor anywhere upon his body, he was cold and dead. His previous employers were wrong in having credited him with no imagination.

Dr. Bourdette on his pedestal watched the dead man unemotionally. He did not move, nor was he capable of motion. But then, after all, he was only a waxwork.

FOR YOUR EYES ONLY

IAN FLEMING

THE MOST BEAUTIFUL bird in Jamaica, and some say the most beautiful bird in the world, is the doctor hummingbird. The cock bird is about nine inches long, but seven inches of it are tail—two long black feathers that curve and cross each other and whose inner edges are in a form of scalloped design. The head and crest are black, the wings dark green, the long bill is scarlet, and the eyes, bright and confiding, are black. The body is a dazzling emerald green, the brightest green in nature. In Jamaica, birds that are loved are given nicknames. *Trochilus polytmus* is called doctorbird because his two black streamers remind people of the tailcoat of the old-time physician.

Mrs. Havelock was particularly devoted to two families of these birds because she had been watching them sipping honey, fighting, and nesting since she married and came to Content. She was now over fifty, so many generations of these two families had come and gone since the original two pairs had been nicknamed Pyramus and Thisbe and Daphnis and Chloe by her mother-in-law. But successive couples had kept the names, and Mrs. Havelock now sat at her elegant tea service on the broad, cool veranda and watched Pyramus dive-bomb Daphnis, who had sneaked in among the nearby bushes of monkeyfiddle that were Pyramus' preserve. The running battle between the two families was a game. In this finely planted garden there was enough honey for all.

Mrs. Havelock put down her teacup and took a cucumber sandwich.

Colonel Havelock looked over the top of his *Daily Gleaner* and said, "It looks to me as if Batista will be on the run soon. Castro's keeping up the pressure pretty well. Chap at Barclays told me this morning that there's a lot of scare money coming over here already. Said that Belair's been sold to nominees. One hundred and fifty thousand pounds for a thousand acres of cattle tick! And somebody's suddenly gone and bought that ghastly Blue Harbor hotel; there's even talk that Jimmy Farquharson has found a buyer for his place—leaf spot and all."

"Where do they get all the money from, anyway?"

"Rackets, government money—God knows. The place is riddled with crooks and gangsters. They must want to get their money out of Cuba and into something else quick. Apparently the man who bought Belair just shoveled the money out of a suitcase. I suppose he'll keep the place for a year or two, and when the trouble's blown over he'll put it on the market again and move off somewhere else. Pity—Belair used to be a fine property."

"Ten thousand acres in Bill's grandfather's day."

"Fat lot Bill cares. I bet he's booked his passage to London already. That's one more of the old families gone. Soon won't be anyone left but us. Thank God Judy likes the place."

Mrs. Havelock said, "Yes, dear," and pinged the bell for the tea things to be cleared away. Agatha, a huge black woman wearing an old-fashioned white headcloth, came out through the white and rose drawing room. Mrs. Havelock said, "It's time we started bottling, Agatha. The guavas are early this year."

Agatha's face was impassive. She said, "Yes'm. But we goin' to need more bottles."

"Why? Only last year I got you two dozen."

"Yes'm. Someone done smash five, six of dose."

"Oh, dear. How did that happen?"

"Couldn't say'm." Agatha picked up the big silver tray and waited, watching Mrs. Havelock's face.

Mrs. Havelock had not lived most of her life in Jamaica without learning that she would not get anywhere hunting for a culprit. So she just said cheerfully, "Oh, all right, Agatha. I'll get some more when I go into Kingston."

"Yes'm." Agatha went back into the house.

Mrs. Havelock picked up a piece of petit point and began stitching automatically. A mockingbird on the topmost branch of a frangipani started on its evening repertoire. An early tree frog announced the beginning of the short violet dusk.

Content, twenty thousand acres in the foothills of Candlefly Peak, had been given to an early Havelock by Oliver Cromwell. Unlike so many other settlers, the Havelocks had maintained the plantation through three centuries, through the boom and bust of cocoa, sugar, citrus, and copra. Now it was in bananas and cattle, and it was one of the richest and best run of all the private estates in the island. The house, patched up after earthquake or hurricane, was a hybrid—a mahogany-pillared, two-storied central block on the old stone foundations, flanked by two single-storied wings with widely overhung, flat-pitched roofs of cedar shingles. The Havelocks were now sitting on the deep veranda, facing the gently sloping garden, beyond which a vast tumbling jungle stretched away twenty miles to the sea.

Colonel Havelock put down his *Gleaner.* "I thought I heard a car."

Mrs. Havelock said firmly, "If it's those ghastly Feddens from Port Antonio, you've simply got to get rid of them. I can't stand any more of their moans about England." She got up quickly. "I'm going to tell Agatha to say I've got a migraine."

Agatha came out through the drawing-room door, followed closely by three men. She said hurriedly, "Gemmun from Kingston'm. To see de colonel."

The leading man slid past the housekeeper. He was still wearing his hat, a Panama with a short, upcurled brim. He took this off with his left hand and held it against his stomach. The rays of the sun glittered on hair grease and on a mouthful of smiling white teeth. He went up to Colonel Havelock, his outstretched hand held straight in front of him. "Major Gonzales. From Havana. Pleased to meet you, Colonel."

The accent was sham American. Colonel Havelock had got to his feet. He touched the outstretched hand briefly and looked over the major's shoulder at the other two men, who had stationed themselves on either side of the door. They were both carrying that new holdall of the tropics, a Pan American overnight bag. The bags looked heavy. Now the two men bent down together and placed them beside their yellowish shoes. When they straightened themselves, their intelligent animal eyes fixed themselves on the major, reading his behavior.

"They are my secretaries."

Colonel Havelock's direct blue eyes took in the sharp clothes, the natty shoes, the glistening fingernails of the major, and the blue jeans and calypso shirts of the other two. He wondered how he could get these men into his study and near the revolver in the top drawer of his desk. He said, "What can I do for you?"

Major Gonzales spread his hands. The width of his smile remained constant. The liquid, almost golden eyes were amused, friendly. "It is a matter of business, Colonel. I represent a certain gentleman in Havana—" He made a throwaway gesture with his right hand. "A powerful gentleman. A very fine guy." Major Gonzales assumed an expression of sincerity. "You would like him, Colonel. He asked me to present his compliments and to inquire the price of your property."

Mrs. Havelock, who had been watching the scene with a polite half smile on her lips, moved to stand beside her husband. She said kindly, "What a shame, Major. All this way on these dusty roads! Your friend really should have written first. You see, my husband's family have lived here for nearly three hundred years." She looked at him sweetly, apologetically. "I'm afraid there just isn't any question of selling."

Major Gonzales bowed briefly. His smiling face turned back to Colonel Havelock. He said, as if Mrs. Havelock had not opened her mouth, "My gentleman is told this is one of the finest *estancias* in Jamaica. He is a most generous man. You may mention any sum that is reasonable."

Colonel Havelock said firmly, "You heard what Mrs. Havelock said. The property is not for sale."

Major Gonzales laughed. He shook his head as if he were explaining something to a rather dense child. "You misunderstand me, Colonel. My gentleman desires this property and no other property in Jamaica. He has some extra funds to invest. These funds are seeking a home in Jamaica. My gentleman wishes this to be their home."

Colonel Havelock said patiently, "I quite understand, Major. And I am sorry you have wasted your time. Content will never be for sale in my lifetime. And now, if you'll forgive me. My wife and I always dine early, and you have a long way to go." He made a gesture to the left, along the veranda. "I think you'll find this is the quickest way to your car. Let me show you."

Colonel Havelock moved invitingly, but when Major Gonzales stayed where he was, he stopped. The blue eyes began to freeze.

There was perhaps one less tooth in Major Gonzales' smile, and his eyes had become watchful. But his manner was still jolly. He said cheerfully, "Just one moment, Colonel." He issued a curt order over his shoulder. The two men picked up their blue Pan American bags and stepped forward. Major Gonzales reached for the zipper on each of them in turn and pulled. The bags were full to the brim with neat, solid wads of American money. Major Gonzales spread his arms. "All hundred-dollar bills. Half a million dollars. A small fortune. There are many other good places to live in the world, Colonel. All I need is half a sheet of paper with your signature. The lawyers can do the rest. Now, Colonel"—the smile was winning—"shall we say yes and shake hands on it? Then the bags stay here and we leave you to your dinner."

The Havelocks now looked at the major with the same expression—a mixture of anger and disgust. The colonel said, "I thought I had made myself clear, Major. The property is not for sale at any price. I must now ask you to leave."

For the first time Major Gonzales' smile lost its warmth. His golden eyes were suddenly brassy and hard. He said softly, "Colonel. It is I who have not made myself clear. My gentleman has instructed me to say that if you will not accept his most generous terms, we must proceed to other measures."

Mrs. Havelock was suddenly afraid. She put her hand on Colonel Havelock's arm and pressed it hard. He put his hand over hers in reassurance. He said through tight lips, "Please leave us alone and go, Major. Otherwise I shall communicate with the police."

The pink tip of Major Gonzales' tongue came out and slowly licked along his lips. He said harshly, "So the property is not for sale in your lifetime, Colonel. Is that your last word?" His right hand went behind his back and he clicked his fingers softly. Behind him the gun hands of the two men slid through the openings of their gay shirts above the waistbands.

Mrs. Havelock's hand went up to her mouth. Colonel Havelock tried to say yes, but his mouth went dry. This mangy Cuban crook must be bluffing. He managed to say thickly, "Yes, it is."

Major Gonzales nodded curtly. "In that case, Colonel, my gentleman will carry on the negotiations with the next owner—with your daughter."

The fingers clicked again. Major Gonzales stepped to one side to give a clear field of fire. The gun hands came out from under the gay shirts. The ugly sausage-shaped guns spat and thudded—again and again, even when the two bodies were on their way to the ground.

Major Gonzales bent down and verified where the bullets had hit. Then the three men walked quickly back through the rose and white drawing room and across the carved mahogany hall and out through the elegant front door. They climbed unhurriedly into a black Ford Consul sedan with Jamaican license plates, and Major Gonzales drove off at an easy pace down the long avenue of royal palms. At the junction of the road to Port Antonio the cut telephone wires hung down through the trees like bright lianas.

Major Gonzales slalomed the car carefully and expertly down the rough road until he came to the outer sprawl of the little banana port. There he ran the stolen car onto the grass verge beside the road, and the three men got out and walked the quarter of a mile to the wharves. A speedboat was waiting, its exhaust bubbling. The three men got in, and the boat zoomed off across the still waters.

The anchor chain was already being raised on a glittering fifty-ton Chris-Craft. The three men went on board, and the speedboat was hoisted up. The twin diesels awoke to a stuttering roar, and the Chris-Craft made for the channel. By dawn she would be back in Havana.

Out on the broad veranda of Content the last rays of the sun glittered on the red stains. One of the doctorbirds whirred over the balustrade and hovered close above Mrs. Havelock's heart, looking down. No, this was not for him. He flirted gaily off to his roosting perch among the hibiscus.

There came the sound of someone in a small sports car making a racing change at the bend of the drive. If Mrs. Havelock had been alive, she would have been getting ready to say, Judy, I'm always telling you not to do that on the corner. It scatters gravel all over the lawn.

IT WAS A MONTH later. In London, October had begun with a week of brilliant Indian summer, and the noise of the mowers came up from Regent's Park and in through the wide-open windows of M's office. They were power mowers, and James Bond reflected that one of the most beautiful noises of summer, the drowsy iron song of the old machines, was going forever from the world.

Bond had time for this reflection because M seemed to be having difficulty in coming to the point. And it seemed to Bond that there was an extra small cleft of worry between M's clear gray eyes. And three minutes was certainly too long to spend getting a pipe going.

At last M swiveled his chair around square with the desk and said mildly, "James, has it ever occurred to you that every man in the fleet knows what to do except the commanding admiral?"

Bond frowned. He said, "It hadn't occurred to me, sir. But I see what you mean. The rest only have to carry out orders. The admiral has to decide on the orders. I suppose it's the same as saying that supreme command is the loneliest post there is."

M jerked his pipe sideways. "Same sort of idea. Some people are religious—pass the decision on to God." M's eyes were defensive. "I used to try that sometimes, but He always passed the buck back again—told me to get on and make up my own mind. Good for one, I suppose, but tough. Trouble is, very few people keep tough after about forty. They've been knocked about by life—had troubles, tragedies, illnesses. These things soften you up." M looked sharply at Bond. "How's your coefficient of toughness, James? You haven't got to the dangerous age yet."

Bond didn't like personal questions. He didn't know what to answer. He did not have a wife or children—had never suffered the tragedy of a personal loss. He had not had to stand up to blindness or a mortal disease. He had absolutely no idea how he would face these things. He said hesitantly, "I suppose I can stand most things if I have to and if I think it's right, sir." He went on, feeling ashamed for throwing the ball back at M, "I suppose I assume that when I'm given an unpleasant job in the service, the cause is a just one."

"Damn it." M's eyes glittered impatiently. "That's just what I mean! You rely on *me.* You won't take any damned responsibility yourself." He thrust the stem of his pipe toward his chest. "I'm the one who has to decide if a thing is right or not." The anger died out of the eyes. He said gloomily, "Oh, well, I suppose it's what I'm paid for. Somebody's got to drive the bloody train."

Bond had never before heard M use as strong a word as "bloody." Nor had M ever given any hint that he felt the weight of the burden he had carried ever since he had thrown up the certain prospect of becoming Fifth Sea Lord in order to take over the Secret Service. M obviously had a problem. Bond wondered what it was. It would not be concerned with danger. If M could get the odds right, he would risk anything, anywhere in the world. It would not be political. M did not give a damn for the susceptibilities of any ministry. It might be moral. It might be personal. Bond said, "Is there anything I can help with, sir?"

M looked thoughtfully at Bond. He said abruptly, "Do you remember the Havelock case?"

"Only what I read in the papers, sir. Elderly couple in Jamaica. The daughter came home one night and found them full of bullets. There was some talk of gangsters from Havana. The housekeeper said three men had called in a car. She thought they might have been Cubans. It turned out the car had been stolen. A yacht had sailed from the local harbor that night. But as far as I remember, the police didn't get anywhere. Were we asked to handle the case, sir?"

"No," M said gruffly, "we weren't. It's personal to me. Just happens"—M cleared his throat; this private use of the service was on his conscience—"I knew the Havelocks. Matter of fact I was best man at their wedding in 1925."

"I see, sir. That's bad."

M said shortly, "Nice people. Anyway, I told Station C to look into it. They didn't get anywhere with the Batista people, but we've got a good man with the other side—with this chap Castro's intelligence people. I got the whole story a couple of weeks ago. It boils down to the fact that a man called Hammerstein, or von Hammerstein, had the couple killed. There are a lot of Germans well dug in in these banana republics. They're Nazis who got out of the net at the end of the war. This one's ex-Gestapo. He got a job as head of Batista's counterintelligence. Made a packet of money out of extortion and blackmail. He was set up for life until Castro began to make headway. He was one of the first to start easing himself out. He cut one of his officers in on his loot, a man called Gonzales, and this man traveled around the Caribbean with a couple of gunmen and began salting away Hammerstein's money outside Cuba. Only bought the best, but at top prices. When money didn't work, he'd use force—kidnap a child, burn down a few acres, anything to make the owner see reason. Well, this man Hammerstein heard of the Havelocks' property, one of the best in Jamaica, and he told Gonzales to go and get it. I suppose his orders were to kill the Havelocks if they wouldn't sell and then put pressure on the daughter. She should be about twenty-five by now. Anyway, they killed the Havelocks. Then two weeks ago Batista sacked Hammerstein. Hammerstein cleared out and took his team with him. Timed things pretty well, I should say. It looks as if Castro may get in this winter."

Bond said softly, "Where have they gone to?"

"America. Right up in the north of Vermont, against the Canadian border. Those sort of men like being close to frontiers. Place called Echo Lake. It's some kind of millionaire's ranch he's rented. Tucked away in the mountains with this little lake in the grounds. He's certainly chosen a place where he won't be troubled with visitors."

"How did you get on to this, sir?"

"I sent a report of the whole case to Edgar Hoover. He knew of the man. He's been interested in Havana ever since American gangster money started following the casinos there. He said that Hammerstein and his party had come into the States on six-month visitors' visas. He was very helpful. Wanted to know if I'd got enough to build up a case on. Did I want these men extradited for trial in Jamaica? I talked it over here with the Attorney General and he said there wasn't a hope unless we could get the witnesses from Havana. But there's no chance of that. It was only through Castro's intelligence that we even know as much as we do. Officially the Cubans won't raise a finger."

M sat for a moment in silence. Then he went on, "I decided to have a talk with our friends the Canadian Mounties. The commissioner has never let me down yet. He strayed one of his frontier-patrol planes over the border and took a full aerial survey of this Echo Lake place. Said that if I wanted any other cooperation, he'd provide it. And now"—M slowly swiveled in his chair—"I've got to decide what to do next."

Bond realized why M wanted someone else to make the decision. Because these had been friends, M had worked on the case by himself. And now it had come to the point when justice ought to be done and these people brought to book. But M was thinking, Is this justice, or is it revenge? M wanted someone else, Bond, to deliver judgment.

There were no doubts in Bond's mind. Von Hammerstein had applied the law of the jungle to two defenseless people. Since no other law was available, the law of the jungle should be applied to von Hammerstein. In no other way could justice be done. If it was revenge, it was the revenge of the community.

Bond said, "I wouldn't hesitate for a minute, sir. This is a case for rough justice—an eye for an eye."

M made no comment.

Bond said, "These people can't be hung, sir. But they ought to be killed."

For a moment M's eyes were blank, looking inward. Then he slowly reached for the top drawer of his desk, pulled it open, and extracted a thin file without the usual title across it and without the top-secret red star. He placed the file squarely in front of him, and his hand rummaged again in the open drawer. The hand brought out a rubber stamp and a red ink pad. M opened the pad, stamped the rubber stamp on it, and then carefully pressed it down on the gray cover. He turned the docket around and pushed it gently across the desk to Bond. The red letters, still damp, said FOR YOUR EYES ONLY.

Bond nodded and picked up the docket and walked out of the room.

Two days later Bond took the Friday Comet to Montreal. He did not care for it. It flew too high and too fast and there were too many passengers. The stewards had to serve everything almost on the double, and then one had a bare two hours' snooze before the hundred-mile-long descent from forty thousand feet. Only eight hours after leaving London, Bond was driving a Hertz Plymouth sedan along the broad

Route 17 from Montreal to Ottawa and trying to remember to keep on the right of the road.

The headquarters of the Royal Canadian Mounted Police is in the Department of Justice alongside the Parliament buildings in Ottawa. Like most Canadian public buildings, the Department of Justice is a massive block of gray masonry built to look stodgily important and to withstand long and hard winters. Bond had been told to ask at the front desk for the commissioner and to give his name as Mr. James. He did so, and a young, fresh-faced corporal took him up to the third floor and handed him over to a sergeant in a large, tidy office. The sergeant spoke on an intercom and showed Bond in through an inner door. A tall, youngish man in a dark blue suit turned away from the window and came toward him. "Mr. James?" The man smiled thinly. "I'm Colonel, let's say—er—Johns."

They shook hands. "The commissioner's very sorry not to be here to welcome you himself. He has a bad cold—you know, one of those diplomatic ones." Colonel "Johns" looked amused. "Thought it might be best to take the day off. I'm just one of the help. I've been on one or two hunting trips myself, and the commissioner fixed on me to handle this little holiday of yours."

The commissioner was glad to help, in other words, but he was going to handle this with kid gloves. Bond smiled and said, "I quite understand. And I haven't seen the commissioner or been anywhere near his headquarters. That being so, can we talk English for ten minutes or so—just between the two of us?"

Colonel Johns laughed. "You understand, Commander, that you and I are about to connive at various felonies, starting with obtaining a Canadian hunting license under false pretenses and going on down from there to more serious things. It wouldn't do anyone a bit of good to have any ricochets from this little plot."

"That's how my friends in London feel too. When I go out of here, we'll forget each other, and if I end up in jail, that's my worry. Well, now?"

Colonel Johns opened a drawer in the desk and took out a bulging file and opened it. The top document was a list. He put his pencil on the first item and looked across at Bond. "Clothes," he said. He unclipped a sheet of paper from the file and slid it across the desk. "This is a list of what I reckon you'll need and the address of a big secondhand clothing store here in the city. Nothing conspicuous—khaki shirt, dark brown jeans, good climbing boots. And there's the address of a chemist for walnut stain. Buy a gallon and give yourself a bath in the stuff. There are plenty of suntans in the hills at this time, and you won't want to be wearing anything that smells of camouflage. Right? If you're picked up, you're an Englishman on a hunting trip in Canada who got across the border by mistake.

"Rifle. It is being put in the trunk of your Plymouth while you are here. One of the new Savage 99Fs, Weatherby 6-by-62 scope, five-shot repeater with twenty rounds of high-velocity .250-3000. Lightest big-game lever action on the market. Only six and a half pounds. It's been tested and it has a range of up to five hundred yards.

"Gun license"—Colonel Johns slid it over—"issued here in the city in your real name, as that fits with your passport. Hunting license ditto, but small game only, as it isn't quite the deer season yet; also driving license to replace the provisional one I had waiting for you with the Hertz people. Haversack, compass—used ones, in the trunk of your car. Oh, by the way"—Colonel Johns looked up from his list—"you carrying a personal gun?"

"Yes. Walther PPK in a Burns Martin holster."

"Right, give me the number. I've got a blank license here."

Bond took out his gun and read off the number. Colonel Johns filled in the form and pushed it over.

"Now then, maps. Here's a local road map that's all you need to get you to the area." Colonel Johns got up and walked around with the map to Bond and spread it out. "You take this Route 17 back to Montreal, get onto 37 over the bridge at Ste. Anne's and then over the river again onto 7 to Pike River. Get on 52 to Stanbridge. Turn right in Stanbridge for Frelighsburg and leave the car in a garage there. Good roads all the way. Whole trip shouldn't take you more than five hours. Make it that you get to Frelighsburg around three a.m. Okay?"

Colonel Johns went back to his chair and took two more pieces of paper off the file. The first was a scrap of penciled map, the other a section of aerial photograph. He said, looking seriously at Bond,

"Now, here are the only disposable things you'll be carrying, and I've got to rely on you burning them just as soon as they've been used. This"—he pushed the paper over—"is a rough sketch of an old smuggling route from Prohibition days. It's not used now or I wouldn't recommend it." Colonel Johns smiled sourly. "The route was used for runners between Franklin and Frelighsburg. You follow this path through the foothills, and you detour Franklin and get into the start of the Green Mountains. There it's all Vermont spruce and pine with a bit of maple, and you can stay inside that stuff for months and not see a soul. You cross over a steep range here and move down into the top of the valley you want. The cross is Echo Lake, and, judging from the photographs, I'd be inclined to come down to it from the east."

"What's the distance? About ten miles?"

"Ten and a half. Take you about three hours from Frelighsburg if you don't lose your way, so you'll be in sight of the place around six." Colonel Johns pushed over the square of aerial photograph. It showed a long, low range of well-kept buildings made of cut stone. The roofs were of slate, and there was a glimpse of graceful bow windows and a covered patio. A dirt road ran past the front door, and on this side were garages and what appeared to be kennels. On the garden side was a flagstone terrace with a flowered border, and beyond this two or three acres of lawn stretched down to the edge of the small lake. There was a group of wrought-iron tables and chairs where the lake's dam wall left the bank, and, halfway along the wall, a diving board and a ladder.

Beyond the lake the forest rose steeply up. It was from this side that Colonel Johns suggested an approach. There were no people in the photograph, but on the flagstones in front of the patio was a quantity of expensive-looking garden furniture. Bond remembered that the larger photograph he had seen in London had shown a tennis court in the garden, and on the other side of the road the trim white fences of a stud farm. Echo Lake looked what it was—the luxurious retreat of a millionaire who liked privacy and could probably offset a lot of his running expenses against the stud farm. It would be an admirable refuge for a man who had had ten steamy years of Caribbean politics and who needed a rest to recharge his batteries.

The two men got to their feet. Colonel Johns took Bond to the door and held out his hand. He said, "Well, so long and the best of luck. I'd give a lot to come with you. But no doubt I'll read all about it in the papers"—he smiled—"whichever way it goes."

A last question occurred to Bond. "By the way, is the Savage single pull or double? There may not be much time for experimenting when the target shows."

"Single pull, and it's a hair trigger. Keep your finger off until you're sure you've got him. And don't get too close. I guess these men are pretty good themselves." He reached for the door handle. His other hand went to Bond's shoulder. "Our commissioner's got a motto: 'Never send a man where you can send a bullet.' You might remember that. So long, Commander."

BOND SPENT THE night and most of the next day at the Ko-Zee Motor Court outside Montreal. He passed the day looking to his equipment and breaking in the climbing boots he had bought in Ottawa. He bought glucose tablets and some smoked ham and bread, from which he made himself sandwiches. He also bought a large aluminum flask and filled this with three quarters bourbon and one quarter coffee. When darkness came, he had dinner and a short sleep and then diluted the walnut stain and washed himself all over with the stuff, even to the roots of his hair. He came out looking like an Indian with blue-gray eyes. Just before midnight he quietly got into the Plymouth and drove off on the last lap south to Frelighsburg.

"Going huntin', mister?" the man at the all-night garage asked.

You can get far in North America with laconic grunts. Bond, slinging the straps of his rifle and haversack over his shoulder, said, "Hunh."

"Man got a fine beaver over by Highgate Springs Saturday."

Bond said indifferently, "That so?" He paid for two nights' storage and left. The garage was on the far side of the town, and now he had only to follow the highway for a hundred yards before he found the dirt track running off into the woods on his right. After half an hour it petered out at a broken-down farmhouse. Bond skirted the house and at once found the path by the stream that he was to follow for three miles.

It was a warm night with a full yellow moon that threw enough light down through the thick spruce for Bond to follow the path without difficulty. The springy, cushioned soles of the climbing boots were wonderful to walk on. Bond knew he was making good time. At around four o'clock the trees began to thin, and he was soon walking through open fields with the scattered lights of Franklin on his right. He crossed a secondary, tarred road, and now there was a wider track through more woods and on his right the pale glitter of a lake.

By five o'clock he had crossed highways 120 and 108. Now he was on the last lap—a small hunting trail that climbed steeply. Well away from the highway, he stopped and shifted his rifle and haversack around, had a cigarette, and burned the sketch map. Already he noticed a faint paling in the sky and small noises in the forest, the rustlings of small animals. Bond visualized the house deep down in the little valley on the other side of the mountain ahead of him. He saw the crumpled, sleeping faces of the four men, the dew on the lawn, and the widening rings of the early rise on the surface of the lake.

With these and other random images Bond steadily climbed upward and obstinately pushed away from him the thought of the four faces asleep on the white pillows.

The round peak was below the tree line, and Bond could see nothing of the valley below. He rested and then chose an oak tree and climbed up and out along a thick bough. Now he could see everything—the endless vista of the Green Mountains stretching in every direction, and below, two thousand feet down, a long, easy slope of treetops broken once by a wide band of meadow, and finally, through a thin veil of mist, the lake, the lawns, and the house.

Bond lay along the branch and watched the band of pale, early morning sunshine creeping down into the valley. It took a quarter of an hour to reach the house, and then it seemed to flood at once over the wet slate tiles of the roof and the glittering lawn. The mist went quickly from the lake, and the target area lay waiting like an empty stage.

Bond slipped the telescopic sight out of his pocket and went over the scene inch by inch. From the edge of the meadow, which would be his only open field of fire unless he went down through the last belt of trees to the edge of the lake, it would be about five hundred yards to the terrace and the patio, and about three hundred to the diving board and the edge of the lake. What did these people do with their time? Did they ever swim? It was Indian summer, still warm enough. Well, if by the end of the day they had not come down to the lake, he would just have to take his chance at the patio and five hundred yards. But it would not be a good chance with a strange rifle. Ought he to get on down to the edge of the meadow now, before the house awoke? It was a wide meadow, and without cover.

A white blind rolled up in one of the smaller windows to the left of the main block. A thin column of smoke began to trickle up from one of the left-hand chimneys. Bond thought of the bacon and eggs that would soon be frying. He eased himself back along the branch and down to the ground. He would have something to eat, smoke his last safe cigarette, and get on down to the firing point.

Tension was building up in him. In his imagination he could already hear the deep bark of the Savage. He could see the black bullet lazily homing down into the valley toward a square of pink skin. As it hit, the skin would dent, break, then close up again, leaving a small hole with bruised edges. The bullet would plow on unhurriedly toward the pulsing heart—the tissues, the blood vessels, parting obediently to let it through. Who was this man he was going to do this to? What had he ever done to Bond?

Almost automatically Bond reached out for the flask. The coffee and whiskey burned a small fire down his throat. He waited for the warmth of the whiskey to reach his stomach. Then he got slowly to his feet, picked up the rifle, slung it over his shoulder, and started slowly off down through the trees.

Now there was no trail and he had to pick his way, watching the ground for dead branches. Under the trees was a sparse undergrowth of saplings and much dead wood from old storms. Bond went carefully down, his feet making little sound among the leaves and moss-covered rocks, but soon the forest was aware of him and began to pass on the news. A large doe saw him first and galloped off with an appalling clatter. A brilliant woodpecker with a scarlet head flew down ahead of him, screeching, and always there were chipmunks, scampering off with chatterings that seemed to fill the woods with fright. With each alarm

Bond wondered if, when he got to the edge of the meadow, he would see down on the lawn a man with glasses watching the frightened birds fleeing the treetops. But when he stopped behind a last broad oak and looked down across the long meadow to the final belt of trees and the lake and the house, nothing had changed. The only movement was the thin plume of smoke.

It was eight o'clock. Bond gazed systematically at the trees, looking for one which would suit his purpose. He found it—a big maple, blazing with russet and crimson, that stood slightly back from the wall of spruce. From there he would be able to see all he needed of the lake and the house.

Somewhere not far off, up to the left on the edge of the trees, a branch snapped. Bond dropped to one knee, his ears pricked and his senses questing. He stayed like that for a full ten minutes, a motionless brown shadow against the wide trunk of the oak.

Animals and birds do not break branches. Dead wood must carry a special danger signal for them. Did these people have guards out after all? Gently Bond eased the rifle off his shoulder and put his thumb on the safety. But then, between him and approximately where the branch had snapped, two deer broke cover and cantered across the meadow to the left. They stopped twice to look back, but each time they cropped a few mouthfuls of grass before moving on, and they showed no fright and no haste. It was certainly they who had been the cause of the snapped branch. Bond breathed a sigh. So much for that. And now to get on across the meadow.

He would have to do it on his stomach, and slowly. A five-hundred-yard crawl through tall, concealing grass is a long and wearisome business. It is hard on knees and hands and elbows; dust and small insects get into your eyes and nose and down your neck. Bond focused on placing his hands right and maintaining a slow, even speed. A breeze combed the meadow, and his wake through the grass would certainly not be noticeable from the house.

From above, it looked as if a big ground animal—a beaver perhaps—was on its way down the meadow. No, it would not be a beaver. They always move in pairs. And yet perhaps it might be a beaver—for now, from higher up, something, somebody else, had entered the meadow, and behind and above Bond a second wake was being cut in the deep sea of grass. It looked as if whatever it was would slowly catch up with Bond just at the next tree line.

Bond crawled and slithered steadily on, stopping from time to time to make sure that he was on course for the maple. But when he was perhaps twenty feet from it, he stopped and lay for a while, massaging his knees for the last lap.

He had heard nothing to warn him, and when the soft, threatening whisper came from only feet away in the thick grass on his left, his head swiveled so sharply that the vertebrae of his neck made a cracking sound.

"Move an inch and I'll kill you." It was a girl's voice, but a voice that fiercely meant what it said.

Bond, his heart thumping, stared up the shaft of the steel arrow whose blue-tempered tip parted the grass stalks perhaps eighteen inches from his head.

The bow was held sideways, flat in the grass. The knuckles of the brown fingers that held the binding of the bow below the arrow tip were white. Then there was the length of glinting steel and, behind the metal feathers, were grimly clamped lips below two fierce gray eyes against a background of sunburned skin. That was all Bond could make out through the grass. Who the hell was this? One of the guards? Bond began slowly to edge his right hand up toward his waistband and his gun. He said softly, "Who the hell are you?"

The arrow tip gestured threateningly. "Stop that right hand or I'll put this through your shoulder. Are you one of the guards?"

"No. Are you?"

"Don't be a fool. What are you doing here?" The voice was hard, suspicious. There was a trace of accent—what was it, Scots? Welsh?

It was time to get to level terms. There was something particularly deadly about the blue arrow tip. Bond said easily, "Put away your bow and arrow, Robina. Then I'll tell you."

"You swear not to go for your gun?"

"All right. But for God's sake let's get out of the middle of this field." Without waiting, Bond rose on hands and knees and started to crawl again. Now he must get the initiative and hold it. Whoever this damned girl was, she would have to be disposed of quickly and discreetly before the shooting match began.

Bond reached the trunk of the tree. He got carefully to his feet and took a quick look through the blazing leaves. Two maids were laying a large breakfast table on the patio. Most of the bedroom blinds had gone up. He had been right. The field of vision over the tops of the trees that now fell sharply to the lake was perfect. Bond unslung his rifle and haversack and sat down with his back against the trunk of the tree. The girl came out of the edge of the grass and stood up under the maple. The arrow was still held in the bow, but the bow was unpulled. They looked warily at each other.

The girl looked like a beautiful unkempt dryad in ragged shirt and trousers. The shirt and trousers were olive green, crumpled and splashed with mud and stains, and she had bound her pale blond hair with goldenrod to conceal its brightness for her crawl through the meadow. The beauty of her face was wild and rather animal, with a wide, sensuous mouth, high cheekbones, and silvery gray disdainful eyes. There was the blood of scratches on her forearms, and a bruise had puffed and slightly blackened one cheek. The metal feathers of a quiver full of arrows showed above her left shoulder. Apart from the bow, she carried nothing but a hunting knife at her belt and, at her other hip, a small brown canvas bag that presumably carried her food. She looked like a beautiful, dangerous customer who would walk alone through life and have little use for civilization.

Bond thought she was wonderful. He said softly, reassuringly, "I suppose you're Robina Hood. My name's James Bond." He reached for his flask and unscrewed the top and held it out. "Sit down and have a drink of this—firewater and coffee. And I've got some smoked ham. Or do you live on dew and berries?"

She came a little closer and sat down a yard from him, with her ankles tucked up high under her thighs like a red Indian. She reached for the flask, drank deeply with her head thrown back, and handed it back without comment. "Thanks," she said grudgingly, and, watching him closely, took her arrow and thrust it over her back to join the others in the quiver. "I suppose you're a poacher. The deer-hunting season doesn't open for another three weeks. But you won't find any deer down here. They only come so low at night. You ought to be higher up during the day, much higher. If you like, I'll tell you where there are some. Quite a big herd."

"Is that what you're doing here—hunting? Let's see your license."

Her shirt had button-down breast pockets. Without protest she took out a white paper from one of them and handed it over.

The license had been issued in Burlington, Vermont, in the name of Judy Havelock. There was a list of types of permit. "Nonresident hunting" and "Nonresident bow and arrow" had been ticked. The cost had been eighteen dollars and fifty cents, payable to the Fish and Game Service, Montpelier, Vermont. Judy Havelock had given her age as twenty-five and her place of birth as Jamaica.

God Almighty! So that was the score! Bond said with sympathy and respect, "You're quite a girl, Judy. It's a long walk from Jamaica. And you were going to take him on with your bow and arrow. Did you expect to get away with it?"

The girl was staring at him. "Who are you? What are you doing here?"

Bond reflected. There was only one way out of this mess and that was to join forces with the girl. He said resignedly, "I've been sent out from London by, er, Scotland Yard. I know all about your troubles and I've come out here to pay off some of the score. In London we think that the man in that house might start putting pressure on you, about your property, and there's no other way of stopping him."

The girl said bitterly, "I had a favorite pony, a palomino. Three weeks ago they poisoned it. Then they shot my German shepherd. I'd raised it from a puppy. Then came a letter. It said, 'Death has many hands. One of these hands is now raised over you.' I went to the police. All they did was to offer me protection. It was people in Cuba, they thought. So I went to Cuba and stayed in the best hotel and gambled big in the casinos." She gave a little smile. "I wasn't dressed like this. I wore my best dresses and the family jewels. And I pretended I was out for thrills—that I wanted to see the underworld and some real gangsters, and so on. And I found out about von Hammerstein."

She gestured down toward the house. "He had left Cuba. Batista had found out about him and he had a lot of enemies. In the end I met a man, a sort of high-up policeman, who told me the rest after I had"—she hesitated and avoided Bond's eyes—"after I had made up to him." She paused. She went on, "I left and went to America. I had read somewhere about Pinkerton's, the detective people. I went to them and paid to find this man's address." Now her eyes were defiant. "That's all."

"How did you get here?"

"I flew up to Burlington. Then I walked. Four days. Up through the Green Mountains. I kept out of the way of people. I'm used to this sort of thing. Our house is in the mountains in Jamaica. They're much more difficult than these."

"And what are you going to do now?"

"I'm going to shoot von Hammerstein and walk back to Burlington." The voice was as casual as if she had said she was going to pick a wild flower.

From down in the valley came the sound of voices. Bond got to his feet and took a quick look through the branches. Three men and two girls had come onto the patio. There was talk and laughter as they pulled out chairs and sat down at the table. One place was left empty at the head of the table. Bond took out his telescopic sight and looked through it. The three men were very small and dark. One of them, whose clothes looked the cleanest and smartest, would be Gonzales. The other two sat together at the foot of the oblong table and took no part in the talk. The girls were swarthy brunettes. They wore bright bathing suits and a lot of gold jewelry, and laughed and chattered like pretty monkeys. The voices were almost clear enough to understand, but they were talking Spanish.

Bond felt the girl standing near him. He handed her the telescopic sight. He said, "The neat little man is called Major Gonzales. The two at the bottom of the table are gunmen. I don't know who the girls are. Von Hammerstein isn't there yet." She took a quick look through the scope and handed it back without comment. Bond wondered if she realized that she had been looking at the murderers of her parents.

The two girls had turned and were looking toward the door into the house. One of them called out something that might have been a greeting. A short, square, almost naked man came out into the sunshine. He walked silently past the table to the edge of the flagstone terrace and proceeded to go through a five-minute program of physical exercise.

Bond examined the man minutely. He was about five feet four with a boxer's shoulders and hips, but a stomach that was going to fat. A mat of black hair covered his chest and shoulder blades. By contrast, there was not a hair on his face or head, and his skull was a glittering whitish yellow. The bone structure of the face was that of the conventional Prussian officer—square, hard, and thrusting—but the eyes under the naked brows were close-set and piggish, and the large mouth had hideous lips, thick and wet and crimson. He wore nothing but a strip of black material hardly larger than an athletic supporter, and a large gold wristwatch on a gold bracelet. Bond handed the scope to the girl. He was relieved. Von Hammerstein looked just about as unpleasant as M's dossier said he was.

Bond watched the girl's face. The mouth looked grim, almost cruel, as she looked down on the man she had come to kill. What was he to do about her? He could see nothing but a vista of troubles from her presence. She might even insist on playing some silly role with her bow and arrow. Bond made up his mind. He just could not afford to take chances. One short tap at the base of the skull and he would gag her and tie her up until it was all over. He reached softly for the butt of his automatic.

Nonchalantly the girl moved a few steps back. Just as nonchalantly she bent down, put the scope on the ground, and picked up her bow. She reached behind her for an arrow and fitted it casually into the bow. Then she looked up at Bond and said quietly, "Don't get any silly ideas. I haven't come all the way here to be knocked on the head by a London bobby. I can't miss with this at fifty yards, and I've killed birds on the wing at a hundred. I don't want to put an arrow through your leg, but I shall if you interfere."

Bond cursed his previous indecision. He said fiercely, "Put that damned thing down. How in hell do you think you can take on four men with a bow and arrow?"

The girl moved her right foot back into the shooting stance. She said through compressed, angry lips, "Keep out of this. It was my mother and father they killed. Not yours. I've already been here a day and a night and I know how to get von Hammerstein. I don't care about the others. They're nothing without him. Now then." She pulled the bow half taut. The arrow pointed at Bond's feet. "Either you do what I say or you're going to be sorry. This is a private thing I've sworn to do and nobody's going to stop me." She tossed her head imperiously. "Well?"

Bond gloomily measured the situation. He looked the ridiculously beautiful wild girl up and down. This was good hard English stock spiced with the hot peppers of a tropical childhood. She had keyed herself up to a state of controlled hysteria. She would think nothing of putting him out of action. And he had absolutely no defense. Her weapon was silent, his would alert the whole neighborhood. Now the only hope would be to work with her.

He said quietly, "Now listen, Judy. If you insist on coming in on this thing, we'd better do it together. Then perhaps we can bring it off and stay alive. This sort of thing is my profession. I was ordered to do it—by a close friend of your family, if you want to know. And my weapon has got at least five times the range of yours. I could take a good chance of killing him now, on the patio. But the odds aren't quite good enough. Some of them have got bathing things on. They'll be coming down to the lake. Then I'm going to do it. You can give supporting fire." He ended lamely, "It'll be a great help."

"No." She shook her head decisively. "You can give what you call supporting fire if you like. You're right about the swimming. Yesterday they were all down at the lake around eleven. It's just as warm today, and they'll be there again. I shall get him from the edge of the trees by the lake. I found a perfect place last night. The bodyguard men don't bathe. They sit around with their guns. I know the moment to get von Hammerstein and I'll be well away from the lake before they take in what's happened. Now then. I can't hang around anymore. I ought to have been in my place already. Unless you say yes straightaway, there's no alternative." She raised the bow a few inches.

Bond shrugged. He said with resignation, "Go ahead. I'll look after the others. If you get away all right, meet me here. If you don't, I'll come down and pick up the pieces."

The girl unstrung her bow. She said indifferently, "I'm glad you're seeing sense. Don't worry about me. But keep out of sight, and mind the sun doesn't catch that scope of yours." She gave Bond the brief, pitying smile of the woman who has had the last word, and made off down through the trees.

Bond watched the lithe dark green figure until it had vanished among the tree trunks, then he impatiently picked up the scope and went back to his vantage point. To hell with her! It was time to concentrate on the job.

The breakfast things were being cleared away by the two maids. There was no sign of the girls or the two gunmen. Von Hammerstein was lying back among the cushions of an outdoor couch, reading a newspaper and occasionally commenting to Major Gonzales, who sat astride a chair near his feet, smoking a cigar. Bond glanced at his watch. It was ten thirty. Since the scene seemed to be static, Bond sat down with his back to the tree and went over the Savage with minute care.

He did not like what he was going to do. He had to keep on reminding himself that von Hammerstein and his gunmen were particularly dreadful men. Many people around the world would probably be very glad to destroy them, as this girl proposed to do, out of private revenge. But for Bond it was different. He had no personal motives against them. He was merely the public executioner appointed by M to represent the community. They had declared and waged war against British people on British soil and—

A burst of automatic fire from the valley brought Bond to his feet. His rifle was up and taking aim as the second burst came. The harsh racket of noise was followed by laughter and hand clapping. A kingfisher, a handful of tattered blue and gray feathers, thudded to the lawn and lay fluttering. Von Hammerstein's red lips grinned with pleasure. He said something which included the words "crack shot." He handed the rifle to one of the gunmen and wiped his hands down his fat backsides. He gave a sharp order to the girls, who ran off into the house; then, with the others following, he turned and ambled down the sloping lawn toward the lake. Now the girls came running back out of the house. Each one carried an empty champagne bottle. Chattering and laughing, they skipped down after the men.

Bond got himself ready. He clipped the telescopic sight onto the barrel of the Savage and took his stance against the trunk of the tree.

He found a bump in the wood as a rest for his left hand, put his sights at three hundred, and took broad aim at the group of people by the lake. Then, holding the rifle loosely, he leaned against the trunk and watched the scene.

It was going to be some kind of shooting contest between the two gunmen. They snapped fresh magazines into their guns and stationed themselves on the flat stone wall of the dam, some twenty feet apart, on either side of the diving board. They stood with their backs to the lake and their guns at the ready.

Von Hammerstein took up his place on the grass verge, a champagne bottle swinging in each hand. The girls stood behind him, their hands over their ears. Through the telescopic sight their faces looked sharp with concentration.

Von Hammerstein barked an order and there was silence. He swung both arms back and counted, *"Uno . . . dos . . . tres."* With the *tres* he hurled the champagne bottles high into the air over the lake.

The two bodyguards turned like marionettes, the guns clamped to their hips. As they completed the turn they fired. The thunder of the guns split the peaceful scene. Birds fled away from the trees, screeching, and some small branches cut by the bullets pattered down into the lake. The left-hand bottle disintegrated into dust; the right-hand one, hit by only a single bullet, split in two a fraction of a second later. The fragments of glass made small splashes over the middle of the lake. The gunman on the left had won.

Von Hammerstein beckoned the two girls forward. They came reluctantly, dragging their feet. Von Hammerstein said something, asked a question of the winner. The man nodded at the girl on the left. She looked sullenly back at him. Von Hammerstein reached out and patted the girl on the rump as if she were a cow.

The group broke up. The prize girl took a quick run and dived into the lake, perhaps to get away from the man who had won her favors. The other girl followed her. They swam away across the lake, calling angrily to each other. Major Gonzales took off his coat and laid it on the grass and sat down on it. He was wearing a shoulder holster, which showed the butt of a medium-caliber automatic. He watched von Hammerstein take off his watch and walk along the dam wall to the diving board. The gunmen stood back from the lake and also watched von Hammerstein, their guns cradled in their arms.

Von Hammerstein had reached the diving board. He walked along to the end and stood looking down at the water. Bond tensed himself and put up the safety. It would be any minute now. His finger itched on the trigger guard. What in hell was the Havelock girl waiting for?

Von Hammerstein flexed his knees slightly. His arms came back. Now his arms were coming forward and there was a fraction of a second when his feet had left the board and he was still almost upright. In that fraction of a second there was a flash of silver against his back, and then von Hammerstein's body hit the water in a neat dive.

Gonzales was on his feet, looking uncertainly at the turbulence caused by the dive. He did not know if he had seen something or not. The two gunmen were more certain. They had their guns at the ready. They crouched, looking from Gonzales to the trees beyond the dam, waiting for an order.

Slowly the turbulence subsided and the ripples spread across the lake. The dive had gone deep.

Bond searched the lake with his telescopic sight. There was a pink shimmer deep down. It wobbled slowly up. Von Hammerstein's body broke the surface. It lay head down, wallowing softly. A foot or so of steel shaft stuck up from below the left shoulder blade, and the sun winked on the aluminum feathers.

Major Gonzales yelled an order, and the two tommy guns roared and flamed. Bond could hear the crash of the bullets among the trees below him. He pulled the trigger. The Savage shuddered against his shoulder and the right-hand gunman fell slowly forward on his face. Now the other man was running for the lake, his gun still firing from the hip in short bursts. Bond fired and missed and fired again. The man's legs buckled, but his momentum still carried him forward. He crashed into the water. The clenched finger went on firing the gun aimlessly up toward the blue sky until the water throttled the mechanism.

The seconds wasted on the extra shot had given Major Gonzales a chance. He had got behind the body of the first gunman and now he opened up in Bond's direction with the tommy gun. Bullets zipped into the maple and slivers of wood spattered into Bond's face. Bond fired twice. The dead body of the gunman jerked. Too low! Bond reloaded and took fresh aim. A snapped branch fell across his rifle. He shook it free, but now Gonzales was up and running forward to the group of garden furniture. He hurled the iron table on its side and got behind it. With this solid cover his shooting became more accurate, and burst after burst, now from the right of the table and now from the left, crashed into the maple tree while Bond's single shots clanged against the white iron.

It was not easy to traverse the telescopic sight quickly from one side of the table to the other, and Gonzales was cunning with his changes. Again and again his bullets thudded into the trunk beside and above Bond. Bond ducked and ran swiftly to the right. He would fire, standing, from the open meadow and catch Gonzales off guard. But even as he ran, he saw Gonzales dart from behind the iron table. He also had decided to end the stalemate. He was running for the dam to get across and into the woods and come up after Bond.

Bond stood and threw up his rifle. As he did so, Gonzales saw him. He went down on one knee on the dam wall and sprayed a burst at Bond. Bond stood icily, hearing the bullets, and squeezed the trigger. Gonzales rocked. He half got to his feet. He raised his arms and, with his gun still pumping bullets into the sky, dived clumsily face forward into the water.

Slowly Bond lowered his rifle and wiped the back of his arm across his face.

The echoes, the echoes of much death, rolled to and fro across the valley. Away to the right, in the trees beyond the lake, he caught a glimpse of the two girls running up toward the house. Soon they would be on to the state troopers. It was time to get moving.

Bond walked back through the meadow to the lone maple. The girl was there. She stood up against the trunk of the tree with her back to him. Her head was cradled in her arms against the tree. Blood was running down her right arm and dripping to the ground, and there was a black stain high up on the sleeve of the dark green shirt. The bow and quiver of arrows lay at her feet. Her shoulders were shaking.

Bond came up behind her and put a protective arm around her. He said softly, "Take it easy, Judy. It's all over. How bad's the arm?"

She said in a muffled voice, "It's nothing. Something hit me. But that was awful. I didn't—I didn't know it would be like that."

Bond pressed her arm reassuringly. "It had to be done. They'd have got you otherwise. Those were pro killers—the worst. Now then, let's have a look at your arm. We've got to get going—over the border. The troopers'll be here before long."

She turned. The beautiful wild face was streaked with sweat and tears. Now the gray eyes were soft and obedient. She said, "It's nice of you to be like that. After the way I was. I was sort of—sort of wound up."

She held out her arm. Bond reached for the hunting knife at her belt and cut off her shirt sleeve at the shoulder. There was the bruised, bleeding gash of a bullet wound across the muscle. Bond took out his khaki handkerchief, cut it into three lengths, and joined them together. He washed the wound clean with the coffee and whiskey, and then took a thick slice of bread from his haversack and bound it over the wound. He cut her shirt sleeve into a sling and reached behind her neck to tie the knot. Her mouth was inches from his. The scent of her body had a warm animal tang. Bond kissed her once softly on the lips and once again, hard. He tied the knot. He looked into the gray eyes close to his. They looked surprised and happy. He kissed her again at each corner of the mouth, and the mouth slowly smiled. Bond stood away from her and smiled back. He softly picked up her right hand and slipped the wrist into the sling. She said docilely, "Where are you taking me?"

Bond said, "I'm taking you to London. There's this old man who will want to see you. But first we've got to get over into Canada and get your passport straightened out. You'll have to get some clothes and things. It'll take a few days. We'll be staying in a place called the Ko-Zee Motor Court."

She looked at him. She was a different girl. She said softly, "That'll be nice. I've never stayed in a motel."

Bond bent down and picked up his rifle and haversack and slung them over one shoulder. Then he hung her bow and quiver over the other, and turned and started up through the meadow.

She fell in behind and followed him, and as she walked she pulled the tired bits of goldenrod out of her hair and undid a ribbon and let the pale gold hair fall down to her shoulders.

THE FOGHORN

GERTRUDE ATHERTON

WHAT AN ABSURD vanity to sleep on a hard pillow and forgo that last luxurious burrowing into the very depths of a mass of baby pillows! . . . Her back was already as straight as—a chimney? . . . Who was the Frenchman that said one must reject the worn counters? . . . But this morning she would have liked that sensuous burrowing, and the pillow had never seemed so hard, so flat . . . yet how difficult it was to wake up! She had had the same experience once before when the doctor had given her Veronal for insomnia . . . could Ellen, good creature, have put a tablet in the cup of broth she took last thing at night: "as a wise precaution," the doctor had said genially. What a curse insomnia was! But she had a congenital fear of drugs and had told no one of this renewal of sleeplessness, knowing it would pass.

And, after all, she didn't mind lying awake in the dark; she could think, oh, pleasant lovely thoughts, despite this inner perturbation—so cleverly concealed. How thankful she was to be tall enough to carry off this new fashion in sleeves! If trains would only come in again, she would dress her hair high some night (just for fun) and look—not like her beloved Mary Stewart, for Mary was almost ugly if one analyzed her too critically. Charm? How much more charm counted than mere beauty, and she herself had it "full measure and running over," as that rather fresh admirer had announced when drinking her health at her coming-out party . . . what was his name? . . . six years ago. He was only a college boy . . . how could one remember? There had been so many.

Ninon de Lenclos? She was passable in her portraits but famous mainly for keeping young. . . . Diane de Poitiers? She must have needed charm double-distilled if she looked anything like an original portrait of her hung at a loan exhibition in Paris: flaxen hair, thin and straight, drawn severely from a bulging brow above insufferably sensual eyes—far too obvious and "easy" for the fastidious male of today—a flaxen complexion, no highlights; not very intelligent.

Madame Récamier? Better-looking than most of the historic beauties: hair piled high—but then she wore a slip of an Empire gown . . . well, never mind. . . .

She ranked as a beauty herself, although perhaps charm had something to do with it. Her mouth was rather wide, but her teeth were exquisite. Something rather obscure was the matter in that region of brilliant enamel this morning. A toothache? She had never had a toothache. Well, there was no pain . . . what matter . . . something wrong, though; she'd go to the dentist during the day. Her nose was a trifle tip-tilted, but very straight and thin, and anyhow the tilt suited the way she carried her head, "flung in the air." Her complexion and hair and eyes were beyond all cavil . . . she was nothing so commonplace as a downright blonde or brunette . . . how she should hate being catalogued! The warm, bright waving masses of her hair had never been cut since her second birthday. They, too, were made for burrowing.

Her mother's wedding dress had a long train. But the delicate ivory of the satin had waxed with time to a sickly yellow. Her mother hadn't pressed the matter when she was engaged to John St. Rogers, but she had always expressed a wish that each of her daughters should wear the dress to the altar. Well, she had refused outright, but had consented to have her own gown trimmed with the lace: yards and yards of point d'Alençon—and a veil that reached halfway down the train. What a way to spend money! Who cared for lace now? Not the young, anyhow. But Mother was rather a dear, and she could afford to be quite unselfish for once, as it certainly would be becoming. When the engagement was broken, the poor old darling cried because she would have another long wait before watching all that lace move up the aisle.

Well, she would never wear that lace—nor any wedding gown. If she were lucky enough to marry at all, the less publicity the better . . . a mere announcement (San Francisco papers please copy) . . . a quiet return from Europe . . . a year or two in one of those impersonal New York apartment houses where no one knew the name of his next-door neighbor . . . no effacement in a smaller city for her!

How strange that she of all girls should have fallen in love with a married man—or, at all events, accepted the dire consequences. With a father that had taken to drugs and then run off with another woman—luckily before Mother had come in for Granddad's fortune—and . . . what was it Uncle Ben had once said? Queer twists in this family since "way back." It had made her more conventional than her natural instincts would have prompted; but, no, let her do herself justice: she had cultivated a high standard of character and planted her mind with flowers both sturdy and fair—that must have been the reason she had fallen in love at last, after so many futile attempts. No need for her to conceal from him the awful truth that she read the Greek and Latin classics in the original text, attended morning classes over at the university . . . odd, how men didn't mind if you "adored" music and pictures, but if they suspected you of being intellectual, they either despised or feared you, and faded away. . . .

Fog on the Bay. Since childhood she had loved to hear that long-drawn-out, almost human moan of the foghorn as she lay warm and sheltered in bed. It was on a night of fog they had spoken for the first time, although they had nodded at three or four formal dinners given to the newcomers who had brought letters to the elect. Bostonians were always popular in San Francisco; they had good manners and their formality was only skin-deep. The men were very smart; some of the women, too; but as a rule they lacked the meticulous grooming and well-set-up appearance of their men. She had been impressed the first time she had met him: six feet (she herself was five feet six), somewhere in the thirties, very spare, said to be a first-rate tennis player, and had ranked as an all-around athlete at Harvard; had inherited a piece of property in San Francisco which was involving him in litigation, but he was in no haste to leave, even before they met.

That had been at the Jeppers', and as the house commanded a fine view of the Bay, and she was tired of being torn from some man every time they had circled the ballroom, she had managed to slip away and had hidden behind the curtains of the deep bow window at the end of the hall. In a moment she was aware that someone had followed her, and oddly enough she knew who it was, although she didn't turn her head; and they stood in silence and gazed together at the sharp dark outlines of the mountains on the far side of the Bay; the gliding spheroids of golden light that were the ferryboats, the islands with their firm, bold outlines, now almost visibly drooping in slumber . . . although there always seemed to her to be an atmosphere of unrest about Alcatraz, psychic emanation of imprisoned men under rigid military rule, and officials no doubt as resentful in that dull monotonous existence on a barren rock. . . . A light flickered along a line of barred upper windows; doubtless a guard on his rounds. . . .

The band of pulsing light on the eastern side of the Bay: music made visible . . . stars as yellow and bright above, defying the thin silver of the hebetic moon . . . lights twinkling on Sausalito opposite, standing out boldly from the black mass of Tamalpais high flung above. Her roving eyes moved to the Golden Gate, narrow entrance between two crouching forts, separating that harbor of arrogant beauty from the gray waste of the Pacific—ponderous, rather stupid old ocean. . . .

For the first time he spoke: "The fog! Chief of San Francisco's many beauties."

She nodded, making no other reply, watching that dense yet imponderable white mass push its way through the Golden Gate like a laboring ship . . . then riding the waters more lightly, rolling a little, writhing, whiffs breaking from the bulk of that ghostly ship to explore the hollows of the hills, resting there like puffs of white smoke. Then, over the cliffs and heights on the northern side of the Bay, a swifter, more formless, but still lovely white visitant that swirled over the inland waters, enshrouding the islands, Sausalito, where so many Englishmen lived, the fulgent zone in the east; but a low fog—the moon and stars still visible . . . the foghorns, one after the other, sending forth their long-drawn-out moans of utter desolation. . . .

With nothing more to look at, they had seated themselves on a small sofa, placed there for reticent couples, and talked for an hour—a desultory exploring conversation. She recalled none of it. A few mornings later they had met on the Berkeley ferryboat, accidentally no doubt, and he had gone on with her in the train and as far as the campus. . . . Once again. . . . After that, when the lecture was over, in the Greek Theater . . . wonderful hours . . . how easy to imagine themselves in Greece of the fifth century B.C., alone in that vast gray amphitheater, the slim, straight tenebrous trees above quivering with the melody of birds!

Never a word of love—not for months. This novel and exciting companionship was enough . . . depths of personality to explore—in glimpses! Sometimes they roamed over the hills, gay and carefree. They never met anyone they knew.

Winter. Weeks of pouring rain. They met in picture galleries, remote corners of the public library, obscure restaurants of Little Italy under the shadow of Telegraph Hill. Again they were unseen, undiscovered.

He never came to the house. Since her mother's death and the early marriages of the girls, Uncle Ben had come to live with her in the old house on Russian Hill; the boys were East at school; she was free of all family restrictions, but her old servants were intimate with all the other servants on the Hill. She barely knew his wife. He never spoke of her.

Spring. A house party in the country, warm and dry after the last of the rains. After dinner they had sat about on the terraces, smoking, drinking, listening to a group singing within, admiring the "ruins" of a Roman temple at the foot of the lawn lit by a blazing moon.

He and she had wandered off the terrace, and up an almost perpendicular flight of steps on the side of the mountain that rose behind the house . . . dim aisles of redwoods, born when the earth was young, whose long trunks never swayed, whose high branches rarely sang in the wind—unfriendly trees, but protective, sentinellike, shutting out the modern world; reminiscent those closely planted aisles were of ancient races . . . forgotten races . . . godlike races, perhaps.

Well, they had felt like gods that night. How senseless to try to stave off a declaration of love . . . to fear . . . to wonder . . . to worry. . . . How inevitable . . . natural . . . when it came! Hour of hours. . . .

They had met the next day in a corner of their favorite little restaurant, over a dish of spaghetti, which she refused to eat as it had liver in it, and talked the matter out. No, she would not enter upon a secret intrigue; meeting him in some shady quarter of the town, where no questions were asked, in some horrible room which had sheltered thousands of furtive "lovers" before them . . . she would far rather never see him again. . . . He had smiled at the flight taken by an untrained imagination, but nodded. . . . No, but she knew the alternative. He had no intention of giving her up. No hope of a divorce. He had sounded his wife; tentatively at first, then told her outright he loved another woman. She had replied that he could expect no legal release from her. It was her chance for revenge and she would take it. . . . A week or two and his business in San Francisco would be settled . . . he had an independent fortune . . . would she run away with him? Elope in good old style? Could she stand the gaff? All Europe for a perpetual honeymoon—unless his wife were persuaded by her family later on to divorce him. Then he would return and work at something. He was not a born idler.

She had consented, of course, having made up her mind before they met. She had had six years of "the world." She knew what she wanted. One might "love" many times, but not more than once find completion, that solidarity which makes two as one against the malignant forces of life. She had no one to consider but herself. Her mother was dead. Her sisters, protected by husbands, wealth, position, would merely be "thrilled." The boys and Uncle Ben, of course, would be furious. Men were so hopelessly conservative.

For the rest of the world she cared exactly nothing.

That foghorn. What was it trying to tell her? A boat . . . fog . . . why was it so hard to remember? So hard to awaken? Ellen must have given her an overdose. Fragmentary pictures . . . slipping down the dark hill to the wharf . . . her low, delighted laugh echoed back to her as he helped her into the boat . . . one more secret lark before they flung down the gage. . . . How magnificently he rowed . . . long, sweeping, easy strokes as he smiled possessively into her eyes and talked of the future. . . . No moon, but millions of stars that shed a misty golden light . . . rows of light on the steep hillsides of the city. The houses dark and silent . . . a burst of music from Fort Mason. . . .

Out through the Golden Gate, still daring . . . riding that oily swell . . . his chuckle as she had dared him to row straight across to China. . . . Her sharp anxious cry as she half rose from her seat and pointed to a racing mountain of snow-white mist.

He had swept about at once and made for the beach below Sutro Heights. Too late. Almost as he turned, they were engulfed. Even an old fisherman would have lost his sense of direction. And then the foghorns began their warnings. The low, menacing roar from Point Benito. The wailing siren on Alcatraz. Sausalito's throaty bass. The deep-toned bell on Angel Island. She knew them all, but they seemed to come from new directions.

A second . . . a moment . . . an hour . . . later . . . a foreign but unmistakable note. Ships—two of them. . . . Blast and counterblast. . . . She could barely see his white rigid face through the mist as he thrust his head this way and that trying to locate those sounds. . . . Another abrupt swerve . . . crash . . . shouts . . . her own voice shrieking as she saw his head almost severed—the very fog turn red. . . .

She could hear herself screaming yet. It seemed to her that she had been screaming since the beginning of time.

She sat up in bed, clasping her head between her hands, and rocked to and fro. This bare small room, just visible in the gray dawn. . . . She was in a hospital, of course. Was it last night or the night before they had brought her here? She wondered vaguely that she felt no inclination to scream anymore, now that she had struggled to full consciousness. . . . Too tired, perhaps . . . the indifference of exhaustion. . . . Even her eyes felt singularly dry, as if they had been baked in a hot oven. She recalled a line, the only memorable line, in Edwin Arnold's "Light of Asia," *Eyepits red with rust of ancient tears.* . . . Did her eyes look like that? But she did not remember crying . . . only screaming. . . .

Odd that she should be left alone like this. Uncle Ben and the girls must have been summoned. If they had gone home, tired out, they should have left a nurse in constant attendance . . . and surely they might have found her a better room. . . . Or had she been carried into some emergency hospital? . . . Well, she could go home today.

Her hands were still clasping her head when another leaf of awareness turned over, rattling like parchment. Hair. Her lovely abundant hair. . . . She held her breath as her hands moved exploringly over her head. Harsh short bristles almost scratched them.

She had had brain fever, then. Ill a long time . . . weeks . . . months, perhaps. . . . No wonder she felt weak and spent and indifferent! But she must be out of danger, or they would not leave her like this. . . . Would she suffer later, with renewed mocking strength? Or could love be burned out, devoured by fever germs? A short time before, while not yet fully conscious, she had relived all the old hopes, fears, dreams, ecstasies; reached out triumphantly to a wondrous future, arrogantly sure of herself and the man, contemptuous of the world and its makeshift conventions. . . . And now she felt nothing. . . .

But when she was well again? Twenty-four! Forty, fifty years more; they were a long-lived family. Her mother had been killed at a railroad crossing. . . . Well, she had always prided herself on her strength. She would worry through the years somehow.

Had the town rung with the scandal when the newspapers flared forth next morning? No girl goes rowing at night with a married man unless there is something between them. Had his wife babbled? Were the self-righteous getting off the orthodoxies of their kind? Punished for their sin. Retributive justice meted out to a girl who would break up a home and take a married man for her lover.

Retributive justice! As if there were any such thing in life as justice. All helpless victims of the law of cause and effect. Futile, aspiring, stupidly confident links in the inexorable chain of Circumstance. . . . Commonplace minds croaking, "Like father like daughter" . . .

How she hated, hated, *hated* self-righteousness, smug hypocrisy . . . illogical minds—one sheep bleating like another sheep—not one of them with the imagination to guess that she never would have stooped to a low secret intrigue. . . .

She had been pounding her knee with her fist in a sudden access of energy. As it sputtered out and she felt on the verge of collapse, her hand unfolded and lay palm down on the quilt. . . . She felt her eyes bulging. . . . She uttered her first sound: a low almost inarticulate cry.

Her hand? That large-veined, skinny thing? She had beautiful long white hands, with skin as smooth as the breast of a dove. Of no one of her beauty's many parts had she been prouder, not even when she stood now and then before the cheval glass and looked critically, and admiringly, at the smooth, white, rounded perfection of her body. She had given them a golden manicure set on one of her birthdays, a just tribute; and they were exquisitely kept. . . .

A delusion? A nightmare? She spread the other hand beside it . . . side by side the two on the dingy counterpane . . . old hands. . . . Shorn hair will grow again . . . but hands . . .

Mumbling. Why mumbling? She raised one of those withered yellow hands to her mouth. It was empty. Her shaking fingers unbuttoned the high nightgown, and she glanced within. Pendant dugs, brown and shriveled.

Brain fever! The sun had risen. She looked up at the high barred window. She understood.

Voices at the door. She dropped back on the pillow and closed her eyes and lay still.

The door was unlocked, and a man and woman entered: doctor and nurse, as was immediately evident. The doctor's voice was brisk and businesslike and deeply mature; the woman's, young and deferential.

"Do you think she'll wake again, Doctor?"

"Probably not. I thought she would be gone by now, but she is still breathing." He clasped the emaciated wrist with his strong fingers. "Very feeble. It won't be long now."

"Is it true, Doctor, that sometimes, just before death, reason is restored and they remember and talk quite rationally?"

"Sometimes. But not for this case. Too many years. Look in every hour, and when it is over, ring me up. There are relatives to be notified. Quite important people, I believe."

"What are they like?"

"Never seen them. The law firm in charge of her estate pays the bills. Why should they come here? Couldn't do her any good, and nothing is so depressing as these melancholia cases. It's a long time now since she was stark-raving. That was before my time. Come along. Six wards after this one. . . . Don't forget to look in. Good little girl. I know you never forget."

They went out and locked the door.

LEININGEN VERSUS THE ANTS

CARL STEPHENSON

"UNLESS THEY ALTER their course, and there's no reason why they should, they'll reach your plantation in two days at the latest."

Leiningen sucked placidly at a cigar and for a few seconds gazed without answering at the agitated district commissioner. Then he took the cigar from his lips and leaned slightly forward. With his bristling gray hair, bulky nose, and lucid eyes, he had the look of an aging and shabby eagle.

"Decent of you," he murmured, "paddling all this way just to give me the tip. But you're pulling my leg of course when you say I must do a bunk. Why, even a herd of saurians couldn't drive me from this plantation of mine."

The Brazilian official threw up lean and lanky arms. "Leiningen!" he shouted. "You're insane! They're not creatures you can fight—they're an elemental—an act of God! Ten miles long, two miles wide—ants, nothing but ants! And every single one of them a fiend from hell; before you can spit three times they'll eat a full-grown buffalo to the bones. If you don't clear out at once, there'll be nothing left of you but a skeleton."

Leiningen grinned. "Act of God, my eye! Anyway, I'm not going to run for it just because an elemental's on the way. And don't think I'm the kind of fathead who tries to fend off lightning with his fists, either. I use my intelligence, old man. When I began this model farm and plantation three years ago, I took into account all that could conceivably happen to it. Now I'm ready for anything—including your ants."

The Brazilian rose heavily to his feet. "I've done my best," he gasped. "Your obstinacy endangers not only yourself but the lives of your four hundred workers. You don't know these ants!"

Leiningen accompanied him down to the river, where the government launch was moored, and the vessel cast off. Long after it had disappeared around the bend, Leiningen thought he could still hear that imploring voice: "You don't know them, I tell you! *You don't know them!*"

But the reported enemy was by no means unfamiliar to the planter. He had lived long enough in the country to see the fearful devastations sometimes wrought by these ravenous insects in their campaigns for food. And he had planned measures of defense accordingly.

Moreover, during his three years as a planter, he had met and defeated drought, flood, plague, and all other acts of God which had come against him—unlike his fellow settlers in the district, who had made little or no resistance. He attributed this success to the observance of his lifelong motto: The human brain needs only to become fully aware of its powers to conquer even the elements.

Dullards reeled senselessly and aimlessly into the abyss; cranks, however brilliant, lost their heads when circumstances suddenly altered or accelerated and ran into stone walls; sluggards drifted with the current until they were caught in whirlpools and dragged under. But such disasters, Leiningen contended, merely strengthened his argument that intelligence, directed aright, invariably makes man master of his fate.

Yes, Leiningen had always known how to grapple with life. Even here, in this Brazilian wilderness, his brain had triumphed over every difficulty and danger it had so far encountered. First he had vanquished primal forces by cunning and organization. Then he had enlisted the resources of modern science to increase miraculously the yield of his plantation. Now he was sure he would prove more than a match for the "irresistible" ants.

That same evening, however, Leiningen assembled his workers. He had no intention of waiting till the news reached their ears from other sources. Most of them had been born in the district; the cry "The ants are coming!" was to them a signal for instant, panic-stricken flight. But so great was the Indians' trust in Leiningen, in Leiningen's word, and in Leiningen's wisdom that they received calmly his curt tidings and his orders for the imminent struggle. They waited, unafraid, alert, as if for the beginning of a new game or hunt which he had just described to them. The ants were indeed mighty, but not so mighty as the boss. Let them come!

They came at noon the second day. Their approach was announced by the wild unrest of the horses, scarcely controllable now either in stall or under rider, scenting from afar a vapor instinct with horror. It was announced by a stampede of animals, timid and savage, hurtling past each other: jaguars and pumas flashing by nimble stags; bulky tapirs, no longer hunters, themselves hunted, outpacing fleet kinkajous; maddened herds of cattle, heads lowered, nostrils snorting, rushing through tribes of loping monkeys, chattering in terror; then followed the creeping and springing denizens of bush and steppe, rodents, snakes, and lizards.

Pell-mell the rabble swarmed down the hill to the plantation, scattered right and left before the barrier of the water-filled ditch, then sped onward to the river, where, again hindered, they fled along its bank out of sight.

This water-filled ditch was one of the defense measures which Leiningen had long since prepared against the advent of the ants. It encompassed three sides of the plantation like a huge horseshoe. Twelve feet across, but not very deep, when dry it was no obstacle to either man or beast. But the ends of the "horseshoe" ran into the river which formed the northern boundary, and fourth side, of the plantation. And at the end nearer the house and outbuildings in the middle of the plantation Leiningen had constructed a dam by means of which water from the river could be diverted into the ditch. By opening the dam he was able to fling an imposing girdle of water completely around the plantation, like the moat encircling a medieval city. Unless the ants were clever enough to build rafts, they had no hope of reaching the plantation, Leiningen concluded.

The twelve-foot water ditch seemed to afford in itself all the security needed. But while awaiting the arrival of the ants, Leiningen made a further improvement. The western section of the ditch ran along the edge of a tamarind wood, and the branches of some great trees reached over the water. Leiningen now had them lopped so that ants could not descend from them within the moat.

The women and children, then the herds of cattle, were escorted by peons on rafts over the river, to remain safely on the other side until the plunderers had departed. Leiningen gave this instruction, not because he believed the noncombatants were in danger but to avoid hampering the efficiency of the defenders. "Critical situations first become crises," he explained to his men, "when oxen or women get excited."

Finally he made a careful inspection of the inner moat—a smaller ditch, lined with concrete, which extended around the hill on which stood the ranch house, barns, stables, and other buildings. Into this concrete ditch emptied the inflow pipes from three great petrol tanks. If by some miracle the ants managed to cross the water, this rampart of petrol would be an absolutely impassable protection for the besieged and their dwellings and stock. Such, at least, was Leiningen's opinion.

He stationed his men at irregular distances along the water ditch, the first line of defense. Then he lay down in his hammock and puffed drowsily at his pipe until a peon reported that the ants had been observed far away in the south.

Leiningen mounted his horse, which at the feel of its master seemed to forget its uneasiness, and rode leisurely in the direction of the threatening offensive. The southern stretch of ditch was nearly three miles long; from its center one could survey the entire countryside. This was destined to be the scene of the outbreak of war between Leiningen's brain and twenty square miles of life-destroying ants.

It was an unforgettable sight. Over the range of hills, as far as the eye could see, crept a darkening shadow, ever longer and broader, until it spread across the slope from east to west, then downward, downward, uncannily swift, and all the green herbage of that wide vista was being mowed as by a giant sickle, leaving only the vast shadow moving rapidly nearer.

When Leiningen's men, behind their barrier of water, perceived the approach of the long-expected foe, they gave vent to their suspense in screams and imprecations. But as the distance began to lessen between the "fiends from hell" and the water ditch, they relapsed into silence. Before the advance of that awe-inspiring throng, their belief in the powers of the boss began to dwindle.

Even Leiningen, who had ridden up just in time to restore their loss of heart by a display of unshakable calm, even he felt a qualm of malaise. Yonder were millions of voracious jaws bearing down upon him, and only a suddenly insignificant, narrow ditch lay between him and his men and being gnawed to the bones "before you can spit three times."

Hadn't his brain for once taken on more than it could manage? If the blighters rushed the ditch, filled it with their corpses, there'd still be more than enough to destroy every trace of that cranium of his. The planter's chin jutted; they hadn't got him yet, and he'd see to it they never would. While he could think at all, he'd flout both death and the devil.

The hostile army was approaching in perfect formation; no human battalions, however well drilled, could ever hope to rival the precision of that advance. Along a front that moved forward as uniformly as a straight line, the ants drew nearer and nearer to the water ditch. Then, when they learned through their scouts the nature of the obstacle, the two outlying wings of the army detached themselves from the main body and marched down the sides of the ditch. This surrounding maneuver took rather more than an hour to accomplish; no doubt the ants expected that at some point they would find a crossing.

Meanwhile, the army on the center, southern front remained still. The besieged were therefore able to contemplate at their leisure the thumb-long, reddish black, long-legged insects; some of the Indians believed they could see, too, intent on them, the brilliant, cold eyes and razor-edged mandibles of this host of infinity.

It is not easy for the average person to imagine that an animal, not to mention an insect, can *think.* But now both the European brain of Leiningen and the primitive brains of the Indians began to stir with the unpleasant foreboding that inside every single one of that deluge of insects dwelt a thought. And that thought was: Ditch or no ditch, we'll get to your flesh!

Not until four o'clock did the wings reach the horseshoe ends of the ditch, only to find these ran into the great river. Through some kind of secret telegraphy, the report must then have flashed very swiftly indeed along the entire enemy line. And Leiningen, riding—no longer casually—along his side of the ditch, noticed by widespread movements of ant troops that the news of the check had its greatest effect on the southern front, where the main army was massed.

An immense flood of ants, about a hundred yards in width, was pouring in a glimmering black cataract down the far slope of the ditch. Many thousands were already drowning, but they were followed by troop after troop, who clambered over their sinking comrades and then themselves served as dying bridges to the reserves hurrying on in their rear. Shoals of ants were being carried by the current into the middle of the ditch, where gradually they broke asunder and then, exhausted by their struggles, vanished below the surface. Nevertheless, the floundering hundred-yard front was remorselessly if slowly advancing toward the besieged on the other bank. Leiningen had been wrong when he supposed the enemy would have to fill the ditch with their bodies before they could cross; instead, they merely needed to act as stepping-stones, as they swam and sank, to the hordes pressing onward from behind.

Near Leiningen a few mounted herdsmen awaited his orders. He sent one to the weir—the river must be diverted more strongly to increase the speed and power of the water coursing through the ditch. A second peon was dispatched to the outbuildings to bring spades and petrol sprayers. A third rode away to summon to the offensive all the men, except the observation posts, on the nearby sections of the ditch, which were not yet actively threatened.

The ants were getting across far more quickly than Leiningen would have deemed possible. Impelled by the mighty cascade behind them, they struggled nearer and nearer to the inner bank. The momentum of the attack was so great that neither the tardy flow of the stream nor its downward pull could exert its proper force; and into the gap left by every submerging insect hastened forward a dozen more.

When reinforcements reached Leiningen, the invaders were halfway over. The planter had to admit to himself that it was only by a stroke of luck that the ants were attempting to cross on a relatively short front; had they assaulted simultaneously along the entire length of the ditch, the outlook for the defenders would have been black indeed.

Even as it was, it could hardly be described as rosy, though the planter seemed quite unaware that death in a gruesome form was drawing closer and closer. As the war between his brain and the act of God reached its climax, he felt like a champion in a gigantic and thrilling contest from which he was determined to emerge victor. Such, indeed, was his aura of confidence that the Indians forgot their stupefied fear of the peril only a yard or two away; under the planter's supervision they began fervidly digging up to the edge of the bank and throwing clods of earth and spadefuls of sand into the midst of the hostile fleet.

The petrol sprayers, hitherto used to destroy pests and blights on the plantation, were also brought into action. Streams of evil-reeking oil now soared and fell over an enemy already in disorder through the bombardment of earth and sand.

The ants responded to these measures by further developments of their offensive. Entire clumps of huddling insects began to roll down the opposite bank into the water. Leiningen also noticed that the ants were now attacking along an ever-widening front. As the numbers both of his men and his petrol sprayers were severely limited, this rapid extension of the line of battle was becoming an overwhelming danger.

To add to his difficulties, the very clods of earth they flung into that black floating carpet often whirled fragments toward the defenders' side, and here and there dark ribbons were already mounting the inner bank. True, wherever a man saw these they could be driven back into the water by spadefuls of earth or jets of petrol. But the file of defenders was too sparse to hold off these landing parties at all points.

One man struck with his spade at an enemy clump, did not draw it back quickly enough from the water; in a trice the wooden haft swarmed with upward-scurrying insects. With a curse, he dropped the spade into the ditch; too late, they were already on his body. Wherever they encountered bare flesh they bit deeply; a few, bigger than the rest, carried in their hindquarters a sting which injected a burning and paralyzing venom. Screaming, frantic with pain, the peon danced and twirled like a dervish.

"Into the petrol, idiot!" roared Leiningen. "Douse your paws in the petrol!" The dervish tore off his shirt and plunged his arm and the ants hanging to it up to the shoulder in one of the large open cans of petrol. Even then the fierce mandibles did not slacken; another peon had to help him squash and detach each separate insect.

Distracted, some defenders had turned away from the ditch. Cries of fury, a thudding of spades, and a wild trampling to and fro showed that the ants had made full use of the interval, though only a few had managed to get across. The men set to work again desperately with the barrage of earth and sand. Meanwhile, an old Indian, who acted as medicine man to the plantation workers, gave the bitten peon a drink he had prepared some hours before, which he claimed would dissolve and weaken the ants' venom.

A dispassionate observer would have estimated the odds against Leiningen at a thousand to one. But then such an onlooker would have reckoned only by what he saw—the advance of myriad battalions of ants against the futile efforts of a few defenders—and not by the unseen activity that can go on in a man's brain. For Leiningen had not erred when he decided he would fight elemental with elemental. The water in the ditch was beginning to rise; the stronger diverting of the river was making itself apparent.

Visibly the swiftness and power of the masses of water increased, swirling into quicker movement its living black surface, dispersing its pattern, carrying away more of it on the hastening current. With shouts of joy, the peons intensified their bombardment of earth clods and sand.

And now the wide cataract down the opposite bank was thinning, as if the ants were becoming aware that they could not attain their aim. They were scurrying back up the slope to safety. Drowned and floundering insects eddied in thousands along the flow, while Indians running on the bank destroyed every swimmer that reached the side. Not until the ditch curved toward the east did the scattered ranks assemble again in a coherent mass. And now, exhausted, they were in no condition to ascend the bank. Fusillades of clods drove them around the bend toward the mouth of the ditch and then into the river, wherein they vanished without a trace.

The news ran swiftly along the entire chain of outposts, and soon a long scattered line of laughing men was hastening along the ditch toward the scene of victory. In wild abandon they celebrated the triumph—as if there were no longer millions of merciless, cold, and hungry eyes watching them from the opposite bank, watching and waiting.

The sun sank behind the rim of the tamarind wood, and twilight deepened into night. It was hoped that the ants would remain quiet until dawn. But to defeat any attempt at a crossing, the flow of water through the ditch was powerfully increased by opening the dam still further, and Leiningen ordered his men to camp along the bank overnight. He also detailed parties to patrol the ditch in two of his motorcars, ceaselessly illuminating the surface of the water with headlights and flashlights.

After having taken all the precautions he deemed necessary, the farmer ate his supper with considerable appetite and went to bed. His slumbers were in no wise disturbed by the memory of the waiting, live, twenty square miles.

Dawn found a thoroughly refreshed and active Leiningen riding along the edge of the ditch. The planter saw before him a motionless and unaltered throng of besiegers. He studied the wide belt of water between them and the plantation. In the comforting, matter-of-fact light of morning it seemed to him that the ants hadn't the ghost of a chance to cross the ditch. Even if they plunged headlong into it on all three fronts at once, the force of the now powerful current would sweep them away. He had got quite a thrill out of the fight—a pity it was already over.

He rode along the eastern and southern sections of the ditch and found everything in order. But when he reached the western section, opposite the tamarind wood, he found the enemy very busy indeed. The trunks and branches of the trees and the creepers of the lianas, on the far bank of the ditch, swarmed with industrious insects. But instead of eating the leaves, they were merely gnawing through the stalks, so that a thick green shower fell steadily to the ground.

No doubt they were victualing columns sent out to obtain provender for the rest of the army. The discovery did not surprise Leiningen. He knew that ants are intelligent, that certain species even use others as milch cows, watchdogs, and slaves. He was aware of their power of adaptation, their sense of discipline, their marvelous talent for organization. His belief that a foray to supply the army was in progress was strengthened when he saw the leaves that fell to the ground being dragged to the troops waiting outside the wood. Then all at once he realized the aim that rain of green was intended to serve.

Each single leaf, pulled or pushed by dozens of toiling insects, was borne straight to the edge of the ditch. Even as Macbeth watched the approach of Birnam Wood in the hands of his enemies, Leiningen saw the tamarind wood move ever nearer in the mandibles of the ants. The situation was now far more ominous than that of the day before.

He had thought it impossible for the ants to build rafts for themselves—well, here they were, coming in thousands, more than enough to bridge the ditch. Leaves after leaves rustled down the slope into the water, where the current drew them away from the bank and carried them into midstream. And every single leaf carried several ants. The farmer galloped away, leaning from his saddle and yelling orders: "Bring the petrol to the southwest front! Issue spades to every man along the line facing the wood!" Arriving at the eastern and southern sections, he dispatched every man except the observation posts to the menaced west.

Then, as he rode past the stretch where the ants had failed to cross the day before, he witnessed a brief but impressive scene. Down the slope of the distant hill there came toward him a singular being, writhing rather than running, an animallike blackened statue with a shapeless head and four quivering feet that knuckled under almost ceaselessly. When the creature reached the far bank of the ditch and collapsed opposite Leiningen, he recognized it as a pampas stag, covered with ants.

It had strayed near the zone of the army. As usual, they had attacked its eyes first. Blinded, it had reeled in the madness of hideous torment straight into the ranks of its persecutors, and now it swayed to and fro in its death agony.

With a shot from his rifle Leiningen put it out of its misery. Then he pulled out his watch. He hadn't a second to lose, but he could not deny his curiosity the satisfaction of knowing how long the ants would take—for personal reasons, so to speak. After six minutes the white polished bones alone remained.

The sporting zest with which the contest had inspired him the day before had now vanished; in its place was a cold and violent purpose. He would send these vermin back to the hell where they belonged, somehow, anyhow. Yes, but how was indeed the question; as things stood, it looked as if the devils would raze him and his men from the earth instead. He had underestimated their might.

The biggest danger now, he decided, was the point where the western section of the ditch curved southward. Arriving there, he found his worst expectations justified. The power of the current had huddled the leaves and their crews of ants so close together at the bend that the bridge was almost ready. True, streams of petrol and clumps of earth still prevented a landing. But the number of floating leaves was increasing ever more swiftly. It could not be long now before a stretch of water a mile in length was decked by a green pontoon over which the ants could rush in millions.

Leiningen galloped to the weir. The damming of the river was controlled by a wheel on its bank. The planter ordered the man at the wheel first to lower the water in the ditch almost to vanishing point, next to wait a moment, then suddenly to let the river in again. This maneuver of lowering and raising the surface, of decreasing, then increasing the flow of water through the ditch, was to be repeated over and over again.

The water in the ditch sank, and with it the film of leaves. The green fleet nearly reached the bed, and the troops on the far bank swarmed down the slope to it. Then a violent flow of water at the original depth raced through the ditch, overwhelming leaves and ants and sweeping them along.

This intermittent rapid flushing prevented just in time the almost completed fording of the ditch. But it also flung squads of the enemy vanguard up the inner bank. These seemed to know their duty well, and lost no time accomplishing it. The air rang with the curses of bitten Indians. They had removed their shirts and pants to detect more quickly the onrushing insects; when they saw one, they crushed it; and fortunately the onslaught as yet was only by skirmishers.

Again and again the water sank and rose, carrying leaves and drowned ants away with it. It lowered once more nearly to its bed; but this time the exhausted defenders waited in vain for the flush of destruction. Leiningen sensed disaster; something must have gone wrong with the machinery of the dam. Then a sweating peon tore up to him—

"They're over!"

While the besieged were concentrating upon the defense of the stretch opposite the wood, the seemingly unaffected line beyond the wood had become the theater of decisive action. Here the defenders' front was sparse and scattered; everyone who could be spared had hurried away to the south.

Just as the man at the weir had lowered the water almost to the bed of the ditch, the ants on a wide front began another attempt at a direct crossing. Rushing across the ditch, they attained the inner bank before the slow-witted Indians fully grasped the situation. Their frantic screams dumbfounded the man at the weir. Before he could direct the river anew into the safeguarding bed he saw himself surrounded by raging ants. He ran like the others, ran for his life.

Leiningen wasted no time bemoaning the inevitable. As long as there was the slightest chance of success, he had stood his ground; now further resistance was both useless and dangerous. He fired three revolver shots into the air—the prearranged signal for his men to retreat instantly within the inner moat. Then he rode toward the ranch house.

This was two miles from the point of invasion. There was therefore time enough to prepare the second line of defense against the advent of the ants. Of the three great petrol cisterns near the house, one had already been half emptied by the constant withdrawals needed for the sprayers during the fight at the water ditch. The remaining petrol in it was now drawn off through underground pipes into the concrete trench which encircled the ranch house and its outbuildings.

There, drifting in twos and threes, Leiningen's men reached him. Most of them were trying to preserve an air of calm and indifference, belied, however, by their restless glances and knitted brows. One could see that their belief in a favorable outcome of the struggle was considerably shaken.

The planter called his peons around him. "Well, lads," he began, "we've lost the first round. But we'll smash the beggars yet. Anyone who thinks otherwise can draw his pay here and now and push off. There are rafts enough and to spare on the river and plenty of time still to reach 'em."

Not a man stirred.

Leiningen acknowledged their silent vote of confidence with a laugh that was half a grunt. "That's the stuff, lads. Too bad if you'd missed the rest of the show, eh? Well, the fun won't start till morning. Once these blighters turn tail, there'll be plenty of work for everyone and higher wages all round. Now run along and get something to eat; you've earned it, all right."

In the excitement of the fight the greater part of the day had passed without the men once pausing to snatch a bite. Now that the ants were for the time being out of sight, and the wall of petrol gave a stronger feeling of security, hungry stomachs began to assert their claims.

The bridges over the concrete ditch were removed. Here and there solitary ants had reached the ditch; they gazed at the petrol meditatively, then scurried back again. Apparently they had little interest at the moment for what lay beyond the evil-reeking barrier; the abundant spoils of the plantation were the main attraction. Soon the trees, shrubs, and beds for miles around were hulled with ants zealously gobbling the yield of long, weary months of strenuous toil.

As twilight began to fall, Leiningen posted sentries with headlights, then withdrew to his office and began to reckon up his losses. He estimated these as large but, in comparison with his bank balance, by no means unbearable. He worked out a scheme of intensive cultivation which would enable him, before very long, to more than compensate himself for the damage now being wrought to his crops. It was with a contented mind that he finally betook himself to bed, where he slept until dawn, undisturbed by any thought that next day little more might be left of him than a glistening skeleton.

He rose with the sun and went out on the flat roof of his house. A scene like one from Dante lay around him; for miles in every direction there was nothing but a black, glittering multitude, a multitude of rested, sated, but nonetheless voracious ants; yes, look as far as one might, one could see nothing but that rustling black throng, except in the north, where the great river drew a boundary they could not hope to pass. But even the high stone breakwater along the bank of the river, which Leiningen had built as a defense against inundations, was, like the paths, the shorn trees and shrubs, the ground itself, black with ants.

So their greed was not glutted in razing that vast plantation; they were all the more eager now for a rich and certain booty—four hundred men, numerous horses, and bursting granaries.

At first it seemed that the petrol trench would serve its purpose. The besiegers sensed the peril of swimming it, and made no move to plunge blindly over its brink. Instead they began to collect shreds of bark, twigs, and dried leaves and dropped these into the petrol. Everything green, which could have been similarly used, had long since been eaten. After a time, though, a long procession could be seen bringing from the west the tamarind leaves used as rafts the day before.

Since the petrol, unlike the water in the outer ditch, was perfectly still, the refuse stayed where it was thrown. It was several hours before the ants succeeded in covering an appreciable part of the surface. At length, however, their storm troops swarmed down the concrete side, scrambled over the supporting surface of twigs and leaves, and impelled these over the few remaining streaks of open petrol until they reached the other side.

During the entire offensive, the planter sat peacefully, watching them with interest but not stirring a muscle. Moreover, he had ordered his men not to disturb in any way whatever the advancing horde. So they squatted listlessly along the bank of the ditch and waited for a sign from the boss.

The petrol was now covered with ants. A few had climbed the inner concrete wall and were scurrying toward the defenders.

"Everyone back from the ditch!" roared Leiningen.

The men rushed away, without the slightest idea of his plan. He stooped forward and cautiously dropped into the ditch a stone which split the floating carpet and its living freight, to reveal a gleaming patch of petrol. A match spurted, sank down to the oily surface—Leiningen sprang back; in a flash a towering rampart of fire encompassed the garrison.

This spectacular and instant repulse threw the Indians into ecstasy. They applauded, yelled, and stamped, like children at a pantomime.

It was some time before the petrol burned down to the bed of the ditch, and the wall of smoke and flame began to lower. The ants had retreated in a wide circle from the devastation, and innumerable charred fragments along the outer bank showed that the flames had spread from the holocaust in the ditch well into the ranks beyond, where they had wrought havoc.

Yet the perseverance of the ants was by no means broken. The concrete cooled, the flicker of the dying flames wavered and vanished, petrol from the second tank poured into the trench—and the ants marched forward anew to the attack.

The foregoing scene repeated itself in every detail, except that on this occasion less time was needed to bridge the ditch, for the petrol was now filmed by a layer of ash. Once again they withdrew; once again petrol flowed into the ditch. Would the creatures never learn that their self-sacrifice was senseless? It really was senseless, wasn't it? Yes, of course—provided the defenders had an *unlimited* supply of petrol.

When Leiningen reached this stage of reasoning, he felt for the first time since the arrival of the ants that his confidence was deserting him. His skin began to creep; he loosened his collar. Once the devils were over the trench there wasn't a chance in hell for him and his men. God, what a prospect, to be eaten alive like that!

For the third time the flames immolated the attacking troops. Yet the ants were coming on again as if nothing had happened. And meanwhile Leiningen had made a discovery that chilled him to the bone—petrol was no longer flowing into the ditch. Something must be blocking the outflow pipe of the third and last cistern—a snake or a dead rat? Whatever it was, the ants could be held off no longer, unless petrol could by some method be led from the cistern into the ditch.

Then Leiningen remembered that in an outbuilding nearby were two old disused fire engines. Spry as never before in their lives, the peons dragged them out of the shed, connected their pumps to the cistern, uncoiled and laid the hose. They were just in time to aim a stream of petrol at a column of ants that had already crossed and drive them back down the incline into the ditch. Once more an oily girdle surrounded the garrison, once more it was possible to hold the position—for the moment.

It was obvious, however, that this last resource meant only the postponement of defeat and death. A few of the peons fell on their knees and began to pray; others, shrieking insanely, fired their revolvers at the black, advancing masses. At length two of the men's nerves broke; Leiningen saw a naked Indian leap over the north side of the petrol trench, quickly followed by a second. They sprinted with incredible speed toward the river. But their fleetness did not save them; long before they could attain the rafts, the enemy covered their bodies from head to foot.

In the agony of their torment, both sprang blindly into the wide river, where enemies no less sinister awaited them. Wild screams of mortal anguish informed the breathless onlookers that crocodiles and sword-toothed piranhas were no less ravenous than ants, and even nimbler in reaching their prey.

In spite of this bloody warning, more and more men showed they were making up their minds to run the blockade. Anything, even a fight midstream against alligators, seemed better than powerlessly waiting for death to come and slowly consume their living bodies.

Leiningen flogged his brain till it reeled. Was there nothing on earth that could sweep this devil's spawn back into the hell from which it came? Then out of the inferno of his bewilderment rose a terrifying inspiration. Yes, one hope remained, and one alone. It might be possible to dam the great river completely, so that its waters would fill not only the water ditch but overflow into the entire gigantic saucer of land in which lay the plantation.

The far bank of the river was too high for the waters to escape that way. The stone breakwater ran between the river and the plantation; its only gaps occurred where the horseshoe ends of the water ditch passed into the river. So its waters would not only be forced to inundate the plantation, they would also be held there by the breakwater until they rose to its own high brink. In half an hour, perhaps even earlier, the plantation and its hostile army of occupation would be flooded.

The ranch house and outbuildings stood upon rising ground. Their foundations were higher than the breakwater, so the flood would not reach them. And any remaining ants trying to ascend the slope could be repulsed by petrol.

It was possible—yes, if one could only get to the dam! A distance of nearly two miles lay between the ranch house and the weir—two miles of ants. Those two peons had managed only a fifth of that distance at the cost of their lives. Was there an Indian daring enough to run that gauntlet? Hardly likely; and if there were, his prospect of getting back was almost nil.

No, he'd have to make the attempt himself; he might just as well be running as sitting still, anyway, when the ants finally got him. Besides, there *was* a bit of a chance.

Leiningen got up on a chair. "Hey, lads, listen to me!" he cried. Slowly and listlessly the men began to shuffle toward him, the apathy of death already stamped on their faces.

"Listen, lads!" he shouted. "There's still a chance to save our lives—by flooding the plantation from the river. Now one of you might manage to get as far as the weir—but he'd never come back. Well, I'm not going to let you try it. No, I called the tune, and now I'm going to pay the piper.

"The moment I'm over the ditch, set fire to the petrol. That'll allow time for the flood to do the trick. Then all you have to do is to wait here all snug and quiet till I'm back. Yes, I'm coming back, trust me"—he grinned—"when I've finished my slimming cure."

He pulled on high leather boots, drew heavy gauntlets over his hands, and stuffed the spaces between breeches and boots, gauntlets and arms, shirt and neck, with rags soaked in petrol. With close-fitting mosquito goggles he shielded his eyes, knowing too well the ants' dodge of first robbing their victim of sight. Finally he plugged his nostrils and ears with cotton wool and let the peons drench his clothes with petrol.

He was about to set off when the old Indian medicine man came up to him; he had a wondrous salve, he said, whose odor was intolerable to even the most murderous ants. The Indian smeared the boss's boots, his gauntlets, and his face with the extract.

Leiningen then remembered the paralyzing effect of ant's venom, and the Indian gave him a gourd full of the medicine he had administered to the bitten peon at the water ditch. The planter drank it down without noticing its bitter taste; his mind was already at the weir.

He started off toward the northwest corner of the trench. With a bound he was over—and among the ants.

The beleaguered garrison had no opportunity to watch Leiningen's race against death. The ants were climbing the inner bank again—the lurid ring of petrol blazed aloft. For the fourth time that day the reflection from the fire shone on the sweating faces of the imprisoned men and on the reddish black cuirasses of their oppressors.

Leiningen ran. He ran in long, equal strides, with only one thought—he *must* get through. He dodged all trees and shrubs; except for the split seconds his soles touched the ground the ants should have no opportunity to alight on him. That they would get to him soon, despite the salve on his boots, the petrol on his clothes, he realized only too well, but he knew even more surely that he must, and that he would, get to the weir.

Apparently the salve was some use after all; not until he had reached halfway did he feel ants under his clothes and a few on his face. Mechanically, in his stride, he struck at them, scarcely conscious of their bites. He saw he was drawing appreciably nearer the weir—the distance grew less and less—dropped to five hundred—three—two—one hundred yards.

Then he was at the weir and gripping the ant-hulled wheel. Hardly had he seized it when a horde of infuriated ants flowed over his hands, arms, and shoulders. He started the wheel—before it turned once on its axis the swarm covered his face. Leiningen strained like a madman, his lips pressed tight; if he opened them to draw breath . . .

He turned and turned; slowly the dam lowered until it reached the bed of the river. Already the water was overflowing the ditch. Another minute, and the river was pouring through the nearby gap in the breakwater. The flooding of the plantation had begun.

Leiningen let go of the wheel. Now, for the first time, he realized he was coated from head to foot with ants. In spite of the petrol, his clothes were full of them, several had got to his body or were clinging to his face. He felt the smart raging over his flesh from the bites of sawing and piercing insects. Frantic with pain, he almost plunged into the river. To be ripped and slashed to shreds by piranhas? Already he was running the return journey, knocking ants from his gloves and jacket, brushing them from his bloodied face, squashing them to death under his clothes.

One of the creatures bit him just below the rim of his goggles; he managed to tear it away, but the agony of the bite and its etching acid drilled into the eye nerves; he saw now through circles of fire into a milky mist, then he ran for a time almost blinded, knowing that if he once tripped and fell . . . The old Indian's brew weakened the poison a bit, but didn't get rid of it. His heart pounded as if it would burst; blood roared in his ears.

Then he could see again, but the burning girdle of petrol appeared infinitely far away; he could not last half that distance. Swift-changing pictures flashed through his head, episodes in his life, while in another part of his brain a cool and impartial onlooker informed this ant-blurred, gasping, exhausted bundle named Leiningen that such a rushing panorama of scenes from one's past is seen only in the moment before death.

A stone in the path . . . too weak to avoid it . . . the planter stumbled and collapsed. He tried to rise . . . he must be pinned under a rock . . . it was impossible . . . the slightest movement was impossible. . . .

Then all at once he saw, starkly clear and huge, and, right before his eyes, furred with ants, towering and swaying in its death agony, the pampas stag—gnawed to the bones. God, he *couldn't* die like that! And something outside him seemed to drag him to his feet. He tottered. He began to stagger forward again.

Through the blazing ring hurtled an apparition which, as soon as it reached the ground on the inner side, fell full length and did not move. Leiningen, at the moment he made that leap through the flames, lost consciousness for the first time in his life. As he lay there, with glazing eyes and lacerated face, he appeared a man returned from the grave. The peons rushed to him, stripped off his clothes, tore away the ants from a body that seemed almost one open wound; in some places the bones were showing. They carried him into the ranch house.

As the curtain of flames lowered, one could see in place of the illimitable host of ants an extensive vista of water. The thwarted river had swept over the plantation, carrying with it the entire army. The water had collected and mounted in the great saucer, while the ants had in vain attempted to reach the hill on which stood the ranch house. The girdle of flames held them back.

And so imprisoned between water and fire, they had been delivered into the annihilation that was their god. And near the farther mouth of the water ditch, where the stone mole had its second gap, the ocean swept the lost battalions into the river, to vanish forever.

The ring of fire dwindled as the water mounted to the petrol trench and quenched the dimming flames. The inundation rose higher and higher; because its outflow was impeded by the timber and underbrush it had carried along with it, its surface required some time to reach the top of the high stone breakwater and discharge over it the rest of the shattered army.

It swelled over ant-stippled shrubs and bushes until it washed against the foot of the knoll whereon the besieged had taken refuge. For a while an alluvium of ants tried again and again to attain this dry land, only to be repulsed by streams of petrol back into the merciless flood.

Leiningen lay on his bed, his body swathed from head to foot in bandages. With applications and salves, they had managed to stop the bleeding and had dressed his many wounds. Now they thronged around him, one question in every face. Would he recover? "He won't die," said the old man who had bandaged him, "if he doesn't want to."

The planter opened his eyes. "Everything in order?" he asked.

"They're gone," said his nurse. "To hell." He held out to his master a gourd full of a powerful sleeping draft. Leiningen gulped it down.

"I told you I'd come back," he murmured, "even if I am a bit streamlined." He grinned and shut his eyes. He slept.

THE INTERRUPTION

W. W. JACOBS

THE LAST OF the funeral guests had gone and Spencer Goddard, in decent black, sat alone in his small, well-furnished study. There was a queer sense of freedom in the house since the coffin had left it—the coffin which was now hidden in its solitary grave beneath the yellow earth. The air, which for the last three days had seemed stale and contaminated, now smelled fresh and clean. He went to the open window and, looking into the fading light of the autumn day, took a deep breath.

He closed the window, put a match to the fire, and, dropping into his easy chair, sat listening to the cheery crackle of the wood. At the age of thirty-eight he had turned over a fresh page. Life, free and unencumbered, was before him. His dead wife's money was at last his, to spend as he pleased instead of being doled out to him in reluctant driblets.

He turned at a step at the door and his face assumed the appearance of gravity and sadness it had worn for the last four days. The cook, with the same air of decorous grief, entered the room quietly and, crossing to the mantelpiece, placed upon it a photograph. "I thought you'd like to have it, sir," she said in a low voice, "to remind you."

Goddard thanked her and, rising, took it in his hand. He noticed with satisfaction that his hand was absolutely steady.

"It is a very good likeness—till she was taken ill," continued the woman. "I never saw anybody change so sudden."

"The nature of her disease, Hannah," said her master.

The woman nodded and, dabbing at her eyes with her handkerchief, stood regarding him.

"Is there anything you want?" he inquired after a time.

She shook her head. "I can't believe she's gone," she said in a low voice. "Every now and then I have a queer feeling that she's still here—"

"It's your nerves," said her master sharply.

"—and wanting to tell me something."

By a great effort Goddard refrained from looking at her.

"Nerves," he said again. "Perhaps you ought to have a little holiday. It has been a great strain upon you."

"You, too, sir," said the woman respectfully. "Waiting on her hand and foot as you have done, I can't think how you stood it. If you'd only had a nurse—"

"I preferred to do it myself, Hannah," said her master. "If I had had a nurse, it would have alarmed her."

The woman assented. "And they are always peeking and prying into what doesn't concern them," she added. "Always think they know more than the doctors do."

Goddard turned a slow look upon her. The tall, angular figure was standing in an attitude of respectful attention; the cold slaty-brown eyes were cast down, the sullen face expressionless.

"She couldn't have had a better doctor," he said, looking at the fire again. "No man could have done more for her."

"And nobody could have done more for her than you did, sir," was the reply. "There's few husbands that would have done what you did."

Goddard stiffened in his chair. "That will do, Hannah," he said curtly.

"Or done it so well," said the woman, with measured slowness.

With a strange, sinking sensation, her master paused to regain his control. Then he turned and eyed her steadily. "Thank you," he said slowly. "You mean well, but at present I cannot discuss it."

For some time after the door had closed behind her he sat in deep thought. The feeling of well-being of a few minutes before had vanished, leaving in its place an apprehension which he refused to consider, but which would not be allayed. He thought over his actions of the last few weeks, carefully, and could remember no flaw. His wife's illness, the doctor's diagnosis, his own solicitous care were all in keeping with the ordinary. He tried to remember the woman's exact words—her manner. Something had shown him fear. What?

He could have laughed at his fears next morning. The dining room was full of sunshine, and the fragrance of coffee and bacon was in the air. Better still, a worried and commonplace Hannah. Worried over two eggs with false birth certificates, over the vendor of which she became almost lyrical.

"The bacon is excellent," said her smiling master. "So is the coffee; but your coffee always is."

Hannah smiled in return, and, taking fresh eggs from a rosy-cheeked maid, put them before him.

A pipe, followed by a brisk walk, cheered him still further. He came home glowing with exercise and again possessed with that sense of freedom and freshness. He went into the garden—now his own—and planned alterations.

After lunch he went over the house. The windows of his wife's bedroom were open and the room was neat and airy. His glance wandered from the made-up bed to the brightly polished furniture. Then he went to the dressing table and opened the drawers, searching each in turn. With the exception of a few odds and ends they were empty. He went out onto the landing and called for Hannah.

"Do you know whether your mistress locked up any of her things?" he inquired.

"What things?" said the woman.

"Well, her jewelry mostly."

"Oh!" Hannah smiled. "She gave it all to me," she said quietly.

Goddard checked an exclamation. His heart was beating nervously, but he spoke sternly.

"When?"

"Just before she died—of gastroenteritis," said the woman.

There was a long silence. He turned and with great care closed the drawers of the dressing table. The tilted glass showed him the pallor of his face, and he spoke without turning around.

"That is all right, then," he said huskily. "I only wanted to know what had become of it. I thought, perhaps Milly—"

Hannah shook her head. "Milly's all right," she said, with a strange smile. "She's as honest as we are. Is there anything more you want, sir?"

She closed the door behind her with the quietness of the well-trained servant. Goddard, steadying himself with his hand on the rail of the bed, stood looking into the future.

THE DAYS PASSED monotonously, as they pass with a man in prison. Gone was the sense of freedom and the idea of a wider life. Instead of a cell, a house with ten rooms—but Hannah, the jailer guarding each one. Respectful and attentive, the model servant, but he saw in every word a threat against his liberty—his life. In the sullen face and cold eyes he saw her knowledge of power; in her solicitude for his comfort and approval, a sardonic jest. It was the master playing at being the servant. The years of unwilling servitude were over, but she felt her way carefully with infinite zest in the game. Warped and bitter, with a cleverness which had never before had scope, she had entered into her kingdom. She took it little by little, savoring every morsel.

"I hope I've done right, sir," she said one morning. "I have given Milly notice."

Goddard looked up from his paper. "Isn't she satisfactory?" he inquired.

"Not to my thinking, sir," said the woman. "And she says she is coming to see you about it. I told her that would be no good."

"I had better see her and hear what she has to say," he said.

"Of course, if you wish to," said Hannah. "Only, after giving her notice, if she doesn't go, I shall. I should be sorry to go—I've been very comfortable here—but it's either her or me."

"I should be sorry to lose you," said Goddard in a hopeless voice.

"Thank you, sir," said Hannah. "I'm sure I've tried to do my best. I've been with you some time now—and I know all your little ways. I expect I understand you better than anybody else would."

"Very well, I will leave it to you," said Goddard in a voice which strove to be brisk and commanding. "You have my permission to dismiss her."

"There's another thing I wanted to see you about," said Hannah. "My wages. I was going to ask for a rise, seeing that I'm really housekeeper here now."

"Certainly," said her master, considering. "That only seems fair. Let me see—what are you getting?"

"Thirty-six."

Goddard reflected for a moment and then turned with a benevolent smile. "Very well," he said cordially. "I'll make it forty-two."

"I was thinking of a hundred," said Hannah dryly.

The significance of the demand appalled him. "Rather a big jump," he said at last. "I really don't know that I—"

"It doesn't matter," said Hannah. "I thought I was worth it—to you—that's all. You know best. Some people might think I was worth *two* hundred. That's a bigger jump, but after all, a big jump is better than—"

She broke off and tittered. Goddard eyed her.

"—than a big drop," she concluded.

Her master's face set. The lips almost disappeared, and something came into the pale eyes that was revolting. Still eyeing her, he rose and approached her. She stood her ground and met him eye to eye.

"You are jocular," he said at last.

"Short life and a merry one," said the woman.

"Mine or yours?"

"Both, perhaps," was the reply.

"If—if I give you a hundred," said Goddard, moistening his lips, "that ought to make your life merrier, at any rate."

Hannah nodded. "Merry and long, perhaps," she said slowly. "I'm careful, you know—very careful."

"I am sure you are," said Goddard, his face relaxing.

"Careful what I eat and drink, I mean," said the woman, eyeing him steadily.

"That is wise," he said slowly. "I am myself—that is why I am paying a good cook a large salary. But don't overdo things, Hannah; don't kill the goose that lays the golden eggs."

"I am not likely to do that," she said coldly. "Live and let live, that is my motto. Some people have different ones. But I'm careful. Nobody won't catch me napping. I've left a letter with my sister, in case."

Goddard turned slowly and in a casual fashion straightened the flowers in a bowl on the table, and, wandering to the window, looked out. His face was white again and his hands trembled.

"To be opened after my death," continued Hannah. "I don't believe in doctors—not after what I've seen of them—I don't think they know enough; so if I die I shall be examined. I've given good reasons."

"And suppose," said Goddard, coming from the window, "suppose she is curious, and opens it before you die?"

"We must chance that," said Hannah, shrugging her shoulders. "But I don't think she will. I sealed it up with sealing wax, with a mark on it."

"She might open it and say nothing about it," persisted her master.

An unwholesome grin spread slowly over Hannah's features. "I should know it soon enough," she declared boisterously, "and so would other people. Lord, there would be an upset!"

Goddard forced a smile. "Dear me!" he said gently. "Your pen seems to be a dangerous weapon, Hannah, but I hope that the need to open it will not happen for another fifty years. You look well and strong."

The woman nodded. "I don't take up my troubles before they come," she said, with a satisfied air. "But there's no harm in trying to prevent them coming. Prevention is better than cure."

"Exactly," said her master. "And by the way, there's no need for this little financial arrangement to be known by anybody else. I might become unpopular with my neighbors for setting a bad example. Of course, I am giving you this sum because I really think you are worth it."

"I'm sure you do," said Hannah. "I'm not sure I ain't worth more, but this'll do to go on with. I shall get a girl for less than we are paying Milly, and that'll be another little bit extra for me."

"Certainly," said Goddard, and smiled again.

"Come to think of it," said Hannah, pausing at the door, "I ain't sure I shall get anybody else; then there'll be more than ever for me. If I do the work, I might as well have the money."

Her master nodded and, left to himself, sat down to think out a position which was as intolerable as it was dangerous. At a great risk he had escaped from the dominion of one woman only to fall, bound and helpless, into the hands of another. However vague and unconvincing the suspicions of Hannah might be, they would be sufficient. Evidence would be unearthed. Cold with fear one moment and hot with fury the next, he sought in vain for some avenue of escape. It was his brain against that of a cunning, illiterate fool—a fool whose malicious stupidity only added to his danger. And she drank. With largely increased wages she would drink more, and his very life might depend upon a hiccuped boast. It was clear that she was enjoying her supremacy; later on her vanity would urge her to display it before others.

He sat with his head in his hands. There must be a way out and he must find it. Soon. He must find it before gossip began, before the changed position of master and servant lent color to her story when that story became known. Shaking with fury, he thought of her lean, ugly throat and the joy of choking her life out with his fingers. He started suddenly and took a quick breath. No, not fingers—a rope.

BRIGHT AND CHEERFUL outside and with his friends, in the house he was quiet and submissive. Milly had gone, and if the service was poorer and the rooms neglected, he gave no sign. If a bell remained unanswered, he made no complaint, and to studied insolence turned the other cheek of politeness. When at this tribute to her power the woman smiled, he smiled in return. A smile which, for all its disarming softness, left her vaguely uneasy.

"I'm not afraid of you," she said once, with a menacing air.

"I hope not," said Goddard in a slightly surprised voice.

"Some people might be, but I'm not," she declared. "If anything happened to me—"

"Nothing could happen to such a careful woman as you are," he said, smiling again. "You ought to live to ninety—with luck."

It was clear to him that the situation was getting on his nerves. Unremembered but terrible dreams haunted his sleep. Dreams in which some great, inevitable disaster was always pressing upon him, although he could never discover what it was. Each morning he awoke unrefreshed to face another day of torment.

Delay was dangerous and foolish. He had thought out every move in that contest of wits which was to remove the shadow of the rope from his own neck and place it about that of the woman. There was a little risk, but the stake was a big one. He had but to set the ball rolling and others would keep it on its course. It was time to act.

He came in a little jaded from his afternoon walk, and left his tea untouched. He ate but little dinner and, sitting hunched up over the fire, told the woman that he had taken a slight chill. Her concern, he felt grimly, might have been greater if she had known the cause.

He was no better next day, and after lunch he consulted his doctor. He left with a clean bill of health except for a slight digestive derangement, the remedy for which he took away with him in a bottle. For two days he swallowed one tablespoonful three times a day in water, without result; then he took to his bed.

"A day or two in bed won't hurt you," said the doctor. "Show me that tongue of yours again."

"But what is the matter with me, Roberts?" inquired the patient.

The doctor pondered. "Nothing to trouble about—nerves a bit wrong—digestion a little bit impaired. You'll be all right in a day or two."

Goddard nodded. So far, so good; Roberts had not outlived his usefulness. He smiled grimly after the doctor had left at the surprise he was preparing for him. A little rough on Roberts and his professional reputation, perhaps, but these things could not be avoided.

He lay back and visualized the program. A day or two longer, getting gradually worse, then a little sickness. After that a nervous, somewhat shamefaced patient hinting at things. His food had a queer taste—he felt worse after taking it; he knew it was ridiculous, still—there was some of his beef tea he had put aside, perhaps the doctor would like to examine it? And the medicine. Perhaps he would like to see that, too?

Propped on his elbow, he stared fixedly at the wall. There would be more than a trace of arsenic in these things. An attempt to poison him would be clearly indicated, and—his wife's symptoms had resembled his own—let Hannah get out of the web he was spinning if she could. As for the letter she had threatened him with, let her produce it; it could only recoil upon herself. Fifty letters could not save her from the doom he was preparing for her. It was her life or his, and he would show no mercy. For three days he doctored himself with sedulous care, watching himself anxiously the while. His nerve was going and he knew it. Before him was the strain of the discovery, the arrest, and the trial. The gruesome business of his wife's death. A long business. He would wait no longer, and he would open the proceedings with dramatic suddenness.

It was between nine and ten o'clock at night when he rang his bell, and it was not until he had rung four times that he heard the heavy steps of Hannah mounting the stairs.

"What d'you want?" she demanded, standing in the doorway.

"I'm very ill," he said, gasping. "Run for the doctor. Quick!"

The woman stared at him in genuine amazement. "What, at this time o' night?" she exclaimed. "Not likely!"

"I'm dying!" said Goddard in a broken voice.

"Not you," she said roughly. "You'll be better in the morning."

"I'm dying," he repeated. "Go—for—the—doctor."

The woman hesitated. The rain beat in heavy squalls against the window, and the doctor's house was a mile distant on the lonely road. She glanced at the figure on the bed.

"I should catch my death o' cold," she grumbled.

She stood sullenly regarding him. He certainly looked very ill, and his death would by no means benefit her. She listened, scowling, to the wind and the rain.

"All right," she said at last, and went noisily from the room.

His face set in a mirthless smile, he heard her bustling about below. The front door slammed violently and he was alone.

He waited for a few moments and then, getting out of bed, put on his dressing gown and set about his preparations. With a steady hand he added a little white powder to the remains of his beef tea and to the contents of his bottle of medicine. He stood listening a moment at some faint sound from below and, having satisfied himself, lit a candle and made his way to Hannah's room. For a space he stood irresolute, looking about him. Then he opened one of the drawers and, placing the broken packet of powder under a pile of clothing at the rear, made his way back to bed.

He was disturbed to find that he was trembling with excitement and nervousness. He longed for tobacco, but that was impossible. To reassure himself he began to rehearse his conversation with the doctor, and again he thought over every possible complication. The scene with the woman would be terrible; he would have to be too ill to take any part in it. The less he said the better. Others would do all that was necessary.

He lay for a long time listening to the sound of the wind and the rain. Inside, the house seemed unusually quiet, and with an odd sensation he suddenly realized that it was the first time he had been alone in it since his wife's death.

He sat up in bed and drew his watch from beneath the pillow. Hannah ought to have been back before; in any case she could not be long now. At any moment he might hear her key in the lock. He lay down again and reminded himself that things were shaping well. He had shaped them, and some of the satisfaction of the artist was his.

The silence was oppressive. The house seemed to be listening, waiting. He looked at his watch again and wondered, with a curse, what had happened to the woman. It was clear that the doctor must be out, but that was no reason for her delay. It was close on midnight, and the atmosphere of the house seemed in some strange fashion to be brooding and hostile.

In a lull in the wind he thought he heard footsteps outside, and his face cleared as he sat up listening for the sound of the key in the door below. In another moment the woman would be in the house, and the fears engendered by a disordered fancy would have flown. The sound of the steps had ceased, but he could hear no sound of entrance. Until all hope had gone, he sat listening. He was certain he had heard footsteps. Whose?

Trembling and haggard, he sat waiting, assailed by a crowd of murmuring fears. One whispered that he had failed and would have to pay the penalty of failing; that he had gambled with death and lost.

By a strong effort he fought down these fancies and, closing his eyes, tried to compose himself to rest. It was evident now that the doctor was out and that Hannah was waiting to return with him in his car. He was frightening himself for nothing. At any moment he might hear the sound of their arrival.

He heard something else and, sitting up suddenly, tried to think what it was and what had caused it. It was a very faint sound—stealthy. Holding his breath, he waited for it to be repeated. He heard it again, the mere ghost of a sound—a whisper of a sound, but significant as most whispers are.

He wiped his brow with his sleeve and told himself firmly that it was nerves, and nothing but nerves; but, against his will, he still listened. He fancied now that the sound came from his wife's room, the other side of the landing. It increased in loudness and became more insistent, but with his eyes fixed on the door of his room, he still kept himself in hand and tried to listen instead to the wind and the rain.

For a time he heard nothing but that. Then there came a scraping, scurrying noise from his wife's room, and a sudden, terrific crash.

With a loud scream his nerve broke, and springing from the bed he sped downstairs and, flinging open the front door, dashed into the night. The door, caught by the wind, slammed behind him.

With his hand holding the garden gate open, ready for further flight, he stood sobbing for breath. His bare feet were bruised and the rain was very cold, but he took no heed. Then he ran a little way along the road and stood for some time, hoping and listening.

He came back slowly. The wind was bitter and he was soaked to the skin. The garden was black and forbidding, and unspeakable horror might be lurking in the bushes. He went up the road again, trembling with cold. Then, in desperation, he passed through the terrors of the garden to the house, only to find the door closed. The porch gave a little protection from the icy rain but none from the wind, and shaking in every limb, he leaned in abject misery against the door. He pulled himself together after a time and stumbled around to the back door. Locked! And all the lower windows were shuttered. He made his way back to the porch and, crouching there in hopeless misery, waited for the woman to return.

HE HAD A DIM memory when he awoke of somebody questioning him, and then of being half pushed, half carried upstairs to bed. There was something wrong with his head and his chest and he was trembling violently, and very cold. Somebody was speaking.

"You must have taken leave of your senses," said the voice of Hannah. "I thought you were dead."

He forced his eyes to open. "Doctor," he muttered, "doctor."

"Out on a bad case," said Hannah. "I waited till I was tired of waiting and then came along. Good thing for you I did. He'll be round first thing this morning. He ought to be here now."

She bustled about, tidying up the room, his leaden eyes following her as she collected the beef tea and other things on a tray and carried them out.

"Nice thing I did yesterday," she remarked as she came back. "Left the missus' bedroom window open. When I opened the door this morning I found that beautiful Chippendale glass of hers had blown off the table and smashed to pieces. Did you hear it?"

Goddard made no reply. In a confused fashion he was trying to think. Accident or not, the fall of the glass had served its purpose. Were there such things as accidents? Or was life a puzzle—a puzzle into which every piece was made to fit? Fear and the wind . . . no—conscience and the wind . . . had saved the woman. He must get the powder back from her drawer . . . before she discovered it and denounced him. The medicine . . . he must remember not to take it. . . .

He was very ill, seriously ill. He must have taken a chill owing to that panic flight into the garden. Why didn't the doctor come? He had come . . . at last . . . he was doing something to his chest . . . it was cold.

Again . . . the doctor . . . there was something he wanted to tell him. . . . Hannah and a powder . . . what was it?

Later on he remembered, together with other things that he had hoped to forget. He lay watching an endless procession of memories, broken at times by a glance at the doctor, the nurse, and Hannah, who were all standing near the bed regarding him. They had been there a long time and they were all very quiet. The last time he looked at Hannah was the first time for months that he had looked at her without loathing and hatred. Then he knew that he was dying.

AN INVITATION TO THE HUNT

GEORGE HITCHCOCK

HIS FIRST IMPULSE upon receiving it had been to throw it in the fire. They did not travel in the same social set and he felt it presumptuous of them, on the basis of a few words exchanged in the shopping center and an occasional chance meeting on the links, to include him in their plans. Of course, he had often seen them—moving behind the high iron grillwork fence that surrounded their estates, the women in pastel tea gowns serving martinis beneath the striped lawn umbrellas and the men suave and bronzed in dinner jackets or sailing togs—but it had always been as an outsider, almost as a Peeping Tom.

"The most charitable interpretation," he told Emily, "would be to assume that it is a case of mistaken identity."

"But how could it be?" his wife answered, holding the envelope in her slender reddened fingers. "There is only one Fred Perkins in Marine Gardens and the house number is perfectly accurate."

"But there's no earthly reason for it. Why *me* of all people?"

"I should think," said Emily, helping him on with his coat and fitting the two sandwiches neatly wrapped in aluminum foil into his pocket, "that you would be delighted. It's a real step upward for you. You've often enough complained of our lack of social contacts since we moved out of the city."

"It's fantastic," Perkins said, "and of course I'm not going," and he ran out of his one-story shingled California ranch cottage to join the car pool which waited for him at the curb.

All the way to the city, like a dog with a troublesome bone, he worried and teased at the same seemingly insoluble problem: How had he attracted their notice? What was there in his appearance or manner which had set him apart from all the rest?

There had been, of course, that day the younger ones had come in off the bay on their racing cutter, when by pure chance (as it now seemed) he had been the one man on the pier within reach of the forward mooring line. He recalled the moment with satisfaction—the tanned blond girl leaning out from the bowsprit with a coil of manila in her capable hand. "Catch!" she had cried, and at the same instant spun the looping rope toward him through the air. He had caught it deftly and snubbed it about the bitt, easing the cutter's forward motion. "Thanks!" she had called across the narrowing strip of blue water, but there had been no sign of recognition in her eyes, nor had she, when a moment later the yacht was securely tied to the wharf, invited him aboard or even acknowledged his continuing presence on the pier. No, that could hardly have been the moment he sought.

Once at the Agency and there bedded down in a day of invoices, he tried to put the problem behind him, but it would not rest. At last, victim of a fretful pervasive anxiety which ultimately made concentration impossible, he left his desk and made his way to the hall telephone (years ago a written reproof from Henderson had left him forever scrupulous about using the Agency phone for private business), where he deposited a dime and rang his golf partner, Bianchi.

They met for lunch at a quiet restaurant on Maiden Lane. Bianchi was a young man recently out of law school and still impressed by the improbable glitter of society. This will give him a thrill, Perkins thought. He's a second-generation Italian and it isn't likely that he's ever laid eyes on one of these.

"The problem is," he said aloud, "that I'm not sure why they invited me. I hardly know them. At the same time I don't want to do anything that might be construed as—well—as—"

"Defiance?" Bianchi supplied.

"Perhaps. Or call it unnecessary rudeness. We can't ignore their influence."

"Well, first let's have a look at it," Bianchi said, finishing his vermouth. "Do you have it with you?"

"Of course."

"Well, let's see it."

Poor Bianchi! It was obvious that he was dying for an invitation himself and just as obvious from his slurred, uncultivated English and his skin acne that he would never receive one. Perkins took the envelope from his wallet and extracted the stiff silver-edged card, which he lay face up on the table.

"It's engraved," he pointed out.

"They always are," Bianchi said, putting on his shell-rimmed reading glasses, "but that doesn't prove a thing. They aren't the real article without the watermark." He held the envelope up against the table lamp, hoping, Perkins imagined, that the whole thing would prove fraudulent.

"It's there," he admitted, "by God, it's there." And Perkins detected a note of grudging respect in his voice as he pointed out the two lions rampant and the neatly quartered shield. "It's the real McCoy and no mistake."

"But what do I do now?" Perkins asked with a hint of irritation.

"First let's see the details." Bianchi studied the engraved Old English script:

The pleasure of your company at the hunt
is requested
on August sixteenth of this year
R.S.V.P. *Appropriate attire ob.*

"The 'ob,'" he explained, "is for 'obligatory.'"

"I know that."

"Well?"

"The problem is," Perkins said in an unnecessarily loud voice, "that I have no intention of going." He was aware that Bianchi was staring at him incredulously, but this merely strengthened his own stubbornness.

"It's an imposition. I don't know them and it happens I have other plans for the sixteenth."

"All right, all right," Bianchi said soothingly, "no need to shout. I can hear you perfectly well."

With a flush of embarrassment Perkins looked about the restaurant and caught the reproving gaze of the waiters. Obviously he had become emotionally involved in his predicament to the extent of losing control; he hastily reinserted the invitation in its envelope and returned it to his wallet.

Bianchi had arisen and was folding his napkin. "Do as you like," he said, "but I know a dozen men around town who would give their right arm for that invitation."

"But I don't hunt!"

"You can always learn," Bianchi said coldly and, signaling for the waiter, paid his check and left.

Meanwhile, word of the invitation had apparently gotten around the Agency, for Perkins noticed that he was treated with new interest and concern.

Miss Nethersole, the senior librarian, accosted him by the water cooler in deep thrushlike tones. "I'm so thrilled for you, Mr. Perkins! There is no one else in the whole office who deserves it more."

"That's very sweet of you," he answered, attempting to hide his embarrassment by bending over the faucet, "but the truth is I'm not going."

"Not going?" The rich pear-shaped tones (the product of innumerable diction lessons) broke into a cascade of laughter. "How can you say that with a straight face? Have you seen the rotogravure section?"

"No," Perkins said shortly.

"It's all there. The guests, the caterers, even a map of the course. I should give anything to be invited!"

No doubt you would, Perkins thought, looking at her square masculine breastless figure. It's just the sort of sport which would entertain you. But aloud he merely said, "I have other commitments," and went back to his desk.

After lunch he found the rotogravure section stuck under the blotter on his desk. Aware that every eye in the office was secretly on him, he did not dare unfold it but stuck it in his coat pocket; and only later, after he had arisen casually and strolled down the long row of desks to the men's room, did he in the privacy of a locked cubicle and with trembling hands spread it out on his knees.

Miss Nethersole had been right: the guest list was truly staggering. It filled three columns in six-point type; titles gleamed like diamonds in the newsprint. There were generals, statesmen, manufacturers and university presidents; editors of great magazines, movie queens and polar explorers; radiocasters, regents, prizewinning novelists—but Perkins could not begin to digest the list. His eyes ferreted among the jumbled syllables, and at last with a little catch of delight he came upon the one he had unconsciously sought: "Mr. Fred Perkins." That was all, no identification, no LL.D. nor Pres. Untd. Etc. Corp. He read his name over four times and then neatly folded the paper and put it back in his pocket.

"Well," he said with a thin-lipped smile, "I'm not going and that's that."

But apparently Emily, too, had seen the paper.

"The phone has been ringing all day," she informed him as soon as he entered the house and deposited his briefcase on the cane-bottomed chair by the TV set. "Of course everyone is envious, but they don't dare admit it, so I've been receiving nothing but congratulations."

She helped him off with his coat.

"Come into the dining room," she said mysteriously. "I've a little surprise for you." The telephone rang. "No, wait, you mustn't go in without me. It will only be a minute."

He stood uneasily shifting from one foot to the other until she returned.

"It was the Corrigans," she announced. "Beth wants us to come to a little dinner party on the seventeenth. Naturally," she added, "the date isn't accidental. They expect to pump you for all the details before anyone else in the subdivision hears about it. Now come on—" and like a happy child on Christmas morning she took his hand and led him into the dining room.

Perkins followed her with mumbled protestations.

"Isn't it gorgeous?"

There, spread out on the mahogany table (not yet fully paid for) were a pair of tan whipcord breeches, a tattersall vest, and a bright pink coat with brass buttons. In the center of the table where the floral piece usually stood was a gleaming pair of boots.

"And here's the stock," she said, waving a bright bit of yellow silk under his eyes. "You can wear one of my stickpins, the one with the onyx in the jade setting I think would be best. And I've ordered a riding crop with a silver handle. It's to be delivered tomorrow."

"You're taking a great deal for granted," Perkins said. He picked up the boots and felt the soft pliable waxed leather. "They must be very expensive. Where did you get the money for them?"

"They're on time, silly. We have twelve months to pay."

"I'll look ridiculous in that coat."

"No, you won't. You're a very handsome man and I've always said you would cut a fine figure anywhere."

"Well," said Perkins hesitantly, "I suppose we can send them back if I decide not to go."

After dinner Bianchi drove by in his old Studebaker, obviously a bit fuzzy from too many cocktails. Emily opened the door for him.

"Fred is in the bedroom trying on his new hunting outfit," she said. "He'll be out in a moment."

"Who is it?" Perkins shouted, and when she answered he hastily took off the pink coat (which was a bit tight under the arms anyway) and slipped on his smoking jacket. He remembered the scene in the restaurant and felt ashamed to let Bianchi see that his resolution was wavering.

"Look, Fred," Bianchi said when they were seated in the living room, "I hope you've finally changed your mind—about—" He glanced at Emily to see how much she knew of the invitation.

"Go ahead. I've told her everything," Perkins said.

"Well, you can certainly decline if you feel strongly about it," said Bianchi in his best legal manner, "but I don't advise it. If they once get the idea you're snubbing them, they can make things pretty unpleasant for you—and in more ways than one."

"But this is ridiculous!" Emily interrupted. "He is not going to decline. Are you, darling?"

"Well . . ." Perkins said.

She caught the indecision in his voice and went on vehemently, "This is the first social recognition you've ever had, Fred. You can't think of declining. Think what it will mean for the children! In a few years they'll be ready for college. And you know what that means. And do you seriously plan to remain in this house for the rest of your life?"

"There's nothing wrong with this house," Perkins said defensively, reflecting that the house was not yet paid for but already Emily was finding fault with it.

"Suppose the invitation was a mistake," Emily continued. "I'm not saying that it was, but suppose it just for a minute. Is that any the less reason why you shouldn't accept?"

"But I don't like hunting," Perkins interjected weakly. "And I'll look ridiculous on a horse."

"No more ridiculous than ninety percent of the other guests. Do you suppose Senator Gorman will exactly look like a centaur? And what about your boss, Mr. Henderson? He's certainly no polo player."

"Is he going?" Perkins asked in surprise.

"He certainly is. If you had paid the slightest attention to the guest list, you would have noticed it."

"All right, all right," Perkins said, "then I'll go."

"I think that's the wisest course," said Bianchi with a slightly blurry attempt at the judicial manner.

Perkins wrote his acceptance that evening, in pen and ink on a plain stiff card with untinted edges.

"It's all right for them to use silvered edges," Emily pointed out, "but they're apt to think it shows too much swank if you do." She phoned a messenger service—explaining, "It's not the sort of thing you deliver by mail"—and the next morning a uniformed messenger dropped his acceptance off at the gatekeeper's lodge.

The ensuing week passed swiftly. Emily fitted the pink coat and the tan breeches, marked them with chalk and sent them out for alterations. The yellow stock, she decided, would not do after all—"A bit too flashy," she observed—so it was replaced by one in conservative cream. The alteration necessitated a change in stickpin and cuff links to simple ones of hammered silver which she selected in the village. The expense was ruinous, but she overrode his objections. "So much depends upon your making a good impression, and after all, if it goes well, you will be invited again and can always use the same clothes. And the cuff links will be nice with a dinner jacket," she added as an afterthought.

At the Agency he found that he basked in a new glow of respect. On Monday Mr. Presby, the office manager, suggested that he might be more comfortable at a desk nearer the window.

"Of course, with air conditioning it doesn't make as much difference as it did in the old days, but still there's a bit of a view and it helps break the monotony."

Perkins thanked him for his thoughtfulness.

"Not at all," Presby answered. "It's a small way of showing it, but we appreciate your services here, Mr. Perkins."

And on Friday afternoon Henderson himself, the Agency chief and reputedly high in the councils of Intercontinental Guaranty & Trust, stopped by his desk on his way home. Since in a dozen years he had received scarcely a nod from Henderson, Perkins was understandably elated.

"I understand we'll be seeing each other tomorrow," Henderson said, resting one buttock momentarily on the corner of Perkins' desk.

"Looks like it," Perkins said noncommittally.

"I damn well hope they serve whiskey," Henderson said. "I suppose hot punch is strictly in the old hunting tradition, but it gives me gas."

"I think I'll take a flask of my own," said Perkins, as if it were his long-standing habit at hunts.

"Good idea," Henderson said, getting up. And as he left the office he called back over his shoulder, "Save a nip for me, Fred!"

After dinner that evening, Emily put the children to bed and the two of them then strolled to the edge of Marine Gardens and gazed across the open fields toward the big houses behind their iron grilles. Even from that distance they could see signs of bustle and activity. The driveway under the elms seemed full of long black limousines, and on the spreading lawns they could make out the caterer's assistants setting up green tables for the morrow's breakfast. As they watched, an exercise boy on a chestnut mare trotted by outside the fence, leading a string of some forty sleek brown and black horses toward the distant stables.

"The weather will be gorgeous," Emily said as they turned back. "There's just a hint of autumn in the air already."

Perkins did not answer her. He was lost in his own reflections. He had not wanted to go, part of him still did not want to go. He realized that he was trembling with nervous apprehension; but of course that might have been expected—the venture into new surroundings, the fear of failure, of committing some social gaffe, of not living up to what they must certainly expect of him. These were causes enough for his trembling hands and the uneven palpitations of his heart.

"Let's go to bed early," Emily said. "You'll need a good night's sleep."

Perkins nodded and they went into their house. But despite the obvious necessity, Perkins slept very little that night. He tossed about, envisaging every conceivable social humiliation until his wife at last complained, "You kick and turn so that I can't get a bit of sleep," and took her pillow and blanket and went into the children's room.

He had set the alarm for six—an early start was called for—but it was long before that when he was awakened.

"Perkins? Fred Perkins?"

He sat bolt upright in bed.

"Yes?"

It was light, but the sun had not yet risen. There were two men standing in his bedroom. The taller of them, he who had just shaken his shoulder, was dressed in a black leather coat and wore a cap divided into pie-shaped slices of yellow and red.

"Come on, get up!" the man said.

"Hurry along with it," added the second man, shorter and older but dressed also in leather.

"What is it?" Perkins asked. He was fully awake now and the adrenaline charged his heart so that it pumped with a terrible urgency.

"Get out of bed," said the larger man, and seizing the covers with one hand jerked them back. As he did so, Perkins saw the two lions rampant and the quartered shield stamped in gilt on the breast of his leather coat. Trembling, and naked except for his shorts, he rose from his bed into the cool crisp morning.

"What is it?" he repeated senselessly.

"The hunt, the hunt, it's time for the hunt," said the older man.

"Then let me get my clothes," Perkins stammered, and moved toward the dresser, where in the dim light he could see the splendid pink coat and whipcord breeches spread out awaiting his limbs. But as he turned he was struck a sharp blow by the short taped club which he had not observed in the large man's hand.

"You won't be needing them." His attacker laughed, and out of the corner of his eye Perkins saw the older man pick up the pink coat and holding it by the tails rip it up the center.

"Look here!" he began, but before he could finish, the heavy man in black leather twisted his arm sharply behind his back and pushed him out the French doors into the cold clear sunless air. Behind him he caught a glimpse of Emily in nightclothes appearing suddenly in the door, heard her terrified scream and the tinkle of glass from one of the panes, which broke as the short man slammed the door shut.

Perkins broke loose and ran in a frenzy across the lawn, but the two gamekeepers were soon up with him. They seized him under the armpits and propelled him across the street to the point where Marine Gardens ended and the open country began. There they threw him onto the stubbled ground and the short one drew out a whip.

"Now, run! You son of a bitch, run!" screamed the large man.

Perkins felt the sharp agony of the whip across his bare back. He stumbled to his feet and began to lope across the open fields. The grass cut his bare feet, sweat poured down his naked chest and his mouth was filled with incoherent syllables of protest and outrage, but he ran, he ran, he ran. For already across the rich summery fields he heard the hounds baying and the clear alto note of the huntsman's horn.

THE VOICE IN THE NIGHT

WILLIAM HOPE HODGSON

IT WAS A DARK, starless night. We were becalmed in the northern Pacific. Our exact position I do not know; for the sun had been hidden during the course of a weary, breathless week by a thin haze which had seemed to float above us, about the height of our mastheads, at whiles descending and shrouding the surrounding sea.

With there being no wind, we had steadied the tiller, and I was the only man on deck. The crew, consisting of two men and a boy, were sleeping forward in their den, while Will—my friend, and the master of our little craft—was aft in his bunk on the port side of the little cabin.

Suddenly, from out of the surrounding darkness, there came a hail:

"Schooner, ahoy!"

The cry was so unexpected that I gave no immediate answer, because of my surprise.

It came again—a voice curiously throaty and inhuman, calling from somewhere upon the dark sea away on our port broadside:

"Schooner, ahoy!"

"Hullo!" I sang out, having gathered my wits somewhat. "What are you? What do you want?"

"You need not be afraid," answered the queer voice, having probably noticed some trace of confusion in my tone. "I am only an old—man."

The pause sounded odd, but it was only afterward that it came back to me with any significance.

"Why don't you come alongside, then?" I queried somewhat snappishly, for I liked not his hinting at my having been a trifle shaken.

"I—I—can't. It wouldn't be safe. I—" The voice broke off, and there was silence.

"What do you mean?" I asked, growing more and more astonished. "What's not safe? Where are you?"

I listened for a moment, but there came no answer. And then, a sudden indefinite suspicion, of I knew not what, coming to me, I stepped swiftly to the binnacle and took out the lighted lamp. At the same time, I knocked on the deck with my heel to waken Will. Then I was back at the side, throwing the yellow funnel of light out into the silent immensity beyond our rail. As I did so, I heard a slight muffled cry, and then the sound of a splash, as though someone had dipped oars abruptly. Yet I cannot say with certainty that I saw anything; save, it seemed to me, that with the first flash of the light there had been something upon the waters, where now there was nothing.

"Hullo, there!" I called. "What foolery is this?"

But there came only the indistinct sounds of a boat being pulled away into the night.

Then I heard Will's voice from the direction of the after scuttle: "What's up, George?"

"Come here, Will!" I said.

"What is it?" he asked, coming across the deck.

I told him the queer thing that had happened. He put several questions; then, after a moment's silence, he raised his hands to his lips and hailed:

"Boat, ahoy!"

From a long distance away there came back to us a faint reply, and my companion repeated his call. Presently, after a short period of silence, there grew on our hearing the muffled sound of oars, at which Will hailed again.

This time there was a reply: "Put away the light."

"I'm damned if I will," I muttered; but Will told me to do as the voice bade, and I shoved it down under the bulwarks.

"Come nearer," he said, and the oar strokes continued. Then, when apparently some half dozen fathoms distant, they again ceased.

"Come alongside!" exclaimed Will. "There's nothing to be frightened of aboard here."

"Promise that you will not show the light?"

"What's to do with you," I burst out, "that you're so infernally afraid of the light?"

"Because—" began the voice, and stopped short.

"Because what?" I asked quickly.

Will put his hand on my shoulder. "Shut up a minute, old man," he said in a low voice. "Let me tackle him."

He leaned more over the rail. "See here, mister," he said, "this is a pretty queer business, you coming upon us like this, right out in the middle of the blessed Pacific. How are we to know what sort of a hanky-panky trick you're up to? You say there's only one of you. How are we to know, unless we get a squint at you—eh? What's your objection to the light, anyway?"

As he finished, I heard the noise of the oars again, and then the voice came; but now from a greater distance, and sounding extremely hopeless and pathetic.

"I am sorry—sorry! I would not have troubled you, only I am hungry, and—so is she."

The voice died away, and the sound of the oars, dipping irregularly, was borne to us.

"Stop!" sang out Will. "I don't want to drive you away. Come back! We'll keep the light hidden if you don't like it."

He turned to me. "It's a damned queer rig, this; but I think there's nothing to be afraid of?"

There was a question in his tone, and I replied, "No, I think the poor devil's been wrecked around here, and gone crazy."

The sound of the oars drew nearer.

"Shove that lamp back in the binnacle," said Will; then he leaned over the rail and listened. I replaced the lamp and came back to his side. The dipping of the oars ceased some dozen yards distant.

"Won't you come alongside now?" asked Will in an even voice. "I have had the lamp put back in the binnacle."

"I—I cannot," replied the voice. "I dare not come nearer. I darc not even pay you for the—the provisions."

"That's all right," said Will, and hesitated. "You're welcome to as much grub as you can take—" Again he hesitated.

"You are very good!" exclaimed the voice. "May God, who understands everything, reward you—" It broke off huskily.

"The—the lady?" said Will abruptly. "Is she—"

"I have left her behind upon the island," came the voice.

"What island?" I cut in.

"I know not its name," returned the voice. "I would to God—" it began, and checked itself as suddenly.

"Could we not send a boat for her?" asked Will at this point.

"No!" said the voice, with extraordinary emphasis. "My God! No!" There was a moment's pause; then it added, in a tone which seemed a merited reproach, "It was because of our want I ventured—because her agony tortured me."

"I am a forgetful brute!" exclaimed Will. "Just wait a minute, whoever you are, and I will bring you up something at once."

In a couple of minutes he was back again, and his arms were full of various edibles. He paused at the rail.

"Can't you come alongside for them?" he asked.

"No—I *dare not,*" replied the voice, and it seemed to me that in its tones I detected a note of stifled craving, as though the owner hushed a mortal desire. It came to me then in a flash that the poor old creature out there in the darkness was *suffering* for actual need for that which Will held in his arms; and yet, because of some unintelligible dread, refraining from dashing to the side of our schooner and receiving it. And with the lightninglike conviction there came the knowledge that the Invisible was not mad, but sanely facing some intolerable horror.

"Damn it, Will!" I said, full of many feelings, over which predominated a vast sympathy. "Get a box. We must float off the stuff to him in it."

This we did, propelling it away from the vessel, out into the darkness, by means of a boat hook. In a minute a slight cry from the Invisible came to us, and we knew that he had secured the box.

A little later he called out a farewell to us, and so heartful a blessing that I am sure we were the better for it. Then, without more ado, we heard the ply of oars across the darkness.

"Pretty soon off," remarked Will, with perhaps just a little sense of injury.

"Wait," I replied. "I think somehow he'll come back. He must have been badly needing that food."

"And the lady," said Will. For a moment he was silent; then he continued, "It's the queerest thing ever I've tumbled across since I've been fishing."

"Yes," I said, and fell to pondering.

And so the time slipped away—an hour, another, and still Will stayed with me; for the queer adventure had knocked all desire for sleep out of him.

The third hour was three parts through when we heard again the sound of oars across the silent ocean.

"Listen!" said Will, a low note of excitement in his voice.

"He's coming, just as I thought," I muttered.

The dipping of the oars grew nearer, and I noted that the strokes were firmer and longer. The food had been needed.

They came to a stop a little distance off the broadside, and the queer voice came again to us through the darkness:

"Schooner, ahoy!"

"That you?" asked Will.

"Yes," replied the voice. "I left you suddenly, but—but there was great need."

"The lady?" questioned Will.

"The—lady is grateful now on earth. She will be more grateful soon in—in heaven."

Will began to make some reply, in a puzzled voice, but became confused and broke off. I said nothing. I was wondering at the curious pauses, and apart from my wonder, I was full of a great sympathy.

The voice continued, "We—she and I, have talked, as we shared the result of God's tenderness and yours—"

Will interposed, but without coherence.

"I beg of you not to—to belittle your deed of Christian charity this night," said the voice. "Be sure that it has not escaped His notice."

It stopped, and there was a full minute's silence. Then it came again. "We have spoken together upon that which—which has befallen us. We had thought to go out, without telling anyone of the terror which has come into our—lives. She is with me in believing that tonight's happenings are under a special ruling, and that it is God's wish that we should tell to you all that we have suffered since—since—"

"Yes?" said Will softly.

"Since the sinking of the *Albatross*."

"Ah!" I exclaimed involuntarily. "She left Newcastle for 'Frisco some six months ago, and hasn't been heard of since."

"Yes," answered the voice. "But some few degrees to the north of the line, she was caught in a terrible storm and dismasted. When the day came, it was found that she was leaking badly, and presently, it falling to a calm, the sailors took to the boats, leaving—leaving a young lady—my fiancée—and myself upon the wreck.

"We were below, gathering together a few of our belongings, when they left. They were entirely callous, through fear, and when we came up upon the decks, we saw them only as small shapes afar off upon the horizon. Yet we did not despair, but set to work and constructed a small raft. Upon this we put such few matters as it would hold, including a quantity of water and some ship's biscuit. Then, the vessel being very deep in the water, we got ourselves onto the raft and pushed off.

"It was later that I observed we seemed to be in the way of some tide or current, which bore us from the ship at an angle, so that in the course of three hours, by my watch, her hull became invisible to our sight, her broken masts remaining in view for a somewhat longer period. Then, toward evening, it grew misty, and so through the night. The next day we were still encompassed by the mist, the weather remaining quiet.

"For four days we drifted through this strange haze, until, on the evening of the fourth day, there grew upon our ears the murmur of breakers at a distance. Gradually it became plainer, and somewhat after midnight, it appeared to sound upon either hand at no very great space. The raft was raised upon a swell several times, and then we were in smooth water, and the noise of the breakers was behind.

"When the morning came, we found that we were in a sort of great lagoon, but of this we noticed little at the time; for close before us, through the enshrouding mist, loomed the hull of a large sailing vessel. With one accord we fell upon our knees and thanked God, for we thought that here was an end to our perils. We had much to learn.

"The raft drew near to the ship, and we shouted on them to take us aboard; but none answered. Presently the raft touched against the side of the vessel, and seeing a rope hanging downward, I seized it and began to climb. Yet I had much ado to make my way up, because of a kind of gray, lichenous fungus that had seized upon the rope and blotched the side of the ship lividly.

"I reached the rail and clambered over it, onto the deck. Here I saw that the decks were covered in great patches with the gray masses, some of them rising into nodules several feet in height; but at the time I thought less of this matter than of the possibility of there being people aboard the ship. I shouted, but none answered. Then I went to the door below the poop deck. I opened it and peered in. There was a great smell of staleness, so that I knew in a moment that nothing living was within, and with the knowledge, I shut the door quickly, for I felt suddenly lonely.

"I went back to the side where I had scrambled up. My—my sweetheart was still sitting quietly upon the raft. Seeing me look down, she called up to know whether there were any aboard the ship. I replied that the vessel had the appearance of having been long deserted, but that if she would wait a little, I would see whether there was anything in the shape of a ladder by which she could ascend to the deck. Then we would make a search through the vessel together. A little later, on the opposite side of the decks, I found a rope side ladder. This I carried across, and a minute afterward she was beside me.

"Together we explored the cabins and apartments in the afterpart of the ship, but nowhere was there any sign of life. Here and there, within the cabins themselves, we came across odd patches of that queer fungus; but this, as my sweetheart said, could be cleansed away.

"In the end, having assured ourselves that the after portion of the vessel was empty, we picked our ways to the bows, between the ugly gray nodules of that strange growth; and here we made a further search, which told us that there was indeed none aboard but ourselves.

"'This being now beyond any doubt, we returned to the stern of the ship and proceeded to make ourselves as comfortable as possible. Together we cleared out and cleaned two of the cabins, and after that I made examination whether there was anything eatable in the ship. This I soon found was so, and thanked God for His goodness. In addition to this I discovered a fresh-water pump, and having fixed it, I found the water drinkable, though somewhat unpleasant to the taste.

"'For several days we stayed aboard the ship without attempting to get to the shore. We were busily engaged in making the place habitable. Yet even thus early we became aware that our lot was even less to be desired than might have been imagined; for though, as a first step, we scraped away the odd patches of growth that studded the floors and walls of the cabins and saloon, yet they returned almost to their original size within the space of twenty-four hours, which not only discouraged us but gave us a feeling of vague unease.

"'Still we would not admit ourselves beaten, so set to work afresh, and not only scraped away the fungus but soaked the places where it had been with carbolic, a canful of which I had found in the pantry. Yet by the end of the week the growth had returned in full strength, and in addition it had spread to other places, as though our touching it had allowed germs from it to travel elsewhere.

"'On the seventh morning, my sweetheart woke to find a small patch of it growing on her pillow, close to her face. At that, she came to me, as soon as she could get her garments upon her. I was in the galley at the time, lighting the fire for breakfast.

"'"Come here, John," she said, and led me aft. When I saw the thing upon her pillow I shuddered, and then and there we agreed to go right out of the ship and see whether we could not fare to make ourselves more comfortable ashore.

"'Hurriedly we gathered together our few belongings, and even among these I found that the fungus had been at work, for one of her shawls had a little lump of it growing near one edge. I threw the whole thing over the side without saying anything to her.

"'The raft was still alongside, but it was too clumsy to guide, and I lowered down a small boat that hung across the stern, and in this we made our way to the shore. Yet as we drew near to it, I became gradually aware that here the vile fungus, which had driven us from the ship, was growing riot. In places it rose into horrible, fantastic mounds, which seemed almost to quiver, as with a quiet life, when the wind blew across them. Here and there it took on the forms of vast fingers, and in others it just spread out flat and smooth and treacherous. Odd places, it appeared as grotesque stunted trees, extraordinarily kinked and gnarled—the whole quaking vilely at times.

"At first it seemed to us that there was no single portion of the surrounding shore which was not hidden beneath the masses of the hideous lichen; yet in this I found we were mistaken, for somewhat later, coasting along the shore at a little distance, we descried a smooth white patch of what appeared to be fine sand, and there we landed. It was not sand. What it was I do not know. All that I have observed is that upon it the fungus will not grow; while everywhere else, save where the sandlike earth wanders oddly, pathwise, amid the gray desolation of the lichen, there is nothing but that loathsome grayness.

"It is difficult to make you understand how cheered we were to find one place that was absolutely free from the growth, and here we deposited our belongings. Then we went back to the ship for such things as it seemed to us we should need. Among other matters, I managed to bring ashore with me one of the ship's sails. With it I constructed two small tents, which, though exceedingly rough-shaped, served the purposes for which they were intended. In these we lived and stored our various necessities, and thus for a matter of some four weeks all went smoothly and without particular unhappiness. Indeed, I may say with much happiness—for—we were together.

"It was on the thumb of her right hand that the growth first showed. It was only a small circular spot, much like a little gray mole. My God! How the fear leaped to my heart when she showed me the place. We cleansed it, between us, washing it with carbolic and water. In the morning of the following day she showed her hand to me again. The gray warty thing had returned. For a little while we looked at one another in silence. Then, still wordless, we started again to remove it. In the midst of the operation she spoke suddenly.

"'What's that on the side of your face, dear?' Her voice was sharp with anxiety. I put my hand up to feel.

"'There! Under the hair by your ear. A little to the front a bit.' My finger rested upon the place, and then I knew.

"'Let us get your thumb done first,' I said. And she submitted, only because she was afraid to touch me until it was cleansed. I finished washing and disinfecting her thumb, and then she turned to my face. After it was finished we sat together and talked awhile of many things; for there had come into our lives sudden, very terrible thoughts. We were, all at once, afraid of something worse than death. We spoke of loading the boat with provisions and water and making our way out onto the sea; yet we were helpless, for many causes, and—and the growth had attacked us already. We decided to stay. God would do with us what was His will. We would wait.

"A month, two months, three months passed and the places grew somewhat, and there had come others. Yet we fought so strenuously with the fear that its headway was but slow, comparatively speaking.

"Occasionally we ventured off to the ship for such stores as we needed. There we found that the fungus grew persistently. One of the nodules on the main deck soon became as high as my head.

"We had now given up all thought or hope of leaving the island. We had realized that it would be unallowable to go among healthy humans with the thing from which we were suffering.

"With this determination and knowledge in our minds we knew that we should have to husband our food and water; for we did not know, at that time, but that we should possibly live for many years.

"This reminds me that I have told you that I am an old man. Judged by years this is not so. But—but—"

He broke off, then continued somewhat abruptly, "As I was saying, we knew that we should have to use care in the matter of food. But we had no idea then how little food there was left of which to take care. It was a week later that I made the discovery that all the other bread tanks—which I had supposed full—were empty, and that (beyond odd tins of vegetables and meat, and some other matters) we had nothing on which to depend but the bread in the tank which I had already opened.

"After learning this I bestirred myself to do what I could, and set to work at fishing in the lagoon; but with no success. At this I was somewhat inclined to feel desperate, until the thought came to me to try outside the lagoon, in the open sea.

"Here, at times, I caught odd fish, but so infrequently that they proved of but little help in keeping us from the hunger which threatened. It seemed to me that our deaths were likely to come by hunger, and not by the growth of the thing which had seized upon our bodies.

"We were in this state of mind when the fourth month wore out. Then I made a very horrible discovery. One morning, a little before midday, I came off from the ship with a portion of the biscuits which were left. In the mouth of her tent I saw my sweetheart sitting, eating something.

"'What is it, my dear?' I called out as I leaped ashore. Yet, on hearing my voice, she seemed confused, and turning, slyly threw something toward the edge of the little clearing. It fell short, and a vague suspicion having arisen within me, I walked across and picked it up. It was a piece of the gray fungus.

"As I went to her with it in my hand, she turned deadly pale; then a rose red.

"I felt strangely dazed and frightened.

"'My dear! My dear!' I said, and could say no more. Yet at my words she broke down and cried bitterly. Gradually, as she calmed, I got from her the news that she had tried it the preceding day, and—and liked it. I got her to promise on her knees not to touch it again, however great our hunger. After she had promised, she told me that the desire for it had come suddenly, and that until the moment of desire, she had experienced nothing toward it but the most extreme repulsion.

"Later in the day, feeling strangely restless and much shaken with the thing which I had discovered, I made my way along one of the twisted paths—formed by the white, sandlike substance—which led among the fungoid growth. I had, once before, ventured along there, but not to any great distance. This time, being involved in perplexing thought, I went much farther than hitherto.

"Suddenly I was called to myself by a queer hoarse sound on my left. Turning quickly, I saw that there was movement among an extraordinarily shaped mass of fungus close to my elbow. It was swaying uneasily, as though it possessed life of its own. Abruptly, as I stared, the thought came to me that the thing had a grotesque resemblance to the figure of a distorted human creature. Even as the fancy flashed into my brain, there was a slight, sickening noise of tearing, and I saw that one of the branchlike arms was detaching itself from the surrounding masses, and coming toward me. The head of the thing, a shapeless gray ball, inclined in my direction. I stood stupidly, and the vile arm brushed across my face. I gave out a frightened cry and ran back a few paces. There was a sweetish taste upon my lips where the thing had touched me. I licked them, and was immediately filled with an inhuman desire. I turned and seized a mass of the fungus. Then more, and—more. I was insatiable. In the midst of devouring, the remembrance of the morning's discovery swept into my amazed brain. It was sent by God. I dashed the fragment I held to the ground. Then, utterly wretched and feeling a dreadful guiltiness, I made my way back to the encampment.

"I think she knew, by some marvelous intuition which love must have given, so soon as she set eyes on me. Her quiet sympathy made it easier for me, and I told her of my sudden weakness, yet omitted to mention the extraordinary thing which had gone before. I desired to spare her all unnecessary terror.

"But for myself I had added an intolerable knowledge, to breed an incessant terror in my brain; for I doubted not that I had seen the end of one of these men who had come to the island in the ship in the lagoon; and in that monstrous ending I had seen our own.

"Thereafter we kept from the abominable food, though the desire for it had entered into our blood. Yet our dreary punishment was upon us; for day by day, with monstrous rapidity, the fungoid growth took hold of our poor bodies. Nothing we could do would check it materially, and so—and so—we who had been human became—Well, it matters less each day. Only—only we had been man and maid!

"And day by day the fight is more dreadful to withstand the hunger-lust for the terrible lichen.

"A week ago we ate the last of the biscuit, and since that time I have caught three fish. I was out here fishing tonight when your schooner drifted upon me out of the mist. I hailed you. You know the rest, and may God, out of His great heart, bless you for your goodness to a—a couple of poor outcast souls."

There was the dip of an oar—another. Then the voice came again, and for the last time, sounding through the slight surrounding mist, ghostly and mournful.

"God bless you! Good-by!"

"Good-by," we shouted together hoarsely, our hearts full of many emotions.

I glanced about me. I became aware that the dawn was upon us.

The sun flung a stray beam across the hidden sea, pierced the mist dully, and lit up the receding boat with a gloomy fire. Indistinctly I saw something nodding between the oars. I thought of a sponge—a great, gray nodding sponge. The oars continued to ply. They were gray—as was the boat—and my eyes searched a moment vainly for the conjunction of hand and oar. My gaze flashed back to the—head. It nodded forward as the oars went backward for the stroke. Then the oars were dipped, the boat shot out of the patch of light, and the—the thing went nodding into the mist.

MIDNIGHT BLUE

ROSS MACDONALD

IT HAD RAINED in the canyon during the night. The world had the colored freshness of a butterfly just emerged from the chrysalis stage and trembling in the sun. Actual butterflies danced in flight across free spaces of air or played a game of tag without any rules among the tree branches. At this height there were giant pines among the eucalyptus trees.

I parked my car where I usually parked it, in the shadow of the stone building just inside the gates of the old estate. Just inside the posts, that is—the gates had long since fallen from their rusted hinges. The owner of the country house had died in Europe, and the place had stood empty since the war. It was one reason I came here on the occasional Sunday when I wanted to get away from the Hollywood rat race. Nobody lived within two miles.

Until now, anyway. The window of the gatehouse overlooking the drive had been broken the last time that I'd noticed it. Now it was patched up with a piece of cardboard. Through a hole punched in the middle of the cardboard, bright emptiness watched me—human eye's bright emptiness.

"Hello," I said.

A grudging voice answered, "Hello."

The gatehouse door creaked open, and a white-haired man came out. A smile sat strangely on his ravaged face. He walked mechanically, shuffling in the leaves, as if his body were not at home in the world. He wore faded denims through which his clumsy muscles bulged like animals in a sack. His feet were bare.

I saw when he came up to me that he was a huge old man, a head taller than I was and a foot wider. His smile was not a greeting or any kind of a smile that I could respond to. It was the stretched, blind grimace of a man who lived in a world of his own, a world that didn't include me.

"Get out of here. I don't want trouble. I don't want nobody messing around."

"No trouble," I said. "I came up to do a little target shooting. I probably have as much right here as you have."

His eyes widened. They were as blue and empty as holes in his head through which I could see the sky.

"Nobody has the rights here that I have. I lifted up mine eyes unto the hills and the voice spoke and I found sanctuary. Nobody's going to force me out of my sanctuary."

I could feel the short hairs bristling on the back of my neck. Though my instincts didn't say so, he was probably a harmless nut. I tried to keep my instincts out of my voice.

"I won't bother you. You don't bother me. That should be fair enough."

"You bother me just *being* here. I can't stand people. I can't stand cars. And this is twice in two days you come up harrying me and harassing me."

"I haven't been here for a month."

"You're an Ananias liar." His voice whined like a rising wind. He clenched his knobbed fists and shuddered on the verge of violence.

"Calm down, old man," I said. "There's room in the world for both of us."

He looked around at the high green world as if my words had snapped him out of a dream.

"You're right," he said in a different voice. "I have been blessed, and I must remember to be joyful. Joyful. Creation belongs to all of us poor creatures." His smiling teeth were as long and yellow as an old horse's. His roving glance fell on my car. "And it wasn't you who came up here last night. It was a different automobile. I remember."

He turned away, muttering something about washing his socks, and dragged his horny feet back into the gatehouse. I got my targets, pistol, and ammunition out of the trunk and locked the car up tight. The old man watched me through his peephole, but he didn't come out again.

Below the road, in the wild canyon, there was an open meadow backed by a sheer bank, which was topped by the crumbling wall of the estate. It was my shooting gallery. I slid down the wet grass of the bank and tacked a target to an oak tree, using the butt of my heavy-framed twenty-two as a hammer.

While I was loading it, something caught my eye—something that glinted red, like a ruby among the leaves. I stooped to pick it up and found that it was attached. It was a red-enameled fingernail at the tip of a white hand. The hand was cold and stiff.

I let out a sound that must have been loud in the stillness. A jaybird erupted from a manzanita, sailed up to a high limb of the oak, and yelled down curses at me. A dozen chickadees flew out of the oak and settled in another at the far end of the meadow.

Panting like a dog, I scraped away the dirt and wet leaves that had been loosely piled over the body. It was the body of a girl wearing a midnight-blue sweater and skirt. She was a blonde, about seventeen. The blood that congested her face made her look old and dark. The white rope with which she had been garroted was sunk almost out of sight in the flesh of her neck. The rope was tied at the nape in what is called a granny knot, the kind of knot that any child can tie.

I left her where she lay and climbed back up to the road on trembling knees. The grass showed traces of the track her body had made where someone had dragged it down the bank. I looked for tire marks on the shoulder and in the rutted, impacted gravel of the road. If there had been any, the rain had washed them out.

I trudged up the road to the gatehouse and knocked on the door. It creaked inward under my hand. Inside there was nothing alive but the spiders that had webbed the low black beams. A dustless rectangle in front of the stone fireplace showed where a bedroll had lain. Several blackened tin cans had evidently been used as cooking utensils. Gray embers lay on the cavernous hearth. Suspended above it from a spike in the mantel was a pair of white cotton work socks. The socks were wet. Their owner had left in a hurry.

It wasn't my job to hunt him. I drove down the canyon to the highway and along it for a few miles to the outskirts of the nearest town. There a drab green box of a building with a flag in front of it housed the highway patrol. Across the highway was a lumberyard, deserted on Sunday.

"TOO BAD ABOUT Ginnie," the dispatcher said when she had radioed the local sheriff. She was a thirtyish brunette with fine black eyes and dirty fingernails. She had on a plain white blouse, which was full of her.

"Did you know Ginnie?"

"My young sister knows her. They go—they went to high school together. It's an awful thing when it happens to a young person like that. I knew she was missing—I got the report when I came on at eight—but I kept hoping that she was just off on a lost weekend, like. Now there's nothing to hope for, is there?" Her eyes were liquid with feeling. "Poor Ginnie. And poor Mr. Green."

"Her father?"

"That's right. He was in here with her high school counselor not more than an hour ago. I hope he doesn't come back right away. I don't want to be the one that has to tell him."

"How long has the girl been missing?"

"Just since last night. We got the report here about three a.m. Apparently she wandered away from a party at Cavern Beach. Down the pike a ways." She pointed south toward the mouth of the canyon.

"What kind of a party was it?"

"Some of the kids from the Union High School—they took some wienies down and had a fire. The party was part of graduation week. I happen to know about it because my young sister, Alice, went. I didn't want her to go, even if it was supervised. That can be a dangerous beach at night. All sorts of bums and scroungers hang out in the caves. Why, one night when I was a kid I saw a naked man down there in the moonlight. He didn't have a woman with him either."

She caught the drift of her words, did a slow blush, and checked her loquacity. I leaned on the plywood counter between us.

"What sort of girl was Ginnie Green?"

"I wouldn't know. I never really knew her."

"Your sister does."

"I don't let my sister run around with girls like Ginnie Green. Does that answer your question?"

"Not in any detail."

"It seems to me you ask a lot of questions."

"I'm naturally interested, since I found her. Also, I happen to be a private detective."

"Looking for a job?"

"I can always use a job."

"So can I, and I've got one and I don't intend to lose it." She softened the words with a smile. "Excuse me; I have work to do."

She turned to her shortwave and sent out a message to the patrol cars that Virginia Green had been found. Virginia Green's father heard it as he came in the door. He was a puffy gray-faced man with red-rimmed eyes. Striped pajama bottoms showed below the cuffs of his trousers. His shoes were muddy, and he walked as if he had been walking all night.

He supported himself on the edge of the counter, opening and shutting his mouth like a beached fish. Words came out, half strangled by shock.

"I heard you say she was dead, Anita."

The woman raised her eyes to his. "Yes. I'm awfully sorry, Mr. Green."

He put his face down on the counter and stayed there like a penitent, perfectly still. I could hear a clock somewhere, snipping off seconds, and in the back of the room the LA police signals, like muttering voices coming in from another planet. Another planet very much like this one, where violence measured out the hours.

"It's my fault," Green said to the bare wood under his face. "I didn't bring her up properly. I haven't been a good father."

The woman watched him with dark and glistening eyes ready to spill. She stretched out an unconscious hand to touch him, pulled her hand back in embarrassment when a second man came into the station. He was a young man with crew-cut brown hair, tanned and fit-looking in a Hawaiian shirt. Fit-looking except for the glare of sleeplessness in his eyes and the anxious lines around them.

"What is it, Miss Brocco? What's the word?"

"The word is bad." She sounded angry. "Somebody murdered Ginnie Green. This man here is a detective and he just found her body up in Trumbull Canyon."

The young man ran his fingers through his short hair and failed to get a grip on it, or on himself. "My God! That's terrible!"

"Yes," the woman said. "You were supposed to be looking after her, weren't you?"

They glared at each other across the counter. The young man lost the glaring match. He turned to me with a wilted look.

"My name is Connor, Franklin Connor, and I'm afraid I'm very much to blame in this. I'm a counselor at the high school, and I was supposed to be looking after the party, as Miss Brocco said."

"Why didn't you?"

"I didn't realize. I mean, I thought they were all perfectly happy and safe. The boys and girls had pretty well paired off around the fire. Frankly, I felt rather out of place. They aren't children, you know. They were all seniors, they had cars. So I said good night and walked home along the beach. As a matter of fact, I was hoping for a phone call from my wife."

"What time did you leave the party?"

"It must have been nearly eleven. The ones who hadn't paired off had already gone home."

"Who did Ginnie pair off with?"

"I don't know. I'm afraid I wasn't paying too much attention to the kids. It's graduation week, and I've had a lot of problems—"

The father, Green, had been listening with a changing face. In a sudden yammering rage his implosive grief and guilt exploded outward.

"It's your business to know! By God, I'll have your job for this. I'll make it *my* business to run you out of town."

Connor hung his head and looked at the stained tile floor. There was a thin spot in his short brown hair, and his scalp gleamed through it like bare white bone. It was turning into a bad day for everybody, and I felt the dull old nagging pull of other people's trouble, like a toothache you can't leave alone.

THE SHERIFF ARRIVED, flanked by several deputies and a highway patrol sergeant. He wore a western hat and a rawhide tie and a blue gabardine business suit. His name was Pearsall.

I rode back up the canyon in the right front seat of Pearsall's black Buick, filling him in on the way. The deputies' Ford and a highway patrol car followed us, and Green's new Oldsmobile convertible brought up the rear.

The sheriff said, "The old guy sounds like a loony to me."

"He's a loner, anyway."

"You never can tell about them hoboes. That's why I give my boys instructions to roust 'em. Well, it looks like an open-and-shut case."

"Maybe. Let's keep our minds open, anyway, Sheriff."

"Sure. Sure. But the old guy went on the run. That shows consciousness of guilt. Don't worry, we'll hunt him down. I got men that know these hills like you know your wife's geography."

"I'm not married."

"Your girl friend, then." He gave me a sideways leer that was no gift. "And if we can't find him on foot, we'll use the air squadron."

"You have an air squadron?"

"Volunteer, mostly local ranchers. We'll get him." His tires squealed on a curve. "Was the girl raped?"

"I didn't try to find out. I'm not a doctor. I left her as she was."

The sheriff grunted. "You did the right thing at that."

Nothing had changed in the high meadow. The girl lay waiting to have her picture taken. It was taken many times, from several angles. All the birds flew away. Her father leaned on a tree and watched them go. Later he was sitting on the ground.

I volunteered to drive him home. It wasn't pure altruism. I'm incapable of it. I said when I had turned his Oldsmobile, "Why did you say it was your fault, Mr. Green?"

He wasn't listening. Below the road four uniformed men were wrestling a heavy covered aluminum stretcher up the steep bank. Green watched them as he had watched the departing birds, until they were out of sight around a curve.

"She was so young," he said to the back seat.

I tried again. "Why did you blame yourself for her death?"

He roused himself from his daze. "Did I say that?"

"In the highway patrol office you said something of the sort."

He touched my arm. "I didn't mean I killed her."

"I didn't think you meant that. I'm interested in finding out who did."

"Are you a cop—a policeman?"

"I have been."

"You're not with the locals."

"No. I happen to be a private detective from Los Angeles. The name is Archer."

He sat and pondered this information. Below and ahead the summer sea brimmed up in the mouth of the canyon.

"You don't think the old tramp did her in?" Green said.

"It's hard to figure out how he could have. He's a strong-looking old buzzard, but he couldn't have carried her all the way up from the beach. And she wouldn't have come along with him of her own accord."

It was a question, in a way.

"I don't know," her father said. "Ginnie was a little wild. She'd do a thing *because* it was wrong, *because* it was dangerous. She hated to turn down a dare, especially from a man."

"There were men in her life?"

"She was attractive to men. You saw her, even as she is." He gulped. "Don't get me wrong. Ginnie was never a *bad* girl. She was a little headstrong, and I made mistakes. That's why I blame myself."

"What sort of mistakes, Mr. Green?"

"All the usual ones, and some I made up on my own." His voice was bitter. "Ginnie didn't have a mother, you see. Her mother left me years ago, and it was as much my fault as hers. I tried to bring her up myself. I didn't give her proper supervision. I run a restaurant in town, and I don't get home nights till after midnight. Ginnie was pretty much on her own since she was in grade school. We got along fine when I was there, but I usually wasn't there.

"The worst mistake I made was letting her work in the restaurant over the weekends. That started about a year ago. She wanted the money for clothes, and I thought the discipline would be good for her. I thought I could keep an eye on her, you know. But it didn't work out. She grew up too fast, and the night work played hell with her studies. I finally got the word from the school authorities. I fired her a couple of months ago, but I guess it was too late. We haven't been getting along too well since then. Mr. Connor said she resented my indecision, that I gave her too much responsibility and then took it away again."

"You've talked her over with Connor?"

"More than once, including last night. He was her academic counselor, and he was concerned about her grades. We both were. Ginnie finally pulled through, after all, thanks to him. She was going to graduate. Not that it matters now, of course."

Green was silent for a time. The sea expanded below us like a second blue dawn. I could hear the roar of the highway. Green touched my elbow again, as if he needed human contact.

"I oughtn't to've blown my top at Connor. He's a decent boy, he means well. He gave my daughter hours of free tuition this last month. And he's got troubles of his own, like he said."

"What troubles?"

"I happen to know his wife left him, same as mine. I shouldn't have borne down so hard on him. I have a lousy temper, always have had." He hesitated, then blurted out as if he had found a confessor, "I said a terrible thing to Ginnie at supper last night. She always has supper with me at the restaurant. I said if she wasn't home when I got home last night that I'd wring her neck."

"And she wasn't home," I said. And somebody wrung her neck, I didn't say.

THE LIGHT AT the highway was red. I glanced at Green. Tear tracks glistened like snail tracks on his face.

"Tell me what happened last night."

"There isn't anything much to tell," he said. "I got to the house about twelve thirty, and, like you said, she wasn't home. So I called Al Brocco's house. He's my night cook, and I knew his younger daughter,

Alice, was at the moonlight party on the beach. Alice was home all right."

"Did you talk to Alice?"

"She was in bed asleep. Al woke her up, but I didn't talk to her. She told him she didn't know where Ginnie was. I went to bed, but I couldn't sleep. Finally I got up and called Mr. Connor. That was about one thirty. I thought I should get in touch with the authorities, but he said no, Ginnie had enough black marks against her already. He came over to the house and we waited for a while and then we went down to Cavern Beach. There was no trace of her. I said it was time to call in the authorities, and he agreed. We went to his beach house, because it was nearer, and called the sheriff's office from there. We went back to the beach with a couple of flashlights and went through the caves. He stayed with me all night. I give him that."

"Where are these caves?"

"We'll pass them in a minute. I'll show you if you want. But there's nothing in any of the three of them."

Nothing but shadows, empty beer cans, and the odor of rotting kelp. I got sand in my shoes and sweat under my collar. The sun dazzled my eyes when I half walked, half crawled from the last of the caves.

Green was waiting beside a heap of ashes.

"This is where they had the wienie roast," he said.

I kicked the ashes. A half-burned sausage rolled along the sand. Sand fleas hopped in the sun like fat on a griddle. Green and I faced each other over the dead fire. He looked out to sea. A seal's face floated like a small black nose cone beyond the breakers. Farther out a water-skier slid between unfolding wings of spray.

Away up the beach two people were walking toward us. They were small and lonely and distinct as Chirico figures in the long white distance.

Green squinted against the sun. Red-rimmed or not, his eyes were good. "I believe that's Mr. Connor. I wonder who the woman is with him."

They were walking as close as lovers, just above the white margin of the surf. They pulled apart when they noticed us, but they were still holding hands as they approached.

"It's Mrs. Connor," Green said in a low voice.

"I thought you said she left him."

"That's what he told me last night. She took off on him a couple of weeks ago, couldn't stand a high school teacher's hours. She must have changed her mind."

She looked as though she had a mind to change. She was a hard-faced blonde who walked like a man. A certain amount of style took the curse off her stiff angularity. She had on a madras shirt, mannishly cut, and a pair of black Capri pants that hugged her long, slim legs. She had good legs.

Connor looked at us in complex embarrassment. "I thought it was you from a distance, Mr. Green. I don't believe you know my wife."

"I've seen her in my place of business." He explained to the woman, "I run the Highway Restaurant in town."

"How do you do," she said aloofly, then added in an entirely different voice, "You're Virginia's father, aren't you? I'm so sorry."

The words sounded queer. Perhaps it was the surroundings; the ashes on the beach, the entrances to the caves, the sea, and the empty sky, which dwarfed us all. Green answered her solemnly.

"Thank you, ma'am. Mr. Connor was a strong right arm to me last night. I can tell you." He was apologizing.

And Connor responded, "Why don't you come to our place for a drink? It's just down the beach. You look as if you could use one, Mr. Green. You, too," he said to me. "I don't believe I know your name."

"Archer. Lew Archer."

He gave me a hard hand. His wife interposed. "I'm sure Mr. Green and his friend won't want to be bothered with us on a day like this. Besides, it isn't even noon yet, Frank."

She was the one who didn't want to be bothered. We stood around for a minute, exchanging grim, nonsensical comments on the beauty of the day. Then she led Connor back in the direction they had come from. Private property, her attitude seemed to say. Trespassers will be fresh-frozen.

I drove Green to the highway patrol station. He said that he was feeling better and could make it home from there by himself. He thanked me profusely for being a friend in need to him, as he put it. He followed me to the door of the station, thanking me.

The dispatcher was cleaning her fingernails with an ivory-handled file. She glanced up eagerly.

"Did they catch him yet?"

"I was going to ask you the same question, Miss Brocco."

"No such luck. But they'll get him," she said with female vindictiveness. "The sheriff called out his air squadron, and he sent to Ventura for bloodhounds."

"Big deal."

She bridled. "What do you mean by that?"

"I don't think the old man of the mountain killed her. If he had, he wouldn't have waited till this morning to go on the lam. He'd have taken off right away."

"Then why did he go on the lam at all?" The word sounded strange in her prim mouth.

"I think he saw me discover the body and realized he'd be blamed."

She considered this, bending the long nail file between her fingers. "If the old tramp didn't do it, who did?"

"You may be able to help me answer that question."

"Me help you? How?"

"You know Frank Connor, for one thing."

"I know him. I've seen him about my sister's grades a few times."

"You don't seem to like him much."

"I don't like him, I don't dislike him. He's just blah to me."

"Why? What's the matter with him?"

Her tight mouth quivered and let out words. "*I* don't know what's the matter with him. He can't keep his hands off of young girls."

"How do you know that?"

"I heard it."

"From your sister, Alice?"

"Yes. The rumor was going around the school, she said."

"Did the rumor involve Ginnie Green?"

She nodded. Her eyes were as black as fingerprint ink.

"Is that why Connor's wife left him?"

"I wouldn't know about that. I never even laid eyes on Mrs. Connor."

"You haven't been missing much."

There was a yell outside, a kind of choked ululation. It sounded as much like an animal as a man. It was Green. When I reached the door, he was climbing out of his convertible with a heavy blue revolver in his hand.

"I saw the killer," he cried out exultantly.

"Where?"

He waved the revolver toward the lumberyard across the road. "He poked his head up behind that pile of white pine. When he saw me, he ran like a deer. I'm going to get him."

"No. Give me the gun."

"Why? I got a license to carry it. And use it."

He started across the four-lane highway, dodging through the moving patterns of the Sunday traffic as if he were playing Parcheesi on the kitchen table at home. The sounds of brakes and curses split the air. He had scrambled over the locked gate of the yard before I got to it. I went over after him.

GREEN DISAPPEARED BEHIND a pile of lumber. I turned the corner and saw him running halfway down a long aisle walled with stacked wood and floored with beaten earth. The old man was running ahead of him. His white hair blew in the wind of his own movement. A burlap sack bounced on his shoulders like a load of sorrow and shame.

"Stop or I'll shoot!" Green cried.

The old man ran on as if the devil himself were after him. He came to a cyclone fence, discarded his sack, and tried to climb it. He almost got over. Three strands of barbed wire along the top of the fence caught and held him struggling.

I heard a tearing sound, and then the sound of a shot. The huge old body espaliered on the fence twitched and went limp, fell heavily to the earth. Green stood over him breathing through his teeth.

I pushed him out of the way. The old man was alive, though there was blood in his mouth. He spat it onto his chin when I lifted his head.

"You shouldn't ought to of done it. I come to turn myself in. Then I got ascairt."

"Why were you scared?"

"I watched you uncover the little girl in the leaves. I knew I'd be blamed. I'm one of the chosen. They always blame the chosen. I been in trouble before."

"Trouble with girls?" At my shoulder Green was grinning terribly.

"Trouble with cops."

"For killing people?" Green said.

"For preaching on the street without a license. The voice told me to preach to the tribes of the wicked. And the voice told me this morning to come in and give my testimony."

"What voice?"

"The great voice." His voice was little and weak. He coughed red.

"He's as crazy as a bedbug," Green said.

"Shut up." I turned back to the dying man. "What testimony do you have to give?"

"About the car I seen. It woke me up in the middle of the night, stopped in the road below my sanctuary."

"What kind of car?"

"I don't know cars. I think it was one of them foreign cars. It made a noise to wake the dead."

"Did you see who was driving it?"

"No. I didn't go near. I was ascairt."

"What time was this car in the road?"

"I don't keep track of time. The moon was down behind the trees."

Those were his final words. He looked up at the sky with his sky-colored eyes, straight into the sun. His eyes changed color.

Green said, "Don't tell them. If you do, I'll make a liar out of you. I'm a respected citizen in this town. I got a business to lose. And they'll believe me ahead of you, mister."

"Shut up."

He couldn't. "The old fellow was lying, anyway. You know that. You heard him say yourself that he heard voices. That proves he's a psycho. He's a psycho killer. I shot him down like you would a mad dog, and I did right."

He waved the revolver.

"You did wrong, Green, and you know it. Give me that gun before it kills somebody else."

He thrust it into my hand suddenly. I unloaded it, breaking my fingernails in the process, and handed it back to him empty. He nudged up against me.

"Listen, maybe I did do wrong. I had provocation. It doesn't have to get out. I got a business to lose."

He fumbled in his hip pocket and brought out a thick sharkskin wallet. "Here. I can pay you good money. You say that you're a private eye; you know how to keep your lip buttoned."

I walked away and left him blabbering beside the body of the man he had killed. They were both victims, in a sense, but only one of them had blood on his hands.

Miss Brocco was in the highway patrol parking lot. Her bosom was jumping with excitement.

"I heard a shot."

"Green shot the old man. Dead. You better send in for the meat wagon and call off your bloody dogs."

The words hit her like slaps. She raised her hand to her face defensively. "Are you mad at me? Why are you mad at me?"

"I'm mad at everybody."

"You still don't think he did it."

"I know damned well he didn't. I want to talk to your sister."

"Alice? What for?"

"Information. She was on the beach with Ginnie Green last night. She may be able to tell me something."

"You leave Alice alone."

"I'll treat her gently. Where do you live?"

"I don't want my little sister dragged into this filthy mess."

"All I want to know is who Ginnie paired off with."

"I'll ask Alice. I'll tell you."

"Come on, Miss Brocco, we're wasting time. I don't need your permission to talk to your sister, after all. I can get the address out of the phone book if I have to."

She flared up and then flared down.

"You win. We live on Orlando Street, Two twenty-four. That's on the other side of town. You will be nice to Alice, won't you? She's bothered enough as it is about Ginnie's death."

"She really was a friend of Ginnie's, then?"

"Yes. I tried to break it up. But you know how kids are—two motherless girls, they stick together. I tried to be like a mother to Alice."

"What happened to your own mother?"

"Father— I mean, she died." A greenish pallor invaded her face and turned it to old bronze. "Please. I don't want to talk about it. I was only a kid when she died."

She went back to her muttering radios. She was quite a woman, I thought, as I drove away. Nubile but unmarried, probably full of untapped Mediterranean passions. If she worked an eight-hour shift and started at eight, she'd be getting off about four.

It wasn't a large town, and it wasn't far across it. The highway doubled as its main street. I passed the Union High School. On the green playing field beside it a lot of kids in mortarboards and gowns were rehearsing their graduation exercises. A kind of pall seemed to hang over the field. Perhaps it was in my mind.

Farther along the street I passed Green's Highway Restaurant. A dozen cars stood in its parking space. A couple of white-uniformed waitresses were scooting around behind the plate glass windows.

Orlando Street was a lower-middle-class residential street bisected by the highway. Jacaranda trees bloomed like low small purple clouds among its stucco and frame cottages. Fallen purple petals carpeted the narrow lawn in front of the Brocco house.

A thin, dark man, wiry under his T-shirt, was washing a small red Fiat in the driveway beside the front porch. He must have been over fifty, but his long hair was as black as an Indian's. His Sicilian nose was humped in the middle by an old break.

"Mr. Brocco?"

"That's me."

"Is your daughter Alice home?"

"She's home."

"I'd like to speak to her."

He turned off his hose, pointing its dripping nozzle at me like a gun.

"You're a little old for her, ain't you?"

"I'm a detective investigating the death of Ginnie Green."

"Alice don't know nothing about that."

"I've just been talking to your older daughter at the highway patrol office. She thinks Alice may know something."

He shifted on his feet. "Well, if Anita says it's all right."

"It's okay, Dad," a girl said from the front door. "Anita just called me on the telephone. Come in, Mr.—Archer, isn't it?"

"Archer."

SHE OPENED THE screen door for me. It opened directly into a small square living room containing worn green frieze furniture and a television set, which the girl switched off. She was a handsome, serious-looking girl, a younger version of her sister with ten years and ten pounds subtracted and a ponytail added. She sat down gravely on the edge of a chair, waving her hand at the chesterfield. Her movements were languid. There were blue depressions under her eyes. Her face was sallow.

"What kind of questions do you want to ask me? My sister didn't say."

"Who was Ginnie with last night?"

"Nobody. I mean, she was with me. She didn't make out with any of the boys." She glanced from me to the blind television set, as if she felt caught between. "It said on the television that she was with a man, that there was medical evidence to prove it. But I didn't see her with no man. Any man."

"Did Ginnie go with men?"

She shook her head. Her ponytail switched and hung limp. She was close to tears.

"You told Anita she did."

"I did not!"

"Your sister wouldn't lie. You passed on a rumor to her—a high school rumor that Ginnie had had something to do with one man in particular."

The girl was watching my face in fascination. Her eyes were like a bird's, bright and shallow and fearful.

"Was the rumor true?"

She shrugged her thin shoulders. "How would I know?"

"You were good friends with Ginnie."

"Yes. I was." Her voice broke on the past tense. "She was a real nice kid, even if she was kind of boy crazy."

"She was boy crazy, but she didn't make out with any of the boys last night?"

"Not while I was there."

"Did she make out with Mr. Connor?"

"No. He wasn't there. He went away. He said he was going home. He lives up the beach."

"What did Ginnie do?"

"I don't know. I didn't notice."

"You said she was with you. Was she with you all evening?"

"Yes." Her face was agonized. "I mean no."

"Did Ginnie go away, too?"

She nodded.

"In the same direction Mr. Connor took? The direction of his house?"

Her head moved almost imperceptibly downward.

"What time was that, Alice?"

"About eleven o'clock, I guess."

"And Ginnie never came back from Mr. Connor's house?"

"I don't know. I don't know for certain that she went there."

"But Ginnie and Mr. Connor were good friends?"

"I guess so."

"How good? Like a boy friend and a girl friend?"

She sat mute, her birdlike stare unblinking.

"Tell me, Alice."

"I'm afraid."

"Afraid of Mr. Connor?"

"No. Not him."

"Has someone threatened you—told you not to talk?"

Her head moved in another barely perceptible nod.

"Who threatened you, Alice? You'd better tell me for your own protection. Whoever did threaten you is probably a murderer."

She burst into frantic tears. Brocco came to the door.

"What goes on in here?"

"Your daughter is upset. I'm sorry."

"Yeah, and I know who upset her. You better get out of here or you'll be sorrier."

He opened the screen door and held it open, his head poised like a dark and broken axe. I went out past him. He spat after me. The Broccos were a very emotional family.

I started back toward Connor's beach house, on the south side of town, but ran into a diversion on the way. Green's car was parked in the lot beside his restaurant. I went in.

The place smelled of grease. It was almost full of late Sunday lunchers seated in booths and at the U-shaped breakfast bar in the middle. Green himself was sitting on a stool behind the cash register, counting money. He was counting it as if his life and his hope of heaven depended on the colored paper in his hands.

He looked up, smiling loosely and vaguely. "Yes, sir?" Then he recognized me. His face went through a quick series of transformations and settled for a kind of boozy shame. "I know I shouldn't be here working on a day like this. But it keeps my mind off my troubles. Besides, they steal you blind if you don't watch 'em. And I'll be needing the money."

"What for, Mr. Green?"

"The trial." He spoke the word as if it gave him a bitter satisfaction.

"Whose trial?"

"Mine. I told the sheriff what the old guy said. And what I did. I know what I did. I shot him down like a dog, and I had no right to. I was crazy with my sorrow, you might say."

He was less crazy now. The shame in his eyes was clearing. But the sorrow was there in their depths, like a stone at the bottom of a well.

"I'm glad you told the truth, Mr. Green."

"So am I. It doesn't help him, and it doesn't bring Ginnie back. But at least I can live with myself."

"Speaking of Ginnie," I said. "Was she seeing quite a lot of Frank Connor?"

"Yeah, I guess you could say so. He came over to help her with her studies quite a few times. At the house, and at the library. He didn't charge me any tuition, either."

"That was nice of him. Was Ginnie fond of Connor?"

"Sure she was. She thought very highly of Mr. Connor."

"Was she in love with him?"

"In love? Hell, I never thought of anything like that. Why?"

"Did she have dates with Connor?"

"Not to my knowledge," he said. "If she did, she must have done it behind my back." His eyes narrowed to two red swollen slits. "You think Frank Connor had something to do with her death?"

"It's a possibility. Don't go into a sweat now. You know where that gets you."

"Don't worry. But what about this Connor? Did you get something on him? I thought he was acting queer last night."

"Queer in what way?"

"Well, he was pretty tight when he came to the house. I gave him a stiff snort, and that straightened him out for a while. But later on, down on the beach, he got almost hysterical. He was running around like a rooster with his head chopped off."

"Is he a heavy drinker?"

"I wouldn't know. I never saw him drink before last night at my house." Green narrowed his eyes. "But he tossed down a triple bourbon like it was water. And remember this morning, he offered us a drink on the beach. A drink in the morning, that isn't the usual thing, especially for a high school teacher."

"I noticed that."

"What else have you been noticing?"

"We won't go into it now," I said. "I don't want to ruin a man unless and until I'm sure he's got it coming."

He sat on his stool with his head down. Thought moved murkily under his knitted brows. His glance fell on the money in his hands. He was counting tens.

"Listen, Mr. Archer. You're working on this case on your own, aren't you? For free?"

"So far."

"So go to work for me. Nail Connor for me, and I'll pay you whatever you ask."

"Not so fast," I said. "We don't know that Connor is guilty. There are other possibilities."

"Such as?"

"If I tell you, can I trust you not to go on a shooting spree?"

"Don't worry," he repeated. "I've had that."

"Where's your revolver?"

"I turned it in to Sheriff Pearsall. He asked for it."

We were interrupted by a family group getting up from one of the booths. They gave Green their money and their sympathy. When they were out of hearing, I said, "You mentioned that your daughter worked here in the restaurant for a while. Was Al Brocco working here at the same time?"

"Yeah. He's been my night cook for six, seven years. Al is a darned good cook. He trained as a chef on the Italian Line." His slow mind, punchy with grief, did a double take. "You wouldn't be saying that he messed around with Ginnie?"

"I'm asking you."

"Shucks, Al is old enough to be her father. He's all wrapped up in his own girls, Anita in particular. He worships the ground she walks on. She's the mainspring of that family."

"How did he get on with Ginnie?"

"Very well. They kidded back and forth. She was the only one who could ever make him smile. Al is a sad man, you know. He had a tragedy in his life."

"His wife's death?"

"It was worse than that," Green said. "Al Brocco killed his wife with his own hand. He caught her with another man and put a knife in her."

"And he's walking around loose?"

"The other man was a Mex," Green said in an explanatory way. "A wetback. He couldn't even talk the English language. The town hardly blamed Al, the jury gave him manslaughter. But when he got out of the pen, the people at the Pink Flamingo wouldn't give him his old job back—he used to be chef there. So I took him on. I felt sorry for his girls, I guess, and Al's been a good worker. A man doesn't do a thing like that twice, you know."

He did another slow mental double take. His mouth hung open. I could see the gold in its corners.

"Let's hope not."

"Listen here," he said. "You go to work for me, eh? You nail the guy, whoever he is. I'll pay you now. How much do you want?"

I took a hundred dollars of his money and left him trying to comfort himself with the rest of it. The smell of grease stayed in my nostrils.

CONNOR'S HOUSE CLUNG to the edge of a low bluff about halfway between the highway patrol station and the mouth of the canyon where the thing had begun: a semicantilevered redwood cottage with a closed double garage fronting the highway. From the grape-stake-fenced patio in the angle between the garage and the front door a flight of wooden steps climbed to the flat roof, which was railed as a sun deck. A second set of steps descended the fifteen or twenty feet to the beach.

I tripped on a pair of garden shears crossing the patio to the garage window. I peered into the interior twilight. Two things inside interested me: a dismasted flattie sitting on a trailer, and a car. The sailboat interested me because its cordage resembled the white rope that had strangled Ginnie. The car interested me because it was an imported model, a low-slung Triumph two-seater.

I was planning to have a closer look at it when a woman's voice screeked overhead like a gull's:

"What do you think you're doing?"

Mrs. Connor was leaning over the railing on the roof. Her hair was in curlers. She looked like a blond Gorgon. I smiled up at her, the way that Greek whose name I don't remember must have smiled.

"Your husband invited me for a drink, remember? I don't know whether he gave me a rain check or not."

"He did not! Go away! My husband is sleeping!"

"Ssh. You'll wake him up. You'll wake up the people in Forest Lawn."

She put her hand to her mouth. From the expression on her face she seemed to be biting her hand. She disappeared for a moment, and then came down the steps with a multicolored silk scarf over her curlers. The rest of her was sheathed in a white satin bathing suit. Against it her flesh looked like brown wood.

"You get out of here," she said. "Or I shall call the police."

"Fine. Call them. I've got nothing to hide."

"Are you implying that we have?"

"We'll see. Why did you leave your husband?"

"That's none of your business."

"I'm making it my business, Mrs. Connor. I'm a detective investigating the murder of Ginnie Green. Did you leave Frank on account of Ginnie Green?"

"No. No! I wasn't even aware—" Her hand went to her mouth again. She chewed on it some more.

"You weren't aware that Frank was having an affair with Ginnie Green?"

"He wasn't."

"So you say. Others say different."

"What others? Anita Brocco? You can't believe anything *that* woman says. Why, her own father is a murderer, everybody in town knows that."

"Your own husband may be another, Mrs. Connor. You might as well come clean with me."

"But I have nothing to tell you."

"You can tell me why you left him."

"That is a private matter, between Frank and me. It has nothing to do with anybody but us." She was calming down, setting her moral forces in a stubborn, defensive posture.

"There's usually only the one reason."

"I had my reasons. I said they were none of your business. I chose for reasons of my own to spend a month with my parents in Long Beach."

"When did you come back?"

"This morning."

"Why this morning?"

"Frank called me. He said he needed me." She touched her thin breast absently, pathetically, as if perhaps she hadn't been much needed in the past.

"Needed you for what?"

"As his wife," she said. "He said there might be tr—" Her hand went to her mouth again. She said around it, "Trouble."

"Did he name the kind of trouble?"

"No."

"What time did he call you?"

"Very early, around seven o'clock."

"That was more than an hour before I found Ginnie's body."

"He knew she was missing. He spent the whole night looking for her."

"Why would he do that, Mrs. Connor?"

"She was his student. He was fond of her. Besides, he was more or less responsible for her."

"Responsible for her death?"

"How dare you say a thing like that!"

"If he dared to do it, I can dare to say it."

"He didn't!" she cried. "Frank is a good man. He may have his faults, but he wouldn't kill anyone. I know him."

"What are his faults?"

"We won't discuss them."

"Then may I have a look in your garage?"

"What for? What are you looking for?"

"I'll know when I find it." I turned toward the garage door.

"You mustn't go in there," she said intensely. "Not without Frank's permission."

"Wake him up and we'll get his permission."

"I will not. He got no sleep last night."

"Then I'll just have a look without his permission."

"I'll kill you if you go in there."

She picked up the garden shears and brandished them at me—a sick-looking lioness defending her overgrown cub. The cub himself opened the front door of the cottage. He slouched in the doorway groggily, naked except for white shorts.

"What goes on, Stella?"

"This man has been making the most horrible accusations."

His blurred glance wavered between us and focused on her. "What did he say?"

"I won't repeat it."

"I will, Mr. Connor. I think you were Ginnie Green's lover, if that's the word. I think she followed you to this house last night, around midnight. I think she left it with a rope around her neck."

Connor's head jerked. He started to make a move in my direction. Something inhibited it, like an invisible leash. His body slanted toward me, static, all the muscles taut. It resembled an anatomy specimen with the skin off. Even his face seemed mostly bone and teeth.

I hoped he'd swing on me and let me hit him. He didn't. Stella Connor dropped the garden shears. They made a noise like the dull clank of doom.

"Aren't you going to deny it, Frank?"

"I didn't kill her. I swear I didn't. I admit that we—that we were together last night, Ginnie and I."

"Ginnie and I?" the woman repeated incredulously.

His head hung down. "I'm sorry, Stella. I didn't want to hurt you more than I have already. But it has to come out. I took up with the girl after you left. I was lonely and feeling sorry for myself. Ginnie kept hanging around. One night I drank too much and let it happen. It happened more than once. I was so flattered that a pretty young girl—"

"You fool!" she said in a deep, harsh voice.

"Yes, I'm a moral fool. That's no surprise to you, is it?"

"I thought you respected your pupils, at least. You mean to say you brought her into our own house, into our own bed?"

"You'd left. It wasn't ours anymore. Besides, she came of her own accord. She wanted to come. She loved me."

She said with grinding contempt, "You poor, groveling ninny. And to think you had the gall to ask me to come back here, to make you look respectable."

I cut in between them. "Was she here last night, Connor?"

"She was here. I didn't invite her. I wanted her to come, but I dreaded it, too. I knew that I was taking an awful chance. I drank quite a bit to numb my conscience—"

"What conscience?" Stella Connor said.

"I have a conscience," he said without looking at her. "You don't know the hell I've been going through. After she came, after it happened last night, I drank myself unconscious."

"Do you mean after you killed her?" I said.

"I didn't kill her. When I passed out, she was perfectly all right. She was sitting up drinking a cup of instant coffee. The next thing I knew, hours later, her father was on the telephone and she was gone."

"Are you trying to pull the old blackout alibi? You'll have to do better than that."

"I can't. It's the truth."

"Let me into your garage."

He seemed almost glad to be given an order, a chance for some activity. The garage wasn't locked. He raised the overhead door and let the daylight into the interior. It smelled of paint. There were empty cans of marine paint on a bench beside the sailboat. Its hull gleamed virgin white.

"I painted my flattie last week," he said inconsequentially.

"You do a lot of sailing?"

"I used to. Not much lately."

"No," his wife said from the doorway. "Frank changed his hobby to women. Wine and women."

"Lay off, eh?" His voice was pleading.

She looked at him from a great and stony silence.

I WALKED AROUND THE boat, examining the cordage. The starboard jib line had been sheared off short. Comparing it with the port line, I found that the missing piece was approximately a yard long. That was the length of the piece of white rope that I was interested in.

"Hey!" Connor grabbed the end of the cut line. He fingered it as if it were a wound in his own flesh. "Who's been messing with my lines? Did you cut it, Stella?"

"I never go near your blessed boat," she said.

"I can tell you where the rest of that line is, Connor. A line of similar length and color and thickness was wrapped around Ginnie Green's neck when I found her."

"Surely you don't believe I put it there?"

I tried to, but I couldn't. Small-boat sailors don't cut their jib lines, even when they're contemplating murder. And while Connor was clearly no genius, he was smart enough to have known that the line could easily be traced to him. Perhaps someone else had been equally smart.

I turned to Mrs. Connor. She was standing in the doorway with her legs apart. Her body was almost black against the daylight. Her eyes were hooded by the scarf on her head.

"What time did you get home, Mrs. Connor?"

"About ten o'clock this morning. I took a bus as soon as my husband called. But I'm in no position to give him an alibi."

"An alibi wasn't what I had in mind. I suggest another possibility, that you came home twice. You came home unexpectedly last night, saw the girl in the house with your husband, waited in the dark till the girl came out, waited with a piece of rope in your hands—a piece of rope you'd cut from your husband's boat in the hope of getting him punished for what he'd done to you. But the picture doesn't fit the frame, Mrs. Connor. A sailor like your husband wouldn't cut a piece of line from his own boat. And even in the heat of murder he wouldn't tie a granny knot. His fingers would automatically tie a reef knot. That isn't true of a woman's fingers."

She held herself upright with one long, rigid arm against the doorframe.

"I wouldn't do anything like that. I wouldn't do that to Frank."

"Maybe you wouldn't in daylight, Mrs. Connor. Things have different shapes at midnight."

"And hell hath no fury like a woman scorned? Is that what you're thinking? You're wrong. Last night I was in bed in my father's house in Long Beach. I didn't even know about that girl and Frank."

"Then why did you leave him?"

"He was in love with another woman. He wanted to divorce me and marry her. But he was afraid—afraid that it would affect his position in town. He told me on the phone this morning that it was all over with the other woman. So I agreed to come back to him." Her arm dropped to her side.

"He said that it was all over with Ginnie?"

Possibilities were racing through my mind. There was the possibility that Connor had been playing reverse English, deliberately and clumsily framing himself in order to be cleared. But that was out of far left field.

"Not Ginnie," his wife said. "The other woman was Anita Brocco. He met her last spring in the course of work and fell in love—what *he* calls love. My husband is a foolish, fickle man."

"Please, Stella. I said that it was all over between me and Anita, and it is."

She turned on him in quiet savagery. "What does it matter now? If it isn't one girl it's another. Any kind of female flesh will do to poultice your sick little ego."

Her cruelty struck inward and hurt her. She stretched out her hand toward him. Suddenly her eyes were blind with tears.

"Any flesh but mine, Frank," she said brokenly.

Connor paid no attention to his wife. He said to me in a hushed voice, "My God, I never thought. I noticed her car last night when I was walking home along the beach."

"Whose car?"

"Anita's red Fiat. It was parked at the viewpoint a few hundred yards from here." He gestured vaguely toward town. "Later, when Ginnie was with me, I thought I heard someone in the garage. But I was too drunk to make a search." His eyes burned into mine. "You say a woman tied that knot?"

"All we can do is ask her."

We started toward my car together. His wife called after him, "Don't go, Frank. Let him handle it."

He hesitated, a weak man caught between opposing forces.

"I need you," she said. "We need each other."

I pushed him in her direction.

IT WAS NEARLY four when I got to the highway patrol station. The police cars had gathered like homing pigeons for the change in shift. Their uniformed drivers were talking and laughing inside.

Anita Brocco wasn't among them. A male dispatcher, a fat-faced man with pimples, had taken her place behind the counter.

"Where's Miss Brocco?" I asked.

"She's in the ladies' room. Her father is coming to pick her up any minute."

She came out wearing lipstick and a light beige coat. Her face turned beige when she saw my face. She came toward me in slow motion, leaned with both hands flat on the counter. Her lipstick looked like fresh blood on a corpse.

"You're a handsome woman, Anita. Too bad about you."

"Too bad." It was half a statement and half a question. She looked down at her hands.

"Your fingernails are clean now. They were dirty this morning. You were digging in the dirt last night, weren't you?"

"No."

"You were, though. You saw them together and you couldn't stand it. You waited in ambush with a rope, and put it around her neck. Around your own neck, too."

She touched her neck. The talk and laughter had subsided around us. I could hear the tick of the clock again, and the muttering signals coming in from inner space.

"What did you use to cut the rope with, Anita? The garden shears?"

Her red mouth groped for words and found them. "I was crazy about him. She took him away. It was all over before it started. I didn't know what to do with myself. I wanted him to suffer."

"He's suffering. He's going to suffer more."

"He deserves to. He was the only man—" She shrugged in a twisted way and looked down at her breast. "I didn't want to kill her, but when I saw them together—I saw them through the window. I saw her take off her clothes and put them on. Then I thought of the night my father—when he—when there was all the blood in Mother's bed. I had to wash it out of the sheets."

The men around me were murmuring. One of them, a sergeant, raised his voice.

"Did you kill Ginnie Green?"

"Yes."

"Are you ready to make a statement?" I said.

"Yes. I'll talk to Sheriff Pearsall. I don't want to talk here, in front of my friends." She looked around doubtfully.

"I'll take you downtown."

"Wait a minute." She glanced once more at her empty hands. "I left my purse in the—in the back room. I'll go and get it."

She crossed the office like a zombie, opened a plain door, closed it behind her. She didn't come out. After a while we broke the lock and went in after her.

Her body was cramped on the narrow floor. The ivory-handled nail file lay by her right hand. There were bloody holes in her white blouse and in the white breast under it. One of them had gone in as deep as her heart.

Later Al Brocco drove up in her red Fiat and came into the station.

"I'm a little late," he said to the room in general. "Anita wanted me to give her car a good cleaning. Where is she, anyway?"

The sergeant cleared his throat to answer Brocco.

All us poor creatures, as the old man of the mountain had said that morning.

THE RETURN OF IMRAY

RUDYARD KIPLING

IMRAY ACHIEVED THE impossible. Without warning, for no conceivable motive, in his youth, at the threshold of his career he chose to disappear from the world—which is to say, the little Indian station where he lived.

One day he was alive, well, happy, and in great evidence among the billiard tables at his club. The next morning he was not, and no manner of search could make sure where he might be. He had stepped out of his place; he had not appeared at his office at the proper time, and his dogcart was not upon the public roads. For these reasons, and because he was hampering, in a microscopic degree, the administration of the Indian empire, that empire paused for one microscopic moment to make inquiry into the fate of Imray. Ponds were dragged, wells were plumbed, telegrams were dispatched down the lines of railways and to the nearest seaport town—twelve hundred miles away; but Imray was not at the end of the dragropes or the telegraph wires. He was gone, and his place knew him no more. Then the work of the great Indian empire swept forward, because it could not be delayed, and Imray from being a man became a mystery—such a thing as men talk over at their tables in the club for a month, and then forget utterly. His guns, horses, and carts were sold to the highest bidder. His superior officer wrote an altogether absurd letter to his mother, saying that Imray had unaccountably disappeared, and his bungalow stood empty.

After three or four months of the scorching hot weather had gone by, my friend Strickland, of the police, saw fit to rent the bungalow from the native landlord. This was while he was pursuing his investigations into native life. His own life was sufficiently peculiar, and men complained of his manners and customs. There was always food in his house, but there were no regular times for meals. He ate, standing up and walking about, whatever he might find at the sideboard, and this is not good for human beings. His domestic equipment was limited to six rifles, three shotguns, five saddles, and a collection of stiff-jointed mahseer rods, bigger and stronger than the largest salmon rods. These occupied one half of his bungalow, and the other half was given up to Strickland and his dog, Tietjens—an enormous Rampur slut who devoured daily the rations of two men. She spoke to Strickland in a language of her own; and whenever, walking abroad, she saw things calculated to destroy the peace of Her Majesty the Queen-Empress, she returned to her master and conveyed the information to him. Strickland would take steps at once, and the end of his labors was trouble and fine and imprisonment for other people. The natives believed that Tietjens was a familiar spirit, and treated her with the great reverence that is born of hate and fear. One room in the bungalow was set apart for her special use. She owned a bedstead, a blanket, and a drinking trough, and if anyone came into Strickland's room at night, her custom was to knock down the invader and give tongue till someone came with a light. Strickland owed his life to her when he was on the frontier in search of a local murderer, who came in the gray dawn to send Strickland much farther than the Andaman Islands. Tietjens caught the man as he was crawling into Strickland's tent with a dagger between his teeth; and after his record of iniquity was established in the eyes of the law, he was hanged. From that date Tietjens wore a collar of rough silver and employed a monogram on her night blanket.

Under no circumstances would she be separated from Strickland; and once, when he was ill with fever, made great trouble for the doctors, because she did not know how to help her master and would not allow another creature to attempt aid. Macarnaght, of the Indian medical service, beat her over her head with a gun butt before she could understand that she must give room for those who could give quinine.

A short time after Strickland had taken Imray's bungalow, my business took me through that station, and naturally, the club quarters being full, I quartered myself upon Strickland. It was a desirable bungalow, eight-roomed and heavily thatched against any chance of leakage from rain. Under the pitch of the roof ran a ceiling cloth, which looked just as neat as a whitewashed ceiling. The landlord had repainted the bungalow when Strickland took it. Unless you knew how Indian bungalows were built, you would never have suspected that above the cloth lay the dark three-cornered cavern of the attic, where the beams and the thatch harbored all manner of rats, bats, ants, and foul things.

Tietjens met me in the veranda with a bay like the boom of the bell of St. Paul's, putting her paws on my shoulder to show she was glad to see me. Strickland had contrived to claw together a sort of meal which he called lunch, and immediately after it was finished went out about his business. I was left alone with Tietjens and my own affairs. The heat of the summer had broken up and turned to the warm damp of the rains. There was no motion in the heated air, but the rain fell like ramrods on the earth, and flung up a blue mist when it splashed back. The bamboos, and the custard apples, the poinsettias, and the mango trees in the garden stood still while the warm water lashed through them, and the frogs began to sing among the aloe hedges. A little before the light failed, and when the rain was at its worst, I sat in the back veranda and heard the water roar from the eaves, and scratched myself because I was covered with the thing called prickly heat. Tietjens came out with me and put her head in my lap and was very sorrowful; so I gave her biscuits when tea was ready, and I took tea in the back veranda on account of the little coolness found there. The rooms of the house were dark behind me. I could smell Strickland's saddlery and the oil on his guns, and I had no desire to sit among these things. My own servant came to me in the twilight, the muslin of his clothes clinging tightly to his drenched body, and told me that a gentleman had called and wished to see someone. Very much against my will, but only because of the darkness of the rooms, I went into the naked drawing room, telling my man to bring the lights. There might or might not have been a caller waiting—it seemed to me that I saw a figure by one of the windows—but when the lights came, there was nothing save the spikes of the rain without, and the smell of the drinking earth in my nostrils. I went back to the veranda to talk to Tietjens. She had gone out into the wet, and I could hardly coax her back to me, even with biscuits with sugar tops.

Strickland came home, dripping wet, just before dinner, and the first thing he said was, "Has anyone called?"

I explained, with apologies, that my servant had summoned me into the drawing room on a false alarm; or that some loafer had tried to call on Strickland, and thinking better of it, had fled without giving his name. Strickland ordered dinner without comment, and since it was a real dinner with a white tablecloth, we sat down.

At nine o'clock Strickland wanted to go to bed, and I was tired too. Tietjens, who had been lying underneath the table, rose up and swung into the least exposed veranda as soon as her master moved to his own room, which was next to the stately chamber set apart for Tietjens. I looked at Strickland, expecting to see him flay her with a whip. He smiled queerly. "She has done this ever since I moved in here," said he. "Let her go."

The dog was Strickland's dog, so I said nothing, but I felt all that Strickland felt in being thus made light of. Tietjens encamped outside my bedroom window, and storm after storm came up, thundered on the thatch, and died away. The lightning spattered the sky as a thrown egg spatters a barn door, but the light was pale blue, not yellow; and looking through my split-bamboo blinds, I could see the great dog standing, not sleeping, in the veranda, the hackles alift on her back, and her feet anchored as tensely as the drawn wire rope of a suspension bridge. In the very short pauses of the thunder I tried to sleep, but it seemed that someone wanted me very urgently. He, whoever he was, was trying to call me by name, but his voice was no more than a husky whisper. The thunder ceased, and Tietjens went into the garden and howled at the low moon. Somebody tried to open my door, walked about and about through the house, and stood breathing heavily in the verandas, and just when I was falling asleep I fancied that I heard a wild hammering and clamoring above my head or on the door.

I ran into Strickland's room and asked him whether he was ill and had been calling for me. He was lying on his bed half dressed, a pipe in his mouth. "I thought you'd come," he said. "Have I been walking round the house recently?"

I explained that he had been tramping in the dining room and the smoking room and two or three other places; and he laughed and told me to go back to bed. I went back to bed and slept till the morning, but through all my mixed dreams I was sure I was doing someone an injustice in not attending to his wants. What those wants were I could not tell; but a fluttering, whispering, bolt-fumbling, lurking, loitering Someone was reproaching me for my slackness.

I lived in that house for two days. Strickland went to his office daily, leaving me alone for eight or ten hours with Tietjens for my only companion. As long as the full light lasted I was comfortable, and so was Tietjens; but in the twilight she and I moved into the back veranda and cuddled each other for company. We were alone in the house, but nonetheless it was much too fully occupied by a tenant with whom I did not wish to interfere. I never saw him, but I could see the curtains between the rooms quivering where he had just passed through; I could hear the chairs creaking as the bamboos sprang under a weight that had just quitted them; and I could feel when I went to get a book from the dining room that somebody was waiting in the shadows of the front veranda till I should have gone away. Tietjens made the twilight more interesting by glaring into the darkened rooms with every hair erect, and following the motions of something that I could not see. She never entered the rooms, but her eyes moved interestedly; that was quite sufficient. Only when my servant came to trim the lamps and make all light and habitable would she come in with me and spend her time sitting on her haunches, watching an invisible extra man as he moved about behind my shoulder. Dogs are cheerful companions.

I explained to Strickland, gently as might be, that I would go over to the club and find quarters for myself there. I admired his hospitality, was pleased with his guns and rods, but I did not much care for his house and its atmosphere. He heard me out to the end and then smiled very wearily, but without contempt, for he is a man who understands things. "Stay on," he said, "and see what this thing means. All you have talked about I have known since I took the bungalow. Stay on and wait. Tietjens has left me. Are you going too?"

I had seen him through one little affair, connected with a heathen idol, that had brought me to the doors of a lunatic asylum, and I had no desire to help him through further experiences. He was a man to whom unpleasantness arrived as do dinners to ordinary people.

Therefore I explained more clearly than ever that I liked him immensely and would be happy to see him in the daytime, but that I did not care to sleep under his roof. This was after dinner, when Tietjens had gone out to lie in the veranda.

"'Pon my soul, I don't wonder," said Strickland, with his eyes on the ceiling cloth. "Look at that!"

The tails of two brown snakes were hanging between the cloth and the cornice of the wall. They threw long shadows in the lamplight.

"If you are afraid of snakes, of course . . ." said Strickland.

I hate and fear snakes, because if you look into the eyes of any snake you will see that it knows all and more of the mystery of man's fall, and that it feels all the contempt that the Devil felt when Adam was evicted from Eden.

"You ought to get your thatch overhauled," I said. "Give me a mahseer rod and we'll poke 'em down."

"They'll hide among the roof beams," said Strickland. "I can't stand snakes overhead. I'm going up into the roof. If I shake 'em down, stand by with a broom and break their backs."

I was not anxious to assist Strickland in his work, but I took the broom and waited in the dining room, while Strickland brought a gardener's ladder from the veranda and set it against the side of the room. The snake tails drew themselves up and disappeared. We could hear the dry rushing scuttle of long bodies running over the baggy ceiling cloth. Strickland took a lamp with him, while I tried to make clear to him the danger of hunting roof snakes between a ceiling cloth and a thatch, apart from the deterioration of property caused by ripping out ceiling cloths.

"Nonsense!" said Strickland. "They're sure to hide near the walls by the cloth. The bricks are too cold for 'em, and the heat of the room is just what they like." He put his hand to the corner of the stuff and ripped it from the cornice. It gave with a great sound of tearing, and Strickland put his head through the opening into the dark of the angle of the roof beams. I set my teeth and lifted the broom, for I had not the least knowledge of what might descend.

"H'm!" said Strickland, and his voice rolled and rumbled in the roof. "There's room for another set of rooms up here, and, by Jove, someone is occupying 'em!"

"Snakes?" I said from below.

"No. It's a buffalo. Hand me up the two last joints of a mahseer rod and I'll prod it. It's lying on the main roof beam."

I handed up the rod.

"What a nest for owls and serpents! No wonder the snakes live here," said Strickland, climbing farther into the roof. I could see his elbow thrusting with the rod. "Come out of that, whoever you are! Heads below there! It's falling."

I saw the ceiling cloth nearly in the center of the room sag with a shape that was pressing it downward and downward toward the lighted lamp on the table. I snatched the lamp out of danger and stood back. Then the cloth ripped out from the walls, tore, split, swayed, and shot down upon the table something that I dared not look at, till Strickland had slid down the ladder and was standing by my side.

He did not say much, being a man of few words, but he picked up the end of the tablecloth and threw it over the remnants on the table.

"It strikes me," said he, putting down the lamp, "our friend Imray has come back. Oh! You would, would you?"

There was a movement under the cloth, and a little snake wriggled out, to be backbroken by the butt of the mahseer rod.

Strickland meditated, and helped himself to drinks. The arrangement under the cloth made no more signs of life.

"Is it Imray?" I said.

Strickland turned back the cloth for a moment and looked.

"It is Imray," he said, "and his throat is cut from ear to ear."

Then we spoke, both together and to ourselves. "That's why he whispered about the house."

Tietjens, in the garden, began to bay furiously. A little later her great nose heaved open the dining-room door.

She snuffed and was still. The tattered ceiling cloth hung down almost to the level of the table, and there was hardly room to move away from the discovery.

Tietjens came in and sat down, her teeth bared under her lip and her forepaws planted. She looked at Strickland.

"It's a bad business, old lady," said he. "Men don't climb up into the roofs of their bungalows to die, and they don't fasten up the ceiling cloth behind 'em. Let's think it out."

"Let's think it out somewhere else," I said.

"Excellent idea! Turn the lamps out. We'll get into my room."

I did not turn the lamps out. I went into Strickland's room first, and allowed him to make the darkness. Then he followed me, and we lit tobacco and thought. Strickland thought. I smoked furiously, because I was afraid.

"Imray is back," said Strickland. "The question is—who killed Imray? Don't talk. I've a notion of my own. When I took this bungalow I took over most of Imray's servants. Imray was guileless and inoffensive, wasn't he?"

I agreed, though the heap under the cloth had looked neither one thing nor the other.

"If I call in all the servants, they will stand fast in a crowd and lie like Aryans. What do you suggest?"

"Call 'em in one by one," I said.

"They'll run away and give the news to all their fellows," said Strickland. "We must segregate 'em. Do you suppose your servant knows anything about it?"

"He may, for aught I know, but I don't think it's likely. He has only been here two or three days," I answered. "What's your notion?"

"I can't quite tell. How the dickens did the man get on the wrong side of the ceiling cloth?"

There was a heavy coughing outside Strickland's bedroom door. This showed that Bahadur Khan, his body servant, had waked from sleep and wished to put Strickland to bed.

"Come in," said Strickland. "It's a very warm night, isn't it?"

Bahadur Khan, a great, green-turbaned, six-foot Mohammedan, said that it was a very warm night, but that there was more rain pending, which, by His Honor's favor, would bring relief to the country.

"It will be so, if God pleases," said Strickland, tugging off his boots. "It is in my mind, Bahadur Khan, that I have worked thee remorselessly for many days—ever since that time when thou first camest into my service. What time was that?"

"Has the Heaven-born forgotten? It was when Imray Sahib went secretly to Europe without warning given; and I—even I—came into the honored service of the protector of the poor."

"And Imray Sahib went to Europe?"

"It is so said among those who were his servants."

"And thou wilt take service with him when he returns?"

"Assuredly, sahib. He was a good master, and cherished his dependents."

"That is true. I am very tired, but I go buck shooting tomorrow. Give me the little sharp rifle that I use for black buck; it is in the case yonder."

The man stooped over the case; handed barrels, stock, and fore end to Strickland, who fitted all together, yawning dolefully. Then he reached down to the gun case, took a solid-drawn cartridge, and slipped it into the breech of the .360 Express.

"And Imray Sahib has gone to Europe secretly! That is very strange, Bahadur Khan, is it not?"

"What do I know of the ways of the white man, Heaven-born?"

"Very little, truly. But thou shalt know more anon. It has reached me that Imray Sahib has returned from his so long journeyings, and that even now he lies in the next room, waiting his servant."

"Sahib!"

The lamplight slid along the barrels of the rifle as they leveled themselves at Bahadur Khan's broad breast.

"Go and look!" said Strickland. "Take a lamp. Thy master is tired, and he waits thee. Go!"

The man picked up a lamp and went into the dining room, Strickland following, and almost pushing him with the muzzle of the rifle. He looked for a moment at the black depths behind the ceiling cloth; at the writhing snake underfoot; and last, a gray glaze settling on his face, at the thing under the tablecloth.

"Hast thou seen?" said Strickland after a pause.

"I have seen. I am clay in the white man's hands. What does the Presence do?"

"Hang thee within the month. What else?"

"For killing him? Nay, sahib, consider. Walking among us, his servants, he cast his eyes upon my child, who was four years old. Him he bewitched, and in ten days he died of the fever—my child!"

"What said Imray Sahib?"

"He said he was a handsome child, and patted him on the head; wherefore my child died. Wherefore I killed Imray Sahib in the twilight, when he had come back from his office and was sleeping. Wherefore I dragged him up into the roof beams and made all fast behind him. The Heaven-born knows all things. I am the servant of the Heaven-born."

Strickland looked at me above the rifle and said, in the vernacular, "Thou art witness to this saying? He has killed."

Bahadur Khan stood ashen gray in the light of the one lamp. The need for justification came upon him very swiftly. "I am trapped," he said, "but the offense was that man's. He cast an evil eye upon my child, and I killed and hid him. Only such as are served by devils"—he glared at Tietjens, couched before him—"only such could know what I did."

"It was clever. But thou shouldst have lashed him to the beam with a rope. Now, thou thyself wilt hang by a rope. Orderly!"

A drowsy policeman answered Strickland's call. He was followed by another, and Tietjens sat wondrous still.

"Take him to the police station," said Strickland.

"Do I hang, then?" said Bahadur Khan, making no attempt to escape, and keeping his eyes on the ground.

"If the sun shines or the water runs—yes!" said Strickland.

Bahadur Khan stepped back one long pace, quivered, and stood still. The two policemen waited further orders.

"Go!" said Strickland.

"Nay; but I go very swiftly," said Bahadur Khan. "Look! I am even now a dead man."

He lifted his foot, and to the little toe there clung the head of the half-killed snake, firm fixed in the agony of death.

"I come of landholding stock," said Bahadur Khan, rocking where he stood. "It were a disgrace to me to go to the public scaffold; therefore I take this way. Be it remembered that the sahib's shirts are correctly enumerated, and that there is an extra piece of soap in his washbasin. My child was bewitched, and I slew the wizard. My honor is saved, and—and—I die."

At the end of an hour he died, as they die who are bitten by the little brown krait, and the policemen bore him and the thing under the tablecloth to their appointed places.

"This," said Strickland very calmly, as he climbed into bed, "is called the nineteenth century. Did you hear what that man said?"

"I heard," I answered. "Imray made a mistake."

"Simply and solely through not knowing the nature of the Oriental, and the coincidence of a little seasonal fever. Bahadur Khan had been with him for four years."

I shuddered. My own servant had been with me for exactly that length of time. When I went over to my own room I found my man waiting, impassive as the copper head on a penny, to pull off my boots.

"What has befallen Bahadur Khan?" said I.

"He was bitten by a snake and died. The rest the sahib knows," was the answer.

"And how much of this matter hast thou known?"

"As much as might be gathered from one coming in in the twilight to seek satisfaction. Gently, sahib. Let me pull off those boots."

I had just settled to the sleep of exhaustion when I heard Strickland shouting from his side of the house—

"Tietjens has come back to her place!"

And so she had. The great deerhound was couched nobly on her own bedstead on her own blanket, while, in the next room, the idle, empty ceiling cloth waggled as it trailed on the table.

JOURNEY BACKWARD INTO TIME

GEORGES SIMENON

IT WAS ONE of those rare cases that can be solved by studying diagrams and documents and by applying police methods. In fact, when Inspector Maigret left the Quai des Orfèvres he had all the facts clearly in mind—even the position of the wine barrels.

He had expected a short jaunt into the countryside. Instead he found himself making a long journey backward into time. The train that took him to Vitry-aux-Loges, scarcely a hundred kilometers from Paris, was a conveyance straight from the picture books of Épinal, which he had not seen since his childhood. And when he inquired about a taxi, the people at the station thought that he was joking. He would have to make the rest of the trip in the baker's cart, they said. However, he persuaded the butcher to drive over in his delivery truck.

"How often do you go down there?" the inspector asked, naming the little village to which his investigation was taking him.

"Twice a week, regularly. Thanks to you, they'll have an extra meat delivery this week."

Maigret had been born only forty kilometers away, on the banks of the river Loire, yet he was surprised by the somber, tragic aspect of this sector of the forest of Orléans. The road ran through deep woods for ten kilometers without a sign of civilization. When the truck reached a tiny village in a clearing, Maigret asked, "Is this it?"

"The next hamlet."

It wasn't raining, but the woods were damp. The trees had lost most of their foliage, and the pale, raw light of the sky bore down heavily through the bare branches. The dead leaves were rotting on the ground. An occasional shot cracked in the distance.

"Is there much hunting around here?"

"That's probably monsieur the Duke."

In another, smaller clearing, some thirty one-story houses were clustered about the steeple of a church. None of the houses could be less than a century old, and their black tile roofs gave them an inhospitable air.

"You can let me off at the house of the Potru sisters."

"I guessed that was where you'd be going. It's right across from the church."

Maigret got out. The butcher drove on a little farther and opened the back of his delivery truck. A few housewives came to look but could not make up their minds to buy. It was not their regular day for meat.

Maigret had pored so long over the diagrams sent to Paris by the original investigators that he could have entered the house with his eyes shut. As it was, the rooms were so dark that he wasn't much better off with his eyes open. As he walked into the shop at the front of the house, he seemed to be stepping into a past century.

The room was as dimly lit as a canvas by an old master. The dark brown tonality of an ancient masterpiece was diffused over the walls and furniture—a monochrome in chiaroscuro broken only by a highlight here and there, on a glass jar or a copper kettle.

The elder of the demoiselles Potru had lived in this house since her birth sixty-five years before—her younger sister was sixty-two. Their parents had spent their lives there before them. Nothing in the shop had changed in all that time—not the counter with its old-fashioned scales and its gleaming candy jars, nor shelves of notions, nor the grocery section with its stale odors of cinnamon and chicory, nor the zinc-covered slab that served as the village bar. A barrel of kerosene stood in a corner next to a smaller barrel of cooking oil. In the rear were two long tables, polished by time, flanked by backless benches.

A door opened at the left, and a woman in her early thirties came in, carrying a baby in her arms. She looked at Maigret.

"What is it you want?"

"I'm here for the investigation. I suppose you are a neighbor?"

The woman, whose apron ballooned over a rounded belly, said, "I'm Marie Lacore. My husband is the blacksmith."

"I see." Maigret had just noticed the kerosene lamp hanging from the ceiling. So the hamlet had no electricity.

The second room, which Maigret entered without invitation, would have been completely dark were it not for the two logs blazing in the hearth. The flickering light revealed an immense bed on which were piled several mattresses and a puffy red eiderdown quilt. An old woman lay motionless on the bed. Her haggard rigid face was lifeless except for the sharp, questioning eyes.

"She still can't speak?" Maigret asked Marie Lacore.

The blacksmith's wife shook her head in the negative. Maigret shrugged, sat down on a straw-bottomed chair, and began taking papers from his pockets.

There was nothing sensational about the actual crime, which had taken place five days earlier. The Potru sisters, who lived alone in the hovel, were believed to have accumulated a considerable nest egg. They owned three other houses in the village and had a long-established reputation as misers.

During the night of Saturday to Sunday their neighbors remembered hearing unusual noises but had thought nothing of it at the time. However, a farmer passing the house at dawn on Sunday noticed that the bedroom window was wide open, looked in, and shouted for help.

Amélie Potru, the elder sister, was lying on the floor in a pool of blood near the window, clad only in a red-stained nightgown. The younger sister, Marguerite, was lying on the bed, her face turned to the wall, dead, with three knife wounds in her chest, her cheek gashed, and one eye torn half from its socket.

Amélie was still alive. She had staggered to the window to give the alarm but, weakened from loss of blood, had fallen unconscious before she could cry out. She had no less than eleven stab wounds in her right side and shoulder, none of them serious.

The second drawer of the dresser had been pulled out and apparently ransacked. Among the linen scattered on the floor was a briefcase of mildewed leather in which the sisters must have kept their business papers. It was empty, but lying nearby were a savings-bank passbook, deeds to property, leases, and bills for supplies.

The Orléans authorities who made the original investigation sent Maigret detailed diagrams and photographs of the scene as well as a transcript of the questioning of witnesses.

Marguerite, the dead woman, had been buried two days after the murder. Amélie had resisted all efforts to take her to a hospital, sinking her nails into the bed sheets, fighting off neighbors who tried to move her, and demanding—with her eyes—that she be left at home. She had lost all power of speech.

The medical examiner from Orléans declared that no vital organ had been injured and that her loss of voice must be due to shock. In any case, no sound had passed her lips for five days; yet despite her bandages and her immobility she followed all proceedings with her eyes. Even now her gaze never left Maigret for a moment.

Three hours after the Orléans authorities finished their investigation, they arrested a man who from the evidence must be the murderer: Marcel, illegitimate son of the dead Potru sister. The late Marguerite had given birth to Marcel when she was twenty-three, so he must be thirty-nine years old. For a while Marcel had worked with the hounds of the Duke's hunt. More recently he had been a woodcutter in the forest and lived in an abandoned tumbledown farmhouse near the Loup Pendu pond, ten kilometers from the village.

The villagers looked upon Marcel as a brute, a miserable wretch who was little better than an animal. Several times he had disappeared, leaving his wife and five children for weeks on end. He beat his family more often than he fed them. What's more, he was a drunkard.

Maigret decided to reread at the scene of the crime the transcript of Marcel's testimony: "I came on my bicycle around seven o'clock just when the old women were sitting down to eat. I had a drink at the bar, then I went out to the courtyard and killed a rabbit. I skinned it and cleaned it and my mother cooked it. My aunt yelled her head off because I ate their rabbit, but she always yells. She can't stand me. . . ."

According to the testimony of other villagers, Marcel frequently came to the Potru sisters for a private spree. His mother never refused him anything, and his aunt, who was afraid of him, did nothing more than complain.

Maigret had stopped off in Orléans to see Marcel in his cell, and got further details.

"There was more argument," Marcel said, "when I took a cheese out of the shop and cut myself a hunk. Seems I shouldn't have cut into a whole cheese."

"What wine were you drinking?" Maigret asked.

"Some of the wine from the shop."

"How was the room lighted?"

"The oil lamp. Well, after dinner my mother wasn't feeling well, so she went to bed. She asked me to get her some papers out of the second drawer in the dresser. She gave me the key. I took the papers over to the bed and we went over the bills. It was the end of the month."

"You took the papers out of the briefcase? What else was in there?"

"A big bundle of bonds. A hundred francs' worth. Maybe more."

"Did you go into the storeroom?"

"No."

"You didn't light a candle to go into the storeroom?"

"Never. . . . At half past nine I put the papers back in the drawer and then I left. I drank another slug of rotgut as I went out through the shop. . . . And anybody says I killed the old lady is a liar. Why don't you talk to the Yugo?"

To the great astonishment of Marcel's lawyer, Maigret broke off his questioning.

Yarko, whom everyone called "the Yugo" because he was from Yugoslavia, was a bit of jetsam who had been washed into the village by the war and who had stayed on. He lived alone in the wing of a house near the Potru sisters and worked as a carter, hauling logs from the woods. He, too, was a confirmed drunkard, although for some time the Potru sisters had refused to serve him; he had run up too long a tab. One night they had asked Marcel to throw him out, and he had given the Yugo a bloody nose in the process.

The Potru sisters had another grievance against the Yugo. He kept his horses in a stable he had rented from them, a dilapidated outbuilding back of their courtyard, but he was always months behind in his rent. At this moment he was probably in the woods with his team.

Maigret continued to match his thoughts with the actual scene of the crime. Papers in hand, he walked to the fireplace where the Orléans men had found a kitchen knife among the ashes on the morning after the murder. The wooden handle had been completely burned, obviously to destroy fingerprints.

On the other hand, there had been plenty of fingerprints on the dresser drawer and on the briefcase—and all of them had been Marcel's.

On a candlestick that stood on a table in the bedroom they had found Amélie Potru's fingerprints—and only hers. Amélie's cold eyes still followed Maigret's every move.

"I suppose your mind is still made up not to speak?" he growled as he lit his pipe.

Silence.

Maigret stooped to make a chalk mark on the floor around some bloodstains that had been indicated on the diagram.

Marie Lacore asked him, "Will you be here for a few minutes? I'd like to put my dinner on the stove."

So Maigret found himself alone with the old woman in the house he already knew by heart, although he had never seen it before. He had spent a whole day and night studying the dossier with its diagrams and sketches, and Orléans had done such a thorough job of groundwork that he was not in the least surprised, except perhaps to find the sordid reality even more shocking than he had imagined.

And yet he himself was the son of peasants. He knew that such things existed—that there were still hamlets in France where people went on living as they had lived since the thirteenth and fourteenth centuries. But to be suddenly plunged into this village in the forest, into this ancient house, into the room alone with the old woman whose alert mind seemed to be stalking Maigret—all this was like entering one of those wretched hospitals where the worst of human monstrosities are hidden away from the eyes of normal men.

When he had begun to work on the case in Paris, Maigret had jotted down a few notes on the original report:

1. Why would Marcel have burned the knife handle without worrying about his fingerprints on the dresser and the briefcase?

2. If he had used the candle, why had he carried it back into the bedroom and put it out?

3. Why didn't the bloodstains on the floor follow a straight line from the bed to the window?

4. Since Marcel might well have been recognized in the street at nine thirty in the evening, why had he left the house by the front door, instead of going through the courtyard, which led directly into open country?

But there was one bit of evidence that worried even Marcel's lawyer. One of Marcel's buttons had been found in the old women's bed, a distinctive button that definitely had come from Marcel's old corduroy hunting jacket.

"When I was cleaning the rabbit, I caught my jacket on something," had been Marcel's explanation, "and one of the buttons must have pulled loose."

Maigret finished rereading his notes. He stood up and looked at Amélie with a peculiar smile on his lips. She was going to be sorely vexed at not being able to follow him with her eyes, for he opened a door and disappeared into the storeroom.

The cubicle was dimly lit by a dirty skylight. Maigret's gaze traveled from the stacks of cordwood to the four wine barrels against the wall—the barrels he had come all the way from Paris to see. The first two barrels were full. One contained red wine and the other white. He thumped the next two barrels. They were empty. On one of the empty barrels several tears of tallow had fallen and congealed. Technicians from Identité Judiciaire reported that the tallow on the barrel was identical with the tallow of the candle in the bedroom.

The report of the inspector in charge from Orléans had this to say about the evidence:

"The candle drippings on the barrel were probably left by Marcel when he came to drink wine. His wife admits that he was quite drunk when he got home that night, and the zigzag tire tracks of his bicycle confirm this fact."

Maigret looked about him for something he had expected to find but which apparently was not there. Puzzled, he stepped back into the bedroom, opened the window, and called to two urchins who were gaping at the house.

"Listen, boys. Will one of you run and get me a saw?"

"A wood saw?"

"Right."

Maigret could still feel the old woman's eyes boring into his back—live eyes in a dead face, eyes that moved only when his bulky figure moved.

The boys came back bringing two saws of different sizes. At the same time Marie Lacore returned from next door.

"I hope I haven't kept you waiting," she said. "I left the baby home. Now I'll have to attend to—"

"Wait just a few minutes, will you?" That was a scene that Maigret intended to skip, thank you! He'd had enough without it. He went back into the storeroom and started sawing one of the empty barrels—the one with the candle drippings on it.

He knew what he would find. He was sure of his theory. If he had had any lingering doubts when he arrived, they had been dispelled by the atmosphere of the old house. Amélie Potru had turned out to be exactly the sort of person he had anticipated. And the very walls of the house seemed to ooze the avarice and hate he had expected.

Another thing. When he first entered the shop, Maigret had noted a pile of newspapers on the counter. That was one important fact the Orléans reports had omitted—that the Potru sisters were also the news dealers of the village. Further, Amélie owned glasses that, since she did not wear them about the house, were obviously reading glasses. So Amélie was able to read—and thus the biggest question mark in Inspector Maigret's theory was eliminated. His theory was based on hate—a festering hate made even more purulent by long years of being shut up together within the same four walls, of sharing the same narrow interests by day, and even the same bed by night.

But there was one experience the two sisters had not shared. Marguerite, the younger, had had a child. She had known love and motherhood. Amélie had shared only the annoying aftermath. The brat had clung to her skirts, too, for ten or fifteen years. And after he had struck out for himself, he was always coming back to eat and drink and to demand money.

It was Amélie's money as much as it was Marguerite's. More, really, since Amélie was the elder and therefore had been working and earning longer.

So Amélie hated Marcel with a hate nourished by a thousand incidents of their daily life—the rabbit he had killed, the cheese he had brazenly cut into, thus spoiling its sales value. And his mother had not said a word in protest—she never did.

Yes, Amélie read the newspapers. She must have read about the scandals, the crimes, the murder trials that take up so much space in certain papers. If so, she would know the importance of fingerprints. Then, too, Amélie was afraid of her nephew. She must have been furious with her sister for showing him the hiding place of their treasure, for letting him touch the bonds he most certainly coveted.

"One of these days he'll come to murder us both."

Surely those words had been uttered in the house dozens of times, Maigret reflected as he sawed away at the wine barrel. He realized that he was perspiring, and stopped sawing long enough to take off his hat and coat. He placed them on the next barrel.

The rabbit . . . the cheese . . . then suddenly the remembrance that Marcel had left his prints on the dresser drawer and the briefcase. And if that was not enough, there was the readily identifiable button, which his mother, having already gone to bed, had not yet sewed back on his jacket.

If Marcel had killed for gain, why had he emptied the briefcase on the floor instead of taking it with him, bonds and all? As for Yarko the Yugoslav, Maigret had learned that he could not read.

Maigret's reasoning had begun with Amélie's wounds—eleven of them. There were too many by far and all of them were too superficial not to be extremely suspicious. Besides, they were all on the right side. She must have been clumsy, as well as afraid of pain. She wanted neither to die nor to suffer. She had expected help from the neighbors after she had opened the window to scream.

Would a murderer have given her time to run to the window?

And fate had laughed at her too. She had lost consciousness before her cries had awakened anyone, so she had spent the night on the floor, with nobody to stanch her bleeding.

Yes, that must have been the way it happened. It could not have been otherwise. She had killed her drowsing sister; then, her fingers wrapped in cloth of some kind to prevent leaving prints, she had opened the drawer and rifled the briefcase. The bonds must disappear if Marcel were to be suspected!

Hence the candle.

Afterward she had sat on the edge of the bed, gashing herself timidly and awkwardly, then had gone to the fireplace (the bloodstains marked her course) to throw the knife into the embers. Finally she had walked to the window and . . .

Maigret stopped sawing. From the other room came the sound of voices raised in argument. He turned abruptly, watched the door opening slowly. The fantastic yet sinister figure of Amélie Potru stood on the threshold, swathed in bandages, wearing a curious petticoat and camisole. She stared hard at Maigret, while behind her Marie Lacore protested shrilly that she had no business getting out of bed.

Maigret did not have the heart to speak to her. He finished sawing open the barrel in silence. He did not even sigh contentedly when he saw the government securities and railway bonds, still curling slightly from having been rolled up and pushed through the bung.

Had he followed his inclination, he would have beat a hasty retreat, first taking a long swig of rum straight from the bottle, the way Marcel would have done.

Amélie still spoke not a word. She stood silent, her mouth partly open. If she fainted, she would fall back into the arms of Marie Lacore, who, in her advanced state of pregnancy, might not be able to catch her.

Well, what of it? This was a scene from another world, another age. Maigret picked up the bonds and walked toward Amélie. She backed away from him.

He dropped the securities on the bedroom table and said to Marie Lacore, "Go get the mayor. I want him as a witness."

His voice rasped a little because his vocal cords were strangely tight. Then he nodded to Amélie. "You'd better get back to bed."

Despite his case-hardened professional curiosity he turned his back to her. He knew that she had obeyed him, for he heard the bedsprings creak. He stood looking out the window until the farmer who served as mayor of the hamlet made a timid, apologetic entrance.

There was no telephone in the village. A man on a bicycle carried the message to Vitry-aux-Loges. The gendarmes arrived at almost the same moment the butcher's delivery truck came rolling out of the woods.

The sky shone with the same pale, raw light. The trees stirred uneasily in the west wind.

"Find anything?" asked the brigadier from the gendarmerie.

Maigret's reply was evasive. He spoke haltingly, without elation, although he knew that the case of the Potru sisters would be the subject of long commentary and review by the criminologists not only of Paris but of London, Berlin, Vienna, even New York.

Listening to him now, the brigadier might well have suspected that Inspector Maigret was drunk—or, at least, a little tipsy.

THE MOVIE PEOPLE

ROBERT BLOCH

TWO THOUSAND STARS.

Two thousand stars, maybe more, set in the sidewalks along Hollywood Boulevard, each metal slab inscribed with the name of someone in the movie industry. They go way back, those names; from Broncho Billy Anderson to Adolph Zukor, everybody's there.

Everybody but Jimmy Rogers.

You won't find Jimmy's name because he wasn't a star, not even a bit player—just an extra.

"But I deserve it," he told me. "I'm entitled, if anybody is. Started out here in 1920 when I was just a punk kid. You look close, you'll spot me in the crowd shots in *The Mark of Zorro.* Been in over four hundred and fifty pictures since, and still going strong. Ain't many left who can beat that record. You'd think it would entitle a fella to something."

Maybe it did, but there was no star for Jimmy Rogers, and that bit about still going strong was just a crock. Nowadays Jimmy was lucky if he got a casting call once or twice a year; there just isn't any spot for an old-timer with a white muff except in a western barroom scene.

Most of the time Jimmy just strolled the boulevard; a tall, soldierly erect incongruity in the crowd of tourists, fags, and freak-outs. His home address was on Las Palmas, somewhere south of Sunset. I'd never been there, but I could guess what it was—one of those old frame bungalow-court sweatboxes put up about the time he crashed the movies and still standing somehow by the grace of God and the disgrace of the housing authorities. That's the sort of place Jimmy stayed at, but he didn't really *live* there.

Jimmy Rogers lived at the Silent Movie.

The Silent Movie is over on Fairfax, and it's the only place in town where you can still go and see *The Mark of Zorro.* There's always a Chaplin comedy, and usually Laurel and Hardy, along with a serial starring Pearl White, Elmo Lincoln, or Houdini. And the features are great—early Griffith and DeMille, Barrymore in *Dr. Jekyll and Mr. Hyde*, Lon Chaney in *The Hunchback of Notre Dame*, Valentino in *Blood and Sand*, and a hundred more.

The bill changes every Wednesday, and every Wednesday night Jimmy Rogers was there, plunking down his ninety cents at the box office to watch *The Black Pirate* or *Son of the Sheik* or *Orphans of the Storm.*

To live again.

Because Jimmy didn't go there to see Doug and Mary or Rudy or Clara or Gloria or the Gish sisters. He went there to see himself, in the crowd shots.

At least that's the way I figured it, the first time I met him. They were playing *The Phantom of the Opera* that night, and afterward I spent the intermission with a cigarette outside the theater, studying the display of stills.

If you asked me under oath, I couldn't tell you how our conversation started, but that's where I first heard Jimmy's routine about the four hundred and fifty pictures and still going strong.

"Did you see me in there tonight?" he asked.

I stared at him and shook my head; even with the shabby hand-me-down suit and the white beard, Jimmy Rogers wasn't the kind you'd spot in an audience.

"Guess it was too dark for me to notice," I said.

"But there were torches," Jimmy told me. "I carried one."

Then I got the message. He was in the picture.

Jimmy smiled and shrugged. "Hell, I keep forgetting. You wouldn't recognize me. We did *The Phantom* way back in '25. I looked so young they slapped a mustache on me in Makeup, and a black wig. Hard to spot me in the catacombs scenes—all long shots. But there at the end, where Chaney is holding back the mob, I show up pretty good in the background, just left of Charley Zimmer. He's the one shaking his fist. I'm waving my torch. Had a lot of trouble with that picture, but we did this shot in one take."

In weeks to come I saw more of Jimmy Rogers. Sometimes he was up there on the screen, though truth to tell, I never did recognize him; he was a young man in those films of the '20s, and his appearances were limited to a flickering flash, a blurred face glimpsed in a crowd.

But always Jimmy was in the audience, even though he hadn't played in the picture. And one night I found out why.

Again it was intermission time and we were standing outside. By now Jimmy had gotten into the habit of talking to me, and tonight we'd been seated together during the showing of *The Covered Wagon.*

We stood outside and Jimmy blinked at me. "Wasn't she beautiful?" he asked. "They don't look like that anymore."

I nodded. "Lois Wilson? Very attractive."

"I'm talking about June."

I stared at Jimmy and then I realized he wasn't blinking. He was crying.

"June Logan. My girl. This was her first bit, the Indian attack scene. Must have been seventeen—I didn't know her then, it was two years later we met over at First National. But you must have noticed her. She was the one with the long blond curls."

"Oh, *that* one." I nodded again. "You're right. She was lovely."

And I was a liar, because I didn't remember seeing her at all, but I wanted to make the old man feel good.

"Junie's in a lot of the pictures they show here. And from '25 on, we played in a flock of 'em together. For a while we talked about getting hitched, but she started working her way up, doing bits—maids and such—and I never broke out of extra work. Both of us had been in the business long enough to know it was no go, not when one of you stays small and the other is headed for a big career."

Jimmy managed a grin as he wiped his eyes with something which might once have been a handkerchief. "You think I'm kidding, don't you? About the career, I mean. But she was going great, she would have been playing second leads pretty soon."

"What happened?" I asked.

The grin dissolved and the blinking returned. "Sound killed her."

"She didn't have a voice for talkies?"

Jimmy shook his head. "She had a great voice. I told you she was all set for second leads—by 1930 she'd been in a dozen talkies. Then sound killed her."

I'd heard the expression a thousand times, but never like this. Because the way Jimmy told the story, that's exactly what had happened. June Logan, his girl Junie, was on the set during the shooting of one of those early ALL TALKING—ALL SINGING—ALL DANCING epics. The director and camera crew, seeking to break away from the tyranny of the stationary microphone, rigged up one of the first traveling mikes on a boom. Such items weren't standard equipment yet, and this was an experiment. Somehow, during a take, it broke loose and the boom crashed, crushing June Logan's skull.

It never made the papers, not even the trades; the studio hushed it up and June Logan had a quiet funeral.

"Damn near forty years ago," Jimmy said. "And here I am, crying like it was yesterday. But she was my girl—"

And that was the other reason why Jimmy Rogers went to the Silent Movie. To visit his girl.

"Don't you see?" he told me. "She's still alive up there on the screen, in all those pictures. Just the way she was when we were together. Five years we had, the best years for me."

I could see that. The two of them in love, with each other and with the movies. Because in those days, people *did* love the movies. And to actually be *in* them, even in tiny roles, was the average person's idea of seventh heaven.

Seventh Heaven, that's another film we saw with June Logan playing a crowd scene. In the following weeks, with Jimmy's help, I got so I could spot his girl. And he'd told the truth—she was a beauty. Once you noticed her, really saw her, you wouldn't forget. Those blond ringlets, that smile, identified her immediately.

One Wednesday night Jimmy and I were sitting together watching *The Birth of a Nation.* During a street shot Jimmy nudged my shoulder. "Look, there's June."

I peered up at the screen, then shook my head. "I don't see her."

"Wait a second—there she is again. See, off to the left, behind Walthall's shoulder?"

There was a blurred image and then the camera followed Henry B. Walthall as he moved away.

I glanced at Jimmy. He was rising from his seat.

"Where you going?"

He didn't answer me, just marched outside.

When I followed I found him leaning against the wall under the marquee and breathing hard; his skin was the color of his whiskers.

"Junie," he murmured. "I saw her—"

I took a deep breath. "Listen to me. You told me her first picture was *The Covered Wagon.* That was made in 1923. And Griffith shot *The Birth of a Nation* in 1914."

Jimmy didn't say anything. There was nothing to say. We both knew what we were going to do—march back into the theater and see the second show.

When the scene screened again we were watching and waiting. I looked at the screen, then glanced at Jimmy.

"She's gone," he whispered. "She's not in the picture."

"She never was," I told him. "You know that."

"Yeah." Jimmy got up and drifted out into the night, and I didn't see him again until the following week.

That's when they showed the short feature with Charles Ray—I've forgotten the title, but he played his usual country-boy role, and there was a baseball game in the climax with Ray coming through to win.

The camera panned across the crowd sitting in the bleachers and I caught a momentary glimpse of a smiling girl with long blond curls.

"Did you see her?" Jimmy grabbed my arm.

"That girl—"

"It was Junie. She winked at me!"

This time I was the one who got up and walked out. He followed, and I was waiting outside, right next to the display poster.

"See for yourself." I nodded at the poster. "This picture was made in 1917." I forced a smile. "You forget, there were thousands of pretty blond extras in pictures and most of them wore curls."

He stood there shaking, not listening to me at all, and I put my hand on his shoulder. "Now look here—"

"I *been* looking here," Jimmy said. "Week after week, year after year. And you might as well know the truth. This ain't the first time it's happened. Junie keeps turning up in picture after picture I know she never made. Not just the early ones, before her time, but later, during the '20s when I knew her, when I knew exactly what she was playing in. Sometimes it's only a quick flash, but I see her—then she's gone again. And the next running, she doesn't come back.

"It got so that for a while I was almost afraid to go see a show—figured I was cracking up. But now you've seen her too—"

I shook my head slowly. "Sorry, Jimmy. I never said that." I glanced at him, then gestured toward my car at the curb. "You look tired. Come on, I'll drive you home."

He looked worse than tired; he looked lost and lonely and infinitely old. But there was a stubborn glint in his eyes, and he stood his ground.

"No, thanks. I'm gonna stick around for the second show."

As I slid behind the wheel I saw him turn and move into the theater, into the place where the present becomes the past and the past becomes the present. Up above in the booth they call it a projection machine, but it's really a time machine; it can take you back, play tricks with your imagination and your memory. A girl dead forty years comes alive again, and an old man relives his vanished youth—

But I belonged in the real world, and that's where I stayed. I didn't go to the Silent Movie the next week or the week following.

And the next time I saw Jimmy was almost a month later, on the set.

They were shooting a western, one of my scripts, and the director wanted some additional dialogue to stretch a sequence. So they called me in, and I drove all the way out to location, at the ranch.

Most of the studios have a ranch spread for western action sequences, and this was one of the oldest; it had been in use since the silent days. What fascinated me was the wooden fort where they were doing the crowd scene—I could swear I remembered it from one of the first Tim

McCoy pictures. So after I huddled with the director and scribbled a few extra lines for the principals, I began nosing around behind the fort, just out of curiosity, while they set up for the new shots.

Out front was the usual organized confusion; cast and crew milling around the trailers, extras sprawled on the grass drinking coffee. But here in the back I was all alone, prowling around in musty, log-lined rooms built for use in forgotten features. Hoot Gibson had stood at this bar, and Jack Hoxie had swung from this dance-hall chandelier. Here was a dust-covered table where Fred Thomson sat, and around the corner, in the cutaway bunkhouse—

Around the corner, in the cutaway bunkhouse, Jimmy Rogers sat on the edge of a mildewed mattress and stared up at me, startled, as I moved forward.

"You . . . ?"

Quickly I explained my presence. There was no need for him to explain his; casting had called and given him a day's work here in the crowd shots.

"They been stalling all day, and it's hot out there. I figured maybe I could sneak back here and catch me a little nap in the shade."

"How'd you know where to go?" I asked. "Ever been here before?"

"Sure. Forty years ago in this very bunkhouse. Junie and I, we used to come here during lunch break and—"

He stopped.

"What's wrong?"

Something *was* wrong. On the pan makeup face of it, Jimmy Rogers was the perfect picture of the grizzled western old-timer; buckskin breeches, fringed shirt, white whiskers, and all. But under the makeup was pallor, and the hands holding the envelope were trembling.

The envelope—

He held it out to me. "Here. Mebbe you better read this."

The envelope was unsealed, unstamped, unaddressed. It contained four folded pages covered with fine handwriting. I removed them slowly. Jimmy stared at me.

"Found it lying here on the mattress when I came in," he murmured. "Just waiting for me."

"But what is it? Where'd it come from?"

"Read it and see."

As I started to unfold the pages the whistle blew. We both knew the signal; the scene was set up, they were ready to roll, principals and extras were wanted out there before the cameras.

Jimmy Rogers stood up and moved off, a tired old man shuffling out into the hot sun. I waved at him, then sat down on the moldering mattress and opened the letter. The handwriting was faded, and there was a thin film of dust on the pages. But I could still read it, every word. . . .

Darling:

I've been trying to reach you so long and in so many ways. Of course I've seen you, but it's so dark out there I can't always be sure, and then too you've changed a lot through the years.

But I *do* see you, quite often, even though it's only for a moment. And I hope you've seen me, because I always try to wink or make some kind of motion to attract your attention.

The only thing is, I can't do too much or show myself too long or it would make trouble. That's the big secret—keeping in the background, so the others won't notice me. It wouldn't do to frighten anybody, or even to get anyone wondering why there are more people in the background of a shot than there should be.

That's something for you to remember, darling, just in case. You're always safe, as long as you stay clear of close-ups. Costume pictures are the best—about all you have to do is wave your arms once in a while and shout, "On to the Bastille," or something like that. It really doesn't matter except to lip-readers, because it's silent, of course.

Oh, there's a lot to watch out for. Being a dress extra has its points, but not in ballroom sequences—too much dancing. That goes for parties too, particularly in a DeMille production where they're "making whoopee," or one of von Stroheim's orgies. Besides, von Stroheim's scenes are always cut.

It doesn't hurt to be cut, don't misunderstand about that. It's no different than an ordinary fade-out at the end of a scene, and then you're free to go into another picture. Anything that was ever made, as long as there's still a print available for running somewhere. It's like falling asleep and then having one dream after another. The dreams are the scenes, of course, but while the scenes are playing, they're real.

I'm not the only one, either. There's no telling how many others do the same thing; maybe hundreds for all I know, but I've recognized a few I'm sure of and I think some of them have recognized me. We never let on to each other that we know, because it wouldn't do to make anybody suspicious.

Sometimes I think that if we could talk it over, we might come up with a better understanding of just how it happens, and why. But the point is, you *can't* talk, everything is silent; all you do is move your lips, and if you tried to communicate such a difficult thing in pantomime, you'd surely attract attention.

I guess the closest I can come to explaining it is to say it's like reincarnation—you can play a thousand roles, take or reject any part you want, as long as you don't make yourself conspicuous or do something that would change the plot.

Naturally you get used to certain things. The silence, of course. And if you're in a bad print, there's flickering; sometimes even the air seems grainy, and for a few frames you may be faded or out of focus.

Which reminds me—another thing to stay away from, the slapstick comedies. Sennett's early stuff is the worst, but some of the others are just as bad; all that speeded-up camera action makes you dizzy.

Once you can learn to adjust, it's all right, even when you're looking off the screen into the audience. At first the darkness is a little frightening—you have to remind yourself it's only a theater and there are just people out there, ordinary people watching a show. They don't know you can see them. They don't know that as long as your scene runs, you're just as real as they are, only in a different way. You walk, run, smile, frown, drink, eat—

That's another thing to remember, about the eating. Stay out of those Poverty Row quickies where everything is cheap and faked. Go where there's real set dressing, big productions with banquet scenes and real food. If you work fast you can grab enough in a few minutes, while you're off-camera, to last you.

The big rule is, always be careful. Don't get caught. There's so little time, and you seldom get an opportunity to do anything on your own, even in a long sequence. It's taken me forever to get this chance to write you—I've planned it for so long, my darling, but it just wasn't possible until now.

This scene is playing outside the fort, but there's quite a large crowd of settlers and wagon-train people, and I had a chance to slip away inside here to the rooms in back—they're on-camera in the background all during the action. I found this stationery and a pen, and I'm scribbling just as fast as I can. Hope you can read it. That is, if you ever get the chance!

Naturally I can't mail it—but I have a funny hunch. You see, I noticed that standing set back here, the bunkhouse, where you and I used to come in the old days. I'm going to leave this letter under the mattress, and pray.

Yes, darling, I pray. Someone or something *knows* about us, and about how we feel. How we felt about being in the movies. That's why I'm here, I'm sure of that; because I've always loved pictures so. Someone who knows *that* must also know how I loved you. And still do.

I think there must be many heavens and many hells, each of us making his own, and—

The letter broke off there.

No signature, but of course I didn't need one. And it wouldn't have proved anything. A lonely old man, nursing his love for forty years, keeping her alive inside himself somewhere until she broke out in the form of a visual hallucination up there on the screen—such a man could conceivably go all the way into a schizoid split, even to the point where he could imitate a woman's handwriting as he set down the rationalization of his obsession.

I started to fold the letter, then dropped it on the mattress as the shrill scream of an ambulance siren startled me into sudden movement.

Even as I ran out the doorway I seemed to know what I'd find; the crowd huddling around the figure sprawled in the dust under the hot sun. Old men tire easily in such heat, and once the heart goes—

Jimmy Rogers looked very much as though he were smiling in his sleep as they lifted him into the ambulance. And I was glad of that; at least he'd died with his illusions intact.

"Just keeled over during the scene—one minute he was standing there, and the next—"

They were still chattering and gabbling when I walked away, walked back behind the fort and into the bunkhouse.

The letter was gone.

I'd dropped it on the mattress, and it was gone. That's all I can say about it. Maybe somebody else happened by while I was out front, watching them take Jimmy away. Maybe a gust of wind carried it through the doorway, blew it across the desert in a hot Santa Ana gust. Maybe there *was* no letter. You can take your choice—all I can do is state the facts.

And there aren't very many more facts to state.

I didn't go to Jimmy Rogers' funeral, if indeed he had one. I don't even know where he was buried; probably the Motion Picture Fund took care of him. Whatever *those* facts may be, they aren't important.

For a few days I wasn't too interested in facts. I was trying to answer a few abstract questions about metaphysics—reincarnation, heaven and hell, the difference between real life and reel life. I kept thinking about those images you see up there on the screen in those old movies; images of actual people indulging in make-believe. But even after they die, the make-believe goes on, and that's a form of reality too. I mean, where's the borderline? And if there *is* a borderline—is it possible to cross over? *Life's but a walking shadow—*

Shakespeare said that, but I wasn't sure what he meant.

I'm still not sure, but there's just one more fact I must state.

The other night, for the first time in all the months since Jimmy Rogers died, I went back to the Silent Movie.

They were playing *Intolerance*, one of Griffith's greatest. Way back in 1916 he built the biggest set ever shown on the screen—the huge temple in the Babylonian sequence.

One shot never fails to impress me, and it did so now; a wide angle on the towering temple, with thousands of people moving antlike amid the gigantic carvings and colossal statues. In the distance, beyond the steps guarded by rows of stone elephants, looms a mighty wall, its top covered with tiny figures. You really have to look closely to make them out. But I did look closely, and this time I can swear to what I saw.

One of the extras, way up there on the wall in the background, was a smiling girl with long blond curls. And standing right beside her, one arm around her shoulder, was a tall old man with white whiskers. I wouldn't have noticed either of them, except for one thing.

They were waving at me. . . .

BROKER'S SPECIAL

STANLEY ELLIN

IT WAS THE first time in a good many years that Cornelius, a Wall Street broker, had made the homeward trip in any train other than the Broker's Special. The Special was his kind of train; the passengers on it were his kind of people. Executives, professionals, men of substance and dignity who could recognize each other without introductions, and understand each other without words.

If it weren't for the senator's dinner party, Cornelius reflected. But the senator had insisted, so there was no escape from that abomination of abominations, the midweek dinner party. And, of course, no escape from the necessity of taking an earlier train home to the tedium of dressing, and an evening of too much food, too much liquor, and all the resultant misery the next morning.

Filled with this depressing thought, Cornelius stepped down heavily from the train to the familiar platform and walked over to his car. Since Claire preferred the station wagon, he used the sedan to get to and from the station. When they were first married two years ago she had wanted to chauffeur him back and forth, but the idea had somehow repelled him. He had always felt there was something vaguely obscene about the way other men publicly kissed their wives good-by in front of the station every morning, and the thought of being placed in their position filled him with a chilling embarrassment. He had not told this to Claire, however. He had simply told her he had not married her to obtain a housekeeper or chauffeur. She was to enjoy her life, not fill it with unnecessary duties.

Ordinarily, it was no more than a fifteen-minute drive through the countryside to the house. But now, in keeping with the already exasperating tenor of the day's events, he met an unexpected delay. A mile or so past where the road branched off from the highway it crossed the main line of the railroad. There was no guard or crossing gate here, but a red light, and a bell which was ringing an insistent warning as Cornelius drove up. He braked the car, and sat tapping his fingers restlessly on the steering wheel while the endless, clanking length of a freight went by. And then he saw them.

It was Claire and a man. His wife and some man in the station wagon roaring past him into town. And the man was driving—seated big and blond and arrogant behind the wheel like a Viking—with one arm around Claire, who, with eyes closed, rested her head on his shoulder. There was a look on her face, too, such as Cornelius had never seen there before, but which he had sometimes dreamed of seeing. They passed by in a flash, but the picture they made was burned as brilliant in his mind as a photograph on film.

He would not believe it, he told himself incredulously; he refused to believe it! But the picture was there before him, growing clearer each second, becoming more and more terribly alive as he watched it. The man's arm possessing her. Her look of sensual acceptance.

He was shaking uncontrollably now, the blood pounding in his head, as he prepared to turn the car and follow. Then he felt himself go limp. Follow them where? Back to town undoubtedly, where the man would be waiting for the next train to the city. Then what? A scene? A public humiliation for himself as much as for them?

He could stand anything, but not such humiliation. It had been bad enough when he had first married Claire and realized his friends were laughing at him for it. A man in his position to marry his secretary, and a girl half his age at that! Now he knew what they had been laughing at, but he had been blind then. There had been such an air of cool formality about her when she carried on her duties in the office; she sat with such prim dignity when she took his notes; she had dressed so modestly—and when he had first invited her to dinner she had reddened with the flustered naïveté of a young girl being invited on her first date. Naïveté! And all the time, he thought furiously, she must have been laughing at me. She, along with the rest of them.

He drove to the house slowly, almost blindly. The house was empty, and he realized that, of course, it was Thursday, the servants' day off, which made it the perfect day for Claire's purpose. He went directly to the library, sat down at the desk there, and unlocked the top drawer. His gun was in that drawer, a short-barreled .38, and he picked it up slowly, hefting its cold weight in his hand, savoring the sense of power it gave him. Then abruptly his mind went back to something Judge Hilliker had once told him, something strangely interesting that the old man had said while sharing a seat with him on the Broker's Special.

"Guns?" Hilliker had said. "Knives? Blunt instruments? You can throw them all out of the window. As far as I'm concerned there is just one perfect weapon—an automobile. Any automobile in good working order. Why? Because when an automobile is going fast enough it will kill anyone it hits. And if the driver gets out and looks sorry, he'll find that he's the one getting everybody's sympathy, and not that bothersome corpse on the ground who shouldn't have been in the way anyhow. As long as the driver isn't drunk or flagrantly reckless, he can kill anybody in this country he wants to, and suffer no more than a momentary embarrassment and a penalty that isn't even worth worrying about.

"Think it over, man," the judge continued. "To most people the automobile is some sort of god, and if God happens to strike you down, it's your hard luck."

There was more of that in Judge Hilliker's mordant and long-winded style, but Cornelius had no need to remember it. What he needed he now had, and very carefully he put the gun back in the drawer, slid the drawer shut, and locked it.

Claire came in while he still sat brooding at the desk, and he forced himself to regard her with cold objectivity—this radiantly lovely woman who was playing him for a fool, and who now stood wide-eyed in the doorway with an incongruously large bag of groceries clutched to her.

"I saw the car in the garage," she said breathlessly. "I was afraid something was wrong. That you weren't feeling well. . . ."

"I feel very well."

"But you're home so early. You've never come this early before."

"I've always managed to refuse invitations to midweek dinner parties before."

"Oh, Lord!" she gasped. "The dinner! It never even entered my mind. I've been so busy all day. . . ."

"Yes?" he said. "Doing what?"

"Well, everyone's off today, so I took care of the house from top to bottom, and then when I looked in the pantry and saw we needed some things, I ran into town for them." She gestured at the bulky paper bag with her chin. "I'll have your bath ready and your things laid out as soon as I put this stuff away."

Watching her leave, he felt an honest admiration for her. Another woman would have invented a visit to a friend who might, at some later time, accidentally let the cat out of the bag. Or another woman would not have thought to burden herself with a useless package to justify a trip into town. But not Claire, who was evidently as clever as she was beautiful.

And she *was* damnably attractive. His male friends may have laughed behind his back, but in their homes she was always eagerly surrounded by them. When he entered a roomful of strangers with her, he saw how all men's eyes followed her with a frankly covetous interest. No, nothing must happen to her; nothing at all. It was the man who had to be destroyed, just as one would destroy any poacher on his preserves, any lunatic who with axe in hand ran amok through his home.

CORNELIUS LEARNED VERY quickly that his plans would have to take in a good deal more than the simple act of waylaying the man and running him down. There were details, innumerable details, covering every step of the way before and after the event, which had to be jigsawed into place bit by bit in order to make it perfect.

In that respect, Cornelius thought gratefully, the judge had been far more helpful than he had realized in his irony. Murder by automobile was the perfect murder, because, with certain details taken care of, it was not even murder at all! There was the victim, and there was the murderer standing over him, and the whole thing would be treated with perfunctory indifference. After all, what was one more victim among the thirty thousand each year? He was a statistic, to be regarded with some tongue clicking and a shrug of helplessness.

Not by Claire, of course. Coincidence can be stretched far, but hardly far enough to cover the case of a husband's running down his wife's lover. And that was the best part of it. Claire would know, but would be helpless to say anything, since saying anything must expose her own wrongdoing. She would spend her life, day after day, knowing that she had been found out, knowing that a just vengeance had been exacted, and standing forewarned against any other such temptations that might come her way.

But what of the remote possibility that she might choose to speak out and expose herself? There, Cornelius reflected, fitting another little piece of the jigsaw into place, coincidence would instantly go to work for him. If there was no single shred of evidence that he had ever suspected her affair, or that he had ever seen the man before, the accident *must* be regarded by the law as coincidence. Either way his position was unassailable.

It was with this in mind that he patiently and single-mindedly went to work on his plans. He was tempted at the start to call in some professional investigator who could promptly and efficiently bring him the information he wanted, but after careful consideration he put this idea aside. A smart investigator might easily put two and two together after the accident. If he were honest, he might go to the authorities with his suspicions; if he were dishonest, he might be tempted to try blackmail. Obviously, there was no way of calling in an outsider without risking one danger or the other. And nothing, nothing at all, was going to be risked here.

So it took Cornelius several precious weeks to glean the information he wanted, and, as he admitted to himself, it might have taken even longer had not Claire and the man maintained such an unfailing routine. Thursday was the one day of the week on which the man would pay his visits. Then, a little before the city-bound train arrived at the station, Claire would drive the station wagon into an almost deserted side street a block from the Plaza. In the car the couple would kiss with an intensity that made Cornelius' flesh crawl.

As soon as the man left the car Claire would drive swiftly away, and the man would walk briskly to the Plaza, make his way through the cars parked at the curb there, cross the Plaza obviously sunk in his own thoughts and with only half an eye for passing traffic, and would enter the station. The third time Cornelius witnessed this performance he could have predicted the man's every step with deadly accuracy.

Occasionally, during this period, Claire mentioned that she was going to the city to do some shopping, and Cornelius took advantage of this as well. He was standing in a shadow of the terminal's waiting room when her train pulled in, he followed her at a safe distance to the street, his cab trailed hers almost to the door of the shabby apartment house where the man lived. The man was sitting on the grimy steps of the house, obviously waiting for her. When he led her into the house, as Cornelius bitterly observed, they held hands like a pair of schoolchildren, and then there was a long wait, a wait which took up most of the afternoon; but Cornelius gave up waiting before Claire reappeared.

The eruption of fury he knew after that scene gave him the idea of staging the accident there on the city streets the next day, but Cornelius quickly dismissed the thought. It would mean driving the car into the city, which was something he never did, and that would be a dangerous deviation from his own routine. Besides, city tabloids, unlike his staid local newspaper, sometimes publicized automobile accidents not only by printing the news of them but also by displaying pictures of victim and culprit on their pages. He wanted none of that.

No, there was no question that the only place to settle matters was right in the Plaza itself, and the more Cornelius reviewed his plans in preparation for the act, the more he marveled at how flawless they were.

Nothing could conceivably go wrong. If by some mischance he struck down the man without killing him, his victim would be in the same position as Claire: unable to speak openly without exposing himself. If he missed the man entirely, he was hardly in the dangerous position of an assassin who misses his victim and is caught with the gun or knife in his hand. An automobile wasn't a weapon; the affair would simply be another close call for a careless pedestrian.

However, he wanted no close calls, and to that end he took to parking the car somewhat farther from the station than he ordinarily did. The extra distance, he estimated, would allow him to swing the car across the Plaza in an arc which would meet the man as he emerged from between the parked cars across the street. That would just about make explanations uncalled for. A man stepping out from between parked cars would be more in violation of the law than the driver who struck him!

Not only did he make sure to set the car at a proper distance from the station entrance but Cornelius also took to backing it into place, as some other drivers did. Now the front wheels were facing the Plaza, and he could quickly get up all the speed he wanted.

The day before the one he had chosen for the final act, Cornelius waited until he was clear of traffic on his homeward drive, and then stopped the car on a deserted part of the road, letting the motor idle. Then he carefully gauged the distance to a tree some thirty yards ahead; this, he estimated, would be the distance across the Plaza. He started the car and then drove it as fast as he could past the tree, the big machine snarling as it picked up speed. Once past the tree he braced himself, stepped hard on the brake, and felt the pressure of the steering wheel against his chest as the car slued to a shrieking stop.

That was it. That was all there was to it. . . .

He left the office the next day at the exact minute he had set for himself. After his secretary had helped him on with his coat, he turned to her as he had prepared himself to do and made a wry face.

"Just not feeling right," he said. "Don't know what's wrong."

And, as he knew good secretaries were trained to do, she frowned worriedly at him and said, "If you didn't work so hard, Mr. Bolinger . . ."

He waved that aside brusquely. "Nothing that getting home early to a good rest won't cure. Oh"—he slapped at the pockets of his coat—"my pills, Miss Wynant. They're in the top drawer over there."

They were only a few aspirins in an envelope, but it was the impression that counted. A man who was not feeling well had that much more justification for a mishap while he was driving.

The early train was familiar to him now; he had ridden on it several times during the past few weeks, but always circumspectly hidden behind a newspaper. Now it was to be different. When the conductor came through to check his commutation ticket, Cornelius was sitting limp in his seat, clearly a man in distress.

"Conductor," he asked, "if you don't mind, could you get me some water?"

The conductor glanced at him and hastily departed. When he returned with a dripping cup of water, Cornelius slowly and carefully removed an aspirin from the envelope and washed it down gratefully.

"If there's anything else," the conductor said, "just you let me know."

"No," Cornelius said, "no, I'm a little under the weather, that's all."

But at the station the conductor was there to lend him a solicitous hand down, and dally briefly. "You're not a regular, are you?" the conductor said. "At least, not on this train."

Cornelius felt a lift of gratification. "No," he said, "I've only taken this train once before. I usually travel on the Broker's Special."

"Oh." The conductor looked him up and down and grinned. "Well, that figures," he said. "Hope you found our service as good as the Special's."

In the small station Cornelius sat down on a bench, his head resting against the back of the bench, his eyes on the clock over the ticket agent's window. Once or twice he saw the agent glance worriedly through the window at him, and that was fine. What was not so fine was the rising feeling in him, a lurching nervousness in his stomach, a too heavy thudding of his heart in his chest. He had allowed himself ten minutes here; each minute found the feeling getting more and more oppressive. It was an effort to contain himself, to prevent himself from getting to his feet and rushing out to the car before the minute hand of the clock had touched the small black spot that was his signal.

Then, on the second, he got up, surprised at the effort it required to do this, and slowly walked out of the station, the agent's eyes following him all the way, and down past the station to the car. He climbed behind the wheel, closed the door firmly after him, and started the motor. The soft purring of the motor under his feet sent a new strength up through him. He sat there soaking it up, his eyes fixed on the distance across the Plaza.

When the man first appeared, moving with rapid strides toward him, it struck Cornelius in some strange way that the tall blond figure was like a puppet being drawn by an invisible wire to his destined place on the stage. Then, as he came closer, it was plain to see that he was smiling broadly, singing aloud in his exuberance of youth and strength—and triumph. That was the key which unlocked all paralysis, which sent the motor roaring into furious life.

For all the times he had lived the scene in his mind's eye, Cornelius was unprepared for the speed with which it happened. There was the man stepping out from between the cars, still blind to everything. There was Cornelius' hand on the horn, the ultimate inspiration, a warning that could not possibly be heeded, and more than anything else an insurance of success. The man swung toward the noise, his face all horror, his hands outthrust as if to fend off what was happening. There was the high-pitched scream abruptly cut off by the shock of impact, more violent than Cornelius had ever dreamed, and then everything dissolving into the screech of brakes.

The Plaza had been deserted before it had happened; now people were running from all directions, and Cornelius had to push his way through them to catch a glimpse of the body.

"Better not look," someone warned, but he did look, and saw the crumpled form, the legs scissored into an unnatural position, the face graying as he watched. He swayed, and a dozen helping hands reached out to support him, but it was not weakness which affected him now, but an overwhelming, giddy sense of victory, a sense of victory heightened by the voices around him.

"Walked right into it with his eyes wide open."

"I could hear that horn a block away."

"Drunk, maybe. The way he stood right there . . ."

The only danger now lay in overplaying his hand. He had to watch out for that, had to keep fitting piece after piece of the plan together, and then there would be no danger. He sat in the car while a policeman questioned him with official gravity, and he knew from the sympathy in the policeman's voice that he was making the right impression.

No, he was free to go home if he wished. Charges, of course, had to be automatically preferred against him, but the way things looked . . . Yes, they would be glad to phone Mrs. Bolinger. They could drive him home, but if he preferred to have her do it . . .

He had allowed time for her to be at home when the call was made, and he spent the next fifteen minutes with the crowd staring at him through the car window with a morbid and sympathetic curiosity. When the station wagon drew up nearby, a lane magically appeared through the crowd; when Claire was at his side the lane disappeared.

Even frightened and bewildered, she was a beautiful woman, Cornelius thought, and, he had to admit to himself, she knew how to put on a sterling show of wifely concern and devotion, false as it was. But perhaps that was because she didn't know yet.

He waited until she had helped him into the station wagon, and when she sat down in the driver's seat, he put an arm tight around her.

"Oh, by the way, Officer," he asked with grave anxiety through the open window. "Did you find out who the man was? Did he have any identification on him?"

The policeman nodded. "Young fellow from the city," he said, "so we'll have to check up on him down there. Name of Lundgren. Robert Lundgren, if his card means anything."

Against his arm Cornelius felt, rather than heard, the choked gasp, felt the uncontrollable small shivering. Her face was as gray as that of the man out there in the street. "All right, Claire," he said softly. "Let's go home."

She drove by instinct out through the streets of the town. Her face was vacuous, her eyes set and staring. He was almost grateful when they reached the highway, and she finally spoke in a quiet and wondering voice. "You knew," she said. "You knew about it, and you killed him for it."

"Yes," Cornelius said, "I knew about it."

"Then you're crazy," she said dispassionately, her eyes still fixed ahead of her. "You must be crazy to kill someone like that."

Her even, informative tone fired his anger as much as what she was saying.

"It was justice," he said between his teeth. "It was coming to him."

She was still remote. "You don't understand."

"Don't understand what?"

She turned toward him, and he saw that her eyes were glistening wet. "I knew him before I ever knew you, before I ever started working in the office. We always went together; it didn't seem as if there was any point living if we couldn't be together." She paused only a fraction of a second. "But things didn't go right. He had big ideas that didn't make any money, and I couldn't stand that. I was born poor, and I couldn't stand marrying poor and dying poor. . . . That's why I married you. And I tried to be a good wife—you'll never know how hard I tried!—but that wasn't what you wanted. You wanted a showpiece, not a wife; something to parade around in front of people so that they could admire you for owning it, just like they admire you for everything else you own."

"You're talking like a fool," he said harshly. "And watch the road. We turn off here."

"Listen to me!" she said. "I was going to tell you all about it. I was going to ask for a divorce. Not a penny to go with it, or anything like that—just the divorce so that I could marry him and make up for all the time I had thrown away! That's what I told him today, and if you had only asked—only talked to me . . ."

She would get over it, he thought. It had been even more serious than he had realized, but, as the saying went, all passes. She had nothing to trade her marriage for any longer; when she understood that clearly, they would make a new start. It was a miracle that he had thought of using the weapon he had, and that he had used it so effectively. A perfect weapon, the judge had said. He'd never know how perfect.

It was the warning clangor of the bell at the grade crossing that jarred Cornelius from his reverie—that, and the alarming realization that the car's speed was not slackening at all. Then everything else was submerged by the angry shrieking of a locomotive, and when he looked up incredulously, it was to the raging mountain of steel that was the Broker's Special hurling itself over the crossing directly ahead.

"Watch out!" he cried out wildly. "My God, what are you doing!"

In that last split second, when her foot went down hard on the accelerator, he knew.

THE SEA RAIDERS

H. G. WELLS

UNTIL THE EXTRAORDINARY affair at Sidmouth, the peculiar species *Haploteuthis ferox* was known to science only generically, on the strength of a half-digested tentacle obtained near the Azores, and a decaying body pecked by birds and nibbled by fish, found early in 1896 by Mr. Jennings, near Lands End.

In no department of zoological science, indeed, are we quite so much in the dark as with regard to the deep-sea cephalopods. A mere accident, for instance, it was that led to the Prince of Monaco's discovery of nearly a dozen new forms in the summer of 1895; a discovery in which the before-mentioned tentacle was included. It chanced that a cachalot was killed off Terceira by some sperm whalers, and in its last struggles charged almost to the prince's yacht, missed it, rolled under, and died within twenty yards of his rudder. And in its agony it threw up a number of large objects, which the prince, dimly perceiving they were strange and important, was able to secure before they sank. He set his screws in motion, and kept the objects circling in the vortices thus created until a boat could be lowered. And these specimens were whole cephalopods and fragments of cephalopods, some of gigantic proportions, and almost all of them unknown to science!

It would seem, indeed, that these large and agile creatures, living in the middle depths of the sea, must, to a large extent, forever remain unknown to us, since underwater they are too nimble for nets, and it is only by such rare unlooked-for accidents that specimens can be obtained. In the case of *Haploteuthis ferox,* for instance, we are still altogether ignorant of its habitat, as ignorant as we are of the breeding ground of the herring or the seaways of the salmon. And zoologists are at a loss to account for its sudden appearance on our coast. Possibly it was the stress of a hunger migration that drove it hither out of the deep. But it will be better, perhaps, to avoid necessarily inconclusive discussion, and to proceed at once with our narrative.

The first human being to set eyes upon a living haploteuthis—the first human being to survive, that is, for there can be little doubt now that the wave of bathing fatalities and boating accidents that traveled along the coast of Cornwall and Devon in early May was due to this cause—was a retired tea dealer of the name of Fison, who was stopping at a Sidmouth boardinghouse. It was in the afternoon, and he was walking along the cliff path between Sidmouth and Ladram Bay. The cliffs in this direction are very high, but down the red face of them in one place a kind of ladder staircase has been made. He was near this when his attention was attracted by what at first he thought to be a cluster of birds struggling over a fragment of food that caught the sunlight and glistened pinkish white. The tide was right out, and this object was not only far below him, but remote across a broad waste of rock reefs covered with dark seaweed and interspersed with silvery shining tidal pools. And he was, moreover, dazzled by the brightness of the farther water.

In a minute, regarding this again, he perceived that his judgment was in fault, for over this struggle circled a number of birds, jackdaws and gulls for the most part, the latter gleaming blindingly when the sunlight smote their wings, and they seemed minute in comparison with it. And his curiosity was, perhaps, aroused all the more strongly because of his first insufficient explanations.

As he had nothing better to do than amuse himself, he decided to make this object, whatever it was, the goal of his afternoon walk, instead of Ladram Bay, conceiving it might perhaps be a great fish of some sort, stranded by some chance, and flapping about in its distress.

And so he hurried down the long steep ladder, stopping at intervals of thirty feet or so to take breath and scan the mysterious movement.

At the foot of the cliff he was, of course, nearer his object than he had been; but, on the other hand, it now came up against the incandescent sky, beneath the sun, so as to seem dark and indistinct. Whatever was pinkish of it was now hidden by a skerry of weedy boulders. But he perceived that it was made up of seven rounded bodies, distinct or connected, and that the birds kept up a constant croaking and screaming, but seemed afraid to approach it too closely.

Mr. Fison, torn by curiosity, began picking his way across the wave-worn rocks, and, finding that the wet seaweed covering them had rendered them extremely slippery, he stopped, removed his shoes and socks, and coiled his trousers above his knees. His object was, of course, merely to avoid stumbling into the rocky pools about him, and perhaps he was rather glad, as all men are, of an excuse to resume, even for a moment, the sensations of his boyhood. At any rate, it is to this, no doubt, that he owes his life.

He approached his mark with all the assurance which the absolute security of this country against all forms of animal life gives its inhabitants. The round bodies moved to and fro, but it was only when he surmounted the skerry of boulders that he realized the horrible nature of the discovery. It came upon him with some suddenness.

The rounded bodies fell apart as he appeared over the ridge, and displayed the pinkish object to be the partially devoured body of a human being, but whether of a man or woman he was unable to say. And the rounded bodies were new and ghastly-looking creatures, in shape somewhat resembling an octopus, and with huge and very long and flexible tentacles, coiled copiously on the ground. The skin had a glistening texture, unpleasant to see, like shiny leather. The downward bend of the tentacle-surrounded mouth, the curious excrescence at the bend, the tentacles, and the large intelligent eyes gave the creatures a grotesque suggestion of a face. They were the size of a fair-sized swine about the body, and the tentacles seemed to him to be many feet in length. There were, he thinks, seven or eight at least of the creatures. Twenty yards beyond them, amid the surf of the now returning tide, two others were emerging from the sea.

Their bodies lay flatly on the rocks, and their eyes regarded him with evil interest, but it does not appear that Mr. Fison was afraid, or that he realized that he was in any danger. Possibly his confidence is to be ascribed to the limpness of their attitudes. But he was horrified, of course, and intensely excited and indignant at such revolting creatures preying upon human flesh. He thought they had chanced upon a drowned body. He shouted to them, with the idea of driving them off, and, finding they did not budge, cast about him, picked up a big rounded lump of rock, and flung it at one.

And then, slowly uncoiling their tentacles, they all began moving toward him—creeping at first deliberately, and making a soft purring sound to each other.

In a moment Mr. Fison realized that he was in danger. He shouted again, threw both his shoes, and started off with a leap forthwith. Twenty yards off he stopped and faced about, judging them slow, and behold! The tentacles of their leader were already pouring over the rocky ridge on which he had just been standing!

At that he shouted again—this time not threatening, but a cry of dismay—and began jumping, striding, slipping, wading across the uneven expanse between him and the beach. The tall red cliffs seemed suddenly at a vast distance, and he saw, as though they were creatures in another world, two minute workmen engaged in the repair of the ladderway, and little suspecting the race for life that was beginning below them. At one time he could hear the creatures splashing in the pools not a dozen feet behind him, and once he slipped and almost fell.

They chased him to the very foot of the cliffs, and desisted only when he had been joined by the workmen at the foot of the ladderway up the cliff. All three of the men pelted them with stones for a time, and then hurried to the cliff top and along the path toward Sidmouth, to secure assistance and a boat, and to rescue the desecrated body from the clutches of these abominable creatures.

AND, AS IF he had not already been in sufficient peril that day, Mr. Fison went with the boat to point out the exact spot of his adventure.

As the tide was down, it required a considerable detour to reach the spot, and when at last they came offshore of the ladderway, the mangled body had disappeared. The water was now running in, submerging first one slab of slimy rock and then another, and the four men in the boat—the workmen, that is, the boatman, and Mr. Fison—now turned their attention from the bearings offshore to the water beneath the keel.

At first they could see little below them save a dark jungle of laminaria, with an occasional darting fish. Their minds were set on adventure, and they expressed their disappointment freely. But presently they saw one of the monsters swimming through the water seaward, with a curious rolling motion that suggested to Mr. Fison the spinning roll of a captive balloon. Almost immediately after, the waving streamers of laminaria were extraordinarily perturbed, parted for a moment, and three of these beasts became darkly visible, struggling for what was probably some fragment of the drowned man. In a moment the copious olive-green ribbons had poured again over this writhing group.

At that all four men, greatly excited, began beating the water with oars and shouting, and immediately they saw a tumultuous movement among the weeds. They desisted to see more clearly, and as soon as the water was smooth, they saw, as it seemed to them, the whole sea bottom among the weeds set with eyes.

"Ugly swine!" cried one of the men. "Why, there's dozens!"

And forthwith the things began to rise through the water about them. Mr. Fison has since described to the writer this startling eruption out of the waving laminaria meadows. To him it seemed to occupy a considerable time, but it is probable that really it was an affair of a few seconds only. For a time nothing but eyes, and then he speaks of tentacles streaming out and parting the weed fronds this way and that. Then these things, growing larger, until at last the bottom was hidden by their intercoiling forms, and the tips of tentacles rose darkly here and there into the air above the swell of the waters.

One came up boldly to the side of the boat, and, clinging to this with three of its sucker-set tentacles, threw four others over the gunwale, as if with an intention either of overturning the boat or of clambering into it. Mr. Fison at once caught up the boat hook and, jabbing furiously at the soft tentacles, forced it to desist. He was struck in the back and almost pitched overboard by the boatman, who was using his oar to resist a similar attack on the other side of the boat. But the tentacles on either side at once relaxed their hold, slid out of sight, and splashed into the water.

"We'd better get out of this," said Mr. Fison, who was trembling violently. He went to the tiller, while the boatman and one of the workmen seated themselves and began rowing. The other workman stood up in the forepart of the boat, with the boat hook, ready to strike any more tentacles that might appear. Nothing else seems to have been said. Mr. Fison had expressed the common feeling beyond amendment. In a hushed, scared mood, with faces white and drawn, they set about escaping from the position into which they had so recklessly blundered.

But the oars had scarcely dropped into the water before dark, tapering, serpentine ropes had bound them, and were about the rudder; and creeping up the sides of the boat with a looping motion came the tentacles again. The men gripped their oars and pulled, but it was like trying to move a boat in a floating raft of weeds. "Help here!" cried the boatman, and Mr. Fison and the second workman rushed to help lug at the oar.

Then the man with the boat hook—his name was Ewan, or Ewen—sprang up with a curse, and began striking downward over the side, as far as he could reach, at the bank of tentacles that now clustered along the boat's bottom. And at the same time, the two rowers stood up to get a better purchase for the recovery of their oars. The boatman handed his to Mr. Fison, who lugged desperately, and meanwhile, the boatman opened a big clasp knife, and, leaning over the side of the boat, began hacking at the spiring arms upon the oar shaft.

Mr. Fison, staggering with the quivering rocking of the boat, his teeth set, his breath coming short, and the veins starting on his hands as he pulled at his oar, suddenly cast his eyes seaward. And there, not fifty yards off, across the long rollers of the incoming tide, was a large boat standing in toward them, with three women and a little child in it. A boatman was rowing, and a little man in a pink-ribboned straw hat and whites stood in the stern, hailing the struggling men. For a moment, of course, Mr. Fison thought of help, and then he thought of the child. He abandoned his oar forthwith, threw up his arms in a frantic gesture, and screamed to the party in the boat to keep away "for God's sake!" It says much for the modesty and courage of Mr. Fison that he does not seem to be aware that there was any quality of heroism in his action at this juncture. The oar he had abandoned was at once drawn under, and presently reappeared floating about twenty yards away.

At the same moment Mr. Fison felt the boat under him lurch violently, and a hoarse scream, a prolonged cry of terror from Hill, the boatman, caused him to forget the party of excursionists altogether. He turned, and saw Hill crouching by the forward oarlock, his face convulsed with terror, and his right arm over the side and drawn tightly down. He gave now a succession of short, sharp cries, "Oh! oh! oh! oh!" Mr. Fison believes that he must have been hacking at the tentacles below the waterline, and have been grasped by them, but, of course, it is quite impossible to say now certainly what had happened. The boat was heeling over, so that the gunwale was within ten inches of the water, and both Ewan and the other laborer were striking down into the water, with oar and boat hook, on either side of Hill's arm. Mr. Fison instinctively placed himself to counterpoise them.

Then Hill, who was a burly, powerful man, made a strenuous effort, and rose almost to a standing position. He lifted his arm, indeed, clean out of the water. Hanging to it was a complicated tangle of brown ropes; and the eyes of one of the brutes that had hold of him, glaring straight and resolute, showed momentarily above the surface. The boat heeled more and more, and the green-brown water came pouring in a cascade over the side. Then Hill slipped and fell with his ribs across the side, and his arm and the mass of tentacles about it splashed back into the water. He rolled over; his boot kicked Mr. Fison's knee as that gentleman rushed forward to seize him, and in another moment fresh tentacles had whipped about his waist and neck, and after a brief, convulsive struggle, in which the boat was nearly capsized, Hill was lugged overboard. The boat righted with a violent jerk that all but sent Mr. Fison over the other side, and hid the struggle in the water from his eyes.

He stood staggering to recover his balance for a moment, and as he did so, he became aware that the struggle and the inflowing tide had carried them close upon the weedy rocks again. Not four yards off, a table of rock still rose in rhythmic movements above the inwash of the tide. In a moment Mr. Fison seized the oar from Ewan, gave one vigorous stroke, then, dropping it, ran to the bows and leaped.

He felt his feet slide over the rock, and, by a frantic effort, leaped again toward a farther mass. He stumbled over this, came to his knees, and rose again.

"Look out!" cried someone, and a large drab body struck him. He was knocked flat into a tidal pool by one of the workmen, and as he went down he heard smothered, choking cries, which he believed at the time came from Hill. Then he found himself marveling at the shrillness and variety of Hill's voice. Someone jumped over him, and a curving rush of foamy water poured over him, and passed. He scrambled to his feet, dripping, and, without looking seaward, ran as fast as his terror would let him shoreward. Before him, over the flat space of scattered rocks, stumbled the two workmen—one a dozen yards in front of the other.

He looked over his shoulder at last, and, seeing that he was not pursued, faced about. He was astonished. From the moment of the rising of the cephalopods out of the water, he had been acting too swiftly to fully comprehend his actions. Now it seemed to him as if he had suddenly jumped out of an evil dream.

For there were the sky, cloudless and blazing with the afternoon sun, the sea weltering under its pitiless brightness, the soft creamy foam of the breaking water, and the low, long, dark ridges of rock. The righted boat floated, rising and falling gently on the swell about a dozen yards from shore. Hill and the monsters, all the stress and tumult of that fierce fight for life, had vanished as though they had never been.

Mr. Fison's heart was beating violently; he was throbbing to the fingertips, and his breath came deep.

There was something missing. For some seconds he could not think clearly enough what this might be. Sun, sky, sea, rocks—what was it? Then he remembered the boatload of excursionists. It had vanished. He wondered whether he had imagined it. He turned, and saw the two workmen standing side by side under the projecting masses of the cliffs. He hesitated whether he should make one last attempt to save the man Hill. His physical excitement seemed to desert him suddenly, and leave him aimless and helpless. He turned shoreward, stumbling and wading toward his two companions.

He looked back again, and there were now two boats floating, and the one farthest out at sea pitched clumsily, bottom upward.

SO IT WAS *Haploteuthis ferox* made its appearance upon the Devonshire coast. So far, this has been its most serious aggression. Mr. Fison's account, taken together with the wave of boating and bathing casualties to which I have already alluded, and the absence of fish from the Cornish coasts that year, points clearly to a shoal of these voracious deep-sea monsters prowling slowly along the subtidal coastline. Hunger migration has, I know, been suggested as the force that drove them hither; but, for my own part, I prefer to believe the alternative theory of Hemsley. Hemsley holds that a pack or shoal of these creatures may have become enamored of human flesh by the accident of a foundered ship sinking among them, and have wandered in search of it out of their accustomed zone; first waylaying and following ships, and so coming to our shores in the wake of the Atlantic traffic. But to discuss Hemsley's cogent and admirably stated arguments would be out of place here.

It would seem that the appetites of the shoal were satisfied by the catch of eleven people—for it turned out that there were actually ten people in the second boat, and certainly these creatures gave no further signs of their presence off Sidmouth that day. The coast between Seaton and Budleigh Salterton was patrolled all that evening and night by four Preventive Service boats, in which the men were armed with harpoons and cutlasses, and as the evening advanced, a number of more or less similarly equipped expeditions, organized by private individuals, joined them. Mr. Fison took no part in any of these expeditions.

About midnight excited hails were heard from a boat about a couple of miles out at sea to the southeast of Sidmouth, and a lantern was seen waving in a strange manner to and fro and up and down. The nearer boats at once hurried toward the alarm. The venturesome occupants of the boat, a seaman, a curate, and two schoolboys, had actually seen the monsters passing under their boat. The creatures, it seems, like most deep-sea organisms, were phosphorescent, and they had been floating, five fathoms deep or so, like creatures of moonshine through the blackness of the water, their tentacles retracted and as if asleep, rolling over and over, and moving slowly in a wedgelike formation toward the southeast.

These people told their story in gesticulated fragments, as first one boat drew alongside and then another. At last there was a little fleet of eight or nine boats collected together, and from them a tumult, like the chatter of a marketplace, rose into the stillness of the night. There was little or no disposition to pursue the shoal, the people had neither weapons nor experience for such a dubious chase, and presently—even with a certain relief, it may be—the boats turned shoreward.

And now to tell what is perhaps the most astonishing fact in this whole astonishing raid. We have not the slightest knowledge of the subsequent movements of the shoal, although the whole southwest coast was now alert for it. But it may, perhaps, be significant that a cachalot was stranded off Sark on June 3. Two weeks and three days after this Sidmouth affair, a living haploteuthis came ashore on Calais sands. It was alive, because several witnesses saw its tentacles moving in a convulsive way. But it is probable that it was dying. A gentleman named Pouchet obtained a rifle and shot it.

That was the last appearance of a living haploteuthis. No others were seen on the French coast. On the fifteenth of June a dead body, almost complete, was washed ashore near Torquay, and a few days later a boat from the marine biological station, engaged in dredging off Plymouth, picked up a rotting specimen, slashed deeply with a cutlass wound. How the former specimen had come by its death it is impossible to say. And on the last day of June, Mr. Egbert Caine, an artist, bathing near Newlyn, threw up his arms, shrieked, and was drawn under. A friend bathing with him made no attempt to save him, but swam at once for the shore. This is the last fact to tell of this extraordinary raid from the deeper sea. Whether it is really the last of these horrible creatures it is, as yet, premature to say. But it is believed, and certainly it is to be hoped, that they have returned now, and returned for good, to the sunless depths of the middle seas, out of which they have so strangely and so mysteriously arisen.

THE CASE OF THE IRATE WITNESS

ERLE STANLEY GARDNER

THE EARLY MORNING shadows cast by the mountains still lay heavily on the town's main street as the big siren on the roof of the Jebson Commercial Company began to scream shrilly.

The danger of fire was always present, and at the sound, men at breakfast rose and pushed their chairs back from the table; others, who were shaving, barely paused to wipe lather from their faces; and those who had been sleeping grabbed the first available garments. All of them ran to places where they could look for the first telltale wisps of smoke.

There was no smoke.

The big siren was still screaming urgently as the men formed into streaming lines, like ants whose hill has been attacked. The lines all moved toward the Jebson Commercial Company.

There the men were told that the doors of the big vault had been found wide open. A jagged hole had been cut into one door with an acetylene torch. This was the fifteenth of the month. The big, twice-a-month payroll, which had been brought up from the Ivanhoe National Bank the day before, had been the prize. The men looked at one another silently.

Frank Bernal, manager of the company's mine, the man who ruled

Jebson City with an iron hand, arrived and took charge. The responsibility was his, and what he found was alarming.

Tom Munson, the night watchman, was lying on the floor in a back room, snoring in drunken slumber. The burglar alarm, which had been installed within the last six months, had been bypassed by means of an ingenious electrical device.

Ralph Nesbitt, the company accountant, was significantly silent. When Frank Bernal had been appointed manager a year earlier, Nesbitt had pointed out that the big vault was obsolete.

Bernal, determined to prove himself in his new job, had avoided the expense of tearing out the old vault and installing a new one by investing in an up-to-date burglar alarm and putting a special night watchman on duty.

Now the safe had been looted of a hundred thousand dollars and Frank Bernal had to make a report to the main office in Chicago, with the disquieting knowledge that Ralph Nesbitt's memo stating the antiquated vault was a pushover was at this moment reposing in the company files.

SOME DISTANCE OUT of Jebson City, Perry Mason, the famous trial lawyer, was driving fast along a mountain road. He had had plans for a weekend fishing trip for some time, but a jury which had not reached its verdict until midnight had delayed his departure and it was now eight thirty in the morning.

His fishing clothes, rod, wading boots, and creel were all in the trunk. He was wearing the suit in which he had stepped from the courtroom, and having driven all night, he was eager for the cool, piny mountains.

A blazing red light, shining directly at him as he rounded a turn in the canyon road, dazzled his road-weary eyes. A sign, STOP—POLICE, had been placed in the middle of the road. Two men—a grim-faced one with a 30-30 rifle in his hands and a silver badge on his shirt, and a uniformed motorcycle officer—stood beside the sign. Mason stopped his car.

The man with the badge, a deputy sheriff, said, "We'd better take a look at your driver's license. There's been a big robbery at Jebson City."

"That so?" Mason said. "I went through Jebson City an hour ago and everything seemed quiet."

"Where you been since then?"

"I stopped at a little restaurant for breakfast." Mason handed him his driver's license.

The man looked at it. "Say," he said, "you're Perry Mason, the big criminal lawyer!"

"Not a criminal lawyer," Mason said patiently, "a trial lawyer. I sometimes defend men who are accused of crime."

"What are you doing up in this country?"

"Going fishing."

The deputy looked at him suspiciously. "Why aren't you wearing your fishing clothes?"

"Because," Mason said, and smiled, "I'm not fishing."

"You said you were going fishing."

"I also intend," Mason said, "to go to bed tonight. According to you, I should be wearing my pajamas."

The deputy frowned. The traffic officer laughed and waved Mason on. Later, when a news-hungry reporter from the local paper asked the deputy if he knew of anything that would make a good story, the deputy said that he did.

And that was why Della Street, Perry Mason's confidential secretary, was surprised to read stories in the metropolitan papers stating that her employer, the noted trial lawyer, was rumored to have been retained to represent the person or persons who had looted the vault of the Jebson Commercial Company.

WHEN PERRY MASON called his office the next afternoon, Della said, "I thought you were going to the mountains for a vacation."

"That's right. Why?"

"The papers claim you're representing whoever robbed the Jebson Commercial Company."

"First I've heard of it," Mason said. "I went through Jebson City before they discovered the robbery, stopped for breakfast a little farther on, and then got caught in a roadblock. In the eyes of some officious deputy, that seems to have made me an accessory after the fact."

"Well, they've caught a man by the name of Harvey L. Corbin and apparently have quite a case against him. They're hinting at mysterious evidence which won't be disclosed until the time of trial."

"Was he the one who committed the crime?" Mason asked.

"The police think so. He has a criminal record. When his employers at Jebson City found out about it, they told him to leave town. That was the evening before the robbery."

"Just like that, eh?" Mason asked.

"Well, you see, Jebson City is a one-industry town, and the company owns all the houses. They're leased to the employees. I understand Corbin's wife and daughter were told they could stay on until Corbin got located in a new place, but Corbin was told to leave town at once. You aren't interested, are you?"

"Not in the least," Mason said, "except that when I drive back, I'll be going through Jebson City, and I'll probably stop to pick up the local gossip."

"Don't do it," she warned. "This man Corbin has all the earmarks of being an underdog, and you know how you feel about underdogs."

A quality in her voice made Perry suspicious. "You haven't been approached, have you, Della?"

"Well," she said, "in a way. Mrs. Corbin read in the papers that you were going to represent her husband, and she was overjoyed. It seems that she thinks her husband's implication in this is a raw deal. She hadn't known about his criminal record, but she loves him and is going to stand by him."

"You've talked with her?" Mason asked.

"Several times. I tried to break it to her gently. I told her it was probably nothing but a newspaper story. You see, Chief, they have Corbin dead to rights. He left her forty dollars, and it was part of the loot. They took it all as evidence."

"I'll drive all night," he said. "Tell Mrs. Corbin I'll be in Jebson City tomorrow."

"I was afraid of that," Della Street said. "Why did you have to call up? Why couldn't you have stayed up there fishing? Why did you have to get your name in the papers?"

Mason laughed and hung up.

PAUL DRAKE, OF THE DRAKE DETECTIVE Agency, sat down in the big chair in Mason's office and said, "You have a bear by the tail, Perry."

"What's the matter, Paul? Didn't your detective work in Jebson City pan out?"

"It panned out all right, but the stuff in the pan isn't what you want. The money your client gave his wife was some of what was stolen from the vault."

"How do they know it was the stolen money?" Mason asked.

Drake pulled a notebook from his pocket. "Here's the whole picture. The Jebson company controls everything in Jebson City except for an old coot by the name of George Addey who lives five miles down the canyon. He has a hog ranch and a garbage-collecting business. He's supposed to have the first nickel he ever earned. Buries his money in cans. There's no bank nearer than Ivanhoe City."

"What about the burglary? The man who did it must have moved in acetylene tanks and—"

"They took them right out of the company store," Drake said. And then he went on. "Munson, the watchman, likes to take a pull out of a flask of whiskey along about midnight. He says it keeps him awake. Of course, no one was supposed to know about the whiskey, but someone did. They doped it with a barbiturate. The watchman took his usual swig, went to sleep, and stayed asleep."

"What's the evidence against Corbin?" Mason asked.

"Corbin had a previous burglary record. It's a policy of the company not to hire anyone with a criminal record. He lied about his past and got a job. Frank Bernal, the manager, found out about it, sent for Corbin about eight o'clock the night the burglary took place, and ordered him out of town. Corbin pulled out in the morning and gave his wife this money. It was part of the money from the burglary."

"How do they know?" Mason asked.

"Now there's something I don't know," Drake said. "This fellow Bernal is pretty smart, and the story is that he can prove Corbin's money was from the vault."

Drake paused, then continued. "As I told you, the nearest bank is at Ivanhoe City, and the mine pays off in cash twice a month. Ralph Nesbitt, the cashier, wanted to install a new vault. Bernal refused to okay the expense. So the company has ordered both Bernal and Nesbitt back to its main office at Chicago to report. The rumor is that they may fire Bernal as manager and give Nesbitt the job. A couple of the directors don't like Bernal, and this thing has given them their chance. They dug out a report Nesbitt had made showing the vault was a pushover. Bernal didn't act on that report." He sighed and then asked, "When's the trial, Perry?"

"The preliminary hearing is set for Friday morning. I'll see then what they've got against Corbin."

"They're laying for you up there," Paul Drake warned. "Better watch out, Perry. That district attorney has something up his sleeve, some sort of surprise that's going to knock you for a loop."

IN SPITE OF his long experience as a prosecutor, Vernon Flasher, district attorney of Ivanhoe County, showed a certain nervousness at having to oppose Perry Mason. There was, however, a secret assurance underneath that nervousness.

Judge Haswell, realizing that the eyes of the community were upon him, adhered to legal technicalities to the point of being pompous both in rulings and mannerisms.

But what irritated Perry Mason was the attitude of the spectators. He sensed that they did not regard him as an attorney trying to safeguard the interests of a client, but as a legal magician with a cloven hoof. The robbery had shocked the community, and there was a tight-lipped determination that no legal tricks were going to do Mason any good *this* time.

Vernon Flasher used his surprise evidence right at the start of the case. Frank Bernal, called as a witness, described the location of the vault, identified photographs, and then leaned back as the district attorney said abruptly, "You had reason to believe this vault was obsolete?"

"Yes, sir."

"It had been pointed out to you by one of your fellow employees, Mr. Ralph Nesbitt?"

"Yes, sir."

"And what did you do about it?"

"I did three things," Bernal said, "to safeguard the payrolls and to avoid the expense of tearing out the old vault and installing a new one. I employed a special night watchman, I installed the best burglar alarm money could buy, and I made arrangements with the Ivanhoe National Bank, where we have our payrolls made up, to list the number of each twenty-dollar bill which was a part of each payroll."

Mason suddenly sat up straight.

Flasher gave him a glance of gloating triumph. "Do you wish the court to understand, Mr. Bernal," he said smugly, "that you have the numbers of the bills in the payroll which was made up for delivery on the fifteenth?"

"Yes, sir. Not *all* the bills. That would have taken too much time. But I have the numbers of all the twenty-dollar bills."

"And who recorded those numbers?" the prosecutor asked.

"The bank."

"And do you have that list of numbers with you?"

"I do. Yes, sir." Bernal produced a list. "I felt," he said, glancing coldly at Nesbitt, "that these precautions would be cheaper than a new vault."

"I move the list be introduced in evidence," Flasher said.

"Just a moment," Mason objected. "I have a couple of questions. You say this list is not in your handwriting, Mr. Bernal?"

"Yes, sir."

"Whose handwriting is it, do you know?" Mason asked.

"The assistant cashier of the Ivanhoe National Bank."

"Oh, all right," Flasher said. "We'll do it the hard way, if we have to. Stand down, Mr. Bernal, and I'll call the assistant cashier."

Harry Reedy, assistant cashier of the Ivanhoe bank, had the mechanical assurance of an adding machine. He identified the list of numbers as being in his handwriting. He stated that he had listed the numbers of the twenty-dollar bills and put that list in an envelope, which had been sealed and sent up with the money for the payroll.

"Cross-examine," Flasher said.

Mason studied the list. "Did you yourself compare the numbers you wrote down with the numbers on the twenty-dollar bills?" he asked Reedy.

"No, sir. I didn't personally do that. Two assistants did that. One checked the numbers as they were read off, one as I wrote them down."

"The payrolls are for approximately a hundred thousand dollars, twice each month?"

"That's right. And ever since Mr. Bernal took charge, we have taken this means to identify payrolls. No attempt is made to list the bills in numerical order. The serial numbers are simply read off and written down. Unless a robbery occurs, there is no need to do anything further. In the event of a robbery, we can reclassify the numbers and list the bills in numerical order."

"These numbers are in your handwriting—every number?"

"Yes, sir. More than that, you will notice that at the bottom of each page I have signed my initials."

"That's all," Mason said.

"I now offer once more to introduce this list in evidence," Flasher said.

"So ordered," Judge Haswell ruled.

"My next witness is Charles J. Oswald, the sheriff," the district attorney announced.

The sheriff, a long, lanky man with a quiet manner, took the stand. "You're acquainted with Harvey L. Corbin, the defendant in this case?" the district attorney asked.

"I am."

"Are you acquainted with his wife?"

"Yes, sir."

"Now, on the morning of the robbery at the Jebson Commercial Company, did you have any conversation with Mrs. Corbin?"

"I did. Yes, sir."

"Did you ask her about her husband's activities the night before?"

"Just a moment," Mason said. "I object to this on the ground that any conversation the sheriff had with Mrs. Corbin is not admissible against the defendant, Corbin; furthermore, that in this state a wife cannot testify against her husband. Therefore, any statement she might make would be an indirect violation of that rule. Furthermore, I object on the ground that the question calls for hearsay."

Judge Haswell looked ponderously thoughtful, then said, "It seems to me Mr. Mason is correct."

"I'll put it this way, Mr. Sheriff," the district attorney said. "Did you, on the morning of the fifteenth, take any money from Mrs. Corbin?"

"Objected to as incompetent, irrelevant, and immaterial," Mason said.

"Your Honor," Flasher said irritably, "that's the very gist of our case. We propose to show that two of the stolen twenty-dollar bills were in the possession of Mrs. Corbin."

Mason said, "Unless the prosecution can prove the bills were given Mrs. Corbin by her husband, the evidence is inadmissible."

"That's just the point," Flasher said. "Those bills *were* given to her by the defendant."

"How do you know?" Mason asked.

"She told the sheriff so."

"That's hearsay," Mason snapped.

Judge Haswell fidgeted on the bench. "We're getting into a peculiar situation here. You can't call the wife as a witness, and I don't think her statement to the sheriff is admissible."

"Well," Flasher said desperately, "in this state, Your Honor, we have a community-property law. Mrs. Corbin had this money. Since she is the wife of the defendant, it was community property. Therefore, it's partially his property."

"Well now, there," Judge Haswell said, "I think I can agree with you. You introduce the twenty-dollar bills. I'll overrule the objection made by the defense."

The bills were produced and received in evidence.

"Cross-examine," Flasher said curtly.

"No questions of this witness," Mason said, "but I have a few questions to ask Mr. Bernal on cross-examination. You took him off the stand to lay the foundation for introducing the bank list, and I had no opportunity to cross-examine him."

"I beg your pardon," Flasher said. "Resume the stand, Mr. Bernal." His tone, now that he had the twenty-dollar bills safely introduced in evidence, was excessively polite.

Mason said, "This list which has been introduced in evidence is on the stationery of the Ivanhoe National Bank?"

"That's right. Yes, sir."

"It consists of several pages, and at the end there is the signature of the assistant cashier?"

"Yes, sir."

"And each page is initialed by the assistant cashier?"

"Yes, sir."

"This was the scheme which you thought of in order to safeguard the company against a payroll robbery?"

"Not to safeguard the company against a payroll robbery, Mr. Mason, but to assist us in recovering the money in the event there was a holdup."

"This was your plan to answer Mr. Nesbitt's objections that the vault was an outmoded model?"

"A part of my plan, yes. I may say that Mr. Nesbitt's objections had never been voiced until I took office. I felt he was trying to embarrass me by making my administration show less net returns than expected." Bernal tightened his lips and added, "Mr. Nesbitt had, I believe, been expecting to be appointed manager. He was disappointed. I believe he still expects to be manager."

In the spectators' section of the courtroom, Ralph Nesbitt glared at Bernal.

"You had a conversation with the defendant on the night of the fourteenth?" Mason asked Bernal.

"I did. Yes, sir."

"You told him that you were discharging him immediately and wanted him to leave the premises at once?"

"Yes, sir. I did."

"And you paid him his wages in cash?"

"Mr. Nesbitt paid him in my presence, with money he took from the petty-cash drawer of the vault."

"Now, as part of the wages due him, wasn't Corbin given these two twenty-dollar bills which have been introduced in evidence?"

Bernal shook his head. "I had thought of that," he said, "but it would have been impossible. Those bills weren't available to us at that time. The payroll is received from the bank in a sealed package. Those two twenty-dollar bills were in that package."

"And the list of the numbers of the twenty-dollar bills?"

"That's in a sealed envelope. The money is placed in the vault. I lock the list of numbers in my desk."

"Are you prepared to swear that neither you nor Mr. Nesbitt had access to these two twenty-dollar bills on the night of the fourteenth?"

"That is correct."

"That's all," Mason said. "No further cross-examination."

"I now call Ralph Nesbitt to the stand," District Attorney Flasher said. "I want to fix the time of these events definitely, Your Honor."

"Very well," Judge Haswell said. "Mr. Nesbitt, come forward."

Ralph Nesbitt, after answering the usual preliminary questions, sat down in the witness chair.

"Were you present at a conversation which took place between the defendant, Harvey L. Corbin, and Frank Bernal on the fourteenth of this month?" the district attorney asked.

"I was. Yes, sir."

"What time did that conversation take place?"

"About eight o'clock in the evening."

"And, without going into the details of that conversation, I will ask you if the general effect of it was that the defendant was discharged and ordered to leave the company's property?"

"Yes, sir."

"And he was paid the money that was due him?"

"In cash. Yes, sir. I took the cash from the safe myself."

"Where was the payroll then?"

"In the sealed package in a compartment in the safe. As cashier, I had the only key to that compartment. Earlier in the afternoon I had gone to Ivanhoe City and received the sealed package of money and the envelope containing the list of numbers. I personally locked the package of money in the vault."

"And the list of numbers?"

"Mr. Bernal locked that in his desk."

"Cross-examine," Flasher said.

"No questions," Mason said.

"That's our case, Your Honor," Flasher observed.

"May we have a few minutes' indulgence?" Mason asked Judge Haswell.

"Very well. Make it brief," the judge agreed.

Mason turned to Paul Drake and Della Street. "Well, there you are," Drake said. "You're confronted with the proof, Perry."

"Are you going to put the defendant on the stand?" Della Street asked.

Mason shook his head. "It would be suicidal. He has a record of a prior criminal conviction. Also, it's a rule of law that if one asks about any part of a conversation on direct examination, the other side can bring out all the conversation. That conversation, when Corbin was discharged, was to the effect that he had lied about his past record. And I guess there's no question that he did."

"And he's lying now," Drake said. "This is one case where you're licked. I think you'd better cop a plea and see what kind of a deal you can make with Flasher."

"Probably not any," Mason said. "Flasher wants to have the reputation of having given me a licking—Wait a minute, Paul. I have an idea."

Mason turned abruptly, walked away to where he could stand by himself, his back to the crowded courtroom.

"Are you ready?" the judge asked.

Mason turned. "I am quite ready, Your Honor. I have one witness whom I wish to put on the stand. I wish a subpoena *duces tecum* issued for that witness. I want him to bring certain documents which are in his possession."

"Who is the witness, and what are the documents?" the judge asked.

Mason walked quickly over to Paul Drake. "What's the name of that character who has the garbage-collecting business," he said softly, "the one who has the first nickel he'd ever made?"

"George Addey."

The lawyer turned to the judge. "The witness that I want is George Addey, and the documents that I want him to bring to court with him are all the twenty-dollar bills that he has received during the past sixty days."

"Your Honor," Flasher protested, "this is making a travesty out of justice. It is exposing the court to ridicule."

Mason said, "I give Your Honor my assurance that I think this witness is material and that the documents are material. I will make an affidavit to that effect if necessary. May I point out that if the court refuses to grant this subpoena, it will be denying the defendant due process of law."

"I'm going to issue the subpoena," Judge Haswell said testily, "and for your own good, Mr. Mason, the testimony had better be relevant."

George Addey, unshaven and bristling with indignation, held up his right hand to be sworn. He glared at Perry Mason.

"Mr. Addey," Mason said, "you have the contract to collect garbage from Jebson City?"

"I do."

"How long have you been collecting garbage there?"

"For over five years, and I want to tell you—"

Judge Haswell banged his gavel. "The witness will answer questions and not interpolate any comments."

"I'll interpolate anything I dang please," Addey said.

"That'll do," the judge said. "Do you wish to be jailed for contempt of court, Mr. Addey?"

"I don't want to go to jail, but I—"

"Then you'll remember the respect that is due the court," the judge said. "Now you sit there and answer questions. This is a court of law." There was a moment's silence. "All right, go ahead, Mr. Mason."

Mason said, "During the thirty days prior to the fifteenth of this month, did you deposit any money in any banking institution?"

"I did not."

"Do you have with you all the twenty-dollar bills that you received during the last sixty days?"

"I have, and I think making me bring them here is just like inviting some crook to come and rob me and—"

Judge Haswell banged with his gavel. "Any more comments of that sort from the witness and there will be a sentence imposed for contempt of court. Now you get out those twenty-dollar bills, Mr. Addey, and put them right up here on the clerk's desk."

Addey, mumbling under his breath, slammed a roll of twenty-dollar bills down on the desk in front of the clerk.

"Now," Mason said, "I'm going to need a little clerical assistance. I would like to have my secretary and the clerk help me check through the numbers on these bills. I will select a few at random."

Mason picked up two of the twenty-dollar bills and said, "I am going to ask my assistants to check the list of numbers introduced in evidence. In my hand is a twenty-dollar bill that carries the number L 07083274 A. The next bill that I pick up is number L 07579190 A. Are either of those bills on the list?"

The courtroom was silent. Suddenly Della Street said, "Yes, here's one—bill number L 07579190 A. It's on the list, on page eight."

"What?" the prosecutor shouted.

"Exactly," Mason said, smiling. "So, if a case is to be made against a person merely because he has possession of the money that was stolen on the fifteenth of this month, then your office should prefer charges against this witness, George Addey, Mr. District Attorney."

Addey jumped from the witness stand and shook his fist in Mason's face. "You're a cockeyed liar!" he screamed. "There ain't a one of those bills but what I didn't have it before the fifteenth. The company cashier changes my money into twenties, because I like big bills. I bury 'em in cans, and I put the date on the side of the can."

A tense silence gripped the courtroom. "I'm afraid I don't understand this, Mr. Mason," Judge Haswell said after a moment.

"It's quite simple," Mason said. "And I suggest the court take a recess for an hour and check these other bills against this list. The district attorney may be surprised."

And Mason sat down and proceeded to put papers in his briefcase.

DELLA STREET, PAUL Drake, and Perry Mason were sitting in the lobby of the Ivanhoe Hotel.

"When are you going to tell us?" Della Street asked fiercely. "Or do we tear you limb from limb? How could the garbage man have—"

"Wait a minute," Mason said. "I think we're about to get results. Here comes the esteemed district attorney, Vernon Flasher, and he's accompanied by Judge Haswell."

The two strode over to Mason's group and bowed with cold formality. Mason got up.

Judge Haswell began in his best courtroom voice. "A most deplorable situation has occurred. It seems Mr. Frank Bernal has—well—"

"Been detained somewhere," Vernon Flasher said.

"Disappeared," Judge Haswell said. "He's gone."

"I expected as much," Mason said.

"Now will you kindly tell me just what sort of pressure you brought to bear on Mr. Bernal to—"

"Just a moment, Judge," Mason said. "The only pressure I brought to bear on him was to cross-examine him."

"Did you know that there had been a mistake in the dates on those lists?"

"There was no mistake. When you find Bernal, I'm sure you will discover there was a deliberate falsification. He was short in his accounts, and he knew he was about to be demoted. He had a desperate need for a hundred thousand dollars in ready cash. He had evidently been planning this burglary, or, rather, this embezzlement, for some time. He learned that Corbin had a criminal record. He arranged to have these lists furnished by the bank. He installed a burglar alarm and, naturally, knew how to circumvent it. He employed a watchman he knew was addicted to drink. He only needed to stage his coup at the right time. He fired Corbin and paid him off with bills that had been recorded by the bank on page eight of the list of bills *in the payroll on the first of the month.*

"Then he removed page eight from the list of bills contained in the payroll *of the fifteenth*, before he showed it to the police, and substituted page eight of the list for the *first-of-the-month* payroll. It was that simple.

"Then he drugged the watchman's whiskey, took an acetylene torch, burned through the vault doors, and took all the money."

"May I ask how you knew all this?" Judge Haswell demanded.

"Certainly," Mason said. "My client told me he received those bills from Nesbitt, who took them from the petty-cash drawer in the safe. He also told the sheriff that. I happened to be the only one who believed him. It sometimes pays, Your Honor, to have faith in a man, even if he has made a previous mistake. Assuming my client was innocent, I knew either Bernal or Nesbitt must be guilty. I then realized that only Bernal had custody of the *previous* lists of numbers.

"As an employee, Bernal had been paid on the first of the month. He looked at the numbers on the twenty-dollar bills in his pay envelope and found that they had been listed on page eight of the payroll for the first. He only needed to extract all the twenty-dollar bills from the petty-cash drawer, substitute twenty-dollar bills from his own pay envelope, call in Corbin, and fire him. His trap was set.

"I let him know I knew what had been done by bringing Addey into court and proving my point. Then I asked for a recess. That was so Bernal would have a chance to skip out. You see, flight may be received as evidence of guilt. It was a professional courtesy to the district attorney. It will help him when Bernal is arrested."

SREDNI VASHTAR

SAKI (H. H. MUNRO)

CONRADIN WAS TEN years old, and the doctor had pronounced his professional opinion that the boy would not live another five years. The doctor was silky and effete, and counted for little, but his opinion was endorsed by Mrs. De Ropp, who counted for nearly everything. Mrs. De Ropp was Conradin's cousin and guardian, and in his eyes she represented those three fifths of the world that are necessary and disagreeable and real; the other two fifths, in perpetual antagonism to the foregoing, were summed up in himself and his imagination. One of these days Conradin supposed he would succumb to the mastering pressure of wearisome necessary things—such as illnesses and coddling restrictions and drawn-out dullness. Without his imagination, which was rampant under the spur of loneliness, he would have succumbed long ago.

Mrs. De Ropp would never, in her most honest moments, have confessed to herself that she disliked Conradin, though she might have been dimly aware that thwarting him "for his good" was a duty which she did not find particularly irksome. Conradin hated her with a desperate sincerity which he was perfectly able to mask. Such few pleasures as he could contrive for himself gained an added relish from the likelihood that they would be displeasing to his guardian, and from the realm of his imagination she was locked out—an unclean thing, which should find no entrance.

In the dull, cheerless garden, overlooked by so many windows that were ready to open with a message not to do this or that, or a reminder that medicines were due, he found little attraction. The few fruit trees that it contained were set jealously apart from his plucking, as though they were rare specimens of their kind blooming in an arid waste; it would probably have been difficult to find a market gardener who would have offered ten shillings for their entire yearly produce. In a forgotten corner, however, almost hidden behind a dismal shrubbery, was a disused toolshed of respectable proportions, and within its walls Conradin found a haven, something that took on the varying aspects of a playroom and a cathedral. He had peopled it with a legion of familiar phantoms, evoked partly from fragments of history and partly from his own brain, but it also boasted two inmates of flesh and blood.

In one corner lived a ragged-plumaged Houdan hen, on which the boy lavished an affection that had scarcely another outlet. Farther back in the gloom stood a large hutch, divided into two compartments, one of which was fronted with close iron bars. This was the abode of a large polecat-ferret, which a friendly butcher boy had once smuggled, cage and all, into its present quarters, in exchange for a long-secreted hoard of small silver. Conradin was dreadfully afraid of the lithe, sharp-fanged beast, but it was his most treasured possession. Its very presence in the toolshed was a secret and fearful joy, to be kept scrupulously from the knowledge of the Woman, as he privately dubbed his cousin. And one day, out of heaven knows what material, he spun the beast a wonderful name, and from that moment it grew into a god and a religion. The Woman indulged in religion once a week at a church nearby, and took Conradin with her, but to him the church service was an alien rite in the House of Rimmon. Every Thursday, in the dim and musty silence of the toolshed, he worshipped with mystic and elaborate ceremonial before the wooden hutch where dwelt Sredni Vashtar, the great ferret. Red flowers in their season and scarlet berries in the wintertime were offered at his shrine, for he was a god who laid some special stress on the fierce impatient side of things, as opposed to the Woman's religion, which, as far as Conradin could observe, went to great lengths in the contrary direction. And on great festivals powdered nutmeg was strewn in front of his hutch, an important feature of the offering being that the nutmeg had to be stolen. These festivals were of irregular occurrence, and were chiefly appointed to celebrate some passing event. On one occasion, when Mrs. De Ropp suffered from acute toothache for three days, Conradin kept up the festival during the entire three days, and almost succeeded in persuading himself that Sredni Vashtar was personally responsible for the toothache. If the malady had lasted for another day, the supply of nutmeg would have given out.

The Houdan hen was never drawn into the cult of Sredni Vashtar. Conradin had long ago settled that she was Anabaptist. He did not pretend to have the remotest knowledge as to what an Anabaptist was, but he privately hoped that it was not very respectable. Mrs. De Ropp was the ground plan on which he based and detested all respectability.

After a while Conradin's absorption in the toolshed began to attract the notice of his guardian. It is not good for him to be pottering down there in all weathers, she promptly decided, and at breakfast one morning she announced that the Houdan hen had been sold and taken away overnight. With her shortsighted eyes she peered at Conradin, waiting for an outbreak of rage and sorrow, which she was ready to rebuke with a flow of excellent precepts and reasoning. But Conradin said nothing: there was nothing to be said. Something perhaps in his white set face gave her a momentary qualm, for at tea that afternoon there was toast on the table, a delicacy which she usually banned on the ground that it was bad for him; also because the making of it "gave trouble," a deadly offense in the middle-class feminine eye.

"I thought you liked toast!" she exclaimed with an injured air, observing that he did not touch it.

"Sometimes," said Conradin.

In the shed that evening there was an innovation in the worship of the hutch god. Tonight Conradin asked a boon.

"Do one thing for me, Sredni Vashtar."

The thing was not specified. As Sredni Vashtar was a god, he must be supposed to know. And, choking back a sob as he looked at that other empty corner, Conradin went back to the world he so hated.

And every night, in the welcome darkness of his bedroom, and every evening, in the dusk of the toolshed, Conradin's bitter litany went up: "Do one thing for me, Sredni Vashtar."

Mrs. De Ropp noticed that the visits to the shed did not cease, and one day she made a further journey of inspection.

"What are you keeping in that locked hutch?" she asked. "I believe it's guinea pigs. I'll have them all cleared away."

Conradin shut his lips tight, but the Woman ransacked his bedroom till she found the carefully hidden key, and forthwith marched down to the shed to complete her discovery. It was a cold afternoon, and Conradin had been bidden to keep to the house. From the farthest window of the dining room the door of the shed could just be seen beyond the corner of the shrubbery, and there Conradin stationed himself. He saw the Woman enter, and then he imagined her opening the door of the sacred hutch and peering down with her shortsighted eyes into the thick straw bed where his god lay hidden. Perhaps she would prod at the straw in her clumsy impatience. And Conradin fervently breathed his prayer for the last time. But he knew as he prayed that he did not believe. He knew that the Woman would come out presently with that pursed smile he loathed so well on her face, and that in an hour or two the gardener would carry away his wonderful god, a god no longer, but a simple brown ferret in a hutch. And he knew that Woman would triumph always as she triumphed now, and that he would grow ever more sickly under her pestering and domineering and superior wisdom, till one day nothing would matter much with him, and the doctor would be proved right. And in the sting and misery of his defeat, he began to chant loudly and defiantly the hymn of his threatened idol:

"Sredni Vashtar went forth,
His thoughts were red thoughts and his teeth were white.
His enemies called for peace, but he brought them death.
Sredni Vashtar the Beautiful."

And then of a sudden he stopped his chanting and drew closer to the windowpane. The door of the shed still stood ajar as it had been left, and the minutes were slipping by. They were long minutes, but they slipped by nevertheless. He watched the starlings running and flying in little parties across the lawn; he counted them over and over again, with one eye always on that swinging door. A sour-faced maid came in to lay the table for tea, and still Conradin stood and waited and watched. Hope had crept by inches into his heart, and now a look of triumph began to blaze in his eyes that had only known the wistful patience of defeat. Under his breath, with a furtive exultation, he began once again the paean of victory and devastation. And presently his eyes were rewarded: out through that doorway came a long, low, yellow-and-brown beast, with eyes ablink at the waning daylight, and dark wet stains around the fur of jaws and throat. Conradin dropped on his knees. The great polecat-ferret made its way down to a small brook at the foot of the garden, drank for a moment, then crossed a little plank bridge and was lost to sight in the bushes. Such was the passing of Sredni Vashtar.

"Tea is ready," said the sour-faced maid. "Where is the mistress?"

"She went down to the shed some time ago," said Conradin.

And while the maid went to summon her mistress to tea, Conradin fished a toasting fork out of the sideboard drawer and proceeded to toast himself a piece of bread. And during the toasting of it and the buttering of it with much butter and the slow enjoyment of eating it, Conradin listened to the noises and silences which fell in quick spasms beyond the dining-room door. The loud foolish screaming of the maid, the answering chorus of wondering ejaculations from the kitchen region, the scuttering footsteps and hurried embassies for outside help, and then, after a lull, the scared sobbings and the shuffling tread of those who bore a heavy burden into the house.

"Whoever will break it to the poor child? I couldn't for the life of me!" exclaimed a shrill voice. And while they debated the matter among themselves, Conradin made himself another piece of toast.

THE NINE BILLION NAMES OF GOD

ARTHUR C. CLARKE

"THIS IS A slightly unusual request," said Dr. Wagner, with what he hoped was commendable restraint. "As far as I know, it's the first time anyone's been asked to supply a Tibetan monastery with an automatic sequence computer. I don't wish to be inquisitive, but I should hardly have thought that your—ah—establishment had much use for such a machine. Could you explain just what you intend to do with it?"

"Gladly," replied the lama, readjusting his silk robes and carefully putting away the slide rule he had been using for currency conversions. "Your Mark V computer can carry out any routine mathematical operation involving up to ten digits. However, for our work we are interested in *letters*, not numbers. As we wish you to modify the output circuits, the machine will be printing words, not columns of figures."

"I don't quite understand. . . ."

"This is a project on which we have been working for the last three centuries—since the lamasery was founded, in fact. It is somewhat alien to your way of thought, so I hope you will listen with an open mind while I explain it."

"Naturally."

"It is really quite simple. We have been compiling a list which shall contain all the possible names of God."

"I beg your pardon?"

"We have reason to believe," continued the lama imperturbably, "that all such names can be written with not more than nine letters in an alphabet we have devised."

"And you have been doing this for three centuries?"

"Yes. We expected it would take us about fifteen thousand years to complete the task."

"Oh." Dr. Wagner looked a little dazed. "Now I see why you wanted to hire one of our machines. But exactly what is the *purpose* of this project?"

The lama hesitated for a fraction of a second, and Wagner wondered if he had offended him. If so, there was no trace of annoyance in the reply.

"Call it ritual, if you like, but it's a fundamental part of our belief. All the many names of the Supreme Being—God, Jehovah, Allah, and so on—they are only man-made labels. There is a philosophical problem of some difficulty here, which I do not propose to discuss, but somewhere among all the possible combinations of letters that can occur are what one may call the *real* names of God. By systematic permutation of letters, we have been trying to list them all."

"I see. You've been starting at AAAAAAA . . . and working up to ZZZZZZZZ. . . ."

"Exactly—though we use a special alphabet of our own. Modifying the electromatic typewriters to deal with this is, of course, trivial. A rather more interesting problem is that of devising suitable circuits to eliminate ridiculous combinations. For example, no letter must occur more than three times in succession."

"Three? Surely you mean two."

"Three is correct. I am afraid it would take too long to explain why, even if you understood our language."

"I'm sure it would," said Wagner hastily. "Go on."

"Luckily, it will be a simple matter to adapt your automatic sequence computer for this work, since once it has been programmed properly, it will permute each letter in turn and print the result. What would have taken us fifteen thousand years it will be able to do in a hundred days."

Dr. Wagner was scarcely conscious of the faint sounds from the

Manhattan streets far below. He was in a different world, a world of natural, not man-made, mountains. High up in their remote aeries these monks had been patiently at work, generation after generation, compiling their lists of meaningless words. Was there any limit to the follies of mankind? Still, he must give no hint of his inner thoughts. The customer was always right. . . .

"There's no doubt," replied the doctor, "that we can modify the Mark V to print lists of this nature. I'm much more worried about the problem of installation and maintenance. Getting out to Tibet, in these days, is not going to be easy."

"We can arrange that. The components are small enough to travel by air—that is one reason why we chose your machine. If you can get them to India, we will provide transport from there."

"And you want to hire two of our engineers?"

"Yes, for the three months that the project should occupy."

"I've no doubt that personnel can manage that." Dr. Wagner scribbled a note on his desk pad. "There are just two other points—"

Before he could finish the sentence the lama had produced a small slip of paper.

"This is my certified credit balance at the Asiatic Bank."

"Thank you. It appears to be—ah—adequate. The second matter is so trivial that I hesitate to mention it—but it's surprising how often the obvious gets overlooked. What source of electrical energy have you?"

"A diesel generator providing fifty kilowatts at a hundred and ten volts. It was installed about five years ago and is quite reliable. It's made life at the lamasery much more comfortable, but of course it was really installed to provide power for the motors driving the prayer wheels."

"Of course," echoed Dr. Wagner. "I should have thought of that."

THE VIEW FROM the parapet was vertiginous, but in time one gets used to anything. After three months, George Hanley was not impressed by the two-thousand-foot swoop into the abyss or the remote checkerboard of fields in the valley below. He was leaning against the wind-smoothed stones and staring morosely at the distant mountains whose names he had never bothered to discover.

This, thought George, was the craziest thing that had ever happened to him. "Project Shangri-La," some wit back at the labs had christened it. For weeks now the Mark V had been churning out acres of sheets covered with gibberish. Patiently, inexorably, the computer had been rearranging letters in all their possible combinations, exhausting each class before going on to the next. As the sheets had emerged from the electromatic typewriters, the monks had carefully cut them up and pasted them into enormous books. In another week, heaven be praised, they would have finished. Just what obscure calculations had convinced the monks that they needn't bother to go on to words of ten, twenty, or a hundred letters, George didn't know. One of his recurring nightmares was that there would be some change of plan, and that the high lama (whom they called Sam) would suddenly announce that the project would be extended to approximately A.D. 2060. The monks were quite capable of it.

George heard the heavy wooden door slam in the wind as Chuck came out onto the parapet beside him. As usual, Chuck was smoking one of the cigars that made him so popular with the monks—who, it seemed, were quite willing to embrace all the minor and most of the major pleasures of life. That was one thing in their favor: they might be crazy, but they weren't bluenoses. Those frequent trips they took down to the village, for instance . . .

"Listen, George," said Chuck urgently. "I've learned something that means trouble."

"What's wrong? Isn't the machine behaving?" That was the worst contingency George could imagine. It might delay his return, and nothing could be more horrible. The way he felt now, even the sight of a TV commercial would seem like manna from heaven. At least it would be some link with home.

"No—it's nothing like that." Chuck settled himself on the parapet, which was unusual because normally he was scared of the drop. "I've just found what all this is about."

"What d'ya mean? I thought we knew."

"Sure—we know what the monks are trying to do. But we didn't know *why*. It's the craziest thing—"

"Tell me something new," growled George.

"Old Sam's just come clean with me. You know the way he drops in every afternoon to watch the sheets roll out. Well, this time he seemed rather excited, or at least as near as he'll ever get to it. When I told him that we were on the last cycle, he asked me, in that cute English accent of his, if I'd ever wondered what they were trying to do. I said, 'Sure'—and he told me."

"Go on. I'll buy it."

"Well, they believe that when they have listed all His names—and they reckon that there are about nine billion of them—God's purpose will be achieved. The human race will have finished what it was created to do, and there won't be any point in carrying on. Indeed, the very idea is something like blasphemy."

"Then what do they expect us to do? Commit suicide?"

"There's no need for that. When the list's completed, God steps in and simply winds things up . . . bingo!"

"Oh, I get it. When we finish our job, it will be the end of the world."

Chuck gave a nervous little laugh.

"That's just what I said to Sam. And do you know what happened? He looked at me in a very queer way, like I'd been stupid in class, and said, 'It's nothing as trivial as *that.*'"

George thought this over for a moment.

"That's what I call taking the wide view," he said presently. "But what d'you suppose we should do about it? I don't see that it makes the slightest difference to us. After all, we already knew that they were crazy."

"Yes—but don't you see what may happen? When the list's complete and the last trumpet doesn't blow—or whatever it is they expect—*we* may get the blame. It's our machine they've been using. I don't like the situation one little bit."

"I see," said George slowly. "You've got a point there. But this sort of thing's happened before, you know. When I was a kid down in Louisiana we had a crackpot preacher who once said the world was going to end next Sunday. Hundreds of people believed him—even sold their homes. Yet when nothing happened, they didn't turn nasty, as you'd expect. They just decided that he'd made a mistake in his calculations and went right on believing. I guess some of them still do."

"Well, this isn't Louisiana, in case you hadn't noticed. There are just two of us and hundreds of these monks. I like them, and I'll be sorry for old Sam when his lifework backfires on him. But all the same, I wish I was somewhere else."

"I've been wishing that for weeks. But there's nothing we can do until the contract's finished and the transport arrives to fly us out."

"Of course," said Chuck thoughtfully, "we could always try a bit of sabotage."

"Like hell we could! That would make things worse."

"Not the way I meant. Look at it like this. The machine will finish its run four days from now, on the present twenty-hours-a-day basis. The transport calls in a week. Okay—then all we need to do is to find something that needs replacing during one of the overhaul periods—something that will hold up the works for a couple of days. We'll fix it, of course, but not too quickly. If we time matters properly, we can be down at the airfield when the last name pops out of the register. They won't be able to catch us then."

"I don't like it," said George. "It will be the first time I ever walked out on a job. Besides, it would make them suspicious. No, I'll sit tight and take what comes."

"I STILL DON'T like it," he said, seven days later, as the tough little mountain ponies carried them down the winding road. "And don't you think I'm running away because I'm afraid. I'm just sorry for those poor old guys up there, and I don't want to be around when they find what suckers they've been. Wonder how Sam will take it?"

"It's funny," replied Chuck, "but when I said good-by I got the idea he knew we were walking out on him—and that he didn't care because he knew the machine was running smoothly and that the job would soon be finished. After that—well, of course, for him there just isn't any 'after that.'"

George turned in his saddle and stared back up the mountain road. This was the last place from which one could get a clear view of the lamasery. The squat, angular buildings were silhouetted against the afterglow of the sunset. Here and there, lights gleamed like portholes in the side of an ocean liner. Electric lights, of course, sharing the same circuit as the Mark V. How much longer would they share it? wondered George. Would the monks smash up the computer in their rage and disappointment? Or would they just sit down quietly and begin their calculations all over again?

He knew exactly what was happening up on the mountain at this very moment. The high lama and his assistants would be sitting in their silk robes, inspecting the sheets as the junior monks carried them away from the typewriters and pasted them into the great volumes. No one would be saying anything, for the Mark V itself was utterly silent as it flashed through its thousands of calculations a second. Three months of this, thought George, was enough to start anyone climbing the wall.

"There she is!" called Chuck, pointing down into the valley. "Ain't she beautiful!"

She certainly was, thought George. The battered old DC-3 lay at the end of the runway like a tiny silver cross. In two hours she would be bearing them away to freedom and sanity. It was a thought worth savoring like a fine liqueur. George let it roll around his mind as the pony trudged patiently down the slope.

The swift night of the high Himalayas was now almost upon them. Fortunately, the road was very good, as roads went in that region, and they were both carrying flashlights. The sky overhead was perfectly clear, and ablaze with the familiar, friendly stars. At least there would be no risk, thought George, of the pilot's being unable to take off because of weather conditions. That had been his only remaining worry.

He began to sing, but gave it up after a while. This vast arena of mountains, gleaming like whitely hooded ghosts on every side, did not encourage such ebullience. Presently George glanced at his watch.

"Should be there in an hour," he called back over his shoulder to Chuck. Then he added, in an afterthought, "Wonder if the computer's finished its run. It was due about now."

Chuck didn't reply, so George swung around in his saddle. He could just see Chuck's face, a white oval turned toward the sky.

"Look," whispered Chuck, and George lifted his eyes to heaven. (There is always a last time for everything.)

Overhead, without any fuss, the stars were going out.

BIOGRAPHICAL NOTES

GERTRUDE ATHERTON
1857–1948
Though not well known today, Gertrude Atherton was a major American writer whose long career spanned the years from 1892 to 1946 and included fifty-six books. She lived most of her life in her native San Francisco, the setting for "The Foghorn," and remained contemporary in her writing down through the years, "entering with gusto into the crowding debates of her time from feminism to communism," as *The New York Times* commented at the time of her death. Page 454

ROBERT BARR *1850–1912*
Barr was born in Glasgow, spent most of his early years in Canada, then began his career as a reporter for the Detroit *Free Press.* Posted to London by his paper, he left it in 1892 to become editor of the fashionable magazine *The Idler.* Barr is now mainly remembered for his detective stories featuring French detective Eugène Valmont, but he also wrote many romances and an occasional tale of terror, such as "An Alpine Divorce," considered by many to be his finest in this genre. Page 326

AMBROSE BIERCE *1842–?1914*
Starting as a newspaperman in San Francisco, Bierce was almost fifty before he gained national recognition with a collection of stories called *In the Midst of Life and Other Stories.* The theme that awakened the full range of his talent was the Civil War, and he returned to it repeatedly. His sharp wit, darkened by bitterness and a sense of the macabre, found permanent expression in *The Devil's Dictionary*, full of cynical definitions. Visiting Mexico while the revolution of Pancho Villa was in progress, he simply disappeared. Page 271

ALGERNON BLACKWOOD
1869–1951
Blackwood's two most absorbing passions were a love of the wilderness and a deep conviction that the average person possesses psychic powers which can surface at odd and unexpected times. He came from a prominent British family in Kent, was educated mainly in Europe, and turned to writing after disappointing ventures as a farmer, hotelkeeper and newspaperman in Canada and the United States. He achieved great fame in his later years as a teller of ghost stories on British television. Page 107

ROBERT BLOCH *1917–*
Author of more than four hundred short stories, several novels, and the radio serial, "Stay Tuned for Terror," Robert Bloch is best known for *Psycho*, which became one of the highest grossing black-and-white films ever made. Born in Chicago and raised in Milwaukee, Bloch was an advertising copywriter for

eleven years before earning enough on his own work to free-lance. He was president of the Mystery Writers of America from 1970 to 1971. Page 570

RAY BRADBURY *1920–*
Since his earliest writing Bradbury has concentrated with remarkable success on fantasy and science fiction. Such imaginative works as *The Martian Chronicles*, *The Illustrated Man* and *Something Wicked This Way Comes* have gained new readers for the field, and new respect. He was born in Waukegan, Illinois, and moved with his family to Los Angeles, where he still resides. Page 207

THOMAS BURKE *1886–1945*
It has been said of Burke that his tendency to write of the lurid aspects of slum life might have been a compensation for his own retiring nature and love of solitude. Born in London, Burke spent part of his childhood in an orphanage and knew the slums well. His first success was *Limehouse Nights*, a short-story collection set in London's Chinese ghetto. His wife was also a writer, who published under the pen name of Clare Cameron. Page 313

A. M. BURRAGE *1889–1956*
With the death of his father, Burrage at the age of seventeen took to writing as a livelihood, and supported his mother and aunt as a free-lancer, like the main character in "The Waxwork." After serving in France with the British forces in World War I, Burrage returned to England and resumed his writing career, contributing to more than a hundred publications. A dwindling market, poor health and World War II brought his writing to an end, and he died in poverty and obscurity. Page 414

TRUMAN CAPOTE *1924–*
A native of New Orleans, Capote lists writing only after conversation, reading and travel as a "preferred pastime." A writer of extraordinary versatility, he has won international acclaim. His novel *Breakfast at Tiffany's* was made into both a Broadway musical and a movie. With *In Cold Blood* he created a journalistic nonfiction style that reads like suspense fiction. Page 156

JOHN DICKSON CARR
1906–1977
The son of a criminal lawyer in Pennsylvania, Carr began reading Sherlock Holmes stories at an early age, and was writing detective stories when still a schoolboy. His first book was published in 1930, after which he wrote prodigiously under his own name and two pseudonyms: Carr Dickson and Carter Dickson, the latter used on books featuring his famous fictional detective, Dr. Gideon Fell. With his English wife, Carr lived many years in Britain before returning permanently to the United States in 1958. Page 331

LESLIE CHARTERIS *1907–*
Leslie Charles Bowyer Yin, born in Singapore of English-Chinese parentage, later changed his name to that of a notorious London rake whom he admired. During his only year at Cambridge University, he wrote his first novel, then abandoned study in favor of writing and a variety of exotic odd jobs. He soon created a detective he called the Saint—a modern Robin Hood whose elegant adventurousness resembled his own. The enormously popular Saint stories that followed over the years led to several Hollywood movies, a comic strip, radio and television programs, and a mystery magazine. Page 222

G. K. CHESTERTON *1874–1936*
In a career that spanned nearly four decades, Chesterton was a prolific writer of serious novels, essays, poetry and criticism. Yet today he is best known for his small collection of detective stories featuring the unique priest-

detective, Father Brown. Born and educated in London, Chesterton first studied art, then switched to literature, launching his career with book reviews. A deeply religious man, he was formally received into the Roman Catholic Church in 1922 by his friend Father John O'Connor, who was the original inspiration for Father Brown. Page 144

AGATHA CHRISTIE *1890–1976*
Dame Agatha's was a colorful life. Born Mary Clarissa Miller in Torquay, England, she went to Paris at sixteen to study voice, then wintered in Cairo with her widowed mother. In 1914 she married Colonel Andrew Christie of the Royal Flying Corps. Mrs. Christie began writing mystery novels, the first of which, *The Mysterious Affair at Styles*, introduced the world to M. Hercule Poirot in 1920. Following a disappearance as bizarre as any of her plots, she divorced Colonel Christie and later married the distinguished archaeologist Max Mallowan. Truly the *grande dame* of detective fiction, she was still producing a book a year when she was well past eighty. Page 54

ARTHUR C. CLARKE *1917–*
A firm grasp of the latest cosmic discoveries, coupled to an enormous imagination, makes Clarke a writer of global influence. The synchronous earth satellites that he proposed in an article in 1945 are now mainstays of worldwide communications. Artistically, his work on the screenplay for Stanley Kubrick's 1968 film *2001: A Space Odyssey* introduced a new dimension of depth to science-fiction cinema. And new ideas flow regularly from his adopted home, the island of Sri Lanka (formerly Ceylon). Page 623

JOHN COLLIER *1901–1980*
British born, Collier began writing verse at nineteen and had his first poetry published when he was twenty. Nine years later his first book appeared, an offbeat satirical novel called *His Monkey Wife*. In Collier's hands witchcraft, sorcery and the wildest fantasies become almost plausible; when a major collection of his short stories, *The John Collier Reader*, was published in 1973, one reviewer advised that it be read only in "broad daylight." Page 136

ROALD DAHL *1916–*
Born in Llandaff, South Wales, of Norwegian parents, Dahl began writing as a result of his experiences as a Royal Air Force fighter pilot in World War II. In short stories published in the 1950s and 1960s he established himself as a master of situations in which the comic and the gruesome combine with devastating results. The author, also, of many widely acclaimed children's books, Dahl is married to the American actress Patricia Neal and makes his home in Britain. Page 196

SIR ARTHUR CONAN DOYLE *1859–1930*
The man who created Sherlock Holmes was born in Edinburgh, attended university there, and later pursued the improbable career of eye doctor before taking up the pen professionally. But it was while studying medicine that Doyle met a thin, angular surgeon named Joseph Bell, whose ability to diagnose occupation and character as well as disease helped provide the model for the immortal Holmes. Knighted in 1902, Sir Arthur also wrote several historical romances in addition to numerous tales involving Holmes, Dr. Watson and their arch-rival, the infamous Professor Moriarty. Page 9

DAPHNE DU MAURIER *1907–*
Granddaughter of George du Maurier, who wrote *Trilby*, daughter of noted actor Gerald du Maurier, Daphne du Maurier was educated at home and in Paris. In 1932 she married Lieutenant

Colonel F. A. M. Browning, who in 1941 became the youngest general in British Empire forces. She now lives in Cornwall, where she combines her writing with her love of gardening, sailing and walking. *Rebecca* and *My Cousin Rachel* are but two of her many haunting books, for which, in 1969, she was created a Dame of the British Empire. Page 280

LORD DUNSANY *1878–1957*
Fox hunter, cricketer, Royal Fusilier, Edward John Moreton Drax Plunkett, 18th Baron Dunsany, once calculated that only three percent of his life was devoted to writing his plays, poems and stories. But that three percent gave Dublin's Abbey Theatre many brilliant evenings, and produced some of the English language's most memorable tales of the macabre—tales whose frequent flashes of humor serve only to make the darkness deeper. Even those who know the solution to Dunsany's classic "Two Bottles of Relish" shiver on rereading it. Page 241

STANLEY ELLIN *1916–*
Born and educated in New York City, Stanley Ellin was a jack of many trades—steelworker, dairy farmer and teacher among them—before he wrote "The Specialty of the House," his brilliant first short story, in 1948. An instant classic, it immediately won a prize in *Ellery Queen's Mystery Magazine*'s prestigious annual contest. He has been writing some of the finest crime stories of modern times and winning prizes, here and abroad, ever since. Page 581

IAN FLEMING *1908–1964*
James Bond has become so closely identified with his creator that it is sometimes difficult to separate their lives. When Fleming first went to Moscow for Reuters in 1929, he was purely a journalist. But when he returned there in 1939 he was working both for *The Times* of London and—secretly—for the Foreign Office. During World War II he was also a secret agent for the director of British Naval Intelligence. His spy stories thus have an authenticity that is a major element in their huge success, both in print and on film. Page 426

C. S. FORESTER *1899–1966*
An Englishman born in Cairo, Forester studied medicine for a time but forsook that for a career in writing, making an auspicious debut in 1926 with the widely acclaimed portrait of the disintegration of a murderer, *Payment Deferred*. However, it was not until 1937 and the appearance of his first Captain Horatio Hornblower stories that Forester took his place as an internationally best-selling author. Many films have been based on his books, including *The African Queen*, for which Humphrey Bogart won an Oscar as best actor of the year in 1951. Page 27

ERLE STANLEY GARDNER
1889–1970
The creator of Perry Mason is possibly the most popular and prolific American writer of all time. To date his thrillers have sold more than three hundred million copies and have been translated into more than fifty languages. The son of a mining engineer, Gardner started out as a trial lawyer in California, and though he soon found writing to be more profitable, he never strayed far from the courtroom. In his later years he helped establish "The Court of Last Resort" to obtain justice for people wrongly convicted of serious crimes. Page 602

GILBERT HIGHET *1906–1978*
A professor of Greek and Latin who was also a master of the language of today, this charming Scot could present the most erudite matters in plain and enjoyable English. Columbia University students benefitted from his talents for almost forty years, and he reached a

wider audience through numerous radio broadcasts, books of literary criticism, and translations of the classics. "Another Solution," which first appeared in *Harper's Magazine* in 1951, is one of his few works of fiction. Page 409

GEORGE HITCHCOCK *1914–*
The author of "An Invitation to the Hunt" is a native of Oregon who has made San Francisco his literary domain for many years. A poet and playwright with a penchant for social satire, Hitchcock has had many plays performed in San Francisco area theaters and is editor of *San Francisco Review.* Page 495

WILLIAM HOPE HODGSON
1877–1918
Hodgson's knowledge of the sea came from many years spent as a ship's officer in the British merchant marine. His first book—one of several with the sea as the setting—was published in 1907, but his brief literary career came to an end with his death in 1918, following injuries sustained while serving as an army officer in World War I. Page 505

WILLIAM IRISH *1903–1968*
William Irish is a pen name for the prolific American mystery writer Cornell Hopley-Woolrich, who also published many books and stories as George Hopley and Cornell Woolrich. His best-known works include *Phantom Lady*, *The Bride Wore Black* and *Rear Window*, whose film version, starring James Stewart and Grace Kelly, was a box-office hit in 1954. Page 388

SHIRLEY JACKSON *1919–1965*
Novelist, writer of short stories and radio and television scripts, Jackson's work reveals a preoccupation with the darker regions of the human experience. Her novel *The Haunting of Hill House* was made into a successful movie, and her story "The Lottery" became a play. But she could also write delightfully about ordinary subjects, as in *Life Among the Savages*, a series of essays on her children. She was born in San Francisco and lived most of her adult life in rural Vermont. Page 36

W. W. JACOBS *1863–1943*
Chiefly a writer of humorous sea tales in which the sailors rarely left port, Jacobs occasionally changed his pace and wrote a totally chilling story such as "The Interruption." Despite the disturbing qualities of this tale, the late W. W. Jacobs was a quiet, gentle man, a former British civil service clerk who turned to writing full time to support his wife and five children. Page 483

M. R. JAMES *1862–1936*
Though he was a distinguished English antiquary and provost of Eton College from 1918 until his death, Montague Rhodes James, with his taste for the bizarre, was widely recognized as a master of the occult and the supernatural, surpassing most writers, as a biographer once said, "in the vindictiveness and malignancy of his ghosts, who had an uncomfortable habit of operating in broad daylight." Page 180

RUDYARD KIPLING *1865–1936*
The author of such masterworks as *The Jungle Books*, "Gunga Din" and scores of other famous stories and poems was born in Bombay, and was sent to England when he was six, his health being extremely delicate. Later he rejected his parents' offer of a university education and went back to India, where he became a journalist. He soon showed himself to be a writer of genius and was the recipient of many honors, including, in 1907, the Nobel Prize for Literature. Page 548

H. P. LOVECRAFT *1890–1937*
Recognition as a master of horror and fantasy tales came to Lovecraft only after he had been writing for twenty years, publishing in such specialized

periodicals as *Weird Tales* and *Amazing Stories*. He was writing newspaper articles on science at the early age of sixteen, but frail health kept him from attending college, and most of his life was spent working in obscurity in Providence, Rhode Island, his birthplace. Much of his writing anticipates the modern vogue of science fiction. Page 370

ROSS MACDONALD *1915–*
After publishing four mysteries under his own name, Kenneth Millar took the pseudonym Ross Macdonald to avoid confusion with his wife, Margaret, who was writing outstanding mystery stories of her own. Macdonald lives in Santa Barbara, California, and his keen interest in probing touchy social issues has given his widely popular novels, featuring detective Lew Archer, special depth and pertinence. Page 518

GUY DE MAUPASSANT
1850–1893
Guy de Maupassant wrote novels, plays and verse, but no other writer is more completely identified with the short story. A consummate master of this form, who learned his craft from Flaubert, Maupassant wrote some three hundred stories, many of them based on personal recollections of his youth in Normandy. Page 86

ANDRÉ MAUROIS *1885–1967*
Biography and history are the fields that won Maurois his fame. His lives of Shelley, Disraeli, George Sand and others were praised in Britain and America as well as in his native France for their keen psychological analyses of persons and periods. But Maurois also wrote more than a dozen volumes of short stories, including many "fantastic tales." One of these, "Thanatos Palace Hotel," displays well his virtues of clarity, brilliance of description and economy of words, as well as an uncanny knowledge of psychology. Page 346

RICHARD BARHAM MIDDLETON
1882–1911
English born and educated, Middleton "endured" six years as an insurance clerk before "escaping" into the literary world. Fellow bohemians knew him as a "dreamer and talker" whose slouch hat and curly black beard gave him a piratical appearance; and the stories he wrote were romantically ghostly. A passionate theatergoer even when penniless, he was just twenty-nine when he made a final theatrical gesture—committing suicide with chloroform. Page 360

ALFRED NOYES *1880–1958*
Few writers of the twentieth century have earned a living from poetry. Noyes did. Great narrative skill and sincere British patriotism won him a large audience; his poem "The Highwayman" became a classroom favorite. Later he added history, biography, essays, novels and short stories to his accomplishments. Far continents intrigued him, especially Asia and America, as is evident in "The Log of the *Evening Star*." Page 168

EDGAR ALLAN POE *1809–1849*
One of America's first important writers, Poe was born in Boston. Orphaned at three, he was reared by foster parents in Richmond, Virginia. Working as an editor, critic, and writer of short stories, he first gained attention in 1833 with his tale "MS. Found in a Bottle." There followed a series of world-renowned stories, including "The Murders in the Rue Morgue," which is considered to be the first true detective story. His poem "The Raven" remains one of the most popular in American literature. Page 48

ELLERY QUEEN *1905–*
Ellery Queen is the pen name of two cousins, Frederic Dannay and Manfred Lee, as well as the name of their elegant and acute fictional detective. The cousins, who were both born in 1905, became Ellery Queen in 1928 with their

collaboration on a mystery story for a contest sponsored by *McClure's Magazine.* They won first prize, and a meteoric writing career was launched. Movie contracts and an Ellery Queen radio series soon followed. In 1941 the cousins started *Ellery Queen's Mystery Magazine*, publishing little-known gems from the past along with an astounding number of new writers who have since become famous. Manfred Lee died in 1971, but Frederic Dannay still carries on the Queen tradition. Page 254

JOHN RUSSELL *1885–1956*
More than six hundred short stories poured from the pen of John Russell, an American journalist born in Davenport, Iowa, and in many of them he turned to the South Seas for his inspiration. He traveled extensively for the New York *Herald* and later for the New York *Sun*, and in 1920 he was adopted as a chief by the Samoans. Page 91

SAKI (H. H. MUNRO)
1870–1916
As a master of humor as well as of the chilling and the macabre, Saki has few peers. Born in Burma but educated in Britain, he learned the writer's craft as a newspaper reporter and foreign correspondent in the Balkans, Russia and France. With World War I intensifying, he enlisted as a private in the Royal Fusiliers, refusing several offers of a commission. A brilliant career ended tragically with his untimely death in battle in 1916. Page 618

GEORGES SIMENON *1903–*
Few writers can match Simenon's production record: more than one hundred and fifty novels under his own name, plus two hundred under various pseudonyms. His best are valued by critics for their psychological probing of human relations, and all are characterized by vivid depiction of varied locales. But his global reputation began in the early 1930s with twenty novels, written in as many months, featuring the formidable Parisian detective Jules Maigret. Simenon was born in the ancient Belgian city of Liège, which he left for Paris at age twenty. He now makes his home in Switzerland. Page 559

CARL STEPHENSON *1886–1954*
A renowned medievalist and author of such books as his 1942 *Medieval Feudalism*, which is still in print, Dr. Stephenson was a native of Indiana who was professor of history at Cornell University for many years. His classic tale, "Leiningen Versus the Ants," is believed by his family to be the only short story that he ever wrote. Page 463

EVELYN WAUGH *1903–1966*
Born in London, where his father was a publisher, Waugh was a brilliantly successful novelist and journalist by the age of twenty-five. From the first, his writing was notable for its "vitality, matchless craftsmanship, audacious imagination and stinging perceptions." After his conversion to Catholicism, followed by a happy family life in the country, he became less the devastating observer of human folly and more the upholder of ancient traditions. "You have no idea how much nastier I would be if I was not a Catholic," he told a friend. Nonetheless, critics much prefer his earlier works, in which he was "defending no one and nothing." Page 72

H. G. WELLS *1866–1946*
Wells was one of the best-known and most prolific authors of his time. An honors graduate in science, he developed a reputation as a master of science fiction with such works as *The War of the Worlds*, *The Invisible Man* and *The Time Machine.* He wrote more realistic novels as well, and for many years no respectable bookcase was complete without his encyclopedic two-volume *Outline of History.* Page 592

ACKNOWLEDGMENTS

THE TURN OF THE TIDE, copyright 1934, copyright © 1961 by C. S. Forester, copyright © renewed 1962 by Dorothy Forester. Used by permission of Harold Matson Company, Inc., and of A. D. Peters & Co. Ltd. THE SUMMER PEOPLE, copyright 1950, copyright © 1968 by Stanley Edgar Hyman, copyright © renewed 1978 by Laurence Hyman, Barry Hyman, Sarah Webster and Mrs. Joanne Schnurer, is from *Come Along With Me* by Shirley Jackson. Used by permission of Viking Penguin Inc., and of Brandt & Brandt Literary Agents, Inc. THE THIRD FLOOR FLAT, copyright 1928 by Agatha Christie, copyright © renewed 1956 by Agatha Christie Mallowan, is from *Three Blind Mice and Other Stories* by Agatha Christie. Used by permission of Dodd, Mead & Company, Inc., and of Harold Ober Associates Incorporated. THE MAN WHO LIKED DICKENS, copyright 1932, copyright 1934, copyright © 1962 by Evelyn Waugh, is condensed from Chapter 6 of *A Handful of Dust* by Evelyn Waugh. Used by permission of Little, Brown & Company, and of A. D. Peters & Co. Ltd. THE WENDIGO, copyright by Sheila Reeves. Used by permission of the estate of Algernon Blackwood. THE TOUCH OF NUTMEG MAKES IT, copyright 1941 by The F-R Publishing Corporation, copyright 1943 by The Readers Club, copyright © renewed 1969 by John Collier. Used by permission of Harold Matson Company, Inc., and of A. D. Peters & Co. Ltd. THE ABSENCE OF MR. GLASS, copyright 1914 by Dodd, Mead & Company, Inc., copyright renewed 1941 by Oliver Chesterton, copyright by Dorothy E. Collins, is from *The Wisdom of Father Brown* by G. K. Chesterton. Used by permission of Dodd, Mead & Company, Inc., and of the estate of G. K. Chesterton. MIRIAM, copyright 1945, copyright © renewed 1973 by Condé Nast Publications, Inc., is reprinted from *Selected Writings of Truman Capote* by Truman Capote. Used by permission of Random House, Inc. THE LOG OF THE "EVENING STAR", copyright by Alfred Noyes, was published by John Murray, Ltd. Used by permission of Hugh Noyes. CASTING THE RUNES, copyright 1919, is from *Collected Ghost Stories* by M. R. James. Used by permission of Edward Arnold Publishers Ltd. MAN FROM THE SOUTH, copyright 1948 by Roald Dahl, is reprinted from *Someone Like You* by Roald Dahl. Used by permission of Alfred A. Knopf, Inc., of Michael Joseph Ltd., and of Penguin Books Limited. THE WHOLE TOWN'S SLEEPING, copyright 1950, copyright © renewed 1978 by Ray Bradbury. Used by permission of Harold Matson Company, Inc. THE ARROW OF GOD, copyright 1949 by The American Mercury, Inc., copyright 1952 by Leslie Charteris, is from *The Saint on the Spanish Main* by Leslie Charteris. Used by permission of Doubleday & Company, Inc., of Hodder & Stoughton Ltd., and of the author. THE TWO BOTTLES OF RELISH, used by permission of Curtis Brown, Ltd., on behalf of John Charles Villiers and Valentine Lamb as literary executors of Lord Dunsany. THE GETTYSBURG BUGLE, copyright 1947 by Ellery Queen, copyright © renewed 1975 by Frederic Dannay and Manfred B. Lee. Used by permission of the author and the author's agents, Scott Meredith Literary Agency, Inc. DON'T LOOK NOW, copyright © 1970 by Daphne du Maurier, is from the book of stories entitled *Don't Look Now* by Daphne du Maurier, published by Victor Gollancz. Used by permission of Doubleday & Company, Inc., and of the author. THE INCAUTIOUS BURGLAR, copyright 1947 by John Dickson Carr, is from *The Men Who Explained Miracles* by John Dickson Carr. Used by permission of Harper & Row, Publishers, Inc., of Hamish Hamilton Ltd., and of David Higham Associates Ltd. THANATOS PALACE HOTEL, copyright © 1967 by Washington Square Press, is from *The Collected Stories of André Maurois* by André Maurois, translated by Adrienne Foulke. Used by permission of the estate of André Maurois. The Reader's Digest Association, Inc., has attempted to clear permission with other possible rights proprietors but, despite best efforts, has been unable to do so. The Rats in the Walls, copyright 1924 by The Rural Publishing Co., copyright 1939, 1945, copyright © renewed 1967, 1973 by August Derleth and Donald Wandrei. Used by permission of the estate of H. P. Lovecraft and the estate's agents, Scott Meredith Literary Agency, Inc. After-Dinner Story, copyright 1936 by William Irish, copyright © renewed 1964 by Cornell Woolrich. Used by permission of the author and the author's agents, Scott Meredith Literary Agency, Inc. Another Solution, copyright 1951, copyright © 1979 by *Harper's Magazine.* Used by permission of Curtis Brown, Ltd. The Waxwork, copyright 1930 by Jarrolds Publishers, London. Used by permission of J. S. F. Burrage. For Your Eyes Only, copyright © 1959, 1960, 1961, 1962 by Glidrose Productions Ltd., is from *Bonded Fleming* by Ian Fleming. All rights reserved. Used by permission of Viking Penguin Inc., of Glidrose Productions Ltd., and of Jonathan Cape Ltd. The Foghorn, copyright 1934 by Gertrude Atherton, copyright © renewed 1961 by Muriel Atherton Russell. Used by permission of Mrs. George S. Russell. Leiningen Versus the Ants, copyright 1938 by Esquire, Inc., is from *Esquire,* December 1938. Used by permission of *Esquire* magazine and the estate of Carl Stephenson. The Interruption, used by permission of the Society of Authors as the literary representative of the Estate of W. W. Jacobs. An Invitation to the Hunt, copyright © March 1960. Used by permission of *San Francisco Review* and George Hitchcock. Midnight Blue, copyright © 1960 by Ross Macdonald. Used by permission of Harold Ober Associates Incorporated, and of Hughes Massie Ltd. The Return of Imray, copyright by The National Trust. Used by permission of The National Trust and Macmillan London Limited. Journey Backward into Time, used by permission of Georges Simenon. The Movie People, copyright © 1969 by Mercury Press, Inc., for *Fantasy & Science Fiction,* October 1969, is from the book *Cold Chills* by Robert Bloch. Used by permission of Doubleday & Company, Inc., and of the author's agents, Scott Meredith Literary Agency, Inc. Broker's Special, copyright © 1956 by Stanley Ellin. Used by permission of Curtis Brown, Ltd. The Sea Raiders, copyright by Professor G. P. Wells. Used by permission of the estate of H. G. Wells. The Case of the Irate Witness, copyright 1953 by Crowell-Collier Publishing Company, copyright © 1975 by Erle Stanley Gardner, is from *The Case of the Irate Witness* by Erle Stanley Gardner, published by William Morrow and Company, Inc. Used by permission of William Morrow and Company, Inc., and of William Heinemann Ltd. The Nine Billion Names of God, copyright 1953 by Ballantine Books, Inc. Used by permission of Arthur C. Clarke and his agents, Scott Meredith Literary Agency, Inc.